The Geocaching Mystery Omnibus

VOLUME 1

Dan DeKoning

The Cacheland Conspiracy, copyright © 2024 by Dan DeKoning

The Quincy Bay Quandary, copyright © 2024 by Dan DeKoning

The Secret of the Seven Valleys, copyright © 2024 by Dan DeKoning

This book is a work of fiction. Names, characters, places, and incidents either are products of the author's imagination or are used fictitiously. Any resemblance to actual persons, living or dead, business establishments, events, or locales is entirely coincidental.

Copyright © 2024 by Dan DeKoning

All rights reserved. No part of this book may be reproduced or used in any manner without written permission of the copyright owner except for the use of quotations in a book review.

Cover Design by GetCovers

ISBN: 978-1-963691-05-4

Contents

The Cacheland Conspiracy..............1

The Quincy Bay Quandary..........233

The Secret of the Seven Valley.......465

The Cacheland Conspiracy

CHAPTER ONE

Drake Decker stepped back from the pine tree, took off his baseball cap, and scratched his head.

"You find the cache? Are you sure it's here?"

Allie Ashe took three steps to her right and peered into the tree. "The secret to finding pine tree geocaches is to stay on the perimeter of the tree and use your eyes to scan the branches. Keep stepping around the tree until you find it."

Drake rolled his eyes. "Yeah, you've told me that like a million times before."

Allie laughed and moved another two steps to her right. "Hey, at least it's not a palm tree, or a holly bush, or a rock pile."

"Well, I'll give you that one."

"Excuse me. What are you doing? Is something wrong with that tree?"

Drake turned around. Behind him was a short and skinny lady who looked to be in her upper eighties. She had a white terrier on a leash, and when the dog tugged at the leash, the woman barely had the strength to hold back the canine. Drake noticed the dog's fur and the woman's hair were the same color, and she could have worn the dog as a wig, and no one would be the wiser.

"No, ma'am, nothing wrong with the tree. We're geocaching. It's a game, like a scavenger hunt," Drake said.

The dog pulled again at the woman's arm, so she picked up the beast, grunting as she did. "What are you looking for?"

"Don't know yet. We haven't found it. A geocache has a container of some sort, with a piece of paper inside we have to sign."

She looked at Drake with a skeptic's eyes, a look he had seen before when encountered by muggles, who were people who didn't know about geocaching.

"Are you sure you can do that?"

"Yes, ma'am. We're in a public park, and the city approved this geocache's placement. So we have permission to be here."

Drake returned to his search. The woman watched for another minute, grew bored, then put her dog back on the ground and walked away.

"She seemed like a pleasant lady," Allie said.

"Yeah. She didn't have her dog chase us off. You spot it yet?"

"Nope. Oh, wait. Marco!"

Yelling out "Marco" was Allie's way of proclaiming she found the treasure, a play on the children's game, Marco Polo.

"Where is it?" Drake asked.

"Okay, move about four steps to your right. And…stop. Touch the branch above your right shoulder."

Drake reached up and took the branch. "This one?"

"No. Other shoulder."

Drake switched arms and grabbed the greenery.

"That's the one. Follow that branch in about three feet.

Got it?"

Drake stayed where he was and stared down the length of the bough, looking for something that didn't belong. At first his eyes failed him, but at last he spotted the container. "I see it. Tricky."

"Can you reach it?" Allie asked.

Drake got his bearings, figured out the best approach, and slid in between the branches. "Yeah, I got it. Come over here. I don't want to lose the spot."

Drake stayed where he was and kept his eye on the geocache as Allie circled the tree to where he entered. He picked the geocache container from the tree and handed it to her. The matchstick holder was the type a camper would use, but the geocache owner covered it with camouflage tape to hide the bright orange color. Once it emulated the color of the tree limbs, the owner added a hook to secure it to a branch.

Allie opened the container and removed a small plastic bag, in which was a piece of paper. She unfurled the piece of paper and signed her geocaching nickname, a play on her own name, then passed the paper and her pen to Drake, who added his nickname to the paper. Drake handed it back to Allie, who folded the paper to the correct size, returned the paper to the bag, and returned the bag to the container. She closed the container, handed the geocache to Drake, and he placed it back on the branch where he found it.

"I saw it before you," Drake teased as he made his way out of the confines of the branches. "I wanted to see if you could find it."

"Right. Sure, you did. Had I not been here, you would've given up on it thirty seconds after you got here. You ready for the next one?"

"Where is it?"

Allie pulled her phone from her back pocket, opened the app, and checked her options. "There's two more in this park.

One is off in that direction, kind of near where that playground is, and one is off to your left along the nature trail."

"Which one's closer?"

"Playground."

"Let's do that one first."

Allie selected the cache in her app and started walking toward the general area of the playground. As she walked, she checked the app's compass and distance to confirm they traveled in the correct direction.

When they got to within fifty yards of the playground, Allie stopped, and Drake halted a second later.

"There are people there," Drake said.

"Yes, I noticed. If I had to guess, the cache is on the slide, or on that bench. Either way, we'll have to come back to it when they leave the area. Let's go do the other one."

"Agreed."

Allie selected the other cache in the park and wandered off to the north, with Drake by her side. They weren't in any hurry, so they kept a leisurely pace as they hiked over toward the woods.

"You get any word back from the Cacheland promotion?" Allie asked.

Drake shook his head. "No. Have you?"

"No. The winners are supposed to be notified today. I hope one of us gets lucky. Watch out for that gopher hole."

Drake looked in the direction Allie alluded to and adjusted his gait to step over the potential ankle-breaker. "It's early yet. There's still plenty of time to hear from them."

"Can you imagine winning? Going on a trip to an old west town dedicated to the sole purpose of geocaching?"

Drake thought about the prospect for half a second. "Personally, I think that would be super cool."

"I read there's a competition for a cash prize of a

thousand bucks. Break right here. Notice that little path?"

Drake saw where Allie was pointing and did a course correction to a deer path that led into the woods. He stepped in line behind her since she had the app and knew where they were headed. "How far?"

"Two hundred feet straight ahead."

Drake looked ahead and took a visual inventory of what he saw. There were a lot of trees in the area, which meant plenty of places to hide a geocache. The most likely spots in the woods were usually old stumps or fallen trees, things that would provide natural cover to hide a geocache under. He spotted a stump off in the distance and headed for it.

"I think you misread the announcement. I'm pretty sure it was a fifty-thousand-dollar prize," he said as he avoided a large branch.

"Oh, wow. Now I really hope one of us gets selected."

Drake stopped at the stump and scrutinized it, looking for a container under the piles of loose bark surrounding the dead tree. "Is there any hint?"

Allie looked it up. "Stick your hand in there."

While Drake checked out the stump, Allie followed the coordinates on her phone another twenty feet away. She stepped behind a large tree, then held out a plastic container before her. "Marco."

"Again?" Drake stood and went to her. "You're on a roll today."

"Yeah, well, it helps that while you guess the location, I rely on the actual coordinates."

"Hey, that's why we make a good team. Where was this?"

"There's a hole in this tree."

Drake moved around Allie and looked. Sure enough, there was a hollow in the tree's center.

Allie handed him the log and container. "Here. Sign the

log and put it back."

Drake did as he was told, and the pair backtracked toward the park and over to the playground. The playground contained a swing set with three swings, two regular sized and one made to accommodate a toddler. Next to the swings stood a fortress with a rope ladder and steps to get to the top. The structure held enough room for a couple of kids, and there were two slides to get back to the ground. Rubber mulch covered the entire playground area, and rubber bumpers contained the mulch to prevent the spread into the grass. Around the play area were three benches, and Drake and Allie sat on one of them.

Allie checked her phone, did a quick calculation in her head, then nodded toward the bench farthest from them. "I think it's over there."

"I guessed that before we got here," Drake said.

"How?"

"Because there's someone sitting there, of course. With my luck, there's always a muggle exactly where I need to be. Let's wait a few minutes and see if they leave."

Allie looked over and spotted the mom. She was sitting on the bench, looking at her phone while she moved a stroller back and forth with her foot. Now and then, the toddler playing on the fort would demand attention, so the mom would glance up for a moment, then turn her attention back to her phone.

While Allie sent a mental command for the mom to take her kids and leave the park, Drake pulled his phone from his pocket and checked his email.

"Holy cow! Here's the notification! Congratulations! You and a guest have won an all-expenses paid trip to Cacheland U.S.A.! This is a once-in-a-lifetime opportunity to explore a town set up as a premier geocaching location! You will also take part in a team challenge where the winning team will walk away with the Golden Horseshoe and fifty thousand dollars! Please note that all participants must be twenty-five years or older." Drake closed the email and looked up from his phone. "Well, I've got that beat. Are you over twenty-five?"

Allie shoved him in the shoulder and almost knocked him from the bench. "You know I am! I'm just a year behind you, you idiot."

Drake laughed, then righted himself on the bench. The exchange had gotten the mom's attention. She looked over at the duo, determined they weren't really a threat, took a quick glance at her toddler, then returned to her phone.

"Are they paying our way out to Arizona? What are the dates again?" Allie asked.

Drake reopened the email and read through all the fine print. "Yes. They'll fly us into Phoenix and provide ground transportation to Cacheland. And the dates are October first through the eighth."

"Southern Arizona in early October? That shouldn't be too bad."

"Certainly much better than the first week of July or August." Drake stretched out his legs, dug the heels of his hiking boots into the ground, and clenched his leg muscles. "I hope they leave soon. I'm getting bored."

Allie frowned. "Gee, thanks. You're sitting on a bench with your best friend having a pleasant conversation, and you're bored? You're a jerk, that's what you are."

Drake put a hand to his mouth to hide his laugh, but he failed. "Come on, you know what I mean. I'd sit and talk to you all day, but I really want to get that cache."

"What's the big deal? This park is only thirty minutes from home. We can come back anytime."

Drake rolled his eyes. "Oh, come on, Allie, you know how I am. I mean, I can't be sitting twenty feet from a geocache and not search for it."

"Why not? You were three feet away from that pine tree one and you wanted to give up."

"That was different. Besides, if we find that one over at the playground, we'll have cleared out the park." As Drake spoke, he pointed at the bench.

The woman on the bench looked up just in time to see Drake gesturing in her direction. Drake noticed her looking at him, pointing at her, so he changed his aggressive point to a friendly wave.

"Hello. Good afternoon," Drake said, loud enough for her to hear.

Allie watched the entire exchange and broke out in laughter, which made Drake laugh as well.

The woman dropped her phone into the stroller and went to the end of the slide. "Come on down here, angel. It's time to leave."

Allie leaned over and whispered into Drake's ear. "Look what you did. You chased them off."

"I should have thought of that sooner," Drake whispered back.

The woman picked up her toddler, passed a dirty look to Allie and Drake, and left with the stroller.

"Have a nice day, ma'am," Drake called after her.

The woman responded with a one-finger salute without looking back.

"Hey, that wasn't nice. You didn't have to be so mean to her."

"What? I wasn't mean. It was a simple misunderstanding."

"Come on, Duck-man."

Drake and Allie got up from their bench, walked over to where the woman was sitting, and began their search.
The bench was a type they'd seen in plenty of parks before.

It was six feet long with a red seat and backrest, and a black frame and legs. A plastic coating covered the seat and back, and both had a hole-punch design, which allowed them to see through both the seat and back to an extent.

Drake started his search by looking through the holes in the seat, especially those near the corners, hoping to find the obvious spot. "I like these types of benches. Really limits the places a cache can hide."

"Then why haven't you found it yet?" Allie asked.

"I will, I will. Are you going to help?"

"Sure, I'll come in and save the day after you give up."

Off in the distance, thunder rumbled. The skies had been cloudy all day, with a threat of rain. The precipitation percentage was low, so neither Drake nor Allie thought twice about going out geocaching all day.

Drake looked at the sky, then at Allie. "Maybe you should help me now. I want to grab this one before we get poured on."

Allie nodded. "I'll take this half."

While Drake continued his search from above, Allie got on her knees and bent over so she could examine the bench from below.

"You know what this thing is supposed to be?" Drake asked.

"No. The description didn't say, but it has to be magnetic, right? Most bench caches are."

The sky darkened, and the thunder rumbled again, this time much closer.

"We need to finish this up. I just got pelted in the head by a raindrop," Drake said.

"At least it hit you where it would do the least amount of damage. Just give me a minute. There's only so many places it can be, right?"

Drake looked up at the sky where he tracked a large

black cloud headed in their direction.

"Got it!" Allie yelled. She got off her knees and sat on the bench. In her hand was a pocket cache, which was a small plastic baggie surrounded by black duct tape and pressed flat to conform to the shape of the bench frame. "That was a tough one. The black tape matched the frame color perfectly. Quick, sign this."

Drake and Allie signed the log. Allie returned the cache to its hiding spot, and the pair started jogging toward Drake's truck. As they moved, a bolt of horizontal lightning traced across the sky, followed by a peal of thunder that echoed along the ground beneath their feet.

With fifty feet to go to reach safety, the skies opened up and heavy rain fell, drenching the friends in the downpour.

Allie got to the truck first. "Open the door!"

Drake thrust his hand into his pocket, pulled out his keys, and dropped them on the ground. It took him a couple of seconds to retrieve them, hit the fob, and unlock the door. Allie and Drake slid into the front seats and watched the deluge through the windshield.

Allie took off her Boston Red Sox baseball cap and set it on the dashboard, then ran her fingers through her long red hair. "Can you turn on the heat? I got a chill from the rain."

In response, Drake started the engine and turned on the heat. "Better?"

"I will be in a bit, thanks."

Drake felt a drop of water hit his nose. He looked in the rear-view mirror and saw the source. A wisp of his blond hair had fallen over his forehead and acted as a funnel point for the extra water in his wet hair. He noticed another drop accumulating, so he wiped it away with his hand. He leaned into the backseat of his truck, found a sweatshirt, and used it to towel his hair dry.

When he finished, he held the damp shirt out to Allie.

"Want to use this?"

Allie took the sweatshirt and blotted the rain from her face with a dry sleeve. When she finished, she handed the sweatshirt back to Drake, and he tossed it back where he'd gotten it from.

"What do you think Cacheland is like?" she asked.

Drake shrugged. "I don't know for sure. From what I heard, some rich guy bought up an old ghost town, spent some money fixing it up, and hid a bunch of geocaches there. I picture it like an old western movie set, but I have seen no photos or anything. All I can find on the Internet is a paragraph about the old town's history, which wasn't much, and a general idea of where it is on the map."

"That's not much help."

"Sorry. But don't worry, we'll find out when we get there."

"True enough. You think we can win that fifty grand?"

Drake checked his hazel eyes in the mirror. He'd missed a drop of rain and wiped it away from his left eyelid. "Why not? We've got twenty-thousand finds between us, so I'll bet we've got just as good of a chance as anyone else there."

"Depends on who else is going to be there. Even around here, we're not the most prolific geocachers. And you know we both have problems with some mystery caches."

Drake made a fist and did a soft double tap on Allie's knee. "Hey, don't worry about it now. It's still six months away, and all we can do is the best we can do. Besides, whether we come in first place or last place, we still get a free week's vacation out of it, right?"

Allie nodded and smiled.

The pair waited a few minutes, and as they did, the rain slowed and eventually stopped altogether. Off to the west, the clouds lightened from dark gray to white, and the sun peeked out between a break in them.

Drake pointed at the sun. "See there, rain is gone. Want to find some more caches?"

"Nah, everything is too wet, and I'm not wearing the right shoes. Let's call it a day, okay?"

Drake agreed, started the truck, and headed for home.

CHAPTER TWO

Allie watched the ground get closer as the plane came in for a landing at Phoenix Sky Harbor International Airport. It overjoyed Allie that Drake had given her the window seat since she loved to watch the clouds roll by the plane. She also liked to doze off occasionally and enjoyed the cool feel of the plane's fuselage she leaned her head against. Drake had lucked out because even though the middle seat was his assigned one, the aisle seat was unoccupied, so he sat in that one and left the middle one empty.

"Everything okay out there?" Drake asked.

"Yep. Looks like the city is still standing, so I think we're good. You ready for the big adventure?"

"I'm ready to get off this plane. It's been a long ride."

It was only a four-hour flight from Nashville to Phoenix, but since Drake didn't like to fly in the first place, it seemed like forever to him.

"The flight wasn't that long," Allie said.

"You're only saying that because you slept most of the way."

Drake clutched the armrests as the plane touched down. Then, unlike most of the people on board, he waited until the plane came to a complete stop at the terminal before undoing his seatbelt and standing up. He removed his backpack from beneath the seat and slipped it over his shoulders. Afterward, he opened the overhead bin and removed his and Allie's carry-on luggage and placed them in the aisle, one in front of him, and one behind him. He waited patiently for the people in front of him to leave, then grabbed both bags and carried them off the plane.

Drake stopped once he got onto the jet bridge, extended the luggage handles, and passed Allie's case over to her when she caught up with him. Together, they walked through the terminal and down the escalator to the baggage claim area.

When they got to the bottom floor, Allie spotted a man with a sign. "Hey, look. Decker, Ashe, and Beasley. That must be us."

Drake and Allie approached the man, and Allie waved to him when they got to within six feet.

"Hi. I'm Drake Decker, and this is Allie Ashe. You are waiting for us?"

"Yes, I am. I'm Andy Johns. I'll be driving you out to Cacheland. If you can take a seat over there by the wall, we're waiting for one other group who should arrive shortly."

"Okay, sure," Drake said.

Allie and Drake wandered over to the seats and sat down to wait. After fifteen minutes, Drake watched as two men stepped off the escalator and approached Andy. They all shook hands, then Andy waved at him and Allie to join them at the door.

"Come with me," Andy said as he gathered the group.

The gang of four followed Andy out into the Phoenix day, across the pickup area, and into the short-term parking garage. He led them to a white Ford eight-passenger van. "Leave your luggage at the rear and climb aboard. There's a cooler with bottled water in there if you like."

While Andy loaded the luggage into the back of the van, Drake and Allie took the bench seat behind the driver, and the two men climbed into the row behind them.

"Hi. I'm Drake Decker, and this is Allie Ashe," Drake said, as he turned in his seat and offered his hand.

"We're the Beasley brothers. I'm Brandon, and this is Ben."

Drake could tell they were brothers, since they were almost identical twins. They had the same oval-shaped face, same brown eyes, and same build. Both had brown hair. Brandon wore his cut short, Ben wore his longer, pulled into a ponytail in the back.

"Are you avid cachers?" Allie asked.

"I've been into it for a few years. Brandon just picked it up like six years ago," Ben answered. "Where are you from?"

"We're from the Nashville area. What about you?"

"Youngstown, Ohio," Brandon answered.

Andy slid into the driver's seat and donned his seatbelt. "We're ready to go. Anyone want to find a few geocaches along the way?"

"How long is the ride to Cacheland?" Brandon asked.

"A little over an hour, depending on traffic."

"Where is it, exactly?" Allie asked.

"It's a little less than halfway between Phoenix and Yuma, not too much off of I-8."

"I don't know where that is."

Andy laughed. "Not too many people do. Bruce will explain the layout over dinner tonight, and you should have a bit of time to wander around, so you'll get a feel for the area. Now, what about those caches?"

"Yes! Let's do it!" Ben yelled from the backseat.

"Great." Andy set a destination into his navigation system and settled in for the drive. "We'll be there in about thirty minutes. In the meantime, sit back and enjoy the ride."

Andy turned on the radio and the group listened to various hits from the 80s as they watched the desert race by. They followed I-10 west, then Andy turned south on state route eighty-five. He drove for a few minutes, then turned off the highway. The van threw up clouds of dust as Andy drove slowly down the dirt road to keep the plume from getting too large. A half mile later, he pulled into a turnoff and shut off the engine.

"Do you guys primarily use phone apps or handheld units for caching?" Andy asked.

Brandon, Ben, and Drake answered they used their phones. Allie mentioned she used both, depending on the environment and circumstances.

"Your phones will suffice for this one," Andy said. "You'll get good satellite reception here. The cache you're looking for is called 'Ridgeway's Ridge Hide'. It's a terrain three, difficulty two. Anyone who doesn't want to go for it can stay with me in the van. Should take you fifteen or twenty minutes to find, depending on how well you navigate the terrain."

The four geocachers left the van and checked their phone apps to look for the correct geocache.

"It's only fifteen-tenths of a mile away," Brandon said, being the first one to find it. "There's no way that will take as long as twenty minutes."

Allie looked at her compass and aligned herself in the correct direction. "Yeah, but it's over that," she said as she pointed to the steep slope that started about thirty yards from the roadway.

"Well, we won't find it standing around here," Ben said. "Let's go."

Ben took a step and stopped when Andy called out. "Hey! Watch out for rattlesnakes, and make sure you've got firm footing going up and down that thing. I don't want any blood in the van."

"You're kidding, right?" Ben asked, turning his head to read Andy's facial expressions. "About the blood?"

Andy scowled. "Of course I'm not kidding. The blood comes off the seats okay, but it's a bear to wash out of the carpet."

Allie glanced at Andy, who passed her a quick wink.

Ready for the adventure, the quartet headed toward the slope. The closer they got, the steeper it looked.

"Oh, man, there's no way I can make it up to the top of that thing," Brandon said.

Ben was quick to offer encouragement. "Chicken. Sure you can. Just lean forward, keep your feet sideways, and keep moving, and we'll be up there in no time."

Drake stepped forward to go with the brothers, but Allie stopped and grabbed his arm. "Let's see how they do."

The Beasleys started off fast enough, but about a third of the way up, they slowed considerably. At one point, Ben windmilled his arms and looked like he was going to hurtle right to the ground, but Brandon saved the day when he pushed Ben toward the slope.

"There's got to be a better way up there," Allie said.

Allie walked along the base of the ridge for fifty yards while Drake stayed where he was and watched the brother's slow ascent.

"Hey, over here. Come on," Allie called out.

Drake looked over and saw Allie beckoning him to join her, and he jogged over to her side. Allie pointed out what looked to be an old wash carved into the rock. The angle of the terrain was much less severe, but there were larger boulders to contend with.

Allie grabbed Drake's arm. "Come on. I want to beat them to the cache if we can."

Drake took the lead and, using his eyes, he mapped out a good trail as he walked with Allie right behind him. About halfway up, they came across a large boulder that stood seven feet high and jutted out into the channel almost to the opposite wall.

"Can we squeeze past it?" Allie asked.

Drake approached the boulder and surveyed the situation. "It looks like it goes through. There's about a two-foot gap here. We should be able to get to the other side without a problem. Want me to go first?"

"Yeah, go ahead. Watch for rattlesnakes."

Drake looked back at Allie and rolled his eyes. "Ha. Ha."

He positioned himself parallel to the rock wall, then sidestepped slowly into the gap. Less than a minute later, he yelled for Allie to join him, so she did just like he did, and a few moments later, she joined him on the other side.

"Easy peasy," Drake said. "And it looks like we're about twenty yards from the top of the ridge. You ready?"

Allie nodded. "Ready."

The angle of ascent lessened the farther they climbed, so they picked up speed as they scampered up the hill. Once at the top, Allie stopped them. She checked her compass and pointed off in the distance. "I think it's in that tree over yonder."

"Over yonder?" Drake teased as they started walking again.

"Yeah. I'm breaking out my western talk."

Drake shook his head as they stepped across the desert, avoiding the brush and watching for snakes as they went.

As they got close, Drake pointed out an oddly stacked pile of rocks at the tree's trunk. "I'll bet it's right there. I'll go get it."

"No, wait," Allie said. "Look at those thorns."

Not having focused on the environment, Drake stepped closer and examined the branches. Sure enough, thorns between two and three inches long covered the full length of each branch. Rather than a normal tree that grew up and out, this tree peaked in height at just over six feet and its branches curled to the ground, like an umbrella.

"What the heck kind of tree is this?" Drake asked.

"I don't know. A prickly one? Walk around it, see if you can find an easier way in."

Drake did as he was told and circled the tree. On the far side of where he had been standing, he found a spot where the branches grew apart from each other. He took a breath, squatted as far down as he could, and duck-walked toward the tree's center. Once there, he removed the top rock from the pile and set it aside.

"It's an ammo can. Come around to this side and I'll pass you the logbook."

Allie moved to the opposite side of the tree. She heard voices, so she looked up and saw the brothers at last approaching ground zero.

"Hello, Beasleys. It took you long enough to get here," Allie teased.

Brandon and Ben joined Allie. Brandon pointed at Allie, then toward the way from which they'd come. "How'd you get up here so fast?"

Allie shrugged. "I don't know. Part mountain goat, I guess."

"Hey, take this," Drake interjected.

Allie looked over at the notebook at the end of Drake's outstretched arm, took it, and signed her nickname to it. "You boys want me to hand it to you, or do you want to go in and get it?"

Ben reached out for a branch and touched the tip of a thorn. A small drop of blood appeared, and he let the branch go. "I'll sign it here."

Allie passed the logbook around, then handed it back to Drake, who returned it to the ammo can, then put everything back the way he found it. He got into his squat position and backed away from the tree. He stood and wiped his hands together to clear away the dust.

"Ready?" Allie asked.

"Yep. Let's go. You guys going the same way down, or do you want to take an easier route?"

Ben answered without collaborating with his brother. "Lead the way."

Five minutes later, the group arrived at the van. Andy had the rear door open and was sitting on the back bumper reading a book. The sunlight gleamed off his bald head, and somehow he had no trouble reading in spite of the dark sunglasses he wore. "You're back already?"

"Have you gotten that cache, Andy?" Drake asked.

Andy slid a dollar bill between the pages to mark his spot. "Yes, of course."

"Did you know about that wash?"

Andy nodded his head. "Yes. I went that way myself when I first searched for that cache."

Brandon stepped forward and pointed at the ridge. "And you let us go up there? Why didn't you tell us there is an easier way?"

Andy gave them a sly smile, closed the back door, and moved to the front. From the cooler on the passenger floor, he extracted four bottles of water and passed them out to the group. "To answer your question, I'm under orders by the boss not to give any geocacher any hints or advice to help them find a cache. That includes offering direction on which way to go."

"And what if one of us would have slipped and fallen?" Ben asked.

"Well, in that case, I would have determined if you received any injuries. If yes, I would have either patched you up myself or taken you to the nearest hospital. If not, I would have suggested you get back at it," Andy laughed. "My orders are to not help you find caches, not to let you die an agonizing death in the desert. Now, if you would, please get in the van. We need to get back on the road."

The crew climbed into the van, Andy did a U-turn and headed back toward the highway.

"Do you know how many groups they invited to Cacheland?" Drake asked.

"Of course. There are ten teams, so twenty geocachers."

"So we have a one-in-ten chance at that big cash prize," Ben said. "I love those odds."

Brandon hit Ben's shoulder. "Don't say that. You don't know who or what we're up against."

"Any of the others here yet?" Drake asked.

Andy shook his head. "No. You're the first to get here, unless a team driving in has arrived since I've been gone."

"You mean we could have driven here?" Ben asked.

"Sure," Andy said, "but we didn't offer that option to everyone. There's a team coming from Las Vegas, and one from Los Angeles. They were close enough that it was more convenient for them to drive. Oh, and the Texas team. They insisted on driving. Those three teams will arrive on their own, and I'll be making two more trips to pick people up from the airport."

"Sounds like a long day for you," Allie said.

"I don't mind. I like to drive."

"What else can you tell us about Cacheland?" Ben asked.

Andy smiled. "Oh, all kinds of things, but unfortunately…"

"Let me guess," Ben interrupted. "You're not allowed to talk about it?"

With an imaginary key, Andy locked his lips, then tossed the key out the window. "Even if I could tell you, I wouldn't. That would spoil all the surprises. Now please, sit back and enjoy the ride."

Thirty-five minutes later, Andy pulled off the highway onto a dirt road. After a fleeting moment, they passed under a stone arch, supported by two columns cut from a gray granite. The arch held a sign with letters made of various colored stones that spelled out 'Cacheland'. Almost immediately after he entered the property, Andy passed over a cattle guard, and for five minutes, they drove on as around them; the landscape changed. The scrub brush gave way to field crops on either side of the road, and where the crops ended, the old ghost town came into view. Andy drove through the town past several buildings until he arrived at the hotel, and once there, he parked, and everyone got out of the van.

"This is amazing," Allie said.

"Yeah, not what I expected at all," Drake added. In his mind, when he heard Cacheland was a converted ghost town, he expected old, rundown buildings with that gray, weathered look of abandonment. Instead, when he turned in a circle, he saw all the buildings that surrounded him, including the hotel, a bank, a general store, and a jail, all wore a fresh coat of paint. He stepped past the van and glanced down the street, and every building looked like it was brand new.

"If you'll all grab your luggage and follow me into the hotel," Andy requested.

The quartet entered the hotel lobby, and again, the sight impressed Drake. Although the furnishings and decorations looked to be right out of the old west, everything had a modern feel to it.

"May I have your name, sir?"

Drake followed the voice and realized it was the hotel clerk speaking to him. He smiled at her, then gave her his name. He noted the clerk checked him in on a modern computer, then slid a large brass key across the counter. Drake picked up the key and saw he was in room seven.

"Please drop off your key with us anytime you leave the hotel, sir. Your room is upstairs and to the right. Mr. Wiens requests you don't leave the hotel until called for dinner, but you're free to use the hotel parlor, which is through that archway to your left."

Drake nodded and stepped aside so the clerk could assist Allie. As he waited, he wandered to the parlor and looked inside. In the room's center stood an old-fashioned pool table. The far wall held a giant fireplace, with leather-bound chairs set in an arc around it. On his left, the wall held floor to ceiling bookcases, each stuffed to capacity. The view to his right surprised him. There was a table setup with two ultra-modern computers, and beyond that was a big screen LCD television hanging on the wall.

"Oh wow, cool room," Allie said.

Drake hadn't detected her approach. "Yeah, it is interesting. All checked in?"

Allie held up her key. "Yep. I'm number eight."

Drake and Allie carried their luggage up the stairs, and Allie waited to get by while Drake unlocked the door to number seven and stepped in.

The room, like the lobby, contained an old west decor, complete with black-and-white photos on the walls. Drake set down his suitcase and pressed his hand against the bed.

He expected an old-fashioned feather bed, but it, along with the lamps and alarm clock, was for certain modern. Although it wasn't as large as the one in the parlor, there was a television mounted on the wall. He stepped into the bathroom. There was a rainfall shower, an LED-backlit mirror, and plush towels folded neatly on the shelf beneath his sink. He heard a tap at the door and turned around.

"You left your door open," Allie said.

"Is your room as nice as this?"

"Exactly the same, except I've got pictures of old locomotives on the walls. Well, we can't leave until dinner. What should we do?"

Drake shrugged. "Well, if you don't want to take a nap or watch TV in your room, I guess we should head on down to the parlor."

Drake and Allie wandered back down the stairs and found the Beasley brothers already in the parlor. Brandon looked up from the pool table, slouched over, stick in hand, ready to sink the eight ball.

"Either of you like a game?" Brandon asked as he stood erect.

Drake nodded and headed for the stand rack that held the pool cues while Brandon circled the table and removed the balls from the pockets.

"You can break," Brandon said as he racked the balls.

While the men started the game, Allie nodded to Ben, who was busy watching a soccer match on television, and made her way to the wall of bookshelves. Allie stopped in the center and scanned through the books. When a title caught her attention, she picked the volume from the shelf, read a few pages, and put it back where she found it.

Andy showed up with the last group of geocachers at ten minutes after five, and at five-thirty, he entered the parlor, cleared his throat, and spoke. "It's time for dinner. Everyone, please follow me."

Drake and Allie held back and followed behind the group that had assembled in the parlor. The number of geocachers swelled to twice as many in the lobby, and Andy stopped everyone there and did a quick count. Once satisfied he had everyone, Andy escorted the large group outside into the warm October sun. They turned left out of the hotel and walked past a doctor's office and a bakery before they arrived at the restaurant.

Inside, the staff had pushed most of the four-person rustic wood tables into the center of the room to make one large table. The table sat twenty-two people, ten on each side, and one at each end, and each place setting contained cloth placemats and napkins, and heavy cutlery. Andy stopped at a spot at the table's head and invited everyone else to sit. Before he sat, Andy gestured to the empty chair at the table's opposite end. "Ladies and gentlemen, I present to you the owner of Cacheland and your host for the week, Mr. Bruce Wiens."

The geocachers applauded as Bruce stepped over to his chair. Bruce was tall, standing a couple of inches over six feet. He had sparkling blue eyes, and hair the color of fresh-fallen snow with a neatly trimmed beard to match. He wore khaki pants and a dark-blue t-shirt with a white compass on the front breast pocket.

"Please, no, stop. You're embarrassing me." Bruce waited until the clapping ended. "First and most important, congratulations for being here and competing in what I hope will be an annual challenge."

A woman at the far end of the table raised her hand to get Bruce's attention.

"Yes?" Bruce asked.

"Can I ask a question?"

"If you could, please hold all your questions for now. What I'd like to do is go around and have you introduce yourselves, and then we'll do the questions and answers during dinner. Let's start with you."

Drake liked the idea of summing up the competition, so he leaned back and focused on the people gathered around the table.

"Of course, I'd have to go first," the woman said, unsure of herself. To her credit, she regained her composure and smiled. "Hi everyone, I'm Penny. I'm from Henderson, which is a Las Vegas suburb. And this is my best friend, Cindy." Penny gently placed her hand on Cindy's shoulder, and in response, Cindy gave the table a half-wave.

Drake looked at the two women. Penny had long, dark brown hair pulled into a tight ponytail and dark brown eyes. She was thin, yet based on the biceps straining against her t-shirt, she looked to be physically fit. Cindy looked shorter and less physically imposing than Penny, and had the same color hair as Penny, but hers had hints of gray throughout. Her eyes were hazel, and she wore red-rimmed glasses.

Next to Cindy were the Texans, Mike Gallagher and Ricky Barker. Both men dressed in sleeveless t-shirts to show off their muscular upper bodies, and both wore blue jeans featuring oversized belt buckles. As they introduced themselves, Drake thought they were the most physically fit team at the table by far. He didn't fear them though, because he also knew that geocaching often involved more than having the ability to bench press a Volvo.

Drake followed along as team after team introduced themselves. After the Texans came a nice, older married couple from Seattle, Jodi and Zach Collier. Drake guessed they were in their upper fifties, or early sixties, and were both soft speakers. If Drake hadn't been sitting right next to Jodi, he probably would have needed to strain to hear her. Drake liked them immediately. Zach wore glasses a little too large for his face, and they kept slipping down his nose as he introduced himself.

Next to the Colliers were Drake and Allie. Rather than do the speaking for the team, Drake nudged Allie in the ribs and prompted her to do all the talking. The last team on that side of the table were another married couple, Will Landry and Julius Connor. As they introduced themselves, they mentioned that besides geocaching; the couple ran ultra-marathons, but Drake could guess that based on the runner's build that each man had.

To Andy's left, who sat at the opposite end of the table from Bruce, were an engaged couple, Marina Blake and Tito Leija, from Los Angeles. Next to them were three sets of friends: Geneva Benson and Ingrid Snyder from Boston, Gilberto Foster and Roy Pace from Des Moines, and Kerry McElroy and Emma Sosa from Raleigh. The Beasley brothers were the last team at the table.

Bruce welcomed everyone individually with greetings and nods as they circled around the table. After Brandon introduced himself and his brother, Bruce rang a small silver bell and five servers came out of the kitchen, each pushing a small cart. Four carts held salads on fine china that were dispersed among the guests. The fifth cart contained several bottles of wine and pitchers of water and tea. When everyone had a drink and a salad, Bruce tapped his fork against his glass to get everyone's attention.

Bruce set down his fork and picked up his wineglass. "Again, I welcome you all, and I offer a toast. To a fun week, and new friendships. Now, dig in." Bruce had a sip, took his seat, and found his fork. The others around the table took the cue and soon silverware clinked against plates as the diners started in on their salads.

Penny put down her fork and raised her hand again. "Excuse me, Bruce. You said we could ask questions during dinner."

Bruce was in mid-chew, so he swallowed his food and set down his fork. "Sure, go ahead."

"What's the story behind Cacheland? Why would you build a place like this?"

"Ah, that's a brilliant question. About ten years ago, I was more than ready to retire, so I sold off all but one of my businesses. Something I hadn't accounted for was what I'd do next. You know, when I didn't have to go into the office every day. Or spend countless hours at board meetings. Or attend those ghastly social events in the evenings that I never wanted to attend to begin with. Just by happenstance, I was sitting on a bench in Central Park in New York, enjoying a warm spring day, when a young man walked by me staring at this phone. At the time, I thought nothing of it, because everyone stares at their phones these days. But the unusual thing was, he wandered over to a nearby tree and started doing circles around it. I realized that was odd, even for New York, and I was curious, so I went over and asked him what he was doing. He said he was geocaching. Of course, I didn't know what that was, so I asked for more information. After he explained it to me, I asked if I could help him find it. To my delight he said yes! Together we looked all around that tree for a good ten minutes, then he recommended we spread out and look at other trees in the area. Can you believe I found it before he did? It turned out to be a pill fob, wrapped in tape that matched the color of that tree's bark perfectly! Let me tell you, from right there I was hooked. The next day, I signed up for my geocaching account and started out on my own adventures."

"Have you found many caches since then?" Roy asked.

"Oh, sure, thousands of them. Since I started, I have geocached in all fifty states, and probably half the countries on the planet. That sound about right, Andy?"

"I'd need to check your profile, sir, but that seems accurate to me."

Marina raised her fork instead of her hand. "But what about Cacheland? How did this happen?"

Bruce grinned and took a big bite of his salad and chowed it down.

"Well, Marla,"

"Marina," she corrected.

"Sorry, Marina. I apologize. I should have passed out name tags. Andy, take a note to add name tags."

Andy nodded, picked up his phone, and noted the request.

"I'd have to blame Cacheland partially on Clint Eastwood. I've always loved those old Clint Eastwood westerns. You know, like The Good, the Bad, and the Ugly, or High Plains Drifter. I loved the western town sets with the old buildings, wooden sidewalks, the saloons, even the horse troughs in front of the buildings. I've always wanted to live in one of those towns. Then, as if willed by the universe, I heard from a friend about an old ghost town that was up for sale, and at a bargain at that! So, I bought it. Then, I imagined how fun it would be to dedicate that town to geocaching. To make it a destination that every geocacher would want to visit. So, over the course of three years, I had a construction team come in and repair and update the buildings to make it an experience people would enjoy."

"Besides the hotel and this restaurant, are any of the buildings functional?" another geocacher asked.

"Oh, yes, um,"

"Emma."

"Emma, of course. Andy, we need nametags. Make a note of that, will you? Most of the buildings are. Inside the general store, you can buy basic supplies and souvenirs. The bakery next door produces the baked goods for the restaurant, or you can go in there and buy things like cookies and other treats. I'd recommend the macadamia nut brownies. In the livery, there are a few horses to take out. At the church, I've arranged for a preacher to come in for Sunday services for those who want to attend. The doctor's office is a fully functioning clinic to handle those geocaching mishaps, anything from a splinter in the finger to a broken leg."

"What about the jail?" Kerry asked.

Bruce laughed. "Actually, the jail can function as a holding cell if there is a need for it. I have a small security team, and the head of it recommended we have the cell as a contingency, although I hope we never need to use it."

The service team came through and cleared away the salad plates, then returned a few minutes later with dinner plates. The server slid a meal in front of Drake, and his mouth watered when he looked down and saw the Cornish Hen paired with a mushroom rice and glazed carrots.

Allie leaned over toward him. "Looks delicious, doesn't it?"

Drake nodded, then grabbed his knife and fork. He cut into the delicate bird, sliced off a piece of meat, and ate it. He leaned back in his chair as he chewed. "This is amazing," he said as he grabbed his wine and drank.

The questions died off as the participants enjoyed the main course, but as they polished off the meals, more hands rose in the air.

Tito's was first. "Mr. Wiens, how were we selected? I mean, to come here and take part in the challenge."

"First off, I insist you all call me Bruce. To answer your question, it was a pure chance. We had over twenty thousand entrants from all over the country, and we randomly drew your names. It turns out we ended up with quite a mix of geocachers. Some of you have geocached for only a year, others have a good decade of experience. Several of you have a few hundred finds, others, ten thousand or more."

Cindy raised her hand. "Won't the geocachers that have a lot of finds over several years have an advantage in the competition?"

Bruce shook his head. "No. We think we've added enough twists and things to make sure that you all have an equal chance of winning the cash prize. For example..." Bruce trailed off his thought, then grinned. "You almost got me to give away a secret or two there, but it will not work! You'll learn how everything will play out after breakfast tomorrow."

"Can we explore the town after dinner?" Drake asked.

Bruce smiled. "Sure, with some limits. I ask that you don't go past the buildings or venture out into the desert. Tomorrow, I'll go over just how big the area is, and until then, I don't want you getting lost. Also, I ask everyone to be in the hotel by ten. Andy will take attendance, and if you're not in the hotel, he'll disqualify you from the competition."

"Why?" Drake asked.

"After ten, my crew will set out tomorrow's geocaches. Each night the game board will change, so we ask that you be inside when that happens. I feel that will keep the game fair for everyone."

Bruce rang his bell again, and the servers appeared and cleared away the dinner plates. A few minutes later, they returned with slices of cheesecake covered with fresh raspberries and a chocolate drizzle.

Once again, forks met the plates, and after she took her first bite, Jodi raised her hand. "Sorry, one last question."

Bruce looked up from his dessert. "Yes?"

"Are we going to eat like this all week?"

If there was any tension in the room, that question broke it, and everyone laughed.

Thirty minutes later, Drake and Allie were back at the hotel. They spent a few minutes after dinner investigating the buildings, but since everything except the hotel was closed, it didn't take long.

At the hotel, the bartender wheeled a portable bar into the parlor. There, the bartender opened a beer bottle for Allie and a can of cola for Drake, and together, they found a small table.

Allie took a long draw of her beer, then swallowed it and let a burp loose.

"That was a good one," Drake said.

"Oh, hush. So, what do you think about the competition?"

Drake shrugged. "Not sure. It's kinda hard to tell, isn't it? Obviously, the Texans are the most athletic here and could possess the clear advantage."

"Yeah, but that doesn't always translate well to geocaching. I mean, look at this morning, for example. The brothers had quite the jump on us, and although they were strong enough to conquer that hill, we still made the find before they did. Brains over brawn will probably be better. Let me ask you this question: how would you feel about teaming up with some of these guys?"

"What? You mean like an alliance?" Drake asked.

"Sure. Who would you take if you could?"

Drake sat back in his chair and took a drink of his cola. He turned the can in his hand as he thought. "Well, I think the first couple I'd take are the married guys. What were their names? Will and James?"

"Julius. Why would you pick them?"

"I liked how they run marathons, and they're experienced cachers. Who would you want?"

"Emma and Kerry really impressed me. He's like a scientist or something, right? And she's a teacher, so they're probably both pretty smart. We could use some smart on the team to make up for what you don't have." Allie laughed.

Drake nodded. "Yeah, we could use more smart for sure. Should we talk to them now?"

"The sooner the better." Allie finished her beer and headed to the bar for another. She soon returned to the table with a fresh bottle in hand. "I don't see any of them. Maybe they retired to their rooms for the night."

"Could be." Drake removed his phone from this pocket and checked the time. "It's a few minutes after ten, so they need to be here in the hotel somewhere. I'll go check with the front desk."

Drake set his cola aside and went to the front desk. When he arrived, he found Andy setting up gold stanchion posts on either side of the front door. Once they were in position, he clipped a red velvet rope between them.

"What are you doing?" Drake asked.

Andy turned around when he finished. "It's after ten, sir. This is just a reminder to not leave the building."

"What if there's an emergency or something? Or we need something to eat?"

"Not to worry. We didn't lock the doors. If there's a fire or something, everyone will get out just fine. If you have another type of emergency, Heather will be at the desk tonight, and she'll be able to help you, or contact the doctor if you need one. As for getting hungry, there's a room service menu in the drawer by your room phone."

"Okay. Sounds like you've got it all worked out. But how do you know someone won't sneak out when Heather uses the restroom?"

Andy pointed toward the ceiling above Drake's head. Drake turned around and spotted the small video camera built into the crown molding in the corner. He would never have noticed it had Andy not pointed it out.

"We have eyes in the sky by all the doors. There are also cameras outside to give us a live street view. So we'll know right away if someone is out and about."

"Seems like you thought of everything."

"We tried to, sir."

"Drake."

"We tried to, Drake. Is there anything Heather and I can help you with right now?"

Drake shook his head. "No, thank you. I guess I'll go grab my partner and head off to bed."

"Great idea. Tomorrow's a big day, Drake. Good luck."

Andy shook Drake's hand, then disappeared down a hallway. Without being overly suspicious, Drake walked past the front desk and scanned the hooks where the keys hung and saw all the hooks were empty.

"Have a pleasant night," Heather said as Drake walked past.

Drake returned to the parlor and scanned the faces in the room before he rejoined Allie. "It looks like a couple of people have left. I'm pretty sure the ones we want are in their rooms already."

Allie finished her beer and set her bottle next to the first one. "We'll catch them after breakfast then and see about an alliance, unless you know for sure which rooms they're in."

"I have no clue, and I'm not about to ask the desk clerk. Let's hit the sack for the night. I have a feeling tomorrow's going to be a tiring day."

CHAPTER FOUR

At seven-thirty, Drake heard a rap on his door, and when he opened it, Allie was standing there in blue jeans, a t-shirt, and a light black jacket. Around her waist was a fanny pack with a multi-colored unicorn on it, so Drake knew she was already prepared for business.

"Good morning. It's time for breakfast," Allie said.

"I'm coming." Drake looked around to check that he had everything he needed, then left the room and closed the door behind him. Geocachers crowded the hallway as everyone headed to the same place at the same time.

Drake and Allie followed the crowd down the stairs, out the door, and over to the restaurant. The large table still dominated the center of the room, but a large, flat screen television now sat on a portable stand behind Bruce's chair. Unlike the day before, Bruce was already there, greeting people as they entered, and directing them to empty chairs. Once everyone had found their seats, Bruce rang his tiny bell, and his army of servers appeared with a choice of coffee, juice, water, or tea. When everyone had a drink, the servers returned with platters of blueberry pancakes, bacon, and sausages.

Once everyone finished their morning meals, Bruce stood.

"Everything ready, Andy?"

At his seat, Andy had a laptop which was connected to the television via a long HDMI cable. "I'm ready any time you are, Bruce."

"I'm glad to see everyone this morning. This breakfast was the last meal we'll share all together until dinner the final evening. Until then, when you eat is up to you. The restaurant will serve breakfast between six and ten, lunch between eleven and two, and dinner from five to eight. If you prefer lunch on the go, there will be sack lunches available for you. There are several coolers set out along the main drag in several places filled with bottled water, so make sure you get plenty to drink. Dehydration is a genuine concern, even during this time of the year. Okay, Andy, first slide."

Andy used a remote to turn on the screen, and a few seconds later, a plat map appeared. There was an irregular-shaped box outlined in red.

"The Cacheland property is just over ten-thousand acres, which translates into over fifteen square miles. That includes this little town, and the crops you drove past on the way in, which is located here."

Bruce removed an extending pointer from his pocket and opened it to its full length. He looked at the map for a moment and pointed out where they were, which appeared to be on the southern edge of the property.

"Next slide."

The image switched. The large map disappeared and was replaced with a hand-drawn map of the Cacheland property.

"Again, here's where we are, and a general idea of the surrounding terrain and landmarks. There are a couple of abandoned mines in the area. Here, and…here. Avoid those and do not enter. To the north, the Gila River bisects the property, and to the northwest, there's a large mesa. Other than the cropland, and the area around the river, the landscape is just what you'd expect to find in the desert. Lots of scrub brush and rocks."

"How do we know where the property ends?" Tito asked.

"It's all fenced in, and every thirty feet, there's a red and blue striped ribbon that looks like this."

Bruce reached into his pocket and extracted a length of nylon ribbon that had red on one half and blue on the other. He held it up for all to inspect, then set it on the table before him.

"The general rule is, if you come across a fence, don't cross it and you'll be good. There will be no geocaches for the competition placed outside of the Cacheland boundaries."

"How do we get around?" Emma asked.

Bruce held up three fingers. "Option one is you walk everywhere. Option two is you go over to the stable and saddle up a horse. A warning, though. The stable boss over there will give you a little test to determine if you can actually handle a horse. If you can't, you'll need to find another mode of transportation. The third option is taking out a UTV, which is a large ATV that will seat both members of your team. Whether you go on horse or UTV, make sure you wear the proper safety equipment. The UTVs are in the large barn behind the stable. Whichever you choose, make sure you return it to where you got it by the end of each day. If you don't, you'll get a penalty. Andy, next slide."

The image flipped to a spreadsheet matrix with different geocache types along the top and team names going down the side.

"Here's how the competition will work. I divided it into five sections, as you can see. Those sections are traditional caches, letterbox caches, mystery caches, multi-caches, and gadget caches. Each day will focus on a different cache type. Today's type will be the traditional caches. There are one hundred geocaches hidden within the borders of Cacheland. They are different sizes, containers, difficulties, and terrains. Between the time I say 'go' in a few minutes here, and nine tonight, your goal is to find as many geocaches as you can. Each geocache is worth a certain number of points, between one and one hundred. We wrote those points on the inside lid of each container for you to keep track of if you like, but we'll do the official scoring so there's no need to track points yourself if you don't want to. Oh, and they're randomized. So don't assume that because a geocache has a higher terrain or difficulty, that cache will be worth more points than the easy one hidden beneath the porch steps of this restaurant. You must be back at the hotel tonight by nine or you'll get a penalty."

"Where can we download the coordinates?" Gilberto asked.

"Because these aren't official geocaches, you can't. Instead, each team will get one of these. Andy, hand me one of those bags, will you?"

Andy passed Bruce a drawstring backpack. Bruce opened the backpack and emptied the contents onto the table. As he explained each item, he held it up for all to see. "Each one of these bags contains the same items. A handheld GPS receiver with all the geocaches preloaded for you, along with a waypoint to tell you where the hotel is. There's a paper listing of all the caches so you can mark off the caches you found, and jot down the point value of each cache should you desire. There's a four-pack of fresh batteries, two gel pens, a self-inking stamp, a small first-aid kit, a compass, a topographic map of Cacheland, a range finder, tweezers, and a compact mirror. If you need any other tools of the trade, you'll have to make do with what you find out there in the wild. There's also a two-way radio if you sustain an injury, your UTV breaks down, you have problems with your horse, you get lost, or some other similar emergency. I'll have staff spread throughout the compound, so they should get to you pretty quickly. We will assign each team a different color, so there are two vests in here to wear. Keep them on during each day. You can't take anything with you, other than the supplies we give you. If you have anything on you like your cell phone or anything you'd normally take geocaching with you, I suggest you return it to your room before you depart. I know you're used to signing logs, but for this competition, we gave each team a unique stamp you will use on the log. Any caches you find that you don't stamp will not count toward your total finds. Understand?"

Bruce looked around the room, and no one responded in the negative.

"Good. After nine tonight, my team will collect all the geocaches, bring them in, and tally up the points. The team with the most points wins that day, and the team with the most points at the end of the last day will win the grand prize, and the illustrious golden horseshoe. Next slide, Andy."

Andy flipped to the following slide, which listed out a few last bullet points.

"Okay, the last of your ground rules. There is no joining up with other teams allowed. Also, you can't geocache without your teammate. So, if one of you breaks a leg, both of you are out of the competition. Only one team at a time can be at a cache, and that's where the range finder comes in. If you encounter a team at a potential geocache, you must stay at least one hundred yards away until the other team has left the area. Also, you must return the geocache to the exact location where you found it, and above all, you cannot remove a geocache and take it with you. Most times, we will secure the cache to make running off with it impossible anyway, but just in case some of you had the thought, forget it. Breaking any of the rules will get you a penalty. There's a full list of the rules and penalties in your backpack, along with the list of caches. Anyone have a question?"

There were none.

"Andy, hand out the bags, will you? Kerry and Emma, you're team black, so please step up here and get your backpack."

Drake and Allie waited until Andy came by and handed them a green backpack. They opened the backpack, checked to make sure they had all the mentioned gear, and put on the supplied vests.

"Well, the alliance idea is out the window," Allie said.

"True, but at least we know that we're all in the same boat. If anyone else had that idea, it's gone for them, too."

"Okay, one last thing," Bruce said. "The time now is fifteen minutes to nine. Make sure you know how to use your electronics. If you don't, come ask me or Andy, and we'll help you out. If you need to return anything to your rooms, you can do that now, but each team will need to leave one member here with us. At nine on the dot, today's challenge will begin."

"I guess I need to take my fanny pack back to my room," Allie said.

"Yeah, here, drop this off for me, will you?" Drake passed her his phone. "And grab my hat off the bed. I forgot it this morning."

Allie left the restaurant while Drake stayed seated. He turned on the radio, asked for a radio check, got one, and turned it off. Then he turned on the GPS and waited while it picked up a signal. When it did, he got into the map view and looked at all the treasure chests on the screen. There looked to be a hundred spread out all over the place, including one that was only a few feet away from where he sat. He found the paper cache list and the topographic map and tried to determine which caches to go for.

"Whatcha doing?" Allie asked when she rejoined him at the table.

"Trying to work out some kind of route here. Here's where we are. Looks like it gets pretty hilly to the northwest."

Allie bent over to get a closer look. "Yeah. Look, here's that mesa Bruce mentioned."

"I propose we do these in a rough circle to the northeast, which doesn't look as hard terrain-wise. We have about twelve hours, right? We'll determine how far we can get going out, then I'd say by two, we should start heading back this way, so we make it here by the deadline."

Allie nodded. "I like the plan. I assume we're taking a UTV?"

"That's a good assumption. I can't ride a horse, and I'm for sure not walking."

"Attention everyone!" Bruce yelled. "It's nine on the dot, so get going, and good luck!"

There was a mad scramble for the door as teams rushed forward and left the restaurant.

"I'll be right back. You pack up the stuff," Allie said.

"We need to leave!" Bruce countered.

"Just give me a minute, okay?"

Allie stepped into the restaurant's depths while Drake marked the first few geocaches he wanted to search for. Afterwards, he packed everything away into the backpack. A minute later, Allie reappeared carrying four brown paper lunch bags. She held them out and smiled. "I guess everyone else forgot Bruce said there were lunches to go. I'm not sure what's in here, but it will be better than nothing six hours from now."

"Good thinking, Al," Drake said. "Let's book."

Drake and Allie left the restaurant and stepped outside. They saw two teams walking toward the cropland, and one team was milling about the church, but no one else was within sight.

Drake stopped, bent over, and looked under the restaurant stairs. "Hey, there is one here. I thought Bruce was just kidding."

Drake reached under and extracted a peanut butter jar. He removed the cap, tipped it over, and a piece of paper fell into his hand. "Get the stamp."

While Drake unfolded the paper, Allie rummaged in the backpack for the stamp.

"Well, we won't get the first to find. Apparently, the black horseshoe team got that one."

"Team black was Kerry and Emma, so that figures."

"Put the log on something and I'll stamp it."

Drake placed the paper on the peanut butter jar cover and Allie stamped it. When she removed her hand, they saw a green four-leaf clover was sitting pretty next to the horseshoe.

"Okay, super," Drake said as he checked the inside of the cover, then put the log back in the jar and returned the jar under the stairs. "That cache was worth two points. We're well on our way to winning this thing! Let's go check out a vehicle and hit the road."

As they walked down the street, a UTV popped out on the road and headed away from them. They passed the stables and saw the Texans decked out in chaps and jeans headed out of the barn.

"Well, that tracks," Allie said as they watched the cowboys ride away.

The duo found the barn holding the UTVs, and when they stepped inside, they saw only four vehicles remaining.

A man wearing overalls appeared, rubbing his hands on a red rag. "I'm Travis. You want to check out a vehicle?"

Drake nodded. "Yes, we do."

"Ever driven one before?"

Allie stepped up in front of Drake. "I have. I used to ride them all the time at our summer place."

Travis nodded once. "Wait here, be right back." Travis went deeper into the barn, and a moment later, an engine came to life. It wasn't long before Travis parked the machine next to the couple and got out of the driver's seat. "This one's yours. Note the green flag on the back, and you've got matching helmets as well. There's a full tank of gas in here, and a spare five-gallon can on the back, so you should have plenty of fuel for the day. If you have any problems with her, contact me on the radio."

"Thanks," Drake said.

"Hey, there's a storage box here." Allie opened the box and set in the lunch bags. Drake put the lanyard of the GPS around his neck and put the backpack in the compartment with the lunches.

They put on their matching green helmets, Allie restarted the machine, and off they went.

"Where's the next stop?" Allie asked.

Drake looked at the unit. "About a half mile to the north-northeast." To help guide her, he stuck his arm out and pointed in the general direction.

Once they were out of the vicinity of town, the road disappeared, and they found themselves on a dirt trail. They followed it for a few hundred yards, then came to a place where the trail split off into a dozen different directions. Wheel tracks showed that five of them had UTV activity recently.

Allie hit the brakes and came to a stop. "Well, which way from here?"

Drake did a quick check and pointed off into the distance. "Follow those tire tracks on the right. We're down to under two-tenths of a mile, so take it slow."

Allie did as directed and drove off into the desert. "I really want to open this thing up and see how it does. It's not as much fun if you're not bouncing all over the place."

Drake looked at her as if she was nuts. "Maybe on the way back, okay? We're getting close. See that enormous pile of rocks? Stop over near those."

Allie slowed, then stopped. The pile of rocks was actually four large boulders that looked like eggs on end. They got out of the UTV and walked to the site.

"Remember, watch for snakes," Allie warned.

When they arrived at the boulders, they walked around them, but noticed nothing that looked remotely like a geocache. On the second circuit, Drake spotted a knotted length of rope stuck between two of the boulders. He grabbed the knot, loosened it from between the stones, and yanked. From the center of the boulders, he heard the telltale sign of metal scraping on rock as he pulled. A moment later, an ammo canister appeared. Drake took it from the hole, then set it on the ground and opened it.

"Nice, a fifteen pointer," he said as he scanned the can's lid. "Got the stamp?"

"Right here."

Allie took the paper and added their clover to the purple arrowhead on the log. "We're not the FTF on this one, either."

Drake closed up the can. "Doesn't matter. First To Finds aren't worth any additional points. All that matters is locating as many of these as we can."

They walked back to the UTV and took their seats. From his pocket, Drake extracted the cache list and checked off the one they just found and jotted down the points. He consulted the GPS to pick which one was next.

"Okay. Next one is a half mile or so to the east."

Allie shifted into Drive. "Just lead the way, man."

CHAPTER FIVE

W hat time you got?" Allie asked.

"Ten after twelve."

The UTV jostled as Allie went over a small hill, followed by a depression before they settled on even ground again. Drake grabbed onto the handle above the door frame, but he was too late, and his shoulder connected hard with the door when he shifted in his seat.

"Ow, hey. Pay attention to the road, will you?" Drake said as he rubbed the pain from his arm.

Allie laughed with a strange giddiness. "What road? You notice anything resembling an actual road around here?"

She slammed on the brakes, and the vehicle skidded to a sliding stop. Allie put the UTV into Park as the trail of dust caught up to the pair, and slowly overtook them before settling back to earth.

"Okay, where are we trying to go?" Allie asked.

Drake consulted the GPS unit and pointed due north. "A half mile that way."

"Give me the map, will you?"

Drake had tucked the map above his sun visor, so he pulled it out and handed it over. "Can you even read this thing?"

Allie shot him a glare and grabbed the map. "Of course I can. I was in the military, remember?" She unfolded the sheet of paper and studied the chart for a couple of minutes. "This would be a lot easier if they put the geocache locations on this thing."

"At least we have latitude and longitude markings on the map, so we can derive some sort of clue," Drake said.

"Great. What were the coords of the last place we were?"

Drake used the handheld to find the coordinates and passed them to Allie. Allie propped the map against the steering wheel and used her left index finger to trace the latitude, and her right to trace the longitude. She moved them inward at the same time until they came to a single point.

"Okay, the last one was here. I followed the trail this way, so we should be right about here now. What are the coords of where we're trying to go?"

Drake looked them up and passed along the information. He pointed his pen at their current position and waited as Allie repeated her exercise with the new coordinates.

"Okay. I have a plan. Somehow, we need to get across the river, which is north of us, and then there's an eighty or hundred-twenty-foot rise to climb depending on this scale. Where's the legend?"

"Doesn't have one."

Allie sighed. "Oh, great. I guess we'll need to worry about that when we get there. Here."

Allie handed Drake the map, which he tucked back above the visor. She put the vehicle in Drive and headed north across the bumpy terrain. A few hundred yards later, she stopped again, parked, and got out. She took off her helmet, placed the headgear on the vehicle's hood, and walked forward another ten feet.

Drake was right behind her and stopped at her side. Before them was the riverbank. Unsurprisingly, the riverbed was bone dry. The lack of water wouldn't be a problem, but in their way was a vertical drop of a good twenty feet in between where they stood and the riverbed before them.

"Well, crap," Drake said. "You can't drive down that. What should we do?"

"We can either continue on foot or drive parallel to the river until we find a place to cross over. Or I guess we could find other caches on this side of the river."

"I don't want to hike that far," Drake said.

"Me neither."

"I'll go check for nearby caches."

Drake returned to the UTV and grabbed the GPS from his seat. He spent a couple of minutes checking the map view and returned to Allie's side. "Nearest one on this side of the river is about two miles to the southwest, but other than that one, there aren't many in that area."

"How many are across the river?"

"There's a cluster of four in about a square mile area."

"So timewise it makes more sense to find a way across the river."

Drake took off his hat and rubbed his forehead with his arm. "I'd say so."

"Okay. Upstream or downstream?"

Drake stepped to the edge of the embankment, dislodging a few stones as he did. He watched them tumble to the bottom, then looked left and right. He realized in an instant that Allie was messing with him. Since there was no water running, the simple task of determining the river's course was impossible. "Um…downstream?"

Allie smiled. "I agree. Let's go."

Allie drove parallel to the river in a direction she thought was downstream, and a quarter mile later she found what she needed. She swung the UTV around and faced the bridge.

"We're going to go over that?" Drake asked. "Seriously?"

"Sure, why not? It looks fine to me."

"Can I get out and walk over first, if only to make sure the thing is sturdy?"

Allie rolled her eyes. "Sure, Duck-man, go ahead if that will make you feel better."

Drake jumped from the UTV and approached the bridge. The structure had a rusted steel frame, and over the frame were wood planks. The bridge looked to be almost wide enough to handle a small compact car. There were ramps on either end to raise the bridge deck an additional two feet above the riverbed, which Drake estimated was fifteen feet below him. Since the bridge had no side rails, Drake stepped cautiously across the bridge directly in the center and turned around when he got to the other side.

"Come on, it should be okay. Make sure you stay in the middle," he yelled.

Allie raised her hand to signal she'd heard him, put it into Drive, and slowly ascended the ramp. As she crossed the bridge at a speed a smidge under a turtle's pace, the boards beneath her wheels groaned and creaked. Drake closed his eyes at one point when he noticed a board tip up and fall back down when the UTV's right rear tire passed over it. Allie descended the ramp on the far side and parked next to Drake.

"You need a ride, stranger?" Allie asked, resting her arms over the steering wheel as if she went over rickety old bridges all the time.

Drake climbed into the UTV, shaking his head. "Was it as bad as it looked from my side?"

"Probably worse because I couldn't see the edge on the passenger side. You'll have to guide me across on the way back."

"Or we need to find another way across. But I agree, if we come back this way, I'll take point. You were veering a bit off to the left. Had the bridge been five feet longer, you'd have gone over."

Allie put the UTV into drive and headed off to the northeast. "I'll guess we'll worry about that when the time comes."

Drake rolled his eyes at her. "Should I be worried you're putting off all the worries into the future?"

Allie took her eyes from the road and winked at him. "Why not? That's where worries belong."

Ten minutes later, they arrived at the edge of a wash. Unlike the river, the wash wasn't nearly as deep, but Allie knew she couldn't traverse it without getting the UTV stuck because of the wash's narrow width.

"What do you think?" Allie asked.

"Well, the cache is only a tenth of a mile away from here. I think if we got to the far side and up that bank, we'd have a better idea of what we're dealing with."

"Okay, so we're walking from here then."

The team got out of the UTV, and Allie retrieved the backpack and slung it over her shoulders. She let Drake go first, and he clambered down the bank, then turned and held out his hand for Allie. They had only a three-foot walk to the other bank, so they closed that distance quickly, then scrambled up fifteen feet of the opposite bank. From there, they saw a large dirt mound, and on top of which was a tree.

"How far do you think that is?"

Allie removed the rangefinder from the backpack and trained it on the mound's base, just below the tree. "Three hundred and one feet. Want to go for this one?"

"Might as well. We're wasting time just standing here."

Allie returned the rangefinder to the bag as they began the walk. The closer they got, the higher the tree looked. When they were only twenty yards from the mound, they stopped again and surveyed their surroundings. The mound, which didn't seem too large from far away, was over thirty feet high and stretched out on either side for a hundred feet and the walls appeared to be nearly vertical.

"The cache is up above us, isn't it?" Allie asked.

"Yep. It is only eighty feet away."

"Yeah, eighty feet straight up. I love those. Let's get closer."

The pair arrived at the mound's face, stopped, and looked up.

"We should have brought our climbing gear," Drake said.

"They didn't issue us any. And neither of us knows how to climb."

"Point taken. I doubt they would have put a cache where no one could get to it. Why don't you go that way and see if there's a way up? I'll head in the other direction."

Drake turned and followed the mound's wall, looking for a slope, or better yet, an elevator, to the top. He had walked for thirty feet when he stopped, didn't believe what he saw, and turned and whistled to get Allie's attention. Allie turned around and jogged to him.

"What's up?"

Drake pointed. "The way to the top."

Allie didn't know what he was talking about, but when she took another step and turned, she saw what Drake found. Stairs cut into the side of the mound. They started offset, carved into a natural fissure within the mound, and appeared to lead to the summit.

"Those don't look natural to me," Allie said.

"I don't think so, either, but I don't think a machine carved them out, either."

Allied leaned over and touched the nearest step she could reach without squatting. It wasn't smooth, and there was a slight indent in the middle where the erosion had worn it away. "Let's go up."

Without waiting for Drake, Allie started climbing the steps. The steps were uneven and deceptively spaced, so Drake and Allie had to pay careful attention as they ascended. Even so, Allie and Drake both tripped on random stairs that were higher or lower than expected. Since someone long ago had carved the stairs inside the mound, the width was just over shoulder wide. In several places, Drake had to climb sideways or risk getting stuck. At last, the space opened up, and the pair stepped out onto the hill's apex.

Drake bent over, put his hands on his knees, and breathed hard. "That was a tough climb."

"Tell me about it. My legs are burning. Come on, let's get this over with," Allie said.

They walked to the mound's center, where the tree stood in a depression that looked like a bowl. Near the tree's trunk, there was an inch of water.

"I was wondering how a tree way up here could have leaves on it," Drake said. "It looks like every time it rains, the water catches in this depression. Pretty cool, actually. Nature finds a way, right?"

"Let's just find the cache," Allie answered. "There's nothing else up here, so it must be in the tree."

Allie and Drake circled the tree. It was about forty feet tall, and the crown was twice that wide.

"There it is," Drake said.

"Where?"

He pointed into the boughs. "Follow my finger. See that fifth branch coming off from the trunk?"

"Yeah, I guess."

"Follow that about five feet out. There's a birdhouse there."

It took Allie a minute, but finally she spotted it. "I see it. How are we going to get it?"

Drake looked at the tree. The closet branch to the ground was a good three feet above his head. "I'll have to give you a boost."

"Me? You want me to climb this tree?"

"I'd do it, but I don't think you can lift me high enough, although we can try if you want to."

Allie considered it for a moment, then decided. "No. You're right, I should go up. I weigh less. You need to catch me if I fall, though."

"Okay, it's a deal. Come on over here."

Drake put his back against the trunk, bent over, and interlaced his fingers. "Alley-oop!"

Allie put her foot into Drake's hand, and he stood straight and lifted her.

"A little higher," Allie said. "I need another foot."

Drake raised his hands until they were just above his abdomen.

"I need a little more," Allie said.

"I can't give you anymore. You're getting heavy. Can you step on my shoulder?"

Allie looked down and set her free foot on Drake's left shoulder. "Okay, ready."

"Go." Drake lifted her foot, and with Allie's leg doing some of the work, she got high enough to grab the bottom branch. She got a grip, swung herself up like a gymnast, and stood on the branch.

"That was easy," Allie said.

"Okay, monkey, climb the tree," Drake said. He stepped back and watched Allie slowly make her ascent in the tree. When she got to the fifth branch, she reached out for the birdhouse.

"Yep, it's a fake birdhouse." It was easy to tell it was a fake since there wasn't a hole for a bird to enter. She lifted part of the hinged roof and checked inside. It was empty. "There's nothing here. No log."

"What? There has to be."

Allie changed her position so she could examine the birdhouse closer. "I'm telling you, it's empty. I'm coming down." Allie made her way toward the trunk, then stopped when she got halfway back. "Hold on a second. There are four more houses up here."

She got back to the trunk and climbed higher. Above her and to her left, she reached the second birdhouse. That, too, was empty. She got back to the trunk, got a quarter way around the trunk, and reached out for the third. This time, she opened the birdhouse and found a small plastic container inside.

"Okay, I got it. Bring up the stamp."

Drake frowned, then started rummaging through the backpack. "It's not here. We must have left it on the UTV or at the last cache." He looked up into the tree and saw Allie making her way down. When she got to the bottom branch, she interlaced her hands around the branch and swung down. Drake rushed to her and grabbed her by the waist. Allie let go of the branch, and he gently set her down.

"Let's hit the trail," she said.

"Wait, we need to go find the stamp and go back up."

Allie laughed and took the stamp from her pocket and showed it to him. "You really think I'd go all the way up that tree without this?"

Drake rolled his eyes and shook his head. "Come on. Let's get down."

"Can we rest just for a minute? That was a tough climb for me."

"Sure."

Allie found a spot where she was under the shade and sat down on the ground and looked at her hand. "Can you get out the tweezers? I got a splinter."

Drake looked for the tool and passed it to her. "You need help with that?"

"No. It's big enough so I can do it myself. I'm pretty sure I could grab it with my fingers, but I might break it. This should take me only a minute or two."

While Drake waited for Allie, he set the backpack next to her and walked to the edge of the mound. From where he was, he had an excellent view, and off in the distance he could see dust kicked up from a UTV.

"There's another team out there."

"Are they headed this way?"

Drake stood for a moment and watched. "Maybe. It's hard to tell."

Allie joined him and looked at the horizon. "I think they are. Look, there's another team over there, too." Allie pointed toward the northwest.

"Maybe we'll run into them. That's toward where the next cache is," Drake said. "Let's get going. Let's hope we don't run into anyone trying to come up while we're going down."

Allie nodded, and the team took the steps back to the ground, then traced their way back to the UTV. Allie stopped to drink half a bottle of water while Drake got out the cache list and checked it off.

"How many points was that one worth?" he asked.

"Twelve."

Drake scoffed. "That's it? We climbed all the way up that killer hill, and up that tree for only twelve points?"

"Tell me about it. You didn't even have to go up in the tree."

"At least tell me others did it, too."

"Um, let's see. There was a heart, a fish, and some sort of paw print on the sheet. So we know there's at least three other teams out here that make questionable decisions."

Allie put the backpack into the storage bin and headed for the driver's door. She was close to it when she reached out and placed her hand against the UTV to keep from falling. She swayed a bit, and Drake rushed around the vehicle to steady her.

"Hey, are you okay?"

"I'm fine. That cache took a bit out of me. I think I'm a bit dehydrated," Allie admitted.

"Here, come around to the other side and sit down in the shade."

Allie let Drake guide her to his side of the UTV, then he brushed away a few rocks, and Allie sat down with her back against the rear tire.

"We should get going," she protested.

"In a minute. Let's take a breather. I'm getting hungry, and there's no way I can eat anything on the road with the way you drive. Hold on."

Drake left Allie and returned a minute later with three bottles of water and two brown bags. He sat down next to Allie, opened a water bottle, and handed it to her. To his delight, she accepted it and drank it without complaint. He opened the sack, looked inside, and dumped the contents into his lap.

"We've got a sandwich of some sort, an orange, and trail mix."

"What's in the other bag?"

Drake opened the other and peeked inside. "Sandwich, orange and a cookie."

Before he could close the bag, Allie reached out and grabbed it from him. "I'll take this one."

The sandwich turned out to be salami with cheddar on fresh-baked bread, and the cookie was oatmeal raisin. Allie, having felt guilty for snatching it from him, shared half the cookie with Drake. Both finished a bottle of water, and Allie started the third. The oranges they both saved for a snack later.

Drake checked his watch. They'd been on break for twenty minutes.

"Are you ready to go?" Allie asked.

"Are you ready? It's not worth it if it means you're going to keel over."

Allie playfully punched him on the leg. "Thanks. I am feeling much better, but let's try to avoid caches like that if we can. We need to play smarter, not harder."

"Okay, deal."

Drake got to his feet, collected all the trash, and shoved it all into a lunch bag, which he stowed in the storage bin. Then he helped Allie to her feet and watched her warily as she walked around the UTV and got into the driver's seat. She didn't stagger and looked as strong as ever.

"Okay, buddy, where to next?" Allie asked.

CHAPTER SIX

W hew, I finally found it." Drake picked up a rock the size of a softball, turned it over and showed Allie the tube that was inserted into the rock.

"Good job," Allie said as she dropped the two rocks she was holding. "I really hate rock pile hides."

"Me too, but we didn't have a choice here. Hand me the stamp, will you?"

Allie tossed him the stamp, and as Drake handled the log, she looked around. "There's another team coming this way. Better make sure the pile is back to the way it was."

Allie started tossing the rocks she'd checked back into the pile they extracted the cache from, and when Drake finished with the log, he helped. Soon, there was an obvious pile of rocks clustered around a small boulder, just like they'd found when they got there.

They got into their UTV and headed off to the next geocache, and stopped when the blue team approached them. Both drivers shut off the engines so they wouldn't have to shout at each other over the din.

"How's it going?" Zach asked.

"Not as good as I expected we'd be doing when we started out this morning," Allie answered. She took off her helmet and ran her fingers through her hair to pull out the snags. "How many finds are you at?"

Zach looked over at his partner, and Jodi checked the sheet and gave him the answer.

"Forty-four," Zach said. "Not that great, considering we've been out here for almost nine hours."

"I can understand that," Drake said. "When we got the sheet this morning, I thought we'd get all hundred of them, but once we found our first five, I knew it was impossible. I guess that's the point of the points."

"How many points do you have?" Jodi asked.

Drake held up the cache sheet. "I don't know. I forgot to capture the points for two caches early on, and after that I didn't bother anymore since we weren't going back to get them. We won't find out until the official tally is done."

"Well, no point in comparing our scores," Jodi said. "Looks like you're headed back to town?"

Allie nodded. "Yep. There's a bunch of caches to the south we haven't grabbed yet, so we're planning on hitting those on the way back."

Jodi turned to Zach. "I told you we should have planned this out better."

Zach smirked and shrugged. "We started in town and worked our way out to here. I figure we'll be fine as long as we head back by eight. "

Allie nodded. "Well, we better get it at it. Good luck and catch you later."

Zach and Jodi both waved and drove off.

"They seem nice," Allie said as she put her helmet back on. "How far away is the next one?"

"A little under a mile."

"Which means a mile and a half or more after accounting for all the wonderful natural terrain we've seen."

"Hey, look at it this way. At least we'll know what to expect for the rest of the week."

Allie didn't respond, and instead kept her eye on her driving. They'd discovered early on that it was ten times easier to take one of the many dirt trails that crisscrossed the property. But they'd also discovered plenty of places where they needed to venture off the trail to get to the cache. And off-trail meant having to slow down to make sure they didn't run straight into a wash or bounce out of their seats when going over the rocky ground. At one point, Allie had tried to go over a dead creosote bush but had misjudged the height and caught the undercarriage of the UTV on the plant. Another time, she'd veered off the dirt path and ran the two wheels on the right side into a sandpit. In each instance, Drake and Allie got lucky. Between the two of them, they got the vehicle unstuck and back on the road without calling in for help, but they lost valuable time by making the mistakes they did.

Drake glanced over at Allie, and even with the helmet's chinstrap obscuring most of her features, he observed the frown on her face.

"Are you having fun?" he asked.

Allie's frown turned upside down. "Actually, yes. Despite how tired I am. It's been an adventure already, and to think it's only the first day! Only one thing though, you're driving this beast tomorrow and I'll take over your simple job."

"Okay. We can do that, but I remind you I offered to drive like three hours ago."

Allie shrugged as she jerked the steering wheel to avoid a ditch. "I wonder how everyone else is doing. You think they're all having the same luck we are?"

Drake considered for just a second before answering. "I'm not sure, since there's nothing we could have done today to make things easier for us, except picking a different route. That was my mistake. Tomorrow we should spend more time first thing and work to come up with a more efficient plan."

"Sounds good to me, although the plan wasn't that bad today. Today, the problem was not knowing what was out here in the back forty. Tomorrow will be a totally different story."

"Hey, watch out for that —" Drake yelled as he put his arms out in front to brace for impact.

Allie interrupted Drake's warning as she slammed on the brakes and pulled the wheel hard to the left to avoid a rock outcropping. When the dust settled, Allie smiled. "Sorry. Wasn't paying attention for a second there. Looks like that's the rise we want. We should veer off a little to the east to get over it."

Drake settled back into his seat. "Okay, if you say so, captain."

Allie did a ninety-degree turn and tracked off in the new direction. After three hundred yards, they came to a large boulder field. Allie stopped the UTV and peered out at the river of large rocks that ranged in size from baseballs to basketballs.

"How wide do you think that is?" she asked.

"I don't know. Quarter mile? Can we drive over that?"

"We probably could, but I don't want to. If we got stuck in there, we'd get stuck for good. So, Duck-man, find me another way around."

Drake studied the map and compared it to the GPS. "Give me a minute, okay?"

"Sure. Take all the time you need."

While she waited for Drake to finish his route planning, she took off her helmet and got out of the UTV. "You want an orange?"

"No, thanks."

Allie dug out an orange, peeled it, and broke it into sections. As she ate it, she leaned against the vehicle and looked out to the west, where the sun was beginning its lazy drop across the sky.

"Hey, Drake, we probably have only three hours of sun left. You think it's safe to be out here night caching?"

Drake didn't look up from his research to respond. "There's no way I want to be out this far at night, but there are some caches closer to town I think we can get, assuming the lights on the UTV work. I can't imagine how dark it will get out here once the sun sets. I have the plan, so I'm ready to go whenever you are."

Allie finished her orange and settled back into the driver's seat.

"The good news is, I think I found a way around. The bad news is we'll have to backtrack almost all the way to the last cache we were at."

Allie exhaled. "You sure? Is there another cache in this direction we can go for instead?"

"Not really. Everything else would take us way off to the west."

"Okay, all right."

Allie turned the wheel and headed back, following the tire tracks they'd made on the way there. Eventually, they came to the place where they'd met Zach and Jodi.

"Is this where I turn off?"

"Yeah, I...wait a minute. Is that smoke?" Drake asked.

Allie stopped the UTV and looked off in the distance. "It looks like it."

"We should go check it out."

"You sure? We'd lose time."

"Yes. Go. Drive."

Allie pointed the UTV at the smoke plume and headed right toward it. Within a few minutes, they found the source. Allie parked twenty yards from the overturned UTV and had not even shut off the engine before Drake jumped out and ran over to the burning vehicle.

"Get the radio, call for help," he screamed back at Allie.

The blue team's UTV was lying on its passenger side, immersed in flames. Drake ran around the heap and discovered it was empty. Then he heard someone calling for help. He turned and saw Jodi ten feet away and reaching out to him.

"Help me, please," Jodi begged.

Drake ran over and kneeled down beside her. "Are you okay? What happened?"

"I think I have a broken leg. I can't feel it. Where's Zachary?"

Jodi was lying on her left side, and Drake winced at the amount of red blood that had discolored her light tan cargo pants.

"Allie! Grab the first-aid kit!" Drake yelled.

In a few seconds, Allie was by his side with the case.

"Help is on the way. Should be here within fifteen minutes," she said.

"See if there's a pair of scissors in the box. She's bleeding. We need to cut away her pants to find where it's coming from."

Allie opened the kit and found a small pair of scissors. As directed, she cut away Jodi's pants, just above the saturated area. Once she pulled away the fabric from Jodi's leg, Drake and Allie noticed the point of a broken bone piercing the skin.

"Are there any bandages in there?" Drake asked.

Allie found a few gauze bandages, unwrapped them, and handed them to Drake.

"Jodi? Listen to me. You're bleeding pretty badly, so I need to apply pressure. It's going to hurt. You understand?"

Jodi nodded. "Do what you need to. Just find Zach, okay?"

"We will. Okay, here we go."

Drake placed the bandages over the fracture and applied pressure. Jodi's scream was immediate and piercing.

"You're doing great, Jodi. Just try to relax. Help will be here soon. Allie, I've got to keep pressure on this leg, or she'll lose too much blood. Go find Zach. He's got to be around here somewhere."

Allie nodded and stood. She walked back toward the UTV and made a short loop but couldn't find him. She widened the circle and then spotted his blue vest. Somehow, he'd ended up face down in a small gully that was just deep enough to obscure his body from a passing glance.

Allie rushed to his side. "Zach? Zach? Can you hear me?"

She got no answer, so she pressed her fingertips against his neck and checked for a pulse and, to her relief, found one. Next, she knew she needed to see if he was bleeding, but to do that, she needed to turn him over. Before she did, she lightly ran her hands over his limbs and neck to see if she could feel anything awry. Praying he didn't have a spinal injury, Allie grabbed Zach's arms, and although he shifted a bit, he didn't roll over. She stepped across his body, then reached over and grabbed his shoulder and rolled him toward her, then laid him flat on his back.

Allie put her hand lightly on Zach's chest and determined immediately he wasn't breathing. She tilted his head back and checked his airway and found it clear. She rechecked his pulse, and when she found it was gone, she started performing CPR without hesitation. Her training quickly took over as she alternated between rescue breaths and chest compressions.

"Come on, Zach. Wake up, buddy," she pleaded as she switched from breaths to compressions.

Her training told her it was unlikely he'd wake up and jump to his feet like in the movies. As she worked, she hoped to at least keep enough oxygen headed to his brain to keep him alive until help arrived.

She stopped for a moment to see if Zach started breathing on his own and to recheck his pulse, and as she did that, she heard Drake calling her name.

"I found him," she yelled. "He's not breathing. Can you come help me?"

"No," Drake yelled back. "I think Jodi's going into shock."

Together, but separately, Drake and Allie continued to render aid. An eternity later, an ambulance pulled up with an ancient pickup truck trailing right behind it.

Two men from the truck jumped out, grabbed fire extinguishers from the back of the pickup and went to work dousing the fire. Of more interest to the injured, a young woman in blue jeans and a white t-shirt exited the ambulance and ran over to Drake. The driver retrieved a medical kit from the ambulance and followed the woman.

"I'm Dr. Liz. What do you have here?" she asked, as she took a pair of rubber gloves from her pocket and snapped them on.

"Jodi's got a broken leg," Drake explained. "Allie is giving CPR to Zach over that way somewhere."

The doctor gave Jodi a quick check. "She's breathing and has a pulse, although it's getting weak. I'll be right back."

Dr. Liz found Allie, who was still giving CPR to Zach.

"I'm a doctor. How long has he been down?"

Allie stopped CPR and let the doctor move in to do a quick assessment. "I don't know how long. I found him with a pulse that stopped, and not breathing, so I've been doing CPR for about ten minutes."

"What's your name?"

"Alyssa. People call me Allie, though."

"Okay, Allie. I'll take over here. Go up to the ambulance and find Joe. Tell him to bring the oxygen and the med kit. Then get on your radio, call the base, and tell them to call in a medical helicopter. Got it?"

Allie did as she was told, then went back to find Drake. He was standing over Jodi, holding a bag of fluid connected to Jodi's arm via an IV, as the two men from the truck gently placed Jodi on a stretcher. Once they strapped Jodi down, the group moved as one to the ambulance and slid her in. Once Jodi was secure, the men grabbed a second stretcher and trotted off to help the doctor.

A few minutes later, the men returned with Zach on the stretcher, who had an IV matching Jodi's, along with an oxygen mask over his nose and mouth. They placed him into the ambulance next to his wife, and then Joe and Dr. Liz drove off.

"Hey, kid, come over here."

Drake turned around and saw the man from the pickup was talking to him. Without question, Drake approached the man standing near the truck's tailgate.

"Let's get you washed up a bit," the man said, gesturing to Drake's hands. Drake looked and saw his hands up to his wrists were red from Jodi's blood.

"Hold your hands out." Drake did as he was told, and the man squirted a soap-like liquid into Drake's palms and Drake rubbed them together and lathered them up. As he did, he checked out the kind man. He was about Drake's height but was at least fifty pounds heavier than Drake. The man had bright blue eyes, and salt-and-pepper hair with a matching scraggly beard.

"Thanks. What's your name?"

"I'm Nick. Here, rinse off your hands."

Drake moved over to a five-gallon water jug attached to the rear of the pickup with a series of bungee cords, and Nick held open the stopper while Drake rinsed.

"What happened here?" Nick asked.

"I don't know. We were on our way to a cache when we spotted the smoke from the fire, so we came over here to investigate. They must have had an accident."

"It wasn't no accident," Nick's partner said as he approached. He set the fire extinguishers in the truck bed, then opened a compartment, pulled out a blue shop towel, and handed it to Drake.

"This is Randy," Nick said.

"Thanks," Drake said as he dried his hands. They still had a pink tinge to them, but he realized he'd have to wait until he got back to town to do anything about it. "I'm Drake. That's Allie."

"What were you saying about it not being an accident?" Allie asked.

"Come on, I'll show you," Randy said.

The three followed Randy to the wreckage site. "Now, I could see something like this happening if they were trying to drive up a steep incline, or if they caught a ridge. Or if they were going too fast and hit a big rock and flipped over, but that didn't happen."

"How can you tell?" Drake asked.

"Look at the tire tracks in the dirt there. They run smooth, straight, and steady, then suddenly they stop where the UTV tipped on its side."

Drake followed the story. He wasn't a trained accident

investigator, but Randy's version made sense to him. "So what happened?"

"I think they got T-boned. Someone came and ran directly into them. Can tell by the denting on the driver's side."

Drake took a couple of steps closer to the UTV, but he could still sense the heat radiating from the vehicle, so he didn't want to get too close. From where he stood, he could see a large dent in the driver's door. "Could it have rolled?"

Randy shook his head. "Nope. It would be away from the tire tracks, and there's nothing on the ground to cause that impression."

"Then I guess you've got a mystery on your hands, fellas," Drake said. "Do you need us around for anything else?"

"Nah," Nick said. "You can go. Taylor Rae might have some questions for you, though."

"Who's he?"

Nick laughed. "He's a woman, and she's the head of security. You can go on ahead. We're going to wait here. Travis is coming out with a flatbed."

Drake and Allie said their goodbyes and got back to their UTV.

"You want to keep caching?" Drake asked.

Allie looked at him. "To tell you the truth, no. I'm mentally stressed and my arms feel like noodles from doing CPR for so long. Would it bother you if we just headed back to town and called it a day?"

"Not at all. I'm emotionally drained myself, and I'd really like to take a nice hot shower for about an hour."

It took almost thirty minutes to get back to town, and as they got closer, they saw a helicopter descend. A few minutes later, it took off and flew in the direction from where it came. Neither Drake nor Allie spoke over the return journey, and when they arrived at the UTV barn, Allie parked the UTV. They placed their helmets and the used first-aid kit on the seat and Drake collected their gear and trash.

Together, they walked from the barn toward the hotel. Drake stopped in front of the restaurant.

"You hungry?"

Allie considered the question for a moment. "My head says no, but my growling stomach says otherwise."

Drake smiled and continued walking. "Great. Let's take a rest and get cleaned up. I'll meet you back at the restaurant in an hour."

"Sounds like a good plan to me, but after I eat, I'm headed right to bed. I've had enough of this day."

"Me too, Allie. Me too."

CHAPTER SEVEN

The following morning, Drake was already in the restaurant, nursing a cup of coffee and paging through an Arizona travel guide, when Allie came in.

"Good morning," Allie said as she pulled out a chair and sat down. "Did you eat already?"

"No, I've been waiting for you. I knocked on your door about twenty minutes ago, but you didn't answer."

"This morning, I got out early and ran over to see Dr. Liz to check on how Jodi and Zach were doing. She wasn't there, so I walked around town for a bit to clear my mind and get my blood moving."

"I hope they're okay," Drake said.

A server came to the table, took breakfast orders, and left.

"I wonder how we did yesterday. Did you hear any rumors about the results?"

Drake shook his head. "No, after you left, I talked to the Beasley brothers for a while, then I headed for bed, too. I'm sure we'll get them this morning before we take off for the day."

The server returned with a plate of French toast for Drake and a Denver omelet and a side of raisin toast for Allie, along with a plate of bacon for them to share.

Drake opened a small bottle of warm syrup and poured it over the toast.

"That looks so good," Allie said.

"Pass your plate over."

Allie did, and Drake cut a slice in fourth, and slid the piece onto her plate. "Would you like more?"

Allie shook her head and took her plate back. She cut her piece in half and ate it. "Oh my, that is the most delicious French toast I've ever had."

Drake was chewing a mouthful but nodded in agreement. He chased it down with a slurp of coffee. "It's gotta be the fresh bread from the bakery. I'll bet your cinnamon toast is the same way."

"Let's find out." She picked up a toast triangle and passed it to Drake and picked one up for herself. She took a bite, chewed, swallowed. "Perfect touch of cinnamon, fresh raisins. I believe that's even home-churned butter on there. I'm pretty sure I want to move into that bakery."

Drake smiled. "I hope they have room for both of us."

As they ate, more teams shuffled into the restaurant for breakfast, a few looking fresh and ready to take on the world, a few obviously not morning people. Forty minutes later, Bruce and Andy entered. As Bruce moved from table to table to greet everyone, Andy set up his equipment for the morning's presentation.

When Andy was ready to go, he pressed a button on the laptop and the spreadsheet appeared on the monitor. Andy had added the competitors' names in the first column with each team's color, so it was easy for Drake to determine his team was more than halfway down the sheet.

"Good morning, all," Bruce said as he walked into the center of the room and attracted everyone's attention. "Before we get started, I want to give you all an update on

Zach and Jodi Collier, who were the blue team. As most of you know, they were involved in an accident yesterday. Jodi suffered a broken leg and blood loss. Zach had a concussion and stopped breathing for a while. I'm happy to report that both are doing well and are on their way to a full recovery in a Phoenix hospital."

A smattering of applause started, and Bruce waited until it subsided.

"Now, back to the action. You can see on the monitor behind me the results of yesterday's event, with the red team in the lead by a bunch. Out of a possible five thousand fifty points, they came in at just over forty-seven hundred. That puts them almost eight hundred points ahead of the second-place team. Don't let that discourage you, though. There is still plenty of game to be played."

Bruce paused for dramatic effect.

"Today's event will be all about letterboxes. Did you know the concept of the letterbox goes all the way back to the 1850s in England? I didn't until Andy here told me. I know you're all used to the common letterbox-hybrids where you go to the coordinates and the cache is there with a stamp inside. These caches today will be a little different. The coordinates programmed into your units will take you to a container. Inside that container will be directions to either another stage or the final container, which may be close to the original coordinates, or may be far away. Either way, it will be up to you to use the clues to find the final cache. As usual, inside that cache, you must stamp the logbook. Also, in the container there will be a stamp that you should use to mark your cache list for today. There are only sixteen caches to find, and you'll need to find them all to give you a leg up on a cache tomorrow. Anyone have questions?"

Tito had one. "Are the caches worth points like yesterday?"

"Good question. No. Today is a timed competition. The first team back with a completed stamped sheet will receive a thousand points. Each team to check in after that will get a hundred points less than the previous team to check in. So, the second team will get nine hundred, the third will get eight hundred, and on and on. Since the blue team is out, the last team in will get two hundred points. Any other questions?"

"Yesterday's rules…" Andy whispered to Bruce.

"Oh, yes, of course. A reminder that all of yesterday's rules are all still in effect. No teaming up, and you have to stay away from a team finding the cache, and all that. We have checked all the gear in your backpack out, the GPS units have today's coordinates entered, and you have a new cache list in there. Since today's a timed event, you can leave as soon as you grab your gear. Be safe, and have a great day."

As soon as Bruce gave the word, several of the teams jumped up at once and headed to the front table to grab their backpacks and rushed out the door.

Drake stood and turned to Allie. "You grab the lunches, and I'll get the backpack. Meet me back here at the table."

Allie nodded and raced to the kitchen. By the time Drake reached the head table, only the green backpack and the brown backpacks remained. Drake grabbed his, returned to the table, and emptied the contents. He turned on the GPS and did his best to mark the starting geocache coordinates on the fresh paper map he had, then studied the map until Allie returned.

"Does this pattern look like anything to you?" Drake asked.

Allie set the lunch sacks on the table and turned the map around so she could see it better. The marks started out beyond the UTV barn and there were two rows of five, and the other six marks made an arc across the top of the map page. "It kind of looks like an arch to me."

"That's what I thought too.   But look here. They staggered the caches in a way where, if you got the closest one, which is near the barn, the next closest one would be the one on the opposite side of the road, yet north of that. They're out there in such a way that if you went in order down the sheet from one to sixteen, you'd be crisscrossing all over the property."

"Hmm," Allie said. "I get what you mean, but what if the final cache location is such that it's closer to the start of the next cache on the list? After all, you don't have the final coordinates on here, only the starting coords."

"That's true. I still think we should start at the cache by the barn, then go around the arch in a clockwise direction. But, to your point, we'll capture the final coords as we go and we should know after that if we've got the right idea. If not, we'll readjust the plan out there."

"Works for me. Pack up and let's go."

Drake looked up and watched Bruce approaching the table. "I guess you two are in a hurry to get on the road, but before you do, I wanted to take a couple minutes and tell you how much I appreciate what you did for the Colliers. Liz told me had you not gotten there when you did, they both would have died."

Allie put her hand on his arm. "There's no need to thank us. It was the right thing to do. I'm grateful we got there in time."

"One last thing, when you get in this afternoon, please stop off and talk to Taylor Rae, my security chief. She has some information she needs from you to write up her report. You can find her at the jail."

"We will," Drake said.

Bruce nodded. "You best be on your way. Have a great day." Bruce turned, took two steps, then stopped, and turned back. "Oh, go counterclockwise." He winked and walked away.

"You heard him," Allie said, "let's get going."

Drake and Allie left the restaurant and walked over to the barn, where they found their UTV waiting for them.

"Got it all ready for us, I see," Drake said as he reached for his helmet.

"It helped that you are the last ones to leave today," Travis answered. "You're all washed up and ready to go, and I replaced the first-aid kit with a new one."

"Thanks," Allie said. "Hopefully, we won't have to use it again."

"Yeah. I heard what you guys did out there. Amazing, I think. How did you learn to do first aid like that? I heard you jumped in the second you got there."

"Easy," Drake said. "I'm an ex-cop, and she was a medic in the Marine Corps."

Travis gave Allie a skeptical look. "You were a Marine medic?"

"Well, technically, I was a corpsman. The Marines don't have medics. We're too tough."

A grinned passed across Travis's face. "Well oorah. How long did you serve?"

"Eight years. Hey, Travis, do you mind if we talk about this later? We're in a competition, you know."

"Oh, right, right? I'm sorry. When you get back later, we can trade stories. I was in the Navy, you know."

"Sure thing. Drake, you ready?"

Allie looked over and saw Drake was already in the driver's seat wearing his helmet, seatbelt, and sunglasses.

"I guess you are," Allie said.

Allie put on her safety gear and picked up the GPS, map, and pen that Drake placed on her seat, and got in. Drake fired up the engine and pulled out of the building. Three hundred feet later, they came to a stop.

"It's right there, over by that power pole," Drake said.

"How do you know?"

"Because that box wasn't on the pole yesterday."

Drake and Allie got out of the UTV and approached the pole, where they found a plastic box that was an inch thick and a square foot in size. Allie spotted a clasp on the top, undid it, and the box opened, revealing a laminated card inside.

Drake read the card. "At three-fifteen you'll find a tree, and that is where you want to be. Three-tenths at zero forty-five, and that is where you'll find the hive. What do you suppose that means? We can't get this one until this afternoon?"

"No, that makes no sense to me. Read it again a little slower."

Drake did, while Allie thought about it.

"Compass points. Three-fifteen and zero forty-five are compass headings," Allie said. "Easy. I'll copy the clue and then we can go."

"Don't bother. That GPS unit has a built-in camera. It will be faster to snap a picture," Drake said.

Allie fiddled with the buttons until she found the correct one to activate the camera, then took a couple of pictures of the card. She took a moment to check the images were clear, then she nodded, and they headed for the UTV.

"Hold on," Allie said. "Let me get out the compass."

Allie took a moment to retrieve the tool and set the direction arrow to three hundred and fifteen degrees.

"Let's go that-away."

Allie sat back and watched the compass and had Drake keep a slow, steady pace as he drove.

"There's a tree ahead. Is that on a line with the heading?" Drake asked.

"Yep. Go for it."

Drake sped up and parked when they got to a large mesquite tree. Once there, Allie stood as close to the tree trunk as she could and reset the direction for forty-five degrees.

"Okay, reset your odometer. We only need to go three-tenths of a mile from here," Allie ordered.

"I already did that."

It didn't take long for Drake to drive the distance, and soon he spotted a wood box resembling a file cabinet sitting by itself in the open desert.

"I'm guessing that's it," Drake said as they got closer. Drake shut off the UTV as Allie jumped out. She lifted the lid on the top of the beehive, glanced inside, and extracted a plastic shoe box. She replaced the hive lid, placed the shoe box on top, and opened it. Inside there was a cache log and a self-inking stamp.

Allie took her team stamp and stamped the logbook with their clover, then used the stamp from the geocache to make the mark on the back of their cache list.

She looked at it for a moment, then shrugged. "This doesn't seem right to me. What do you think?" Allie passed the paper over to Drake while she put the geocache back together and returned it to the beehive.

"I have no clue. It looks like a couple of random lines to me. Maybe it will make more sense when we get the rest of them."

"I hope so," Allie said. "Well, one down, fifteen to go."

Allie looked at the map and set the GPS for the next cache. "Half a mile to the east for the starting coordinates."

As Drake drove, Allie studied his face.

"What are you thinking about?" she asked.

"What makes you think I'm thinking about anything?"

"Because you don't hide your expressions, and that makes you easy to read. Is it the Colliers?"

"Indirectly. I've been reflecting about what Randy said about it not being an accident. If that's true, it means there's a team out here willing to kill people to win the prize money."

"Are you sure that's not just the suspicions of an ex-cop kicking in?"

"That could be. I wish I could have examined the Collier's UTV a little closer. Or gotten out early enough to check the other UTVs. Perhaps I could have found some sort of clue, like a damaged front end, or paint chips, or something."

"You're not a cop anymore, detective. You're out of that life, remember?"

"I get that, but I can't help it. I don't have the badge anymore, but I still have the instincts. Just like you when you jumped in and started doing CPR yesterday. We left those jobs, but the skills didn't leave us."

Allie sighed. "I get it. This afternoon when we meet with Taylor Rae, maybe she'll have some answers to your questions."

"I hope so."

Drake spotted a flag waving from the back of a UTV in the distance and rolled to a stop. "Who do you think team pink is?"

"I'm guessing those guys from Texas. When I parked the UTV yesterday, the pink one was the only one in the barn, and we know they traveled out on horseback, so I guess it had to be theirs."

Drake nodded. "That's a pretty good assumption there. You'd make a good detective yourself."

Allie laughed at the idea. "No way. Hey, they're driving off. Let's go."

"Why bother? Why not just follow them?" Drake asked.

"We could, but what if they misinterpret the directions and get us off course?"

Drake couldn't argue with her logic. "Good point."

He drove to the coordinates and parked next to a cactus. Leaning against the far side was a plastic box, similar to the one they'd found before. Allie got out, took a picture of the clue inside, and returned to her seat.

"Well?"

"Go due north until you come to a wall, then turn right and drive until you reach the fall. Another right, go until you see the ridge, and what you seek is under the bridge."

"This one seems even more vague than the previous one," Drake said.

"True, but it least it still rhymes. North is that way."

Drake drove until they came to a small mesa roughly the size of a two-story house, then turned right. As he drove along, he spotted a jackrabbit running across the ground, and followed it with his eyes as he drove forward.

"Stop!" Allie screamed suddenly.

Drake slammed on the brakes, and the UTV skidded to a halt.

Allie hit him on the shoulder. "Pay attention to where you're going. You could have killed us."

Drake looked forward and saw what Allie meant. Five feet in front of him was the edge of a cliff. He turned to Allie and gave him his best apologetic smile. "Sorry. I guess that's the fall."

"You guess that's it? Really? Do you need me to drive?"

"No, I'm good. I'm getting even from when you almost killed us yesterday."

Allie shook her head. "Just be careful."

Drake backed away from the edge, put it in Drive, and turned right and followed the rim until he saw a ridge, and as he got closer, a bridge came into view. He moved close, then parked.

"I guess this is the place," Drake said as he got out of the vehicle. He took off his helmet and went to the bridge. It was an ancient pedestrian bridge that spanned the thirty feet gap across the wash. The frame was rusted metal, and the deck comprised corrugated metal planks. Unlike the bridge from the day before, this one had waist-high rails all the way across.

Allie got to Drake's side and surveyed the situation. "It's under the bridge. You want to crawl under there and get it?"

Drake hesitated.

"You remember when I had to climb that tree yesterday?"

"Yeah, yeah. Okay."

Drake stepped closer to the bridge, crouched, grabbed a bridge brace, and leaned as far over as he could. Below him, he saw a small concrete ledge, so without letting go of the brace, he stepped down onto the ledge.

"Don't look down," Allie said.

Drake looked down. There was a straight twenty-five-foot drop to the ground. "Gee, thanks."

He repositioned his hand on the deck and bent over to look under the bridge. Tucked under the bridge on a small stone ledge was a small plastic box. He removed the box and passed it to Allie.

"Do your thing, girl."

Allie stamped the logbook and her cache sheet, closed everything up, and passed it back to Drake.

"Only two other teams have been to this one," Allie said as Drake climbed back up to her.

"Does that mean we're ahead of the pack, or behind it?"

Allie shrugged and got into the UTV.

CHAPTER EIGHT

S low down. It looks like there's another team up ahead," Allie said.

"I see them." Drake slowed, rolled forward a few more feet, and stopped well outside the one-hundred-yard range. "When should we have lunch? It's almost one."

"Looks like we have time for a sandwich now. It doesn't seem like they're moving fast on this one," Allie said.

Drake got out of the vehicle, grabbed two lunch bags and bottles of water from the storage compartment, sat back down, and passed a sack to Allie. He opened it up and looked inside.

"Same as yesterday. Sandwich, cookie, orange." Drake removed the sandwich from the bag, slid it from the plastic, and took a bite.

"Salami again?" Allie asked.

Drake nodded.

"Too bad. I'm not the biggest fan of salami."

"Why don't you ask the kitchen to make you something else?" Drake asked once he took a swig of water.

"They have these bags pre-made and lined up on the

counter. I simply grab and go and never thought to ask for anything different."

"Tomorrow you should. No sense eating something every day that you don't enjoy."

Allie unwrapped the sandwich and was about to take a bite when she noticed something unusual.

"Are they trying to get our attention?" she asked.

Drake looked through the windshield at the team ahead of them. He couldn't quite make out who it was, but one was standing on the hood of their UTV, and the other was on the ground. Both were waving their arms in the air.

"I believe they are. Let's go check what's going on." Drake shoved his sandwich back in the bag and passed it to Allie. He started the UTV, drove toward the team, and parked within five feet of them.

"Oh, thank you so much," said the brunette in shorts as she jumped down from the hood. "We've been stranded here for at least an hour."

"You're Cindy, right?" Allie asked.

"No. I'm Penny. She's Cindy. Good guess, though."

"Why are you stranded?" Drake asked.

"Car won't start. Can you help us out?"

"I can try, but I'll warn you ahead of time. I'm not the best mechanic in the world," Drake said.

Drake got behind the wheel and turned the key. The machine made a groaning noise, but it didn't turn over. He tried a second time and got the same result. He got out, opened the hood, and wiggled the wires.

"You know what you're doing there?" Allie asked.

"Checking that everything looks okay. Actually, why am I doing this? You're the one with experience with these things. You know I know absolute zero about machines."

Drake stepped out of the way to make room for Allie. She checked the battery connections, spot checked every connection she could, and inspected the hoses.

"Everything seems fine in here." Allie stepped away and walked toward the rear of the UTV. When she got to the rear, she bent over and looked underneath.

"Penny, put the thing in neutral. Drake and Cindy, help me push this beast forward a bit."

With everyone's help, they successfully moved the UTV. After they pushed it two feet, Drake glimpsed what Allie had seen: a puddle of liquid on the ground. Drake put his finger in the liquid and sniffed it.

"That's gas. You must have ruptured the tank somehow. Did you go over a rock or something?"

Cindy shook her head. "No. I was driving. I didn't roll over anything larger than a pebble."

Drake walked around to the passenger side where the fuel tank was located. He didn't spot any damage from the side, so he dropped to the ground and slid under the tank as far as he could.

"Allie, get me our GPS, will you?"

Drake laid where he was, and soon Allie's hand appeared with the handheld. Drake took it, turned on the camera, and snapped a couple of pictures. Satisfied, he slid out from under the machine, sat up, and looked at the results.

"Yep, you've got four punctures in your gas tank." Drake held up the unit, so everyone had access to the pictures.

"There's no way I ran over something to cause that," Cindy said. "We haven't so much as gone over a large bump all day."

"No, you didn't. Those were deliberately done." Drake got to his feet and brushed the dirt from his pants. "Has anyone else been by?"

"No, we didn't notice anyone," Penny said. "But this

cache is down at the bottom of this gully, and we were down there for a while. I imagine someone might have come and gone in our absence."

"You should call in to base and get Travis out here to help."

"We can't. Our radio's gone," said Penny.

"What? Are you sure?" Allie asked.

"Yes, we looked all over the place and can't find it anywhere."

"Where's the last place you had it?" Drake asked.

"In the bin on the UTV. I know we had it at one point. I spotted it only an hour ago when I dug into the backpack to get some fresh batteries for the GPS," Cindy said.

Drake headed to his UTV and retrieved the radio from the pack. "This is team green to base. Over."

The radio crackled, and a moment later, a voice came over the airwaves. "Base to green. Go ahead."

"Base, I'm here with team orange at the final location for cache eight. Their vehicle is inoperable. They need a replacement. Over."

"New UTV. Copy that. Does anyone need medical help?"

"No base. No medical required. They need a new radio, though. Over."

"New radio, new vehicle, near the endpoint of geocache eight. Got it. Anything else?"

"Negative. Over."

"Okay, sit tight. We'll dispatch Travis out right away. Should be twenty minutes to a half hour. Base out."

Drake turned off the radio and put it back into his UTV.

"Okay, ladies, help is on the way."

"Thanks again for your help," Cindy said. "We appreciate everything you've done for us. I'm sure you're eager to get back on the hunt. So, in return for your kindness, if you go down into this gully behind us, you'll find five large piles of rocks stacked like pyramids. They hid the cache container behind a rock in the fourth pile near the top, on the south side."

Drake nodded, then he and Allie made their way to the edge of the gully.

"Looks pretty steep," Allie said.

"And with plenty of loose rocks besides? What could go wrong?" Drake asked. "Want to go down first or second?"

Without answering, Allie positioned herself sideways and stepped down the slope. Beneath her feet, stones slid away as she made her way slowly down the hill. Three-quarters of the way down, the ground underneath Allie's feet gave way, and she fell, landing on her right hip. She yelled out of fear and pain as she slid down the hill and came to a rest at the bottom, unmoving.

"Allie!" Drake yelled. "Allie! Are you okay?"

Allie didn't move. Drake ran ten feet along the edge of the gully, then started down. Like Allie, he was sideways to the hill, but half-jumped, half-slid down in a hurry. Several times he almost lost his own footing, but he used his arms as a counterbalance and relied on a lot of luck to make it to the bottom unscathed. Once down, he ran to Allie, and before he got to her, Allie sat up and shook her head.

"Hey, are you okay?" he said as he got to her side.

"I…I think so. That was stupid. I should have been more careful, gone slower."

Allie stretched out her limbs and ran her hand over her head. "Am I bleeding anywhere?"

Drake gave her a once-over. "Only your leg. You tore your pants by your right knee."

Allie bent her knee and looked at her leg. Her favorite pair of geocaching pants had a hole that started mid-thigh and extended down to her knee. She placed her hand inside the hole, extracted it, and looked at her fingers. The blood was already tacky.

"I think it's only a scrape. Help me up, okay?" Allie said.

Allie reached out her hands, and Drake clasped them and pulled her to her feet. She walked a few steps, slow and limping at first, but eventually she got faster, and the limp transformed into a normal walk.

"I'm good. Let's go."

Undaunted, Allie spotted the rock piles in the distance and headed toward them with Drake a step behind her. They skipped the first three piles and headed right to the fourth.

Together, they checked the six-foot high rock pile, and eventually Drake found the prize. Allie stamped each sheet, then Drake re-hid the cache, and they headed back to the slope.

Allie stopped when she arrived at the spot where they were going to start their ascent and looked up at the hill. "Any chance you can just carry me up this little hill?"

Drake laughed. "No way. But you go first, and I'll be a step behind you if you fall."

Allie took a deep breath and started up the slope. True to his word, Drake stayed a step behind with a light hand on her lower back the entire time.

As they walked back to their UTV, they saw Cindy and Penny still waiting for their rescue. They all said their goodbyes in passing, and Drake and Allie drove away.

When they had gotten out of eyesight of everyone, Allie had Drake pull over and stop.

"I'm getting out. Turn around and don't peek," Allie said.

Drake did as he was told as Allie stepped to the rear of the UTV. She undid her pants and pulled them down below her knees and examined the scrape on her leg.

"That doesn't look too good. Hold on, I'll get some water and we'll wash it off," Drake said.

"Hey, I told you not to peek!" Allie protested.

"Come on, Al, I've seen you in your favorite bikini, and that's much less fabric than you're wearing now."

Allie shrugged. "Good point. Pass me a bottle of water, will you?"

Drake retrieved the water and Allie rinsed off her wound. It wasn't bleeding, but besides the long, red scrapes, the surrounding skin displayed a variety of color shades ranging from an angry pink to a round, purple bruise on her right buttock where she'd obviously encountered a sharp rock.

Satisfied she wouldn't die just yet; she pulled her pants up and drank the remaining water in the bottle.

"You good?" Drake asked.

"I think so, but I'd better visit Dr. Liz when we return to town. Let's go. I want to finish up these caches and get back."

Drake was about to enter the vehicle when he stopped and backed out.

"What's going on?" Allie asked.

"I'll be right back. I think I have something."

Drake wandered from the dirt trail twenty-five feet off into the brush. He bent over to examine what he'd found, then stood, and called to Allie. "Hey, bring me my lunch sack."

Allie approached, favoring her right leg, and gave him the bag. "Odd spot to have lunch. What's going on?"

"Hold out your hands," Drake said.

Allie cupped her hands, and Drake tipped over the bag. The sandwich and cookie fell into Allie's hands, but the orange hit the meat of her palm and dropped to the ground.

"I also need your pen." Drake reached out and grabbed

the pen that was tucked under Allie's hat, just above her ear.

"What's going on, Drake?"

"I think I found their radio. Take a gander."

Drake bent over and pointed at the broken mass of electronics.

"What happened? Looks like someone smashed it."

"That's my guess, too."

"Are we sure it belongs to Cindy and Penny?"

"Don't know. I'm hoping Taylor Rae can tell us."

Drake put the paper bag on the ground and used the pen to push the broken unit inside, then he searched the area for other parts, and as he found them, he added those as well. Satisfied he'd collected everything, he put the bag in the storage compartment, and climbed back into the UTV.

"Come on. We've wasted too much time already. Where to next?"

A few hours later, Allie navigated their way to the starting coordinates of the sixteenth cache. "Go due north, then six little cacti sitting in a row, line them up, then left you will go. Another left turn when you get to the fence, when you come to the flag, you can come to a rest."

"I wonder how long it took them to come up with all the bad rhymes," Drake said as he glanced at the compass to get the correct bearing.

Allie giggled. "I know. Although I bet you could have come up with worse in half the time."

Drake grinned. "Just keep your eye out for the cactus, okay?"

They drove on in silence, and eventually came to a large saguaro that stretched a good twenty feet into the air. Just beyond it were several more.

"Oh, wow, that's beautiful," Allie said.

"Sure is. Looks like it's not alone. Looks like there are over six, though."

Allie did a quick count, pointing at each cactus as she did. "There are eleven I can count from here. How do we pick out the right six?"

"I don't know. These aren't exactly little cacti as described in the clue, either. Let's get out and investigate the area on foot, see if we can make sense of anything."

Drake jumped out of the UTV and headed directly into the midst of the desert giants.

Allie turned and grimaced the second she put weight on her right leg. She exhaled through her teeth, then took a few slow, tentative steps to follow Drake. Her leg was stiff, and she could tell by touch that the area around her knee had swollen over the last few hours.

"Damn," she whispered under her breath as she made her way between the cacti toward Drake. When she reached his side, she could see they were on the top of a ridge, and below them in the valley were hundreds of cacti. "Oh, man, this may take forever to find the right ones."

Drake nodded. "I was just thinking the same thing. Maybe we're missing something. Let's look around more up here before we trudge down there, okay?"

"Sounds like a plan to me."

Drake turned around and saw Allie struggle to pivot on her right foot. She lost her balance and almost toppled over, but Drake caught her shoulder and steadied her.

"Are you okay?"

"I'm good. Come on, let's get this done."

"Allie, look at me."

Allie's eyes came up and met his.

"You look really pale. Are you lying to me?"

She gave him a weak smile. "Maybe a little. Let's get this last one done. I want to go lay down, okay?"

Drake nodded. "I'd send you back to the UTV to wait there, but I really can't do this by myself. There's just too much ground to cover. Are you okay with helping?"

Allie nodded.

"Good. You cover the cacti closest to the UTV. I'll handle the rest. If you see anything that resembles the clue, give me a shout."

Drake jogged off to the other side of the cacti field while Allie surveyed her zone from where she stood. Within a fifty-foot circle of her position were at least eight cacti of various heights. She lurched to the closest one, got behind it, and peeked around the trunk to see if it aligned with any of the others. It didn't, so she went to the next cactus and repeated the exercise. Still no luck.

Thinking she was missing something simple, Allie walked to the outer edge of the cacti, where there was a large boulder the size of a sedan. The side sloped down like a ramp, so Allie climbed up, turned, and looked behind her to see if she could line up any of the plants.

"Nothing," she said. "Great."

Allie looked down to check her footing as she stepped off the rock and glimpsed a reflection of sunlight off of metal to her left. When she reached the ground, she walked around the boulder and at its side she found a steel feed trough. In the trough were six plastic solar-powered cacti dancing in the sun. Each of the cacti resembled a part of a mariachi band and had a small plastic instrument. One held a large bass, one a guitar, one a violin, one a trumpet, one a flute, and one an accordion. All wore sombreros and had googly eyes that shifted as they moved.

Allie whistled, and Drake was soon by her side.

"Found them," Allie said.

Drake watched the cacti as they moved. "I guess someone's been shopping for tourist trinkets."

Allie grinned. "I love them! I hope they sell them in the general store."

Drake rolled his eyes. "Come on. Get out the compass and set the heading."

"Okay, but as I do, you take a picture of them."

Allie set the compass, Drake took the picture, and soon they were back on the road. It didn't take long to get to the fence, and based on the attached colored ribbons, they were certain they had hit the property boundary.

At the fence, Drake turned left and drove along the fence line.

"What kind of flag do you think it is?"

"Beats me, but I hope there's only one," Allie said.

Ten minutes later, Drake discovered the answer to his question when he spotted a large pirate flag featuring the skull and crossbones waving in the breeze. Propped against the flagpole was a plastic box meant to fit a sandwich. Leaving Allie inside the UTV, Drake got out, stamped the logbook and their cache list, and returned to the vehicle.

"That's it. We're done for the day," he said.

"Good," Allie said. "I was ready to quit three hours ago. What time is it?"

Drake checked his watch. "Just after three. Let's get back and check in. Hopefully, we're near the front of the pack and made up some points from yesterday."

Drake drove as fast as he dared, parked in front of the restaurant and turned in the team's gear while Allie waited in the UTV.

"How'd we do?" Allie asked when Drake returned.

Drake shrugged. "Don't know. They didn't say."

He put the UTV in Drive, then stopped a few dozen feet later.

"What's going on?" Allie asked.

"Here's the plan. You're going in there to see the doctor. I'm going to return this to the barn, then go see Taylor Rae."

Allie was too beat to argue, so without a word, she

stepped out of the UTV and into the doctor's office.

CHAPTER NINE

To Allie's surprise, Dr. Liz herself was sitting at the small wooden reception desk paging through a magazine when Allie entered. She saw Allie take a step and rushed to her side to help.

"Oh, my, what happened?" the doctor asked as she helped Allie into an adjacent room and boosted her onto an examination table.

"I slid down a hill. I assumed it was only a scrape, but my leg started getting stiff a few hours ago."

"Let's get you out of those pants."

Allie giggled. "I haven't heard that in a long time."

Dr. Liz laughed. "Hey, I mean professionally. I'm not hitting on you or anything." The doctor gave Allie an exaggerated wink, and they both laughed.

Allie watched as Dr. Liz put on a pair of gloves. The doctor had short blond hair brushed straight back and blue eyes. She was taller than Allie by a couple of inches and had a slighter build. The doctor was, in a word, classically beautiful.

Allie undid her pants and lifted her butt to slide them

down. The doctor helped by removing Allie's hiking boots, then gently took off Allie's pants.

"Ouch," Dr. Liz said as she got her first look at Allie's leg. "That must hurt. Would you like something for the pain?"

Allie looked down at her leg and saw it for the first time since earlier in the day. The scrape she'd gotten was red and ugly, and the area from her mid-thigh to her mid-calf was swollen and discolored. She hadn't realized how much pain she was actually in until that moment. "Yes, please."

"Okay. And I'm going to have to take an X-ray of that knee."

Disappointment appeared in Allie's eyes. "No. We can't be out of the competition."

Liz gave Allie a reassuring pat on the shoulder. "Don't put the cart in front of the horse. Let's see what the diagnosis is before we work on a solution, okay? Lay back and try to relax. I'll be right back." The doctor retrieved a bed sheet from a drawer of the table, folded in half, draped it over Allie, and rushed from the room.

Allie stared at the ceiling and sat back up when Liz returned with something that looked like a laptop with a robot arm connected to a rolling golf pull cart.

"What's that?"

"Portable X-ray machine. Lay back, okay. Don't move unless I tell you to."

The doctor plugged in the machine, fired it up, and took several shots of Allie's leg. She took a few moments to study the images, then adjusted the table so Allie could sit up. She rolled the machine closer to Allie and pointed at the pictures.

"The good news is, you didn't break or fracture anything. The bad news is, you've got a moderate knee sprain."

Allie opened her mouth to speak, but Liz held up a

hand. "No, this shouldn't knock you out of the competition, but we'll have to keep a close eye on it. Let me get some things, and I'll clean up your leg and stitch you back together."

Allie's eyes got wide. "I need stitches?"

"No. You don't. It's a phrase I use. A bad habit, considering most of the things I do for patients don't involve stitches. Sit tight."

Allie waited as Dr. Liz removed the X-ray machine and returned a few minutes later with several items on a rolling tray.

"You don't have to watch this part if you get queasy. I can put your head back down."

"No, it's okay. I used to be a corpsman in the Marines."

The doctor stopped and looked at Allie. "No. Really?"

Allie smiled. "Hospital Corpsman First Class. Of course, that's a Navy rank, but I spent eight of my ten years assigned to a Marine unit, so I consider myself a Marine."

"Wow. I'm impressed. Did you see any combat?"

Allie dropped her head. "I did, but I don't like to talk about it."

Liz smiled. "I understand. Let's get this leg cleaned up. Are you allergic to anything?"

"No."

"Good. I'm going to give you a shot of a general antibiotic and something for pain. There's lots of nasty stuff you can pick up in the desert. So, you sit back and try to relax, and I'll show you what a brilliant doctor I am."

While Dr. Liz worked on her leg, Allie wondered what Drake was up to.

After Drake dropped Allie off and returned the UTV to the barn, he made a beeline for the town jail. The jail looked like he'd expect an old western jail to look. Wooden, one-story building, rusted iron bars in all the windows, and a sign with the word 'JAIL' in capital letters above the door.

When he stepped over the threshold, things jumped from old west to modern times in a heartbeat. The desk that Taylor Rae sat behind looked rustic enough, but beyond her was a wall that was made of glass, starting halfway from the floor to a foot below the ceiling. Through the glass, Drake saw a man surrounded by electronic equipment sitting with his feet on a chair and reading a *Superman* comic book.

"Can I help you?" Taylor Rae asked.

"I'm Drake Decker. I understand you wanted to speak to me?"

Taylor Rae stood and extended her hand. Drake took it and noted her strength when they shook.

"You're…" Drake started.

"I know. I'm big. Trust me, I've heard it a billion times before."

Drake agreed. She stood at least four inches taller than him, and although the desk hid her legs and a light jacket covered her torso, Drake could tell she was built of pure muscle and power. The sleeve on her jacket identified her as head of the security detail. The embroidered initials on the front suggested she preferred to go by T.R. instead of her full name. Her eyes were steel gray, and she wore her chestnut brown hair pulled back into a ponytail that rested on her right shoulder.

"Actually, I was going to confirm that you were the security chief."

"Oh. Yes, I am. Have a seat."

Taylor Rae sat, and Drake settled into the seat in front of the desk.

"Can I call you Taylor Rae?" he asked.

"You could, although I prefer T.R., or some around here call me chief, but I'm trying to squash that too. I'm not big on titles."

"What questions do you have for me?"

T.R. opened a desk drawer and pulled out a legal pad. She flipped a couple of pages, folded them over the top, and set it down on her desk.

"Why didn't your partner come in?"

"She had a fall this morning. I dropped her off at the doctor's office."

"Tell me about how you found the Colliers yesterday."

Drake took a breath and recounted the entire adventure. After ten minutes, he stopped speaking and looked across the desk. T.R. stared at Drake, tapping her pen on her pad. She put the pen down and leaned back in her chair.

"I have to admit, that was a pretty thorough report. You don't tell it like a civilian."

Drake blushed. "Okay, I'm busted. I was in the police force for eight years."

"I could've guessed that. What did you do?"

"Patrolman for four years. Detective for the other four."

"Why did you get out?"

Drake pointed to his stomach. "I was on scene late at night at a homicide case when a couple of gangbangers wanting payback drove by and sprayed the area with bullets. I caught two in the stomach and one in the leg. The leg wasn't so bad, but the belly wounds almost killed me."

T.R. winced. "So, what did you do?"

"After I got out of recovery, I switched to a career in marketing. I found the benefit of that change is not one person has ever shot at me while I was making a commercial for cat food."

T.R. laughed. "No, I suppose not."

T.R. turned in her chair and looked into the other room. The man in there had the comic over his chest and was in the middle of a nap.

"He looks busy," Drake said.

T.R. swiveled back around. "It's better that way. That's the radio room and I keep someone in there at all times when there are players out in the field."

Drake nodded. "That's a good idea. Have you gotten many calls?"

T.R. frowned. "Actually, only two, and you'll never guess who they came from."

Drake pointed his index finger at himself.

T.R. nodded. "You got it, detective." She leaned forward in her chair and dropped her voice to a hair above a whisper. "I don't think what happened to the Colliers was an accident. In fact, my guess is someone out there tried to get them out of the way to get a leg up on the prize money. I'm hoping we can partner up here — unofficially, of course. You can keep an eye on things out there in the field, and I can work it on my end. What do you think?"

"Why not use some of your own security detail?"

T.R. waved his question away. "They couldn't handle it. Don't get me wrong, they're all good people, but they don't have the background. The closest one to a real investigator I have is a dropout from the police academy."

Drake thought about it for a moment. "What do you want me to do?"

"Like I said, keep your eyes open. Let me know if you see anything out of the usual, or if you come up with a lead suspect or two. In exchange, I'll share any information with you I have."

Drake nodded. "Sounds fair."

"We need to keep it on the down-low, though, only between us."

"Why?"

"First, if people know, that may make you a target. Second, if you come out the winner of the grand prize, I don't want people to assume that you had any inside information about the competition."

"Makes sense."

"So then, we keep this to the two of us. You shouldn't even tell your partner."

Drake shook his head. "Nope, you're wrong there. Whatever I know, she knows. She's retired military, so you can trust her. Allie is also one of the smartest people I've ever known and often picks up things I don't. She can be an asset to the team."

T.R. considered it for a moment, then nodded. "Okay, but that's it. No one else, other than the three of us, got it? No other competitors, no staff at Cacheland, including Bruce and Andy, okay?"

"Okay, deal. What can you tell me about the Collier's UTV? Randy seemed to think another team rammed into it. Did you check that out?"

"He said the same thing to me. I checked all the other UTVs last night and other than some scuffed tires, lots of dust, and one broken taillight, there was no other damage to any of them."

"Any chance some other vehicle from here hit them? Like a pickup truck or something?"

"It's possible," T.R. said, "but I can't say for sure. Every vehicle here is a working vehicle and has their share of scrapes and dents, regardless of how much Travis tries to keep up with the repairs."

Drake rubbed his chin and scratched his neck. "What I hear you saying is we haven't started yet, and we've already hit a dead end?"

"Yeah, pretty much."

"Maybe this will help." Drake picked his lunch bag off the floor and placed it on T.R.'s desk.

"What's this?"

"Remember, I called in earlier about team orange's vehicle being disabled?"

"Yeah. I heard it come through and we got Travis right on it. Why?"

"I think someone deliberately punctured their gas tank. They couldn't call for help because they lost their radio, so I had to call in on ours."

"So?"

"So, about a half mile from where they were stranded, we found this."

Drake grabbed the bottom of the bag and lifted it. The smashed radio and the broken-off parts tumbled onto the desk blotter.

"Is this what I think it is?" T.R. asked.

"I believe so. Do you have any way to check it's theirs?"

"No problem."

T.R. pulled the blotter toward her, then looked closely at the radio and jotted down the last four digits of the serial number onto her legal pad. Drake watched through the window as she went into the radio room, pulled a binder from a shelf, and compared the number on her pad to a page in the binder. She slipped the binder back into position and left the room. The napping man never stirred. T.R. returned and sat down in her chair.

"Yep, it's theirs. I assume you didn't handle it?"

"No, I didn't touch it. I was hoping you could pull some fingerprints from it."

T.R. shook her head. "Great idea, but I don't have the technology here. I'd have to run it over to the county sheriff's office. Even if we did get prints, it's not like I have everyone's fingerprints on file here to compare them to."

"Sorry, yeah, you're right. I guess I got a little overzealous there," Drake said.

"Don't worry about it. It was a great thought, and

maybe it will come into play later."

T.R. used her pen to push the radio back into the lunch bag, stapled the bag closed, then stashed it away in her bottom desk drawer.

Just then, the door opened and Allie hobbled in, wearing a large compression bandage and walking with a cane.

Drake scrambled to his feet and went to her. "Allie! Are you okay? Come in here, sit down." Drake guided her to his chair, and she sat.

"The doc says it's just a sprain. I'm supposed to do ice and elevation, keep the compression on until the swelling goes down, and use this stupid cane when I need to. That's it. No big deal."

Allie turned to the security chief. "I assume you're Taylor Rae?"

"Please, call me T.R. I guess since you're here, can I ask you a few questions?"

Allie nodded yes, so T.R. referenced her legal pad and asked the questions while Drake stood against the wall and stayed out of the way.

After Allie finished telling her tale, T.R. looked past Allie and directly at Drake. "I see what you mean about her."

Allie turned around. "What does she mean?"

Drake smiled. "I'll tell you later. Are you done with us for now?"

T.R. nodded. "Sure, but let's keep in touch with each other."

"Sure. Come on, Allie, let's get that knee on ice."

Drake helped Allie to her feet and escorted her across the street to the hotel.

"You want to go up to your room, or hang out in the parlor?"

"What time is it?"

"Almost five."

"Parlor. We'll stay there for an hour, then head over to the restaurant for dinner."

Drake agreed and helped Allie into the parlor. She sat on the couch, and Drake propped her leg on some pillows and got a bag of ice from Heather at the front desk. While Allie sat on the couch, rested her leg, and paged through a book, Drake amused himself by shooting pool. A smile came to his face when the Beasley brothers appeared.

"Hey Ben, hey Brandon. What's going on?"

"We're just headed over for dinner," Ben said.

"How about a quick game?" Drake asked.

Ben and Brandon looked at each other and communicated in the secret telepathy that twins seem to share.

"Sure. I'll play," Brandon said. "Rack 'em up."

Drake collected the balls and loaded them into the triangle while Brandon picked out a cue.

"What happened to you?" Ben asked Allie.

Allie closed her book and set it beside her. "I did my best Jack and Jill impression and tumbled down the hill."

Ben smiled. "Let me guess, the one with the pyramids?"

"How'd you guess?"

He smirked. "I had a minor problem with that one myself. I slipped and tore the pockets right off the back of my jeans as I slid on my butt all the way to the bottom. Are you okay?"

"Yeah. Just a minor sprain. Nothing that should hold me back. I'll be good tomorrow. How did you guys do today?"

Ben frowned. "Not too well. It would really surprise me if we didn't come in dead last. Neither one of us is good with a compass, and that lack of skill really cost us today."

"Eh, don't worry about it. Still got three days to come in second place."

"Second place? You mean first."

"Oh, no. I'm going to win. You'll have to accept first runner-up."

Ben grinned. "You know, I wouldn't mind losing to you one bit."

"Do you know who came in first today?" Allie asked.

An unnatural cracking sound came from the pool table, followed by Drake with a swearing spasm that he probably meant to keep internal. Ben and Allie looked at him, so he shrugged and apologized.

"I don't know for sure, but scuttlebutt around the hotel is that it was the red team, same as yesterday," Ben said.

"What's the deal with those guys?" Allie asked. "Have you talked to them at all?"

"Just a little. Will and Julius. Married guys from Seattle? Boston? I don't remember, exactly, but they're from somewhere between those two places. They seem nice enough, but they don't speak much. I can tell you they're super competitive and, in their minds, they've already spent the prize money."

"So, they're the team to beat, huh?"

"Yep. That's what everyone's saying."

"Son of a biscuit-sailor!" Drake yelled.

"What do you think that was about?" Ben asked.

Allie smiled. "That one's easy. Drake lost."

A few seconds later, Drake and Brandon joined Allie and Ben.

"What was the deal with the biscuit-sailor?" Ben asked.

Drake took a sudden interest in the carpet. "Brandon beat me."

Allie winked at Ben. "Told ya so. Come on fellas, let's go get some dinner."

CHAPTER TEN

Drake looked around the room for the red team and spotted them sitting at a table off to the side of where Bruce typically did his morning briefing. Unlike most of the other teams who were working on the last bites of breakfast, the red team was already sitting at attention and had their game faces on.

At eight-forty on the dot, Bruce and Andy appeared. Once again, Bruce greeted people while Andy set up his laptop. The teams applauded when Andy was ready to go, and Bruce took his spot.

"Good morning, everyone. I hope everyone enjoyed the letterboxing yesterday, and based on some stories I've heard, some of you had some difficulties. That's okay though because today is a brand-new day. Before I send you out, does anyone want to hear the results of yesterday's leg?"

Bruce waited for the chorus of yeses to die down and picked up a note from the table.

"Team red came in first with a time of four hours and seventeen minutes. Team pink was second at five hours thirty minutes, and team black was third with a time of five hours and forty-two minutes. Here are the updated standings."

Bruce turned around and pointed at the monitor, which was blank.

"Andy, come on, I thought you were ready."

"Sorry, Bruce, technical problem."

Andy checked a couple of things on his laptop, and as a last resort, got up and wiggled the HMDI cord running into the monitor. After a second, the spreadsheet appeared on the screen.

"Looks like we moved up," Allie said to Drake.

Drake noticed it as well. Their team had jumped from ninth to fifth. The red team had the overall lead by an increasing margin over the second-place team.

"Yeah, but we're still almost three thousand points behind the lead team," Drake said.

"Geocachers, today is all about my favorite geocache type, the mystery cache," Bruce said.

The crowd's reaction to Bruce's statement was mixed. Some people cheered; others moaned.

"There are fifty geocaches hidden out in the field, but to find them, you'll have to solve fifty puzzles. To help you do that, you'll have to rely on your own intelligence with a helpful assist in what information you find in the schoolhouse. Because you'll have to do some work on the front end, chances are you'll be caching after dark. Since that's the case, we have added two flashlights to your backpacks. By now, I shouldn't have to remind you that the terrain out there is dangerous, so watch where you're driving if you're out past sundown. The deadline has been extended by an hour, so you have until ten tonight to turn in your sheets. Instead of a cache list, today you have a booklet. Each geocache has its own page describing the puzzle you need to solve to get the coordinates. And there are plenty of blank pages in the back of the book to use as scrap paper. Don't lose the book though, you'll have to submit it when you check in, and all the pages will need to be there. So, if you tear some pages out of the book, make sure you hold on to them. Like the first day, each cache has random points assigned to it, but since there are only fifty of them, we doubled the points. You'll have a minimum of two points and a maximum of a hundred points in the caches. Any questions?"

Bruce looked over at the crowd. There were no questions, only the looks of determined geocachers ready for the next challenge to begin.

Suddenly, Roy's hand shot up in the air.

"Yes?"

"How will we know if the solutions are correct?"

Bruce smiled. "That's the question I was waiting for. I know you're used to having an online checker to verify you have the puzzle answer right, but you won't have that luxury today. Instead, when you want a solution checked, take the puzzle to Andy, who will wait for you next door in the church. Present him the puzzle you want verified and he'll give you either a green checkmark or a red X on that page. Green means you got it right, red means it's wrong. Here's the rub. You can only get a puzzle checked once. If you have it wrong, you're welcome to figure out the correct answer, but you can't ask Andy for a recheck. At that point, you'll have to rely on your solving skills and best guesses. Also, you can only get one puzzle checked at a time. If there's a line behind you, you get a check on one puzzle only, then go to the back of the line if you need any additional puzzles verified. Another thing, you're not required to get a check, so if you're confident you have the right answer the first time around, run with it. Are there any other questions?"

The group remained silent.

"Okay, everyone. Come and get your backpack, and

good luck!"

The teams rushed forward to collect their gear. Allie got theirs while Drake headed to the kitchen to grab the lunches.

Allie was at the table making sure all their equipment was in the backpack when Drake returned carrying a large silver bag.

"What's that?"

Drake smiled. "Our lunches. I was right, there are more options than just salami. They put everything in this bag to stay cool. Hey, are you sure you're going to be okay today?"

Allie put everything back in the bag and stood up. She had the leg brace on, which hindered her movement, even with the cane. "I should be. I admit, I'm a little stiff, and I took a couple of pills this morning, so I'm not feeling any pain yet. Let's just hope there aren't any trees to climb or mountains to slide down. Come on, let's go."

Drake took the gear and the lunch sack and held the door for Allie as they left the restaurant.

"Schoolhouse was next to the church, wasn't it?" Drake asked.

"Yep," Allie answered.

They stepped out into the street and headed toward the tall white steeple at the end of the road. As they passed a barrel, Drake extracted a half dozen bottles of water and added them to the large lunch bag.

"I can carry something. I'm not a frail old woman," Allie protested.

"Not yet, anyway," Drake said.

Allie raised her cane and whacked Drake on the butt. Drake laughed and ran a few steps ahead to get out of the way of her reach. When they pulled even with the UTV barn, Drake left Allie alone for a few minutes. He stored the lunches and water into their vehicle and caught up to her as she was getting to the schoolhouse door.

A single, large room dominated the schoolhouse. There were two rows of six tables each, with enough seating for twenty-four people in all. Around the perimeter of the room were bookshelves from floor to ceiling, except for where the windows let in the sunlight. Board games and jigsaw puzzles of all types stuffed one six-foot section of shelves from top to bottom, and another held stacks and stacks of comic books. Non-fiction books dominated a large section of shelf space, and another area held rows of textbooks on every subject imaginable, from algebra to zoology. The centerpiece of the non-fiction section was a complete twenty-five volume encyclopedia set from 1972.

At the room's front was a teacher's desk, and atop the desk sat a single plastic red apple and a wooden paddle with holes drilled into it to lessen wind resistance. Hanging on the walls on either side of the desk hung sepia toned portraits of George Washington and Abraham Lincoln. Directly behind the desk, an American flag was on display, complete with thirty-seven stars.

Teams occupied eight of the tables, so Drake and Allie settled into an empty one and Drake took the booklet from the backpack and set it on the table.

"We both know you're better at these puzzles than I am. How should we handle it?"

Allie took the book and paged through it to get an idea of what they were dealing with. "This doesn't look as bad as it could be. There are several ciphers to solve, of course. And quite a few math puzzles, and I know how much you love those. There's a few where we only need to find information on several topics. I guess we should probably divide them up. You take the easier ones, and I'll work on the ciphers. Are any of the whiteboards free?"

Drake looked around the room and spotted a group of portable whiteboards lined up along one wall. He got up and rolled one back to the table. The board was four feet high and two feet wide, and they could write on both sides. Drake took off again and returned with a coffee mug filled with dry erase markers, as well as two erasers.

"I don't suppose the teacher has a ruler or a pair of scissors in her desk drawer?" Allie asked.

Drake left for a third time and returned with a plastic tub a little larger than a shoe box. "Here you go."

Allie opened the box and looked inside. She found a random smattering of supplies, including a pair of scissors, a roll of tape, paper clips, rubber bands, rubber cement, a foot-long wooden ruler, a ball of yarn, and a single violet crayon.

"Here, I've got an easy one for you to start with," Allie said.

Allie grabbed the ruler from the box, lined it up against the spine of the booklet, tore out a page, and handed it to Drake.

Drake looked at the page, which looked like a checkerboard with sixteen squares, four high by four wide. He turned the page over and saw it was blank.

"What am I supposed to do with this?" he asked.

Allie rolled her eyes and pulled the cache list from the previous day out of the backpack and turned it over. On the page were the sixteen stamps from the letterboxes with random line patterns on them.

Drake looked at the cache sheet, then at the puzzle page. "I got it now. Like a jigsaw puzzle?"

Allie smiled. "That's right. Go for it."

He grabbed the pair of scissors and carefully cut out the stamps from the cache sheet and laid them out on the table. Once he had them all free, he shuffled the pieces until they aligned with each other. Within five minutes, he had the correct combination and used the rubber cement to paste the squares onto the cache page. Once he had them in the correct order, the random lines combined to reveal the corrected coordinates for the puzzle. When he finished, he picked up the paper and grinned at Allie.

"Done!" he proclaimed with a good deal of pride.

"Sweet. One down, a bunch to go," Allie answered without looking away from the whiteboard where she was trying to work out a cipher. "There are two puzzles in there based on the periodic table of elements. Go see if you can find a chemistry book."

Drake took off for the reference section and, after a few minutes, returned with a volume from the encyclopedia. "All the textbooks were gone, so I brought this."

Allie looked at the book. "That'll do."

She capped her dry erase pen, set it aside, and flipped through the booklet until she found the first element puzzle, and read through it.

"Okay, to get the coordinates for this one, simply read through the story. See those words where there are two bold letters together?" She pointed at an example on the page.

"Yeah, sure."

"Good. All you need to do is find those, and I'm guessing the atomic number of the element it represents. For example, He is helium, so the atomic number is two. All the puzzles will have north coordinates starting with thirty-two and west coordinates starting with a hundred twelve, so you don't need to bother with the degrees. You good?"

Drake nodded and started on the puzzle. He found a highlighter in the supply box, then read through the short story on the page and found all the instances of bold text. As he discovered them, he added a stripe of yellow through the elements. Once he had the list, he copied the elements from the story and converted them to their atomic numbers. Within seven minutes, he was done and set that one aside.

As he was paging through the book to find the other

chemistry puzzle, Allie clapped her hands, grabbed the page she was working from, and jotted down the coordinates.

"That one took you a bit," Drake said.

"Too long. I recognized it right away as a Caesar Cipher, but I had to figure out the right rotational. I'm never going to complain about the speed of an online solver again."

"Maybe we should stay away from the cipher puzzles and pick off the low-hanging fruit first?"

"Good idea, Drake."

Allie took the book, paged through it, tore out pages as she scanned them, and made three piles on the table. "Okay. The first pile are things I think we can get through fairly fast. It's about half the caches. The second pile had about fifteen puzzles I think are doable, but will take some time. The last pile are ones I'm not so confident on and may take a while for us to solve."

Allie grabbed the first one off the easy pile and handed the second one to Drake.

Allie's was a Pigpen Cipher, which was a breeze for her to figure out, while Drake took one look at his puzzle and realized it was a message in Morse Code. As Drake ran to find a Morse Code table, Allie finished her puzzle and gathered the next one on the pile.

Drake returned and set a book on the table.

"Can you go find me a book with a Braille table in it?" Allie asked.

Drake nodded and took off again. While he was gone, Allie opened the book he had retrieved, found the Morse Code table, and had translated a dozen letters in the message before Drake returned.

"How's it going?" Drake asked.

"So far, I have 'the coordinate', but I just started. You want to continue with this one, or work on the Braille?"

Drake reached for the puzzle Allie had started. "I'll take

this one. And I'll race you. Whoever loses takes the next puzzle no matter what it is."

"Okay, then go," Allie said as she opened the book Drake had and looked for a Braille table. Once she found it, she broke the dots on the puzzle sheet into groups of six and started translating them into letters.

"I like these puzzles," Drake said. "They're not as bad as I thought."

"I think you dislike mystery caches because you don't want to take the time and get impatient with them if you can't figure them out in ten seconds or fewer. I, on the other hand, like the thought process that goes into creating them, and then solving them. How many of these do you think we should do before we go out searching for the caches?"

Drake glanced at his watch. "It's quarter after nine now. Let's work on the puzzles for another hour and see how many we get done. Then we'll judge if it's time to go or not. I mean, if we run out of caches, we can always come back here and do more of the puzzles."

"We can, but would traveling out and back save us any time?"

Drake shook his head. "Probably not. But like the first day, I don't think these were all meant to be found. There's no sense spending the whole day doing puzzles for caches we wouldn't find in time, anyway."

Allie checked her puzzle page, added the last three letters, and placed her sheet face down on the table. Then she collected the other few puzzles they'd finished and added them to the completed pile.

"That was quick," Drake said.

"Mine had fewer words than yours did."

Allie selected the next page and looked at it. There was a line that went through the center of the page. Above the line, there were seven logos of professional baseball and football teams. Below the line were logos of eight basketball and hockey teams. As quickly as she could, she penciled in the team names she knew below the logos.

"Chicago Cubs, Buffalo Bills, Green Bay Packers… hey, Drake, have you seen this logo?"

She pointed at the one she meant. It was a letter B with what looked like spokes around a circle.

"Yeah. Boston Bruins. Ice hockey. My dad was a big fan of theirs."

Allie wrote the answer on the page.

"What about this one? It says Oilers. Isn't that Houston?"

Drake smiled. "Not anymore. They moved to Nashville and are the Titans now. How could you not know that? We went to three games last year. Try Edmonton Oilers. Hockey again."

"The hockey ones are hard."

"That's only because you don't want to go to any Predators games with me. You need any more help with that one?"

"Nope. I got it."

Allie looked at her scribbles and noticed that all the city names started with letters from A through I, which she then converted to numbers one through nine. She replaced the team logos with the number corresponding to the first letter of the city name, then added the puzzle to the completed pile.

As she picked up the next one, she noticed the red team was already packing up and heading for the door.

"Are they finished already? How can that be? We've all been here less than thirty minutes," she said.

Drake looked up in time to see the door close. "I have no clue." He looked around to see if anyone was close enough to overhear him. "Remember what you and I and T.R. talked about yesterday? I think we need to monitor that team if we can. Something to me just doesn't sit right with the way they're blowing through this competition every day."

Allie nodded. "I agree. It's like they already know where everything is. We'll keep them in mind as our top suspects, but for now, get back to work, mister!"

CHAPTER ELEVEN

At eleven o'clock, Allie and Drake left the schoolhouse and headed to the church. Of the thirty-five puzzles they completed, they only needed to get two answers checked. Allie sat in the last pew while Drake got in line behind three other teams and waited for his turn. Ten minutes later, they had a plan plotted and were on their way.

"I don't believe we can catch up with the red team," Allie said.

"I agree, considering we're almost two hours behind them. The best we can do is run into them with pure luck. In the meantime, we'll need to do our best to get these caches."

"I've got an idea. Why don't we radio T.R. and have her find out where the red team is? Then we could go straight to their location and see what they're up to?"

Drake veered the UTV around a tumbling tumbleweed and got back on course. "Good idea, except for two things. First, the radio is on an open channel, so everyone would hear what we were up to, including the red team. And second, we would seem suspicious to Bruce and Andy if we checked in, having found only a dozen caches over the course of a whole day. No, we need to keep to the plan. Besides, have you forgotten we have fifty grand on the line?"

Allie didn't answer, and instead studied her map. As they had completed puzzles, Drake entered the corrected coordinates for each one into their GPS. Along with that task, he made a small mark on the paper map where the general area of the cache was. Once Allie finished solving puzzles and Drake drew two lines, which divided the map into a grid of four squares. They were currently on route to the southeast corner of the grid, which had eleven caches within it. From there, the plan was to go to the southwest, the northwest, and finally finish with the northeast, which only held four caches.

"How close are we?" Drake asked.

Allie checked her GPS. "Three tenths of a mile dead ahead."

Drake slowed the UTV to go over a small ditch. Although he barely crawled over the obstruction, the jostle was enough to cause a bolt of pain to run through Allie's leg. In reflex, she inhaled sharply and grabbed her knee. Once Drake was back on solid ground, he parked the UTV.

"Okay, no lies. Are you going to be okay today to do this?"

Allie rolled her eyes. "Of course. I'll be fine. I simply wasn't expecting that big lurch."

"Big lurch? We slinked through something only three times the size of an average sidewalk crack. Hey, if you can't cache today, say the word and we'll go back to the hotel and spend the day by the pool. I'd be fine with that, really."

Allie shook her head. "No. If we did that, we'd have no chance at the money. Keep going."

"Allie, the money doesn't matter if it means you're going to be in pain all day."

Allie looked straight ahead and pointed in the general

direction of the cache. "The geocache is that way, Drake. Hit the gas and go."

Drake shook his head in disbelief as he put the UTV into Drive. "You know, you're the most stubborn person I've ever met."

Allie smiled. "You're only saying that because you've never met my mother. Go. We're burning daylight."

Drake took his foot off the brake and headed for the cache. It wasn't long before they arrived at a large mesquite tree.

"There's something you don't see every day," Drake said.

The tree itself was a normal-looking tree. Except for baseball-sized Christmas ornaments hanging from its branches.

"Looks pretty," Allie said. She approached the nearest ornament, unhooked the orb from the branch, and studied it. "Plastic. I was expecting glass."

Allie shook the ornament, and something rattled inside.

"You don't think..." Allie unscrewed the ornament's top where the hook connected to the ball and tipped the ornament upside down. A small plastic vial the size of a pen cap dropped into her hand. She put the ornament on the ground, opened the vial, and fished out the piece of paper inside.

"Oh, boy."

"What does it say?" Drake asked.

Allie read the note aloud. "Congratulations. You have found a fake log. This log will not count as a find for this geocache. Find the official log for credit."

"I'd guess there are over fifty ornaments here," Drake said as he looked through the branches.

"Well, I guess we should get to work on them," Allie said. "Let's not put the ornaments back until we've found the right log. I don't want to waste time checking ones we've already looked at."

Drake nodded and grabbed the nearest ornament. He fished out the vial, read the note, and put the container all back together before he set the ornament on the ground. "This is going to take us forever," Drake said.

"Just keep going," Allie answered.

On the thirty-third ornament, Allie struck pay dirt when she unrolled the log and noticed the team stamps on the paper. "I got the right one!" she said as she waved the log in the air.

"Great. Any chance the red team has been here?" Drake asked.

"No. Only purple and gray. I'll take care of the log. You hang the ornaments back up. Make them look pretty, okay?"

Drake laughed. "Yes, ma'am. I'll do my best."

Allie stamped the log, put the geocache back together, and hung the ornament back on the branch where she found it. Rather than help Drake hang the rest, she limped back to the UTV and dug out the bottle of prescription pain killers that Dr. Liz had been kind enough to give to her. She dumped the contents into her hand and counted them. She had six to last her the entire day, but she hoped she wouldn't have to rely on all of them. Allie dumped all six back into the bottle, removed one, and took the white pill, followed by a drink of water. While she waited for Drake to return, she plotted the way to the next geocache.

At the fourth geocache, they found themselves at the top of a tall ridge. Allie studied the compass and looked off into the distance. "Yep, it's down there somewhere."

"How far?"

"Quarter mile. What would you guess?"

Drake looked to his left and over to his right. "We should pick a direction and see if there's a way to drive down this thing. Otherwise, we're going to skip it."

"Skip it? Why? We need the points."

Drake shot her a look. "There's no way you can climb up and down this thing, and I can't carry you, so if we can't drive there, we're going to cross it off the list."

Allie sighed. "I understand, even though at the moment I feel like I'm personally costing the team any chance we have at the grand prize."

Drake glared at her, wordless.

In the end, she capitulated. "Okay. You're right."

"Left or right?" Drake asked.

Allie consulted the map. "Left. If we can't find a way down, that's the direction of the other caches in this sector."

Drake followed the ridge for ten minutes, and by the time he came to a stop, they were already almost two miles from the cache. "Scratch this one off the list. Unless you can see something on the topo map to get us down there."

Allie studied the map for a moment. "No. Actually, it looks like that cache is in the middle of a big bowl. I'm not sure there's a way down there besides walking."

"Okay, put a line through this one and pick out the next," Drake said.

"Are you sure? I don't like the idea of skipping caches, especially since we're so far behind in the point count."

"We talked about this, Allie. It's not worth you further injuring yourself. Tell me, if we were back home and one of us wasn't fit enough to go after a cache, would we do it?"

Allie answered right away. "Of course not. We would leave whoever couldn't make it behind and the other would go for it."

She meant her response as a joke, but it didn't hit. Drake ignored her response.

"We'd skip it. So why is it different here? Because there's a prize on the line? Not worth the risk. What's the next one?"

Allie consulted the sheet, set the GPS, and pointed the way.

"I wish this thing had a radio."

Drake glanced over at Allie. "What?"

"A radio. You know, tunes? Music? An adventure around the desert would be more fun if we had music."

"I don't know. That's more your thing than mine. Hey, there's another team up ahead."

Drake stopped a hundred yards short of the cache and shut down the UTV.

"Come on, I bet you'd love it if I sang to you all day while we were out here," Allie said.

Drake looked at Allie. "Really? I honestly don't think you recognize how bad you sing."

Allie laughed. "You're jealous. The people at the bar tell me I'm great when we go for karaoke."

"Yeah, but those people are always drunk and don't know any better. They'd say a goat bleating along with an old country song was great. Can I look at the map?"

Allie passed the map to Drake, and he studied it. "This isn't working out. We need to pick up the pace. What's taking the gray team so long?"

Allie took the map back and slid it above the sun visor, then took off her helmet. "I don't know. It looks like another tree cache. They're both in the tree."

Drake got out of the UTV, took off his helmet, and set it on the hood. He moved a few paces closer to the gray team, then stopped. "Listen. Can you hear something?"

Allie tilted her head and concentrated. "It seems they're calling for help. We'd better go over."

"I'll go. You stay here," Drake said.

Drake left Allie and walked toward the tree. When he got to within twenty feet, Geneva called out to him.

"Stop! Don't come any closer!" she yelled.

Drake froze. "What's wrong? Do you need help?"

"There are snakes! Don't come any closer."

Drake's eyes shot from the women clinging to the tree trunk to the ground. He did a quick scan and saw nothing, so he took a few steps closer. When he was eight feet from the tree, he spotted the serpent. A rattlesnake sat coiled at the tree's base. It moved, then Drake heard the distinctive rattle.

"It's no problem. I'll throw some rocks at it and chase it away."

"No. Wait. There are two more," Geneva said.

Drake watched his step as he slowly crept around the tree. He sighted three additional snakes, not just two.

"Where the hell did they come from?" Drake asked.

"I pulled on a rope I thought was the geocache, and a tarp fell from a limb and the snakes were inside. As soon as we saw them, we jumped into the tree," Ingrid said.

Drake had overlooked the tarp at first since it was the same hue as the ground surrounding the tree, but once he saw it, he couldn't unsee it.

"You're going to be okay. Can you climb up a little higher?" Drake asked.

Ingrid nodded and started up the branches right away. Geneva, however, stayed where she was.

"Geneva, can you go up more?"

"I'm… I'm afraid of heights."

Drake nodded. "I understand. I'm not a fan of heights either, but right now, these snakes can harm you more than a fall from the tree would. Going up is the lesser of two evils for you. Understand?"

Geneva nodded, then looked up.

Ingrid wrapped her legs tightly around a branch and held out her arm. "Come on, Geneva, grab my hand. I'll help you up."

Drake watched and waited while the women climbed up as far as they could go. He had the thought of warning them that snakes could climb trees, but he didn't want to panic Geneva more than she already was.

"I'll be right back, okay? Don't move and you'll be fine."

"No, don't go," Ingrid begged.

"I'll be right back. I'm just going back to the UTV for a minute, okay? Don't worry, I will not leave you. Trust me."

Drake jogged back to his UTV.

"What's going on?" Allie asked.

"You're not going to believe this, but they're stuck up a tree and surrounded by rattlesnakes."

"You're right. I don't believe you. What's really going on?"

Drake gave her a look that conveyed to her he was serious.

"Should I call for help?" Allie asked.

"No. I think I can handle it myself." Drake got into the UTV and drove it half the distance to the tree, then parked it. "Hand me your cane, will you, and if I give you the signal, then radio for help."

"What's the signal?"

"A blood-curdling scream after the snakes have bitten me."

Drake took the cane with him and went back to the tree. When he got to within eight feet, he picked up a large rock and threw it five feet from the nearest snake. It landed with a thump, and the vibration it caused when it hit the ground caught the snake's attention. Drake picked up another rock and tossed it toward the first. The second rock hit the initial stone with a clatter and came to rest right next to it. He was about to throw a third rock, but the snake took the hint and slithered away into the desert.

Drake watched the snake move away and after he

determined the reptile left the area, he circled the tree again. As he did, he stomped hard against the ground and waved his hands in the air. In doing so, two of the other snakes left of their own accord.

"There's one coming!" Geneva screeched.

Drake looked up and watched the last snake slowly making its way up the tree trunk. "It's okay. Don't move. I got it."

He approached the tree, and he reached toward the snake with the cane. Using the handle as a hook, he dragged the snake's head slowly away from the trunk. The snake rattled its tail and Drake was momentarily worried the snake would hasten its journey up the tree. Drake pulled on the cane a little harder, and the snake separated from the tree and dropped back to the ground.

The unhappy snake rattled louder, picked its head up and reared, ready to strike. It flicked its forked tongue a few times, then lost interest in the humans, turned, and disappeared into the underbrush.

"Is it safe to come down?" Ingrid asked.

"Hold on just another minute," Drake answered.

Drake went to the tarp laying on the ground, found the end of the rope, then pulled the tarp away from the tree. He walked backwards, and as he did, he eyed the tarp as he pulled it along to make sure no other critters came out of it. Once he was a respectful distance away, he grabbed a corner of the tarp and flipped it over. It was empty.

"Okay, it's safe to come down now," Drake called up to the women in the tree.

He waited at the trunk and helped Geneva and then Ingrid out of the tree. As they got their feet on the ground, they each gave him a hug, and Ingrid kissed Drake on each cheek like they were old friends.

"Thank you so much," Geneva said. "I thought we

would be stuck up there forever."

"You're welcome. I'm glad neither of you got hurt."

"What happened?" Allie asked as she limped over to the group.

"I pulled on a rope expecting the cache to drop from the tree and got a tarp filled with rattlesnakes instead," Ingrid said.

"That doesn't sound like a pleasurable surprise. Do you know if another team was here before you?" Allie asked.

"We didn't see anyone, and we didn't find the geocache, so I couldn't tell you," Geneva said.

Allie checked her GPS. "Are you sure you've got the right coordinates? Mine is pointing a hundred feet to the west."

"Let's go that way then," Geneva said.

"I'll be right behind you," Drake said as he handed Allie her cane.

As the women walked away, Drake returned to the tarp to examine it further for any clues that it might have. The tarp itself was only four feet square and had grommets at every foot. The rope was tied to one corner, and Drake suspected it had looped through the other corners as well before being placed in the tree, but he knew it was only a guess. He noticed nothing else of consequence, so he folded the tarp as small as he could get it, then stuffed it into the storage unit of his UTV. He turned and was about to head toward the geocache when he saw Allie, Geneva, and Ingrid coming his way.

"You find it?" Drake asked when Allie got close.

"Yeah. Ammo can beneath a rock pile."

"Who else has been here today?"

"Purple, pink, and red."

A look of surprise passed over Drake's face like a lone cloud passing over the sun on a summer's day. "The red team, huh? Can you tell which team they were to stamp the log?"

Allie shook her head. "No. They weren't in a line. They are stamped in random places all over the log."

"Too bad. It might have told us something."

"Like what?"

"Like who might have hung a tarp full of rattlesnakes in that tree? I doubt Bruce did it. It wouldn't make sense to have Cacheland kill the people they're trying to target as tourists."

CHAPTER TWELVE

Eight caches later, Drake and Allie got to where they were consistently seeing little red hearts stamped on the geocache logs. There was little chance the red team was following the same cache order that Drake and Allie were, but Drake remained optimistic they'd encounter the other team within the next hour.

Three caches later, a smile crept across Drake's face as he pulled up right next to the red team's UTV.

"Look who we found. I wonder where they are." Drake said.

Allie glanced at the handheld. "The cache is four-tenths of a mile to the northwest from here. Perhaps it's down that hill."

Drake left the vehicle and walked to the edge of the ridge. It resembled the one they had skipped earlier in the day, but this one was twice as steep but had a switchback path going down the side.

"Hey, you think you can handle this one?" Drake asked.

Allie joined him at the ridge and looked down the hill. "I think I could get down there and back up again, but to be honest, I'm not sure if my knee can handle the mile round-trip hike."

"How's the leg doing?"

"It's throbbing on par with my heartbeat. I should take another pill."

"Okay. That's fine. We should take a break; let you rest up. Are you hungry? We could have a snack as well."

Allie smiled. "I'd like that."

"I hate to be a jerk, but I'd like to have a peek at their UTV. Could you stay here for a bit and be my lookout? Let me know if you see them coming?"

"Sure. No problem."

The way the path cut into the ridge allowed Allie to walk a few feet down the trail and sit on the top of the ridge. It was like she was sitting on the top of a wall, so she got as comfortable as she could and scanned the area below her.

Drake, in the meantime, approached the UTV and started looking through it. He checked the storage compartment first. Inside was their backpack, two empty brown lunch sacks, and four bottles of water. He emptied the backpack and found all the same items he had in his, excluding the GPS, the map, the stamp, and a pen. Drake returned everything to the backpack and placed everything in the storage compartment.

Next, Drake checked the front of the UTV. He spotted the puzzle booklet standing between the two seats and grabbed it. He flipped through the booklet, scanned each page, then put it back.

"I can see them coming," Allie called. "They're a way off yet though. Hurry up with your investigation."

Drake made sure everything was the way it was before he got there. He was about to leave when something caught his eye. He rushed to his UTV, grabbed his GPS, and snuck back to the red team's vehicle to snap a picture. Drake shoved the GPS into his pocket, then retrieved a bottle of water, continued to where Allie was sitting, and joined her. He opened the bottle, then passed it to her.

"Thanks." Allie took a drink and capped the bottle. "What are we doing now?"

"We're taking a break. Enjoying the view."

Drake watched the red team make their way to the bottom of the ridge. He estimated they had another hundred yards before they reached the start of the switchback trail.

"What are we really doing?" Allie asked.

"I found their puzzle booklet. They had every puzzle solved."

"They must be smart."

Drake looked at her. "No, they must be geniuses. Notice our booklet. We've got pages torn out, notes in margins, solutions scribbled out in places and reworked. Big X marks through the ones we couldn't figure out."

"Yeah, so?"

"So, they don't. Their book is pristine except for the coordinates written in the expected place on each page. No notes, no false starts, no wasted ink at all. Not so much as a doodle."

"You think they're cheating?"

"Oh, I guarantee they're cheating. Take a gander at this."

Drake fished the GPS out of his pocket, brought up the pictures, and showed Allie the last photo he snapped.

"What is that?" she asked.

"That, my dear, is a charging cable for a smart phone."

"How could they even get coverage out here?"

"That I can't answer. When they get up here, I'm going to make some friendly geocaching small talk with them. While I'm doing that, you stay back and try to see if there's anything in their pockets that looks like a phone."

"Sounds like a plan."

Drake and Allie watched the red team ascend the slope. They got to their feet and moved to the top of the ridge as the men got closer to them.

"Hey, how's it going?" Drake asked.

"Good," one man said.

"You're Will and Julian, right?"

"Julius."

"How was the hike on this cache?" Drake asked.

As Will talked about the route they took to the geocache, Allie leaned against their UTV and sipped at her water while she studied the men. Will was an inch shorter than Julius. He had a cowboy's frame and looked like he just stepped out of the May page of a cowboy calendar. His brown hair hung to just below his shoulders. His eyes, which were surrounded by crow's feet from spending too much time in the sun, were ice blue. She noticed he had a small scar on the left side of his neck, and that stood out as a white blemish against his deep-tanned skin.

Julius had chestnut skin and dark eyes. He wore his hair in a closely shaved fade, and had a full mustache and beard, tightly trimmed. He looked like he had stepped out of the calendar as well, but she imagined him more like a Mr. September. Both were handsome, fit, trim, and polite, and they wore matching wedding bands on their left hands.

She had a straight-on view of Julius, so she took another drink of water and tried to appear disinterested as she looked him up and down. Allie blushed when he caught her looking at him and coughed and looked away when he winked at her.

She moved over toward her seat and sat down so her legs were hanging out and waited for a lull in the conversation. It appeared Will was the storyteller of the two, because not only did he go into great detail about finding the cache, he included a lot of hand gestures as he did so.

"Hey, y'all, I hate to interrupt, but can we eat, Drake? I need to take my pills and can't do it on an empty stomach."

He turned to Allie. "Of course. Right away." Then he pivoted back to address Will. "I'm sorry, but I'm sure we can talk later tonight. I don't want to hold you up anyway since you've probably got a lot of caches to find yet."

Will nodded and slipped into the seat of his UTV without a word. Julius approached Allie. "I hope your leg gets better soon, ma'am. I broke mine once while busting a bronco. It was horrible. I was in a cast for an entire summer, and let me tell you, you don't want to be on a west Texas ranch in a hot cast during the summer."

Will interrupted. "Are you telling your broken leg story again? Get over here and leave those people alone. If you want to, you can bore them over dinner."

Julius smiled, left Allie, and joined his partner. Allie watched the couple drive away while Drake retrieved the lunch bag. From inside, he extracted two chicken salad sandwiches and passed one to Allie.

"Well?" he asked as he reached into the bag and found the chocolate chunk cookies he was searching for.

"Julius has it. I think he thinks he caught me checking out his man-package, but I was really much more interested in the rectangle-shaped bulge in his pants pocket. He should know that when people wear jeans that tight, they can't hide anything."

Allie opened the sandwich and took a bite. The chicken salad was creamy, but not overly so, and had chunks of apple, red grapes, and pineapple in it, on fresh wheat bread.

"This is so good."

"Yeah," Drake agreed. "When we leave here, I'm going to miss the food. How many caches do we have left to go before we're finished today?"

"About half. Fifteen, I'd guess."

"You going to be up for them?"

"Sure thing. As long as my pills hold out, I'll be fine."

A warm breeze came up from the south. Drake closed his eyes and enjoyed the wind blowing through his hair. He had spent little time in the southwestern part of the country before, but he liked it. There was something about the wide-open spaces and the desolation that appealed to him somehow.

Drake and Allie finished lunch and cleaned up their site, and it wasn't long before they were in pursuit of their next cache. Fortunately for them, the first seven were simple grabs, but the eighth involved a tree climb. Since Drake was too short to reach the bottom branch, he pulled the UTV next to the tree and scaled the vehicle's frame to get started with his ascent. To encourage him, Allie acted as cheerleader and clapped and hooted as he scurried up the branches like a squirrel. After a quick search, he found the container, stamped the log, and joined Allie back on the ground.

On the way to the next location, Drake stopped at the foot of a large hill circled by boulders.

"How far from here?" Drake asked.

Allie checked the distance. "Just under three hundred feet."

"Doesn't look too steep. Want to give it a go?"

"Absolutely. I feel stiff and I need to walk around a bit. I might as well do it here."

Allie passed Drake the GPS, then slipped out of the UTV. She didn't want to use her cane, but she thought it was safer to use the extra support it afforded, and she certainly didn't want to topple down another hill.

She took a moment to check her path, visually picking out the steps ahead of time she wanted to take, then started down. Normally something like the hill wouldn't bother her, and three hundred feet would take her only two minutes at a leisurely pace. But as she took one tentative step after another, she recognized she wasn't in her best condition. Even though she'd taken another pain pill, her knee throbbed, and she admitted to herself that she should have taken up Drake's offer for a relaxing day by the pool. Allie needed rest, not a hike through the desert. Still, she trudged on.

"There's a cairn up ahead," Drake said.

"I see it."

"Can you make it that far?"

Allie stopped and looked behind her. She'd walked more than halfway already. "I came this far, so I might as well finish it." She put her head down and limped the entire way to the cache. Near the cairn was a boulder the approximate size of an easy chair, so while Drake unstacked the rocks to expose the cache container below them, Allie sat down with a grimace.

"It's getting worse, isn't it?" Drake asked.

Allie reluctantly nodded.

"Okay, that's it then. You're not getting out of the UTV for the rest of the day. If we can't park within twenty feet of a cache, we're not going for it, okay? Same goes for the competition. Unless you're good, we should drop out. For us, the competition will be over, and we can consider the rest of the week a casual vacation."

Allie shook her head in disagreement, but quit when she realized Drake was right.

"Are you sure?" she asked. "About all of it?"

"Of course. Look, it's nuts trying to keep up this frantic pace. We're already in the back of the pack anyway, so it would probably be impossible to catch up. And now that we figured out it's the cowboys who are the team that's cheating, the pressure is off as far as the investigation is concerned."

Drake stamped the log, put it back in the container, and stacked the rocks into the cairn. He sat down on the rock next to Allie and rubbed her shoulder. "Let me know when you're ready and we'll start heading up. Take all the time you need."

"I am ready. So, we can go now," Allie said.

Drake took Allie's cane from her. "Too bad. I'm not ready. I'm getting tired, too. And to be honest, I really don't like that UTV. It's only been a couple of days, and I feel like my spine turned to pudding. I don't know how people ride these things every weekend."

Allie smiled. "Those people probably say the same thing about us. They don't know how we can spend our free time looking for film canisters in the woods and magnetic key holders in guardrails and on signs."

Drake laughed. "Yeah, you're probably right. Different strokes for different folks, right?" He handed her the cane. "If you're really ready, we can go. No rush. I meant it when I said take all the time you need."

"Help me up then. I don't want to stay here all day. My leg will stiffen up, then you'll have to carry me."

Drake helped Allie to her feet, and they walked back to the UTV.

Two hours later, Drake pulled up to the hotel and helped Allie into the parlor. Once he got her settled in, he grabbed the tarp from the UTV and headed to the jail. He went through the door, saw T.R. in the communications room, and when she waved him in, he joined her. As he walked through the room, he handed her the tarp.

"What's this?" T.R. asked.

"This was hanging in a tree, with rattlesnakes in it, waiting for an unsuspecting geocacher to pull it down."

T.R.'s brow furrowed as she frowned. "You're kidding? Was anyone hurt?"

"No, but it caused Geneva and Ingrid of the gray team to climb up a tree and wait for someone to come along to save them."

"My goodness. Good thing you did."

"No doubt. Are there any other teams back yet?"

T.R. picked up a clipboard and showed the page to Drake. T.R. had all the teams listed in alphabetical order by color, and all had a check mark in a box labeled out. No team had a check mark in the box labeled in. He handed the clipboard back to T.R.

"Team green is here."

She winked at him. "No, you're not. At least not until I get the call from Andy that you've officially checked in. Get it?"

Drake smiled. "Got it. I've got something else, too. I think the red team is the one you're looking for. We caught up to them when their UTV was unattended. They had a phone charger in there, and their puzzle booklet had nothing in it but the coordinates for each cache."

"What do you mean?"

Drake reached around and pulled his booklet from his back pocket and handed it to T.R. "Here's ours for comparison."

As she opened it, several pages fell to the floor. Drake picked them up as T.R. looked through the rest of it. "I don't understand what you're showing me here."

"I'm showing you the work that went into solving the puzzles. See those pages that have scribbled out numbers? Highlighter marks? Code tables that were written out, then scratched off?"

"Yeah? So?"

"So that's Allie and I, solving the puzzles. Their book wasn't like that. They only had the answers."

T.R. held out a sheet with only the north and west

coordinates on it. "What about this one?"

"Allie worked that one out on a whiteboard, then wrote the answers on the page."

"Couldn't the other team have done the same?"

Drake shook his head. "No. You're looking at over two hours of work there. They left the school after only thirty minutes. They would have had to do every puzzle in forty-five seconds to accomplish that. There's another thing. Allie saw the outline of a cell phone in Julius' jeans pocket. I'd bet my last dollar that they're getting outside help."

T.R. handed the booklet back. "I'll look into it. In the meantime, you'd better go check in if you're done for the day."

Drake nodded and left the jail. He got into the UTV and drove it back to the barn. He parked in their assigned spot and unloaded his gear.

"You're back early."

Drake turned around and saw Travis standing there, socket wrench in hand.

"Yeah. I know. Allie's not feeling well, so we only did the easy ones today."

"She sick?"

"She sprained her knee yesterday, and all the bouncing around today didn't help her much. Too many miles to cover on the rough road. Speaking of mileage, do you track these things?"

"Sure. Every day. Helps me keep a record of the maintenance schedule."

"You mind if I see that?"

"Why in the world would you want to? Trust me, I check them every day before they go out, and again when they come in. They're safe."

"No, I'm sorry. I didn't mean to imply you're not doing your job. It's just that back home I keep a log of how many miles we travel when we're geocaching, and I just realized I haven't done that in the last couple of days. Come on, could you help me out?"

Travis shoved the socket into his back pocket. "You geocachers sure are strange, but come on, I'll show you."

Drake followed Travis into the office, where Travis produced a three-ring binder.

"How can I tell which one is mine?"

"There's a sticky note on the page with the team color on it. I think I hear another team coming in. Come find me if you need anything else."

"Okay, thanks, Travis."

Travis left, and Drake opened the binder. Inside he found tabbed section dividers with numbers written on the tab, and Drake flipped it open to the first page. The first sheet of the section contained a page with the serial number of the UTV at the top, along with columns that showed the date, the mileage, and a line for comments. The third line on the sheet had the words 'broken axle' written in, and since it had no note with the team color on it, Drake assumed it was a vehicle not being used. He turned the page and saw a receipt and order slip for a new axle that apparently hadn't arrived yet.

He flipped through the binder until he found the red team's sheet, then found a spare sticky note and scribbled down the mileage for the last couple of days. Then he found the sheet for his own UTV and did the same. Once done, he set the notes side by side to compare the numbers.

"Holy cow," he said. "There really is something rotten going on in the city of Cacheland."

CHAPTER THIRTEEN

Hey you," Allie said as she pulled a chair out and sat down. "What did you do last night?"

Drake grinned when he saw her. "Allie. How are you doing today? I didn't want to wake you, so I came here."

"Honestly, I'm much better than yesterday. I was so tired and my leg hurt, so I headed right to bed."

"I know. Heather told me when I got back from dropping off the UTV. What about dinner? Did you eat?"

Allie nodded. "I ordered room service. Nothing fancy, just a grilled ham and cheese sandwich and fries. What did you do?"

"When we first got back, I talked to T.R. about our suspicions of the… other team. Then when I turned the UTV in, I had Travis show me the odometer readings, and discovered this."

Drake pulled the sticky notes from his pocket and handed them to Allie. "The one with the larger numbers is us. The other is the red team."

Allie glanced at the numbers. "Ours are almost twice as much."

Drake nodded. "Exactly. Somehow, they magically found more geocaches with less distance traveled. There's no way that could happen unless they have access to a wormhole. Here comes the server."

Allie folded the notes in half and shoved them in her back pocket. "Good. I'm starving. French toast today for me. You never told me what you did last night."

Drake and Allie ordered breakfast, then Drake answered. "Not much. Since we got back so early, I spent some time walking around town, then I talked with people as they came in. I ended up having dinner with Ingrid and Geneva. They're really nice."

"They're from out east somewhere, aren't they?"

"Boston."

"Oh, nice. I've always wanted to go geocaching in Boston. I hear they have a fantastic history trail there," Allie said.

"Yeah, me too. We'll have to get their information before the week is out and maybe plan a trip up there."

The server dropped off two plates of French toast, along with orange juice and a plate of bacon. They had barely taken a bite when Geneva stopped by, and Allie invited her to join them.

"Did you catch the news?" Geneva asked. She looked giddy, like a pre-teenager with a secret to tell. "They busted one team for cheating. I don't know which one, but I'm sure we'll find out soon enough, won't we? I heard they got arrested or something."

Allie looked at Drake, who took a sudden interest in moving the fresh strawberries around on his plate.

"No, I hadn't heard that," Drake said without looking up.

Ingrid trailed in and joined them at the table. She was

about to say something when Bruce and Andy made their daily appearance. Unlike the previous days, when Bruce greeted everyone, he stayed close to Andy. His face looked like he was in the middle of a twelve-hour marathon of sucking on a lemon. Bruce's eyes darted across the room as he surveyed the teams there, determined they had a quorum, and started.

"Good morning, everyone. Before we begin today, I'd like to make an announcement. Yesterday, when the red team checked in, our security chief did a brief investigation and determined they had been cheating. For full transparency, I will tell you they were getting outside help. They had a smart phone with them and were in contact with a third person. That person gave them puzzle solutions yesterday, as well as provided direct routes to geocaches the previous two days. Subsequently, I've removed the red team from the competition, and they earned themselves a lifetime ban from Cacheland. Like I said on the first day, we will not tolerate any form of cheating in these games. Now that the bad news is out of the way, here are the updated standings. Andy?"

Andy turned on the monitor and displayed the spreadsheet. Team pink was now in the lead, team black was in second place, and the Beasley brothers, representing the yellow team, had moved up to third. Drake scanned the list and saw he and Allie were holding firm in fifth place. With the red team off the board, it encouraged him that the point spread between all the teams was a lot closer together. He smiled when he calculated that the green team was less than two hundred points behind the leaders. On the downside, fifth in an eight-team race looked worse than with ten teams on the list. Drake felt better when he looked at the chart when he was in the middle, rather than trending toward the bottom as they were now.

"Today is all about the multi-cache," Bruce said. "Today

there are ten multi-caches for you to find. Each multi-cache will have ten segments. You'll receive the starting coordinates for each multi on your cache sheet today. Those coordinates will lead you to a container with the coordinates to the next set, and so on, until the tenth, where there will be a container with the log ready to receive your stamp. For each geocache log stamped, you'll get points depending on when you sign each log. First to find will get a hundred points, second to find will get ninety, and points will go down ten points per finder. The last team to sign the log, assuming you all find it, will get thirty points minimum since two teams are now out of the competition. Also, for today only, I'm allowing team-ups. If you want to, you can work with another team, but only one other team. How you choose to work with them is up to you. Each team must still sign the log to get the points available. Check-in deadline for today is eight tonight, so be safe out there, and have a great day!"

Bruce left the room and Andy shut down the monitor and passed the backpacks out to the teams.

Ingrid was the first to speak. "Do you guys want to work together?"

Drake looked over at Allie. "I'd be up for it. How would you feel about a collaboration?"

Allie shrugged. "I'm fine with it. Like the old adage says, four heads are better than two."

Drake pushed the team backpack toward Allie. "Can you get out the map and start on a plan? I'll go grab lunch."

"Can I come with you?" Geneva asked.

Drake nodded, and he and Geneva got up and headed toward the kitchen.

"I bet Geneva has a crush on him," Ingrid said as she watched the pair traverse the dining room. "She's been talking about him nonstop since yesterday."

"I can see why. He's a good guy," Allie said.

"Are you two… together?"

Allie smiled. "No. We're caching partners and friends, nothing more. We've never even been on an actual date. Like I said, Drake's a good guy, but he's not really my type."

"How did you two meet?"

Allie smiled. "I was driving by when I spotted him on the side of the road looking for a cache near a billboard outside of town. I always like meeting other cachers, so I parked behind his truck and waited for him to finish. After five minutes, I realized he was having some difficulty finding it. So, I walked right to where the geocache was, pulled it out, pretended to write my name, put it back, and returned to my car and waited for him."

"Why did you only pretend to sign?"

"Because I found that cache the week before. I didn't tell him that at the time, so he thought I was a cache finding genius since it was a such a tough hide. Anyway, since we were both out caching, we teamed up and went out together."

"How long have you been friends?"

Allie thought about it for a moment. "Not sure exactly. Four years? Five? I can't really pin a date on it. I guess I could find out for sure by looking at past logs or something."

"Nah, no need to go through all that trouble. I was just curious. All that time together, and you never went on a date?"

"Nope. Why ruin a great relationship by dating someone?"

Ingrid tittered, and Allie joined her in laughter. They were still giggling when Drake and Geneva returned, each with a thermal lunch bag in hand.

"What's so funny?" Geneva asked.

"Oh, nothing," Ingrid said. "We're just sharing geocaching stories."

Drake rolled his eyes and took his seat. "Have you mapped out the plan?"

"No. We thought we'd wait for you. Do you have a suggestion?" Allie answered.

Drake started the GPS and plotted out the best route based on the starting locations for each of the ten multi-caches. Unlike the previous day, where the puzzle caches mapped out nicely into a grid, they spread the caches today out all over the property. "I'd say that four sets of eyes are better than two. We could do each cache together. We might go faster that way."

"I've got a better idea," Ingrid said. "We split the team in two, with one of us and one of you in each UTV. The stamps for both teams travel in one UTV. Then, we split up, and each team goes and finds a cache. When the team with the stamps gets to the final location and signs a log, they stamp for both teams. When the team without the stamps gets to a final, they radio the coordinates of the final to the team with the stamps."

"Oh, I like that idea much better," Allie said.

"Me, too," Drake said. "And when you stamp, you could alternate the finds, so each team gets a fair shot at the higher points."

"One question," Geneva interrupted, "what will prevent the other teams from listening in and getting the final coordinates as we find them?"

The four sat at the table, not speaking as each thought about that problem. Allie reached over and grabbed her map and looked at it. "Okay. Eight caches, eight planets. We give each cache a random planet name, so when we call out over the radio, we can say something like Jupiter three one one, nine two seven. The first set of numbers can be the last three digits of the north coords, and the second set will be the last three numbers of the west coords."

"Good. Why don't we switch it up and give the west numbers first, then the north?" Drake asked.

"That works," Geneva said. "As long as we're consistent, we shouldn't have a problem."

"What about naming the first two caches?" Ingrid asked. "Don't they get names?"

"Don't need them," Allie said. "Whoever has the stamps will know which one they're at, and we'll know which one the other team goes for when we start out."

"All in favor of the plan?" Geneva asked.

Four hands reached into the air.

"Okay, it's settled then. Ingrid, why don't you and Allie take our UTV and both stamps, and I'll go out with Drake."

The four geocachers picked out the two closest caches to search for, then broke into teams and headed out.

Drake drove their UTV to the second-furthest cache. When they got to the posted coordinates, they found a place where there were four bricks laying on the ground with a single rock on top. Geneva jumped out of the UTV, picked up the rock, and turned it over in her hands. Nothing.

"Try under a brick," Drake said.

Geneva picked up a brick and looked underneath, where she again discovered nothing. The second brick was the same, but the third brick she hefted had a small plastic pocket glued to it. In the pocket were the coordinates they needed for the next stage. Drake jotted down the numbers on his cache page, then entered them into the GPS. Geneva lined up the bricks the way she found them and returned the stone to the center.

When they arrived at the third set of coordinates, there were eight bricks waiting for them. Geneva flipped bricks over, and on the fourth one, she got lucky and found the next set of numbers she needed. From then on, for every leg, the number of bricks doubled until finally, at the ninth stage, there were over a thousand bricks. The bricks were in rows of fifty that looked to stretch all the way to an emerald city. Drake dropped Geneva off at the beginning, then hiked to the other end and, for an hour, they flipped over bricks until they found the specific one they wanted. Drake recorded the coordinates, walked over to the radio, and transmitted the six numbers. When Allie acknowledged the call, Drake picked out the next cache to find as Geneva walked back to the UTV.

Before they took off, Geneva removed her helmet and ran her fingers through her short brown hair, then reached around with her right hand to her left shoulder. "Hey, can you help me out here? I think there's something sticking me in the back, and I can't reach it."

Drake got out of the UTV and faced her shoulders. "I don't see anything."

"Look down the back of my shirt. Come on. It's prickly and annoying."

Drake moved closer and pulled on the neck of Geneva's teal t-shirt. He thought he saw something, so he got close enough to smell the floral scent of her shampoo and the linger of the body lotion she used.

"*Easy, tiger,*" he thought.

Drake let go of her shirt. "I see something, but I don't believe I can reach it from here. Can I pull the back of your shirt up?"

"Please. Whatever is there is driving me nuts!"

Geneva pulled her t-shirt loose from her jeans and Drake lifted the back of her shirt. When he reached the area a half-inch above the olive-green sports bra she wore, he spotted the offending object.

"Hold still," Drake said.

He reached up, plucked the item from her perfect skin, and let her shirt fall back into place.

Geneva spun around and her hazel eyes met his, and he noticed for the first time the specks of gold and green she had in them. He stared at her, awkwardly lost for a moment, and missed the words she spoke.

"I'm sorry, what?"

"I said, what was it?" Geneva repeated.

"Oh. This." Drake held up the inch long thorn he had plucked from her flesh.

Geneva took it from his fingers and looked at the offending thing. "That's what I guessed it was. I had a close encounter with a cactus yesterday, something I wouldn't recommend."

She got up on her tiptoes and kissed him on the cheek, a kiss that lingered. "Thanks. You're my hero."

Drake was dumbfounded and could respond only with a stupid grin. He cleared his throat and pulled away from her, even though he didn't want to. "Ready to head for Saturn?"

"Sure thing. I've never been there before."

Drake and Geneva got back into the UTV and headed toward the next cache. The silence was awkward, and Drake felt the need to break it.

"Can I ask you a question?" Drake asked.

"Of course."

"Why don't you sound like a Boston girl?"

"Probably because I didn't grow up in Boston. I attended college there and never left."

"Let me guess, you studied at Harvard?"

"Close. Berklee. I got a master's degree in music."

"Wow, that's impressive," Drake admitted.

"Eh. My parents don't think so. They wanted me to be a doctor, not a composer."

"For like a symphony?"

"That's my goal, but lately I've been doing mostly

songwriting and music production."

Drake was about to answer but stopped when he saw a small stake with an orange ribbon blowing in the breeze ten yards ahead. He pulled up next to the stake, examined it, and discovered the coordinates written on the ribbon. He recorded the numbers and headed off to the next waypoint.

"I like Allie. She's nice." Geneva said.

"Yeah, she is."

"I bet she makes a good girlfriend."

Drake smiled, since he recognized Geneva's fishing expedition right away. It wasn't the first time a lady questioned his status with Allie. "I wouldn't know. She's not my girlfriend. We're only friends and geocaching buddies, nothing more. The most romantic thing we've ever done is to be each other's date at a Valentine's Day event last year."

"So, then, you're not…"

"Nope. I'm not her type, and we're nothing more than best friends and won't ever be more than that. Oh, no."

"What?"

"More stakes ahead." Drake drove another fifty yards and parked near the five stakes with orange ribbons. He got out and examined them.

"Well?" Geneva asked when he returned.

"Four have random numbers on them. The fifth had the coordinates."

"Do you think there's any significance to the random numbers?"

"I hope not, because I didn't write any of them down. My guess they were there to make finding the coordinates harder since I had to look at every ribbon and couldn't simply find the one with the writing on it. We'll see if the theory holds when we get to the next location."

The third waypoint had fifteen stakes with ribbons, and with Geneva's help, they quickly found the correct one. From there, the number of stakes increased with each step, until, at the ninth spot, they found hundreds of stakes spread out in an area that covered half of a football field. After thirty minutes, Geneva found the right stake, so she jotted down the coordinates for the final cache location and handed the sheet to Drake.

Drake got the radio and spoke. "Allie, come in, over."

It took a few seconds, but eventually she answered.

"Allie, Saturn six one seven, eight eight three. Over."

Allie repeated back the coordinates and signed off.

"I hope all the caches aren't like this," Geneva said. "So far, finding the coordinates has been like finding a specific needle in a haystack made with needles."

"Yeah, I know what you mean. Hopefully Allie and Ingrid are having an easier time at it. Where should we go next? It looks like Neptune and Venus are equidistant from here."

"Let's go to Venus," Geneva said.

CHAPTER FOURTEEN

S aturn six one seven, eight eight three. Got it, Drake. Over and out."

Allie wrote the coordinates for the Saturn geocache on her paper, clipped the radio onto her belt, and went back to the sunflowers.

"That's the second one they've finished," Ingrid said. "And we're still on our first."

"Don't worry about it. That's the way we planned it, remember? Besides, we're almost done."

They were on the ninth stage looking through a patch of fake sunflowers, searching for the coordinates that were written on one of its petals. Like the first multi-cache the other team did, the first stage presented a single flower, but the number of flowers at each stage increased in number. Checking each flower was long, tedious work, but eventually it paid off.

"Got it!" Ingrid squealed with delight. "Finally."

Allie jotted down the numbers as Ingrid read them off. Then, three minutes later, they arrived at the location of the geocache. From beneath a pile of rocks, Ingrid extracted an ammo can. They opened the can, pulled out the log, and saw the sheet of paper without a mark on it other than boxes labeled from one to ten.

"Who should we stamp first?" Ingrid asked.

"Yours. You found the coords to this one," Allie said.

Ingrid pulled the stamp from her pocket and applied a gray moon in the number one box, then passed it to Allie, who added her green clover to the number two space. She handed the sheet back, and Ingrid put it away and tucked the can back under the rocks.

"And now, the simple part begins. Where to next?" Ingrid asked.

Allie entered the coordinates for the first geocache Drake called in and mapped the route. "That way," she said as she pointed toward the northeast.

"What do you do for work?" Ingrid asked as she drove along a dirt trail.

"I teach classes at a gym. Aerobics, yoga, stuff like that."

"That's going to be hard with that knee," Ingrid said.

Allie rubbed her leg. The night before, Dr. Liz stopped by, had a look at it, and didn't seem concerned. She'd also given Allie two additional pain pills, which Allie appreciated. "It's feeling better today. The swelling is way down since yesterday, so I think I'll be fine in the long run, but you're right, I probably won't be teaching the high-impact stuff for a while. I might have to concentrate on the water exercise classes for a couple of months."

"Oh, I love those," Ingrid said. "I go to them all the time at my gym. I love all the water stuff. Swimming, kayaking, sailing, snorkeling. My mom always said I was part mermaid."

Allie nodded. "I can see that." And she could. Ingrid had long hair that was so blond it was almost white, and she had ice-blue eyes that sparkled like the stars over Iceland.

Her summer tan was fading, so her skin was fading back to its alabaster shade. "You remind me of that mermaid in Copenhagen."

"You've been to Denmark?" Ingrid asked with a pitch in her delivery that showed her excitement.

"Yes. I embarked for a cruise there, so I got there a couple of days beforehand to explore the city."

"My parents are from Denmark. A little city called Aalborg, which is in the Jutland region in the north. Have you been there?"

"No. Just Copenhagen. Can you speak Danish?"

"Ja jeg kan. I learned Danish before I learned English. I still speak it at home when I visit my parents."

"Do they still live in Denmark?"

"No. They live near Boston."

"So, what do you do?" Allie asked.

"Oh, I'm a teacher, too."

"You teach aerobics?"

Ingrid smiled. "No. English and American literature to high schoolers. It's almost the same thing, though."

Allie laughed. "Almost."

Allie checked her GPS and had Ingrid slow down since they were almost at ground zero. Ingrid parked next to an area where there was a small cactus field, and both women got out and started the search.

"Be careful in here. Geneva wasn't paying attention yesterday and backed right into a saguaro." Ingrid laughed.

"You found that funny?"

"No. I'm just remembering all the choice words she said afterward. It was funny at the time, and of course, much funnier if you were there in person."

The radio gave a squelch, and then Allie heard her name.

"Allie here, copy."

"Venus nine two one zero three eight. Copy," Drake said over the radio.

Allie recorded the numbers and repeated them to Drake, and when he confirmed they were correct, she ended the call.

"That was a quick one," Ingrid said. "I feel like we're getting behind them."

"Don't panic. We're only two back, and they have the hard work. We'll catch up to them soon enough. Relax. Keep looking for this one."

Together, they carefully picked their way around the cacti, and eventually Allie stumbled upon a small rock pile.

"Hey, it's over here."

Allie undid the pile and found a small plastic pencil box underneath. She opened the log and saw a mark already in the one position. "Looks like the Beasley brothers beat us to this one."

Allie placed her mark at number two, and Ingrid stamped hers at number three.

"Well, we can't expect to be the first at every cache, right?" Ingrid said as she placed the paper back in the box and stacked the rocks on top. "Let's go get Saturn."

They had traveled half the distance when they came across the Beasley brothers. Ingrid stopped the UTV when they pulled even with them. Brandon was sitting on the front bumper; Ben was sitting on the ground with his back to the vehicle in the UTV's shade.

"Hi Ben, Brandon," Allie said. "Need help?"

Brandon pointed his thumb at Ben. "Genius here kissed a rock formation and blew the sidewall out of the front tire."

"Oh, no. Are you guys okay?"

"We're fine. Just embarrassed, since I should know better," Ben said.

"You need us to radio base?" Ingrid asked.

Brandon shook his head. "No thanks, we already did that. They should be here anytime now. I think within twenty minutes we'll be back on the road. Where are you coming from?"

Allie held out an arm in the direction they came from. "That way. We just found your mark on a log. First to find. Not bad."

Ben shrugged. "Not that impressive. Ten caches and eight teams mean the odds are good that everyone will get one, right?"

"Good point. Well, I guess we'd better get at it then. Have a good day."

"See you later," Brandon said as he saluted to the women.

Ingrid pressed the accelerator and drove off.

"I like those guys. They're fun. We were hanging out at the pool together a couple of nights ago," Ingrid said.

"Yeah, they're a hoot. Watch out for Brandon, though. He's a pool shark. Like eight-ball, I mean, not swimming."

"Do you know if they're single?"

Allie shrugged. "It beats me. I didn't think to ask."

"Why not? They're dreamy."

"Not my type. You're a little off track. Look off to the north, see that mesa way out in the distance? Head for that."

Ingrid got her bearings and made the course correction. They soon arrived at the top of a ridge, stepped out of the vehicle, and walked to the edge.

"Based on the distance to the cache, I'm guessing it's by that gigantic tree down there," Allie said as she pointed to the large mesquite near the bend of a dry river. "I don't think I can make that hike."

"Why walk when we can ride? If we follow the ridge, it dips down to that level."

Allie turned and traced the landscape with her eyes. Just

as Ingrid said, the ridge lowered as it went, and eventually it bottomed out at near the same ground level as the tree.

"Let's go," Allie said.

They got in the vehicle, and Ingrid followed the ridge. Near the end, they got to a fairly steep slope, but it wasn't so bad that they needed to abandon the UTV and walk. Instead, Ingrid took her time and drove to the bottom of the hill without incident. From there, she motored across the riverbed, and made a direct line for the tree.

"I hope it's not up in there. I wouldn't be able to climb it," Allie said.

Ingrid parked next to the tree and looked for the telltale rock pile, but there wasn't one. She started scanning the branches, looking for a container, but didn't see one.

"I can't get up there, either. The branches are too high," Ingrid said.

"Don't have to. It's around here," Allie said.

Ingrid moved her vision from the boughs to the ground and spotted Allie on the opposite side of the tree. She walked to Allie's side and noticed a thin plastic case stuck in where the two main trunks joined to become one. Allie pulled out the case and opened it up.

"Drat. Pink and yellow have both been here," Allie said as she checked the log.

"No worries. Third and fourth are worth points too."

The women stamped the logs and were on their way. Over the next three hours, they found Venus, Neptune, and Uranus, and were on their way to Earth when the radio cackled.

"That must have been an easy one. Drake just called like ten minutes ago," Ingrid said.

Allie picked up the radio and turned up the volume.

Drake's voice came over the radio. "Team green to base. Team green to base. Over."

"This is base. Go ahead."

"Base, I'm here with the black team. They've been involved in an accident and need medical attention. Over."

"Where are you?"

Drake rattled off his coordinates, and Allie jotted them down and entered them into the GPS.

"He's less than a mile from here. Go due west. Fast."

Ingrid nodded and pressed the pedal to the floor, leaving a trail of dust behind them. A few minutes later, Allie spotted the green flag of Drake's UTV next to the sheer wall of a thirty-foot high mesa that had an uncanny resemblance to Devil's Tower in Wyoming. Ingrid got as close as she dared, then skidded to a stop. The women jumped out of the vehicle and rushed to the scene of the accident.

Allie couldn't believe her eyes. A rock pile completely covered the black team's UTV. "What happened?"

Drake hadn't noticed their approach, but he looked relieved when he looked back and spotted a couple of extra people to help.

"Rockslide. Can you two help pull some of these smaller ones aside? I can't reach them."

Ingrid got right to work next to Geneva and pulled stones away from the UTV. Drake wedged his way to the front of the UTV and cleared the rocks the size of basketballs away from the windshield.

"Can you see them?" Allie asked.

"Move over," Drake ordered.

Allie stepped aside and Drake pushed the rocks over to the side of the UTV, then lifted them enough so they'd topple over the top of the pile. From there, it took only another push for gravity to take over and the rocks rolled off the pile and farther down the hill they were on.

Once he cleared the hood and windshield area of debris, he had enough space to sit down and use his legs to push away the larger rocks that settled near the driver's seat.

"Okay, Allie, get in here. Take a look at him while I see if we can get to her."

Allie approached the driver and realized immediately he was unconscious. She checked for a pulse and determined he was breathing.

"His vitals are okay, but I don't want to move him until the ambulance gets here. He may have a spinal injury. What about her?"

"I can't get to her. That side is pushed all the way against the wall, and I can't get through the windshield."

Allie looked past the driver at the passenger. She, too, was out cold, but based on the wheezing sound she was making as she breathed, Allie suspected the woman had a broken rib or two.

"Allie, her head is bleeding pretty good."

"Can you reach around from where you are to the inside?" Allie asked.

"No. The wall's in the way."

"Why don't we push them out?" Geneva asked. "We'll move the UTV. Allie, put it in Drive and steer, and the rest of us will push it from behind."

Allie looked at Drake. "You think that will work?"

"Can't tell that until we try."

Drake got off the hood and made sure the ground was clear in front of the UTV. He rushed around to the back, where he kneeled and checked the ground around the back wheels. Once he cleared away a few smaller rocks, he got to his feet.

"Okay, let's do this. Put it in Drive, Allie."

"It already is."

Drake got in the middle of the UTV, and with Geneva and Ingrid on either side of him, he counted to three, and they pushed. It didn't move.

"Let's try to rock it," Geneva said. "That always works when I get my car stuck in the snow."

Drake nodded, and the trio pushed the car, and after it budged and settled back, they pushed again. After the fourth push, there was a screech of metal on stone and the UTV broke away from the wall and rolled forward, first a foot, then another.

"Keep pushing!" Allie yelled.

Allie cranked the steering wheel to the left, so it turned away from the mesa, then got worried that the thing would take off down the hill.

"Okay, stop," Allie ordered.

The three stopped pushing, but the UTV kept rolling and even though it was only going as fast as a quick walk. It was gaining some speed as it rolled down the incline. Allie tried to reach the brake but couldn't. Instead, she straightened the steering wheel and aimed the UTV at a boulder that was ten feet away. Confident it would hit, she stepped away from the vehicle and let it hit the boulder.

"Did you plan it that way?" Drake asked.

"Calculated risk, unless you wanted to chase them all the way down the hill. Come on."

Allie and Drake ran to the UTV. Geneva and Ingrid, who didn't know what to do, stayed where they were and watched.

Allie moved to the passenger and checked the side of the passenger's head. Just as Drake had described, her head was gushing blood. "I need a compress or something. Get the first-aid kit."

Drake checked the black team's UTV for the kit, couldn't find it, and retrieved the one from his own UTV. When he got back to Allie's side, he opened it.

"What do you need?" he asked.

"Give me all the gauze pads you have there."

While Allie waited for Drake to hand her the pads, she checked for additional injuries. She noticed by the contorted angle of the woman's hand she had at least a broken wrist.

"Here," Drake said as he passed Allie the gauze.

Allie took the gauze and, while supporting the woman's head with her left hand, pressed the cotton pads firmly against the scalp laceration.

In response, the woman woke immediately and started to scream and cry at the same time.

"No. Stay still. You have to stay as still as you can. What's your name?"

"Her name is Emma," Ingrid said.

"Emma, can you hear me? You need to calm down, okay? I know you're in pain, and help is on the way, but until then, you need to stay still. Understand?"

Emma tried to nod, but Allie held her head firm. "Can you speak?"

"Yes," Emma whispered in between sobs.

"I'll give it to you straight. You have a big gash on your head and a broken arm. If you move, you may injure something else, so don't move, okay?"

"Yes."

To Allie, Emma's voice sounded soft, like the plea of a wounded kitten.

"What about Kerry? I can't see him. Is he okay?" Emma said.

"He's unconscious, but his pulse and breathing are strong. I don't want to move him either until the ambulance gets here. Drake, you got any more bandages in there? These are beginning to seep through."

Without a word, Drake ran to the gray team's UTV and returned with their kit. Within seconds, he scrounged from there any bit of cotton he could find.

"Here."

"I'm going to remove this one, and when I do, put the new one against her head, okay?"

"Got it."

Drake moved in close to Emma's head, and when Allie removed the bloody bandage, he replaced it with the clean one. Allie dropped the used one to the ground and replaced Drake's hand with her own.

"This isn't going to work. She needs stitches like right now. Where's the ambulance?"

Drake was about to ask Geneva to radio base again when, off in the distance, he heard a siren. He knew his time was short, so he leaned into the UTV, close to Emma's face.

"Emma? Can you understand me?"

"Yes." Her voice was trailing off, and Drake could tell she was getting weak.

"Can you tell me what happened? How did the rocks fall on you? Do you remember? Emma?"

"Not fall… Hit… Truck…"

"Emma? What does that mean? Emma?"

"She passed out, Drake. She's not going to tell you anything else."

"Damn. Hold on a couple more minutes, Allie. They're almost here."

"I know. There's one other thing I'd really like to know."

"What's that?"

Allie turned to look at Drake. She had a small streak of Emma's blood on her cheek. "What the hell is going on around here?"

D r. Liz popped out of the ambulance and rushed to the UTV. "This wasn't what I meant by taking it easy, Allie. What do we have here?"

Allie gave a succinct report on the condition of Emma and Kerry. Afterwards, she, Drake, Geneva, and Ingrid all stepped out of the way while the professionals got to work. Dr. Liz quickly stabilized her patients, and after ten minutes, the ambulance took off, leaving the four alone.

"So now what do we do?" Geneva asked.

Drake checked his watch. "We've got plenty of time left, and I recognize it sounds insensitive, but I think we should get back at it. We've only got two geocaches left. How far behind us are you guys?"

Ingrid sauntered to the UTV and retrieved the cache sheet and handed it to Drake. "One. We were going to Earth when we picked up your call over the radio."

"Okay. You go back and get Earth, and we'll carry on the way we were. We'll call in Mercury, and we'll wait at the Mars final for you to get there."

The team split and headed for their respective

geocaches.

"That was really impressive the way you jumped in there," Geneva said. Although she pretended to watch the landscape roll by, she secretly stole occasional glances at Drake.

"It was the right thing to do, that's all. When people need help, I believe you have to help them if you can. My dad taught me that."

"Your dad sounds like a good man."

Drake glanced over and caught Geneva looking at him. "He had his moments. Where are we going?"

"South by southwest, one point two miles. You ever visit your dad?"

"No. He died when I was a kid."

"I'm sorry."

Off in the distance, Geneva watched a small dust devil kick dirt into a horizontal cone. As quick as it appeared, it dissipated, and the cone turned into a cloud of dirt that soon settled back to the ground.

"You ever been to Boston?" she asked.

"Only the airport," Drake answered. He spotted a pair of fresh tire tracks, determined they headed in the same direction he was, took a chance, and started following them.

"That doesn't count," Geneva said.

"I figured it wouldn't. Have you ever been to Nashville?"

"Only the airport. In Memphis." Geneva laughed.

Drake grinned. "That counts even less than my trip to Boston."

Drake navigated around a large bush, and as he got back on course, he stole another look at Geneva. Even though her helmet obscured most of her face, he still envisioned her without, and liked what he saw. She had an oval-shaped face, a button nose, and natural lips. Best of all, though, he thought she was intelligent, funny, and was easy to talk to.

"Would you like to have dinner with me tonight?" he asked.

"Sure. I can't wait to hear how Ingrid and Allie got along."

"No. I mean, just the two of us." Drake swallowed hard, not believing what he was doing.

Geneva thought about it for a bit before she answered. "No, I don't think that would be a good idea. I came out here to spend time with Ingrid, and it wouldn't be right to ditch her."

"Oh. Okay." Drake tried, but he realized he had failed at hiding the disappointment in his voice.

"Funny thing about Ingrid is, after dinner, she always likes to curl up with a book, which means I'm stuck not doing anything. Perhaps tonight I could do nothing by the fire pit behind the hotel?"

Drake smiled. "What a coincidence. I was thinking I could use a little fire pit time tonight myself. With perhaps a bottle of red wine?"

"White," Geneva countered.

"Did I say red? I meant white. Of course, white wine always goes best with fish and fire pits."

"Excellent," Geneva said. "I'll save you a seat. Turn off to the left a bit. We're almost there."

Drake did as he was told and stopped. Directly in front of them was a cemetery marker, reminiscent of Boot Hill.

Geneva took off her helmet and read the text. "Here lies Geo. Cash. Use his clue to find your stash. Oh, happy day, a riddle."

They got out and checked behind the marker, found nothing, and started turning over rocks to find the next set of coordinates. They couldn't find them, so they expanded their circle around ground zero to increase their search radius, but still came up empty. After several minutes, they returned to the marker.

"It's got to be there," Drake said. He approached the marker, crouched down in front of it, and looked at it closer. He ran his fingertips along the surface of the wood. "Bring me the cache sheet, will you?"

Geneva handed him the paper, and he held it against the marker, a quarter of an inch below the last word. Drake then gathered some grit from the ground and pressed it against the paper. After a few iterations, he removed the paper and gently blew away the lighter particles. Left on the paper were small indentations of numbers, stained tan.

"That's evil," Geneva said.

"No doubt. Give me a pen."

Geneva handed Drake a pen, and he carefully transcribed the digits, stood up and handed the paper back to Geneva, and she entered the new coordinates into her GPS.

At the second location, they found another marker with the same inscription as before. This time, Geneva found the coordinates hidden above the first word, not under the last word. And on they went. At each waypoint, they found one marker with the same wording, with the coordinates engraved in a unique spot on the wood. At the ninth location, after twenty minutes of searching, Geneva found them on the marker's side, near the bottom of the left edge.

She jotted down the final set of numbers, passed them to Drake, and he radioed the information to Allie.

"That's it. One last multi and we're done for the day," Drake said.

"Good," Geneva said. "I'm not really made for bouncing around in these vehicles all day."

Drake smiled. "Allie said the same thing yesterday. I agree with you, though. My favorite daily activity has become my end of day shower when I wash all the dust away."

Fifteen minutes later, Drake and Geneva came to the starting coordinates of the last multi-cache of the day. It surprised both of them to see three other teams milling about, including the yellow team.

Drake exited the UTV and approached Ben, who was standing off from the crowd and staring at his GPS. "Hey, what's going on?"

"Can't find the coordinates to the second waypoint."

"How can that be?" Drake asked.

"I don't know. We've only been here for a few minutes. Tito says they've been looking for almost an hour."

"Who's Tito?"

Ben pointed over his left shoulder. "The guy on the purple team."

Drake left Ben and walked over toward Tito, who was involved in a conversation with one man from the brown team. Since it was entirely in Spanish, Drake couldn't make out exactly what they were saying, but based on the body language and hand gestures, he guessed they were discussing the current geocache.

"Hey guys, what's going on? I'm Drake."

Drake held out his hand, and the man closest to him reached for it first. "Gilberto."

Gilberto released his grip, and Tito introduced himself.

"Ben tells me you've been here for a while," Drake said.

"Almost an hour," Tito said. "We were the first team here. Gilberto and Roy showed up about fifteen minutes later, and the yellow boys got here a few minutes before you did."

"And there's no sign of the second stage?" Drake asked.

"Dude, if we found it, we wouldn't be here now," Gilberto said.

"Excellent point. Okay, where have you checked so

far?"

"We've looked under every rock and bush in a forty-foot radius," the other member of the brown team said as he approached. "I'm Roy Pace."

Drake nodded at him, said hello, then turned in a small circle. He stepped away from the small group and surveyed the area. He noticed uncountable footprints all over the area, as well as places where people had flipped rocks and examined the bushes. Drake did his own quick circle around the area and surmised there was nothing more to see.

"Hi," Drake said as he approached the purple team's UTV. "Marlena?"

The woman behind the wheel smiled at him. "Close. It's Marina."

"Sorry. I'm horrible with names. Listen, would you mind pulling your vehicle ahead a few feet?"

Without a word, Marina started the machine, moved forward eight feet, and shut it off again, all without letting go of the bottle of water she was drinking from.

Drake examined the ground that was underneath the UTV.

"I already thought of that," Tito said as he joined Drake. "I bent over and looked under there, but there wasn't anything big enough to hold coordinates."

"Did you see this?" Drake picked up a stone that was covering a small hole two inches square.

"That's just an animal burrow. I've seen dozens of them over the last few days. The desert's full of them."

"True, but this one's perfectly square. The burrows are round, not square."

Tito kneeled and examined the hole closer. "Sure enough, it is." He took the pen from his pocket and explored the hole with it. "It goes down pretty deep, too."

Drake nodded. "I'd guess a foot or so. There was a sign

here at one point."

"Son of a gun," Brandon said as he leaned over and looked at the hole. "I think you're right, Drake. Someone must have pulled the sign after they got the next stage coordinates from it."

Drake nodded. "Logical assumption."

"I guess it's back to town for us then," Brandon said.

"Not necessarily. Which way did y'all come from?"

Tito, Ben, Brandon, and Marina all spoke at once, and each gave a different answer.

Drake stopped them by holding up his hand. "Better yet, each of you go find your tire tracks, about fifty or sixty feet from here."

"How can I do that? I'm a city boy, not a tracker. Never even been in the boy scouts." Ben said.

"Easy," Gilberto said. "Look for the coordinates of the geocache you just came from, then walk in that direction. You'll spot your tracks soon enough."

"Great idea, Gilberto," Drake said.

Ben and Tito followed Gilberto's advice, grabbed their GPS units, and followed the arrow out into the desert. Roy and Geneva, who had both come in on a straight line, easily picked up their own tire tracks and followed them away from the site.

"That's good," Drake yelled once he saw everyone had found the tracks. Roy and Ben were standing about fifteen feet from each other to the northeast, Geneva was due east, and Gilberto was off on his own to the southeast. "Everyone, stay where you are."

Noting that each of the teams were all in easterly directions, Drake walked forty feet due north, looked around to get his bearings, then strolled in a wide arc. When he reached north-northwest on the compass, he spotted a set of UTV tire treads. He walked a few more feet and discovered another set, this one wider than the first. Drake followed the second set for a few feet, and the two tracks turned into three, so he knew there were two separate UTVs that headed in that direction.

He stood where he was and whistled to get everyone's attention, then waved everyone over. "Bring the UTVs!"

Within three minutes, the four teams gathered around him.

"The next waypoint is that way," Drake said as he pointed behind him.

"How do you figure that?" Marina said.

"We all got here from more or less the same direction, and these tracks are too well concentrated to have come from that way. Ben, you guys follow the tracks over there, I'll follow these tracks, and Tito, you follow that other set."

"What about us?" Gilberto asked.

"You can follow me. If I'm right, we'll all end up at the same place at the same time, anyway."

Everyone got in their vehicles and started the engines, then pulled out Drake in the lead. Drake drove slowly while monitoring the trail. Like he suspected, the other teams stayed close to him. After four-tenths of a mile, all four teams lost the trail momentarily when the road went over a patch of bedrock. The whipping winds wiped the trail free of dirt and dust, but after a quick search, Gilberto found the trail again and they continued on.

Three minutes later, they spotted an arrow-shaped sign on a three-foot-high stake. Although the sign pointed to the direction from which they'd come, there were coordinates clearly displayed on the sign's back.

From those coordinates, they easily found the next waypoint, but instead of one arrow, there were two right next to each other.

"Each one of these has numbers," Roy said.

"Let me see," Geneva said.

She loaded the first set of coordinates into her GPS and looked at where they were, then she repeated the process with the second set. "These are the correct coords for the next leg," she said as she pointed to the second arrow. "The other set takes us backwards to where the second stage is."

"So, whoever removed the sign from the initial waypoint planted it here to get us to go the wrong way?" Roy asked.

"Looks that way. Although it would only work once. When you got back here, you'd take the second set, right? At the least, you'd only lose some time," Geneva said.

Roy reached out, grabbed the arrow with the wrong coordinates, pulled it from the ground, and threw it down. "Come on, let's get back on the road."

The four teams had no further issues and soon they arrived at the location for the geocache. Everyone gathered around the ammo can they plainly saw hidden beneath a pile of rocks.

"Go ahead, Drake. You stamp the log first. We wouldn't be here without you," Tito said.

"Um, we can't. We don't have the stamps."

"What do you mean?" Ben asked.

"Geneva and I were going from cache to cache. Once we had the coordinates to the last location, we'd radio them to the other halves of our team, and they go to the final stages and stamp the logs."

"So you're the person who's been calling out planets and random numbers all day? That's pretty smart, actually," Ben said. "How many have you found so far?"

"This is our last one," Geneva said.

"Last one? That can't be! We have three left!" Marina said.

"We still got two more to go," Brandon added.

"Still, on this one, you go first," Tito said. "Anyone here got a problem with that?"

No one said a word, so Drake radioed the final coordinates to Allie. Fifteen minutes later, they drove up.

"There's a party, and you didn't invite us?" Ingrid said as she left the vehicle.

"We're just waiting for you," Gilberto said.

Roy removed the rocks from the ammo can, took it to Ingrid's UTV, and opened it on the hood. He dug out the log and handed it to Ingrid.

"Before you stamp that, which teams have already been here?" Drake asked.

Ingrid looked at the paper. "The orange team was first, and the pink team was second."

Drake nodded, and Ingrid handed the paper to Allie. Allie stamped the paper, then handed it back to Ingrid, who added her mark.

"Who gets it next?" she asked.

"Purple, then brown, then us," Ben said. "That's only fair, to stamp it in the order the teams arrived, isn't it?"

Everyone agreed and passed the log sheet around. Brandon was the last to stamp it, so he returned it to the ammo can and hid it under the pile of stones.

"Probably didn't need to do that," Drake said. "There are no other teams to sign the log."

"What do you mean?" Brandon asked.

"There are five teams here. Two already signed, and three teams aren't competing today." Drake said.

"I know the red and blue folks are out, but what about the black team? They haven't been here yet," Marina said.

"Didn't you hear? They were in an accident," Drake said. "Emma and Kerry were both injured and had to be removed via an ambulance."

"That's horrible," Ben said. "Are they going to be

okay?"

"Don't know. I'm sure we'll hear more when we get back to town," Drake said. "Speaking of which, we're burning daylight, and I know y'all want to get on to the next one."

"One last question," Ben said. "Can you give us all the final coordinates to the rest of the geocaches?"

Allie laughed, then lifted her butt and sat on the geocache sheet. "Sorry. You know that's against the rules."

Allie got out of the gray team's UTV, made sure she had all her stuff, and joined Drake.

"I guess we should get back to town. T.R. is going to have questions for you," Allie said.

"I have some questions myself. Number one is, if the red team were the cheaters and Bruce kicked them out, how is it we're still having mysterious accidents and moved stages?" Drake said.

"That's one I'd like the answer to myself. Is there any other reason you're in a hurry to get back?"

Drake shrugged. "Just need to prepare for a date I have tonight. I should at least shower and put on a clean shirt. But before all that, we do need to see T.R."

CHAPTER SIXTEEN

You get anywhere with T.R.?" Allie asked just before she put a forkful of the breakfast special, a breakfast casserole, into her mouth.

"No. When I talked to her, it was pretty much a one-way conversation. I told her what we found and what we did, but she had little chance to investigate it. According to Travis, something may have hit Emma and Kerry's UTV. It was hard to tell with all the damage that occurred by having a rock pile fall on top of it," Drake answered.

"Can I have a bite of that?" Allie asked.

Drake slid the plate holding a cinnamon roll over to her, and Allie used her knife and fork to cut away a small section. She took a bite and grinned.

"That's amazing."

"I agree with you, but it's way too big. What is that? Eight inches in diameter? If I ate the whole thing, it would have me spinning in circles all day."

Allie washed the tasty treat down with a drink of orange juice and moved back to her own breakfast. "So, what else do you have to tell me?"

Drake looked away. "About what?"

Allie pointed her fork at Drake. "You get what I'm talking about. Don't play stupid. Your big date with Geneva. How did that go?"

"Oh, fine. We just hung out by the fire pit for an hour or so. Watched the stars come out. Talked. Nothing major."

"Okay, Duck-man. If you say so. I guess if I want the truth, I'll have to ask her." Allie used her fork to point at the door.

Drake turned in his chair and his eyes followed Geneva as she walked into the restaurant. She wore a light blue shirt with her khakis, and when she spotted him, it caused a hitch in his chest. Geneva approached the table, and Drake rose and pulled out a chair for her. He spotted Ingrid following a few steps behind, so he repeated the action for her as well.

Once the pair settled into their chairs, the server came over. The women ordered breakfast, and once that task was over, Geneva leaned over and handed Drake his watch.

"You'll probably need this. I found it this morning when I was getting dressed," Geneva said.

Allie raised an eyebrow. "Nothing major, huh? You want to stick to that story?"

Drake slipped the band over his wrist. "No. I want to plead the fifth if it's okay with you. Um Ingrid, I understand you like books. Allie likes books. What are you currently reading?"

Ingrid smiled. "It's called How to Get Out of Uncomfortable Conversation Topics by Drake."

"Sounds like something I'd enjoy," Drake said.

The friends at the table laughed, and the server approached with pancakes for Geneva and a quiche for Ingrid.

"You hear anything about how the members of the black team are doing?" Ingrid asked.

"Not yet," Allie said. "I visited Dr. Liz when we got back yesterday for my daily knee check, but she said she hadn't heard. She said she'd check in with the hospital later and tell us how everyone is doing."

"How is the knee?" Geneva asked. "Ingrid said you were quite the trooper out there yesterday and she could barely tell you had a problem with it."

"Ingrid must be a good fibber then because I sure did. I could only get the really simple stuff. She probably got seven of the ten containers."

Ingrid smiled. "Surely you understand that teamwork makes the dream work."

Allie smiled. "It sure does. My knee is getting better. The swelling is going down every day. I won't be running any marathons or hiking up mountains anytime soon, but I'll be fine, eventually. Just need to take the time and not rush it, is what Dr. Liz tells me."

"That's good," Geneva said. "I'm glad you're feeling better."

"Show's about to begin," Drake said.

The women looked over and saw Bruce and Andy taking their morning positions. Allie looked around the restaurant. They were three teams down, and with the six people missing, the room looked even larger than it was.

"Again, I have to start the morning off with some bad news," Bruce said once the side conversations ended and everyone gave him their focus.

"As you all probably heard by now, the black team had an accident yesterday. Emma has a broken wrist and had to have several stitches in her head. Kerry has yet to regain consciousness, and that's all I know about them. Please, let's give them a moment of silence for well wishes and prayers if you prefer."

Bruce bowed his head, and the rest of the people

followed suit. After twenty seconds, Bruce took his normal stance.

"I can tell you that the nature of their crash is under investigation, but as for now, we don't have a lot of information. We also learned there was an issue with one of the geocaches yesterday where someone moved a waypoint marker. This is also under investigation, and we have already questioned some teams about it. Remember, we take cheating seriously, and we don't want to disqualify another team. In the meantime, Andy, can you bring up the standings?"

Andy brought up the spreadsheet on the monitor, and Drake studied it. The black team found a couple of geocaches before their incident, but even so, they dropped from second to seventh. The yellow team Beasley brothers were now in first place, followed by the pink team, and in a surprise move, the orange team had jumped up to third. Drake and Allie were in fourth, well within striking distance of first place. Geneva and Ingrid were right behind Drake and Allie, and the purple and brown teams were right on the gray team's tail. Really, it was still anyone's game.

"We're getting closer," Allie said to Drake. "Only eighty points away from the top."

Drake nodded. "Yep. Hopefully, we can make that up today and the other three teams have a tough outing."

Bruce took a drink from his mug of coffee, took a second sip, then placed the mug down on the table next to him.

"Today will be all about gadget caches," Bruce said. "This town comprises thirty buildings and outbuildings. The largest ones are the hotel and church, and others as small as the replica outhouse behind the school. Each one of those buildings has a geocache in or next to it. All you need to do is to locate and open the cache. Inside, instead of a log, you'll find a token like this."

Bruce fumbled in his left pocket, came up with nothing, then pulled the token from his right pocket. Drake couldn't see any detail from where he was, but he could tell it was the approximate size of a casino chip.

"So, at the end of the day, we'll count up the tokens, and the team with the most wins a thousand points. Second place gets seven hundred points, and subsequent teams go down from there."

"What if there's a tie?" Tito asked from the back.

"In the case two or more teams have the same number of tokens, the team who checks in first wins the higher points available."

"How will we know if the cache still has a token?"

Bruce smiled. "You won't until you open it up and find out. There are a couple of other special rules just for today. If you find a door locked, don't try to unlock it. The cache won't be behind any locked doors. Also, if you come across any areas roped off, the caches won't be behind those either. For example, you won't find the geocache in the kitchen of this restaurant, or on the guest floors of the hotel. Those areas are off limits as far as geocaching is concerned, and you'll find more in town. The deadline for today is sundown since you won't be able to open most of these caches in the dark. Are there any other questions?"

"What about our backpacks?" Roy asked.

"You won't need them today. Everything you need will be at the cache location, but not necessarily in plain view. Also, since the town itself is a small, contained area, we'll expect you to do today's geocaches by walking. No UTVs or horses today. If there are any of you who have trouble getting around, like Ms. Allie over there, you can borrow a portable wheelchair from the doctor's office. Anything else?"

No hands appeared in the air, and no one said a word.

"Okay, then, it is now a quarter to nine, so finish your

breakfast quick if you're still eating because the round starts at nine on the dot. Good luck, everyone."

Bruce sat down in front of his coffee, and a second later, a server appeared with a carafe of java to refill his mug and a fresh cinnamon roll. Bruce smiled, thanked the server, and dug into the sweet treat.

"Are you going to want that wheelchair, Allie?" Drake asked. "Clearly Bruce meant that comment for you."

"You think?" Geneva said. "He only mentioned her by name."

Allie was good-natured and laughed at the remark. "No. I think I'll be fine with the cane. If worse comes to worse, Drake can always run and get the chair for me."

Drake finished his coffee, set the mug down, wiped his mouth with a napkin, and stood. "Excuse me, ladies. I need to run to the restroom."

The second Drake left the area, Ingrid and Allie focused their gazes on Geneva. After a period of uncomfortable silence, Geneva's cheeks reddened into a blush.

"What?" Geneva asked.

"We're waiting for you to spill the proverbial beans," Ingrid said.

"Nothing happened. After dinner, we went out back and had some wine and talked. No big deal."

"And you got his watch how?" Allie asked.

Geneva's cheeks turned redder. She picked up a napkin and fanned herself with it, which was a giveaway since the room was cool. "I can't say," she said with her best southern belle accent, "because I'm a lady and Drake is a gentleman."

"So, you kneppet all night?" Ingrid asked.

Allie was in mid-swallow when Ingrid spoke. She laughed, which caused her orange juice to dribble from her mouth. She covered her mouth with a napkin and coughed violently and couldn't stop until Geneva slapped her on the back a few times.

"Kneppet?" Allie asked.

"Yah," Ingrid said. "It's a Danish word. It means they—"

Allie held up a hand and stopped Ingrid. "I can guess what it means."

"You can guess what what means?" Drake said as he returned to the table.

"Never mind. You had to be here to get it," Geneva said, hoping it would squash the conversation.

"Good," Drake said. "It's almost time to go. You ready, Allie?"

Allie nodded. "Yep, let's do this."

Drake and Allie said goodbye to Geneva and Ingrid, then waited for the rush of people to leave the building at the stroke of nine.

"Where should we head first?" Allie asked.

"How about the jail?" Drake said. "Give me a couple of minutes to grab my sunglasses from the room, and we'll go."

Allie agreed, waited for Drake to return, then the pair ambled across the street and stepped into the jail. Thankfully, no other geocachers were in there. T.R. was behind her desk reading a magazine when they entered, and Drake glanced through the radio room and saw it was empty.

"No one minding the radio today?"

"Nope," T.R. said as she closed the magazine and tossed it to the corner of the desk. "No radios issued to cachers, so no need. Besides, I have my security team out in town. Bruce asked me to make sure nothing hinky went on today. Hinky was his word, not mine."

"Have any more details about the accident the black team had yesterday?" Drake asked.

"There's nothing more I can tell you than what you already know. I tried to contact Emma this morning to see if she could give me any more details, but she was still pretty out of it. Their UTV was pretty banged up, so Travis wasn't much help, either."

"Bruce said you talked to some teams about the missing waypoint marker yesterday?" Allie asked.

T.R. nodded. "Yep. I talked to the four members of the orange and pink teams individually, I should add. They all claim the marker was right where it should have been when they left the area."

"Could they have collaborated their stories before you talked to them?" Drake said.

"Nope. I talked to each team as they pulled in, and since you're an ex-cop, you know as well as I do when people are lying, and I don't think any of them were."

"We're still pretty much nowhere. I was wrong about the red team," Drake said.

"No, you weren't. You thought they were cheating, and they got caught. What we didn't know is that apparently there's something else going on we haven't quite put our finger on yet."

"You have a battery? Double A?" Allie asked as she walked over to the desk.

T.R. opened her shirt pocket, took out a battery, and handed it to Allie.

"What do you need that for?" Drake asked.

"Watch and prepare to be amazed!" Allie said.

She walked over to a shadow box that hung on the wall next to the jail's window. The box held an old sepia-toned photo and a pair of handcuffs from the mid-eighteen hundreds.

"They used those handcuffs on Salty Pete when they captured him and brought him to justice. He was a big outlaw around these parts," T.R. explained.

"Interesting, but I'm more interested in this."

Allie placed the battery between two metal points on the box's side that were barely noticeable. Something hummed inside, but nothing else happened. Allie turned the battery upside-down. The hum started again, and this time, a pill fob attached to a length of fishing line slowly descended from the box's bottom. Taped to the fob was a token. Allie removed the token, turned the battery right-side up, and watched as the pill fob disappeared into the shadow box.

"Nice job," T.R. said. "Two other teams rushed in here, took a quick look around, and rushed right out again. Neither group so much as glanced at that box."

"Thanks. It helped that I had a chance to look around while you two talked."

Allie handed the battery back to T.R., who slid it back into her pocket.

"Thanks," T.R. said. "And if you two see anything hinky out there, let me know, okay? Since I've got my crew wandering around town, I'm not expecting any more trouble, but you never know."

Drake and Allie left the jail, and at Allie's insistence, walked across the street to the doctor's office.

"You here for the wheelchair?" Dr. Liz asked when they entered.

"No, but could you give me a couple of aspirin? The day just started, and I want to have something with me in case I start to ache," Allie said.

"Did you take all the painkillers I gave you?"

"No. They're in my room. I think I'll be fine with some over-the-counter stuff."

The doctor smiled and excused herself. There was a velvet rope separating the front room of the office from the back, so she removed one end of the rope and let it fall to the ground.

"Don't let anyone back here, okay? I'll return in a

second."

While the doctor was gone, Drake and Allie looked around the room for where the cache might be hiding. They were still searching when the doctor returned.

"I'm not supposed to tell you this, but don't bother. Pink team got it already." Dr. Liz handed a half-dozen small packets of aspirin to Allie. "Here you go. There are two pills in each packet, so that should keep you going for the entire day if you need them."

"Thanks," Allie said. She stuffed all but one packet into her jeans pocket, then tore one open. She popped the pills into her mouth and swallowed them dry.

Liz held out her hand, and when Allie placed the empty packet into it, the doctor balled it up and tossed it into the waste can next to her desk. "You two be careful out there. And don't be a martyr, Allie. If you aren't up to all the walking, come back for the chair, okay?"

"Sure thing. Let's go, Drake."

Drake held the door for her, and they stepped out into the street.

"Where to next?" Allie asked.

Drake looked up and down the street. At the general store, he saw Tito and Marina messing with what looked to be an over-complicated gumball machine, and he noticed Geneva and Ingrid walking in the middle of the main street.

"I don't think they agree on where to go next," Drake said.

"Who? Why?"

"Geneva and Ingrid. Geneva keeps pointing at the schoolhouse, Ingrid keeps pointing at the horse barn."

"Hey, come with me," Allie said.

Together, they walked back into the restaurant and stopped just inside the door. Three of the servers were busy cleaning up after breakfast, but other than the staff, they were alone.

"Everyone left here in a rush, remember? We were the last ones to leave. Take a loop around the room and see if you notice anything."

Allie found a nearby chair and sat while Drake wandered around the perimeter of the room. For the most part, there wasn't much to see. Between the windows on the walls were old-fashioned wall sconces that, although appeared to be oil, threw off electric light instead.

In the corner stood an enormous grandfather clock. To Drake, it looked like the real thing. Even so, he attempted to open the glass door housing the weights and pendulum, but the door was locked and wouldn't budge. He gave up on the clock and stepped over to the fireplace.

The fireplace was large enough where Drake could have curled into a loose ball and nap inside the firebox if he wanted to. There was a large wood mantel that stretched the length of the fireplace, and on the mantel were a collection of old German-style beer mugs.

Drake bent over, looked into the throat of the chimney, saw no sign of anything out of the ordinary, and stood up. He was about to discount the fireplace completely, but then he noticed one stone didn't quite look like the others. He pulled on it, and an entire square foot section of a false stone-front detached from the fireplace.

"Hey, Allie, come take a look at this."

Allie limped to his side and looked at what Drake had uncovered. There were fifteen wood squares in the exposed space, in rows of four. In the bottom row, there were only three squares.

"This looks like one of those slider puzzles," Allie said. "You know, where the image is all there, and you have to slide the little plastic pieces around until you get the picture in order?"

"It does indeed." Drake tested the theory by moving one square into the empty slot, then slid another to where he removed the first square from. "Okay, that seems to work, but how do we know what the order should be?"

Allie leaned in and scrutinized the squares. "Look at this. The grain looks wavy to me, and some of them are wider than others. Maybe that's it."

Drake did a closer inspection. "Yeah, you're right. Okay. Stand back and let me work my magic."

Allie pulled a chair up from the nearest table and let Drake focus on the puzzle. A few minutes later, Drake let out an extended sigh, like a balloon slowly losing all its air.

"Usually I suck at these things, but this one wasn't too bad."

Allie stood back up and looked at the puzzle. Drake had aligned all the grains, but there was nothing but a black-painted piece of wood where the empty slot was. She saw something that piqued her interest.

"Hand me one of those fireplace matches, will you?"

Drake looked above him and grabbed a metal container that held the long matches. He removed one and handed the eleven-inch match to Allie.

Allie turned it over and shoved the end into a small square hole she found. She pushed it in two inches until she felt resistance, and after she applied a little pressure, they both heard a click and the black panel moved. Allie removed the matchstick, swung open the little door, reached in, and removed the token from its hiding spot.

"Good one, Allie," Drake said. While Allie waited for him, Drake set everything back the way they found it, and together, they left the restaurant.

CHAPTER SEVENTEEN

I guess I'd like to head over to the UTV barn now," Drake said as they stepped into the sunshine.

"Why do I get the idea that today is becoming less about finding tokens and more about snooping around?" Allie asked as she started up the street.

"Hey, we've got two already. That's a great start," Drake said as he trotted to catch up with her. "Want some water?"

"Sure."

Drake detoured over to where an old horse watering trough was standing next to the general store. The trough had ice on the bottom and held dozens of plastic bottles of water to the brim.

"Where do you think this pipe goes?" Allie asked.

"Huh?" Drake looked up after extracting two bottles of water. He handed one to Allie and shoved the other into the leg pocket of his cargo pants.

"Look at this setup."

Next to the trough was a rain barrel. The general store had a section of downspout that dropped from the edge of the gutter and into the rain barrel. Attached to the rain barrel was a section of PVC pipe that was two inches in diameter and was three feet long, with caps on both ends.

"What's the PVC for, you're wondering?" Drake asked.

"Yep."

Drake stepped to the PVC and tried to pull the top cap off, but the cap wouldn't budge. He got a better grip on it and pulled with enough force that the cap flew into the air and landed in the trough. Allie retrieved it while Drake tried to peer into the pipe.

"See anything?" she asked.

"I can't tell. Too dark in the pipe. If there is something, it's way down at the bottom. We need to find a stick or something to probe down to the bottom and check."

"No, we don't. Step aside, Duck-man."

Drake moved to the side, and Allie took his place. Using the pipe's cap, she scooped water from the rain barrel and poured the liquid down the pipe. She knew she was adding only a couple inches of water at a time, but she scooped cap full after cap full until at last the orange tip of something floated to the top.

"Grab that," Allie said.

Drake grabbed the item and lifted it out of the water. "It's a float. Used for fishing. Good job, Allie."

There was a line attached to the bottom of the float, and when Drake pulled on a line, a small waterproof box came to the surface. Drake opened the box. Inside the box was a small plastic baggie filled with fishing weights and a token.

"Yes!" he said as he grabbed the token. "Now we've got three!"

Drake put the box back in the pipe and watched it sink from view. He fed the line in, and soon the float was back in the water as well.

"There's got to be a way to get the water out of there," Drake said. He bent over, examined the pipe's bottom, and discovered a clean out adapter. He unscrewed the adapter and waited for the water to drain out. Once the water stopped, he screwed the pipe back together and returned the cap to the top of the PVC.

"Okay, now let's go to the barn," Drake said.

They walked down the street and passed the riding stables and headed to the UTVs. The large door was open, and   Drake spotted Mike and Ricky from the pink team and Penny and Cindy of the orange team wandering around the enormous building.

Drake continued to Travis' office and noticed the door was closed, and when he tried the doorknob, he found it locked. They walked farther into the barn. The twelve marked spaces that held the UTVs took up the front section, and   Drake zigzagged through them until he stopped in front of the blue team's UTV. There were several parts that were taken off and set alongside the vehicle. Two spots from where he was, he found the black team's UTV. The UTV looked horrible. There wasn't a spot on it that looked normal. The sides and hood all contained several dents, both seats were torn to shreds, and there was a large puddle of something underneath the left rear tire. He slowly stepped around the vehicle and tried to determine if indeed it had been rammed by another vehicle, or if they were just the victim of an accidental rockslide.

"Spot anything obvious?" Allie asked.

"No. It's too beat up. Let's check out the rest of the barn and hopefully find the cache."

Past the UTVs, Drake and Allie found several parked work vehicles. Among them there was a pickup truck missing an engine, and another up on a lift with missing tires.

"Wow. Take a gander at this," Allie said. She grabbed

Drake's hand and rushed him across to the far end of the barn.

When she stopped, they were in front of a stagecoach that looked like it belonged in an old western movie.

"Beautiful, isn't it?" Travis said as he approached the pair.

"Yes, I love it," Allie said.

"I'm not supposed to do this, but go on in, take a seat." Travis opened the door and took Allie's hand to keep her steady as she climbed the steps and sat down inside. "This is an old Western Concord from around 1890. Bruce bought it at an auction in California and had it shipped here."

"It's amazing. Why isn't it on display?" Allie asked.

"Oh, no, you misunderstand. It's not meant to be a museum piece. We're going to use it for guests. Can you imagine riding in that stagecoach pulled by a team of horses?"

"No way."

"Yep. It will be horse-drawn and everything. The plan is to take it out three times a day for sunrise, noontime, and sunset tours. Each one would come with a meal, of course. I'm just waiting on some brake parts, and it needs another coat of paint, and then it will be ready to go."

Allie held out a hand, and Travis helped her down. "I hope I can come back when it's done and go for a ride," she said.

"We'd love to have you," Travis answered.

"What's that over there under the tarp?" Drake asked.

"It's a road grader," Travis answered without hesitation.

"Can I look at it?"

Travis shrugged, then approached the grader, and pulled off the tarp.

Unlike the massive machine that he was used to seeing

on highways, this grader looked like a baby in comparison. It was an older model, and Drake realized it was well-used, but what he was really interested in was the bucket on the front.

"What's it used for?" Drake asked.

"I'm sure you've been on the maintained trails out there. We use this to do the job. We take it out every six weeks or so to smooth the trails, especially if there's been rain or high winds."

Drake kneeled, reached forward, and ran his fingers over the pitted surface of the bucket. "How fast can one of these things go?"

Travis shook his head. "You don't want to go more than five miles an hour, otherwise the blade will jump, and you'll get pits and whatnot in the ground."

"No, I mean, what if you weren't grading? If you had the blade up?"

Travis scratched his chin as he thought about it. "I'd say right around thirty miles an hour, give or take five."

"Okay, thanks, Travis. We'd better get back to our search."

Travis waved and left the couple.

"What was that all about?" Allie asked.

"Remember what Emma said yesterday about being hit? I think this hit them. If it was going full speed, it could certainly disable those little UTVs, and then the bucket could dump the rocks on top so the damage would be harder to identify."

Allie looked over at the machine. "Yeah, I get what you mean. I bet it pushed the Colliers over the edge, too. But wouldn't those big tire treads give it away?"

"Nope. See that box behind the back tires? They can put that down and it would wipe away the tracks, and all you'd have in the end is a pristinely groomed trail. Come on, let's go talk to T.R. again."

As they made their way to the front of the barn, they caught up with Mike and Ricky, who were just leaving as well.

"Why so glum, chums?" Allie asked when she noticed the frowns on both of their faces.

"Aw, the girls beat us to that one," Ricky admitted.

As they stepped into the sunlight, Allie tripped. She stuck out her cane and pinwheeled her left arm for balance, but in the end, she fell to the dirt, face first. At the last second, she repositioned her hands and caught most of her weight on her palms.

"Allie!" Drake yelled as he leaned over her. "Are you okay? What happened?"

Allie turned over and sat. "I stepped on a rock and twisted my ankle."

"You're bleeding. Help me get her up."

Ricky and Mike stepped in, and between the three of them, they got Allie back on her unsteady feet. Ricky and Mike held onto Allie while Drake brushed the dirt from her jeans and gave her a once-over for injuries.

"We can carry her to the doctor's office," Mike said.

"No, it's too far. Just take me across the road and put me on that bench," Allie answered.

Ricky was the largest of the men, so he scooped up Allie into his arms as easy as lifting a bundle of tissue paper. He carried her across the road and placed her gently on the bench next to the schoolhouse.

"You good?" Ricky asked.

"Yes. Thanks, you're my hero."

Ricky and Mike took their leave as Drake sat down next to Allie. "How bad are you hurt?"

"Other than the stigmata, you mean?" Allie held her palms up and Drake noticed blood where stones had pierced her flesh.

"You've got a cut on your forehead, too. I'm going to run down to the doctor's office and get you something to clean you up."

"What about talking to T.R.?"

"Allie, that can wait. I'll be right back, okay? Don't talk to any strangers."

"There's no one here any stranger than you."

Drake rolled his eyes at the often-heard remark, and without another word, Drake jogged off toward the doctor. A few minutes later, Allie saw Dr. Liz pushing a wheelchair up the street.

"You can't get enough of me, can you?" Dr. Liz said when she got to Allie.

Allie smiled. "I guess not."

Dr. Liz had a plastic tub of medical supplies in the wheelchair, and from it she took a large bottle of saline and opened it, then she unwrapped some gauze pads. She wet the pads with the water.

"Tip your head back. I'm going to wipe off your forehead first. This might sting a little."

Allie sat still while the doctor did her thing.

"It's only a minor cut. It stopped bleeding already. Let me see your hands."

Allie held out her hands, and the doctor examined them. The left one wasn't so bad, and Liz easily washed it clean. The right one, however, was a different story. From inside her coat, she extracted a pair of magnifying glasses and put them on.

Allie giggled. "You look silly."

"Hold still, you've got some embedded particles here, and I need to tweeze them out. This may sting a bit."

Allie held her hand as still as possible, and Dr. Liz leaned over and started her work. Allie grimaced when the doctor removed the first particle and flinched when she dug for the second.

"Hold still, I'm almost done."

Dr. Liz got even closer to Allie's hand, spread her wound, and went in with the tweezers.

Allie screamed and pulled her hand away. "Hey! That stung!"

"I warned you it could. Come on, let me see it again. I want to make sure I got it all."

Allie was tentative, but she held up her hand.

Dr. Liz gently took it, looked it over, then washed it off with the saline. "I think you're good. Drake said you twisted your ankle."

Allie waved it off. "It's nothing. I simply stepped on a rock and lost my balance."

"Can you stand?"

Allie got to her feet, took a step, then immediately retreated, and sat back down.

"Sit over here." Dr. Liz removed the plastic bucket from the wheelchair and put it on the bench beside her, then helped   Allie into the wheelchair and raised the right leg. She removed Allie's shoe and sock and examined her ankle. "No redness, no swelling. I think you'll survive."

Dr. Liz helped Allie redress, then had Allie stand and walk around a little. It took Allie a couple of minutes, but eventually she got her normal stride back and returned to the bench.

"See, I told you," Dr. Liz said. "Just be careful with it the rest of the day, okay?"

"I will, thank you."

"Do you want to keep the wheelchair?"

"No, I'll be fine with just the cane. I'll send Drake for it if I really need to. Where is Drake, by the way?"

"Once I said I'd come over and look at you, he said he needed to go over to see T.R. about something. I hope you're not too hard on him."

"Why would I be? You're much better qualified to help me out than he is."

Liz nodded in agreement. "You're right. I am. I'd better get back. Good luck with your finds. I'm rooting for you."

"Thanks, Doc."

Allie watched as the doctor gathered up all her gear and pushed the wheelchair away and waited for Drake to return. In the meantime, she watched as the other teams moved from building to building. From where she sat, she had an excellent view of the UTV barn, the riding stables, the schoolhouse, the general store, and the church.

She was looking toward her left, watching the yellow team enter the church, when she felt someone sit down next to her. She thought it might be Drake returning, but when she turned her head, she saw Geneva.

"Hey you!" Geneva said. "Taking a rest?"

"Yeah. I took a bit of a tumble, so I'm on timeout for a few minutes. At least until Drake returns from wherever he ran off to. What are you up to?"

"Ingrid had to make a pit stop, and I noticed you over here alone, so I thought I'd keep you company. Have you found any tokens so far?"

"Only three."

"Three, wow. That's great. We only have one. It seems everywhere we go; someone grabs it ahead of us. Where'd you find your three?"

Allie was hesitant to share her secret. After all, it was a competition. In the end, she relented. "Restaurant, jail, and the rain barrel next to the general store. I think the ones in the doctor's office and the UTV barn are gone, too."

Geneva nodded. "Yep. We found the cache in the UTV barn. Took us a good ten minutes to figure out how to open it, only to find that the token was already gone. Talk about frustrating. We found ours at the bank. Other than that, we searched everywhere you have."

"I'm surprised these are so hard to find. Usually, the thing about gadget caches is that they're easy to find, but hard to open."

"I said the same thing to Ingrid. Every gadget cache I've found in the wild has always been a fake birdhouse. Drake's coming back."

Allie looked down the street and saw him headed straight for them. "You want me to leave you two alone?" Geneva laughed. "Don't tell me you're jealous. I thought he wasn't your type."

"No. He's not. He's kinda dull-witted, not very smart, impatient, and often smells like overripe fruit," Allie said. Drake protested. "Hey, I'm standing right here, you know. I can hear you."

"And he's over-sensitive," Allie added, then laughed, soon joined by Geneva and Drake.

"Did the doctor check you out?" Drake asked with serious concern in his voice.

"Yep. She cleaned me up and gave me the green light. I'm ready to rock whenever you are."

"Where to next?"

Allie pointed off to the north. "I think it's time we went to church. Since I've been sitting here, I've seen three teams go in and out quickly. So, I think either that one's really easy and we can discount it pretty fast, or it's too hard and no one's found it yet."

"Sounds logical to me. Are you good, Geneva?"

"Oh, yes. I'm just waiting for Ingrid to return. You two go on. No need to wait on me."

Drake and Allie headed for the church and stopped when they got in front of it. The church was small and had the same A-frame design as the school. The only thing that set the two buildings apart was the bell tower in the church.

"Wait," Allie said. She walked over to the sign in front of the church's main door, which was really an outside message center. The frame was painted green, and along the top were white letters that said 'Cacheland Church'. The sign was divided into two sections, each with its own acrylic door.

"Welcome to Cacheland. Non-denominational services Sun eight a.m.," Allie read aloud.

"Yeah? So?"

"So why did they put that on only one side of the sign? They could have easily spread the message out."

Allie limped over to the right-hand side of the sign. Since it was see-through, it appeared to be an empty corkboard behind the acrylic. When she opened the door, the corkboard swung free and revealed an outline of the church created in a heavy copper wire. At the bottom left-hand side of the church was a handle with a loose loop around the copper wire. In the middle of the clock tower was a red button, and beneath that was a digital display. In the sign's corner was a small metal box secured with a four-digit padlock.

"There are instructions here," Drake said. "Push the button to begin. Touch the wand at the bottom to start. Move the magic wand from one end to the other without touching the coil, touch the end of the maze, and it will display the answer to you."

Allie pushed the red button, and the display flashed green zeroes. She moved the wand, but only got an inch before it touched the copper wire. The display beeped and showed red zeroes and then shut off.

"You'd be better at this than me," Allie said as she stepped aside and made way for Drake.

Drake stepped in, hit the red button. On his first turn, he got to the top of the bell tower before he slipped and got the red light.

"Hurry, the Beasleys are coming over," Allie said.

Drake returned the wand to the start position and tried again. This time he got three-quarters of the way through before he erred.

"Our turn," Ben said.

Drake and Ben traded places, and Ben tried for the first time. Like Allie, he only made it an inch before the machine shut off.

Drake got back into position, took a deep breath, and restarted the machine. This time, he blocked everything else out, concentrated, and moved the wand at a snail's pace around the outline. At last, he got to the end, touched the end position, and the display beeped and displayed four numbers.

"Three one four seven," Allie said.

Drake adjusted the numbers on the padlock, pulled, and heard the pleasant sound of the lock coming free. He removed the lock, opened the box, and retrieved the token from inside.

"Nice job, Drake," Ben said as he clapped him on the back.

Drake locked the box and returned the puzzle to the starting position, then stepped back and closed the door.

"Well, that was a fun one. Where to next?"

CHAPTER EIGHTEEN

Geneva said they were going to the post office next. Why not try there?"

"Has anyone gone in the schoolhouse?"

"No one did while I was sitting there."

"Let's stop off there on the way to the bank."

When Drake and Allie entered the school, they were not alone. Tito and Marina were busy going book by book on the shelves.

"Find anything?" Allie asked.

"Nope," Marina answered.

"Have you looked through all the bookcases?"

"Yes. Been here about an hour now."

Allie and Drake split up to explore the room. Allie tried the teacher's desk drawers, which were locked, while Drake examined the various items hanging from the walls. The presidential photos were real, as were several of the various displays around the room. There were several dioramas Drake examined. There were depictions of a Native American settlement, the Grand Canyon, the shootout in Tombstone, and one displaying the fictional town of

Cacheland, Arizona.

From there, Drake wandered across the room where several science-related displays sat on tables. There was a display of various desert animals and plants. He spotted one that showed the rivers and water tables of the region, and one that featured the constellations in the night sky. One display looked empty, except for a hole in the board, and the letters ABCD printed above the hole. At the base of the display was a small toolbox, and next to the toolbox was a small wooden box attached to the display with a padlock on it.

"Whatcha got?" Allie asked as she stepped to Drake's side.

"Look familiar?" Drake asked, as he pointed to the padlock.

"What's in the toolbox?"

Drake opened it and took out the items inside. There were five stainless steel hex bolts in various lengths, a handful of steel washers, and a piece of wood that resembled a small diving board. The wood was eight inches long, an inch thick, and an inch wide. On one end of the wood was a hole, and on the other was a small screw embedded in the wood. There was also a hole that passed through the side of the tiny plank.

"What do you make of all this?" Drake asked.

Allie picked up a bolt and examined it. On top of the bolt, the letter C was written in permanent marker. "Are there nine washers there by chance?"

Drake took a couple of seconds and counted them out. "Yep. How'd you guess?"

Allie looked at the heads of the rest of the bolts and found the longest one was without markings. She picked up the board, pushed the bolt through the hole in the side, and screwed the bolt into the display board. She removed it, turned the board over, and screwed it back in. "I had it upside-down," she explained when Drake gave her the look of confusion.

"Find the bolt with the letter A on it."

Drake did as he was told, and gave it to Allie, who slipped the bolt into the hole in the board's end. Like a teeter totter, the heavy side with the bolt dropped low, and raised board's side with the screw attached.

"Okay, now put the washers over the screw until the plank balances even," Allie ordered.

Drake picked up a washer and slipped it over the screw head. The plank moved a little. He continued to add washers, until finally, the board looked even when he added the fourth washer.

"Four," Drake said.

Allie looked at the padlock and set all the numbers to one and moved the first digit to four.

"Okay, keep going."

Drake removed the washers and replaced the letter A bolt with the B bolt. "Seven." He moved on to the next two bolts and determined the last two numbers were six and nine.

Allie entered the numbers into the padlock as he called them out and then opened the lock. Inside the box, the token was waiting for them.

"Sweet," Drake said. While Allie retrieved the token and replaced the lock on the box, Drake gathered all the items and returned them to the toolbox. "Didn't Bruce say something about the outhouse? Why don't we check that out next?"

They left the school and walked around back to the outhouse. When they got there, Drake opened the door. Although they expected to see and smell an authentic outhouse experience, they were pleased to find out that although the seat was there; the hole was plugged, and therefore unusable. Drake entered and checked all the walls, then stood on the seat to check the structure where the roof met the sides and left a ledge all the way around. He still found nothing. Exasperated, he stepped outside and did a circle around the outhouse, and when he got to the back, he discovered a large door, closed with a hook and eye latch.

"Allie, back here!" he yelled as he undid the hook and opened the door.

"Oh, that's cool," Allie said when she joined him.

Before them, built into the back wall of the outhouse, was a large maze behind a sheet of acrylic. In the bottom left-hand corner of the maze was a large metal ball, and at the top right-hand corner was a tube with an arrow pointing to it. On the maze's side, on a small hook, hung a foot-long wooden dowel with a large magnet attached to one end. Drake took the dowel from the hook and touched the magnet to the acrylic where the ball was and determined he could move the ball. He took a few seconds to plot his way through the maze, then moved the ball up, then over one of the maze walls to the right. He needed to go up again, but he hit the ball against the side, the magnet disconnected, and the ball dropped. The maze had slightly slanted paths, so when the ball hit the slant of a wrong ledge, gravity took over and it bounced all the way to the bottom of the maze.

"Shoot," Drake said, exasperated.

He tried again, connected the ball to the magnet, and gently lifted. He moved the ball up to where he needed to rejoin the correct path, but once again, he hit the ball against the wall, and it fell to the bottom.

"Damn. You want to give this a try?" Drake asked, offering the magnet to Allie.

"No. I figured out the last one. You can do this one," Allie said.

Drake exhaled, then tried again. The third time was almost the charm, and he navigated the ball three-quarters of the way through the maze before it dropped. On the fifth try, Drake raised the ball high enough and dropped it into the tube. They heard the ball as it fell through the tube, and it stopped at the bottom with a thunk. Next to the bottom of the tube, a small compartment opened.

"Did we get it?" Allie asked.

"No. It's empty. Other than the ball." Drake removed the ball and closed the door, then put the ball in a hole at the top left side of the maze. From there, the ball dropped to its original starting spot. Drake hung up the magnet and closed the door.

"I have to admit, that was a pretty cool cache," Drake said. "Even if it didn't pay off for us. Where should we go next? The post office?"

Allie nodded, and the pair took off. As they approached the front of the schoolhouse, they saw Geneva still sitting on the bench.

"Ingrid not back yet?" Allie asked.

"No," Geneva answered.

Drake checked the time on his watch. "It's been close to an hour since we saw you last."

"I know. I've been worried for a while now. It doesn't take a person over an hour to use the restroom. I think I'll go check her room."

"If you need us, we'll be at the post office."

Geneva left without saying goodbye and jogged off toward the hotel.

"I hope everything is okay," Allie said. "I really like Ingrid. She's sweet."

Drake walked on without saying a word.

"You think there's a problem, Drake?"

Drake shook his head. "I don't think so, but I'm not a hundred percent sure about it, especially with everything that's gone on the last few days. We'll go for this next cache, and if Ingrid hasn't shown up by then, we'll go over and get T.R., okay?"

Allie nodded, and they plodded in silence to the post office. The post office was one of the smallest buildings on the street. From the outside, it looked to be at most fourteen square feet in size, but it was also one of the most elegant buildings as well. The building carried a coat of cerulean blue paint, with white trim around the windows and black shutters. Standing outside the post office was a tall flagpole from which the stars and stripes were blowing in the breeze.

When they entered the building, they encountered a fusion between old and new. On the new side, there was a counter manned by a person with a modern computer, printer, and postage scales. On the wall by the counter was a display with postcards for sale, and a small display of greeting cards.

"Hello, folks, how are you today? Need anything postal, or just looking for the geocache?" the man behind the counter said.

"You have postal services?" Drake asked.

"Yep. Although we're not an official post office, we're still fully functional. I can hook you up with stamps, and even mail packages for you."

"I can't imagine a mail truck coming all the way out here," Allie said.

"You're right about that. I close this building every day at four and take whatever outgoing mail we have over to Gila Bend. We've got a post office box for the incoming mail, which I bring back with me the next day."

"Sounds like quite a business model. I can't imagine manning this keeps you busy all day," Drake said.

"Sure doesn't, especially since we're just getting the town up and running. I'm also a part of the maintenance crew, so I also tend to things and do painting and whatnot."

"Tell me, Murry," Drake said, reading the man's name tag. "Can you tell me if anyone found the cache in here?"

Murry laughed. "No, sir, I certainly can't tell you that. Wouldn't be fair, you know."

"Murry," Allie said as she batted her big green eyes at him, "could you please tell me if someone got the cache in here? I won't tell anyone if you tell me."

Murry stared at Allie, then rolled his eyes. "Funny thing, ma'am, all day there's been people coming in here, and no one has left with anything more than they came in with." Then Murry did an odd thing and gestured with his head toward the safety deposit boxes on the far wall.

Allie gave him her sweetest smile. "Thanks, Murry. I appreciate it."

Allie joined Drake, and they moved to the far wall where there were forty post office boxes lined up. The wall was eight boxes wide and five boxes high and numbered from one to forty. The first box had a key in it. Drake turned the key, opened the box, and pulled something out. He looked at it, then sighed.

"Great. An algebra problem. This is on you. You're much better at math than me."

Drake held out the laminated card and Allie took it.

"This is just simple math, not algebra. Letters A through D are what we need to solve for, and some letters are the results of other equations. You have a pen and piece of paper?"

Drake went over to Murry, who had a notebook and a pencil ready to go. Drake handed the book and pencil to Allie, who copied the formulas from the card to the page.

"Is there anything else in that box?" Allie asked.

Drake bent over slightly and peered into the open box. "Nope. It's empty."

"Does that key open any other boxes?"

Drake closed the door and removed the key from the first box, then systematically tried the key in the other thirty-nine boxes. None of them opened until Drake got to the fortieth one. He opened that one and pulled out a smaller box with a familiar-looking padlock.

"That explains the need to solve for A through D. Now we just need to find digits to represent the other letters we have here."

"Which letters do we need?" Drake asked.

Allie scanned through the equations and circled the ones that were the initial values needed to figure out the problem. "E, J, K, Q, R, X, and Y. Of course, you always must solve for X and Y."

Drake started examining the other items in the post office. The old-time side of the post office contained an old wooden table. On that table was an ancient postal scale, and several various sized boxes wrapped in plain brown paper. The packages had string wrapped around them, and they all featured addresses of random historical figures such as Doc Holliday and Calamity Jane. He picked up each of the boxes, determined they were red herrings, and placed them back where he found them. Then he scrutinized the scale and got nothing from that, either.

"What's in those binders?" Allie asked.

There were four royal blue binders on the table. Drake grabbed the first one, opened it, and paged through the contents. "This one's full of old letters."

Drake passed the binder to Allie, and she scanned the letters. They all dated to the eighteen-hundreds, and most were written in a cursive script that was hard to read. She paged through them, but nothing jumped out at her as being useful for figuring out the puzzle.

"E is five," she said as she went back to the fifth letter in the binder. Other than the date, there were no other numbers, or anything that would match the letter E with any numbers. Frustrated, she closed the binder.

"What's in the other ones?"

Drake passed her the second binder, which was also filled with letters. Again, she tried to map them back to her puzzle, and again, she failed.

The third and fourth binders contained postage stamps and postage cancelation stamps. Allie paged through them and noticed they dated from the late seventeen-hundreds until eighteen-eighty. As she finished each binder, she handed them back to Drake, who put them back into place.

"My knee is getting tired. I need to sit down for a bit. Can we go outside for a while?"

Drake was about to speak, but Murry beat him to it.

"Here, take my chair," Murry said as he came around his counter with a metal folding chair. He opened it up, set it against the wall, and motioned for Allie to sit down.

"Thank you, Murry, you're very kind. We shouldn't be long," Allie said. "Give me that stamp binder again, Drake."

Drake passed her the binder, and she opened it up, using her lap for a table. She studied the stamps on the first page for a while, waiting for inspiration to strike. When it didn't, she turned to the next page and started the search over again.

"Anything ring a bell?" Drake asked.

"No. Not yet."

Allie shifted in the uncomfortable seat, and when she did so, the binder slid off her lap. With a huff, she bent over to pick it up. When she rose, the charm on her necklace, which was a steel compass with a needle that always pointed north, slipped out from beneath her shirt, came in contact with box number thirty-seven, and stuck there.

"Drake. Look. My lucky compass."

When Allie saw Drake looking at her, she used her free

hand to pull the charm from the mailbox and tucked it back under her shirt. "Give me that key."

Drake handed her the key, and she put it on the box where the charm had stuck. The key, too, was stuck to the front of the box, two inches below the box number. "I think there's a magnet in here. Try another one."

Drake took the key and ran it along the front of box thirty-six, but nothing happened. He tried several other boxes at random, and when he waved the key in front of box seventeen, he again got a reaction. "I think we're on to something here."

"Start at one and do every box in order. Every time you get a hit, tell me the box number. There should be seven of them," Allie ordered.

"Okay, boss." Drake ran the key from box to box, and on number seven, the key stuck for the first time. He gave her the number, and Allie jotted the number seven next to the letter E on her sheet. He continued the exercise until he got to number thirty-seven, which Allie wrote next to the letter Y.

"Okay. That's all the numbers I need. Now give me some time to do the math here."

Allie got up, moved her chair to the table, and sat again. There, she put her head down and worked on the calculations. Five short minutes later, she called the combination numbers. "Two seven, nine three."

Drake put the numbers into the padlock and pulled. "Nope. It didn't open."

"Hold on, then." Allie double-checked her work and soon found her error. "Sorry. It's two seven, nine four. Math is hard."

Drake set the three to a four and pulled, and this time, the lock released. He opened the box and removed the token. "Number six. We're on a roll."

"You mind if I keep this sheet, Murry?" Allie asked.

"It's all yours, and congratulations. None of the other teams ever got half as far as you did."

Allie tore the page from the notebook and stuffed it into her pocket while Drake closed the box and put everything back the way it was before they got there.

"Let's go see about Ingrid," he said.

Allie nodded, and together they stepped into the late-afternoon sunlight.

CHAPTER NINETEEN

Drake jogged back to the schoolhouse while Allie waited by the post office.

"Geneva wasn't there," he said when he returned.

"Let's check the hotel," Allie said.

Drake nodded, and they walked over to the hotel. Heather was behind the desk, and when Drake inquired about the whereabouts of Geneva and Ingrid, all Heather could tell him was that she hadn't seen either of them, and that their room keys were hanging on their respective hooks behind her.

From the hotel, they crossed the street to the jail, but when Drake twisted the doorknob, he found it locked.

"What's going on here?" Drake asked. "You would think someone would be here."

"I don't know. Where to next?"

"If you're up for it, why don't we walk up this side of the street and down the other? We'll talk to anyone we meet. Find out if anyone has seen our friends," Drake said.

"Sounds like a plan, but I've got a better one. You take this side, I'll take the other, and we'll meet in the middle."

The team split up, and Drake walked up the street. He checked the bank, the general store, and the post office and didn't come across a soul. When he arrived at the horse barn, he thought he heard voices, so he stepped into the building.

"Hello?" he called as he walked past the stalls. A couple of horses huffed at him as he passed, and one stuck his head over the gate and demanded a scratch on the head. When he arrived at the barn's far end, he found the tack room. Inside the tack room, he found Cindy and Penny of the orange team working on rearranging a bunch of blocks and trying to make a cube.

"Hey, excuse me, I'm looking for Geneva and Ingrid. Have you seen them?"

Penny put down the block she held. "The girls from the gray team?"

"Yes, that's them."

"Sure. We saw them. When? Three or four hours ago? Before lunch, right Cin?"

Cindy looked up from her cube. "I think so. Yeah. I remember now. We traded pleasantries with them, coming out of the restaurant when we headed in. We found the cache there and had a quick bite. Why? Is something wrong?"

"No, not really. We were supposed to meet up for a drink. Thanks anyway. Good luck with that puzzle. It looks tricky."

"Did you do this one? Can you give us a hint on how to solve it?" Penny asked.

"No, sorry. We haven't gotten around to it yet."

"Good luck finding your friends," Penny said.

"Thanks."

Drake left the room and stopped for a second when he heard the women laugh. It wasn't a quiet giggle, but an outright belly-buster, and Drake couldn't help but wonder if he appeared as the punchline of some joke.

From the horse barn, he walked around the UTV barn. He thought that was empty as well, but he found Travis way in the back working on the engineless pickup. Travis gave Drake the same amount of help as the orange team had. When he entered the church, he found Allie waiting in the last pew for him.

"Well?" Allie asked.

"The only people I found were Penny, Cindy, and Travis. None of them have seen Geneva or Ingrid."

"Well, that's three more people than I talked to."

"No one? Not even Dr. Liz?"

"Nope. The doctor's office was closed and locked up tight as a drum."

"Stranger and stranger," Drake said.

"We should go back and check the restaurant and the hotel again in case we missed them, and after, check the buildings on the south side of the town. We haven't been there all day."

When they entered the restaurant, it surprised Drake that the brown and purple teams were at one table, talking and enjoying bottles of beer.

"Hey, y'all," Drake said as he approached them. "Have any of you seen Geneva or Ingrid?"

"Drake!" Tito yelled as he stood. "Pull up a chair and join us. We're having pizza and beer."

"Why aren't you guys out finding tokens?" Drake asked.

"Eh, we weren't having much luck," Gilberto said. "Every geocache we found; someone had already been there before us."

"Same with us," Marina said. "You watched us at the school, right? Way off track. After we left there, we thought we'd try our luck on the other end of town, but that didn't work out for us either."

"Allie, come over here, sit down," Tito insisted.

"We really can't Tito, we're looking for Ingrid and Geneva. Have you seen either of them?"

"We saw Geneva over by the school. She sat on a bench there," Marina said.

"No, after that. We saw her there, too. She was waiting for Ingrid to return, but now we can't find either of them," Drake said.

"Gil, didn't we spot them over by the equipment barn?" Roy asked. "You asked the blond girl to meet you for drinks later."

Gilberto took a swig of his beer. "Hey, that's right. When she turned me down, I put it right out of my mind."

"He doesn't handle rejection well," Roy said.

The four at the table laughed, but the laughter quickly subsided when they caught the serious expression of concern on the faces of Drake and Allie.

"Sorry. Bad joke," Roy said. "Last place we saw them was by the barn. About two hours ago, maybe a little more."

"What barn?" Drake asked.

Roy pointed off to the south. "We passed it when we got here. It's over by the crop fields. It's got all the farm machinery in there, like the plows and the other big machines. Sorry, I don't know what they are. I'm a mechanic, not a farmer."

Two servers appeared, each carrying a large pizza, one with pepperoni and extra cheese, the other decked out with pepperoni, sausage, onions, mushrooms, and green peppers. The aroma from the freshly baked pies wafted up and hit Drake in the face, causing his stomach to rumble.

"Come on, there's plenty here," Tito said as he took his seat and reached for a slice.

"We'll be back. Save us some beer," Drake said.

"Not likely with this group," Marina said.

The group erupted into laughter once again, and while they did, Drake and Allie slipped away.

"They haven't been here," Heather said when she saw Drake enter the hotel.

"You're sure?" Drake asked.

Heather nodded. "Sorry. I haven't left the desk since the last time you asked."

"Perhaps they're out back?" Allie offered.

"Stay here," Drake said.

Drake left Allie with Heather, took a peek in the parlor, saw it was empty, and headed down a hallway toward the back door of the hotel. He opened the door and stepped outside. The entire area was deserted. No one by the pool, no one by the fire pit.

"You mind if I check their rooms?" Drake asked when he returned.

"I'm sorry, sir, that would be highly inappropriate," Heather said.

"Please?" Allie said. "Heather, we're worried about our friends. We were supposed to meet up with them and it's like they've disappeared."

"Perhaps they took a horse ride, or took out a UTV, or decided on a walk."

"I accounted all the horses and UTVs for when I checked the barns. And they wouldn't have forgotten all about the competition to take a walk. Please help us," Drake said.

Heather stared at them for a moment with her sparkling brown eyes and turned and picked a couple of keys from the board behind her. "I'm not supposed to leave the desk, so here. And make it quick. This could get me fired."

Drake accepted the keys. "Thanks. I won't be a minute."

"I'll be timing you. Go. I hope you find them."

Drake dashed up the stairs. He rushed to Geneva's room first, located down the opposite hallway from his. He unlocked the door, entered the room, and stopped when he got inside. Nothing looked out of place. The bed was made, and a pair of shoes sat neatly next to the dresser. There was a light jacket folded neatly over the back of an easy chair. He spotted the book that had fallen to the floor when they'd bumped into the nightstand the night before. Without thinking, he retrieved the book and placed it on the bed, then moved into the bathroom. Everything there was in order, too. Geneva's hairbrush lined up on a washcloth with her toothbrush and toothpaste, the exact way he remembered seeing it the night before. Drake found nothing awry.

He left Geneva's room and continued a few doors down to Ingrid's. Someone neatly made her bed as well, but that's all she had in common with Geneva's room. There were two pairs of shoes near the window in a pile. Dirty and wrinkled clothing, presumably everything she'd worn over the course of the week, covered Ingrid's easy chair. To Drake's trained eye, it looked more messy than ransacked.

"Anything?" Allie asked as Drake rejoined them at the desk.

"No. Thanks, Heather, I appreciate it. Come on, Allie." Drake returned the keys. Then the duo left the building and turned south.

"I hope they're in the barn," Allie said, "because I don't recall there being anything else much this way."

"I remember we passed a guard shack, and I think there was a chicken coop. I don't remember for sure since I wasn't paying that close of attention when we came in."

They walked down the road a few hundred yards and eventually the view of the big barn came into view. They cut off the road and headed diagonally for the barn. When they got there, the sight of two small green tractors greeted them, along with various attachments, just inside the door. Drake recognized a plow based on its blades but didn't know what the other ones were for.

Drake and Allie passed the equipment and came to a small room. He opened the door and found the hand tool storage. There were several shovels, along with pickaxes, hoes, scythes, rakes, and spading forks, but no sign of Geneva or Ingrid.

Drake closed the door, and they passed deeper into the barn. When they got to the back third of the barn, they found a pickup truck with a small wagon attached to the back. Stacked against the walls on either side of the door were rectangular bundles of hay. Near one stack of hay were large bags of horse feed, and next to those were several bags of chicken feed. On a workbench nearby were several pairs of work gloves and three stainless steel buckets.

"What about up there?" Allie asked, pointing to a ladder along one wall.

"I'll go check."

Drake climbed the ladder to the loft, which extended the full length of the barn. Near where he had gone up were more hay bales and more bags of animal food.

When he got to the far side of the barn, he found Brandon trying to work out a three-dimensional puzzle.

"You alone?" Drake asked.

Brandon dropped the piece he was holding and spun around. "Oh, Drake, it's you. You scared me."

"Sorry. Where's Ben?"

"He wasn't downstairs? He said he had to pee, so he was going to find a discrete spot to do his business then come right back."

"No, he wasn't there. How long has he been gone?"

Brandon shrugged. "I don't know. Maybe five or ten minutes. Why? What's going on?"

"Have you seen Ingrid or Geneva?"

Brandon shook his head. "Not since this morning."

"They appear to be missing, and now that your brother is late in returning, it's safe to assume he is, too."

"Missing? How can that be? Where would they go? We're out in the middle of the desert."

"That's what I'm trying to figure out. Why don't you come with us?"

Drake and Brandon left the loft and rejoined Allie on the ground floor, and they left the barn.

"Where else can we check?" Allie asked.

"Why don't we find someone in security?" Brandon asked. "Wouldn't they be the better option to look for missing persons?"

"I have seen no security at all. We stopped by the jail, and it was locked up tight," Drake answered.

"What about Andy or Bruce? Surely, they're around somewhere."

Drake shook his head. "Haven't seen them either. Wouldn't know where to look for them."

"Have you seen anyone?" Brandon asked.

"The orange team was in the horse barn, Travis was in the UTV barn, and the purple and brown teams were in the restaurant," Drake answered.

"And Heather was at the front desk of the hotel," Allie added.

"How about I run back to the hotel and see if Heather can rustle up anyone else, and in the meantime, you two keep up your search?" Brandon said.

"Okay. Go," Drake said.

They watched Brandon run off toward town, then they stood for a moment and surveyed the land before them.

"Now what? Walk up and down the crop rows and hope we literally trip over someone?" Allie asked.

"I don't know, but I wish we'd paid more attention to

this end of town. I don't know what's out here."

"Let's go back to the main driveway then and hike down to the guardhouse, and we'll stop at any building we find along the way."

"I think that will be a long hike for you. Will your knee handle it?" Drake asked.

"I don't know, but I can try. I'll go as far as I can, then send you off alone if I feel like I can't make it."

They made their way to the main road, then headed south. Along the way they passed five freestanding windmills, and then came upon a small building, eight feet square and made of cinder blocks. At one end was a wooden door with a shiny new padlock, holding it closed.

"I'd sure like to get a look in there," Drake said.

"I think there was a window on the other end," Allie said. "Come and give me a boost."

They walked around the building, and sure enough, there was a long, skinny window that was on the side opposite the late afternoon sun, so there wasn't enough light for Allie to get a good look when Drake lifted her up. The pair returned to the door, and Drake looked around until he found a rock the size of a softball. He hoisted the rock and smashed at the lock until the wood from the old door splintered and the lock assembly dropped to the ground.

Drake pushed the door open and stepped inside with Allie a single stride behind.

"What is this place?" Allie asked. She spotted a light switch on the wall beside her and flipped it. Four single bulbs lit up in various places in the room, then one of them flickered and went out.

There was still enough light to see the inside of the building had a thick layer of dust and cobwebs.

"It's a pump house. Probably powered by the windmill to move water around the cropland," Drake explained.

"There's a tarp covering something ahead. I'm going to check it out."

Drake made his way to the tarp, grabbed an edge, hesitated, then flipped it over. It was a piece of machinery sitting on a wooden pallet. He turned and was about to speak when the pump fired up, made a whining sound at first, then spurted into life, sounding like a diesel train engine.

Allie left the building with Drake, a step behind her.

"I didn't like it in there. Way too creepy."

Drake turned off the light, then shut the door, but since he busted the lock away, the door swung open an inch, then stopped.

"Let's keep moving. The sun will be gone soon, then we'll really be in trouble out here."

They walked on another quarter mile, and Drake noticed Allie's pace was getting slower and slower with each few steps she took.

"Why don't you rest here, and I'll go to the guardhouse and come back. It shouldn't be more than half a mile from here, and I'll be back in no time," Drake offered.

Allie nodded, stepped over to a large rock that lined the road, and sat down on it to wait.

Drake ran up the road, trying to keep up a steady pace, even though he wasn't much of a runner. Within five minutes, he saw the guard house up ahead, so he picked up his speed. As he got closer, he felt comforted by the light peering from the windows, and soon after, he got there and opened the door. Drake rushed inside and almost collided with a guard sitting with his feet up on the desk, drinking a cup of coffee.

"Where did you come from?" The guard asked once he got his feet to the floor and stood.

"From town. Can you help me? Some of my friends have been missing most of the afternoon and I can't find them."

"It's a big town, son. I'm sure you could have just missed them."

Drake shook his head. "No. Please. Can you at least call T.R. and get her or some of her security detail to help me out?"

"I would, but we got an S.O.S a few hours ago from a pair of hikers out in the desert. Apparently, one had a fall with major injuries. Most everyone is out there trying to find them."

"A pair of random hikers, huh?" Drake asked.

"Yep. It happens from time to time. There are quite a few public trails to the north, and sometimes hikers get lost and end up on our side of the fence. I'll call out on the radio and see if someone can come back to help, though. You want to wait here?"

"No, thanks, I've got to get back to my partner. We'll head back to town and wait by the jail."

Drake left the guard, jogged back to Allie, and told her everything he'd learned.

They walked back to town and were just about there when Allie spotted a roof.

"There's another building over there. Come on." Without waiting for a response, Allie limped off to the northeast, and soon they arrived at a large chicken coop.

Drake had never seen a coop so large. It looked like the horse barn, except it was only a tenth of the size. It was even painted red with white trim. There was a human-sized door in the center, and several windows lined the sides. In a half dozen places, there were little ramps where the chickens could enter or leave the coop of their own accord.

There was twenty feet of grass and earth around the coop, then there was a perimeter fence made of chain link, and above the chain-link fence was a tin roof.

"Go in," Allie said.

"I really don't want to."

"Come on, Duck-man, what are you? Chicken?"

"Ha, ha, very funny, Allie. Okay. I'll go."

Drake undid the clasp of the fence, stepped through the gate, and closed it behind him. There were chickens out in the yard, and they scampered away from him as he walked toward the coop's main door. It was unlocked and opened outward, so he stepped in, leaving the door open.

There was a corridor that stretched from the door to the end of the coop, and along the sides were nesting and sleeping areas. As he walked forward, the wooden floor creaked below him, and although the coop smelled musty, it didn't give off the pungent ammonia smell he expected.

Drake thought he heard something, so he stopped to listen. Among the clucking, he heard someone calling for help.

"I'm coming!" Drake yelled. He rushed forward, and suddenly the floor dropped away, and he descended into darkness.

CHAPTER TWENTY

Drake? Drake? Can you hear me?"

Drake's eyes fluttered open, but it was dark, so he couldn't tell who was cradling his head. "Geneva? Is that you?"

"Yes."

"Where are we?"

"Underneath the chicken coop. You fell through a trapdoor."

"Is he okay?" another voice asked.

"He's fine," Geneva answered.

"Who else is here?" Drake asked.

"Ingrid and Ben," Geneva answered.

"What the hell is going on?"

"Your guess is as good as mine."

"Hello? Drake? Where are you?"

It was Allie, her voice muffled by the floor.

"Allie! Stop. Don't come in any farther!" Drake yelled. "Can I stand up in here?"

"Sure. From what we can tell, the floor is about nine feet above us," Ben said.

"Allie! Can you hear me?" Drake yelled.

"Drake? Is that you? It's hard to understand you. Where are you?" Allie answered.

"I'm down here. There's a trapdoor on the floor! Stomp on the floor if you understand me."

Drake listened and a couple of seconds later, two thumps resounded on the ceiling above them, then he heard creaking, followed by silence.

"Where did she go?" Geneva asked.

"Hopefully to get help," Ben said.

"Help probably won't be here for a while," Drake said, then he added what the guard had told him. "Is anyone injured down here?"

"No. Only mostly cold and miserable," Geneva said.

"Ingrid, what about you?" Drake asked, concerned he hadn't picked up a peep from her.

"I don't like the dark and I want to get out of here. I feel like I'm going to lose my mind," she said.

"It's okay. Be calm and hold on. Allie will get us out of here if anyone will."

The conversation died off as they waited in the dark.

"Hey," Ingrid said to get everyone's attention. "Why do you never see elephants hiding in trees?"

"What? Why?" Geneva asked.

"Because they're so good at it," Ingrid answered.

There was silence for a second and suddenly, Ben let out a moan, followed by a guffaw. "That was horrible. Not funny at all."

"So, why are you laughing?" Drake asked, trying to hold back a chuckle.

Ben began to answer, but stopped when they sensed stomping on the ceiling, followed by a scraping noise.

"What is that?" Geneva asked.

The appearance of a light above them answered her

question. Suspended over their heads was a bucket tied to a rope, and on top of the bucket were two flashlights. As the bucket spun, the flashlights lit up the space above them like a lighthouse beam. A second later, a third light appeared and shined down into the hole. As one, the four captives held up their hands to block out the bright light.

"Hey everybody," Allie said as she moved the direct beam of her light to a wall just over their heads. "How y'all doing?"

Drake looked up and noticed Allie was on her stomach, leaning precariously over the edge of the hole.

"We're great," Drake answered. "You got a ladder or something to get us out of here?"

"No. No ladder, but I have a plan. First, I'm going to lower down the bucket, okay?"

"Lower away," Drake said.

Allie slowly lowered the bucket, and Drake and Ben removed the flashlights. Drake noticed the bucket was full of chicken feed to give it weight.

"Is there any way to get out from down there?" Allie asked.

Drake shined his light around the room, which almost had the look of an old root cellar. There was a crumbling set of wood shelves leaning crookedly against the far wall of the six-foot-square space. But other than that, the walls and floor were rock, dirt, and dust. "Nope. It's only a big hole down here."

"Okay. No problem. Plan B it is then," Allie said. "Step aside."

Everyone moved over closer to the shelves, and Allie pulled up the bucket. A few seconds after it disappeared from the hole, a thicker rope dropped in. It stopped two feet above the floor.

Allie's head reappeared, and she shined her light down

into the hole. "Is that long enough? I knotted it, so you should be able to climb up. Easy peasy."

Drake moved to the rope and checked it over. Sure enough, there was a knot about three inches above the end, and a knot every nine to twelve inches all the way up the rope. "It's good. Is it tied off securely?"

"Of course it is, Drake. This isn't my first daring rescue, you know. Send someone up. Let's get the show on the road."

"Ingrid? You want to go first?" Drake asked, but before he finished speaking the last syllable of his sentence, Ingrid already had her hands on the rope.

Drake grabbed the rope's bottom to hold it steady, and Ingrid began her climb to the top. He thought she'd have trouble with it, but to his surprise, she scampered up like she'd done it a hundred times before. There was a slight delay when she got to the top. Then he saw Allie lean over and grab Ingrid by the belt and pull her up and out.

"Who's next? Geneva? Ben?" Drake asked.

"I'll go next in case they need some more muscle up top," Ben said. He handed his flashlight to Geneva and stepped up, grabbed the rope, and started his climb. He was a third of the way up when he lost his grip and fell back to the ground.

"Wow, that's harder than it looks," he said. "Ingrid made it look so easy."

"She's a natural born climber," Geneva said.

Ben stepped back up to the rope, spit on his hands for effect, and started again, this time at a slower pace, so he wouldn't repeat his mistake. A few minutes later, his legs disappeared from view.

"I guess we're all alone now," Drake said.

"Yeah, it's almost romantic. Could get a bottle of wine and a blanket down here, and it would be downright homey." Geneva leaned in and gave him a soft kiss on the lips. "Thanks for saving me, hero."

Drake returned the smooch. "Allie's going to save you. I'm only here by proxy."

A light shined down on them. "Hey, you two, can you play kissy-face after we get you out of there?" Allie asked.

Geneva smiled, clutched the rope, and started her ascent. Like Ingrid, she had no trouble getting to the top. Once she was clear, Drake shut off both flashlights and tucked one into each of his back pockets. He'd had some training climbing ropes that weren't knotted, so getting up the one Allie had prepared was as simple for him as climbing a ladder.

When he got to the top, Allie helped him out of the hole.

"Thanks, you're a lifesaver," he said to Allie.

"I know," Allie said as she pulled up the rope, passing the slack to Drake as she did.

"What are you doing?"

"Closing the trapdoor, of course. I don't want the chickens to fall into the hole. That would be cruel."

Once Allie removed the weight of the rope, the door sprung back up into position, and Allie leaned over the door and moved two braces into position.

"Okay, we can go now. And hurry, I think I'm allergic to chicken feathers," Allie said.

Drake, still holding the rope, left the coop. He spotted the other three people congregating outside the fence, near a pickup truck with the wagon attached. He dropped the rope on the ground and followed the other end with his eyes. Drake noticed Allie had threaded it through the fence and tied it off to one of the support posts. Allie walked past Drake and held the fence gate open for him while he exited.

"Where did you get all this stuff?" Drake asked.

"The feed barn, of course. You mind driving us back to town? My knee's really bothering me, and it's getting stiff."

Drake got into the driver's seat and started the truck. Geneva slipped into the passenger seat next to him, and Ben helped Allie and Ingrid into the wagon. Ben leaned over the side and waved, and Drake slipped the pickup into Drive and slowly headed to town. When they had gotten about halfway, Drake spotted Brandon walking down the road toward them.

"Need a ride, mister?" Drake asked when he got even with Brandon. "There's someone in the back waiting for you."

Brandon walked to the wagon, but before he got there, Ben jumped to the ground and gathered his brother into a bear hug. They both climbed onto the wagon, and Drake drove off again and didn't stop until he pulled up alongside the hotel. As he got out of the truck, the jail door flew open and T.R. rushed to him.

"What's going on? I got a call from the guard shack."

Drake took her aside. "Did you know there's a trapdoor in the chicken coop's floor that leads to a cold, dark pit?"

"Of course not," T.R. said.

"Yeah, well, you know now. Four of us were stuck in there for about an hour, and I don't think it was an accident."

T.R. leaned in closer and whispered. "I know for sure it wasn't. I need to let one more thing play out, okay? Trust me for another hour or two."

Drake looked at her for a second, then nodded. "We've come this far, so sure. Can you find the doctor for us? I think Allie aggravated her knee."

"She's already back, so check her office."

"What about the search party?"

"It's been called off. Looked for almost five hours out there and didn't find a single thing. We're thinking it's a hoax, and everyone is on their way back now."

Drake found Allie and escorted her over to see Dr. Liz.

Within a half hour, Allie left the doctor wearing a knee brace that made her look like a cyborg, and she was on crutches instead of a cane.

Slowly, Drake walked with her over to the restaurant and sat her down in the first chair she came to.

He looked around the room for Geneva and Ingrid and, by the time he spotted the pair, they were already on their way to join them.

"My goodness, Allie, what happened?" Ingrid asked.

"The doc thinks I either strained or tore a ligament. Won't know for sure until I see a specialist and she already set an appointment for me to see one in Nashville on Monday morning."

"You need anything?" Geneva asked.

"Well, how about some food and drink for a start?"

A server came over and Drake ordered three pizzas and beer for everyone except Allie, who had taken prescription painkillers and was under doctor's orders not to drink alcohol. She ordered a diet cola instead.

They made small talk until the pizzas arrived, and each person had devoured a slice when Bruce and Andy unexpectedly entered the room.

Andy took a moment to connect his laptop to the display while Bruce chatted with the pink team, who sat at the table closest to him. Eventually, Andy was ready and showed the spreadsheet.

"Everyone has checked in, so it's time to determine the winner!" Bruce said. He paused to allow the applause to fade. "Each team should select a representative to step forward and hand over the tokens you collected today."

Mike from the pink team was the first to stand, and since he was close to the front, he only needed to lean over to pass his tokens to Bruce.

"Official count for the pink team is two tokens," Bruce

said.

Tito and Marina played a quick round of rock paper scissors to determine the winner. Tito got up and walked over to Bruce, followed by Gilberto. Ben made his way to the front of the room from his seat near the back.

"Purple team, one token. Brown team has one token. Yellow team has four tokens. Well done, geocachers," Bruce said.

There was a smattering of applause for Ben, who took a mock bow and got laughter and louder applause in return.

"I guess we should get up there," Geneva said to Drake.

Allie dug through her pockets to extract the tokens she carried and passed them off to Drake. Drake bowed and gestured ahead of him. "Ladies first," he said.

"Ooh, how gallant," Geneva mocked.

Before Geneva or Drake pushed away from the table, Penny rushed to Bruce and made a show of putting her stack of tokens on the table before him. Bruce divided the stack in half and did a quick count.

"Orange team has ten tokens. That's amazing, folks. Ten tokens!" Bruce said, then led the applause.

Ten tokens, to Drake, not only seemed amazing but also improbable just based on, well, math, but he kept his mouth closed as he followed Geneva to the head table.

"The gray team has two tokens, and finally, the green team has six tokens. There you are, folks. Just give us a moment to factor the points and accumulate the final totals."

"Wait," Marina said, "that's only twenty-six. What about the other four?"

Bruce looked at her for a moment, then looked down at the tokens he'd placed on the table before him. He looked over at Andy, and they had a few quick, whispered words.

"Good question. No one found the other four geocaches,

so twenty-six is the correct count. Okay?"

Marina nodded, then went back to her drink.

"It'll be just a couple more minutes, and we'll announce the winner," Bruce said. While he waited, he filled the silence with empty banter as he stretched the time to allow Andy to enter the final scores and calculate the victor.

Drake sensed the door open behind him, then looked up when someone got to his side. T.R. was standing there holding a piece of paper. She nodded at him, then stepped a few feet away.

"Okay folks, we're ready. The team in seventh place is…" Bruce waited for the answer to flash on the screen. "The brown team. Congratulations Gilberto and Roy. Well done, fellas. In sixth place is… the gray team. Geneva and Ingrid, good for you. Fifth place is… the purple team. Way to go, Marina and Tito. In fourth place is… the pink team. Mike and Ricky, you put in a great effort out there. Now for the top three! In third place is… the yellow team. Ben and Brandon. Let's hear it for them."

Bruce waited until the applause dissipated for the well-liked Beasley brothers.

"And the winner of the first annual Cacheland competition is… the orange team. Cindy and Penny! Please come forward!"

Cindy and Penny jumped from their chairs, screamed in delight, and hugged each other while their fellow geocachers cheered for them.

"I'm sorry, Drake," Allie said. "It's my fault we didn't win. We would have if I wasn't stupid and injured myself."

Drake shook his head. "No, there's no reason to apologize. It was an accident, and I'm both proud and amazed at how hard you still went at it. You're a trooper."

T.R. caught Drake's eye as she moved from the back of the room to the front, then passed the paper to Bruce. He took it and read it. As he processed the words on it, he looked from T.R. to Andy, to the still-hugging orange team, back to T.R. He asked her a question, and she nodded, then stepped off to the side.

"Settle down, please. Everyone take your seats."

The room quieted, and all those who were standing sat.

"First off, I'd like to offer an apology. On day one, I talked about the integrity of this game and how I wouldn't allow cheating of any kind, and that is why I had the rules I laid out. You know full well I was serious about it when we found out the red team was indeed cheating, and we expelled them from the property immediately. In the spirit of full transparency, T.R. has brought to my attention that another team has been cheating. The orange team."

There were sounds of unexpected shock throughout the room, and everyone turned to look at Penny and Cindy. Cindy, without a word, got up from her chair and made a quick run for the exit, with Penny on her heels a second later.

Drake felt the breeze as they both rushed past him, and he turned in time to see Cindy throw the door open and stomp out of the building. From where he was, he could see members of T.R.'s security team waiting outside for them. The door closed, and Drake gave his attention back to Bruce.

"It appears they were getting help from the inside. Andy, it turns out, is Cindy's brother."

Andy looked up at Bruce, then looked away. He pushed his chair back, but T.R. had maneuvered behind him and placed her foot behind his chair leg so he couldn't move.

"Even worse, according to the investigation report I have here, the accidents the blue and black teams had weren't accidents at all. It turns out Andy did it. It goes without saying, but Andy, you're fired."

Bruce passed the paper back to T.R. "T.R., would you be kind enough to give Andy a ride to the county sheriff's office?

Make sure he's charged with assault and attempted murder. And please make sure he never sets foot on this property again."

To thunderous applause, T.R. grabbed Andy by the shirt collar and pulled him from his chair. She marched him through the dining room as easily as if he were a marionette.

"Based on all that, I apologize again, and since I have disqualified the orange team, that means Allie and Drake, the green team, are the winners. Come forward and collect your prize."

The applause started again, and Tito jumped up, rushed over to Drake, and gave him another hearty clap on the back. The rest of the geocachers rose to congratulate the winners and then made way so Allie and Drake could reach the head table. Once there, Bruce handed Drake an oversized check and Allie the Golden Horseshoe.

"Congratulations to you all and thank you for a great week!" Bruce said. "Let's bring out the bubbly!"

Three hours later, Drake was sitting on a chair beside the fire pit when he sensed a presence.

"I'm going to miss these western skies at night," Geneva said. "You can't see all these stars in the city."

"You're right about that, for sure. I'm also going to miss all the peace and quiet."
Geneva sat on Drake's lap and wrapped her arms around his neck. "How's Allie doing?"

"She's been asleep for a couple of hours already. The drugs the doc gave her kicked in and knocked her right out. She probably shouldn't have had those two glasses of Champagne."

"I hope she'll be okay," Geneva said.

"She will. She's strong, and believe me, she's been through much worse than a bum knee."

"And what about you?" she asked.

"I don't have a bum knee," Drake joked.

"Sure, but aren't you going to have a broken heart after tonight when you won't see me anymore?"

"I was thinking about that. Boston and Nashville aren't that far apart."

"I guess, probably only eighteen hours or so by car," Geneva agreed.

"There are lots of geocaches to find along the way."

Geneva stopped him by putting a finger over his lips. "Do me a favor before you plan out that trip in your head."

"Sure, what?"

"Take me upstairs to my room."

The Quincy Bay Quandary

CHAPTER ONE

D rake Decker was so busy watching the plane's shadow pass over the houses, office buildings, and highways below them, he didn't catch the question.

His seatmate, Allie Ashe, tapped him on the shoulder to get his attention. At first, he didn't react, so Allie had to tap progressively harder to get him to notice her.

"Earth to Drake. Hello? Anyone home?"

Drake's head turned toward her, and his hazel eyes met her green ones.

"Are you nervous?"

"About what?" Drake asked.

"Seeing her again. It's been a long time."

Drake made a face like he'd bitten into a lemon stuffed with tart cherries.

"It's only been eight months. That's hardly any time at all."

"Yeah, but perhaps she's forgotten about you by now," Allie teased. Aside from working out, going to Broadway musicals, and geocaching, messing with Drake was one of her favorite activities.

"It's not like we never talk. We text every day, and video chat at least four times a week," Drake said.

He looked at Allie, who, despite trying to keep her straight face, cracked a wide grin, and finally he recognized she was trying intentionally to rile him up.

"Thanks, Allie," Drake said as he rolled his eyes. "As if this flight isn't long enough, you're going to torture me even more by messing with my head?"

Allie giggled, then slapped Drake on the thigh. "Sorry, just trying to entertain myself."

"And you couldn't do that by reading that in-flight magazine? The one with the cover hanging half off and the crossword puzzle already done, usually completed by two different people?" Drake said.

Allie rummaged through the seat pocket for the magazine and when she pulled it out, she noted the cover was indeed missing the top corner. She skipped right to the last page and paged backward through all the airport terminal maps until she came to the crossword. Sure enough, it was already done. Someone with a red pen filled out more than a dozen answers, all the simple ones, she noted, and a different passenger had completed the rest in black ink.

"How did you guess?" she asked.

"Because they're always like that. And chances are, if you're flying into a city that's featured in an article, someone has torn that article out as well."

"That makes no sense to me. Why not just take the entire magazine at that point?"

Drake shrugged. "No clue. I've never done it. I also don't understand why we didn't drive instead of fly."

Allie released her ponytail from the dark blue scrunchy she wore. She gathered her long red locks together, including the strands that had wrestled themselves free over the course of the last few hours. She pulled her hair tight and bundled everything back into a ponytail.

Drake watched her, and in return, he took off his Tennessee Titans baseball cap. He ran his fingers through his military precision cut blond hair and returned his hat to his head.

"You know why. There's a convention I'm going to in two weeks and it would take us forever to drive to Boston and back," Allie said.

Drake shook his head. "We've been through this. Nashville to Boston is only seventeen hours one-way. Had we taken turns driving, we would have gotten there in one long day."

Allie nodded and gave him a sarcastic smile. "Would you have wanted to find some geocaches along the route?"

Drake shrugged. "Probably. Only to get out of the car and stretch our legs. Or there might be one at a gas station or restaurant we would normally stop at, anyway."

"Mmm hmm, sure. Remember that time we traveled to Knoxville, only a two-hour trip from home? How long did that take us?"

"I don't remember," Drake said, then turned back to the window.

"I remember. Six hours. We almost missed the event because you wanted to stretch your legs so much."

Drake returned to looking at her and smiled. "Hey, that wasn't all me. You're the one who wanted to visit those EarthCaches along the way."

"That was different," Allie said.

"How?" Drake pressed.

Allie's nose crinkled as she attempted to find an answer in her head. "Well, because they were pretty. Don't you remember how gorgeous those waterfalls were?"

"Thanks for proving my point. It's not all me, and you know it. So, you ask, how long would it take to travel seventeen hours across what, seven states? I'd guess three days."

"That's not too bad," Allie said. "I would have guessed five days. Six at the most."

Drake laughed and patted her leg. "Yeah, that's probably more like it. It's all right though, we've got the money, so it was good to treat ourselves to a flight."

The previous fall, Drake and Allie took part in an exclusive geocaching competition. They were one of only ten teams vying for a fifty-thousand-dollar grand prize. Although a couple of teams tried to cheat their way to the prize money, Drake and Allie had come out on top. More important than the cash, though, Drake had met his new girlfriend.

"You still would have preferred to drive, right?" Allie asked.

Drake nodded, then shrugged.

"What's the plan if we ever get there?" Drake asked. "I mean, other than geocaching."

"Well, I love history, especially American history. Since Boston is crucial to the birth of America, I'd like to spend a couple of days taking in the touristy sites. I've never been to Boston before. What about you?"

"I'd like to check out the Salem witch trial locations. And isn't Lizzie Borden from up there somewhere? I'd like to see her house," Drake said.

"You want to delve into the macabre? Is Geneva into all that creepy stuff?"

"Not really, but she said she'd be up for whatever. We're the tourists in her city, after all. I'd like to do other stuff, too. Maybe go see the Red Sox if they're in town. Or take a boat tour. I've never been on a boat tour. Oh, and of course, we absolutely must eat some authentic Boston clam chowder."

Allie stuck out her tongue. "Yuck, you can keep the chowder. Clams are nasty. I'd rather have a nice Boston creme pie."

"I've heard people say you can tell if the clams are fresh if there's sand in the chowder."

Allie made a soft retching noise, then smiled at the person across the aisle from her who was eying her warily. "As if the chowder wasn't bad enough, you want sand in it? No thanks, I'll stick to a burger. Medium rare. No sand."

"Oh, I forgot, Tuesday night we're going to the symphony. Geneva's playing that night and she wants us to go," Drake said.

"What? You should have told me that before we left Nashville. I didn't pack my symphony dress!" Allie protested.

"Symphony dress? Does it come with long white gloves, high-heeled black designer shoes, a clutch purse, and a pearl necklace?"

"Of course," Allie said. She tried to hold the moment, then laughed. "Okay, I don't own a symphony dress."

"Do you own any dress?"

Allie slapped Drake's arm. The report was louder than she expected, and when she looked over at the man across the aisle, she caught him glancing at her over his business magazine.

"Of course. I own a dress," she whispered to Drake. "Well, okay, maybe not a dress, per se. It's more of a long skirt. But I have a really nice blouse and jacket to go with it."

"Really? I've never seen you in that outfit."

"That's probably because I only wear it to funerals and weddings, and we don't go to those together, do we?"

"Well, we might someday." Drake threw Allie a wink that she easily caught.

"Drake Decker, you're not thinking of proposing, are

you? After eight months? Are you serious?"

Drake nodded.

"No? Really?"

Drake nodded again, but he couldn't hold his straight face and chuckled. "Got you."

"You're such a jerk. Just for that, I might have to drop some hints that you are indeed thinking about the idea of a wedding."

"You wouldn't?" Drake said, as a look of deep concern passed over his face.

Allie nodded. She took an interest in straightening the materials in the seat pocket in front of her.

"No. really?"

Allie smiled. "Got you back."

"You're such a jerk," Drake said.

"And that's what you love about me."

Drake turned back to look out the window to see if they were any closer to their destination. He hated to fly, partially because he didn't like being cooped up in a tin can, and partially because he had to give all his control over to someone he'd never met. Of course, he'd heard all the statistics about flying being the safest form of travel. However, between the events of 9-11, the Miracle on the Hudson, and a lifetime of movies he'd seen involving air crashes, he was always leery about getting on a plane. His canned response was if the engine failed in his car, he could always pull over to the side of the highway and call for roadside help. The pilot couldn't really do that at thirty thousand feet in the air.

Drake closed his eyes and leaned his head against the cool, oval plane window. Allie was right. It would take them several days to make the drive a third of the way across the country. He was also excited, yet anxious, about seeing Geneva. It was true they talked in one form or another every day and shared text messages and video chats over the last few months. Drake's biggest concern was if the passionate flame they kindled in the Arizona desert had died off. He also worried if they were still as good a match being together in the real world as they were in the virtual one.

Drake glanced over at Allie and secretly wished she'd declined his invitation to go with him. He wasn't worried she'd interfere with his private time with his girlfriend. Rather, Drake worried she would get the third-wheel feeling that people often got in situations in this. He had to invite her along for the ride. She'd talked about visiting Boston for forever, and he believed if she found out he went there without her, she'd never speak to him again. And that was after she buried him in a hard to get to holler in the Appalachians of eastern Tennessee.

Drake had a surprise for her, though. Geneva's friend and geocaching partner, Ingrid, planned on joining them for lunch. He saw that Allie and Ingrid had sparked a pretty wonderful friendship when they first met back in October. According to Allie, they'd only kept in touch a few times a month via text, but Drake was certain Allie would be happy to see Ingrid. Also, if he could convince Allie and Ingrid to venture off together to find caches or explore the city, that would be all the better. It would be more time alone for him and Geneva.

Drake focused on the landscape and watched the city leave his view, replaced by the blue of the Atlantic Ocean. Even from as high as they were, he could see the whitecaps atop the waves, and the uncountable number of boats either heading away from or toward the shore. His adventurous side wanted to get on one of those boats and feel the power of the ocean beneath his feet. Realistically, though, he was prone to seasickness, so he sensed he'd spend most of the voyage with his head over the side of the boat.

The overhead bell dinged, and the captain's voice came over the intercom with the message that they'd be landing in fifteen minutes. Around him, the passengers and crew impatiently got their respective acts together.

"Did you know that most airplane accidents happen during takeoffs and landings?" Allie asked.

"Does that go along with most accidents happening within five miles of your house?" Drake countered.

"I don't know. It was just a statistic I read once," Allie said.

"What do you want to do when we land?" Drake asked, desiring to drop the plane crash topic.

"Get off the plane," Allie deadpanned.

Drake gave her a grin. "No. I mean after that."

"Go to the second women's room I find."

"Second? Why not the first?" Drake asked.

"The first one will have a line out the door. At the second one, I'd have a decent shot at actually getting a toilet. You wouldn't understand the struggle since you're a man."

Drake took some mock offense at the comment. "Hey, what's that supposed to mean?"

"It means you're a guy and you can pee anywhere. I've seen you mark so many trees, I think you're part beagle. You probably go into a men's room and share urinals, but women don't have that luxury."

Drake thought about it. He had been to more than one stadium where the men's room featured one wall to wall stainless steel trough for men to do their business into. He thought twice and smartly dropped the conversation topic all together.

"No. I mean when we're out of the airport. Want to get some food, or find some caches, or see some sights?"

"What time is it?" Allie asked.

Drake checked his watch. "Almost nine. We've got the

entire day ahead of us."

"I don't need food. I can hold out until lunch. What if we can find a cache or two near something historical and kill three birds with one stone?" Allie asked.

Drake nodded. Since geocachers often hid geocaches near sites of historical interest, they could usually do both at once. It was an excellent strategy they often applied whenever venturing away from home. Otherwise, they'd never think of visiting Abraham Lincoln's boyhood home in Kentucky or the world's largest ball of twine in Kansas. Based on how scenic the spot was, either the geocache or the location took top billing. They'd found a magnetic keyholder in a guardrail in Wyoming once. Although the geocache wasn't all that unique or spectacular, the view of Devil's Tower from ground zero was.

"Sure. We can see if Geneva has any suggestions," Drake said. "She'd know a spot right off the top of her head."

There was a slight jolt as the wheels hit the runway, followed by the whine of the air brakes being deployed. They coasted straight until they slowed, then the pilot navigated the plane to the terminal. Drake watched as the gate numbers continued to rise and knew, based on his luck, the plane would stop at the gate farthest away from everything.

The plane slowed as it approached the jet bridge and around him the distinctive metallic sound of seat belts unfastening filled the air. The plane had barely come to a stop when people around Drake and Allie rose from their seats.

"Aren't you going to stand up?" Drake asked.

Allie leaned over so she could see down the aisle. "Not yet. Relax. The door hasn't opened yet, and since we're way back here, it'll be a good ten minutes before we can move, anyway."

"How can you be so sure?"

"Experience. Because of FAA regulations, there has to

be an older person in the first five rows who needs help to retrieve their bag from the overhead bin. And then we have to wait for them to get into the aisle and put on their hat and coat before anyone can pass them."

"That's a regulation, huh?"

Allie nodded. "We're just lucky this is our final destination and we're not connecting with a half hour or less to catch the next flight. In that case, the law says there has to be an elderly person and a single mother with a baby and multiple bags somewhere in the first five rows."

Drake shook his head at her.

"Hey, don't blame me. Look it up."

The duo sat still. When Allie noticed the line move, she rose and retrieved Drake's carry on and set it behind her and then pulled down her suitcase and set it in front of her. Then she fished her backpack out from under the seat and threw it over her shoulders. As she waited for her turn, she extracted the handles on both pieces of luggage. Once the aisle was clear, she pushed hers ahead and dragged Drake's bag behind her until he was out of his seat and ready to haul his own suitcase.

Once they were out of the jetway and in the gate area, Allie removed her backpack. She did a couple of yoga poses to stretch her limbs as Drake fished his phone from his pocket and texted Geneva.

Ready to go, they pulled their luggage behind them as they navigated their way through the terminal and the hordes of people walking in their direction. Drake noticed Allie didn't even hesitate when she passed the first women's room they found, which had a line stretching out into the open space of the corridor. They hiked on for five more minutes. When they came to the next women's room, Drake moved off to the side and watched over Allie's bags while she took care of business.

"Did you hear from her?" Allie asked upon her return.

"Yeah. She's waiting for us at the cell phone lot. I'm supposed to text her again when we get outside. Apparently, security likes to keep the pickup zones moving along quickly."

They followed the signs to baggage, went down an escalator, and a few seconds later they were outside in the warm June weather. Sure enough, airport security personnel were at several places waving their hands and blowing their whistles. They tried to keep the flood of passenger cars, taxis, and airport shuttle buses moving at a good clip. All the while keeping a close eye on the pedestrians trying to cross the road to the parking garage.

"She'll be here in like thirty seconds," Drake said.

"You know what she drives?"

"Navy blue Nissan Rogue."

Drake had barely finished answering when a blue blur swung up to the curb next to them. Geneva popped out of the SUV, opened the trunk, then greeted Drake with a hug and a kiss, and then gave Allie a hug as well.

A security guard whistled at Geneva to get her attention, then pointed at her car and motioned for her to pull away. In response, Geneva gave him an air kiss, then got back in the driver's seat while Drake and Allie tossed their bags in the trunk. Thirty seconds later, everyone had their seatbelts on, and Geneva drove toward the airport exit.

"Where to?" Geneva asked.

"Allie likes American history. Do you know of a geocache we could visit with a historical angle to it?"

Geneva looked in the rear-view mirror and glanced at Allie. "Of course. We'll go where it all started. Perfect way to begin your trip."

CHAPTER TWO

D id you have a pleasant flight?" Geneva asked as she raced along the interstate, weaving in and out of traffic like a NASCAR driver. Drake held on to the grab handle above the door with a grip tight enough to whiten his knuckles.

"We got here without incident, so I consider it a great success," Drake said.

"Allie, how's your knee? Ingrid told me you're one hundred percent now."

Allie leaned forward from the backseat so she could hear better. The windows were open, so the whoosh from the passing air combined with the highway noise made it difficult to hear anything in the front seat.

"It's more like eighty percent. I had to have surgery to fix a tendon in there, and it'll take another few months until I'm fully recovered. Until I heal, no more long hikes, climbing mountains, or running marathons for me."

"You won't have to do any of those things this week,

and I can guarantee you won't have to worry about a scree pile the height of a five-story building."

"Good," Allie said and settled back into her seat. It had been eight months since the accident, but she still dreamed of tumbling down that giant hill out in the desert. Unfortunately, her fall was only a couple of days into the competition. Her stubbornness and competitive nature kept her going at it for the rest of the week, and although they'd won the top prize, Allie often wondered if it was worth it. She realized she only had herself to blame. Drake, as her geocaching team partner, had asked her multiple times if she wanted to keep going, and she agreed to press on. She couldn't quit. In a previous career, she spent ten years as a U.S. Navy medical corpsman, and for eight of those years, she served with a Marine unit. If it was one thing she learned in those eight years, it was Marines didn't quit.

In the front seat, Geneva offered her hand to Drake, and he took it without a hint of hesitation.

"I'm happy you guys came out here. It's good to see you in person," Geneva said.

"Me too. I'm sorry I didn't have time to come out earlier." Drake squeezed her hand, but not too hard. There was an incongruity in her touch. Her hands were silky and supple, yet each fingertip on her left hand wore the rough telltale calluses of a musician.

"Where are we headed?" Drake asked.

"Out to Lexington, where the revolution began. There's a multi-cache out there that should take us an hour, maybe a little more, then we'll head downtown. Ingrid is meeting us in the city for dinner tonight."

Geneva laid on her horn to let the driver in the Mercedes beside her know she existed and bullied her way over to the exit ramp and left the highway. After another five minutes of assertive driving, Geneva turned into a parking lot and grabbed the first spot she saw. She turned off the car and sat back in her seat.

"Welcome to the Lexington Battle Green, where the initial shots kicked off the Revolutionary War. There's a multi-cache here that will take us to a few of the historic sites in the area. Here, I copied down the geocache code for you."

The trio got out of the car, and Drake and Allie went for their cell phones and opened their favorite geocaching apps. It wasn't long before they each found the geocache page for the multi-cache.

"Oh, my, this is a five-part cache," Allie said as she read the description. "We need to get some numbers from the monument and then use those to calculate the coordinates for the next stage."

Drake shook his head. "That's on you. You know how I feel about math."

Geneva laughed at him. "Come on, my big hero. You can handle some addition for me, can't you?"

"I'm not so sure about that, Geneva. There's multiplication in here too, although since it's by zero, I think Drake may have a chance of figuring it out without the calculator," Allie said. She hit Drake on the shoulder and tugged him toward the large monument in the center of the green.

"Can you imagine being here when the first shots of the war rang out?" Allie said when they got to the monument. Geneva nodded. "It must have been a scary time. One day you're carrying on with your normal life, and the next you're in the center of a huge armed conflict."

While the women chatted, Drake circled the monument,

searching for the numbers needed for the geocache. Once he'd completed the circle, he had a list of values written in a pocket-sized notebook. He passed his notes to Allie, who responded with a mock huff, then dramatically rolled her eyes. Without asking, she leaned forward and snatched the pen Drake had protruding from his baseball cap right above his ear.

To be helpful, Drake read out the calculations from the geocache description while Allie did the math. Soon, she had all the numbers they needed to go to the next stage. She added a waypoint with the new coordinates into her app and looked at the updated location.

Allie showed her screen to Drake and Geneva. "Next stop is over two miles from here. That can't be right."

Geneva borrowed Allie's phone and opened the map function. She studied it for a second, then handed the phone back. "Nope, that's right."

"How do you know?" Drake asked.

Geneva smiled. "Because I've already done this multi-cache."

"So why don't you take us right to the final, and we can skip all the steps?" Drake asked. "It would save us a ton of time and energy."

Allie stepped in and grabbed him by the arm. "No way. That would take away half the fun. Where's your sense of adventure?"

They got back in the car, and with no need for directions, Geneva drove them five minutes up the road and pulled into a parking lot with room for only four vehicles. They left the car and sauntered over to a small area surrounded by a short rock wall in the shape of a horseshoe. At the top of the horseshoe was an old plaque, green with oxidation. The story written on it recounted the tale of when British troops captured Paul Revere while out on his famous midnight ride. To the left and right of the plaque were more recent informational signs that added additional details to the event.

Drake looked at the cache description and alternated between his phone and the signs. He jotted down the needed numbers as he found them, and while he did that, Allie immersed herself in the history at the site.

Since there was no math to do for this puzzle, Drake entered the coordinates into his phone and projected the next waypoint.

"You ready to go?" he asked.

"Don't rush me, Duck-man, I'm learning something here. For example, did you know Paul Revere wasn't alone on the ride? There were a couple other guys with him, and of the three, he was the only one caught by the British?"

"So how did he get all the glory, then?" Drake asked. The stone wall was only a couple of feet tall, so he sat down on it and waited for Allie to finish reading the three markers there. He knew from previous experience that she liked to slow it down sometimes and take in the things surrounding her.

Drake was the opposite from her in that he usually liked to rush from geocache to geocache to increase his find numbers as fast as possible. Allie often had to insist that he stop for a few minutes so she could pause and read a historical marker or wander around a cemetery. Allie liked to take pictures of the scenery, or step into a local history museum for a few minutes. Since she did it, regardless of whether he wanted to, Drake had no choice but to wait for her.

"Where are we going next?" Allie asked as she turned to him.

"About a mile away. Are you okay to hike that?" Drake said.

"No need," Geneva said. "I can get you closer. Where we're going next is part of the national park, so we can get into the parking lot nearby, but there's still enough of a walk involved to stretch your legs."

Less than three minutes later, the trio were strolling up a paved lane. Drake periodically checked this phone to make sure the distance was getting shorter, an indication they headed in the correct direction. Within ten minutes, a saltbox style two-story building came into view. The exterior wood stain matched the same color brown as many of the trees that surrounded it. The only hint of color was the small panes of glass in the large windows that were bordered with white trim.

"This is amazing," Allie marveled as they stepped up to the main door of the tavern. "I love old buildings like this. I wonder if it's original."

"It is, indeed, ma'am," a park ranger answered. He stood just inside the door waiting for them. Rather than the typical tan and green of the National Park Service uniform, the ranger wore an outfit of full colonial garb, from the tricorn hat on his head, right down to the wide buckles on his shoes.

"About sixty-five percent of the tavern's original structure is here. Although it had some changes over time, the NPS restored it back to the way it looked in 1775," the ranger explained. "Care to come in and look around?"

"Would I? I'd love to. Can you give me a quick tour?" Allie asked.

The ranger took off his hat and bowed. "It would delight me to no end. Please, step this way."

Before entering, Allie turned back and addressed Drake and Geneva. "Are you guys coming with me?"

Drake waved her off. "Nah. Knock yourself out. While you take the tour, Geneva and I will find the coordinates for the next leg."

Allie smiled, then stepped over the threshold and into the building.

"Shall we?" Drake asked.

"Sure. What do we need?"

Drake scanned the description. "Let's see. We need the number of panes of glass above the entry door. The number of cross beams on the tavern room ceiling. The number of barrels in the pantry. Um, the number of spokes of the spinning wheel in the kitchen. The number of windowpanes in the parlor divided by five, and the number of large windows on the front of the tavern. These are some odd things to count."

Geneva nodded. "Yeah, but this building is closed for half of the year. When I did this cache, I had to look inside the windows to get the answers. It would probably be easier if we just walked through, well, except for the last one. We can get that answer from here."

Drake took a few steps away from the building, quickly counted the number of windows, and jotted down the answer.

"I can do the first one from here, too. It's seven. Come on, let's go inside."

Drake and Geneva passed the ranger and Allie as they rushed through the third room they got to. They stopped long enough to get the information they needed, then stepped back out into the sunlight.

Drake completed a few quick calculations and entered the numbers into his app as a new waypoint. "Four miles?"

Geneva cocked her head while she thought, then nodded. "That seems about right."

Drake took her hand, pulled her close into an embrace, and leaned in and kissed her. "I can't tell you how much I've missed you."

"Even though we talk to each other almost every day?"

"No, silly, I mean, I've missed seeing you in person. Holding your hand, kissing those soft lips of yours."

Geneva gave him a kiss, then pushed him away. "You're such a goofball, you know that?"

"He knows it, but he can't help himself," Allie said as she exited the tavern. "Where are we headed next?"

"Another tavern. It's a few miles from here, so we'll drive it," Geneva answered.

A quarter of an hour later, the three stood outside of the Munroe Tavern, a two-story wooden building painted red with white-trimmed windows.

"All the numbers we need will be on the outside of the building," Geneva said to Allie. "Drake and I can look for those answers while you go on in. There's a little museum in there that houses, among other fascinating things, the very table George Washington sat at when he ate here."

"The actual table? No way," Allie said.

"Way," Geneva answered.

"Okay with you if I go in and take a peek, Drake? I won't be too long. I promise."

Drake looked at his watch. "Okay, I'll give you five minutes. If you're not out in five, we're leaving without you."

Without responding, Allie made her way to the entry and went into the building.

"That was mean. Five minutes?"

Drake smiled. "I've got to put a time limit on her, or she'll be in there all day. Don't worry, I'm sure that five will stretch into twenty or more. She'll rush, but she'll do her version of rush and come out when she's ready. Let's get the information we need while we wait on her."

Drake and Geneva circled the building and got the numbers they needed, which included the number of chimneys and how many doors. They also had to count the number of windows on the west side of the building, and the number of words on the fourth line of the sign hanging by the driveway's entrance.

After they got all the required data, Geneva and Drake returned to the car and waited for Allie to appear, and ten minutes later, she did. She slipped into the backseat, excited by what she'd seen, and regaled the couple with all the details of what they'd missed. Of course, she spent most of the time discussing the Washington table and several documents relating to his trip.

"Are you going to be like this all week?" Drake asked as Geneva started the car and maneuvered her way across the driveway to the main road, checked for traffic, then pulled out.

"Like what?" Allie asked.

"Fangirling, every time we come across some trivial item related to the Revolutionary War?"

Allie sat back in her seat and crossed her arms. "You simply don't appreciate history. You never do."

"No. I do. I just like it in moderation is all," Drake said.

Allie didn't have time for a retort, because Geneva

turned again, then parked the car in a large public park.

"Here you go, last stop for this cache. I'll wait here while you two venture off into the trees," Geneva said. She rolled down all the windows, then shut off the engine.

Drake and Allie exited the car, and Drake checked his app and headed off toward the large grove of trees in the distance. The park was a nice one, with gentle, rolling hills, a walking trail, and several benches and picnic tables scattered throughout. There were a hundred yards of a grassy area with tall, individual oak trees that stretched to the sky, and the grass gave way to a dense pack of trees in the park's rear.

"How many more feet?" Allie asked when they reached the spot where the grass ended, and the grove began.

"Fifty," Drake answered. "Okay, into the fray, we go."

Drake stepped into the woods with Allie following three feet behind him. She learned from experience to keep far enough back so that if he moved a branch out of his way to get through, it wouldn't spring into its original position and hit her.

Drake walked for ten feet, stopped, checked the direction and range, then started again. After fifteen more feet, he stopped again, looked up to get his bearings, and started again. The app he used sent out a ping like a submarine's sonar, and as they got closer to ground zero, the pings resounded faster. When they arrived at the coordinates, the pings came rapidly, one after another, so Drake clicked off the app and slid his phone into his pocket.

"We should be right on it, so look around and see if there's anything that jumps out at you," Drake said.

"Sure, of course. There's like twenty trees in a thirty-feet radius, along with five stumps that I can see from here. This should be a simple one to find. Were there any hints on the cache page?"

Drake retrieved his phone and checked the hint. "It says wooden you like to know, and it's spelled like tree wood, not like the would you would."

"That's zero help," Allie said.

"The cache is a small size, so that should tell us at least something," Drake said.

Drake and Allie split up and started examining the trees in the area for a geocache hanging from a limb, or perhaps a large hole in a tree in which to place a container. Allie also checked the tree stumps, which is a favorite hiding spot for many geocachers in the woods.

After ten frustrating minutes of not finding anything, Allie walked around a tree and stopped.

"It's over here."

Drake crossed over to her, and she pointed at the birdhouse attached to the tree when he got near her.

Fake birdhouses are also a favorite hiding spot. Typically, the first sign that it wasn't a real birdhouse was that the cache owner blocked off the entry hole with wood or a mesh. The hole was almost always painted black. From the glance of a casual hiker, it looked like a real birdhouse, and they'd be none the wiser that there was a secret treasure inside.

The birdhouse had a hinged roof, so Drake lifted it and extracted a small plastic box. He opened the box and took out the paper log from inside, signed it with his geocaching name, and passed it to Allie, who added her nickname below Drake's. She handed the paper back to Drake, who then put everything back the way they found it.

Mission accomplished, they took a more direct route out of the woods and started their walk back to the car.

CHAPTER THREE

How was that for you?" Geneva asked when Drake and Allie took their seats and belted up.

"Good," they said, almost in unison.

"Oh, wait, I forgot to tell you something. The final is a birdhouse," Geneva said, then grinned.

Drake took off his hat, removed a small stick that was stuck in it, and tossed the stick out the window. "Thanks for the hint. Where are you going to take us next?"

"We can head downtown right away, but I was wondering if either of you wanted to go to Bunker Hill or tour the USS *Constitution* before we do. They're fairly close to each other."

Drake checked his watch. There was plenty of daylight left. "Would we have time for both?"

"Of course, depending on how long you'd want to spend at each location. They both have museums nearby, and you can climb to the top of the Bunker Hill monument and go on the *Constitution* and explore the vessel."

"Let's do both," Drake said.

Geneva went back into beast-mode as she navigated the

local roads and dipped back onto the interstate that circled the northern part of the city. Within forty minutes, she pulled into a spot next to a park and rolled up all the windows.

"We can walk to both from here. Where to first?"

"Which one is farther? Let's do that one first," Allie said.

"That would be the boat. Everybody out. Make sure you don't have any valuables showing through the windows."

They got out and stepped into the park.

"What's up with the red brick road?" Drake asked.

Cutting through the park in a straight line was a path of red bricks, set two wide, in the concrete.

"That's the Freedom Trail," Geneva explained. "Tourists primarily use the trail to get to most of the primary historical sites in Boston. The route we're on will take us to the ship. Had we gone that way," Geneva turned around and pointed at the bricks headed in the opposite direction, "we would end up at Bunker Hill."

"That's a good idea," Allie said. "I bet it really cuts down on people getting lost."

"True. It also cuts down on traffic. It's less than three miles long, so the trail is pretty easy to walk. Of course, some people still drive it."

Allie spotted a memorial in the distance and attempted to veer off toward it, but Geneva caught her by the shirtsleeve and brought her in close.

"It'll still be there when we get back. I'm in a two-hour parking spot, so we need to move it along," Geneva said.

Allie nodded, then stepped back on the road. Geneva guided them down Adams Street and turned on Chestnut. They walked a couple of blocks, then followed a pedestrian underpass which took them under a highway. When they got to the other side, they spotted the mast of the three-hundred-year-old frigate in the distance. They followed the red bricks, and soon they were at the entrance to the ship.

They secured tickets for the next tour, but had fifteen minutes to wait, so Drake pulled up his geocaching app and checked for nearby caches in the area. "Hey, there's a virtual twenty feet from here."

"Sweet," Allie said, "what do we need to do to claim it?"

Virtual geocaches, unlike the other geocache types, had no physical container to locate. Instead, it had other qualifications to mark the geocache as a find. Sometimes a geocacher had to answer questions specific to the location. Other times, they needed to post a photograph of themselves, and often there were other requirements. Virtual caches were such that geocache owners could place them in areas where regular caches couldn't go, such as in federal lands.

"You need to upload a photo of yourself with Old Ironsides in the background. That's it," Drake said.

"Easy enough," Allie said.

Drake held up his phone, got into position, and was ready to snap a selfie when Geneva stopped him.

"Hey, why don't you two get close, and I'll take a photo of both of you," she said.

"You sure?" Drake asked. "Would you want to get one too, or…"

Geneva nodded. "Yep, I already logged this one."

Drake and Allie positioned themselves, so the USS *Constitution* was in the background, then stood shoulder to shoulder.

"Okay, smile," Geneva said.

The pair smiled, and while they waited for Geneva to take the picture, Allie formed a V with her fingers and put her hand behind Drake's head to give him rabbit ears. Geneva noticed it coming, and waited a second until the fingers were in place, and snapped the picture.

"Okay, you're done," Geneva said as she handed Drake his phone back.

Drake glanced at the picture long enough to spot the ship in the background and sent the picture via text to Allie before he logged the geocache as a find for himself. Once Allie received the photo, she used it to claim the find on the virtual for herself.

"C'mon, time to board," Drake said.

The three queued up in line to get on the ship and waited to be called aboard. Once there, they were free to roam around the ship. True to her nature, Allie rushed ahead to see everything she could see.

Below deck, they saw the white canvas hammocks that acted as beds for the sailors. Beyond that, they found the captain's cramped quarters, and a small dining parlor, among other rooms and areas on board. Most impressive were the well-maintained cannons that gave them the impression the ship was ready for war at any second.

Back on the top deck, they walked among the cannons and took in the sights of the Boston skyline in the distance.

"What's that over there? The thing that looks like the Washington Monument?" Allie asked as she pointed to an obelisk.

Geneva walked over to her side to see what she was pointing at. "Ah. That's Bunker Hill, our next stop."

"I have to admit, I'm really impressed by this ship," Allie said, leaning in closer to Geneva. "And don't tell Drake I said that."

"Why not?"

"He loves these things, and I can't tell you how many battleships, submarines, and aircraft carriers he's had me tour with them. I find some of them interesting, but after the third hour of hiking up and down the stairs across ten decks, it gets to be a little much. You get what I mean?"

Geneva laughed. "Yeah, I get you. I visited the *Yorktown* in Charleston with a friend once, and I was ready to leave there after thirty minutes. It got so hot down in those lower decks I felt like I was in an oven. It wasn't even a warm day out, and I still sweated right through my shirt."

"This one I don't mind. I like the wood, and it's so well maintained. Did you see that leather furniture down below?"

"Not bad for the oldest ship in the fleet," Geneva said.

"What are you ladies talking about?" Drake asked as he joined them.

Geneva winked at Allie. "Simple girl stuff. Ready to head over to the museum?"

They disembarked the ship and followed the wharf to the museum, where they walked through exhibits on the history of the USS *Constitution*. They also learned what it was like to be a sailor during the early years of the U.S. Navy. After forty-five minutes of reading practically everything and a brief visit to the gift shop, the trio left the museum. They stepped back on the red brick road and headed back in the direction from which they came.

"Hey, there's a cache here," Allie said as they approached the underpass.

"Really?" Drake stopped and opened his app, and Geneva did the same.

"You sure?" Geneva said. "I haven't found one around here."

"Yep, there it is. A brand new one," Drake said. "Looks like it's in the middle of the tunnel. Has a terrain rating of one-and-a-half, and a difficulty rating of four. Cache container is the other type."

The three slowed their gait as they walked into the underpass. Since there were no obvious places to hide a geocache, they concentrated on the walls. They checked for any cracks, holes, or depressions; anywhere something could hide. After ten minutes of looking, Geneva turned the light of her cell phone on and pointed it at the wall, lighting up a small pink object attached to the wall.

"Is that it?" she asked.

Allie got closer. "It looked like used chewing gum to me, but I'm not going to touch it. You touch it."

Geneva shook her head. "I'm not going to touch it, you touch it."

Allie shook her head. As one, both women glanced over at Drake, who was busy looking over another area of the wall five feet from them. "Drake!" they both said as one.

"What?"

"Come check this," Allie said.

Drake joined the women and saw the gum. "I don't want to touch that."

"You're too late. Allie and I both called it before you."

Drake rolled his eyes, then examined the surrounding ground. Not finding what he wanted, he left the underpass and returned a few seconds later with a stick in hand.

"Stand back. I'll take care of this."

Drake put the stick end next to the gum and pushed on it. It wiggled a bit but didn't pop away from the wall like he expected. He tried again from a different angle, got the same results, and handed the stick to Allie. He reached up, put his thumb and forefinger around the gum, and pulled. The gum pulled free, and Drake found he wasn't holding gum at all, but a rubbery pink plastic that only looked like chewed gum. Attached to the fake gum was a small plastic vial.

"That was sneaky," Geneva said.

"Thus the difficulty of four," Drake answered. From inside the vial, he extracted the logbook, and jotted down his geocacher handle and passed the paper and pen to Geneva and Allie. Once everyone signed the log, he rolled it up, stuck it back in the vial, and closed the lid.

"Put your light up against the wall, Geneva."

When she did, Drake looked over the area again until he

found the small hole from where he pulled the cache. He inserted the vial into the hole and pushed the fake gum against the wall, so it looked like a careless person had stuck it there.

They continued their walk and stopped when they reached the open air and took a moment to log their finds. When they got back to Winthrop Square, Geneva checked her watch and saw they were short on time. While Drake and Allie checked out the nearby soldier's monument, Geneva moved her SUV around the block and found another parking spot. Within ten minutes, she rejoined her friends.

It didn't take them long to walk the three blocks to the Bunker Hill area, and they stopped at the corner.

"The museum is right behind us," Geneva said. "That's the monument over there, obviously. There's a virtual geocache at the top, and all you need to do to claim it is take your picture with the 294th step."

"What if you lose count?" Allie asked. "Have to come down and start all over again?"

Geneva laughed. "That would be cruel, wouldn't it? No need to worry about that. They painted the number on the top stair. All you need to do is climb up all the stairs, take a picture, enjoy the view, and come back down."

"I assume you've already done this one, too?" Drake asked Geneva.

She nodded. "Last summer."

Allie scanned the monument from the bottom to the top. "That's like a twenty-story building."

Geneva nodded again. "Yeah, a little more, probably."

"You want to do it, Drake?" Allie asked.

"You know I do. I'm never one to stand down from a challenge. What about you?"

Allie looked over the monument again. "You know I like an easy virtual. However, in this case, I think I'm going to pass. There's no way I'm going to put my knee under the strain of six-hundred steps."

Drake nodded. "I don't blame you. Do you mind if I go?"

"Of course not. Knock yourself out. While you're doing that, I'm going to check out this museum. If you're not back by the time I'm finished, I'll go across the street and sit on those stairs and wait for you."

"Sounds like a plan. What about you, Geneva? Coming with me, or staying with Allie?"

Geneva didn't hesitate with her answer. "Sorry, Drake, you're on your own with this one. The second I got down from doing that climb, I vowed I'd never do that again. Make sure you take it easy, okay? Don't try to be a hero and run up and down it in five minutes. It's a lot harder than it looks."

"Okay." Drake leaned over and kissed Geneva on the cheek. "I'll be back when I'm back, and I'll see you guys later. Enjoy the museum."

Drake turned, crossed the street, and bounded up the stairs toward the monument.

"Shall we?" Geneva asked.

Allie and Geneva stepped into the museum. After thirty minutes of learning about the Battle of Bunker Hill, the monument's construction, and the obligatory visit to the small gift shop, they exited.

"That was pretty interesting," Allie said.

"It was. I've never been in there before," Geneva admitted. "Ice cream?"

Allie looked where Geneva was pointing and started walking toward the vendor. "How can I resist getting ice cream from a food truck featuring a smiling ice cream cone on the side?"

A few minutes later, Allie and Geneva were sitting on the steps where they said they'd meet Drake. Allie had a waffle cone filled with mint chocolate chip soft serve while Geneva preferred a cup stuffed with rocky road.

Allie concentrated on her cone and quickly rounded off the ice cream to prevent it from melting and dripping over the edge. Once she was certain she had prevented the crisis, she looked over at Geneva.

"You don't have to worry about me. Like I told you in Arizona, Drake and I are only friends, and nothing has changed about that over the last eight months. I'm not a threat to your relationship."

Geneva finished her bite of ice cream, then took a moment to play with the rest of the dessert in her dish. "I know. He's said the same thing to me. I don't think there's anything romantic going on between you two."

"Good," Allie said. "You should also know that while we're here this week, I'm perfectly capable of entertaining myself, so don't let me offend you if there are some nights when I want to have dinner with myself and a good book or catch a movie with me and me alone. You can't expect that I'm going to be with you guys twenty-four hours a day while we're here."

Allie winked, and Geneva snickered.

"Well, okay. You're being kind of tough on us, but if you insist on leaving the two of us by ourselves, then I guess we'll just have to accept that." Geneva scraped the rest of her ice cream into the spoon, then ate it. She set the spoon into the cup, wiped her hands with a napkin, then balled it up and added it to the cup as well.

"Is there anything special you want to do while you're here?" Geneva asked. "I tried to get some ideas from Drake, but he wasn't helpful."

Allie was close to finishing her cone, so she waited until she'd eaten the final bit of it before she answered. "Well, I could go for more ice cream."

Geneva smiled. "You'll ruin your dinner."

"Yes, mom," Allie said. "Seriously, I'm just along for the ride. Find some geocaches, see some historical stuff, that's good enough for me. Maybe take in a Red Sox game. Are they in town this week?"

"I'm not sure. I could check, though. Are you a big baseball fan?"

Allie shrugged. "Not huge, but I enjoy going to a game now and then. I've been to Cincinnati, St. Louis, and Atlanta for games, so I'm always looking for other parks to visit. It's fun to see what the locals do at ballparks. You know what I mean?"

"Not really. I've always assumed that everyone just sings "Take Me Out to the Ballgame" during the seventh-inning stretch."

"Well, there is that, but some places do more than only sing the song. For example, in Milwaukee, they have sausage races."

Geneva's brow crinkled. "What's that?"

"They dress people up as sausages, like a bratwurst and a hot dog, then race around the field."

"Sounds weird," Geneva said.

Allie shrugged. "It's what they do."

Allie wiped her mouth with a napkin, then stood and picked up Geneva's empty cup. She walked over to the trash can, threw out the refuse, and walked back.

"I wonder what's taking him so long," Allie said.

"He's probably half-way up, regretting his life choices," Geneva said.

Allie smiled. "I know I would be. I hate doing stairs. You know, I hated stairs even before I hurt my knee. Hey, here he comes."

Geneva stood and looked toward the monument and picked Drake out of the crowd. He was walking slowly; the pep lost from his step. It took him much longer to get to them than it normally would.

"Hey, honey, how was that?" Geneva asked when he finally got to them.

"I have to admit, it was a magnificent view."

"How are you feeling?" Allie asked.

"My legs feel like jelly. I never want to do that again."

"Hopefully you remembered to take the picture," Allie said.

Drake turned and looked at the monument, then slapped his forehead. "Actually, I did forget. There were so many people up there, I couldn't have if I had remembered. I probably would have been trampled had I sat on the steps for a photo. I'm going to get some ice cream from that truck over there."

"No, you can't," Geneva said.

Drake scowled. "Why not?"

Allie smiled at him. "Because you'll ruin your dinner."

CHAPTER FOUR

They ambled back to Geneva's SUV, with Drake protesting the entire time. With a sigh, he collapsed into the passenger seat while Geneva started the car.

"What would you guys like to do next? I know of a great multi-cache in a park south of Boston. It's about a five-mile round trip," Geneva said.

In response, Drake groaned like a giant had hauled off and kicked him in the family jewels.

Geneva turned and smiled at him. She glanced in the rearview and saw Allie holding a hand over her mouth, trying not to break out into laughter.

"So that's a no?" Geneva asked. "How about something easier?"

Before anyone could answer, Geneva's phone rang. She pushed a button, and it connected to the car's Bluetooth.

"Hello?"

"Geneva? This is Stacy. Jonathan just called. He's going into surgery early tomorrow morning to get gallstones removed. Gallstones. Can you believe it? I didn't think people still got those. Anyway, he won't be available on

Friday, so can you step in for him?"

A wide grin crossed Geneva's face, but she tried to hide the excitement in her voice. "Oh. I'm so sorry about Jonathan. I can sit in for him."

Stacy's sigh of relief came over the car speakers. "Thank you. Hey, do you think you could come down to the theater? I'm here now, and it shouldn't take more than a couple of hours to go over everything."

"Right now?" Geneva confirmed.

"Yes. Would that be a problem?"

Geneva looked over at Drake, who shook his head no. "No. That's fine. I'll be there within an hour. Does that work?"

"Certainly. See you soon." Stacy clicked off without saying goodbye.

"Yes!" Geneva yelled as she tapped excitedly on the steering wheel. "Yes, yes, yes, yes, yes, yes!"

"Good news? What's going on?" Drake asked.

"Jonathan has gallstones! That's great!"

"Yes. We overheard, and I think Jonathan would disagree on how great gallstones are," Drake said.

"Yeah, yeah," Geneva said. "Anyway, Jonathan's our normal conductor, and the backup is out of the country, so I'm going to do it. Can you believe it? I'm going to conduct a symphony!"

"Great, honey, I'm proud of you. It's the big break you've been waiting for."

"I'm happy for you, too," Allie said from the backseat. "It sounds like an excellent opportunity."

"Anyway, you know I need to go in for a couple of hours. We need to review the program, and oh, my, I just realized I'll need someone to replace me. I was supposed to be the first chair cello. I guess I can move everyone up a chair and have Brad fill in the open seat, right?"

Geneva looked over at Drake, but he simply shook his head. "I have no clue what you're talking about. Would you be able to drop us at our hotel before you go?"

Geneva laughed. "Of course. I won't kick you out at the next corner and expect you to find your way. The hotel is a couple of miles from here, will take less than five minutes to get there."

Geneva had covered half the distance when the Boston traffic converged around her like a tight blanket. Geneva cursed herself when everything slowed to a glacial pace, and her hand went to her forehead in frustration. She tried to adapt by honking her horn a few times, but only got honks from other cars in return.

"Sometimes I really hate this town," she said as she slammed on the brakes as someone cut her off.

As they inched along, Geneva played tour guide and pointed out sights of interest. She also mentioned restaurants she'd eaten at, complete with reviews of what she thought of each of them. After twenty minutes, she finally turned off into the guest check-in area of the hotel.

"Boston Common is like three blocks from here. There are a few geocaches scattered around, mostly virtuals, but there are a couple of mystery caches, and other types as well. If you don't want to geocache, there are plenty of attractions to check out. And of course, tons of stores if you want to go shopping," Geneva said as Allie and Drake pulled their luggage from the trunk.

"I'd be fine with a shower and a nap," Drake said. "I'm a little tuckered after that climb."

"Great." Geneva leaned over and gave him a kiss. "I'll call you as soon as I'm finished and we can all go to dinner, okay?"

Without waiting for an answer, she waved goodbye, got back in the SUV, and inched back into traffic.

Drake and Geneva walked into the hotel, and although it was still a little before three, it delighted them to discover that their rooms were ready for them. They took the elevator to the fourteenth floor, and Allie unlocked the door to 1432, while Drake moved on to the room next door.

Drake pulled the folding luggage rack from the small closet, placed it next to the dresser, and set his bag on top of it. He zipped it open and pulled out the travel kit and hauled it to the bathroom sink. Drake was about to strip off his shirt when he heard a knock on the door. He moved to the door, opened it, and stuck his head out. He looked both ways down the hall, but he saw no one. As he closed the door, he heard another knock and realized it came from the inner door to his left. He unlocked the deadbolt and opened the door.

"We have adjoining rooms, isn't that cool?" Allie said.

"Yeah, sure."

"I've never had adjoining rooms before. I'll leave my door unlocked, but knock first if you want to come in, okay?"

"Sure thing," Drake said. "I'll do the same. I, uh, was going to take a shower and lay down for a bit."

"Yes, I know. You said that downstairs. I only wanted to let you know I'm going to go out for a while. I want to take a walk, see what there is to see. Give me a jingle when Geneva calls, and I'll meet you back here, okay?"

"Okay, be careful out there."

Allie closed the door, turned on the lamp next to the bed, checked to make sure she had her room key, then left the room.

She walked out of the hotel and stopped when she got to the sidewalk. There, she had to decide which way to go. Left or right. Since they had come in from the left, she turned right, walked to the end of the block, then looked down all the streets at her hiking options. Things seemed to open up a bit to the right, so she headed in that direction. Allie passed several restaurants and stores as she walked, but nothing captured her attention until she came to a bookstore.

It was a small bookstore, and the picture window was barely eight feet wide. She was walking at a good clip, and her brain finally registered what she'd seen in her peripheral vision once she'd already passed it. Allie came to a stop, then walked backward, and turned to look in the window.

The window display showed only one book she recognized as a recent release. The other books in the window were older editions of classic literature. She spotted a copy of *A Tale of Two Cities*, *Robinson Crusoe*, and a *Batman* comic book that looked to be from the late sixties.

Intrigued, Allie opened the door and stepped into the shop. Above her, a bell rang when the door opened, and rang again when she closed the door behind her.

"Can I help you?" the store owner asked.

She'd been so focused on looking at all the potential treasures on the shelves, she didn't notice the small man sitting behind a counter.

"Not really. Is it okay if I just look around? I love old bookstores."

"Certainly. If there's anything I can show you, let me know."

Allie took a brief look around at the layout of the store. The bookshelves were made of wood, well-stained and polished, and were six feet tall. They reminded Allie more of library shelves rather than those normally found in a retail bookstore. They stood close enough together such that only one person could comfortably be in an aisle at a time. Handwritten labels on the ends announced the type. The fiction labels had subclasses of genres; the non-fiction titles divided into subjects.

Usually, Allie liked to roam bookstores in a snaking pattern. She'd go down one aisle and up the next, but in this store, each aisle ended at the wall, so Allie had to go down and come up the same aisle.

The first aisle she stepped into enveloped her in a cocoon of old-book smells. The aroma, a mixture of a faint odor of vanilla combined with the scent of old leather book covers and glued spines. As she walked along, she noticed the owner cared for the books, at least in the first aisle. There was no dust present on either shelf or spine, and there was no musty odor present. She was in the mystery section, surrounded by Agatha Christie on her left and Arthur Conan Doyle on her right. She noticed several copies of *And Then There Were None*, the first Christie book she remembered reading, and the one that got her hooked on the author. Although there were at least a dozen copies on the shelf, none were the same. Roughly a third was hardcover, and she pulled from the shelf what she considered the prettiest one of those. It had a maroon binding, and the title stamped in gold on the spine. Allie opened the cover to the title page. Inside was a bookmark featuring the store's name, Stanford's Stories. On the bookmark was a sticker with the book's name, the publication year, which was 1940, and the price, which was one hundred and fifty dollars.

Allie gently closed the book, returned it to the shelf, and selected a paperback version with a creased spine instead. The bookmark inside told her that printing was from 1991, and was only five dollars, much more in line with her budget for a used book.

She put the book back on the shelf, continued to the end of the row, waiting for something to catch her eye. When she got to the wall, she turned around and strolled up the other side.

The next aisle's label told her she was in for romance and westerns. Since she was a reader of neither, she skipped it and stepped over to the next, which featured biographies.

Allie often enjoyed a fun biography, so she ventured down the aisle hoping to find something interesting on one of the founding fathers she hadn't yet read. She saw volumes on George Washington, John Adams, Paul Revere, and Benjamin Franklin. Every book she pulled had a price tag of twenty dollars or more, even for later printings and editions that weren't in the best shape. For comparison, she turned around and picked a book at random. It was a leather-bound edition from 1931 on the life of Richard I, and that volume carried a cost of a more modest fifteen dollars.

In the history section in the next aisle over, she discovered the same thing. The cost of a book about the thirteen original colonies' history was fifty percent higher than a book about the history of Texas or England.

The last aisle was what Allie really enjoyed: the world of discount, mass-market paperbacks. She picked up the first book she found, opened the cover, and without regard for any other information, looked at the price. Two dollars! She returned the book to the shelf, then scanned the spines for authors she enjoyed. Allie spotted several, and since they all wrote mysteries or thrillers, they were all clumped fairly close to each other. She bypassed the ones she'd already read, and pulled out a few that she either hadn't read, or couldn't remember if she'd read or not. It didn't take her long before she had a stack of ten books to choose from.

Allie had a bad habit when picking a book off her to-be-read pile at home. She'd start reading without checking the title, and sometimes she'd read an entire book without knowing what it was called. Allie picked up the first book, read the back cover blurb, then the first couple of pages. She realized it sounded familiar to her, so she placed it back on the shelf where it belonged.

Allie repeated her process until she was down to just three books she hadn't read. Thinking that three books was one too many, and unable to decide which one to cut, she closed her eyes and shuffled the books as she counted aloud. Once she reached ten, she opened her eyes, removed the top book from the stack, and placed it on the shelf. Satisfied, she carried her two selections to the counter.

"Did you find what you wanted?" the bookseller asked as she approached. He was a short, rotund man, with hair swept over one side of his head to hide his bald spot. He wore gray slacks, a dark green dress shirt, and had a pair of reading glasses that dangled from a chain around his neck.

"Sure did," Allie answered. "Just some light bedtime reading for the week while I'm in town."

"I noticed you spent a lot of time in the history section. Did you not find anything to your liking?"

"To be honest, Mr...."

"Stanford Edison. You can call me Stan if you like."

"Okay. To be honest, Stan, I thought the books on local history and biography were a little overpriced for my liking. Sorry, I didn't mean to offend you if I did."

Allie expected Stan to get angry, but to her surprise, he just smiled at her. "Sorry, my dear. Most people who come in here don't even bother to check the price. They're more than happy to pay for whatever I ask, so why not get what I can for my books? It helps me keep the lights on."

"I understand," Allie said. "Trust me, if I lived here, I'd be in here all the time buying things, but I'm just here for some easy reads to get me through the week."

"If I may be so bold, perhaps I can interest you in this." Stanford reached to a stack of books behind him and handed one to Allie.

"*The Mystery of Quincy Bay.* What's this about?" Allie asked.

"It's part local history, part lore, part urban legend. It tells the story of a group of patriots who hide a treasure from the British during the early days of the revolution. According to local legend, the treasure is still out there, hidden in the area somewhere."

"Didn't Nicolas Cage make a movie about that?"

Stan smiled. "Well, similar concept, but this book is based on research done right here in Boston. It's more fact than fiction."

Allie flipped through the book. It was smaller in dimension than an average magazine, and she estimated it was fifty or sixty pages long. Inside, she saw several maps and photocopies of original source material, seemingly to support the printed text. She closed it, set it on the counter, and pointed at the author's names.

"S. Edison and H. Handon. Is S. Edison you?"
Stan grinned. "Yes. Hailey Handon is my co-author. She runs a local history museum not too far from here."

"Have you looked for the treasure yourself?"

"Oh, yes. Many times, in fact. The story has intrigued me since I first heard it as a little boy. Even now, when I get a day to myself, I chase down leads. I'll find it someday, I'm certain of it."

Allie thought about it for a second, then pushed the book forward. "No, thanks. Lost treasure stories aren't really my thing."

Stan pushed it back toward her. "Trust me. With all the local history in here, you'll love the book, even without the treasure aspect of it. Besides, it's only ten dollars."

Allie shook her head. "No. But thank you. I'll just take these two paperbacks."

Stan took the books from her and rang them in on his register. "How about five dollars? Come on, you'd be helping an independent author."

Allie gave him a deep sigh. "Okay, five dollars, but you'll have to sign it for me."

"Excellent," Stan said. He grinned as he found a pen, opened the front cover, and signed his name in a large, fancy script. As he did so, Allie dug a ten-dollar bill from her wallet and placed it on the counter.

"That will come to nine twenty-five," Stan said as he took the ten and replaced it with three quarters. As he placed her books into a plastic bag, Allie slid the coins into her pocket.

"Thank you," Allie said.

"No, thank YOU," Stan responded. "If you have questions about that book, any at all, I'd be happy to talk with you about them. You can stop by in person while you're in town. Or, if you prefer, contact me via phone or email on the bookmark I put in your bag."

Allie smiled and did a hasty exit from the shop. She gave a large exhale, thought about going back to the hotel, changed her mind and jaywalked across the street to the Boston Common. There, she found a bench in the sun, took out one of her new paperbacks and turned to the first page.

CHAPTER FIVE

"Allie? Hey, Allie?"

Allie opened her eyes, and it surprised her to see Drake standing over her with a concerned expression on his face.

"What are you doing here?" she asked. She looked around, confused at first, then she realized she'd fallen asleep. Napping was something she often did when she read in her backyard at home. She looked down at the book she was still holding in her cramped hand. She'd made it all the way to page four.

"I called you. Several times, in fact, so I got worried and came out looking for you."

"How did you find me?"

Drake held up his phone. "Location sharing. Remember?"

"Oh, yeah. Sure. The Great Kentucky Incident of 2020."

A few years earlier, they had been out in a geocaching road rally and had become separated. The group Allie was traveling with forgot about the rally all together and instead took a tour of the local bourbon distilleries. She lost cell service and could not call Drake to come and save her. Eventually, a worker at the third distillery she entered took pity on her and let her use the shop's phone to call out. After that experience, Allie and Drake agreed to download a location sharing app on each of their phones so they could find each other if one of them ever turned up missing again.

Allie dug her phone out of the back pocket of her jeans and checked it. She saw the seven missed calls from Drake, then turned the ringer up. "Sorry. I had it on silent."

"No worries. Geneva called. She's going to be a little later than projected, but recommended we head over to the restaurant to get a table. It's a popular place."

"Where are we going?"

"For Mexican food. Are you hungry?"

At the thought of a burrito, her stomach rumbled. "Yes. I suppose I could eat. Is the restaurant walkable from here, or do we need to catch a cab?"

Drake checked the map app on his phone, found the restaurant, and determined the distance from the bench to the front door. "It's about a half mile from here."

"Alrighty, mister, let's go." Allie got up from the bench, stretched, and followed Drake.

"How was your nap?" Allie asked.

Drake rubbed the back of his neck and turned sideways to avoid a woman pushing a stroller toward him. "It was good. I didn't even intend to take a nap. I wanted to rest my legs for a while. You were right to not climb that tower. My calves are still stinging!"

Allie chuckled. "That's what you get for being a nut. We're on vacation here. Let's try to take it easier for the rest of the trip."

"Sounds good to me."

They walked in silence the rest of the way to the restaurant, and once they arrived, the host escorted them to a table right away. The server dropped off menus, glasses of water, a bowl filled with tortilla chips, and individual bowls of salsa for each of them.

"I discovered the coolest little bookstore," Allie said as she dunked a chip into the salsa and ate it. "The guy there sold me the oddest thing."

Allie dipped into her bag and passed the book over to Drake. "According to the owner, who is also the writer of this book, there's a secret buried treasure out there somewhere."

"Who buried it? Pirates? You realize that's only an old wives' tale. Pirates never buried their treasure, and now that I think about it, that makes little sense to me, anyway. Why would a pirate bury a treasure so far from home? That would be like us putting our money in a local bank in Denver instead of Nashville."

"He claims the patriots did it to hide it from the British," Allie said.

"Isn't that the plot of some old movie?"

Allie laughed. "That was the same thing I said, except I didn't remember the name of the movie."

Drake was about to pass the book back when someone appeared at the table.

"Can I take your order?"

Allie looked up and grinned. "Ingrid! I'd forgotten Geneva told me you'd be joining us for dinner!" Allie jumped up from the booth and took Ingrid into a big embrace.

"You forgot? How would you forget about me? I'm hurt," Ingrid teased.

"How have you been? I haven't talked to you in

forever," Allie said.

"I've been good. Sorry, I've been busy with final grades at school. Those are always a nightmare for me, and they're even worse now."

A server dropped off a glass of water for Ingrid and refilled the glasses for Drake and Allie.

"Why is that?" Allie asked.

"I have a two-part final exam in my classes. The first part is a test with questions that span what I taught in class for the entire school year. It's multiple choice, so it's not that bad. The horrible part is I also ask students to submit a thousand-word term paper with references. Apparently, it's vogue now to ask the artificial intelligence programs on the Internet to write the paper for you. I had to fail a quarter of the class for plagiarism."

"No way," Allie said, shocked. "How did you catch them?"

Ingrid smiled. "It's easy when half of my students are too lazy to change anything that comes out of the computer. I must have had a dozen copies of the same essay, right down to the title and footnotes. Next, I always check the word count. Typically, the word count won't come in exactly at a thousand. Sometimes it's nine-eighty, or, more commonly, is over by a few sentences. Students often think that adding an extra hundred words will get them on my good side. Those dozen copies, and several others, had exactly a thousand words. No more, and no less. After that, it was a matter of checking the phrasing and the voice, you understand. These kids have been writing papers for me all year, so I can tell at this point who sounds authentic, and who doesn't."

"That's too bad. I always enjoyed writing essays in school," Allie said.

"You would," Drake teased. Drake, not really a part of the conversation, had the book open in front of him, and went back to scanning through the material.

"I suspect you'll have a lot of angry students and parents," Allie continued.

Ingrid shrugged. "All my students understand the consequences of cheating. It's right there in the class rules, and they all must sign an ethics pledge at the beginning of the year. I'm thinking of getting out of teaching, anyway. Too many headaches for too little pay."

Allie nodded. She couldn't blame Ingrid for that one bit.

"Anyway, enough of that. What did you do today?" Ingrid asked.

"After Geneva picked us up from the airport, she took us to a multi-cache out in Lexington."

"The one at the old taverns? Where the final is the birdhouse in the woods?" Ingrid asked.

"Yep. That's the one. Afterwards we went and explored the USS *Constitution*, and after that, we visited Bunker Hill."

"Did you climb the monument?"

Allie shook her head. "Not with my knee. He did, though." She had a chip in her hand and pointed it in Drake's direction. She had a bit of salsa on it, which dripped back into the bowl.

"How was that for you, Drake?" Ingrid asked.

"It was fine," Drake answered without looking up from the book.

Allie laughed. "Fine. Sure. Afterwards Geneva and I practically had to carry him back to the car, and he had to take a nap."

Ingrid joined in on the laughter. "That sounds exactly like what happened to me. I didn't walk right for three days after making that climb. I'm never doing that again."

"Join the club," Drake murmured.

"You're looking super good. You cut your hair." Allie said.

"How could you notice? We haven't seen each other in almost a year, and I only took off about an inch." Ingrid ran her fingers through her hair that barely touched her shoulders. It was so blond it almost looked white. She was a Danish beauty, with ice-blue eyes and alabaster skin that was just beginning to tan with the help of the early summer sun. "Enough about me. How are you? Are you back to teaching your full slate of classes? The last time we talked, you weren't."

Allie shook her head. "Not yet. I'm still only doing water aerobics. It'll be another couple of months before I start on anything more strenuous."

Ingrid frowned. "I'm sorry."

Allie patted Ingrid's hand. "No need to be sorry. It was my own carelessness that caused it to happen."

"Are you ready to order?" the server asked as she approached the table, order pad in hand.

"I'm sorry. We're still waiting for one more person. She should be here soon," Allie said. "Won't she Drake?"

The server turned her attention to another table.

"Drake? Hello?"

"Hmm. Oh, sorry. I didn't mean to ignore you. This book is fascinating. I wonder if this is actually real."

"What book?" Ingrid asked.

Drake closed it and passed it across the table. Ingrid set her water glass aside to make room and opened the book on the table and started paging through it. After a few minutes, she closed the book and handed it back to Drake.

"I've heard of this treasure before, but it's not always referring to Quincy Bay. Sometimes it's Broad Sound, or Mystic River, or Dorchester Bay. Regardless, the story is mostly the same. During the revolution, a group put together a big treasure that was buried somewhere. So far as I know, no one has ever come close to proving anything other than it's simply a story."

"Yeah, but look at these," Drake said as he flipped the book open to a picture of a handwritten letter. As with most letters of that age, the script was difficult to read.

Ingrid shrugged. "Yeah, so? I saw a photograph once of the Loch Ness Monster, but no one has ever proved it's really in that lake, either."

"Okay, that's a valid point," Drake said. He held the book across the table for Allie to take, but she waved him off.

"You can keep that if you're interested. I only bought it to get away from the guy," Allie said.

Drake took the book and set it down on the floor, leaning it against the chair leg.

"I wish Geneva was here so we could eat," Drake said as he pulled another chip from the basket.

"Wish granted, sweetie pie," Geneva said as she appeared as if from out of thin air. She leaned over and gave Drake a kiss and moved to her chair.

Allie and Ingrid looked at each other and giggled. "Get a room," they teased in unison.

Geneva picked up her menu and swatted Ingrid with it, then looked at it, turned it right-side up, and looked at it again. "Did you order yet?"

"Nope. We were waiting for you," Ingrid said.

"Do you at least know what you want?" Geneva asked as she drummed her fingers on the table as she read through the menu.

"Steak fajitas," Drake said.

"Shrimp tacos," Allie answered.

"I'm having the beef enchiladas with Mexican rice. No beans. She's having the classic burrito with sour cream and guacamole on the side," Ingrid said.

"How did you guess that?" Geneva asked.

Ingrid smiled and reached for a chip. "We've been here a dozen times, and you always get the same thing."

"Will there be anything else? Anything besides water to drink?" the server asked, jotting the last of the order down.

Allie ordered a Diet Coke, while the other three opted for frozen strawberry margaritas.

Geneva had a smile on her face the size of a Ford Bronco, but everyone stared at her without saying a word for a good while.

"Okay, I'll get it going," Drake said. "How was your day, honey?"

Geneva excitedly clapped four times, loud enough to attract glances from the surrounding tables. "It's official! I'm conducting the symphony on Friday! Look, I'm sorry it took so long for me to get here, but I had to work over arrangements, timing, and material and I had to figure out what to do with the cello chairs. I'm so excited!"

"I'd be excited too, conducting for the world-famous Boston Symphony," Allie said.

Geneva smiled, and her cheeks blushed. "It's not the Boston Symphony, Allie. I thought you guys knew that. I'm with the Boston Common Symphony. We do shows throughout the summer in the Boston Common park. Under the stars, it's really quite nice."

"It sounds nice," Allie said. "I didn't mean to offend

you, and I'm sorry if I did."

Geneva dismissed her with a wave of the hand. "You didn't. Sure, it's not as prestigious, but that doesn't mean the musicians aren't any less talented. Besides, the whole idea of our symphony is to bring the classics to the people in a new way, and since it's in the park, it's more relaxing and much more fun."

"I'm looking forward to it," Drake said. "Are you sure you're going to be ready? Friday is only a couple of days away."

Geneva waved him off, too. "Of course. I was already the second backup for the conductor anyway, so I was in on all the show planning from the beginning."

Drake looked up and saw the server approaching with plates in hand, followed by a second server. Once they passed out all the meals, Drake picked up his glass to toast. "Here's to a great week with great friends."

Everyone touched glasses, took a sip, then turned their attention to their meals. Drake settled in as he usually did, which was like an underfed wild hyena that hadn't eaten in weeks. Even though he had to assemble his fajitas, he did so quickly. Then he ate them with haste, as though he expected someone to swoop in and take his fork and his plate away from him. He could eat slower, and did so when occasion dictated him to, like at special occasion dinners like weddings, but for the most part, he inhaled his food.

Ingrid almost gave him a run for the money. She had three enchiladas on her plate resting on a bed of Mexican rice. Ingrid used her spoon to cover her enchiladas with additional salsa from her bowl, then used the same spoon to cut off an end of one enchilada and eat it. She looked up and saw Allie watching her. "What?"

Allie took a drink of her Diet Coke to knock down the chunk of taco she'd just eaten, then cleared her throat. "I noticed in Arizona, but I didn't ask then. Why do you eat everything with a spoon?"

Ingrid swallowed, then held her spoon out before her. "Because. The spoon is the perfect utensil. All you need to do is scoop and eat. You can eat anything with a spoon. You can't say the same of a fork. Can you eat soup with a fork? No. The spoon is superior. There isn't anything you can't eat with a spoon."

"What about spaghetti?" Drake asked. "You can't eat any noodle dish with a spoon."

"You can if you cut them up first," Ingrid argued.

"And just exactly how do you use a spoon and knife rather than a fork and knife?" Drake asked.

Ingrid showed everyone by pushing down on the top of her enchilada with her spoon and slicing off a piece with her knife. "Tah-dah!"

Drake shook his head, rolled his eyes, and returned to vacuuming his meal.

"Why aren't you two eating?" Ingrid asked as she pointed her spoon in Allie and Geneva's direction.

The women looked down at their plates. While Drake was a bite away from finishing, and Ingrid had but one enchilada to finish, the burrito and shrimp tacos had barely moved. Allie and Geneva looked at each other, silently sharing the secret of the late afternoon ice cream treat, then at Ingrid.

"Too many chips?" Allie said.

Geneva nodded enthusiastically. "Yes! Too many chips. And I'm really excited about the symphony, and my adrenaline hasn't calmed down yet, so I'm sure I'll be hungry any time now."

Ingrid was suspicious, but she let it drop and concentrated on her own meal. "So what's the plan for after dinner?"

"Good question. Actually, maybe the four of us can go back to the hotel and play cards all night. The four of us. All night long," Allie said.

Drake's attention was on something across the room, but he turned and focused in on Allie long enough to pass her a dirty look.

Ingrid saw Drake's evil eye and doubled down to further antagonize him. "You know what would be even better? A nice long game of Monopoly. Four is the perfect number of players. Why, I bet the game would last until breakfast. Lunch, perhaps."

Drake expelled a loud sigh that was meant only for his inside voice, then coughed quickly to cover it up. Geneva didn't say a word. She just sat back in her chair and enjoyed the entertainment.

"Actually, you know what, Ingrid? I haven't been to the movies in a long time. Do you know if there's a theater around here?" Allie said.

"There's one about three blocks from this restaurant," Ingrid answered. "It's got just short of a million screens."

"What do you say you and I go over there after dinner? I'm sure there's a nice chick-flick we can see."

Ingrid wrinkled her nose. "Ack. I'm more of an action or sci-fi kind of girl."

Allie's countenance brightened. "Even better. I don't really like chick-flicks either. Or anything that would cause me to cry. If I wanted to cry out in public, I'd stand on the corner and check my bank balance."

Everyone at the table laughed.

"So, what do you say? Want to go on a movie date with me, Ingrid?"

She nodded. "I do. Provided we can get some popcorn with extra butter. And as long as these two sticks in the mud don't come along. I couldn't stand to hear another word about the symphony."

"And if I have to suffer through another word about Drake's aching legs, I think I'll throw up. Nope, it's just you and I tonight," Allie said.

Allie looked over at Drake. He mouthed some words, and although she couldn't hear them, she knew what they were. Thank you.

CHAPTER SIX

The group arrived at Paul Revere's house twenty minutes before it opened after almost a mile hike from the hotel. Drake and Geneva took the lead on the walk since Geneva knew the area well and could get there without a map. Not that they needed a map, since once they got on the Freedom Trail, all they had to do was follow the familiar red bricks. However, Geneva also showed them a couple of shortcuts, which saved some walking time for them all.

"There's a virtual cache here," Geneva said as she slid her sunglasses up onto her head. "It's a fairly easy one. When the building opens, we can go in and glance around."

Drake opened the geocaching app on his phone and searched for the cache. When he found the correct one, he read off the description. "Take a picture in front of the building and provide the count of the number of stones in the foundation beneath the door. That seems simple enough. What can go wrong? It's only a virtual."

Allie snickered. "Are you kidding? Plenty can go wrong. Remember that time we were trying to find the answers to the questions at that war memorial by that county courthouse? The one where the police stopped us and questioned us?"

"Really? What happened?" Geneva asked.

Drake rolled his eyes. "It wasn't anything major. The local sheriff caught us scouring the war memorial for information and wanted to find out what we were doing."

"You forgot to mention it was the middle of the night, and he thought we were terrorists intent on blowing up the courthouse," Allie said.

"Okay, okay," Drake said. "We were coming back from a geocaching event in Alabama—"

"It was in Georgia," Allie interrupted.

"Come on, Allie, I'm trying to tell the story. Like I said, we were coming back from an event in Georgia. Allie was driving, and I was looking for nearby caches and spotted this virtual cache coming up. It seemed easy enough, find a few names on the war memorial and send them to the cache owner to get the credit. No big deal. We get to the courthouse at just after sunset—"

"It was one in the morning, Drake," Allie said. "Right after sunset? You need to get your memory checked."

Drake threw Allie a glare and continued. "We arrived at a few minutes after one in the morning. Because it was night out, I got out my flashlight and headed to the dimly lit memorial and started looking for names. Little did we know, the police station was right across the street. Apparently, the town's sheriff noticed us and wandered across the street to see what we were up to. No big deal."

"Is he missing any other important details, Allie?" Ingrid asked.

Allie smiled. "Only the part where neither one of us spotted the sheriff coming across the street toward us. Drake had found a name and was writing it down in his notebook when a light bright enough to use in a lighthouse appeared and the sheriff yelled 'freeze'. Drake dropped his notebook and pen and froze. Me being me, I started laughing so hard, the gum I was chewing flew out of my mouth and landed smack dab on the sheriff's right boot."

"That didn't happen," Geneva said. She glanced at Drake, who raised an eyebrow and nodded.

"What happened next?" Ingrid asked.

"Same thing that always happens when we encounter a LEO," Drake said.

"What's a LEO?" Ingrid asked.

"Law enforcement officer," Allie answered. "We explained what we were doing there and what geocaching is. The sheriff had never heard of it before and thought we were there to vandalize the monument. Then backup showed up, and fortunately, the deputy who arrived was also a geocacher. Once she validated everything we said, we were off the hook."

"Only after Allie retrieved her gum from the man's boot," Drake said.

"He wanted to cite me for littering, but didn't," Allie said. "Crisis averted. After that adventure, we found the last couple of names we needed. We logged the cache and rolled out of town, never to return."

"Can we end it with the stories and do this thing?" Drake asked.

Drake turned around and looked at the building. The two-story wood house looked out of place in its environment. It was well-maintained, with a coat of dark gray paint, clean windows, and all the shingles on the roof lined up perfectly and seemed accounted for. Even though it was immaculate, it looked alien abutted against a coffee shop, and dwarfed by the four-story buildings in the surrounding area.

"Take our picture?" Drake asked of Geneva.

Geneva nodded, and Drake handed her his phone, and

grabbed Allie to get into the frame. Together they gave a thumbs up as Geneva snapped the photo. The picture part was complete, so Geneva and Ingrid walked across the street. There, they found a small, three-foot high wall surrounding the parking lot of another building, so Geneva and Ingrid sat. While the women rested, Drake and Allie counted the stones and joined their friends.

"Ten." Geneva said as Drake sat down next to her. He took his backpack off and put it on the ground next to his feet.

"We were arguing if it was nine or ten. We're not sure whether to count that real little one," Drake said.

"It's ten. We disagreed about it, too. I logged nine when I answered the question, but the cache owner messaged me that the answer was incorrect and urged me to try again. So, go with ten."

Drake continued to work, logging the find for the geocache. Once complete, he sent the photo to Allie so she could do the same. He stretched his legs out in front of him and took Geneva's hand. "I feel like it's going to be an interesting day filled with fun and wonder."

"That's a goofy thing to say," Geneva teased.

"I'm a goofy guy. Hey, did we drive by this place yesterday?" Drake asked.

Geneva reached over and took Drake's hand in hers. "No, why?"

"I think I've seen this building before."

"You probably noticed it in some travel brochures. It's not uncommon to recognize pictures of it in this town."

"Yeah, I suppose you're right. There's a mural of Freedom Trail locations on a wall in the hotel lobby. I probably spotted it there." Drake gave Geneva's hand a gentle squeeze. He felt so good being so close to her.

A half-dozen tourists lined up to enter the house, and Ingrid and Allie stood intending to join the queue. Allie stretched and put her backpack on her shoulders.

"You two coming?" Ingrid asked.

"Hold on a second," Drake said. He grabbed his backpack, unzipped it, and pulled out the book Allie gave him. He flipped through the pages and stopped when he came to the photo of the house. "See, I knew I saw it somewhere."

"What does it say?" Geneva asked.

Drake scanned the text, turned the page, and flipped back. "Not much. Only speculation that Paul Revere was one of the few people who knew the location of the treasure. According to the book, the secret to the find lies inside the house. Is this really his house?"

Geneva shrugged. "I think so, but I've never been inside, so I couldn't tell you for sure."

Drake stowed the book back into the backpack and returned the pack to his shoulders. "Let's go. We'll see if there's anything to see. Perhaps we'll get lucky and there will be an unattended treasure map inside, complete with GPS coordinates and an X to mark the spot."

The four queued up and waited to enter the building. Once they got inside, Drake spotted a tour guide and walked over and said hello.

"Is this the original building where Revere lived?" Drake asked.

The guide handed Drake a brochure. "The building itself is about ninety percent original. There are some furniture and personal items that are from the Revere family. Of course, there are several reproductions and other original period pieces that didn't belong to the Reveres."

Drake took the pamphlet, glanced at it, then shoved it in his back pocket. "Thanks."

They wandered around the house at their own speeds. Drake, who wasn't as interested in the history behind things, rambled around, giving only casual glances at items as they passed through the house. To her credit, Geneva stayed by his side the entire time.

Allie, who was a history buff, lingered in each room, and stopped to inspect every item in each room, regardless of the room's purpose. When she and Ingrid got to the kitchen, they found Drake and Geneva standing in front of the gigantic fireplace that dominated the room.

"All these cool things, and you're concentrating on the fireplace?" Allie asked when she got to them.

Without looking at her, Drake spoke. "The fire of revolution starts in the home's hearth."

"Huh?" Allie asked.

"There. Above the fireplace."

Allie's eyes went from the fireplace to above it. On the mantle there were several items, including bellows, what looked to be a small butter churn, and a few silver plates on display. Above them all, attached to the wall, was a needlepoint featuring the words Drake had just read.

"I'll be right back." Drake left the three women standing there and disappeared from the room.

"That was odd," Allie said, "even for him."

A few moments later, Drake reappeared with the tour guide in tow. He pointed to the embroidery. "What can you tell us about that?"

The tour guide smiled. "Ah, good eye. Can you guess how often I get asked about that piece? Once or twice a year at most. We can trace that embroidery back to Rachel Revere, Paul's second wife. The story goes that as the talk of revolution warmed up, Paul had her create that embroidery to remind them of the time they lived in."

"Wow, that's been hanging on that wall for almost two-hundred and fifty years?" Allie asked.

"Not quite. The Reveres took it with them when they

sold the house in 1800. When Revere's great-grandson got this house, he returned the piece to that spot above the mantle where it's hung since the early 1900s. Other than being cleaned and framed for its protection, it's hanging like it was back then. Sadly, that artwork is probably one of the most overlooked and under-appreciated items in the entire house."

"Thank you. That was a great story," Drake said. The guide nodded at the group and then stepped away.

"You've got that look in your eye, Drake. What are you thinking?" Allie asked.

"I'm thinking, since we're here anyway, we should check out this fireplace and determine if there's anything odd about it."

"Are you saying there's a hidden compartment in the fireplace, like that one at Cacheland?" Geneva said. "If you are, we certainly can't go looking for it. There are security cameras in this room, and I doubt they would catch us on the monitor and continue to let us tear apart a piece of American history."

"No. I'm not saying that at all. No need to touch. Just use our eyes."

The four spread out to the width of the fireplace and examined the entire thing. After a few minutes, Drake stepped away. "This isn't working. We've got too many chefs in the fire, and we're just getting in each other's way."

"Why don't Allie and I go check the one upstairs?" Ingrid said. "You two give this one a thorough searching. If we have found nothing in, let's say, ten minutes, we'll swap fireplaces. If we still can't find anything, then we just need to agree that there's nothing to be found and go on about our day, okay?"

"I think that's a good idea," Allie said. "After all, there's zero chance that there's something here to be found after all this time."

Drake considered it for a moment, then relented. "Okay. Sounds like a plan to me."

Allie and Ingrid left the room, leaving Drake and Geneva to search the ground floor fireplace on their own. They spread out, and each took a side of the fireplace that stood four feet tall and eight feet wide.

Drake started with the topmost brick in the firebox and scanned each one in the row, and once he got to the end, he moved on to the second row. He continued his methodical search until he finished the last row, then did the same with the back of the fireplace. There was a cutout that looked like a 1700s version of a pizza oven, and a cutout below that held firewood. Unlike a modern-day fireplace, the bricks weren't perfectly flush with each other. That construction caused nooks, crannies, and depressions that he couldn't closely examine. In places, the bricks jutted out slightly, which caused shadows to cover other bricks, making some areas impossible to investigate.

Besides the bricks, the fireplace also had items in it. There was an iron grate holding a small pyramid of wood, and a long bar which spanned the length of the fireplace. From the bar, a kettle and a cast iron cooking pot hung on hooks, making it impossible for Drake to examine the bricks behind them.

"Any luck?" Drake asked Geneva.

"Nope. The only thing I see are the strange looks we're getting from other people who enter the room. They probably think we're nutty."

"Maybe we should switch sides," Drake offered.

Geneva agreed, so they changed positions. Drake started his search all over again, except this time he felt even less likely he'd locate something. He trusted that if there was something to find where he was looking, Geneva would have found it already. After another five minutes of staring at stones, Drake stepped back and shook his head.

"Maybe we should swap with Ingrid and Allie," Geneva said.

Drake opened his mouth to answer, but before he could say anything, Allie entered the room and grabbed him by the shirtsleeve. "Come on, let's go. I'm bored. Ingrid's already outside waiting for us."

Drake let his mouth hang open for a moment, then closed it and allowed himself to be led from the house. As they exited, they spotted Ingrid sitting on the wall where they had rested earlier.

"Did you show them?" Ingrid asked.

"Show us what?" Geneva said.

Allie pulled her phone from her pocket, sat down, and opened the photo gallery. She passed the phone to Drake. "Take a gander at that."

Drake looked at the phone. It showed a firebox that looked similar, but not exactly the same, to the one he'd spent several minutes staring into.

"The upstairs fireplace?" he asked.

"Yep. Swipe to the next picture."

Drake did as ordered. There was a closeup area of three bricks in particular.

"What do you see?" Allie asked.

Drake shrugged. "Soot?"

Allie took her phone back and expanded the photo. "Ingrid spotted it. She's the hero. Look again."

Drake took the phone back, and with Geneva looking over his arm, he spotted what looked like letters crudely scratched into the brick. "Are these initials? Looks like an L, a V with a dot in it, and a backward C. Who is LVC?"

"Could have been anyone," Geneva said. "The brick maker? The guy who built the fireplace? A random piece of graffiti?"

"That's what I figured too, but the dot was bothering me. That's when I realized it was pigpen cipher, also known as a Freemason's cipher," Allie said.

"Paul Revere was a Freemason," Ingrid added.

"In pigpen, the first L would be a C, the V with the dot would be a W, and the backward C would be a D. CWD," Allie said.

Drake handed the phone back. "Okay. So, we're back to three initials. CWD? Who's CWD?"

"Why go through the trouble of a cipher for just initials? What if the C wasn't the letter, but see as in look? Like go see WD."

"Makes sense," Drake said, "but how to you know which WD would be associated with Paul Revere?"

Ingrid smiled and raised her hand. "I know that one. William Dawes. He was on the ride with Revere that night."

"You sure?" Drake asked.

Allie put her hands on her hips. "Of course, she's right. We were just at his capture site yesterday. Don't you remember reading the signs?"

Drake grinned.

"I'll take that as a no. Clearly, we're meant to go find William Dawes. Anyone know anything about him?"

Ingrid used her phone to find some information. "He was born in Boston, baptized at the Old South Church, and was a tanner, did the midnight ride and became a major in the militia. Any of this helpful?"

Drake and Allie looked at each other. "Not really. When did he die?"

"In 1799. Said to have been buried in King's Chapel Burying Ground, but then now they think he's buried in Jamaica Plain." Ingrid looked up from her phone and saw the blank faces looking back at her. "We're not getting anywhere with this, are we?"

Drake, Allie, and Geneva shook their heads in unison.

"Any chance his house is a tourist attraction?" Geneva asked.

Ingrid went back to her phone. "Says here he lived at 64 Ann Street. I wonder where that is." Ingrid clicked at the keys for several more minutes until she spoke. "Okay. Got it. Ann Street doesn't exist anymore, but now it would be at around 6 North, which is about a half mile from here back near Faneuil Hall. Should we go?"

Drake smiled. "Why not? It's a beautiful day for a walk."

Ten minutes later, they arrived at the location.

"This doesn't look promising," Drake said as the four stood shoulder to shoulder, staring up at the plaque attached to the building about ten feet above them. According to the marker, William Dawes had a house at the location at one point. Where Dawes' house once stood was now a series of large red brick buildings that spanned the length of the entire block. The spot where William Dawes lived now nestled nicely in between a bank and a Korean restaurant.

"Well, now what?" Ingrid asked. "Is this the end of the road?"

Allie huffed, and her shoulders hunched. "I have an idea, but I don't really like it much."

Drake rubbed her back. "What is it?"

She looked up into his eyes. "I think we should take a trip to the bookstore."

CHAPTER SEVEN

The tiny brass bell above the door jingled as Allie entered the bookshop. The day before, the shop didn't seem all that small, but as Ingrid, Geneva, and Drake entered behind her, the space quickly filled up. Allie imagined with the skinny aisles it could accommodate only two more people inside before a line needed to form outside.

"You came back. And brought friends," Stan said when the group approached the counter.

"Yes," Allie said. She noticed right away he was wearing the same clothes as the day before. This morning, as she got closer to the man, she noticed an unpleasant smell about him. The stench reminded Allie of the odor stale fast food French fries left in the car after being closed up in the scorching sun all day.

"We're looking for information on William Dawes. Is there anything you can tell us?" Drake asked.

Stan was so fixated on Allie, he barely noticed that Drake and the others were there. It was only when Drake cleared his throat and repeated the question that Stan looked at him.

"William Dawes? The one who rode with Paul Revere?"

"Yeah, that's the one," Drake said.

"Hold on, let me check." Stan moved from the back of the counter and purposely bumped into Allie. On his way past her, gave her the creepiest smile she'd ever seen, and slipped into the aisle containing the local history.

"Drake, come up here," Allie yell-whispered.

Drake pushed his way past Geneva and Ingrid and switched places with Allie.

"You saw that, huh?" Allie asked in a quiet voice.

"Which part? The guy staring at your boobs, or trying to cop a feel?"

When Stan came around the corner, the smile dropped from his face when he noticed Allie was no longer standing where she had been. He approached the counter slowly. Rather than pushing his way through like he did on the way out, he excused himself and waited for Drake to step aside before he returned to his stool by the register.

"Well, did you find anything?" Allie asked.

"No. There were no books on Dawes himself. I checked a couple of local history volumes as well, but there was nothing in them you couldn't learn from the Internet."

"I guess we struck out," Drake said. "Let's go."

The four turned to leave. Geneva was now the first one in line, and she opened the door and stepped outside with Ingrid right on her heels.

"Wait!" Stan said. "If you still want to know more, go visit my colleague, Hailey Handon. She's the head of the Minuteman Museum, which is only a few blocks from here. She's also the co-author of the book I sold you. I can give you directions."

"What do you think?" Drake asked Allie.

"This is your quest. I'm up for it if you still are."

A few minutes later, as the group was walking down the street. Drake referred to the handwritten directions he'd received to make sure they were on the right path.

"The book guy was really creepy," Geneva said from out of nowhere.

"Yes, wasn't he?" Ingrid said. "I wouldn't worry, Gen, it seemed he only has eyes for Allie." Ingrid laughed and placed her hand on Allie's shoulder.

Allie playfully swatted Ingrid's hand away and huffed. "He certainly wasn't my type."

"Would you three knock it off? We're here," Drake said as he came to a stop.

Although the sign above the door proclaimed it to be the correct place, from the outside, it looked more like a dentist's office than a museum. The museum was in an ill-maintained red brick building. The front stoop had a chunk of concrete missing from the corner. In front of the building, the sidewalk had more pieces of litter on it than it had pedestrians walking by. The highlight was a black circle of spray paint on the wall where someone had covered some graffiti.

"You sure this is the right place?" Ingrid asked.

"It's the correct address, and there's that nice historical display in the window," Drake said.

In the window was the top half of a mannequin. Draped over its armless shoulders was the blue coat associated with the Continental Army, and on the head was the distinctive three-corner hat. Drake smiled when he noticed the soldier was wearing a Bruce Springsteen Born in the U.S.A. concert T-shirt under the coat.

"We're here. Might as well go in," Drake said. He stepped up two stairs and turned the doorknob, but it didn't open. Then he spotted a doorbell with a sign above it that read 'ring bell for entry'. The writing had letters so small, they could well have had a mouse write them. Drake pressed a button and heard a buzz inside. He waited for perhaps fifteen seconds, then pushed the doorbell again.

The door opened, and a woman's head appeared. Her round face contained brown sparkling eyes, a button nose, chipmunk cheeks, and the most welcoming smile Drake had ever seen. She had her dirty-blond hair combed back and secured in a ponytail.

"Can I help you?" she asked.

"Um. We're here to see Hailey Hendon."

"That's Handon. Are you the folks from the bookshop?"

Drake nodded, and the woman threw open the door. "Well, come on in then. I'm Hailey. Stan called and said you'd be coming over. Said you wanted to know about William Dawes?"

Drake entered the museum and saw the body that accompanied Hailey's head. She was roughly six inches shorter than Drake, and she wore a pair of white capris pants, a teal t-shirt, and a pair of untied teal Converse shoes with no socks.

Before Drake could answer, a phone rang.

"I'd better get that. I'm expecting a call from the state archives. Please take a tour of the place while I'm gone," Hailey said.

Hailey flashed Drake another smile, then turned and walked down the hallway and disappeared behind a door marked private.

Drake turned around and bowed to the three women who hadn't even cleared the threshold of the door yet. "Come on in and have a look around."

Drake stepped past a small desk that acted as an entry point. There was a small wood donation box on the edge of the desk, surrounded by brochures for historic sites in the area, and a stack of bookmarks from Stan's bookshop.

Hailey had divided the museum into four main rooms, each one twelve-foot square. The first room they entered was the one that had the mannequin in the window. The featured piece was a diorama in the room's center that was four feet square and three feet high and featured the Battle of Lexington and Concord. Along the edge were descriptions of the troop movements and significant events of the battle, and next to each description was a red button.

As the resident history buff, Allie followed the entire perimeter of the diorama, read all the descriptions, and pushed all the red buttons. When a button got activated, a light would appear to direct your eye to that position in the diorama, but only roughly half of the buttons actually worked.

Considering it was a museum, Hailey had the rest of the first room furnished strangely. The display cases popular at jewelry stores lined most of the walls. Safely inside the cases were a mishmash of items. The treasures included coat buttons, clothing, musket balls, military supplies, and common household items. Overall, the room seemed more like a flea market than a museum.

The second room contained a diorama of the Battle of Bunker Hill. Like the first room, jewelry store cases lined the walls, but only half of them contained artifacts, and the others were empty.

The third and fourth rooms had no dioramas at all, and instead of display cases, file cabinets lined the walls, all of them locked.

It didn't take long for the quartet to make their way around the museum. They ended up back in the first room since it seemed to be the most spacious, well-lit, and least dreary of the four.

"Well, Allie, what do you think of the place?" Drake

asked.

"Certainly not the most impressive museum I've been in," Allie answered.

"I know, and I apologize for that," Hailey said as she entered the room. "We're not much of a museum for physical artifacts as a repository for information related to the Revolutionary War."

"But the sign outside literally says Minuteman Museum," Ingrid argued.

Hailey's wide smile returned. "I know. I actually bought the building from the previous owner and since I liked the alliteration of the name, I kept it. The dioramas and the few artifacts we have were left over from him."

"So, you're not really a museum then?" Allie asked.

"No, but what I am is one of the most respected historians on the east coast. And only the Library of Congress rivals my collection of Revolutionary War documentation."

"My apologies, I didn't mean to offend you," Allie said.

"No apologies needed. It's a common mistake. It was my fault. I should have changed the name when I took over the place, but I didn't. Now so many people know of my work, I'm stuck with it. So, now, what can I do for you?"

"We're searching for information about William Dawes. Specifically, if there is anything around the area that is still here from when he was alive," Drake said.

"I'm not sure what you mean," Hailey admitted.

"For example, we toured Paul Revere's house this morning, then thought it would be fun to see where William Dawes lived."

"And you walked all the way there and found a Mexican restaurant and a donut shop?"

Allie smiled. "Donut shop is still there, but it's a Korean restaurant now."

"Really?" Hailey said. "I should go try that out.

Anyway, as far as locations are concerned, the only things that come to mind are the Old South Church, where his parents baptized him, and his grave, of course. Other than that, there are a few monuments around, mostly dedicated to the ride. I'd have to check my archives on him."

"Would you mind? We're really interested."

Hailey hesitated, then agreed. "Okay, fine. Come along with me."

Hailey led the group into the fourth room, went directly to the third file cabinet on the east wall, and tugged at the second drawer from the top. Realizing she locked the files, she swore softly under her breath, then produced a single key from her pocket and unlocked the cabinet. As she slid open the correct drawer, Drake noticed a single small plastic golden retriever dangling from the keychain.

"What's your dog's name?" he asked.

"Daisy," she said without hesitating her search for the correct file.

"Ah, nice name," Drake said. His observation explained the short blond hairs on the back of Hailey's shirt.

"Here, take this." Hailey held out a three-inch-thick hanging file folder. Drake grabbed it and set it on top of the cabinet. Several manila folders and individual pages slid out, attempting to make as escape, so he put his hand on top of it to prevent anything from spilling onto the floor.

Hailey passed a second file folder to Drake, who handed it off to Allie. When Hailey found the third bundle, she stood up and closed the file drawer, and flashed an apologetic smile. "Sorry, but this is all I have on William Dawes. Come on, let's take these into the other room."

Drake gathered up his bundle, and everyone followed Hailey down the hallway and through the private door. One look around, and Drake believed they were in the room where all the action happened. It must have been a large storage and receiving room at one point because there was a large steel loading dock door on the north wall. Besides file cabinets, there were four aisles of makeshift shelving units. Altogether, Drake guessed, they held hundreds of books. In one corner were two old desks pushed together, on which there were enough newspapers stacked to provide each person in Boston their own copy.

The highlight of the room was two conference tables that were joined in the middle of the room to make one big table. There were five folding chairs around the table, and one leather rolling office chair. At one end of the table was a microfiche reader, and a small cart overflowing with reels of microfiche.

"Grab a chair, everyone," Hailey said. She made a beeline for the good one for herself. "Now, what are you looking for? Anything physically related to Dawes that might still stand today?"

"Yes, that's right," Drake said.

Hailey opened the folder in front of her and started dividing it into small stacks. "Okay, everyone, grab something from the pile and we'll see what we can see."

"Aren't you worried about us touching old documents?" Allie asked.

Hailey grabbed the first sheet off the top of the pile and held it up. "Not at all. These are all copies made from the originals. I keep all the source material in an off-site location for preservation, so don't worry about it. I'd die if I ruined a three-hundred-year-old ledger or something like that." She passed the piles around to everyone in the room, and they all got started looking through the documents.

Drake set the small stack of papers in front of him and squared the corners. The top page was a copy of Dawes' baptismal record, and since Drake knew the church was still standing, he set that aside. Letters Dawes had written to various people made up the next four sheets. Since they didn't mention any physical places, Drake turned them upside-down as he discounted them and stacked them neatly in their own pile. The last sheet he studied was a quartermaster's inventory of supplies with Dawes' signature on it. Since Drake didn't think the amount of turnips Dawes had on hand applied to his search, he added the sheet on top of the reject pile. Drake looked down and saw the only page he had was the initial one he found. As he surveyed the stacks of the others around the table, he saw they weren't faring much better.

Once they made their way through the first folder, Hailey took all the non-relevant documents and put them back. Then she divvied up the stack from the second folder and they repeated the process all over again. By the time they were through the third and final folder, they had around a dozen possibilities left before them.

"Okay, let's merge the notes," Hailey said. "What do you have?"

Drake started. "I've got the Old South Church. Anyone else have anything on that?"

Ingrid did, so she passed the page over to Drake, who set it with his sheet.

Geneva held up the only page she had. "I've got something related to the tannery he ran. There's an address mentioned here, but I can't read it." She passed the paper to Hailey, who studied it carefully.

Hailey's chair squeaked as she got up. She went to a bookshelf, ran a finger along the spines, then pulled out the book she was looking for and returned to the table. Hailey set the large atlas down and paged through it until she found what she wanted. She searched for the tannery's old location, then closed the book. "Nope. This is a park now. Quite a nice one down by the harbor. Next?"

"I've got a deed to his house, and a picture of his grave marker," Allie offered as she passed the papers forward.

"We all know the house doesn't exist anymore," Hailey said as she added that sheet to the discard pile. She held up the picture for all to see. "This marker is in King's Chapel Burying Ground, but it's speculated he's really buried with his first wife in Jamaica Plain."

"In New York?" Drake asked.

"No. It's a neighborhood in Boston, a couple of miles southwest of here. Anything else?"

"I've got some pictures of portraits," Allie said as she held them up.

"Ah, yes. Nice, aren't they? The portrait in your left hand is in Ohio. The other is in Illinois."

"Who's this?" Allie asked, setting down the papers she was holding and displaying a picture of a woman.

"That's a portrait of Mehitable May, Dawes' first wife. That's in Illinois as well."

"Last thing I have is this picture of a cannon," Allie said.

Hailey smiled. "Yes, of course. My favorite stories involving William Dawes weren't about the horse ride he took with Revere. Nope, it was his propensity for heisting cannons from the British that are my favorites. It's believed that is one of the many cannons he swiped. On the bottom of that page, it should tell you where they took the picture."

Allie turned the sheet around and looked. "Bunker Hill Museum." Allie passed the page to Hailey, who passed it to Drake.

"So here you are, everything that exists today related to William Dawes," Hailey said.

Drake spread out the items before him. A church, a grave marker, a cannon. Not much to go on.

"Hopefully, you have the answer you wanted?" Hailey

asked.

"Not the one I wanted, but the one I got," Drake answered. He stood from the table and offered his hand. "Thank you for your time and the information. We really appreciate your help."

Hailey shook his hand. "No problem. That's what I'm here for. Come back anytime."

Drake nodded and ushered his friends from the room. They passed through the museum, out the door, and huddled together when they got to the street corner.

"Well, folks, what's the plan?" Allie asked.

"Where's the church from here?" Drake asked.

Geneva looked around to get her bearings. "Four or five blocks, I'd guess. Not far."

"And what about the cemetery?"

"A few blocks east of Boston Common."

Drake nodded. "Okay. Let's go check out the church, pick up Geneva's car from the hotel, then go to the cemetery and to the museum. Sound logical?"

Everyone agreed, and Geneva took Drake's hand and led him off toward the Old South Church.

CHAPTER EIGHT

So you have nothing here that would be from William Dawes?" Drake asked.

Drake waited for an answer. The pastor sitting behind the librarian's desk of the Old South Church library took off his reading glasses and placed them on the blotter.

"I'm sorry, son, but no. We have the records from back then in our off-site archives, but we have nothing else from that far back at this location."

Drake's eyes shifted from the pastor's eyes to the stained-glass window behind him. In it was the depiction of a blue summer sky, white clouds, and two doves sitting in a tree. Off on one side was a lone apple.

Drake readied himself to stand but settled back in his chair. "Wait, what do you mean by at this location?" Drake asked.

"True, this is the Old South Church, but this isn't the building that William Dawes and the rest of Boston used in the 1700s. They didn't build this church until 1837. If you want the physical location where Dawes worshipped, you want the Old South Meeting House."

"Old South Meeting House?" Drake repeated.

"Yes, although before you go, you should know that the British practically gutted the interior during the war. Also, it almost burned down in 1872, but they restored it to its formal glory in 1877."

"Doesn't sound like I'll find what I'm searching for," Drake admitted.

The pastor shrugged. "Depends on what you're looking for. If you want to learn what life was like back in the beginning of the country, it's well worth a visit. Do you need directions?"

Drake shook his head. "No thanks. I'm visiting someone who's from here. And if she weren't around, I'll bet it's right on the Freedom Trail."

The pastor laughed. "That it is, son. That it is." He stood, shook Drake's hand, wished him well, and ushered him to the door.

"Well? What did he say?" Ingrid asked when Drake joined the others outside.

"He said we need to go to the Old South Meeting House. He said they built this church in the 1800s."

"That's my bad," Geneva said. "I should have realized that."

Drake took her hand, and they started walking toward the hotel. "Don't worry about it. It was a pleasant walk over here. Should we get your car and travel in style, or should we walk around all day?"

"With all the places we need to check, the car would be faster," Geneva said.

"And my knee's bothering me," Allie interjected.

Drake stopped, turned around, and looked at Allie. "Are you okay to get back to the hotel? Or we could get you a cab or an Uber."

"Or I could run ahead and get the car and pick you up here," Geneva said.

"How far is it to the hotel?" Allie asked.

"Less than half a mile," Geneva said. "We can cut through Copley Square. That would reduce some distance as well."

"Okay, I can make that." Allie said.

They maintained a slow, even pace to accommodate Allie's gait, and by the time they reached the hotel, she had a visible limp.

"Are you sure you don't want to rest for a while?" Drake asked Allie as Geneva retrieved the car from the parking garage.

Allie smiled at him. "I'll be good once I sit for a bit. I can do that in the car. Besides, what would you do without me? We both know I'm the brains of this operation."

Drake returned the smile without a word. When Geneva appeared, Drake opened the front passenger door and waited for Allie to take the seat. "You'll be more comfortable up front. Besides, I've been hoping for some alone time with Ingrid."

"I heard that!" Geneva yelled from the driver's seat. "And I've got a mirror here too, so I can keep my eye on you. Where to first?"

"Whichever one is closer."

"That would be the meeting house by about two blocks. Hold on, everyone."

Geneva didn't ease out into traffic as much as she bullied her way between cars that were waiting for the traffic light to change. She made two right turns and was finally satisfied she headed in the correct direction.

"I hope you two aren't too comfortable back there," she said as she glanced into the mirror.

Within a few minutes, the meeting house came into view. Geneva bypassed it, continued on for two blocks and sat on her brakes while she waited for a guy in a white pickup truck to pull out. The second he left she swooped in to claim his spot.

"There's a no parking sign here," Drake said.

"Don't worry, it's for street sweeping. We're good until two in the morning. If we're here that long, we've got bigger problems than a traffic ticket," Geneva said. "Are you coming along, or do you want to stay here?" she asked Allie.

"I'm going to sit this one out," Allie said.

Geneva smiled. "I don't blame you. I'll leave you the keys so you can roll down the windows, or run the air, or listen to the radio. There are some non-aspirin pain relievers in the unmarked pill bottle in the center console if you want them."

"Good luck you guys," Allie said.

Drake, Geneva, and Ingrid got out of the car, and once they turned around, they immediately spotted the tall clock tower two blocks away. They covered the ground quickly, and within a couple minutes, they were standing outside the red brick building, looking up at the structure.

"It sure is impressive," Drake said. "To think that William Dawes was here once."

"As was Ben Franklin and Samuel Adams," Ingrid said.

"The beer guy?" Drake asked.

Geneva rolled her eyes and pulled Drake toward the entrance, and the three stepped into the building.

Drake expected to look at an ordinary church on the inside, and it surprised him when it was more than that. He stepped in far enough to get away from the door so others could enter and exit, and he stopped to glance around.

The color white dominated the interior. All around him, the walls, ceiling, railings of the second-floor balcony, window shutters, pulpit, and the pew backs were all painted white. The only other real splash of color was that of the stained wood that accented the top of the pew backs, the seats, and the well-worn floor. Along the outside walls there were several displays explaining the Boston Tea Party, along with other historical events from the time. The floor creaked beneath Drake's pacing feet as he studied the site.

Drake, Ingrid, and Geneva spread out and did a circle around the interior. Once they completed the ground floor, they followed the arrow downstairs. There, they discovered more exhibits and the obligatory gift shop. At the shop, they spotted the exterior door, stepped up a short flight of stairs, and found themselves outside the building.

"What do you think?" Geneva asked.

"I believe this stop was a waste of time. I discovered nothing to help us. Did you?" Drake said.

"No. Although there were a lot of places that were off limits to us. Should we go back in? Ask if we can get access to those areas?"

Drake shook his head. "No. Let's go over to the cemetery next."

They turned around and headed back to the car. A few minutes later they arrived and spotted Allie right where they had left her, windows down, her nose in a book. She finished the page she was on, inserted a bookmark, and stuffed it into her backpack. "How was it?"

"No luck. On to the next spot," Geneva said as she fired up the engine. She moved only a few blocks and found another space on the street to park her car. "It's about three blocks from here," she announced. She didn't bother to ask Allie if she was going along since Allie was already pulling the paperback from her bag.

They made quick work of the hike and found themselves at the main cemetery gate. Ingrid read aloud the signs attached to the fence listing the notable people buried before them.

"Too bad Allie's not here. She really enjoys visiting old cemeteries," Drake said. "Let's spread out and find the marker."

The three took different paths into the cemetery, and while Drake and Geneva headed off right away, Ingrid lingered and took a few photos with her phone. After she got some pictures she expected Allie would like, she strolled about five feet into the cemetery, then came to a stop. Before her was a square cement pillar, about three feet high, on which was placed a bronze plaque covered with a green patina. She took a picture, then read the inscription. "William Dawes Jr. Patriot, Son of Liberty, and first messenger sent by Warren from Boston to Lexington on the night of April 18-19, 1775 to warn Hancock and Adams of the coming of British troops. Born April 6 1745, died February 25 1799. Placed by the Massachusetts Society Sons of the Revolution April 19, 1899."

Ingrid looked to her side and discovered the person she'd felt approach a few seconds earlier was Geneva.

"I guess this is strike two," Geneva said. "He died well after the war was over."

Ingrid nodded in agreement. "Yeah. There isn't

anything for us here. Where's Drake?"

Geneva spotted him in the far corner of the small cemetery, got his attention, and waved him over. "We rushed right past it," Geneva said when Drake got to their side.

Drake stopped for a second and read the inscription. "I guess this spot's a bust, too."

"That's what we felt as well," Geneva said.

"How did you guys make out?" Allie asked as the others climbed into the SUV.

"We had no luck there either," Drake said. "One last spot to try."

Geneva swerved in and out of stop-and-go traffic until finally, twenty minutes later, she spied a prime parking spot right in front of the museum. "Is this close enough for you?" she asked Allie as she undid her seatbelt and shut off the ignition.

Allie smiled and undid her belt as well. "I suppose I can make it that far. I have to use the restroom, anyway."

Geneva locked up the SUV, and the group filed into the museum. Allie made a beeline for the ladies' room, while the other three fanned out to search for the cannon. The museum wasn't a large one, and it didn't take long for Drake, Geneva, and Ingrid to meet up in the last room. There, they found the cannon. It was a small one, only four feet long and only a foot tall.

"Hailey said Dawes stole a cannon, and I didn't understand how he could," Drake said. "Of course, I was picturing those big guns we encountered on the *Constitution*. I didn't know they came mini-sized. I can understand how two men could easily pick this up and run away with it."

"Do you think Dawes handled this one?" Ingrid asked. "That's what the sign right there says. This cannon, rescued from the British by William Dawes, and so on," Drake said. "I was hoping we'd be able to get a good view of it, but clearly that's out of the question."

"Why?" Allie said as she entered the room.

Drake stepped aside so Allie could see what the rest of them did. The cannon, in its full glory, was covered by a glass display case to protect it from harm.

"Oh. I see," Allie said. "You can't see anything on it?"

Drake crouched and leaned in close enough for his breath to fog the glass. He examined as much of the cannon as he could, then stood. "I see nothing unusual. And of course, we won't see anything on the other side since it's pushed up against the wall."

Drake kneeled, and inspected the cannon again, and came up empty.

"I guess that's strike three. Game's over," Geneva said. "The game was fun while it lasted, though."

The four left the museum and stepped into the warm summer sun. Drake spotted the ice cream truck and jerked a thumb at it. "Who wants a treat? I'm buying."

Geneva and Allie looked at each other and laughed at the same time.

"What's so funny? What is it with you two?" Drake asked.

"Nothing," Allie said. "Get me a mint chocolate chip waffle cone, will you? I'll be over on the steps."

As Allie headed for the stairs, Ingrid gave her order to Geneva and rushed to Allie's side. While they waited, they both sat down in the shade.

Ingrid took out her phone, unlocked the screen, and offered Allie her phone. "Drake told me you like cemeteries, so I snapped some photos for you."

"Thanks, that's sweet of you," Allie said as she took the phone. She looked at the photos, then passed the phone back. "Looks like I missed the fun."

"You think cemeteries are fun?" Ingrid asked.

"I actually do. Just think about it. You stood a foot away from William Dawes' remains. Whenever I'm in that situation, I like to wonder about what that person's life was like, and how they got to be the person they were. I know it's silly, but hey, that's me."

Ingrid shook her head. "I don't figure that's silly at all. Besides, he wasn't really there."

Allie took a moment to brush a strand of hair over her ear. "What do you mean?"

"Remember what Hailey said? That they originally thought they buried him in that cemetery, but he's actually buried with his first wife? Or he was in that cemetery and then moved to be with the wife. I don't remember which."

"How many wives did he have?" Allie asked.

Ingrid shrugged, then looked for the answer on her phone. "Two. He was with his first for about twenty years, and the second he married after the first died."

"And he's buried with the first one? Where?"

"Forest Hills Cemetery in Jamaica Plain. In the May family plot."

"Sounds odd to me."

"What does?" Drake asked as he handed Allie her cone.

"We were just trying to figure out why they would bury Dawes in his first wife's family plot rather than with his second wife."

"I don't know, you tell me," Drake said as he licked from the side of his chocolate hazelnut cone.

"You know, I think I know where she's going with this.

Are you thinking that we should check out his grave there?" Geneva asked.

"Yep, that's what I'm thinking."

"Well, let's go then," Drake said, taking a step toward the car.

"Whoa, there, tiger," Geneva said. "No ice cream in the car. Let's finish eating first and then continue the mission."

An hour later, Geneva pulled into the cemetery and parked next to the office. "I've been here before. The cemetery is huge, so I'm going to go in and see if I can get directions to where we're headed, and maybe a plot map."

Geneva left the car and stepped toward the building. She was about to walk up the stone steps to get to the office door when a small plastic box caught her attention. From inside, she pulled a map of the cemetery, glanced at it briefly, then carried it back to the car. She passed it over to Allie.

"Here's a map. I saw Dawes on there. Can you navigate us to the site?" Geneva asked.

"Of course. Give me a second to get my bearings." Allie studied the map for a moment. "Okay, I got it. Hey, did you know that E. E. Cummings and Eugene O'Neill are in here, too? Can we make a side stop?"

"After we're done with Dawes, we can make all the stops you like," Drake said.

"Yay!" Allie exclaimed with excitement. "Okay, go straight, then turn left at the third street you come to."
It wasn't long before they discovered the May family plot, with a small hill acting as a backdrop. They exited the car and approached the markers, ten of them lined up all in a row. Although some of the writing on some stones had been erased by nearly three hundred years' worth of sun, rain, wind, and snow, there was one that was easily read, a small,

rectangle slab with the words "W. D. 1774".

"Is this the right one?" Allie asked.

"It can't be. Dawes didn't die until 1799," Ingrid said.

Drake shuffled from stone to stone, reading the names and dates that he could, then put his attention on the marker in the middle. "I agree. It seems odd, but let's check it out, anyway, okay?"

Drake approached the marker, crouched before it, and ran his fingers over the stone, as if some tactile impression would answer the questions he had in his mind. Besides the initials and the single date, there was no other information on the marker's front. Drake stood and walked to the back, crouched again, and examined the back. Again, he saw nothing but smooth stone. He lost his balance, and on instinct, he reached for the top of the stone to right himself.

He stood, then bent over, and looked at the stone's edge.

"Allie, come here a moment."

Allie made her way to the grave and when she arrived, Drake pointed at the top edge of the marker. "Run your hand along there. Feel any depressions?"

Allie rubbed the marker, then stopped. She looked around, found a small stick on the ground, and used it to clean the many decades' worth of debris from the stone. She wet her finger, then rubbed it over the spot. "It's an X."

She moved her fingers to the right, and an inch later came upon another depression.

"Hey Geneva, do you have any water in your car, and perhaps a towel I can use?" Allie asked. While Geneva went back to the SUV to look for the items, Allie used her stick and wet finger method to expose the next item. "E? Does that look like an E to you, Drake?"

Drake leaned over and looked. "Yeah, I think so. XE.

Does that mean anything to you?"

"Not yet," Allie said, "but I'm hoping it will soon."

Geneva returned carrying a red shop towel, two bottles of water, and a toothbrush.

"I hope you're not going to want that back," Allie said.

Geneva laughed. "Of course not. I get them free from the dentist every time I go for a cleaning, so I must have two dozen of them under the bathroom sink at home."

Allie went to work on the stone. She used a gentle touch with the toothbrush to pick away at the debris, followed by a rinse and dry, and after several minutes of work, she finished.

"Anyone have a pencil?" Allie asked.

"Go ahead. I'll write it down on my phone," Ingrid said.

"Okay. N, G, G, H, P, X, F, E, R, F, G, F. Got it?"

Ingrid read the letters back to Allie, and Allie confirmed they were correct.

"They make no sense to me," Geneva said.

Allie ran her fingers over the letters once more, then smiled. "Are you sure? You see these every single time you look at a hint on the geocaching website. It's a ROT13 Caesar cipher."

"I have an app to decode that," Geneva said.

"No need," Allie said. She stood up straight and pointed the toothbrush at the headstone. "It says Attucks rests."

CHAPTER NINE

"A ttucks rests. Another riddle?" Drake asked.

"At least it's an obvious one," Ingrid said. "Historians believe Crispus Attucks was the first person killed in the Revolutionary War during the Boston Massacre."

"Does he have anything from the day? House? Gravestone?" Drake asked.

"I've never heard of him having a house in Boston, but I think there's a grave marker for him in the Granary Burying Ground," Geneva said.

"Good. Let's go there," Drake said.

Geneva took out her phone and checked the Internet for something, then shoved her phone back in her pocket. "We can't today. It closes at four, and we wouldn't make it there in time. Speaking of which, this place closes at four-thirty, and we promised Allie a visit to the other graves."

Allie nodded enthusiastically. "That's right, you promised. And you're not supposed to break a promise."

"You're right. Okay, everyone back in the car, and let's make this quick. I don't want to get locked in here for the night," Drake said.

Geneva grabbed Drake's arm and pulled him in close. "It's okay, darling. I'd protect you from the ghosts."

Drake laughed. "Thanks. I appreciate that. Let's get a move on. After this, I'd like to see if we can find something for dinner."

With Allie navigating, they searched the cemetery and found the last resting places of Cummings and O'Neill. At her insistence, they also stopped at several other interesting monuments as they drove past them. They realized it was time to leave when security caught up with them, reminded them of the time, and politely asked them to leave and return the next day if they wished.

Rather than fight the rush hour traffic back to the hotel, Geneva spotted a microbrewery with a restaurant a few blocks from the cemetery entrance. Although the parking lot was jam-packed with people who shared the 'it's five o'clock somewhere' mindset, Geneva found a spot for her SUV. Inside, they had a brief wait before they got a table for four in front of a large Plexiglas window. Behind the window were large stainless-steel vats and holding tanks. Above each of them were signs displaying the name of the beers being produced within.

Before long, Drake, Geneva, and Ingrid were sipping beers while Allie nursed a glass of water with lemon.

"What's the plan for tonight's activities?" Ingrid asked.

"I've got a rehearsal tonight at eight," Geneva said. "It's a run-through of Friday night's concert. You're welcome to come and sit in if you want to. It should only last a couple of hours, three at most."

"Don't most symphonies rehearse during the day?" Drake asked.

Geneva took a drink of her beer, a light apple ale, the specialty of the brewery. She smacked her lips, then took a second sip. "Oh, my, that's good. I have to remember this place exists and come here more often. Anyone got a pen?"

Allie had been playing with one of the brewery's heavy paperboard coasters. She had it standing on a corner beneath an index finger, then hitting it with the other finger and watching it spin. She stopped and handed the coaster to Geneva. "Here, take this home with you so you don't forget."

"Thanks." Geneva accepted the gift and shoved the coaster into her back pocket. "To answer your question, Drake, professional symphonies practice during the day. We're composed of mostly volunteers. We have benefactors and do fundraising to cover the expenses, and at the end of the year, any cash we've made above the budget gets split up among everyone. Although, it's rare someone will take the cash and run. Usually, we pool it and have a party, then roll the remainder to the next season. We're in it for the love of the music we play."

"Sounds nice. Would you mind if I joined you tonight?" Drake asked.

Ingrid and Allie passed a glance between them. Neither one seemed surprised that Drake wanted to go.

"Of course, I wouldn't mind. What about you two?"

"I think I'm going to rest up the knee," Allie said. "The hotel has a rooftop pool. Perhaps I'll hang out up there and read a book."

"I was going to go home, wash my hair, and watch television, but I guess I'll go hang out by the pool with Allie," Ingrid said.

Allie was in mid-drink, so she tipped her glass at Ingrid. "Come on over, you're more than welcome. What do you like to read?"

"Oh, you know, the classics. Like John Grisham."

"Sounds great. We can have a book club!" Allie exclaimed. She clapped a couple times, then leaned over, and gave Ingrid a high five.

Drake placed his hand on his forehead and shook his head. "Oh my. You two have a great time with that."

The group laughed, and soon they settled back down into casual conversation. A few minutes later, the server appeared with a tray filled with three burgers and a pulled pork sandwich for Geneva.

They were only half-finished eating when a man approached their table. Allie recognized his smell before he said a word.

"Hello, Stan, fancy meeting you here," Allie said without looking at him.

Stan stepped in closer to Allie, and in response, she leaned closer to Ingrid.

"You want to take a step back there, bud?" Drake ordered as he reached his arm out to shield everyone at the table. "What do you want?"

Stan shrugged. "I just wanted to see if Hailey gave you all the information you needed. She called me, you know, after you left her. Said you were interested in William Dawes. That's interesting. Is that why you were here at the cemetery? To see his grave?"

Drake was about to respond when Allie held up her hand and stopped him.

"Not that it's any of your business, but I was interested in Dawes because I love history. I learned all about the midnight ride, and never knew Revere wasn't the only one involved, so I wanted to know more about the others he rode with. You know all this. We asked you about it earlier, remember? And as far as our visit to the cemetery, I was there to see the graves of O'Neill and Cummings. As far as I know, they buried Dawes downtown. Now, if you'll excuse us, we have places to be later, so my friends and I need to finish dinner."

Stan sneered at her, then pulled away.

"Stan? One more thing," Allie said, her voice tempered with the sweetness of honey.

Stan turned back around and got close enough for Allie to feel his breath on her neck.

"You've got ketchup on your shirt."

Stan stepped back, looked at his left sleeve, and finding nothing looked at his right. Sure enough, there was a bright red blob on his forearm. He took a napkin from the stack the server had left the group, wiped off the condiment, and dropped the napkin on the floor. He gave Allie a ghoulish smile, then turned and left.

"Odd coincidence seeing him here," Geneva said.

"Especially since his shop doesn't close until seven," Allie said.

"Do you think Hailey tipped him off on where we were going?" Geneva asked.

"I guess it's possible. Maybe he picked up our trail and followed us," Drake said.

"And what happens when he goes into that cemetery and finds the same code we did?" Allie asked.

Drake drained his beer and leaned back in his chair. "I'm not too worried. He'll be there, and we'll be a step ahead of him at the other cemetery. Also, you know I'm a stickler for the geocacher's code, right?"

The three women stared at him, each with a blank look on their face.

Drake smiled. "We're supposed to leave an area the same way we found it, right? He won't find those letters except by accident, the way I did, because I filled them all back in with mud, the exact way we found them. Anyone want another beer?"

*

The next morning, at five after nine, the four friends were in the Granary Burying Ground. They clustered in front of the granite memorial that marked the burial plot of Crispus Attucks.

"The remains of Crispus Attucks, victim of the Boston Massacre, March 5th, 1770, were here interred," Allie read. "Well, here he is."

"Not what we need, though. It's the last line that bothers me," Drake said. "Placed by Boston Chapter S.A.R. 1906. 1906. The marker's not original."

"I guess we need to find something else related to him. What about where the Boston Massacre took place?" Allie asked.

Geneva shook her head. "No. There's a historical marker embedded in the ground there, nothing else. I've walked past it myself like a hundred times."

"Do you guys mind if I stroll around the cemetery and look at some other markers while we're here?" Allie asked.

Drake rifled his fingers through his hair and yawned. "Sure, why not? We're on vacation. Knock yourself out."

Allie thanked them and strolled off toward the tallest marker in the cemetery, a twenty-five-foot-tall obelisk.

"I thought they buried Benjamin Franklin in Philadelphia," Allie said, sensing someone beside her.

"He is buried in Philly," Ingrid said. "This marker is for his parents. I had a good time last night hanging out with you."

Allie looked over at Ingrid and smiled. "You know, I did too. Even though we did nothing but sit around and read and talk. It was nice. I don't have a lot of female friends with the same interests I have, so it's nice to spend time with someone who does."

Ingrid's cheeks turned a light pink from the complement. "Come on, let's find more dead people."

Ingrid interlocked arms with Allie and led her off to the next tall pillar they saw. When they got to the resting place of

Paul Revere, Allie snapped a photo before they moved on to the large stone memorial for John Hancock.

"I like this one," Allie said as she stopped and pointed at the marker. The grave was above ground and looked large enough to contain a coffin. At the foot end was an intricate carving of what looked like a coat of arms. It included a family crest with a heart in the middle, and a knight's helmet with a bird standing on top of it.

Ingrid nodded. "Yeah, they don't make them like that anymore. The closest modern marker I've seen to this is a gravestone with granny's secret chocolate chip cookie recipe on the back."

"Whose grave is this?" Allie asked. "Peter Faneuil? I never heard of him."

"Oh, he was a rich guy who…" Ingrid trailed off and stared into Allie's eyes.

"Is there something on my face?" Allie asked.

Without responding, Ingrid took out her phone and looked up the history of Peter Faneuil, and then the building he gave to the city.

"What are you doing?" Allie asked.

Ingrid held up a finger to pause Allie, finished reading, then spoke. "Faneuil was this rich business guy who built Faneuil Hall, which was a market and a meeting place. After the British shot Crispus Attucks during the Boston Massacre, they took him to Faneuil Hall. He laid in state there until they buried him here, three days later."

"I'm not following you."

"Attucks rests. The message. Not his eternal rest here, but his temporary rest at Faneuil Hall."

Allie let out a squeak of excitement, then drew Ingrid in for a hug. "You're a genius! Let's go round up the lovebirds."

A half hour later, the quartet was standing before the tall statue of Samuel Adams. Despite Geneva's efforts, Drake continued to refer to him as 'the beer guy'. Beyond the statue stood the impressive three-story, red brick Faneuil Hall.

"Fancy," Drake said as he admired the architecture.

"Come on, there's a visitor's center inside. Let's go see what we can find out," Geneva said.

They stepped into the meeting hall and stopped just inside the entry and looked around. Like the name implied, the meeting hall had fifteen rows of wood chairs on either side of an aisle that ran from the entry door to the stage. Off in the wings was additional seating, and the second-floor balcony contained seats along the outside walls. A stage five feet high and faced with red, white, and blue bunting dominated the front of the room.

A wood lectern stood center stage in the front. Behind the lectern were several wood chairs to accommodate speakers. Behind the chairs along the back wall were marble busts of several Bostonians, including John Adams and Daniel Webster. Dominating the entire wall behind the stage was a massive painting of Daniel Webster debating Robert Hayne. Four other portraits hung on the walls, including one of Peter Faneuil himself.

Drake spotted a park ranger standing in the back corner of the room, looking bored. As Allie, Ingrid, and Geneva went off to explore the exhibits, Drake approached the ranger.

"Hello, quick question. Could you tell me if this is the original building from the 1700s?"

The young ranger shifted his stance and scratched his beard as he thought about it. "Well, there are elements of it that are original, but they redid most of the building over the years. It burned down in 1761, and they rebuilt it the next year. They expanded the building then, and added the third floor in 1806, and in 1898 they completely rebuilt it. They did the last major restoration in 1992. Does that answer your question?"

Drake's shoulders slumped in resignation, and he sighed. "Yes, thanks."

"You sound disappointed. Not get the answer you were looking for?"

Drake thought for a moment. "Not really. My redheaded friend over there is really interested in authentic artifacts from the American Revolution. We've come all the way from Nashville to see what we could see from that time period."

The ranger looked where Drake was pointing, which was at Allie, who was busy snapping pictures of the artwork near the stage.

"Wait here, I'll be right back," the ranger said. He left the room and returned a couple minutes later, followed by another ranger.

"Steve here says I should give you and your friend the special tour," the new ranger said.

"Hold on, let me get my friend." Drake rush-walked across the room, grabbed Allie by the arm, and returned to the ranger.

"Allie, this is…"

"Folks called me Ranger Red for the longest time, because my hair is the color of yours." He ran his fingers through his white hair. "Of course, not so much anymore. Now I look like when the founding fathers wore those wigs, but twenty-five years ago, we'd have been mistaken for twins, you and I. Ready to go? Follow me."

Drake and Allie stepped behind the skinny ranger and followed him to the elevator. Once inside, he pushed the button for the fourth floor, and they waited patiently during the ride. The door opened, and Drake thought they were going to the Ancient and Honorable Artillery Company Museum that occupied the fourth floor. When they exited the elevator, Ranger Red took them down a corridor, then behind a door that was marked for employees only. Red flipped a light switch, and they found themselves in a large storage room. The building caretakers over time had stuffed the room with file cabinets, storage shelves, boxes, and crates of all shapes and sizes.

"This is where we hide the good stuff," Red explained. "Mostly items that people aren't interested in, or things we use for rotating displays. If you're looking for authentic artifacts that date back to the war, I've got two that may interest you. Follow me."

Red guided Drake and Allie over to the side of the room, where a large granite stone sat on a pallet. The engraving on the side read 1740.

"This was the original cornerstone when it was first built. The workers removed it in 1806 when the building underwent its first major renovation. Fortunately, someone had the foresight to save it."

"Can I touch it?" Allie asked.

Ranger Red grinned at her. "Go on ahead. It's survived three hundred years' worth of fires, construction, and wars, so I doubt you giving it a touch will cause it to crumble to dust at this point."

Allie smiled back, then crouched down to get a closer look at the stone. It looked pitted and well-worn, but she neither saw nor felt any indications of markings on it other than the date.

"What's the other item?" Allie said as she got back to her feet.

"The crown jewel, and my absolute favorite." Red waved them along and picked their way through a tight aisle of metal shelves.

"Wait," Drake said as he stopped and pointed at a box. "Are these really Paul Revere's shoes?"

Red backtracked, picked the plastic storage box from the shelf, opened it up, and held it so everyone could see inside. The box contained a pair of black leather shoes with a rectangular silver belt on the front. "Looks like it to me," Red said. He closed the box, returned it to the shelf, and continued on.

In the far corner of the room, set into a concrete block, was a four-foot-high weathervane with a giant grasshopper on top, gilded in gold leaf.

"What do you think?" Red said. "Impressive, isn't it?"

"Isn't this the same as the one on top of the building?" Allie asked.

Red leaned in closer, and whispered, as if there was someone else around who could hear them. "I'll let you in on a secret. This one's the original, made in 1742. After thieves returned it in 1974, we put up a reproduction instead. Go ahead. Look at it. It's an amazing work of art."

"Can I touch this?" Allie asked.

Red laughed a hearty laugh. "Lightning has struck it several times. I'm sure it can handle you!"

Allie leaned in and examined the vane closely. Something caught her attention, so she looked back at Drake and gave him a nod.

Drake caught the meaning, turned around, and pointed back into the heart of the room. "Hey, Ranger Red, besides Revere's shoes, what other treasures did you hide away up here?"

Drake and Red stepped away from the weathervane and disappeared among the shelves. Once they were gone, Allie quickly retrieved her phone and snapped off a few pictures. She reviewed them, and, satisfied with what she had, rejoined the others where she found Ranger Red showing Drake a small box of uniform buttons.

"Hey, Drake, we should get a move on. Geneva and

Ingrid are probably wondering where we are. Red, thank you. This has been wonderful."

Rather than wait for the elevator, Allie and Drake rushed down the stairs, and found Geneva and Ingrid sitting on chairs inside the hall.

"Where have you been?" Geneva asked.

"Let's go outside," Allie said. "I could really use some sun."

CHAPTER TEN

Allie led the group outside, and they found an empty park bench near the statue of Samuel Adams to sit on. "Where did you guys disappear to?" Geneva asked.

"Got a special tour to check out Paul Revere's shoes. They were pretty fancy," Drake answered.

Geneva stared at Drake with an expression of disbelief on her face.

Drake reached over, took her hand in hers. "It's true. I asked the ranger in there if they had any artifacts from back in the day, and he got one of the other rangers who gave Allie and me a backstage tour of the place. They have like a billion pieces of history tucked away behind a door on the top floor."

"Including one that had these on it," Allie said. She passed her phone around and showed everyone the small, hand-etched letters, looking like graffiti in the golden gilding.

"Where did you find this?" Ingrid asked.

"On the original weathervane. The one that's up there

now is a replica."

Ingrid looked back at the pictures and thought about the letters scratched into the grasshopper: SVRUQ MCGIL VCFMS FDWIW QRTPW GJKG. "Another cipher?"

Allie nodded. "For sure. Not Caesar, though. This one's a little harder."

"Let me see if can run it through a few code breakers and see what we come up with," Ingrid said.

Ingrid dug out her phone, transcribed the letters into the notepad, and handed Allie's phone back to her. She brought up her favorite puzzle solving app and copied the letter string from the clipboard to the app and started the decryption. She looked up and caught her friends watching her.

"You know, this would go faster if everyone helped," Ingrid said.

"Yeah, probably," Drake admitted. "What's the letters?"

Allie brought up the picture again and held out her phone for Geneva and Drake to see. Withing a minute, all four of them were trying out different ciphers and ideas for solutions. As they failed, they called out the ones that didn't work, and after thirty minutes, they gave up.

Allie set her phone down and leaned back on the bench. She stretched her arms above her head, interlaced her fingers, and tried to touch the sky. She twisted her torso to the left, to the right, and finally released her hands and let them fall to her sides.

"Maybe we should give this up. Do something else, like visit other touristy things, or perhaps find some more geocaches," Allie said. "I mean, it's not like any of us are actually expecting to find a king's ransom worth of buried treasure that is still out there after three hundred years."

Drake shook his head. "Tsk, tsk, Allie. Where's your sense of adventure?"

Allie picked up her phone and opened her geocaching app to see if there were any geocaches nearby. "Hey, there's a virtual cache only point one-one from here. I'm going to go for it. Anyone want to come?"

"Is it the Boston Massacre site one?" Geneva asked.

Allie checked the app. "Yep. You already have that one?"

"Yes. I'll keep trying to crack the code. I'll wait for you here."

"I'll stay here, too," Drake said. "I'm sure I can figure this out."

Allie rolled her eyes and shook her head. Drake was good for some puzzles, but he hated things like ciphers with a passion and usually relied on her to crack the code and get the answers.

"I'll go with you," Ingrid said as she got to her feet. "My back is getting stiff from too much sitting. Let's go."

Allie went to check the compass for the directions to the geocache, but Ingrid stopped her.

"There's no need for that. I've been there before," she said.

After they were out of earshot of the others, Ingrid whispered to Allie. "You know, he wasn't even trying to solve that cipher. I noticed him looking at sports scores on his phone instead."

Allie laughed. "I don't know. Maybe he's on to something. Perhaps the founding fathers were so smart, they included a message about the Red Sox - Yankees game and they hid the next clue by the left field foul pole at Fenway."

Ingrid smiled. "I'm sure that's the line he's taking. He's not so good with the puzzles?"

"You could say that. He's my good friend, and I love him to death, but he's honestly not that great at them. He doesn't mind the simple things, like finding coordinates in word searches, or Sudoku grids. And he's pretty good at the ones where you only need to look up answers on the Internet, but when you get into cipher territory, he tunes out. It's simply not in his wheelhouse."

"Are there any geocaches that aren't your thing?" Ingrid asked.

"Of course. I don't like it when EarthCaches are overly complicated. I mean, I know you're supposed to learn something from them, but I don't like it when the cache owner gets carried away. Estimate the height or width of a waterfall? I can do that. Determine the flow rate of a natural spring? I can do that, too. I visited one in Tennessee where I had to count the fossils in a wall, which I was good with. But man, when you get questions about having to determine the specific type of rock in an area. And come up with the exact measurement and a scientific theory of how the rock formed over a billion years? Nope, that's when I draw the line. If I read the description and I think it's something that I'd only be able to answer with a doctorate in geology, I skip it."

Ingrid nodded. "Believe me, I know what you mean. I'm not a fan of geocaches placed on a ledge, or on a high bridge. I'm always afraid I'm going to fall, even if my rational mind tells me I'm perfectly safe."

"Oh, and I dislike caches that are in caves, or underground. I mean, I'll do them, especially if I can still sense sunlight, but I try to avoid those," Allie admitted.

"That we can agree on. I don't like them either," Ingrid

said. "We're almost there. Notice that ring over there in the concrete? That's the site."

They stopped at the outer edge of the marker, and Allie reopened her app to check the qualifications for the find. "Upload a picture of you or your GPS at the site of the Boston Massacre and answer the question of what animals are watching you. Do not post the answer in your log or I will delete it. Seems easy enough."

Allie turned in a circle and checked if any animals were around. Other than a woman walking a Pekingese with golden fur, she didn't observe any non-humans. She spun around a second time, still saw nothing, but she heard Ingrid giggle.

"Are you enjoying watching me make a fool of myself?"

Ingrid giggled again. "Of course. You look so cute when you do it."

"Okay smarty-pants. What's the answer?"

Ingrid stepped behind Allie, grabbed her shoulders, and turned her until she faced a red brick building. Then she lifted Allie's right arm and pointed it at the roof. "How's that for a hint?"

Allie looked up, and above her there were two statues, one on each corner of the roof. "A lion and a horse?"

"It's not a horse. It's a unicorn," Ingrid corrected.

Allie squinted, and saw that indeed, a long horn extended from the horse's forehead. "Okay. It's a unicorn." Allie typed the answers into the app and sent them off. "Picture time. Get in here with me."

Allie turned so her back was to the marker and held the phone high so she could get a selfie with it. Ingrid moved into the shot.

"You need to get closer. I only have half of your face in frame," Allie said.

Ingrid moved in closer still, and a moment later, Allie could feel the heat coming from the soft flesh of Ingrid's cheek.

"Perfect," Allie said. "Now smile."

They did, and after Allie snapped the photo, Ingrid pulled away. "Let's get one more."

Ingrid moved in close again, and a second before Allie pushed the button, Ingrid turned her head and kissed Allie lightly on the cheek. Allie snapped the shot, and Ingrid pulled back away, embarrassed.

Allie, unflinching, brought up the photo and showed it to Ingrid. "Looks good. You take a splendid picture."

Ingrid smiled. "It's in the Danish genes I have."

Allie reached out and grabbed Ingrid's hand. "Let's go back. If we leave those two alone, who knows what trouble they'll get into?"

Without speaking, the two walked back to Faneuil Hall and took their original seats on the bench.

"You find what you were looking for?" Drake asked without looking up from his phone.

"Oh, yes I did," Allie answered. "How's the code breaking going?"

Geneva shook her head. "Not so good. I've hit a brick wall every time I've tried something."

"Did you try a Vigenère cipher?" Ingrid asked.

"No," Geneva said. "Those are impossible to crack without a keyword."

From where they were sitting, Allie could barely see a large golden insect that appeared to be standing on the roof of the building. "Try grasshopper."

Geneva shrugged, then put the word grasshopper in as the keyword. "Well, I'll be a monkey's aunt. You got it. Mercy for the woman with many words."

"Mercy for the woman with many words? What does that mean?" Drake asked. "What woman needs mercy? For what words? All we've done is uncover another riddle."

"True, but at least this one's in English. I'll go ask Red and see if he can shed any light on it," Allie said.

"Did she find her cache?" Drake asked Ingrid as they watched Allie walk toward the building's entrance.

"Oh yeah," Ingrid said.

"Did she have any trouble with the animals?" Geneva asked.

"She only spun in a circle twice before I helped her out."

Ingrid and Geneva laughed, knowing what they'd gone through.

"What's so funny?" Drake asked.

"You should have seen us when we did that cache. We must have looked in every window within viewing distance of that site before Ingrid had the common sense enough to just look up," Geneva said.

"And that was an accident. I was following a helicopter that was flying over us," Ingrid admitted. "She's coming back fast. Must not have gotten what we need."

The three peered at Allie as she walked toward them, then she stopped without sitting back down. "Red is incredible. I think he knows everything about the American Revolution."

Drake snickered. "He's old enough to have probably lived through it."

Allie ignored the comment. "It turns out we were on

the wrong track. It's not to give mercy to a woman with many words. There was a woman back then named Mercy who used a lot of words. She was a big-time revolutionary who was heavily into politics, and was also a writer who published several articles, poems, and plays. Mercy Warren was her name."

"I don't suppose Red had her complete bibliography tucked away in a dusty box up there, did he?" Drake asked.

"No. But he suggested we go visit a library nearby. Apparently, they digitized a lot of her writings, and they are available with the touch of a button. Let's get going. It's only a few blocks from here."

After a five-block hike, they stepped into the local library, and had a brief chat with the head librarian, who directed them to the local history section. It wasn't a large room, considering the sheer amount of local history that Boston and the surrounding region had accumulated over the roughly four hundred years of Boston's existence. But there was enough space for three walls worth of shelves. The shelves held everything from city directories, to handwritten journals, to volumes of homemade family genealogies, and ship's passenger manifests. The room held anything related to local history that didn't fit in nicely on the neat stack in the main library.

Also in the room were four small cubicles, two of which held desktop computers, and two which held microfilm machines. A quick round robin of rock-paper-scissors determined that Drake and Ingrid would search through the digital records. Geneva, in third place, got to handle the microfiche. Allie, the first one out of the game, got the arduous task of checking the physical stacks to see if there was anything to find on the mysterious Mercy Warren.

Ingrid was more computer-savvy than Drake and quickly found a treasure trove of information. "Hey, I've got lots of hits here," she said as she leaned back in her chair and pointed at the screen. "You said she was a writer, Allie, but I didn't expect her to be this prolific. There are references to several plays, as well as a bunch of poems, and a few books as well. I don't even know where to start."

Drake leaned over and looked at Ingrid's screen and the list of search results it contained. "Can you sort that by date?"

Ingrid poked at the keys and, after a few seconds, got the list in ascending order by publication date, then moved aside so Drake could get a closer look.

"I'd say based on the other clues we've followed, you should probably concentrate on anything published before, let's say, 1776. What do you get then?"

"I've got four plays for sure. Some poetry had early dates. And there was a book published of some of her personal letters to some of the heavy hitters of the day, including Washington and Jefferson."

Drake nodded. "Hold on." Drake got up and walked over to a small table just inside the entrance of the room and selected from it a sheet of paper and a pencil. He rejoined Ingrid and copied down the file names of the first three items on the list, then sat at his own computer. "You start from line four on down. Whoever finishes first helps the other."

Ingrid nodded, clicked on the first file, and began to scan through the play *The Adulateur*.

"How are you doing, Allie?" Drake asked.

Allie was busy at one shelf of books, running her fingers from spine to spine as she read the titles. "Fine. Have found nothing remotely related to her yet. I found a copy of an old family cookbook, so if you need a good recipe for corn porridge, or instructions on how to make your own cheese, I've got you covered."

Drake laughed and turned his attention to Geneva, who was getting irritated with a microfilm reader that wasn't working correctly. Every time she fed the spool of film through the machine and tried to advance it with the control knob, the end would slip. Then it would feed back out and spin around until it dropped off the spool. Watching her fight with the machine was like viewing an old Charlie Chaplin movie.

"Hey, Geneva?" Drake said.

Geneva turned and gave Drake the death stare she'd been using on the machine for the past few minutes.

"Um, never mind," he said as he turned his attention back to his computer.

Geneva turned her attention back to the microfilm and removed the spool from the spindle. She carefully rewound the spool to get the film back on, then pulled it taut so it wouldn't spill off again. Keeping it taut, she took her time feeding the film between two rollers, between the glass plates, then through two rollers on the other side. For the last step, she tucked the film end into the slot, applied tension on the receiving wheel, then spun it with her fingers until the reel took up film. She crossed her fingers, then turned the fast-forward knob just a touch. The film finally cooperated, and the front page of the *Boston Gazette* appeared on the screen.

Geneva had her own notepad, and she checked the list of five entries for the first date, then compared the date on the paper's masthead to that on her list. She fast-forwarded through two years' worth of weekly newspapers before she slowed the machine and eventually got to the issue she wanted. There, on the first page, was a poem that argued for independence over twenty-seven lines. Although it was stirring, there was nothing about it that looked peculiar. Geneva moved on to the second one, published only three months later, and that poem took an unkind view of George III. The third poem spoke of the evils of taxation without representation, and the fourth, published in the first week of December 1776, was an ode to an old church. Next to the entry, she jotted down the microfiche page number, then moved forward until she got to the fifth and final poem. The last poem turned out to be a rousing call for the citizens to take up arms against injustice.

"Hey, guys, I think I found something odd," Geneva said.

Allie sat down in the unoccupied chair, and Drake and Ingrid shifted their seats so they could see better.

Geneva fed the fiche backward until she found the page number for the fourth poem. "I looked up five poems in the *Boston Gazette* that were attributed to Mercy Warren. Four out of the five were all rallying cries to spur the locals into war with Britain, but she titled the fourth *The Crypt 'Neath the Church*."

"Can you make that bigger?" Drake asked.

Geneva adjusted a couple of knobs, and the text became larger on the screen. Silently, and at their own pace, the four read the poem.

"You're right, this poem seems out of place," Drake admitted. "Why would a newspaper print this, especially with a war right around the corner? What church is this referring to even? It's a little vague, isn't it?"

"Not really. Based on the year, I'd say it's Christ Church," Ingrid said.

"Is there a chance it's still standing?" Allie asked.

Geneva grinned. "You bet your boots it's still standing. It's one of the oldest churches in America, although now it's commonly known as the Old North Church. You know, of one if by land, two if by sea fame."

CHAPTER ELEVEN

A half an hour later, they were in line, waiting to gain entry into the old church. Slowly, they traveled the cobblestone sidewalk between the church and the gift shop, and they waited patiently until it was their turn to enter.

Drake waited in line behind an old couple wearing American flag shirts. When they shifted, he spotted a brochure on the counter that attracted his attention, so he reached out around the man and took one. He only had a few seconds to scan the brochure before the person behind the counter called him forward to pay the entrance fee.

"Can we do the crypt tour?"

"How many?" the teenage ticket seller asked.

"Four."

She clicked a couple of buttons on the computer. "There's room for four on the tour that starts in a half hour. Does that work for you?"

"Sure does," Drake said as he dug his credit card from his wallet and passed it to her.

The transaction completed, she handed him back his card, along with four tickets. "Inside you'll see a sign where the tour starts. I recommend you get there five minutes early because the tour starts right on the hour. No refunds."

"Thanks," Drake said. He turned and passed a ticket out to everyone in his group. "We've got twenty minutes to kill before we enter the crypt, so we can go in and look around in the meantime."

They stepped into the church proper and looked around. White was the dominant color inside the church. The entire floor contained box pews, which resembled modern day office cubicles. Only three aisles running from the back to the front of the room broke up the space.

Each box pew had waist-high walls, painted white with wood trim on the tops. And each had a small door that swung out, and every door contained a brass plaque. The plaques listed the pew number, along with the name of the parishioner who owned them, and the year they owned it. Inside the box were white-painted wood pews, along with modern hymnals for worshippers to use during modern Sunday services.

The front of the church held the altar and an elevated pulpit. In the back were stairs that led to the upper gallery, which contained additional pews, as well as an impressive-looking organ.

Along the walls between the open windows were various historical displays, and memorials dedicated to past members. Allie, being Allie, made a tour around the room, reading every available sign.

Drake checked the time, saw he still had twenty minutes to wait until the crypt tour, opened a door to a box, and sat down on the pew. Geneva slid into the spot next to him, and he reached for her hand.

"Fancy church, huh?" Drake said. "Can you picture them throwing a lantern up in the belfry and starting Revere's ride?"

"No, not really," Geneva admitted.

Drake chuckled. "Yeah, me neither. I'll bet Allie can, though. Visualizing herself in historical contexts is like her superpower."

"That's not necessarily a bad thing," Geneva said.

"Oh, no, I didn't say it was. It only becomes a problem when we're on a time schedule. Actually, I've been quite proud of her for the past couple of days. She seems focused, and isn't wandering off to check out every statue, plaque, and historical marker she sees."

Geneva let go of Drake's hand and scratched the back of his neck gently. "It seems we have been rushing through this town. Doesn't seem like the laid-back vacation experience I had in my head."

Drake nodded. "Yeah, same here. I think I've gotten a little nutty with the treasure thing. Perhaps it's best if we pull back the throttle on that and get back to finding geocaches and seeing the sights."

"And don't forget about going to the symphony."

Drake grinned. "There's no way I would forget about that! It's what I'm looking forward to the most!"

"What's that?" Ingrid asked as she entered the box and took the seat next to Geneva. Allie, who also appeared from nowhere, stood outside the box and leaned over the wall.

"Heading to the symphony on Friday night," Drake answered. "Aren't you looking forward to it?"

"For sure I am," Ingrid gushed. "I wouldn't miss it for the entire world."

Geneva laughed. "You're such a liar."

Ingrid put a mock look of taken offense on her face. "Who? Me?"

"Yes, you. You hate classical music. The only time you like to hear violins is when they're used as fiddles in country music," Geneva teased.

"Ooh, you'd fit right in Nashville," Allie said with a smile. "Come to town and I'll take you around to all the country bars."

"I enjoyed the symphony concert you took me to a couple of years ago," Ingrid said.

"You mean when we went to see the Fourth of July show?" Geneva asked.

Ingrid nodded. "Yes, that was the one."

"First off, that was the Boston Pops, not the Boston Symphony. And, as I recall, you liked the fireworks show more than any of the music they played that night."

Ingrid shrugged. "Okay, so I like the fireworks. So, sue me."

"Hey," Drake interrupted, "Geneva and I were just talking about this treasure thing, and we both agree that I've gotten out of control trying to pursue it. I mean, it's probably been gone for forever, if it even really existed at all. I think we should slow down and get back to geocaching and being tourists. What do you say?"

Allie looked at Ingrid, then at Geneva.

"Don't all speak at once," Drake said. "It's hard to hear you over the others. Ingrid, what do you think?"

Ingrid pointed at Allie. "Ask her. She's a guest here."

Allie felt the weight of three sets of eyes staring at her. She gathered her thoughts, then exhaled slowly. "Actually, I don't think the treasure hunting thing has been too bad. I mean, so far, it's taken us to these historical places I wanted to visit while we were here. Like right now, I mean, we're already here, and we already have tickets for the tour, so why would we not hunt for clues while we're down there?"

"So, to clarify, we're still on the hunt?" Drake asked.

Allie thought for a moment. "Okay, new rules. One, we slow down the pace. We don't have to rush around like mad. Let's take it easy, stop for lunch, enjoy the nice day. And we find caches, and we see more things of interest. And if any of us decides it's too much, we give it up."

Drake nodded. "That's reasonable. Okay with y'all?"

Geneva and Ingrid nodded.

"Good," Drake said. "New plan. We'll finish with the crypt tour, then find something else to do besides chase a mystery all over town." Drake looked at his watch. "Speaking of the tour, it's about time we head over there."

Allie walked up the aisle to give the others enough room to leave the box, and they made their way to the sign pointing the way to the crypt tour. Five minutes before the tour was about to depart, a guide appeared and starting checking tickets. It was a light tour. Besides the four friends, the only other couple interested in the macabre adventure was the couple who had entered the museum just before them.

"Can I have your attention, please? My name is John and I'll be your guide down into the crypts. Just a few comments before we go. The stairs and the floor are uneven in spots, so please watch your footing. And there are areas down there that can be tight, so if you're claustrophobic, I recommend you stay up here. In places it's also dimly lit, so please be cautious. There's no eating or drinking on the tour, and out of respect for those interred below, please don't touch. Anyone have questions before we go?"

Allie raised her hand. "Can we take pictures, John?"

"Photographs are fine, but please, no selfie sticks because of the tight quarters," John answered.

"Are selfie sticks still a thing?" Ingrid whispered to Allie.

Allie shrugged. "I have no clue."

"Please, now follow me, be careful, and stick together," John ordered.

The group followed John through a corridor, and that corridor led to a flight of stone stairs. As they descended, their footsteps echoed against the stone walls, and the temperature decreased. When they finally arrived at the bottom, John stepped a few feet into the main corridor to give everyone room to enter.

"Please remember to watch your footing," John advised, as he waited for people to cluster around him.

Drake was the last one down the stairs. When he got to the bottom, he joined the group and looked around. The floor was a gray concrete that reminded him of his garage floor at home. The walls were brick, but not a consistent color. They ranged from a deep maroon to red, to brown, to white, and there was a light film of dust that covered everything and swirled around people's feet as they stepped. Above the corridor, a line of single-bulb lights strung along at several-foot intervals provided the only light.

"Just a little background," John said. "Here beneath the church, there are thirty-seven brick vaults and each one can hold twenty to forty coffins. Burials down here started in 1732 and ended in 1860."

"How many people did they bury down here?" the woman asked.

"Around eleven hundred is the best guess, although

there could be more," John answered. "Please, step this way."

"And they don't bury people down here anymore?" the woman asked.

John stopped in his tracks. "No. The city of Boston ordered that all burials in crypts stop, and all the vaults sealed in 1853. It ended because of ongoing health concerns for the general population. But the church didn't halt burials until 1860, when the courts stepped in and compelled every cemetery and church to comply with the new law."

"It must not have smelled very good with the bodies down here," the lady said.

A sly smile crossed John's face. "No. It must not have. In fact, there are air vents that lead from the crypt to below the windows upstairs to allow for air circulation down here. It doesn't take much of an imagination to guess what it was like to be at church in the heat of the summer. Come, follow me."

The group shuffled along behind John, stopped when he did, and formed a semi-circle around the tomb he was standing before.

"Before you is the tomb of Major John Pitcairn, who got shot six times during the Battle of Bunker Hill, including once in the head. His son ferried him across the river, and he later died of his wounds."

"Why would they bury him here and not send him back to England?" Geneva asked.

"Back then, this was an Anglican church, connected to the Church of England, so it wasn't unusual for British subjects to be buried in one. In fact, they interred several other British officers here with Pitcairn. If you'll notice, right next door is the tomb of Samuel Weekes. His wife, Elizabeth, died in 1721 while at sea on the way to America, leaving

Samuel without a wife or any children. So, when he bought this tomb, he shared it with his friends, as seen in the old inscription there. Note the differences between the two markers. The Weekes marker is most likely to be original to the era, while the one for Major Pitcairn was most likely placed here in the early to mid-1800s."

John waited for the group to take photographs, then moved down the corridor.

Since he was at the back of the pack, Drake waited until the group left, then turned and rushed along the short corridor behind him. He scanned each tomb door, looking for any clues that had anything to do with the poem by Mercy Warren. He rushed his way through, not wanting to take too much time away from the group. Because of the tight quarters and the fact that they sealed each tomb closed, he felt confident that he didn't miss a thing. Just in case, he snapped photographs of every piece of writing he came across. Drake rushed his way back to the group and slowed as he caught up to them. He tried to pretend that he'd been with them the entire time, and he returned to find John in mid-lecture.

"So, if you'll compare this tomb door to some others we've seen, you can see that this one, leading to the tomb of Shubael Bell, is clearly made of iron. Stone, iron, and wood were the three options for creating tomb doors down here, and no one is clear why there were different materials for the different doors. Sir, did you find what you were looking for?" Everyone turned and looked at Drake, since he was the only other sir in the group.

"Yeah. Sorry. I was just taking pictures of the different tombs. History nut. Sorry."

"Okay, fine. If you want to take photos, please do so,

and if I'm going too fast for you, I'm happy to slow down, but please keep up with the group," John said.

"Okay. Sorry again," Drake said.

John nodded, then guided the group farther down the corridor.

Allie waited for Drake to catch up to her, then elbowed him in the ribs. "You got busted!" she whispered.

Drake snickered. "Yeah, I did. Come on. We need to get moving. I don't want to get sent to the principal's office."

Drake stopped long enough to snap a picture of the tombs as they walked past, but he was never over five feet behind the tour.

"Here's an interesting one. Number fourteen, the stranger's tomb, from 1813. Who's behind the door? Who knows? Some say it's one of the many ghosts that inhabit the crypt," John said.

John turned and went on with the tour, and Drake waited until everyone had cleared the area before he stepped in and snapped a photo of the crypt.

"Well? What do you think?" Allie asked.

"I think we're probably at a dead end here. I mean, for all we know, they sealed the next clue inside a tomb. John was unhappy with me leaving the tour for three minutes. I can't imagine it would thrill him if I started breaking down walls and disturbing the dead."

"Probably not. There would be ghosts haunting you forever then," Allie agreed.

"I can't have that. I can barely put up with you haunting me every day," Drake teased.

"You're such a turd!"

"I know. Come on, we're falling behind."

Drake and Allie rushed to catch up with the group, but

Drake still stopped several times to click photos of various tombs along the way. When they rejoined the others, they got there just in time to see the American flag wearing woman pointing to a small iron door. It was two-feet square, near the bottom of the floor.

"What's that?" The woman asked.

"Good eye. Of all the tombs in the place, that is the one that garners the most questions. Open the door," John said.

"Wait, what? We're not supposed to touch anything."

"This is the one exception to the rule. Go ahead."

The woman bent at the waist and opened the door. The small iron door opened freely, although not without a squeak reminiscent of every haunted house movie ever produced. Everyone bent over to look at what was behind the door, but it was dark and hard to see. John pulled a flashlight from a belt clip and illuminated the area.

Behind the door was a small tomb marker, just a shade smaller than the door that hid it. Carved into the center of a marker were five concentric circles. The inner circle was about the size of a quarter, the others radiated out every inch. At the center of the inner circle, six shapes resembling flower petals reached out with their outer tips that ended at the outer circle.

Above the crude etching were the initials 'O.D.E.', and beneath the etching were the words 'G.C., Witch Man'.

"What the heck is that?" Geneva asked.

"According to our researchers, that is an apotropaic mark, also known as a witch mark. It's a pattern used to protect from witchcraft," John explained.

"You're saying there's a witch buried in there? Why would someone bury a witch in a church? And why is that door so little?" Ingrid asked.

"No one knows for sure. Experts have x-rayed the wall, and there is indeed something in there that looks like it could be a small urn, but we've never opened or disturbed it."

"Why not?" Ingrid asked.

"There's never been a reason to. We opened many of the tombs when we upgraded the church with power, water, and fire suppression systems, but because this one wasn't in the way, we didn't touch it. This is still a crypt, so we don't like to disturb the remains unless it's absolutely necessary. Besides, folklore has it that if you disturb the grave of a witch, the witch will rise again."

John leaned forward, shut the door, and turned off his flashlight. "And with that, we've come to the end of the tour. Are there questions I can answer for anyone?"

No one said anything, so John pointed to the exit. "Good. I hope you enjoyed yourselves down here, and I hope you learned something. Watch yourselves on the stairs up, and I hope you all have a great rest of the day."

The stairs were behind them, so Drake was first in line to climb up to the street level. Without speaking, he left the church. In the church's courtyard, he sat down on a stone bench and waited for the others to join him.

"What's going on, Drake?" Geneva asked, the first to reach him.

Drake took out his phone, opened it to the last picture he took, and enlarged the photo. "Who can tell me something about witches?"

CHAPTER TWELVE

Sure. I'll bet if we took a trip up to Salem, we would learn all we wanted to know about witches. But not today," Geneva said.

"No, I didn't mean today," Drake said. "What I meant was—"

Drake stopped speaking when Ingrid raised her hand to cut him off.

"Can we walk? I'd like to leave," Ingrid said.

Without a word, Drake stood, the others followed suit, and they trudged out of the courtyard.

"Where to? Should we return to the hotel?"

Ingrid looked around her as she hesitated. "Sure."

They strolled along Salem Street, following the narrow sidewalk, Drake and Geneva in front, Ingrid and Allie a few steps behind. They set a leisurely pace, not in a hurry to get anywhere, which allowed them to more appreciate the eclectic mix of shops as they wandered.

Ingrid stopped at a bakery and looked in the window.

"Those cakes look good, don't they?" Ingrid said as she

pointed to a three-tiered wedding cake with pearls piped in around the base of each layer. "Do you like cake, Allie?"

Allie joined Ingrid at the window and peered in. "Of course. As long as it has buttercream frosting. I'm a snob that way."

"I agree. If it doesn't have buttercream, I'd rather not have it."

Ingrid made a show by pointing to something else in the window. "I think your boyfriend is following us."

Allie tilted her head in confusion. "I'm not sure what you mean."

"The book guy," Ingrid clarified.

"Stan? The one who showed up at the restaurant yesterday?"

"Yep."

"Are you sure it was him?"

"Pretty sure. He was peeking around the corner when we were sitting in the courtyard. I only spotted him for a second and he stopped. I didn't know if I should mention it or not."

Allie gave a quick glance in the direction from which they came. She didn't recognize anyone who looked familiar among the many pedestrians traveling in either direction on both sides of the street.

"Can you tie my shoes for me? My knee hurts and I don't want to bend down," Allie asked.

Ingrid looked down at Allie's shoes. She had both perfectly tied, double knotted, with each loop the same size as the others. "Your shoes are fine."

"Please, don't argue, just do it." Allie turned her body, so she was facing down the street, and Ingrid crouched and pretended to retie Allie's shoes. As Ingrid pulled at the loops, Allie studied the street. Most people were walking with a purpose. She spotted a two-man crew washing the windows of a bank a half of a block away, and a steady stream of people going in and out of a delicatessen. She counted three people in suits chatting on cell phones as they rushed to their destinations. Down the street walked a small group of tourists being led by a guide using an old car antenna with a red ribbon tied to the top as a flag. The tourists were coming toward Allie. She thought the group of eleven were going to squeeze past them on the sidewalk, but at the last second, they took a left and walked across the intersection. As the last of the group cleared Allie's sight line, she spotted Stan, trying to look like a tourist interested in whatever window he was peering into.

"I got him. He's about a block back from us," Allie said. "You can stand up now."

Ingrid stood and brushed off the knees of her pants, even though they hadn't touched the concrete. "What should we do?" Ingrid asked.

"I guess carry on with our day. Maybe it's a coincidence that he's here."

"A coincidence? I'm sure it is. And during the winter, I play quarterback for the New England Bills," Ingrid said.

Allie grinned. "Patriots. Buffalo is the Bills."

"Whatever. You understood what I meant."

"Yes, I get your drift. Come on, let's catch up to the others."

Allie and Ingrid walked quickly until they caught back up with Drake and Geneva two blocks later, and once there, Allie told the others they had a tail.

"Okay, so what are we going to do about it?" Geneva asked.

"I think we should confront him," Drake answered without hesitation. "It's obvious to me he's stalking Allie, and we should put an end to it right now, before this goes any further."

Allie placed a hand on Drake's chest to stop his rant. "Hold on there, big fella. How can you be sure it's all about me?"

"Um, because I've got eyes, and I noticed the way he leered at you at the restaurant yesterday. He was practically drooling over you."

"I'm still not convinced it's all about me," Allie said. "Look, there's a crowded bookstore up ahead. Let's keep walking, and when we pass it, I'll dip in there and hide and you three keep going. Then we can see if he comes after me for sure, or if it's all of us he's interested in."

"Or it might be a coincidence," Ingrid said.

"Right, or he simply ends up going his own way."

"What happens if he follows you, and we're not there to protect you?" Drake asked.

"Simple. I go up to the counter and ask someone to call the cops. It's a crowded building. Even if he was the stalker supreme, I doubt that he'd pull something with dozens of witnesses around."

Drake thought about it and nodded. "Okay. I'm not stoked about the idea, but let's see what happens."

The group started walking again, and Allie stepped a little faster to take the lead position. When they passed the large bookstore, Allie slipped into the door, and the other three kept strolling right on by without so much as a pause.

The bookstore had a large picture window at the front of the building. In full view of that window were two large wooden tables on which were displays of new arrivals, and a sign that announced an upcoming author signing event. Beyond the table display were shelves that came to two inches below Allie's shoulder height, so Allie placed herself behind the bookcase. She picked a random book from the shelf and propped it open and stood it up on end to use it as cover. Allie checked her position and determined she had not only a good view of the window and saw everyone that passed by, but she also had a view of the door. She examined anyone who entered, and all the while, she was confident that no one could see her. Just in case, she surveyed her surroundings and plotted out the best route to reach the checkout counter if anything wrong happened.

Allie waited. She ignored anyone outside walking from her right to her left and concentrated on those coming from the other way. The door opened, and Allie watched as a grandmother with a young girl in tow stepped into the store. Less than a minute later, a teenage boy wearing a basketball jersey and carrying a skateboard entered.

Allie counted off the seconds in her head, and she got all the way to ninety-three when Stan walked past the window without stopping. Allie did a ten count and was about to leave her hiding space, when suddenly, Stan reappeared and walked to the center of the window. He held his hand over his eyes to ease the glare as he looked into the store. He scanned from left to right and reversed direction, and a heartbeat later, he was gone again.

Allie didn't realize she had been holding her breath, but based on the burning in her lungs, she knew she was for at least forty seconds. She waited another few moments for Stan to return, and when he didn't, Allie made for the front door.

She wanted to play it coy, open the door, stick her head out, and make sure the coast was clear. A large man with two bags bulging with books foiled that plan when he practically pushed Allie out into the street as he exited. Allie panicked, knowing she'd blown her cover, but when she looked up the street, she saw Stan nowhere in sight.

Allie walked to the end of the block, stopped and peeked around the corner to discover if Stan was there, but he wasn't. She continued on, knowing the route Drake and the others were planning to take to the hotel, and increased her rate of speed. She knew the others had planned to dally, so she guessed she'd encounter them sooner than later.

The buildings fell away when she left the claustrophobic feeling of Salem Street and stepped across the road onto the Rose Kennedy Greenway. Her knee ached, and she spotted a table where there were two men playing chess. She thought about asking to sit down at one of the two spare chairs near them when a woman with a stroller vacated a park bench only a few feet away.

Allie sat on the bench and swung sideways so she could put her leg up on the seat and rubbed her sore knee. She considered for a moment calling for an Uber, but being the stubborn soul she was, resolved to keep going. Allie knew all she needed to do was get back to her room, and the rest of the night would be one with little tromping around the city.

As she rested, Allie took her backpack from her shoulders, fished out a bottle of water, and had a drink. She checked through all the various pockets for the small bottle of ibuprofen she usually carried but couldn't find it. Allie closed her eyes, thought for a moment, and remembered it was sitting on the sink in the hotel bathroom where she'd last taken some pills. She took another drink, swished the water around in her mouth to knock back some of the dryness, swallowed, and returned the bottle to her pack.

She looked across the park and, wanting to not push it too much, eyed her next potential spot to sit. It was where the brick path dipped to become flush with the next street over. Next to the path was a wall that she estimated would be hip height, a perfect spot to rest once she got across the park. Allie swung her leg over and got to her feet. She took three steps and stood stone still when she spotted Stan.

Allie had been so focused on the wall, she hadn't noticed the large bush that separated the park from the street. Just at the edge of that bush, she spotted Stan standing there.

To her surprise, he didn't focus on her. Rather, he paid close attention to something ahead of them. She watched him for a while, and not once did he glance behind him.

She opened her backpack again and fished out a light blue windbreaker and a Tennessee Titans baseball cap. She put them on, added her sunglasses to complete her disguise, and ambled toward the other end of the park. Allie made it halfway through the space when Stan looked both ways, then crossed the street against the light.

Although her knee was throbbing, Allie picked up the pace and rushed to the corner. The light turned green, and the little man on the walk signal said to go, so Allie stepped out into the street. Before she could take a second step, someone grabbed her by the shoulder and pulled her back onto the sidewalk. She was about to turn around and confront the stranger, but before she could, a taxi blew the light and sped through the crosswalk.

Her anger dissipated, and Allie turned around and saw a woman in shorts and a sports bra running in place.

"Thanks," Allie said.

"No problem," the woman said. "We have to protect each other out here." The woman checked for cars, then ran across the road, and Allie followed her.

Once across the street, Allie picked up sight of Stan again. Although he had a fifty pace lead on her, Stan didn't seem like he was walking with a purpose, more like he was taking a leisurely stroll through the city.

When they got to the park dedicated to the New England Holocaust Memorial, Allie stopped at the entrance. Before her stood six glass square towers under which visitors could walk. Stan stopped underneath the fourth tower and pretended to read something. At the far end of the park, she saw Drake pacing back and forth. Allie pulled her phone from her pocket. She brought up the messaging app and sent a group text.

I'm at the entrance to the memorial. I can see you. He's not following me, he's following you.

She watched the phone screen, then little bubbles appeared, so she knew someone was responding. It was Drake.

What should we do? Should we come to get you?

Allie thought for a second, then responded. *No. You three split up, each one take a different route back to the hotel. I'll follow him.*

She looked up from her phone, and as soon as she did, Ingrid and Geneva stood, and the three left together. They were near the corner already, so once they were there, Ingrid made a left turn and disappeared around the corner. Geneva waited for the light, then turned right, and Drake continued on straight ahead.

Allie kept her eyes on Stan, and when he walked, she did too. When he got to the corner, he stopped, looked left, right, and straight, as if trying to decide which way to go, then continued straight on down Congress Street. When she got to the corner, she crossed the street and realized that she was right back at Faneuil Hall.

Allie had made it a half block from the hall when she sensed someone fall into step behind her.

"You know you stand out like a reject from the F.B.I., right?" Ingrid said.

Allie laughed. "Don't mock me. This is my secret disguise. It fooled you, didn't it?"

"Not for a second. Where is he?"

Allie pointed up the street. "A hundred yards ahead. Gray pants, gray sweater."

"Okay, I see him."

"Weren't we just here?" Allie asked when they stopped for a moment in front of a building. She looked up into the air and pointed. "Yep. Unicorn. Is it me, or does Boston involve walking around in a lot of circles?"

"It only seems that way. You won't think that tomorrow when we go up to Salem. It'll get us a little outside of this area, and you'll be able to see some different things."

Allie took a step, stumbled, staggered, and almost fell face down in the center of the Boson Massacre memorial. Ingrid reached over, caught her, and prevented Allie from falling.

"Are you okay?" Ingrid said. There was a concrete planter holding a small fir tree nearby, and Ingrid helped Allie over to the planter and boosted her up so she could sit. "You didn't answer me. Are you okay?"

"I'm…fine. I just lost my balance. That's all. Help me down," Allie said.

"You shouldn't lie to me, Allie. I'm trying to help you. You're practically in tears. I'm going to get us an Uber to take us back to your hotel, okay? Don't answer. It wasn't a question, and I'm not giving you a choice, so just sit there and be quiet."

Allie did as she was told and waited in silence until a car pulled up. The driver rolled down the window and Ingrid stuck her head in. "I'm sorry. It's such a brief ride. My friend hurt her leg. Do you mind if I put her in the front?"

The driver nodded, then moved his personal items from the front seat to the back.

Ingrid returned to Allie, helped her off the planter, and got her in the car. Once everyone buckled in, the driver took off like a shot, and within five minutes, they were at the hotel. Ingrid helped Allie from the car, then Allie leaned on her friend's shoulder and let her guide her past the lobby and to the elevator bank.

"I hope Drake and Geneva are okay," Allie said. "I feel like I abandoned them."

"Oh, don't you worry about them," Ingrid said. "They're big kids, and they'll be fine."

The door dinged, slid open, and the two trekked down the hallway. Allie fished the keycard from her pocket, and a few seconds later, Ingrid plopped Allie on the bed like she was dropping off her luggage.

"Drop your pants, let me look at your leg," Ingrid ordered.

"Excuse me?" Allie said.

"You heard me."

Allie hesitated and unbuttoned her jeans and slid them under her butt. She tried to reach for the right leg but couldn't do it. Ingrid stepped over, grabbed one pant leg in each hand, and pulled off Allie's pants in one smooth motion, folded them, and set them on the dresser.

"Wow," Ingrid said, "you've got some really nice legs. Well, except for that knee. It looks swollen."

Allie locked eyes with Ingrid for a moment, blushed slightly, and looked down at her leg. Her knee was indeed swelling rapidly. It wasn't yet twice the size of the other knee, but it was getting there.

"I'm going to get you some ice, okay? Don't go anywhere," Ingrid said.

Ingrid went into the bathroom and came back out with the plastic ice bucket.

"Ice and vending are one floor up," Allie said as Ingrid left the room.

Ingrid was back in a flash. "You wouldn't have a resealable bag on you, would you?"

Allie pointed to the floor. "There's one in my backpack."

Ingrid checked through the backpack and found an empty, gallon-sized plastic bag. She filled it with ice, then handed it to Allie, who placed it gently on her knee.

"Ooh, that's cold. You think you could grab me a

towel?"

Ingrid did, and Allie wrapped the ice bag in the towel, then reapplied it.

"I wonder how Geneva and Drake are doing," Allie said.

Before she even finished the sentence, Ingrid's phone dinged. She checked and gave the report. "Geneva's waiting outside for Drake, and he's just a couple of blocks away. They'll be here within ten minutes."

"Well, shoot," Allie said, "can I ask for one more favor?"

"Sure, anything."

"Can you help me slide into a comfortable pair of sweatpants? They're in the top drawer over there, blue ones that say 'honey' on the butt."

Ingrid smiled and turned toward the dresser.

CHAPTER THIRTEEN

Allie was shivering. In her dream, she was adrift on an ice floe that was ten feet in diameter and shrinking by the minute. Swimming laps around the floe were a colony of penguins. Although there were only a dozen birds circling around her, every time one of them passed, her anxiety level rose. As she watched, one bird flew out of the water and landed on its feet only five feet from her. Allie knew her birds, and she could tell by the black and white tuxedo it wore that it was a Magellanic penguin.

The bird waddled a foot toward her and squawked, but she wasn't as concerned about the two-foot-high bird as she was about the ice that was rapidly melting. She noticed simply by looking that the ice had shrunk by another foot. Allie figured she had five minutes at most before the ice was gone, and she'd plunge into the freezing water. Since she was wearing only a pair of black panties, a black sports bra, and a pair of black socks, she assumed she'd become frozen as a fish stick as soon as she submerged for the first time.

The penguin took another step and opened his mouth. That's when Allie noticed that the penguin's mouth didn't contain papillae, but rows and rows of razor-sharp shark's teeth. The bird stepped forward again. Allie took an instinctive step back, slipped on the ice, and fell on her butt. She struggled to get up but got no traction from her socks. Her legs worked overtime trying to get purchase, but she kept losing her footing. Allie rolled over on her hands and knees, and she was about to push to her feet when she sensed the strange sensation of webbed feet on her bare back. She stopped moving and felt the beak push past her ear and open. Allie smelled the scent of digested fish coming from the penguin's mouth, and she looked over her shoulder in time to see the bird poise for the killing strike.

Allie shrieked and woke herself from her nightmare.

The yell surprised Ingrid, who was sitting in the easy chair reading a book. She dropped her book, jumped to her feet, and ran to Allie's bedside.

"Hey, Allie, are you okay?"

Allie opened her arms, and Ingrid moved in and embraced her. After the coldness in her dream, Ingrid's closeness was warm and safe.

"Yeah. Only a bad dream. I was on a shrinking ice floe surrounded by penguins with shark teeth. I was so cold."

"Probably has something to do with this." Ingrid slid the covers from Allie's legs and picked up the bag, which was filled with frigid water from the melted ice. She removed the plastic bag and returned the bedspread.

"It seemed so real," Allie said.

"Yeah. I've had dreams like that, ones that stay with you the rest of the day."

"I hope this one doesn't. How long have I been asleep?"

Ingrid checked the bedside table clock. "Almost an hour and a half. How are you feeling?"

"Better, I think. I need to use the bathroom."

Allie threw back the covers and swung her legs over the

side, setting her feet on the floor. She hesitated for a minute, worried that her knee would buckle, and she'd collapse to the floor the second she put any weight on it. She surprised herself when she stood tall, with nothing more than a slight ache. Allie limped into the bathroom and a few minutes later, limped back to the bed and sat on the edge.

"Where are Drake and Geneva?"

"They left for dinner about an hour ago. I imagine they'll be back soon."

Allie's stomach rumbled at the mention of food. "Have you eaten? I think the hotel has a restaurant we can eat at."

Ingrid put her hand on Allie's knee. "I'm sorry, I misspoke. I meant to say that they're out getting dinner for all of us. There's a pizza place that Geneva really loves, but the place doesn't deliver, so they had to go pick it up."

Allie's stomach rumbled again. "Good. I really like pizza. It's one of my favorites."

"Me, too."

They heard a knock on the door, and Ingrid rose to answer it. Geneva entered first with a canvas sack in each hand, followed close behind by Drake, carrying two pizzas. They made their way to the small, two-seat table in the corner of Ingrid's room, and Drake set the pizzas on the table. With a grunt, Drake moved the heavy table toward the center of the room so they could all sit around it. After he adjusted the two chairs they had, he disappeared into his room to get his chairs.

While Drake was rearranging the furniture, Geneva unpacked the bags. From one, she pulled three six-packs of Diet Coke, and from the other she produced a pack of paper plates, napkins, and a handful of silverware.

When everything was ready, Drake and Geneva took seats, and Ingrid and Allie joined them at the table.

"Thanks for getting dinner. I'm starving," Allie said.

"What do we have here?"

Drake placed the pizzas so they were next to each other, and flipped open the tops. "You can have a boring one with pepperoni, sausage, mushroom, and onion, or you can have the slightly less boring barbecue chicken with onion and bacon."

"How about a slice of each?" Allie said. "And why are they boring?"

Drake reached for a plate and pointed it at Geneva. "Ask her. She wanted to get something called a seafood special. I talked her out of it."

"Seafood? On a pizza? Yuck," Allie said as Drake passed her a plate.

Geneva shrugged. "No worse than pineapple on a pizza."

"I like pineapple on pizza," Ingrid and Allie said at the same time. They looked at each other, smiled, and giggled like teenagers.

Drake folded a slice of the barbecue chicken pizza in half and took a bite. He chewed a few times and nodded, as if he were agreeing most heartedly with a point someone made. He swallowed and took a drink of Coke. "Oh my, that's a good pizza," he said a second before he moved in for a second bite.

"I told you so. Best in town. Worth the trip and the wait," Geneva said. "How are you doing, Allie?"

Allie swallowed the bite she'd been eating and wiped her mouth with a napkin. "Much better, thanks. The rest did me a world of good. I'm sorry to you all that I had to give up my end of the pursuit."

Drake shook his head. "Don't worry about it. Splitting up was actually a good idea that you had. We all made a bad assumption that he had the hots for you, but it turns out I'm the one he's interested in."

"Are you sure? Did he follow you the entire way back?" Allie asked. "He never veered off, or kept on walking, or headed in a different direction?"

"Nope, he tailed me the entire time. At one point I slowed down, and he didn't and came within twenty yards of me. Once that happened, it was easy to keep him spotted."

"How did you do that? Do you have eyes in the back of your head?" Geneva asked.

"No. I used this." Drake dug into his pants pockets and took out two items: a pair of tweezers, and a compact mirror. "No good geocacher leaves home without them. I tracked him in the mirror. He followed me all the way back to the hotel."

"Perhaps he was headed to his bookstore," Ingrid said.

Geneva shook her head. "Nope. The hotel is out of the way. He took the long route if he intended to go to his shop."

"But why would he follow Drake and not Allie?" Ingrid asked. "It was Allie who went to his store, and it was Allie he was making lovestruck eyes at yesterday. Why Drake?"

The room fell silent as everyone considered the question while they ate, but no one could come up with any logical or illogical answer to the question.

Allie finished her third slice of pizza, picked up a second napkin, and thoroughly wiped her hands and mouth. She crumpled the napkin into a little ball and placed it on top of her plate. "Okay, I've got another question for you all. We've been following these clues for the last couple of days, and what I don't understand is why all the hassle? Why bother going through the trouble of setting up all these convoluted clues in these random locations? Why not just have one cipher somewhere that tells the last location of the treasure, complete with a little X that marks the spot?"

Drake pushed his plate aside as well. "I've been thinking about that myself, and the conclusion I've come to is that I do not have a clue. Maybe it was a way to obscure the trail. It's possible there were only one or two people who had the treasure's hiding spot, and they backtracked it. You get it? They hid the treasure somewhere and told someone to hide a clue to get there. Afterwards, they got someone else to make a clue to find the previous person's clue. That way not everyone realized where it was, but everyone contributed to the elaborate scheme to hide it."

"Or more likely, it was a giant ruse to get the British to spend time and effort trying to track down a secret treasure that never existed," Geneva said.

"That could be as well," Drake admitted.

"Or it's all an elaborate fairy tale," Ingrid said.

"Could be that too," Drake said.

"What's the book say?" Geneva asked.

"Which book?"

"Which book? Come on, Drake, the book that started this whole baffling adventure. What does it say? Are we on the right track? Are the places we've been to even in the book?" Allie said.

"I'm not sure. I'll go get it," Drake said.

Drake disappeared into his room and returned a minute later, carrying his backpack. He placed it on the floor, opened it up, and rifled through it. He pulled out two empty water bottles and placed them on the table and underneath those found the book. In the process of putting the book on the table, he knocked the bottles, and they fell to the floor and bounced away.

Drake took a drink of Diet Coke, shook the can to confirm it was empty, and set it on the table. He opened the cover, then in dramatic fashion for the enjoyment of the others, he licked his finger and turned the page. He started reading, then started scanning the pages, flipping through them in a hurry, and skipping large chunks of information.

Finally, he pushed the book across the table.

"Engaging reading?" Geneva said as she picked up the book.

"From what I can tell, it's mostly rumors and theories. Paul Revere is in there, but not a word about William Dawes. They mentioned the Old North Church, and Bunker Hill, Faneuil Hall, the USS *Constitution*, but only just in passing."

Geneva picked up the book and started going through it. "That wasn't much of a book report. I'm sure Ingrid wouldn't give you a good grade on that one. What do you think? A 'D'?"

Ingrid smiled. "D-plus, at best. Could have been a C if he pronounced Faneuil correctly."

Geneva slowly paged through the book. "Okay, according to this, John Adams and Samuel Adams had the brainchild of hiding the treasure to prevent it from falling into British hands. From what this says, George Washington himself decided where to hide it, and sent Paul Revere to pass the message."

"If the treasure was so valuable, why not simply take it with them?" Ingrid asked. "You know, when Washington left town and started moving his headquarters farther and farther down the east coast? Clearly, he had the troops to make it happen."

Geneva shrugged without looking up and kept reading. "There are several theories in here, but all of them seem to agree that they buried the treasure on an island in the Atlantic Ocean. However, where the island is seems to be anywhere from the coast of Gloucester in the north to Martha's Vineyard in the south, and about a dozen points in between."

"Is there any information at all in there to narrow it down?" Allie asked.

Geneva continued through the last few pages, then

closed the book and passed it back to Drake. "I don't think so. Even by my amateur eye, it seems to contain a lot of conjecture and a fair amount of sloppy research."

"How can that be?" Allie asked. "I thought that Hailey person we met with is one of the premier authorities on the American Revolution this side of the Mississippi. And she's on here as the co-author. You would think with all the documentation she has at her fingertips; she could figure this thing out without an issue."

"I don't know," Drake said. "I still think we're missing something on that end, but I don't know what. Either way, what about going to Salem tomorrow?"

"That depends. Are we going as tourists, geocachers, or treasure hunters?" Geneva asked.

Drake looked across the table. "Allie? What do you say?"

Allie got out her phone and checked her geocaching app. "It looks like there are four virtual caches up there, and a handful of traditional caches. Have y'all done any of these?"

"I haven't," Geneva said. "Have you done any caching up there, Ingrid?"

Ingrid shook her head. "No."

"Alrighty then. It looks like some of these caches correspond with historical locations anyway, so we'll go as geocachers first, tourists second. If we accidentally run into anything that would give us the next step to the treasure, then we'll do that," Allie said. "Oh, and lunch. We need to stop for lunch. How long will it take us to get up to Salem?"

"On a perfect day, a half hour. On a usual day, maybe an hour. All depends on how bad traffic is," Geneva said.

"Why don't we do breakfast at seven and try to be on the road by eight? Is that too early?" Drake asked.

No one objected.

"Next concern," Drake said as he stared down Allie. "Are you going to be okay, or should we take a rest day and hang out by the pool?"

Allie rolled her eyes at him in the most mocking manner she could. "I'll be fine. We'll have a car tomorrow, right? So, if I get tired, or the knee acts up, I'll just hang back and take it easy. It would also be helpful if we didn't do what amounts to a death march tomorrow."

"Okay, so what do y'all want to do with the rest of tonight?" Drake asked. He looked from Allie to Ingrid to Geneva, but no one spoke. "We could play cards. Or go to the movies. Or just hang out."

"What about the club? Why don't we go dancing?" Allie asked.

"Are you serious?" Drake asked.

Allie laughed. "Of course not, you goofball. Actually, I'd just like to curl up with a book and get some rest. That way I'll be ready for tomorrow."

"I get it," Drake said. "I'm good if we call it an early night."

Drake looked down at the pizza. "You want the leftovers with you?"

"Nah, you can have it," Allie said.

Drake consolidated the remaining five slices into one box and closed it. "I'll put it in my room fridge. If you get hungry during the night, just knock on the door and I'll slide a slice under."

Allie smiled. "That's so nice of you. Don't worry, I'll be good."

"Okay. Party's over. Geneva, can you help me with the chairs?"

Drake and Geneva each grabbed a chair that belonged in Drake's room and carried them through the door. While they were gone, Allie and Ingrid cleaned up the used plates and napkins and dumped them into the empty pizza box. While Ingrid took the trash and removed it from the room, Allie put the clean plates and napkins into a sack. She withheld a couple of cans of soda and put the rest in the other sack, then looked around. Satisfied everything was in order, Allie took a seat.

Drake came back into the room and gave Allie a hug. "I'm sorry about your knee. I still feel bad about that, you know."

Allie hugged him back. "You really shouldn't. I was the one who was careless on that hill, and I'm the one who has to pay the piper. I just need to accept the fact that I need to slow down for a while and try not to be super-woman all the time."

"Hey, I can help by not pushing you so hard, but you know how I get when I have a goal in sight. I just can't help myself."

"I know. That's how you always end up with briers on your pants, poison ivy on your hands, and random bloody holes from thorn encounters. You never look before you leap, but that's okay. We balance each other out that way."

"We do," Drake said. He released the hugs and grabbed the sacks. He said goodnight, then stepped through the door into his own room.

"Are you sure you two are just friends? You seem much closer than that," Ingrid said as she stepped back into the room.

Allie turned and smiled at her. "We are close. But just friends. I think I told you a long time ago that he's not my type."

"What is your type?" Ingrid asked as she moved closer.

Allie reached out her hand, and Ingrid took it. "To be honest, I prefer blondes. Preferably smart ones, with a good sense of humor. Oh, and someone who's easy to talk to."

"Anything else?" Ingrid asked as she took a step closer.

"Hmm. Sparkling blue eyes. A kind heart."

"You have quite a laundry list of expectations," Ingrid said. "I'm not sure that person exists in real life."

"I think they do," Allie said.

Ingrid took a step closer and wrapped her arms around Allie. "Are there any other qualifications?"

Allie smiled. "A good kisser. They need to be a good kisser. Are you a good kisser?"

Ingrid batted her sparkling blue eyes and whispered into Allie's ear. "Kiss me and find out for yourself."

CHAPTER FOURTEEN

"Is this a traditional or a virtual?" Ingrid asked.

Geneva checked the app. "It's a virtual. We need to either take a photo showing ourselves with the stones in the background, or—"

Drake interrupted Geneva in mid-sentence. "Hold that or, darling. I'm not sure why anyone would ever go beyond the photo part and actually do the task. The photo is so easy to take. Snap one shot, and you're done!"

"Not everyone likes to post a picture of themselves on the Internet, you know," Geneva said.

"True, but it's not like you're posing nude or anything. And most people post nothing besides selfies, anyway."

Geneva shook her head and snuggled close to Drake and snapped a picture with him. "There. Satisfied?"

She showed him the picture, and when he nodded his approval, she sent it to him and logged the geocache as a find for herself. "You guys want a picture, too?" she asked Ingrid and Allie.

"No. I'm already done with this one," Ingrid said, "and Allie seems preoccupied."

Geneva looked to her left and noticed Allie studying the nineteen names engraved into stones. "Allie? You want a photo for the cache requirements?"

Allie looked up from the marker she was reading. "No thanks. I took care of that the minute we got here. Can you imagine hanging nineteen people here for being witches? I mean, with no evidence other than the wayward claims of young girls? I can't wrap my brain around that."

"Well, it was three-hundred years ago. Definitely a different time," Geneva said.

"How did people let that happen?" Allie asked.

"I don't know," Geneva answered. "I'm sure when we get to the museum, someone could probably answer that question for you."

"Drake, do you think… what are you doing?"

Everyone turned their attention to Drake, who was looking at his phone and comparing it to the markers. "I'm looking to see if any of these people had the initials G.C., like what we found in the crypt yesterday."

Geneva passed her gaze quickly along the stones. It only took a few seconds to determine no one there had those initials. "I don't see a match."

Drake frowned and shoved his phone back into his pocket. "I didn't either."

"Wouldn't matter if you did," Ingrid said. "You wouldn't find any treasure clues here."

Drake looked up. "How do you know?"

Ingrid pointed to a small sign nearby. "Because they did not dedicate this park until 2017. I doubt the patriots would have had the foresight to hide clues in a location that wouldn't have a memorial until two hundred years later."

"Okay, that's a valid point."

"Besides, we're treasure hunters third today, remember?" Geneva said. "Let's get in the car and move on to the next geocache. It's only a half mile from here."

They all got back in the car, and Geneva drove a few blocks, found street parking, and they all got out again. Drake checked his app and pointed to a stop sign fifty feet ahead of them. "I'll bet it's there," he said.

The four walked to the corner, and Drake checked all over the sign and the pole from as high as he could reach to the ground. Despite his search, he had no luck in finding it. He was about to give up when Ingrid handed him a small plastic box meant for hiding spare keys.

"Where was it?" he asked as he slid open the box and removed the paper log.

"Over there, behind the downspout attached to that building. You only missed it by less than fifteen feet," Ingrid said.

Drake signed the log and passed the sheet to the other three, and Ingrid put the geocache back together and returned it to where she found it.

Five minutes later, they parked outside of a three-story white mansion.

"Cool house," Allie said.

"Wait until you discover the garden around back," Geneva answered as she turned off the engine. "Unless plants aren't your thing, and in that case, we can grab the cache and leave."

"I'd vote for cache and go," Drake said.

"Me, too," Ingrid agreed.

"Okay, okay, I'll come back and enjoy the flowers on my own. This is another virtual. We need to find the sundial in the garden. The gnomon points to an information sign, and we need to grab the fifth word from the second sentence on the sign."

"What's a gnomon?" Drake asked.

"I think it's the pointy part of the sundial," Geneva

answered. "Let's go find out."

The four walked into the maze. While Geneva stayed a step behind to take pictures of the vegetation, the other three quickly found the sundial. Sure enough, the point of the sundial led to the sign with the answer they needed.

For their next stop, they visited the statue of Roger Conant, who was the person credited with founding the community of Salem. Together, they took a group photo for the requisite picture and logged the virtual geocache. Afterwards, Drake pointed to the large brick building across the street that resembled an old Gothic cathedral.

"Can we go over there?" Drake asked.

"The Salem Witch Museum?" Allie clarified. "Sounds fun, let's do it."

The quartet headed across the street and stepped into the museum. Lucky enough to secure a spot, they passed through the presentation that gave an in-depth examination of the Salem witch trials in 1692. They spent an hour going through the museum, then left the building and found a seat on the bench.

"Did you see what I did?" Drake asked.

"Um, like the history of the witch trials?" Allie answered.

"No. I think I figured out who G.C. is. Giles Corey, the dude who got pressed to death."

"Okay, I'd have to admit, that's a pretty good guess. What do we know about him?" Geneva asked.

"Other than a pressing was the grossest thing I would ever imagine? Not much. I'll find some info on him," Ingrid said as she pulled out her phone. As the others watched the tourists wander back and forth, Ingrid dug up all she could find on Giles Corey. After ten minutes, she set the phone on her lap and turned to the others.

"Well?" Drake asked.

"I found nothing we didn't already learn from the presentation we just saw. Originally from England, married three times, accused of being a wizard. During the trials, they pressed him to death when he didn't plead either guilty or not guilty to the charges against him."

"I don't suppose he's got a house around here that was perfectly preserved as a historical site," Drake said.

"Nope," Ingrid said.

"Did you find out where they buried him?"

"Sure," Ingrid said. "In an unmarked grave in what is now the Howard Street Cemetery. You'll be happy to know that it's rumored his ghost haunts the cemetery."

Drake leaned forward so he could hear Ingrid better over the din of the crowd. "And why would that make me happy?"

Ingrid grinned. "We simply go there tonight, and you can ask him all the questions you have about him."

Drake laughed. "That's a great idea, but I doubt he'd be able to tell me what clues people may have planted eighty years after he died. Is there anything else that connects him physically to the area?"

"No. Only a marker over at the memorial. That's all I found. I'm sorry," Ingrid dropped her head, and Allie leaned over and rubbed her shoulder.

"There's no need to be sorry," Drake said. "It's not your fault. If there's not a lot of information out there, then there's nothing you can do. Why don't we go over to the memorial? It's sounds touristy."

"Would you like to walk or drive over there?" Geneva asked.

"How far is it?" Drake asked.

Ingrid picked up her phone and mapped it out. "Three-tenths of a mile."

"Allie? Are you up for the hike? You're the only one

who gets a vote."

Allie glanced from Drake's face to Ingrid's to Geneva's. "I'm kind of torn. On one hand, I'm afraid I'll injure myself again, but on the other, I'd really like to stretch my legs. I'm leaning toward walking."

"Let's do that. And if I need to go back to the car and pick you up, that's not a problem for me," Geneva said.

"Thanks. Okay, Ingrid, lead the way."

Ingrid got up from the bench, brushed off the seat of her jeans, got her bearings, and started walking. Although their destination was only a five-minute walk away, Ingrid walked at a slow pace. She made a show of looking at the architecture of buildings as they passed them.

"Are you moving like a snail for my benefit?" Allie asked as she slid into step next to Ingrid.

Ingrid glanced over and smiled without stopping. "Would I do that?"

"Probably."

Ingrid grew silent and kept the same gait of her stroll.

"Is there something on your mind?" Allie asked. "You've seemed kind of distant today."

"No. I just have some things on my mind. Plural," Ingrid said.

Allie stepped closer and lowered her voice. "I just asked you that. Did you hear me? Is it anything about last night?"

"Yeah, I guess."

"We can talk about it. You don't need to hide from me, Ingrid."

"No, it's not that. It's just… complicated. And I want to talk to you about it, but I need to wrap my head around what it is I want to say, so I can say it without sounding like an idiot."

"You wouldn't sound like an idiot. I won't judge you that way," Allie said.

"I know, but I'd also prefer if we talked when it was just the two of us. I have a feeling I won't get any guff from Geneva or Drake, but…"

"…but you don't want an audience. I can understand that. We can talk by ourselves whenever you feel that you're ready. Okay?"

"Okay. Thank you for understanding," Ingrid said.

"What are you two whispering about?" Drake asked.

"I get your point," Allie said to Ingrid. Allie stopped, turned around, and waited for Drake and Geneva to catch up to them. "We were talking about you."

"Oh yeah? About how I'm the greatest guy around? Besides being the world's greatest geocacher?"

Allie rolled her eyes. "Yep, that was it exactly. I was telling her about the time you were looking for that cache at the only probable location in a one-hundred-foot area."

"Oh? Did he have trouble finding it?" Geneva asked.

"He sure did. Drake lifted the light pole skirt and didn't find it. He stepped to the other side of the pole, lifted it again, couldn't find it. Then gave up. It turned out to be a fake electrical cover attached to the pole with magnets. I had spotted it right away, but he was so focused on assuming it was under the skirt, he looked nowhere else. He logged it as a DNF and then got mad at me when I walked right to it and slid it right off the pole."

"I think I see the memorial up ahead. Let's keep moving," Drake said as he pretended not to hear the conversation.

Allie smirked, then turned back around and kept walking. After another fifty feet, they arrived. The memorial was rectangular, and on each of the one-hundred-foot-long sides were four-foot-high stone walls. Attached to the walls were twenty granite benches. Etched into each bench was the name, means of execution, and execution date of a victim of the trials. A grassy patch and several large locust trees made up the middle of the memorial.

The four walked up the dirt path and reflected on the names carved into the granite. They passed the first ten benches without spotting the one they were searching for, then started down the other end of the rectangle.

Drake stopped when he finally found it. "Giles Corey. Pressed to death, September 19, 1692. Amazing, isn't it?"

"Sure is," Geneva said.

"I would have loved to learn more about him," Allie said.

"We could give Hailey a call. Maybe she could tell us something," Geneva suggested.

"Nah, I would think this might be outside of her area of expertise," Drake said.

"Excuse me, do you mind if I squeeze in here?"

Drake turned to look at the speaker. Before him was a man in jeans, a brown windbreaker, and a brown herringbone flat cap that matched the color of his jacket.

"I'm sorry. I wouldn't normally be this rude, but I'm on a deadline and I need to get some photos snapped of the benches," the man explained as he held up his Nikon for his credentials.

"No problem," Drake said as he stepped back from the bench. Ingrid and Geneva followed suit to give the man room, and Allie was already reading the details of the next victim.

The photographer looked into the viewfinder, then brushed away some grass from the top of the bench. Satisfied, he snapped the photo.

"Thanks again. Oh, and I didn't mean to eavesdrop, but if you're looking for anything about Giles Corey, there's an art gallery a block down Charter Street. They specialize in objects related to the witch trials. They might help you out."

"Thanks. We'll go down there for a look," Drake said.

The photographer moved on to the next bench, and Drake turned to the group. "Well? What do you say?"

"If it's only a block down, we might as well take a gander," Geneva said.

The four finished looking at the remaining benches, then left the memorial. Within three minutes, they were standing inside the art gallery.

"Can I help you?" the gallery owner asked as he came out from a back room. He looked right at home in the area where the witch trials took place, since the man resembled a witch himself. He wore a black suit, black shirt, and a black tie. On his feet were black shoes, and on top of his head was a mop of raven-black hair. He even painted his fingernails black. The only trace of color on him was a lapel pin of a red rose.

"Yes, we're interested in seeing any pieces you may have about Giles Corey," Geneva said.

"I have a few prints of some of the more famous etchings of the time, like him being accused, or one of his pressing."

"Just prints? You have nothing original?" Drake asked.

"No. Sorry. I don't think anyone does from back then. It's not like it was a well-known event during that time. And once the trials were all over, the town tried their best to put that nasty piece of history behind them."

"Do you have anything from later, like maybe dating back from the 1700s?" Geneva asked.

The man in black looked at Geneva, as if trying to size her up. After two minutes of silence, he finally spoke. "I have one item, but it's not for sale. It's in my private collection."

"Can we see it? Pretty please? We won't be more than a moment."

The man considered it for a bit, then nodded. "I'll be

back in a few minutes. Browse the shop while I'm gone if you wish."

Allie went off to get a closer look at the art on the walls, but the other three stayed clustered together, and within ten minutes, the man came back pushing a wood cart. A silver ewer protected by an acrylic box was on the cart. The man stopped near the group, and when Allie came back over, the man spoke.

"Paul Revere himself created this item. It's a solid silver ewer. It was a commissioned piece, and you can see engraved upon it, the pressing of Giles Corey."

"For real? Revere made this?" Geneva asked.

The man nodded. "I have the provenance on the paperwork going all the way back to 1775, including the sketches Revere made before he started the work."

"That's amazing. Can we see that?" Drake asked.

The man shook his head. "I'm sorry. It's not in the gallery. I keep the documentation in an off-site storage facility to keep it safe."

"I'm surprised you keep the ewer here," Geneva said.

The man smiled. "It's much too beautiful to be locked away." He looked beyond them when the door opened, and a couple entered the shop. "Please excuse me, I'll be right back."

"Keep a close eye on him and let me know when he's coming back," Drake said as he took out his phone. With as much haste as he could muster, he snapped photos of the ewer from all four sides. Once he finished, Drake stowed his phone back into his pocket and resumed the stance of a casual observer.

"It's a remarkable piece, isn't it?" Drake asked Geneva when he noticed the man coming back toward them.

"It is," Geneva agreed. "I've seen nothing like it anywhere before."

"Well, what do you think?" the man asked.

"Beautiful. Why isn't it in a museum?" Allie asked.

The man grinned. "Pure selfishness on my part. I couldn't stand the thought of it being out of my possession for even a moment. Is there anything else I can help you with?"

Drake shook his head, and as the man pushed the cart back from where he got it, the four left the gallery. They walked up the block, then Drake spotted a bar and grill with outdoor seating. "Anyone hungry?"

Every one of the three women replied in the affirmative, so they went to the tavern and got a table outside under an umbrella. They took a moment to examine the menu before ordering drinks and burgers, and once that bit of business was out of the way, Drake passed his phone over to Allie.

"Can you look at the pictures and see what you can see?"

Allie took the phone and started scanning through the photos. She took her time and enlarged each one as she looked through them. She hadn't finished by the time the server arrived with burgers for all, so Allie passed Drake's phone back to him, and the four settled into small talk as they ate.

A few blocks away, while the four friends were busy enjoying lunch, Stanford Edison stepped into the art gallery. He wasn't usually a patron of the arts, but he was interested in knowing why Drake and his friends had been there.

CHAPTER FIFTEEN

After Allie finished her burger, she pushed her plate aside, wiped her mouth and fingers with a napkin and asked Drake for his phone. Drake handed it back over, and Allie continued looking through the pictures.

"Are you seeing anything?" Drake asked. He dipped an onion ring into a puddle of ranch dressing while he waited for the answer.

"I'm working on that," Allie said. "If there is anything here, it's pretty well hidden."

"There has to be something. I can't believe that someone would really get Paul Revere to create that ewer with such an odd subject," Geneva said.

"I would love to find out who commissioned the piece. Perhaps it would tell us something to know who the piece went to," Ingrid said.

"Yeah, that would have been nice," Drake said as he finished the last bite. "All we would need to do is go back into the gallery and demand that he show us the documentation."

"Or we could go all ninja and break into the storage place and get the records ourselves," Geneva said.

"Did he mention where it was?" Drake asked.

Geneva grabbed her iced tea and took a sip. "I was being sarcastic. You may have noticed that although each of us brings a particular set of skills to the table, none of us are cat burglars."

"We don't need to go back," Allie said. "Anyone have a pen?"

Allie knew it was a rhetorical question because all geocachers carried a pen, sometimes even when they weren't geocaching. She herself had a half dozen of them in her backpack, but she was too lazy to go digging for them. Instead, she took the first one to appear in front of her, which turned out to be Ingrid's. The server left a stack of extra paper napkins on the table, so Allie took the one off the top. She unfolded the napkin and started copying symbols from the pictures to the napkin.

"What did you find?" Drake asked.

Allie ignored the question until she finished jotting down the symbols. "Clever of old Paul. He engraved these in the bottom edge of the ewer, made to seem like a decorative border." She expanded the photo she was referring to and held the phone so everyone could examine the picture. "See? I'm positive that's a code."

"How can you tell?" Geneva asked.

"The border doesn't repeat. Usually when you see a border around anything, it's a repeating pattern, right? It's human nature to want a sense of evenness, and this border doesn't have it. It's unnatural."

Ingrid asked for the phone and looked closer at the

pictures. "I think you're right."

Drake motioned for his phone back, then slipped it into his pocket. "She usually is. The next logical question is, can you break the code? I mean, all I spot are random symbols, and if you say there's a code hidden in that base, then there is. The question is, how do you break the thing?"

"We could start by taking a picture of it and seeing if any of the symbols pop up in an image search online," Geneva suggested.

"That's a good idea," Allie said. She passed the napkin over to Geneva, who took several photos of it, then gave the napkin back. "In the meantime, I'll try to break the code the old-fashioned way. Trial and error."

Allie put the napkin down and stared at the symbols for a moment, then took a fresh napkin and made a copy of the first. Once she had a backup, she leaned over and tapped the pen on the table while she inspected the napkin. All the symbols were etchings of animals. On a third napkin, Allie copied a symbol, then wrote the number of times it repeated next to the symbol. There were two different snakes, one facing left, the other right, and each had a count of ten. She made out two bird heads, one with a short beak, one with a long beak, both of which had two instances. Allie recognized a turtle, which showed up twice, and a frog, which had only one entry.

"I think we have only four letters here, based on the repeating images," Allie said.

"How do you figure that?" Drake asked.

Allie pointed at the snakes. "There are too many instances of these to be letters. I think they are just here to take up space." She grabbed another napkin and rewrote the symbols, leaving the snakes off of the napkin. When she finished, there were only seven symbols left.

"There's only one non-repeating letter in here, the frog. One letter has two instances, but not doubled, and two places where I think are double letters. Ingrid, can pull up one of those word finder apps?"

Ingrid fussed with her phone for a minute. "Okay, got one. Give me some parameters."

"Hold on. Let's assume that the first letter is a consonant, and the second and fifth letters are vowels. Then there are two separated double letters. Seven letters only. Hold on. Let me see if I can map this out. Can you pull me up a list of common repeating letters?"

Ingrid made a query and had the answer in an instant. "The most common repeating letters are E, L, S, O, T, F, R, N, P, and C."

"What about at the end of a word?"

Ingrid worked for almost thirty seconds to get the information. "E, L, S, and F."

"I'm going to guess that is an L or S at the end. The E wouldn't make sense."

"If you're knocking out the E as a double, I'd get rid of the O as well. What does that leave us with?" Geneva said.

Allie checked her scratching. "Starting with A, blank, A, L, L, A, S, S. Does that mean anything to anyone?"

No one said a word.

"Okay, how about blank, A, S, S, A, L, L?"

"'Assall'? That doesn't sound like anything," Drake said.

"You need to put a letter in front. Like a C to get 'cassall', or G to get 'gassall'."

Drake waved his hand at Allie. "Yeah, but those aren't words."

Ingrid smiled, as if a light bulb came on. "Yeah, but if you add a V, you get vassall. There's a name I've heard before, but I can't remember where. Give me a second." She checked for a hunch. "Got it. The Vassall House is where George Washington had his first headquarters in 1775."

"Any chance it's still standing?" Geneva asked.

"Not only is the building still standing, but it's now a part of the National Park Service. It's in Cambridge."

"Where's that from here?" Drake asked.

"Back toward Boston, about an hour from here," Geneva answered. "You want to go for a drive, don't you?"

Drake looked at her, then gave her a smile. "It is a historical site, right?"

"It is," Ingrid said. "Not only did Washington use the house as his headquarters, but Longfellow owned it as well."

"Longfellow the poet?" Allie asked.

"Yep."

"That is interesting. I'm in if you guys are," Allie said.

Geneva smiled. "Okay. Let's go get the car and hit the road."

An hour in the mid-afternoon traffic took an hour and a half, but eventually Geneva found her way to Cambridge and parked in front of the Longfellow house. The house was a three-story mansion, painted yellow with a large white door, white window trim, and black shutters. There was a large yard in front, and the quartet walked up the front sidewalk and stood before the house's door.

Drake took off his hat, scratched his head, and put his hat back on. "Looks too good for being so old. They must have rebuilt it at some point."

Geneva pulled on Drake's arm to move him along. "Let's go find out."

"Welcome to the Longfellow House," the park ranger said as the friends entered the visitor center. "Are you interested in a tour?"

Drake stepped forward to represent the group. "Sure. Could you tell us a little about the house's history first?"

"Of course. As you can see from the outside, they built the house in the Georgian style in 1759 for John Vassall, Jr., who used the home as a summer residence. In 1774, patriots confiscated the house, and General George Washington used it from 1775 to 1776 as his house and headquarters. The house passed through various hands after the war. Ultimately, poet Henry Wadsworth Longfellow received it as a wedding gift from the father of his new bride Frances Appleton. After his death, the surviving Longfellow children put the house into a trust in 1913, and in 1972 the trust donated the property to the National Park Service."

"What's in the house now?" Geneva asked.

"Since the Longfellow family held the property for so long, the house is as when Henry lived and worked here. There's also an excellent exhibit based on some guests the Longfellow family had come through. The dignitaries included Charles Dickens, Ralph Waldo Emerson, and Oliver Wendell Holmes. The emperor of Brazil once visited as well."

"That all sounds cool, but we're primarily interested when Washington used the house as his headquarters. Are there any exhibits highlighting that era?"

"Yes. There is one room that was used as Washington's office when he was in the house that is set up the way we believe it was back then."

"Can we check out that one?" Drake asked.

"You're not interested in the rest of the house?" the ranger asked. "Usually when people visit, they want to experience what it was like in the time of the Longfellows."

"Oh, you see, our friends here are visiting from Nashville. They came all the way here to learn about the American Revolution. We wanted to show them something associated with General Washington," Geneva explained.

"You don't want to tour anything else, just the Washington room?"

"Not unless it was authentic to the time Washington was here," Geneva clarified.

"Well, why don't you four follow me and I'll take you over," the ranger said.

"Are you sure you can leave your post? What if someone else comes in?" Allie asked.

The ranger smiled at her, then stood, and reached for his hat. "Not a problem. My partner should be back soon, and it won't take us long to see the one room."

He led the group from the visitor's center and locked up behind him. He led the party to the entry door of the mansion, and they stepped into the blue entryway. They walked directly through the front parlor and into a room dedicated to Washington's stay at the house.

Along one wall was a fireplace, and above the fireplace were portraits of George and Martha Washington. There stood a simple wood table underneath the lone window. Scattered on the tabletop were several maps and pieces of correspondence. On a mannequin in the corner was a reproduction of Washington's coat and hat, and a side table held a few old books.

"Not much to learn here," Drake said.

"That's why there's only the one room," the ranger explained. "When Washington left the house, they took pretty much everything with them when they moved on to the Dexter House in Dedham. What we have here is a basic recreation based on what few items we had from the time."

"Is there anything original?" Drake asked.

The ranger shook his head. "No, I'm sorry. Even the portraits are reproductions. If you want to see the originals, you'd have to go down to D.C."

Ingrid pointed at a framed hand-written document on the wall. "What's this?"

The ranger walked over to it and straightened the frame. "This is actually an original. A poem written by Phillis Wheatley entitled 'To His Excellency, George Washington' that she sent to Washington himself in 1775. What you see on the wall there is what the *Pennsylvania Gazette* republished in 1776."

"I've never heard of Phillis Wheatley," Geneva said.

"I'm not surprised, although more people should. Historians consider Wheatley the first African-American author of a published book of poetry. She was born in West Africa, kidnapped, and sold as a slave. When she came to North America, the Wheatley family bought her. She learned to read and write and started writing poetry. After she published her first book, she got emancipated. Rumor has it she and Washington corresponded with each other several times, and newspapers published several more of her poems."

"What happened to her?" Ingrid asked.

"She died young and poor in Boston." The ranger's radio squawked, and he stepped out of the room to take the call.

"While we have a moment alone, look around and check if we missed anything important," Drake ordered.

The four split up and inspected everything in the room. Drake dedicated his effort to the fireplace. They looked for clues, but there was nothing to be found. Dejected, they left the room, walked out of the house, and found the ranger outside, still having a conversation over the radio.

The ranger spotted the group, waved at them, then headed back toward the visitor's center.

"Well? What now?" Geneva asked. "Should we do a loop around the exterior? Check out the carriage house?"

Drake scrunched his face and shook his head. "I don't know if it's worth it. I think we finally hit the end of the road here. So, with that, back to geocaching. Is there anything around here to find?"

Ingrid was the first to open her app and check. "There's an EarthCache and a multi-cache nearby. Those are the two closest. Anyone interested?"

"You know I'm not a fan of EarthCaches," Allie said. "How hard does the multi look?"

Ingrid brought up the cache detail and checked it out. "Doesn't look too bad at all. Looks like stage one gets you the call number, and they hid the final inside of the library."

Allie's face brightened. "You should have led with that. I love library caches!"

Five minutes later, they were in the parking lot of the library, and were looking for stage one around the library's bulletin board.

Drake spotted it first. "I have it. It's 796.233."

"You sure?" Geneva asked.

Drake pointed at the sheet he was reading from. "They have a list of the most popular books of the month. One is titled *Finding Tupperware in the Woods* by G. Cacher."

Geneva nodded. "Good enough for me. Let's go in."

Drake held the outer door and let the ladies enter the library before him. As with entering any library for the first time, it took them a couple of minutes to get their bearings. It wasn't long until they headed for the 796 section of the stacks. Once there, all four of them scanned the shelves until Allie pointed at the book they needed.

Geneva pulled the volume from the shelf and opened the book. They had all seen geocaches in libraries before. Some were fake books; some were plastic containers hidden in book sleeves. The most common was the one they had before them. Someone had gone through the work of cutting a hole in the inner pages, leaving just enough on the edges to make it resemble an actual book. They glued the title page to a thin piece of cardboard, and when Geneva turned the page, they found the goodies inside. The contents included a green plastic army man, a pair of red dice, and a coupon for a free ice cream cone. Geneva pulled the paper log from inside and passed it around. Once everyone signed, she tucked it back into the book and returned the book to the shelf.

Together, they all left the section and headed toward the door. On the way out, Allie stopped when she got to a computer, hit the spacebar to activate the screen, and brought up the library catalog. Once she got in there, she did a name search on Phillis Wheatley, and found a grand total of one book in her name. She jotted down the Dewey Decimal number for the book on a scratch pad next to the computer and ripped the page from the pad. She turned to ask a question, but discovered all her friends were gone.

Allie shrugged, glanced at the note, and headed back to the stacks to find the American poetry section. When she got to the eight-elevens, she scanned the shelf but couldn't find the book she wanted. Allie took a step back, put her fingers on the book a few spots ahead of where she expected the volume to be, and touched each book in sequence to make sure she hadn't missed it. Once satisfied she hadn't just passed it over, she checked the shelf above where the book should have been. When that was unsuccessful, she checked the shelf below. There, in the American Drama section, was the book she wanted.

Allie opened the book and checked the table of contents. In there she noticed the same poem she saw hanging on the wall of the Longfellow House, and several others as well.

"There you are. Where did you disappear to?" Ingrid said as she appeared in the aisle. "Allie? Are you there?"

Allie looked up from the book, then closed it. "Sorry, what?"

"We got back to the car and realized you weren't there. Drake wanted to leave you behind, but I said I'd come in and look for you."

Allie grinned. "He's such a dork, isn't he? Hey, do you have a library card that works for this library?"

Ingrid held up her phone. "Sure. There's an app for that."

"Can you check out this book for me?" Allie handed the volume of poetry over to Ingrid, who took it and glanced at the spine.

Ingrid raised an eyebrow and held the book up. "What's this about? A little light reading?"

Allie smiled. "Just a hunch. Can you get it for me, pretty please?"

"I don't know. Checking out a book for someone else can be a dangerous thing. You never know if they will return it, and the next thing you know, you've racked up a dollar's worth of late fees and your card gets disabled."

"You're just as big of a dork as Drake is. Come on, let's get out of here before they really leave us behind."

CHAPTER SIXTEEN

It was a few minutes after eight, and Allie had settled into bed with the Phillis Wheatley book when she heard a gentle knock at her door. She threw the covers off her, plodded over to the door, and opened it, and discovered Ingrid standing there.

"I'm sorry. Hey, I get I should have called first, but I thought since I was nearby anyway, I'd stop by. I have a question for you."

"Sure, what is it?"

Ingrid smiled. "Would you like to meet my cat?"

"Your cat? I didn't know you had a cat. Want to come in?"

Without waiting for the answer, Allie backed away from the door to allow Ingrid room to enter. "Are you serious about me meeting your cat?"

Ingrid nodded. "I realize it seems silly."

"Is your cat here?"

"Of course not. She's back at my apartment. It looks like you're ready for bed. I'm sorry. I'll leave you be and catch you tomorrow."

Ingrid turned to leave, but Allie reached out and grabbed her arm. "No, wait. I'd love to meet your cat. Give me a moment to get dressed."

Allie grabbed her jeans that were folded over the back of the chair, took off her sweats, and got into her jeans. She tucked her t-shirt into her pants and zipped them up. She grabbed her room key from the top of the dresser and slipped into her shoes.

"Okay, I'm ready. Lead the way," Allie said.

Forty-five minutes later, Ingrid slipped the key into the lock of her apartment door. "Watch out. She likes to make a break for it sometimes."

Allie took a step back and waited for a little ball of fur to rush her way the second that Ingrid opened the door a crack, but no cat appeared.

"And sometimes she doesn't." Ingrid stepped over the threshold and flipped a light switch.

There was a small bench next to the door in the entryway, and Ingrid slipped out of her shoes and tucked them under the bench. To be polite, Allie followed suit.

Ingrid walked into the living room and turned on another light. "Come on in and make yourself at home. I'll go find Roxie."

Allie sat down on the couch and looked around the room. There was a television set and three bookshelves, crammed with books, on the opposite wall from the couch. In front of the couch was a small coffee table holding a laptop, and in front of the balcony windows was a small easy chair. From where she sat, Allie could look at the area set aside as the dining area, which contained a small square table and two chairs, and a door she assumed led to the kitchen.

A shadow crossed the room and the next thing she knew, Allie's breath was knocked out of her chest as the largest cat she'd ever seen jumped into her lap. She tried to push the beast away, but instead, the cat reached up and put its paws over Allie's shoulder and nuzzled in her ear. The cat's purr was loud enough to make Allie believe she was on an airplane.

"Oh, you found Roxie!" Ingrid said as she came back into view.

"More like Roxie found me. I was expecting a house cat, not a full-grown tiger."

"She's part Maine Coon, part Russian Blue."

"She's gorgeous is what she is," Allie said as she petted the cat's slate gray fur. "Is she going to get any bigger?"

"Oh, I hope not. She's almost like having an elephant for a pet as it is. Here, let me take her from you."

Ingrid grabbed Roxie and with a grunt, lifted the cat and placed her on the chair. The cat stood, did a lazy circle, and laid down. Roxie put her head on her paws and closed her green eyes.

"Thanks for coming over. You want something to drink? Beer? Soda? Water?" Ingrid asked, mindful of being a good host.

"I'd take a glass of water, thanks."

"Ice?"

"No. Straight out of the tap is fine."

Ingrid traipsed into the kitchen and returned with two bottles of room temperature water and passed one over to Allie, opened the other, and took a drink.

Allie waited. She sensed Ingrid wanted to say something. She didn't, and instead, Ingrid played with the bottle cap and stared at her cat. "Everything okay, Ingrid?"

Ingrid turned her attention from Roxie and gave it to Allie. "Can we talk about last night?"

"Of course. What's on your mind?" Allie put her bottle on the floor and turned sideways in her seat, so she was facing Ingrid.

Ingrid looked from Allie to the floor, picked a spot on the carpet, and stared at it. "I wanted you to understand that I realized last night was really special. It was a first for me, for sure, and I didn't want you to think that I did it just because I think you're pretty. I really like you, and I've never had these feelings for anyone the way I feel them for you."

Allie reached over, placed her fingers beneath Ingrid's chin, and gently lifted her head to force her to make eye contact.

"Wait. You said I'm pretty?" Allie asked.

Ingrid hesitated and nodded.

"I think you're pretty, too. Beautiful, in fact. You should know that I've never felt this way before, either. I've been in quasi-relationships with both men and women, but never anything serious. I've never thought about wanting anything serious. At least, until I met you."

Ingrid took Allie's hand in hers. "I'm in love with you, Allie. Since the moment I first saw you last year."

Allie squeezed Ingrid's hand. "I love you, too."

Ingrid's face turned from uncertainty with a side of fear to exuberance in a heartbeat. "So now what?"

Allie leaned forward and gave Ingrid a gentle, lingering kiss. "I have no clue. You tell me."

The next morning, Allie's eyes fluttered open, and she was aware of three things. First was the sunlight peering in through the window. The second was the sensation of an enormous weight on her lower legs. The third, and best, were Ingrid's blue eyes looking at her.

"Good morning," Allie said. "How long have you been awake?"

"Only a few minutes. I wanted to glance at you to make sure last night wasn't a dream. Now that I say it out loud, that sounds super creepy."

Allie smiled. "No. Not creepy at all. Why can't I move?

Did you drug me? Because that would be super creepy."

Ingrid laughed. "Nope, that never crossed my mind. You're sleeping on Roxie's side of the bed, and she decided that you're only a lumpy part of the mattress. Roxie, time to get up. Roxie, up."

Allie sighed when the blood came rushing back to her legs as the cat stood, stretched, and finally jumped down to the floor with a loud thump. She leaned over, gave Ingrid a kiss.

"I have to use the bathroom," Ingrid said. She threw off the covers, slid out of bed and padded off into the other room, naked.

Allie got out of bed, found her clothes, and got dressed while she waited for Ingrid to reappear. She heard the toilet flush, and the sink run for an extended time. When Ingrid finally appeared, she had brushed her hair and when she gave Allie a kiss, Allie tasted the fresh mint of Ingrid's toothpaste.

"Would you mind feeding Roxie while I get dressed? The food is in the cabinet next to the fridge, and her bowl is in the sink. Then I'll run you back to the hotel so you can get ready for the day."

Allie moved into the kitchen, had a drink of water, then found Roxie's dish. She found a can of chicken and rice cat food in the cabinet and dumped the contents into the bowl. Before she uttered the first syllable to call the cat, Roxie was at her feet, looking up at her. Allie put the bowl on the floor and let Roxie go to it.

"Ready to go?" Ingrid asked as she came out of the bedroom, ready to take on the day.

"Sure thing. What time are we meeting the others for breakfast?"

"Nine," Ingrid answered. "But you know how they are. It will be closer to ten before we get a peep from them."

Allie saw her phone and hotel key on the coffee table and retrieved them. She checked the phone and saw she had no text messages or missed calls overnight. She also noticed it was going on six-thirty.

Allie shoved the phone into her pocket. "Do you always get up this early?"

Ingrid pushed her way into the kitchen, checked the water level in Roxie's fountain, and topped off her bowl of dry food.

"Yeah, usually. I've always been an early riser. Is that a problem?"

"Not in the least. I'm the same way," Allie said.

By seven-fifteen, Ingrid and Allie were back in Allie's hotel room. While Ingrid watched the morning news, Allie took a quick shower, brushed her teeth, and got into fresh clothes.

"Okay, I'm ready to go," Allie announced as she zipped up her jeans. She checked her phone and saw it was not yet a quarter to eight. "Although I guess I'll sit for a bit. You want some coffee?"

Ingrid shook her head. "No thanks. I can't stand the stuff."

"Something else we have in common. So now I guess we wait until we hear from the others."

"I hope Geneva set an alarm. She could sleep all day if you let her."

Allie walked over to the nightstand where she'd left the Wheatley book the night before and carried it over to the table and sat. "There's something else she has in common with Drake. I can't tell you how many times we've been late to things because he has trouble getting out of bed. Want a Diet Coke?"

"Sure. Wait, I got it." Ingrid got up from the bed and retrieved the cans of Diet Coke they had saved from the night before and joined Allie at the table. "Mind if I sit with you?"

Allie opened a can and took a drink. "Of course, you can. Do you mind if I read for a while? I want to see if there's anything in this book that leads to the treasure."

"Go ahead. I can entertain myself."

Ingrid moved her chair so she could watch the television while Allie read. An hour and a half passed without either of the women saying a word. The only sounds in the room were the noise from the television and the sound of paper scraping across paper as Allie turned the pages.

"The fires of freedom from Boston burns. From Salem to Concord, from the Graveyards to the Steeples. From Houghs Neck to Hayman's, and again to Rainsford. Follow the march to Freedom's Ring."

Ingrid found the clicker and turned down the volume of the television. "Can you read that again?"

Allie repeated the passage she'd just read, then put a marker in the book and closed it.

"Okay? And? What's so special about those lines?" Ingrid asked.

"I don't accept Phillis Wheatley wrote that, even though a Boston paper published it under her name in 1775."

"Why not?"

Allie pushed the book toward Ingrid. "Read it. But before you do, read a few of the poems before, and a few after. I don't have a doctorate in literature, but I can tell the same person didn't pen those poems. You teach lit, right? Read them and tell me what your thoughts are."

Ingrid picked up the book and did as Allie suggested. It was Allie's turn to remain silent while Ingrid studied the pages. Rather than turn to the television or her phone to amuse herself, Allie sat patiently and waited for Ingrid to finish.

A half an hour passed before Ingrid put the bookmark

back and set the book on the table. "You're right. There's no way that Wheatley wrote that poem. The tone and cadence and voice are all significantly different from any other work in the book. And it's certainly not as good as any of the other poems in there."

"And it doesn't rhyme," Allie pointed out.

"No, it did not."

"Now we need to ask, why would a newspaper print this poem, and attribute it to Wheatley, even though it clearly wasn't hers? Can you read it again? Aloud?"

Ingrid picked up the book, found the place, and read. "The fires of freedom from Boston burns. From Salem to Concord, from the Graveyards to the Steeples. From Houghs Neck to Hayman's, and again to Rainsford. Follow the march to Freedom's Ring."

"You've got a lovely reading voice," Allie said. "Boston to Salem to Concord. Graveyards to church steeples. Any of that seem familiar to you?"

"You mean like the various places we've found clues?"

Allie took another drink. "Exactly. Now, what about the rest of it? Someone's neck, a hay man, and a dude named Rainsford? Are those more clues?"

"Houghs Neck isn't a body part. It's a land mass at the south end of Quincy Bay. Did you know they interred John Adams and John Quincy Adams and their wives in the same crypt in a Quincy church?"

"No, I didn't. We should stop by there if we have the chance. I'd love to see it. What about Hayman's? Is that a person?"

Ingrid did a bit of magic on her phone and quickly came up with the answer. "Hayman's is an island. Today it's called Hangman Island. It's a chunk of rock northwest of Houghs Neck. And before you ask, Rainsford is also an island in the bay."

"What do we know about that one?"

Ingrid looked it up. "In the olden times, the Native Americans used it. During the 1700s, settlers used the island for farming and cattle."

"Is that it then? Is that the last clue? Rainsford is the location of the treasure?" Allie asked.

"I don't think so. I imagine we're missing something else. Every other clue we found one at a time, so why list out three locations at once?"

"I don't know. Perhaps we need to get Geneva and Drake involved. I'm sure they can figure this out," Allie said.

Without waiting for a reply, Allie walked to the connecting door and knocked. Much to her surprise, Geneva opened the door right away.

"Hey, Geneva. Are you guys up?"

"For the most part. Drake is in the shower. Are you hungry already? Are we going to the pancake place for breakfast?"

Allie's stomach rumbled at the mention of pancakes. "I'd love to, but I wonder if we found the next clue to the treasure. We think we're on to something but can't quite figure it out. We were hoping that you and Drake could look at what we found."

"Okay, sure."

Allie stepped back into her room, and Geneva followed her over to the table. Once Geneva settled into a chair, Allie explained her suspicions and Geneva took the book and read through the passages.

After a few minutes, Geneva set the book down. "I'm not saying you're wrong, but I don't see it."

"Surely you agree Wheatley didn't write the poem," Ingrid said.

Geneva gave a loud, long exhale. "I honestly couldn't tell you. But I'm not an expert on literature or 1700s poetry.

All I can tell you is it didn't rhyme. It's probably just a coincidence and you're reading too much into it. What's that old saying, if all you have is a hammer, then everything you see is a nail? I just don't know. Maybe you should wait and get Drake's opinion."

"About what?" Drake asked as he came through the door, his hair still wet from the shower.

"Allie thinks she found a clue to the secret treasure in a poem published in a Boston newspaper for all to see," Geneva said.

Drake turned to Allie. "Really?"

Allie nodded.

"Show me what you got."

Allie passed Drake the book and had him read a few poems before pointing out the one of interest. While he read, the women watched him, and he glanced up several times while he was reading, a look of discomfort on his face. When he finished, he gave them his full attention. "I don't get what you're looking at."

Allie sat down on the bed and subconsciously rubbed her knee. "It's best if you take it one line at a time and compare it to where we've already been. Boston, Salem, churches, cemeteries, those are all written in the poem, right? Then you have those next three places, Houghs Neck and two islands. Surely that can't be a coincidence."

"Where are these located?" Drake asked.

Ingrid pulled out her phone and opened a map. "They're all close to Quincy Bay. Here, look."

Ingrid handed Drake the phone, and he studied it for a moment.

"I'm guessing the next three steps to the treasure are at those three points," Allie said.

Drake shook his head. "Why would they put three clues in one place when they've been so careful about doing them one at a time?"

Ingrid smiled. "That's the same thing I said."

Drake looked at the phone again, then stared at the ceiling for a full minute. He came out of his trance, then looked at the women. "Nobody move. I'll be right back."

Drake left the room, went through the door into his room, and a few seconds later, the exterior door to his room opened and closed.

"I guess we'll wait here," Geneva said.

Allie raised her hands above her head and stretched. "I hope he's not gone too long. You've got me thinking about those pancakes."

Ten minutes later, there was a knock at the door, and when Ingrid answered it, she found Drake on the other side.

"Sorry, I forgot my key." Drake made his way to the table and laid down three sheets of paper on the table, then adjusted them so they lined up the way he wanted them to. "I went down to the business center and printed out some enlarged maps of the areas listed in the poem."

Allie got up from the bed and joined the others, and Ingrid pointed out the three locations.

Drake took a pen from the bedside table. "I was thinking, why three at once? Maybe because they needed three points." He grabbed the book, placed it on the paper, then used it as a straightedge to draw a line. He repeated the process twice more, then set the book aside. "What do you see now?"

"A triangle." Geneva said.

Drake drew a circle on the page. "Yeah. What's in the center?"

Geneva leaned in, then took the paper from the table and held it up. "It's an island."

CHAPTER SEVENTEEN

Allie poured warm maple syrup over her blueberry pancakes. Once she had the entire pancake covered in the gooey substance, she passed the bottle to Ingrid. Allie used her fork to cut off a wedge of pancake and ate it. She smiled as she chewed and happily swallowed.

"Oh, my, that's one of the best pancakes I've ever eaten," she said. "I assume these blueberries are fresh. Anyone want a bite?"

Everyone was engaged with their own breakfasts, so no one took her up on it. Ingrid had a plate of French toast in front of her. Geneva was working on a Denver omelet, and Drake had a plain plate with a couple of eggs over easy with a compliment of bacon, toast, and hash browns.

"There are two things we should probably talk about," Drake said as he mopped up some egg yolk up with a piece of bread. "First thing, we need to talk about the secret treasure. Should we go for it or should we not? Should we spend a day geocaching? Be normal tourists and go to a museum or something? What's the temperature of the room here? Everyone gets a vote today."

"What do you want to do?" Geneva asked.

Drake dabbed at his mouth with a napkin. "Nope. No, no, no, no. I'm not saying. In fact, here's an idea." Drake pulled a small notepad from his back pocket and ripped out a page. "Everyone, take a sheet and write your preference. The option with the most votes wins."

Drake passed the pad around and everyone ripped out a page.

"What if there's a tie?" Ingrid asked.

"If it's a tie, we have the server do a blind pick. Fair enough?"

Drake produced a pen, recorded his choice, folded the paper in half, and passed the pen to Geneva. Geneva took the pen, hid the paper as she cast her vote, and sent the pen to Ingrid. Ingrid let the pen and the paper lay where they were until she finished eating the rest of her breakfast. When she finished the last bite of her toast and had a drink of orange juice to wash it down, Ingrid pushed her plate to the side, picked up the pen, and wrote her vote.

Allie had already finished eating by the time she finally got the pen. She looked from face to face until she finally marked the paper and passed the pen back to its owner.

Drake dropped the pen on the table the second he touched it. "Oh gross! Who got syrup on this? It's my favorite pen!" Drake dipped his napkin in his water and used it to wipe down his writing utensil. Once he was confident he had dealt with the stickiness, he clipped it down the front of his T-shirt.

Ingrid and Allie looked at each other, then at Drake. "Sorry," they said in unison.

Everyone passed their votes to Drake, and he opened them up and showed them to the others as he did. It was a unanimous vote to go for the treasure.

"I have to admit, these results surprised me," Drake

said. "I thought for sure you'd vote for something else, Allie."

"I almost did, but I figured we've come this far. Besides, it's been fun tromping all over town, trying to determine if we can solve the puzzle. It's certainly unlike any adventure that we've ever had before."

"That's for sure," Drake agreed.

"Now what's the second thing you wanted to discuss?" Allie asked.

Drake and Geneva looked at each other and back at Allie and Ingrid.

Geneva shifted in her chair and sat a little straighter. "Is there anything you two would like to share with the rest of the table?"

Allie's jaw dropped, and Ingrid blushed immediately, her cheeks turning a lovely pink.

"Like what?" Allie asked innocently.

"Oh, let's see. Like maybe an update in the relationship status on any social media apps?" Drake said.

"Okay, we give. What gave it away?" Allie asked.

"Um, perhaps the way you two look at each other gives us the entire story," Geneva said. "Also, there's the way you walk next to each other, close, but not too close, like you both have this desire to reach out for the other's hand but are too hesitant to do it."

Drake drained the last of his coffee and pointed at Allie. "And you weren't in your room all night. I doubt you spent the entire night up by the pool reading."

"How do you know I was gone?" Allie asked.

"The walls are paper thin. I can always tell when you're watching television, or listening to music while you're reading at night, but last night, it was stone quiet the entire time. Oh, and you left your room light on all night. I noticed it under the adjoining door every time I got up. Then this morning, the light went out, and the TV came on," Drake

said.

"Okay, you got us, detective. We're busted," Ingrid said. "So what?"

"So what?" Geneva asked. "So what?" she repeated, raising her voice. "So, congratulations. It took long enough for you two to get together. Geez, Allie, every time I see Ingrid, she talks about you, and it only takes a single look to understand that you two belong together."

Allie reached over and took Ingrid's hand. "I guess the jig is up. So now what?"

"Now we see about getting to that island," Drake said.

*

"You don't think they'll be mad at us since we took a minor detour, do you?" Allie asked.

Ingrid took her hands off the steering wheel just long enough to wave Allie's question away. "Of course not. We're only five minutes away from the marina. Besides, how long will it take us to look at a grave? Five, ten minutes at most? We'll just say we got held up at the market."

"I like where you're going with that. Someone paying with a check, holding up a really long line. Or maybe someone who used cash, with a ton of coins."

Ingrid grinned. "Exactly. Besides, we're already here." Ingrid pulled into a parking space in front of the church, threw Geneva's SUV into Park, and got out and joined Allie on the sidewalk. "You ready?"

Allie looked at the granite church, took a quick picture, then headed for the door. Once inside, the pair paid a donation to enter, then stepped into the building. Inside the church proper, the first stop was at box pew number fifty-four. There they found a simple brass plaque that read 'The Adams Pew', and the pew decorated with a red, white, and blue carnations, and a small American flag.

"What are you thinking?" Ingrid asked.

"Can you believe two presidents sat right here? I think that's amazing," Allie answered.

"Don't be amazed for too long. Remember. We're on the clock."

"Okay, you're right. Let's go downstairs."

Allie took a few pictures of the pew and the church's interior, then followed Ingrid to the steps to the crypt. Down below, Allie stopped and gazed at the graves of John Adams, John Quincy Adams, and their wives, Abigail and Louisa. She stared at the vaults for the longest time, lost in her thoughts about the American history that corresponded with only four people. She broke from her trance, took a few photos, and turned back to Ingrid.

"You know what we should do, you and me? We should go on a quest to visit the graves of every dead president."

"I thought maybe we might go to Paris or Rome, but okay, I suppose wandering around the country looking for dead people could be fun," Ingrid said.

Allie kissed Ingrid on the forehead. "I like your idea, too. I'm sure I could find plenty of famous graves to look at in Rome and Paris. There are probably plenty of geocaches to find there, too."

"But I'm not discounting your idea. We should rent an RV and make a really fun road trip out of it, right?"

Allie checked the time on her phone. "We need to get back to the marina. They're going to be waiting for us. I appreciate the side trip, though, sugar. Thanks for bringing me here."

Ingrid giggled.

"What?" Allie asked.

"You called me sugar."

The church was only ten minutes away from the marina, and for once, traffic worked for them rather than against them. Once they parked, Allie grabbed two bags of bottled sodas, and Ingrid retrieved a Styrofoam cooler from the back of the SUV and headed down the dock to the boat.

From the pier, Allie saw Drake and Geneva sitting in the rear seats of the boat, not moving. "Hey, you two, mind giving us a hand down here?" Allie shouted from the dock.

Neither one responded, so Allie put her bags down and climbed aboard. "What's up? Didn't you hear me? Hello?"

Both Drake and Geneva looked at Allie but didn't speak.

"Please, join them," a voice said from behind her. Allie turned. Sitting on the deck, half-hidden by the console, was Stan. It took only a couple seconds to recognize he was holding a 9mm in his right hand. Allie's eyes darted from the gun to the deck between Stan and herself.

"No, don't think about it. There's no way you can cover that distance before I pull the trigger first. Please have your other friend come aboard and take a seat with the others," Stan said.

Allie put her hands out before her and turned toward the dock. "Ingrid. You want to come aboard, please?"

Ingrid stepped on the boat and set the cooler down next to the hull. "What's up?"

Allie cocked her head in Stan's direction, and Ingrid mimicked Allie's hands.

"Sit. I won't ask you again."

Although the rear seat could only comfortably seat three, Drake and Geneva squeezed in together to make room for Ingrid and Allie to sit down.

"What's the deal, Stan?" Allie asked. "What's this all about?"

Stan got to his feet and moved closer to the four. "The treasure, of course."

"You mean your book? Do you want it back?"

"No. You don't understand. Throughout the years, I've only sold a few dozen copies of that book. Although most go unread, now and then some ambitious people will take it upon themselves to track down the treasure. Of all of them, you four have gotten further along than anyone else ever."

"How could you possibly know that?" Drake asked. "How did you even know to find us here?"

"The same way I've been tracking you ever since the cemetery. At first, I thought you were just normal tourists. But then your movements seemed a little too odd to be just seeing the sites. Especially the way you'd skip some of the most-visited tourist attractions, only to visit places not as well known."

"You didn't answer the question. How did you guess we were here?" Drake asked.

A sly smile crossed Stan's face. "There's a tracker in your book. Following you is as easy as looking at an app and reading a map."

"So then meeting you at the restaurant wasn't a coincidence?"

Stan shook his head. "Nope. In fact, I knew you would head there before you figured it out yourself. I was lucky enough to get there before you. I'm surprised you didn't see me in the next booth."

"And it was you I spotted following us that day," Allie said.

"Yes, it was. It was a good move for you to dip into that bookstore. I saw you, you know, peering around those books like you were playing hide and go seek. Although it hurts to admit it, I also must give you credit. It was smart for the four of you to go four different ways, but then again, I had the upper hand. I was following the book, regardless of who had it."

"So why make yourself known now?" Drake asked. He attempted to move a little to his right but couldn't.

"Because I saw you use the business center at the

library, and it only took me a few keystrokes to figure out you were interested in an ocean voyage. The only problem is, you printed too much area for me to figure out where you were going to next, so I decided it was time to make myself known."

"We're just going out for a day on the water," Ingrid said.

Stan tipped his head back and expelled a hearty laugh. "I'm sure you are. I'm not quite the idiot you think I am."

"Fine. So then what's the plan, Stan?" Geneva asked.

Ingrid couldn't help herself and started giggling at the quip. Allie tried to hold back, but she laughed too.

Stan held the gun out and took a step forward. "You, you stop laughing at me! Now! I mean it."

Allie stopped right away and elbowed Ingrid in the ribs to stop her. Ingrid got the hint and contained herself.

"Seriously, what's next?" Drake asked.

"I figured I'd tag along on your little adventure. You wouldn't mind a third, would you?"

"Third? You mean fifth, don't you?" Geneva said.

Stan took a couple of steps back and leaned on the console. "No. I know how to count. I need to make sure I have some insurance out there, and that means splitting you up. Half of you will stay here. Half of you will go with me. If anyone steps out of line, I will assess penalties. You get me?"

"We get you. You expect us to play nice," Drake said. "If all goes as planned, how do you see this turning out?"

"Simple. We go out there and find the treasure, which you will turn over to me. Then we come back here, and I release all four of you. I get what I want, you get your freedom."

"What guarantee will you have that we won't go to the cops?" Geneva asked.

Stan rushed over and grabbed a handful of Geneva's

hair, pulled her head forward, and pointed the gun at her temple. "Because I've discovered where you and the blond live. If any of you make the mistake of going to the police, one of you is going to have a deadly accident. You get me?"

Geneva whimpered, so Stan thrust her head back and went back to his position.

"Who stays and who goes?" Ingrid asked.

"We'll figure that out soon. In the meantime, you sit there and be quiet."

For the next twenty minutes, no one moved, and no one spoke. Then, unexpectedly, Hailey appeared and stepped onto the boat, hoisting the bags that Allie had left on the dock.

"What's in here?" Hailey asked as she opened the bag and looked in. "Ugh. No beer? I suppose that's being a responsible boater. It would be a shame if some of you had too much to drink and fell overboard, right, Stan?"

"Yep, that's a fact."

"How are you sure the treasure is even out there?" Drake asked. "For all you know, it's but another step in the goose chase. There's no guarantee it's the end of the line, and nothing for sure says it even exists."

"Oh, I have my ways," Hailey said. "We've been chasing these ghosts for a long time. I always believed that it lies out there in the Atlantic somewhere, but we've never been able to figure out exactly where. That was the whole point of the book. To get people to do all the tough legwork for us, and from what Stan tells me, you're the closest anyone has ever come. Enough chat. Let's get this show on the road. Stan, who are you taking out to sea with you?"

Stan pointed in Drake's direction. "Him for sure. I don't care who else. You pick who stays."

Hailey approached the group and looked them over. Finally, her eyes settled on Allie. "You. Up."

When Allie didn't move, Hailey reached behind her and

pulled a gun from the waistband of her pants and waved it in Allie's direction. "Perhaps you didn't understand me. I said up."

Allie slowly got to her feet, but when she didn't move fast enough, Hailey reached out for Allie's arm, and spun her toward the edge of the boat. Hailey stuck out her foot, tripped Allie, and Allie screamed as she flipped over the gunwale and landed face down on the dock. Ingrid made a move to jump up, but Hailey held out a hand and pushed her back into the seat. "You stay, you go."

Hailey pointed her gun at Geneva and motioned for her to get up. Geneva looked at Drake for reassurance, and he nodded. "Go on. Take care of Allie. Everything will be okay."

Geneva moved quickly, left the boat, and dropped to Allie's side. Allie was grabbing her right knee and writhing in pain.

"Are you okay?" Geneva asked.

"Forget all that. Pick her up and let's go. Remember that I'm armed, and your friends will be in trouble if you don't comply," Hailey said as she stepped onto the dock.

Geneva crouched and helped Allie to her feet. Allie took a tentative step and almost fell again. Had Geneva not caught her, Allie would have fallen into the water.

"Come on, lean on me," Geneva said as she placed Allie's arm around her neck. Although it took a few minutes, Geneva struggled to get Allie to land. There was a bench nearby, and Geneva made for it and sat Allie down.

"Keep going," Hailey demanded.

"Come on, let her rest for a minute," Geneva pleaded.

"I said get up."

Geneva leaned over so Allie could put her arm around her again. "Hopefully it's not much farther, and you can sit down and rest."

"It's that white cargo van over there," Hailey said as she

pointed to the parking area.

Geneva half-carried Allie to the van. Hailey opened the back doors, and Geneva and Allie got in. Hailey produced two pairs of handcuffs. She put one handcuff around Geneva's wrist and attached the other to a ring welded to the van wall and repeated the process with Allie.

Allie looked out the back door, hoping to see if she could get someone's attention. All she saw was the fishing boat carrying Drake and Ingrid leaving the harbor.

CHAPTER EIGHTEEN

As Drake drove the boat, he ran options through his mind about how to get out of the situation he was currently in. He checked the GPS on his phone to make sure he was still headed in the right direction and stole a glance behind him. Ingrid was sitting on the bench seat in the back, but Stan had handcuffed her to the gunwale. Their eyes met, and to Drake's surprise, he recognized anger and frustration behind her beautiful blues, but not fear. Stan was sitting on the far side of Ingrid, with his gun pointed at Drake's back.

Drake daydreamed about certain escape scenarios, but his ideas were limited to those he'd seen in the movies. He considered for a second, turning the engine to full throttle. Drake thought of steering violently from side to side, hoping to throw Stan overboard. Just as soon as he imagined it, he dismissed his plan because he didn't know how that would affect either himself or Ingrid. Likewise, he couldn't aim for the nearest patch of sand and beach the boat for the same reason. He believed Stan was more than capable of pulling the trigger, and expected that for now, he had to play the game straight.

"How long until we get to that island?" Stan yelled over the roar of the engines.

Drake didn't respond, so Stan stood, made his way to the captain's chair, and thrust his gun into Drake's side. Drake responded by pulling away, and when he did so, he jerked the wheel and almost fell. He feared he was going to dump the boat, so he eased the throttle back, switched into Neutral, straightened the wheel, and regained his footing.

Stan jabbed Drake in the side again. "What are you trying to pull?"

Drake bared his teeth and leered at Stan. "What do you mean? You snuck up on me. You're lucky I didn't tip this thing."

Stan stepped back. "I asked you a question. How long until we get to the island?"

"I have zero clue. Half an hour, maybe more. I'm not a sea captain. We'll get there when we get there."

"Go," Stan ordered.

Drake spun around and looked at Ingrid. She'd taken the worst of the jostling. She had tears streaming from her eyes, and she was rubbing her shoulder with her free hand. Drake left the wheel and rushed to her side.

"Are you okay?"

Ingrid shook her head. "When the boat lurched, I felt my shoulder pop."

"Okay, sit tight, okay. I'm going to look at it."

Drake reached for her, but Stan intervened. "Hey, get back to the wheel."

"Not until I check her out."

Stan considered pushing the issue and changed his mind. "Do it, but quick. We need to get back at it."

Drake turned his attention back to Ingrid and slowly inched his fingers along Ingrid's shoulder. She flinched at his touch and took a deep breath and tried to relax.

"It doesn't seem like you dislocated it. Probably pulled a muscle, though. I'm sorry for my bad driving," Drake said. "Any chance you can lose the cuffs on her? She promises she'll be nice."

Drake stared at Stan, but Stan didn't move.

"Come on, where's she going to go? Jump overboard and swim back to shore?"

Stan didn't move.

Drake held his phone over the side of the boat. "Take off the cuffs or I drop my phone into the ocean and the coordinates to the treasure will go with it."

Stan considered it for a second and fished the handcuff keys from his pocket and tossed them to Drake. In a moment, Drake unlocked the cuff on Ingrid's wrist.

"Thanks," Ingrid said as she rubbed her wrist. "That was painful."

Drake smiled. "I'd suggest some ice and a couple aspirin, but I'm afraid we have neither. Can you hold on for a couple of hours? We'll be back to shore soon enough."

Ingrid gave him a tentative nod, and Drake moved back to the wheel. He rechecked his position, opened the throttle, and started out again. Ahead of him was nothing but open water, but eventually the land came into view. After a few more minutes, he throttled back.

"Why are you slowing down?" Stan asked.

Drake looked at the depth finder and watched as the numbers dropped. "I don't want to run aground anywhere. Unless you'd like to be stuck on a deserted island. I'll need to circle the island to discover if there's a place to go ashore. I really don't want to swim for it. "

"Just do what you need to do. Don't try anything funny, though. I've still got the gun."

Drake took it easy as they circled the island, and when they got to the far side, Drake spotted a jetty that extended out a hundred feet into the bay. Monitoring the water depth, Drake moved closer.

"Can you step off and take the line and find a place to tie up to?" Drake asked Stan.

"Yeah, right? I get off the boat so you can take off? Nice try. Let Blondie do it."

Drake turned and addressed Ingrid. "Do you think you can handle it?"

"I think so," Ingrid said.

"Can you at least toss her the bow line?" Drake asked.

"Okay. No quick moves from either of you. Got it?" Stan moved to the front and gathered the line while Ingrid opened the boarding door. She carefully stepped from the boat to the jetty, got her footing and caught the line that Stan threw to her.

"Where should I put this?" she asked.

Drake pointed to a spot a few feet to her left. "Wrap it around that part of the rock that's sticking up. I'll secure it better when I get there."

Once Ingrid secured the line, Drake cut the engine. Stan motioned with the gun for Drake to disembark, so Drake stepped over the side and joined Ingrid. He double checked the line, determined Ingrid had done a good enough job and waited while Stan got off the boat.

"Okay, move."

The rocks of the jetty were loose, so the three had to pick their way carefully to the shore.

"Now where to?" Stan asked once they got to the beach.

Drake shrugged. "I don't know. I guess we need to explore the island and see what we can see."

"That would take us all day," Stan said.

"I don't think so. It can't be any greater than two or three acres at most, and the vegetation isn't all that heavy. Seems to be mostly trees and small brush. It shouldn't take long to navigate around the entire island. Just pick a direction into the woods and go from there."

"Go then," Stan said.

Drake stood on the beach and looked at the tree line for a moment, picked out a spot to begin the search and started walking with Ingrid matching him step by step. Stan held back a few feet, then followed.

"Everything will be fine," Drake said.

"I hope so. I'm worried about Allie, though," Ingrid said. "She had a nasty fall, and I hope she's okay."

"Geneva will take good care of her. Allie is tough. She'll be good."

Ingrid looked over at Drake as she brushed her hair from eyes. "And what about us? Do you have a plan to get us out of this mess?"

"Honestly?" Drake asked.

"This would be a great time for it," Ingrid said.

"No. I don't have one. Do you?"

Ingrid picked up her pace by a half step. "Get in front of me and enter those the trees over to your right where that sapling is. Once we get into the trees, I'll give the signal, and we'll run. You go left, I'll go right, and I'll meet you back at the boat."

"Wait, no, what are you planning to do?"

Ingrid didn't answer, but Drake did as she asked and passed into the trees. When Ingrid passed by the sapling, she grabbed hold of the branch and bent it forward as she walked. When she estimated Stan had entered, she let go of the sapling. It snapped back and caught Stan right in the face.

"Drake, run!" Ingrid yelled.

Drake took off like a rabbit. He'd taken only three steps at most when he heard a gunshot ring out and he stopped dead in his tracks.

"Ingrid? Ingrid? Answer me!" Drake screamed.

Drake turned around and jogged back to where he'd entered the woods. When he returned to the scene, he saw Ingrid lying on the ground on her side. He rushed to her and dropped to his knees. "Ingrid? Hey? Can you hear me?"

He gently rolled her onto her back, felt the warm wetness, and saw the blood on her hand.

"Oh no, Ingrid," Drake said.

"She got what she deserved for pulling a stunt like that," Stan said.

Drake looked over and spotted Stan on his butt. Stan had the gun still extended, and whether Drake actually saw the smoking muzzle, or if that part was all in his imagination, he didn't know.

Drake's muscles tensed, and he wanted to rush the man, but held off when Stan raised the gun.

"She was an accident. You won't be," Stan muttered, a tinge of boredom in his tone.

Drake hesitated and turned his attention back to Ingrid. He lifted her T-shirt and winced at the blood coming from her side. Another inch, and the bullet would have missed her completely.

"This is going to hurt. I'm sorry." Drake rolled Ingrid to him and checked her other side, noticed no exit wound, and gently placed her back down. In response, Ingrid moaned.

"Can I go get a first aid kit from the boat?" Drake asked.

Stan got back to his feet but kept his distance. "You know the answer to that. Come on. It's time to go."

"Wait. Give me a minute." Drake took off his T-shirt, folded it in quarters and pressed it to Ingrid's wound. "Ingrid? Can you hear me? Ingrid?"

Ingrid moaned and her eyes fluttered open. "Drake? What happened?" Her voice was barely over a whisper, and Drake had to lean close to her mouth to hear her.

"You got shot. You'll be okay, but I need to leave you

for a few minutes. Can you hold this tight?" Drake took Ingrid's hand and placed it on top of his shirt, but her hand dropped away immediately. He scanned the ground and found a large, flat rock a foot in diameter. "Lay still," he said.

Drake placed the rock on top of the T-shirt. He watched it for a moment and thought it would tip off. Drake stacked more rocks next to Ingrid's side to give the rock's weight something else to lean against without falling.

"Let's go," Stan said.

Drake leaned in close to Ingrid. "I'll be back for you. I promise. We'll get out of this."

Drake got to his feet and wiped his bloody hands on his jeans, then walked into the woods with Stan.

"What are we looking for?" Stan asked.

"I don't know. Anything that looks man-made would be a good start. Of course, since we're looking for something from the 1700s, it might only be a pile of rocks by now."

Drake walked forward through the trees, and as he did, he scanned to the left and right. He searched for anything around other than natural rocks, trees, and bushes, but he noticed nothing else as he went. After a hundred yards, he stepped out of the tree line and found himself on the rocky beach on the opposite side of the island.

"Left, or right?" Drake asked aloud, mostly to himself.

"I'd go right," Stan said, answering the rhetorical question.

Out of spite, Drake turned left and started walking along the shoreline. A gull pierced the silence, and on instinct, Drake looked out at the water until he spotted the bird. He stopped for a moment and closed his eyes. Despite his current situation, it was a nice day. Blue sky, warm sun, nice and quiet. The way he liked it.

"What are you doing? Keep moving," Stan said.

"I was only reflecting on what a great day it is. Weather-wise, at least. Of course, being kidnapped and having my friend shot has put a damper on it pretty quick. I don't know what you're expecting to find out here, and you will not get away with shooting Ingrid."

"I will if I shoot you, too. Then you can die out here with her, and I take the boat back, and no one will ever be the wiser."

"You can't shoot me. You need me to find your treasure. Imagine the book sales you'll make when you do a second edition and explain how you found it."

Stan scratched his temple with the gun barrel. "Thanks for the idea. I hadn't even thought about that. It would be an excellent ending to the book."

"Yeah, but you'll have to keep me alive to tell you how we got this far."

"You're wrong about that. I only need to keep one of you alive. Or did you forget I have two others back on shore that I'm sure I could get the information out of, especially when you and the blond don't return?"

Drake scanned the beach and considered finding a rock large enough to hit Stan with. Deep inside, he understood he didn't have the reflexes to do it without getting shot, and if he was going to keep his promise to Ingrid, he needed to keep his head.

"What's that up there?" Stan asked.

"Huh?" Drake snapped out of his reverie and spotted the structure Stan was referring to. "Beats me. Let's go see."

As they approached, Drake saw it was the foundation of a long-destroyed building. Whatever was there before was just a pile of rubble in the center surrounded by walls that were part brick, part island stone. He walked around the remains and determined it had been eight feet square, and the walls that surrounded it ranged in height from four feet to nothing.

"Is this what you want?" Stan asked.

"Hard to say. It's not like there's a certificate of authenticity with the date of creation stuffed under a rock. The best we can do is check out the site and see if there's anything to tell us how long it's been here."

Stan sat on a portion of the wall and pointed his gun at Drake. "You best get at it, then. Remember, you're on the clock. I don't know how long the blond will last with the bullet in her belly."

Drake started at a corner and duck-walked his way along the wall, looking for any indications of what it was and when whoever made it. It wasn't until he got to the third corner that he found a brick that captured his attention. He tried to move it with his hands, and although it shifted, it didn't come free from the structure. He found a small, sharp-edged rock to use as a chisel, and another to use as a hammer, then went to work chipping away the stones from around the brick.

For ten minutes, he tried to free the brick, then finally, with a great yank, he freed it from the stone. Written on the side of the brick were the words 'Boston 1775', and when he turned it over, a small silver snuffbox slid away from the hollowed-out brick.

He opened the box, and inside was a small piece of an animal hide and written on the hide were words he couldn't make out in the shade under which he'd been working. Drake closed the snuff box and shoved it into his pocket, and put the hide inside the brick, and clambered to his feet.

"I've got something here," Drake said as he held up the brick.

Stan stood. "Toss it over."

Drake threw the brick toward Stan, and although he thought Stan was going to catch it, he let it drop, and the brick broke in half when it hit the ground. Stan saw the hide, bent over, and picked it up.

"What does it say?" he said as he examined the writing.

"I'm not sure. I couldn't make it out."

Stan threw the hide back at Drake. "It would be in your best interest to figure it out."

Drake caught the hide and stepped into the sunlight. Even then, he couldn't make out the words. He touched the writing, and noticed although the ink was age-worn, the depressions from whatever tool etched the words were still sharp.

Drake thought for a moment, then walked past Stan and halted at the edge of the woods. He stopped in front of a bush that had a crop of bright red berries growing on it. Drake tucked the hide into his back pocket, then started picking berries from the bush, and when he had a good handful, he carried them to the water's edge. He found a flat stone large enough to hold the three-inch by two-inch piece of hide. He put the hide on the rock then covered it completely with the berries. Drake folded the hide in half, simulating a berry sandwich, then placed another rock on top of the hide. He pressed as hard as he could, grinding the top rock down into the hide. He took off the top rock, unfolded the hide, brushed away the smash berry residue, and gave the hide a quick rinse in the water.

Drake held up the hide and looked at it again. Although he had erased the remaining writing on the hide, the berry juice had leeched perfectly into the depressions. The writing looked as if someone had written it in a red pen only a few moments before.

"Did that work? What does it say?" Stan asked.

"The script is still hard to make out, but I believe it says two-hundred paces into the sun, then into the maw three man's lengths."

"What does that mean?"

"I'm pretty sure it means we found another clue to find the treasure. Hopefully, this one will lead to the treasure itself and we can be done with this."

"It better, for your sake," Stan said.

CHAPTER NINETEEN

Two hundred paces into the sun." Drake looked up at the sky, but the sun was almost directly overhead. He dug his phone out of his pocket, opened a compass app, and determined where the east was.

Stan noticed Drake was using his phone, so he moved forward like a snake's strike and pulled Drake's phone from his hand.

"Texting for help, are you?"

"No. That's not the case at all. I'm trying to locate the next spot. I needed to determine where the directions were sending us."

Stan raised his gun and pointed the firearm at Drake's head. "I told you no games."

Drake put his hands out in front of him. "It's not a game. There's a way we can find the place without wandering blindly all over the island."

"How?"

"There's an app for that. Look, I'm a geocacher. I have an app on my phone that can project a waypoint. You don't even have to give me the phone back. You can do it."

"How?"

"Open up the phone. If the lock screen is on, the code is zero three one six. On the main screen, there's an app called 'Tools'. Go into that. All you need to do is enter the starting coordinates, angle, and distance, and it will calculate the coordinates of where we need to go."

Stan unlocked the screen, found the app, but couldn't figure it out. Instead, he passed the phone back to Drake. "You do it. But I'm going to watch. No funny stuff."

"Right. No funny stuff. Follow me."

Drake returned to the corner of the building where he'd found the brick and held the phone so Stan could watch his every move. He opened the app, selected an option to use his current coordinates, and entered ninety as the angle to represent an eastern heading. "How long do you suppose a pace is?"

Drake looked at Stan for an answer, but Stan didn't know.

"Let's assume a yard. Three feet. Three times two is six, so I'll enter six hundred for the distance." Drake waited for the microsecond it took for the app to do the calculations. When he looked at the screen again, he noticed not only the projected coordinates, but a line to guide him to the location.

"That's where we need to be. Almost to the far end of the island. We need to hurry, though."

"Why?" Stan asked.

"I'm down to four percent charge on my phone. It's going to die soon." Drake winced at the poor choice of words he'd selected. "Come on."

Drake glanced at the app to estimate the general area of the projected location, then started swiftly walking along the shoreline.

"Hey," Stan yelled, "this isn't due east. Where are you going?"

Drake pointed up at the shoreline. "We'll walk along the beach for a few hundred feet and cut over into the trees. It'll save us time and effort without having to pick our way around bushes and whatnot."

They walked four hundred feet up the beach. When he noticed the shore was going to curl around in the opposite direction from where they needed to go, Drake stopped. He got his bearings and pointed into the trees. "We need to head that way. It looks like there's a hill to go up, but it doesn't seem too bad from here."

Drake looked at his battery percentage, and as he did, the number dropped from four to three. He selected a bent over tree fifty feet in the distance as a waymark and headed toward it, paying close attention to his footing as he did. Once he got to the tree, he picked another unique tree and picked his way through the underbrush until he reached it.

Drake checked his app and adjusted his position, so he was facing the direction he needed to go. He realized his battery had dropped to two percent, so he shut it off, hoping he would have enough power to make one phone call for help if he got the chance.

"We need to hike up this little mound," Drake said to Stan. The mound was more of a hill, and a steep one at that as it rose to an apex thirty feet above their heads. Unlike the rolling hills Drake climbed in the area around Nashville, the one before him was primarily rock. There was an intermittent tree or bush that had taken root over time, and Drake eyed their positions for use as potential handholds.

"I'm glad Allie's not here," Drake whispered to himself as the hill reminded him of the one Allie had injured herself on the previous year.

Drake leaned over, and using his hands and his feet, he began his ascent. Remembering Allie's tumble, Drake was careful to make sure that he planted each foot securely before he put weight on it and pushed his way up. The climb up the hill took him eleven minutes, and when he finally arrived at the top, it surprised him to find a large tree a few feet to his left. He walked to the tree and sat down in its shade.

As he waited for Stan to appear, he looked around. The hilltop was crescent-shaped and was forty-five feet at its widest point. He viewed the ocean and two other landmasses, although he didn't know what they were. Drake got back to his feet and looked over the side to check on Stan, hoping he'd fallen down the hill, but he was slowly but surely making progress toward him.

Drake figured he had another couple of minutes, so he hustled to the end of the point and looked out into the distance. From where he was, he barely made out the boat's stern in the distance. He figured it was maybe a quarter of a mile away.

"What are you doing?" Stan shouted.

Drake turned around and noticed Stan getting his second foot up and beneath him.

"Checking the view while waiting for you."

"Fine. I'm here. So now what?"

"The thing said into the maw, so look around for a maw, a hole, or something," Drake said.

Drake held back and watched as Stan walked back and forth across the hilltop. As Stan looked away, Drake glanced down the hill from where he stood. He thought about making his escape from there. When he took a better look, he acknowledged the ten-foot vertical drop to solid stone, so he knew he couldn't go that way. He followed the perimeter and hoped for an area he could scramble down in a hurry, but based on what he saw, the best way down was the way they'd come up.

"Hey, over here," Stan yelled.

Drake glanced in Stan's direction and saw him standing

next to a depression in the stone, and as Drake approached, he saw that the depression opened into a hole.

"Here's your maw," Stan said as he pointed to the hole. "Go check what's in that."

Drake looked at the hole and groaned. It was a rough oval with the center about four feet wide, and he could tell from where he stood it dropped three feet and slanted away into the darkness.

"Go."

"There's no way. I'm not going into that thing," Drake objected.

Stan rolled his eyes, racked the slide of his gun, aimed it close to Drake's feet, and pulled the trigger. The report was loud and there was an audible ricochet off the rock, and Drake jumped back a foot out of instinct.

"Oops," Stan said. "Accident. If you don't want me to have another accident, one that ends up in your chest, I suggest you get in that hole."

Drake stared into Stan's eyes, then when Stan racked the slide again, Drake turned his attention to the hole. He got down on his knees, dropped his head into the gap, and prayed there was nothing in there that didn't like company.

"It's too dark in there. I can't see anything after, like, three feet. We'll have to go back to the boat and check if there's a flashlight aboard."

"Nope. No way," Stan said. "Use the light on your phone."

Drake shook his head. "Sorry, man, no can do. My battery is dead like a doornail. The only way I'm getting light from my phone is if I set it on fire."

"Use mine then," Stan said as he produced his phone. He unlocked the screen and turned on the light, then relocked the screen before he handed it over to Drake.

Drake took the phone, hung his legs over the hole, and

dropped in. He shined the light forward and saw that the sides and ceiling had grooves, like tool marks, in them. Drake also sensed that the tunnel slanted forward for about four feet before it ended. The tunnel was spacious enough for him to duck walk to the end, and when he got there, he found the tunnel didn't end abruptly, but ended in another hole.

Drake shined the light into the hole and saw a small cavern ten feet below him. He thought about turning around and going to get some rope when the light caught a reflection on the wall below him. He leaned into the void and reached the phone out as far as he dared. The light was enough for him to see that there were iron bars embedded in the walls, starting three feet below him and ending a foot or two above the floor.

Drake turned around, got on his belly, and inched backward until his legs dropped over the edge. He flailed his feet until one of them connected with the iron rod, and he put his foot on top of it. Without fully committing, he tested to see if the rung would hold his weight, and when he trusted it would, he went for it and stood. The rod held, so holding on to the tunnel floor for support, he dropped and found the next rung on which to put his other foot. Slowly, he stepped from rung to rung until, finally, his feet hit the stone floor of the cavern.

Once in the cavern, Drake took a better look around. The cavern was almost a perfect circle, and the floor sloped downward to the center of the circle. Drake followed the slope and in the center of the room he found nine holes, each an inch in diameter, drilled into the floor. The floor was completely empty, save for a pile of brown leaves and small sticks near the holes. He left the center and stepped to a wall at random and followed the arc of the circle. Halfway around the circle, he found an area where the arc jutted out slightly from the rest of the wall, overlapping itself. Where the arc stopped was an enormous pile of stones and rubble that stood almost all the way to the ceiling. Drake thought he was at a dead end and was going to leave when he spotted a sideways brick in the stone pile. He cleared away enough rocks to free the brick, and using the light, he saw an imprint of Boston 1775, just like the other he found.

He set the brick aside and got to work clearing away the stones, and after twenty minutes, he'd removed enough to see the debris was concealing a small hallway. Once he opened a hole big enough to pass through, he moved forward, having to shuffle sideways to do so. After twenty feet, the hallway opened into another room.

The room was only twenty-five feet square and six feet high, and bricks, not stone, made up the walls. Each brick had a marking from being made in Boston. He pushed on the wall closest to him, hoping to find a secret door, but the wall was firm. Drake moved to the wall opposite, and pushed on that one, too, but again, nothing budged. He eyed one brick that looked unlike the others, since it had a marking of 'Boston 1775'.

Drake tapped on the brick and found it made a distinct sound from its neighbor. He slid back into the passageway far enough to find a baseball-sized rock, then headed back into the room. Drake located the brick again, then smashed the rock against it. It took three hits before the brick gave way and fell to the floor. Behind where the brick had been Drake discovered a depression. Drake used the phone's flashlight to peek inside, and he saw another piece of hide.

He removed the hide from the hole, unwrapped it, and found a large iron key. He wrapped the key back in the hide, then examined the remaining bricks. On the back wall, Drake discovered four other bricks that weren't like the others and used the rock to break them. Behind each of the broken bricks, he found an indentation, and within the indentation, he found an iron bar. He reached in, pulled on the bar, and a corner of the facade broke away from the wall. Once he pulled all the bars, the bottom part of the wall fell away.

Once the dust settled, Drake looked where the wall had been and found a large wooden chest. He struggled to pull the chest out of the wall and into the room, but with extra effort, he managed the task. Drake found the chest locked but based on the size of the lock hole in the front, Drake guessed he already had the key.

Drake extracted the key from his pocket, slid it into the keyhole, and turned it. At first it wouldn't go, but after a couple minutes of wiggling it back and forth, the key finally turned all the way, and the lock popped open. Drake opened the chest, took a deep breath, and looked inside.

The only item in the chest was a silver snuffbox, a duplicate of the one he had in his pocket. He removed the box from the chest and opened it. Inside the cover were a few engraved words, and inside the box was a silver key, the size of a modern house key. Drake closed the snuffbox and put it in his back pocket, then he removed the key from the chest lock, wrapped it back up in the hide, and stowed that in his front pocket.

He left the room, backtracked to the cavern, and used the iron bars to climb up to the main tunnel. Soon after, he sensed daylight, crawled to the entrance, and poked his head up into the fresh air.

"You've been gone long enough," Stan said. "What did you find?"

"It's down there. The treasure. Loads of it," Drake said.

Stan looked at him, disbelieving.

Drake pulled the snuffbox from his front pocket. "For real. Here. I brought this back." Drake held the box out and Stan greedily grabbed it.

Stan examined the box, then put it in his pocket. "That's

it? Silver?"

Drake shook his head. "No. There's silver and gold. Lots of gold. I only brought that up because it was easy for me to carry."

"Get back in there, then. Show me where it is. I'll follow you."

"No, you can't. There's not enough room. Whoever built this place made sure it would only handle one person at a time. You got it though, all the treasure. All you need to do is go down there and get it."

Drake got out of the hole and took a few steps away to the edge of the hill. Stan took the box from his pocket and marveled at how it reflected the sun.

"Thanks for the help," Stan said. He lifted the gun, and without really aiming, fired a bullet in Drake's direction.

Drake fell over the hill and disappeared. Stan walked over to the edge and looked at Drake's prone, unmoving body, then went back to the hole and entered the way Drake had done.

While hiking in the woods, Drake once came across an opossum. When the possum spotted him, the animal rolled over and played dead, and that was the exact thing Drake was doing. The bullet had come close enough to his face for him to hear the buzz as it passed, and he threw himself over the edge. Although he didn't fall far, landing on the rocks was enough to knock the breath out of his lungs. He wanted to cry out, but he bit his lip and stayed as still as he could, hoping that Stan wouldn't pepper his body with more shots. If he did, Drake knew he was dead for sure.

He felt Stan's shadow fall over him. It hesitated for a few seconds, then Drake felt the warmth of the sun on his back again. Drake waited and slowly counted to ninety, then slowly turned his head and moved slightly so he could glance up the hill. Stan wasn't there, so Drake noiselessly got to his feet and climbed down the hill as silently as he could.

When he got to the bottom, he looked up at the hill to the spot where the point of the crescent was to give him an idea of the boat's direction. He started running as fast as he could through the woods, which wasn't faster than a slow jog. As he ran, the bush and tree branches slapped against his legs and his bare chest, and twice he fell when he wasn't paying attention to his footing. Finally, he broke through the trees and spotted the boat only fifty feet away.

Drake ran toward the boat, then changed direction and made for the spot where he'd left Ingrid. He dropped to his knees, and at first glance, noticed Ingrid hadn't moved a centimeter since he'd left her side.

"Ingrid? Can you hear me?" Drake reached for her neck and exhaled when he found a pulse. It was weak, but it was there. Drake removed the rock from Ingrid's belly and lifted his shirt. When he did, the wound oozed a little, but Drake knew it was time to go. He pushed the shirt back over the wound.

"I'm going to lift you up now."

As gently as he could, Drake lifted Ingrid from the ground and carried her to the jetty. He hesitated for a moment, picked his path with his eyes, then started slowly walking over the uneven rocks to the boat. Once there, he laid Ingrid across the back seat, jumped back onto the jetty to untie the bow line, then got back on the boat. Drake started the engine, reversed away from the island, then put it into gear and pointed the bow toward the mainland.

CHAPTER TWENTY

When he was a few hundred yards away from the island, Drake put the boat in Neutral and checked all the compartments of the boat until he found the first aid kit. From that, he dressed Ingrid's wound with something more than just a dirty T-shirt.

"Ingrid? Are you still with me?" Drake asked as he checked her pulse again. He shook his head and realized he had to get her medical attention as quickly as he could.

Drake pushed the engine as fast as he dared, fearful that the boat bouncing over the waves would throw Ingrid off the seats and onto the deck. As he steered back toward the marina, he tried to use the marine radio to call for help, but since he had never used one before, he quickly gave it up out of frustration.

Drake finally spotted the marina and made for it, and when he felt he was close enough, he pulled his phone from his pocket. The cracked screen made him worry he'd broken it, but when he pressed the power button, the phone came to life. He looked at the battery percentage and grew immediately concerned that he had enough life left in it for only one call. With one hand on the wheel, he called for help.

As Drake came into the marina, he spotted Hailey waiting for them on the dock. When he got close enough to drift, Drake killed the engine. A few seconds later, the boat jarred when it came into contact with the old car tires that acted as bumpers on the dock. He threw the bowline to Hailey, and while she tied off the bow, he opened the side door, left the boat, and tied off the stern line.

"Where's Stan?" Hailey asked as Drake rushed to step back on the boat.

"Where are my friends?" Drake asked in return.

"Where's Stan?" Hailey pulled the gun from her waistband and pointed it at Drake.

Drake stopped and raised his hands in the air. "He's back on the island waiting for you. We found the treasure."

He wondered for a moment if he should rush Hailey, rip the gun from her hands, and give her the same treatment Ingrid had received.

"Why did he send you back?" Hailey asked.

"Stan shot my friend, and as a sign of appreciation, he sent me back with her. He wants you to come back with the boat. All I want is an ambulance. Y'all can have the boat and the treasure. It means nothing to us."

Hailey looked over the edge of the boat and glanced at Ingrid's prone body in the back seat, but she seemed skeptical and wasn't buying a word of it. "Why didn't he call me? He said he would call if he found something."

"The treasure's hidden underground in a cavern. Surrounded by stone. Couldn't make a call from there."

"I think you're lying," she said, point blank.

"No, wait, I can show you." Drake dug into his pocket and removed the hide. He uncovered the key and showed it to Hailey. "He sent me back with this as proof. This is the key that opened a giant chest filled with gold and silver. Let me get my friend medical attention. You take the boat, and that will be the end. We'll go our separate ways from here."

Off in the distance, sirens pierced the mid-afternoon peace.

"Your time is running out, Hailey. That's the police and, hopefully, an ambulance. I called them when we got close to the shore. You still have time to get on the boat and get out of here. Tell me where my friends are and take the boat. For both of our sakes."

Hailey looked in Drake's eyes, then out toward the parking lot, then back at Drake. "Get your friend off my boat."

Drake dropped his arms, then jumped back on the boat. He picked up Ingrid. She moaned but had the strength to put an arm around his neck. By the time Drake stepped off the boat, Hailey was there holding the bow and stern lines and when Drake cleared the door, Hailey got on the boat and closed the door.

"Your friends are in the white van. Keys are in the ignition." Hailey started the engine, shifted into Reverse, and pulled away from the dock.

Drake carried Ingrid to the end of the pier and into the parking lot. Just as he got to the van, two squad cars tore into the lot and stopped in a V-shape behind the van.

The officers erupted from each car and pointed their guns at Drake. "Put down the girl!" one of them screamed at Drake.

Drake complied, kneeled, and placed Ingrid gently on the ground, then dropped to his knees and put his hands behind his head. "I'm the one who called you. There's one getting away on a boat, the one who shot her is on an island out in the bay. I have two more friends locked in this van here. The keys are in it."

While one officer held a gun on Drake, the other placed him in handcuffs, took him away from Ingrid's side, and leaned him over the hood of his squad car. Once Drake was in custody, the other officer called for an ambulance, then crept to the back door of the van and, gun drawn, threw it open. He put his gun back in his holster, unlocked the women from their handcuffs, and helped them out of the van.

Allie saw Ingrid laying on the ground and made a move toward her, but when she put weight on her right leg, she screamed, lost her balance, and fell to the ground.

Geneva watched Allie lying on the ground, writhing in pain as she clutched her knee. She knew she had a decision to make, and neither choice was the correct one. She chose the unconscious friend, ran to Ingrid, dropped to her knees, and put her hands on Ingrid's face. "Ingrid! Ingrid? Drake, what happened to her?"

"Stan shot her," Drake yelled.

Geneva glanced at Drake, handcuffed and sitting on the pavement, his back to the squad car's front tire.

Geneva looked back down at her friend and took Ingrid's hand. "You'll be okay. Help will be here soon. Hang on."

A few seconds later, an ambulance pulled into the parking lot. The EMTs got out and immediately attended to Ingrid, determined she was stable enough for transport, got her on a gurney, and placed her into the ambulance. Once Ingrid was secure, the EMTs came back for Allie and attended to her as well. Within five minutes, two out of four of the friends were on their way to the hospital.

Geneva stepped over to Drake and told the officer holding him about everything that had happened that day. Eventually, the trooper removed the handcuffs from Drake. It took an hour between the two of them to give a statement to the police and have it validated. Finally, the police put a

BOLO out on Stan and Hailey, and Drake and Geneva retreated to the SUV.

Once they were alone, they embraced, each not wanting to let the other go.

"Well, now what?" Geneva asked. "Should we go to the hospital?"

Drake shook his head. "I don't think we have time. Don't you have a concert tonight that you can't miss?"

Geneva checked the clock in the car. "Yes, you're right. I'd forgotten it was Friday today. I don't need to be there for another three hours."

"It might take that long to get Ingrid through surgery, and for Allie to get looked at. We wouldn't be able to visit them before then."

"So, what do you propose?"

"Let's take a quick ride out to Lexington."

"Lexington? Why do you want to go there?"

Drake reached around and took the snuffbox from his back pocket, opened it up, and handed it to Geneva. She took it and looked inside. "Oh, my." She passed the box back to Drake and put the car in gear.

Forty-five minutes later, Geneva pulled her car into an old Lexington cemetery. She followed the road until they found the mausoleum they were looking for. They got out of the car, and as they walked to the entrance, Drake removed the key from the box.

"You don't think this is really going to work, do you?" Geneva asked as Drake put the key in the lock.

Drake attempted to turn the key, but it didn't budge. "I guess not." Dejected, Drake climbed down the three steps and sat down.

Geneva sat by his side and took his hand. "Well, we've had a good run. It's time to give it up. There's been enough blood, sweat, and tears shed over this adventure."

"Yeah. I feel bad for Ingrid. And for Allie. I hope they're going to be okay."

Drake had barely finished the sentence when Geneva's phone rang. She looked at the screen, then took the call. Once it connected, she fumbled with the buttons until she activated the speaker.

"Hello? Are you there?" Allie said from the box.

"Allie? How are you doing?" Drake asked.

"I'm okay. They gave me something for the pain. I'm waiting for x-rays and to see a doctor. I'll probably be here a few hours yet."

"What about Ingrid?" Geneva asked.
"That's why I'm calling. She woke up in the ambulance and told me to give you a message. It's Friday, don't forget about your concert. Then she passed out again."

"Is she okay?" Drake asked.

"I don't know. The last update I got was she was going into surgery, and that was forever ago. I have to go. I'll call back later."

Without saying goodbye, Allie ended the call, leaving Geneva staring at her phone.

"Come on, let's go. We should probably head for the show." Geneva got to her feet and tugged Drake's arm. As he got up, he took one last look at the mausoleum, then took three steps toward the car, and stopped.

"What is it?" Geneva asked.

Drake went back to the mausoleum and kneeled. He ran his fingers along a brick. "Boston, 1775."

"Yeah, so?"

"You wouldn't have a hammer and a chisel in your SUV, would you?"

"No chisel. But I probably have a hammer and a screwdriver in the toolbox in the trunk. Would that do?"

Drake smiled.

Fifteen minutes later, Drake freed the brick from the mausoleum. He turned it over, and a key slid out of the hollow brick. He placed the brick back in the wall, then returned to the mausoleum door. He put the key in the lock, turned it, and unlocked the door.

Inside the mausoleum were two six-sided oak coffins, each one with a silver lock on the front. Geneva took the silver key Drake had given her. She slipped the key into the lock and hesitated.

"I hope there's not a squishy body in here," she said.

"If there is someone in there, they'd just be bones by now. You want to go outside while I do this?" Drake asked.

"No," Geneva said. "I'm good."

Geneva turned the key, unlocked the lock, and together, Geneva and Drake opened the coffin.

Geneva had her eyes closed, and when she opened them, she didn't see a body at all. Instead, she saw several leather pouches. Drake pulled the top one from the pile and carefully opened it. He pulled out the first document and set it on the pouch. Silently, they both read the document for a few moments.

"Holy cow. Is that a letter from George Washington?" Geneva asked.

"Yeah, I believe it is. Allie's going to freak when she sees this."

"Are these bags all filled with correspondence?"

Drake shrugged. "Your guess is as good as mine. The only way to find out is to go through them all."

Drake opened each of the pouches enough to glance inside to see what they contained. Every pouch held documents.

"I don't think we should disturb these. I wouldn't want to destroy anything," Geneva said.

"Yeah, I agree. We need to turn this over to a museum

or something."

"What's in the other coffin?" Geneva asked.

"I don't know. The squishy body you're hoping for?" Drake teased.

Geneva took the key from the coffin and unlocked the other one. When they lifted the lid, they discovered more pouches, but instead of being filled with documents, they found gold, silver, and precious stones.

"Oh, my," Geneva said. "I think we're rich."

"Well, someone is for sure," Drake said. "I'm fairly certain once we call this in, it won't be a case of finders, keepers. I can only imagine that the cemetery or the city will claim ownership."

"You're probably right. Still, we have to call someone about all this, right?"

Drake rubbed his chin. "Yes. This is a treasure that we should share with the country. But not today. We've got a concert to go to. Let's put everything back together and head out."

* * *

"Hey, you," Ingrid said softly.

Allie looked up from the book she was reading. She smiled when she saw Ingrid looking at her, then put the book down and picked her crutches up. Allie maneuvered to Ingrid's bedside and took Ingrid's hand. "Hey yourself. How are you feeling?"

"I'm exhausted. What time is it?"

"It's three in the afternoon on Sunday."

The information confused Ingrid. "Sunday? What happened?"

Allie sat on the bed awkwardly, unable to get her full-leg brace into a suitable position. "You got shot, remember? Drake brought you back. You didn't lose any organs, but you lost a lot of blood. I was so scared when I first saw you. You were so pale."

"I'm a Dane," Ingrid joked weakly.

"You were paler than a Dane should be. They got the bullet out without any problems. You're still getting intravenous fluids and antibiotics. You'll be fine though and should be out of here in a couple of days."

"Do I have a big scar?"

"I don't know. I haven't seen it. It's okay, though. I think scars are sexy."

"Can I have some water?"

Allie got off the bed, found the bed's controls, raised the head of the bed, and pressed the call button. When the nurse answered, Allie requested water for her friend.

"What's up with your leg?" Ingrid asked.

"I whacked it pretty good when I got thrown off the boat. Lucky for me, it's just another terrible sprain, and I won't require surgery, but I won't be out skiing or mountain climbing for a long time."

A nurse entered the room carrying a Styrofoam cup. "Good to see you awake, Ingrid. Do you mind if I check your vitals while I'm here?"

"Go ahead," Ingrid said.

As the nurse gave Ingrid a once-over, Allie stepped back to the chair and sat down. The nurse checked Ingrid's pulse, temperature, respiration, and blood pressure. Afterwards, she checked the fluid levels Ingrid was getting.

"All is good here," the nurse said. She handed Ingrid the cup. "Here are some ice chips for you. Once you get through these, we'll see if we can get you something fancy, like Jell-O or some broth."

"Ooh," Ingrid said, "I can't wait. I hope it's orange."

The nurse smiled, patted Ingrid on the shoulder, then left the room.

"Where are Geneva and Drake? Are they okay?" Ingrid

asked.

"Yeah, they're fine. They're busy cleaning out a crypt." Allie said.

"What?"

"On the island, Drake found a key, and the key led to a cemetery mausoleum. Inside two coffins, they found papers and gold and other stuff dating back to the revolution."

"Wouldn't that all belong to the cemetery?"

"You'd think so, but when they built the mausoleum, the builders wrote a five-hundred-year contract with the cemetery. It stated whoever had the key was the rightful owner of whatever was held within. Drake found that key, which made him the owner." Allie explained.

"That sounds really suspect," Ingrid said.

"I agree. I imagine it's all going to end up in court at some point, but Geneva, Drake, and I all agree that we need to donate most of the stuff to a museum, anyway. If we're lucky, we'll get a nice finder's fee out of it."

Ingrid spooned an ice chip out of the cup and chomped on it. "What happened to Stan and Hailey? Did they get caught?"

"Oh yeah. I almost forgot about them. The story's been all over the news. The Coast Guard picked Hailey up. She didn't know where the island exactly was, so she just did laps in the Atlantic until she eventually ran out of gas. What an idiot. They found Stan in the dark in a cave on the island. I heard when they finally found him, he was crying like a baby. Either way, she's facing charges for kidnapping and theft of the boat, and he's on the hook for kidnapping and attempted murder."

Allie's phone buzzed, so she picked it up to check the message. "Your parents will be back soon. They went out to get a bite to eat."

"My parents are here?"

"Yep. They came in yesterday, remember?"

Ingrid shook her head.

"Yeah, I didn't think so. You were pretty out of it. I really like them. They've been telling me stories about you."

"Oh, no," Ingrid moaned.

"Don't worry. Nothing too embarrassing. I asked them to save that stuff until you were back with us so I could watch your expression as they talked."

"That's evil," Ingrid said.

"I know. I learned it from Drake," Allie said. "Well, I guess that wraps everything up. You're all up to date."

"Just one more question. Where should we go next?" Ingrid asked.

Allie shrugged. "I don't know. How about Rome or Paris like you wanted? We couldn't possibly get into trouble over there."

Ingrid smiled. "Well, we could try."

The Secret of the Seven Valleys

CHAPTER ONE

The elevator bell dinged, the doors slid open, and Drake Decker exited the elevator carrying a cardboard box loaded with white paper bags filled with Chinese takeout food. He navigated the hallway until he at last reached room four hundred and stopped before the door. He attempted to hold the box in a way to allow him to dig the room key from his front pocket, but the bundle was too far off balance for that. Afraid to spill the box and too lazy to set it down on the floor, Drake kicked the door three times.

He waited a few seconds, and at last heard the chain slide away from the door and the security lock disengage. The door opened, and he saw the bright hazel eyes of his girlfriend.

"Sorry, wrong room. We didn't order anything,"

"Come on, let me in, Geneva. This box is getting heavy."

Geneva stepped aside and held the door for Drake. He entered the room and made a beeline for the only table at which two women were overlooking one laptop and taking notes. The blonde noticed his approach, gathered up the papers, and moved them and the computer to a nearby dresser.

Drake set the box on the table, and the three women began extracting the bags from the box. Once it was empty, Drake dropped it on the floor.

The blonde opened a bag, extracted the white cubed container, and opened it. "Who ordered the noodles?"

The redhead half-raised her hand. "I did."

Ingrid passed the Lo Mein and a pair of chopsticks to Allie and selected another bag to open. It didn't take her long to distribute the remaining meals, and soon they all dove into dinner, chopsticks waving wildly, except for Drake, who took the less-traditional route and used a fork.

"This reminds me of Chinatown," Geneva said. "Every time Ingrid and I go to the theater, we stop either after or before the show in this little restaurant on Oxford Street. I love Chinese food."

"Did you gals get far in the planning?" Drake asked before selecting his next piece of honey chicken.

Allie sucked in a noodle, quickly chewed and swallowed. "We're getting there. I wish we'd done more research over the last few months."

"Are you getting stuck on anything I might help with?" Drake asked.

Ingrid shook her head. "Not really. Fortunately, where we're going, there aren't a ton of geocaches to select from. Maybe a hundred in all. We made a first pass and removed anything greater than a terrain rating of four since we don't want to do anything Allie would have trouble with because of her knee."

"My knee is fine," Allie said.

"Then why didn't you want to do that marathon with me?" Ingrid asked.

"Because I couldn't make it out here that weekend, remember? I had that other thing going on. The one I told you about," Allie tried to explain, generating the least lame excuse she could think of.

"I'm surprised she agreed to this trip," Drake said. "She is still wary about steep hills since she wrecked her knee a couple of years ago."

"Drake, I'm not wary. I simply don't bound up and down them like a mountain goat anymore. I like to take my time," Allie countered.

Ingrid shoved her chopsticks into the takeout container and placed it on the table. "Anyway, once we knocked out anything greater than terrain four, that narrowed it down to about fifty."

"That many?" Geneva asked.

Allie nodded. "Apparently, they like the geocaches challenging in the Alps. Now it's simply been a matter of translating the descriptions from Italian to English."

"Are there any puzzle caches?" Drake asked.

Allie grinned. "We're saving those for you since we realize you love figuring those out."

Drake groaned, and his lips formed into a pout. "Really?"

The three women laughed.

"Of course not. Geneva's been working on those," Allie said. "Maybe you would give her a hand after lunch."

Drake produced a grin that would make any sly fox proud. "Of course. I'd love to."

"She meant a hand with the puzzle," Allie clarified.

The women laughed again, and Drake joined in this time.

"We should have gone to Denmark instead," Ingrid said. "I would have translated for you, and we wouldn't have to do all this pre-work. And I could show you the village my parents are from."

"I don't know. I liked the way we came up with this

idea. Everyone submitting three ideas, then picking one at random from a hat seemed the fairest way to select this year's geocaching trip," Geneva said.

Ingrid capitulated. "Okay. I suppose. You've got food on your chin, buddy."

Drake rose and ambled to the mirror. He took a close look and spotted a smudge of orange sauce just below his chin that he wiped away with the back of his hand. He continued his inspection to make sure he was clean, and his hazel eyes drifted to his blond hair. Drake normally kept it in a tight, close cut, but since Geneva liked it longer, he was attempting to grow it out. Instinctively, he patted his belly. Normally, he liked to keep his average build at a hundred and ninety pounds, but he'd ballooned to three pounds heavier over the summer. Satisfied that he looked okay, he returned to the table.

"Did anyone learn how to explain geocaching in Italian?" Drake asked.

"I can barely explain it in English," Ingrid said.

"What do you tell people?" Drake asked.

"That I'm looking for things people have hidden."

"I always compare it to a high-tech scavenger hunt. That seems to help," Allie said. "I only get into the details if people seem interested, but usually that simple explanation works the best for me."

"So does anyone know how to say scavenger hunt in Italian?" Drake asked.

"I learned how to say I don't speak Italian," Geneva said.

Drake thought for a second, then shrugged. "That will work. Everyone done eating?"

No one said otherwise, so Drake and Allie cleared the mess from the table, and Drake gathered it all into the box.

"I'll take this to the garbage outside," he said.

"I got it," Allie offered. She took the box and left the room.

As soon as the door clicked shut, Drake turned to Ingrid. "You're not looking for anything higher than a terrain of three, right? Allie plays off that injury, but she's still having problems with that knee, even though that accident was two years ago."

"Of course. I set the filter at four, since that's what she said, but I've been ignoring every terrain rating more than a three. Most of the ones I've written down are lower than that. I don't enjoy the thought of seeing her in pain either, Drake."

Drake nodded. "Good. I wasn't happy about this location at first. I was hoping we'd pick something flatter, like Florida, but who could have guessed Allie herself would have submitted a challenging place?"

"Why did she do that?" Geneva asked.

"She's always trying to push herself, even though there's nothing for her to prove. So, that said, what do y'all need help with?"

"You could check the equipment. Make sure we're not forgetting anything," Geneva suggested. "While you're doing that, we'll continue with the list and solving any puzzle caches."

Drake nodded. On the dresser were four matching mini backpacks. He gathered them up and carried them to the bed. To get comfortable, he pulled his chair from the table and sat at the bed's edge. Although the backpacks were identical, he could tell who owned which one based on the pins they'd attached to the flap on the front. Allie had a Marine Corps emblem, based on her time in the service. Geneva's pin was a treble clef, which was apropos since she played cello in the symphony and often conducted. Ingrid was a bit more on the nose with a pin of the Danish flag, a field of red with a white Nordic cross. Drake when the obvious route with a geocaching pin and a compass.

Drake heard a knock at the door, and since he was closest, he got up from his seat, opened it, and found Allie standing there.

"I locked myself out," Allie explained.

Drake let her in and returned to the bags while Allie returned to the computer.

Drake opened his bag first and dumped all the contents onto the bed. As he picked items from the pile, he placed them in a neat row. In order, he lined up a handheld GPS, four extra batteries, tweezers, a compact mirror, a mini notebook, a half dozen gel pens with black ink, a small flashlight, a multi-tool, and a compass. He studied the pile for a moment.

"I feel like we're missing something here," he said, looking up from his stash. "Can someone else come take a look?"

Ingrid and Allie seemed focused on the laptop. "I got it," Geneva said. "I'm just looking over shoulders, anyway."

Geneva joined Drake and went through each of the items, pointing at each of the items as she called them out.

"Do you think this is everything?" Drake asked. "After all, it's been four months since we put this list together."

Geneva snapped her fingers, the pop loud enough to get Allie's attention. "You're missing the cache list and the maps. Hopefully Allie and Ingrid will finish the list soon, and we'll pick up the maps when we get to Italy."

Drake scanned the pile again. "I feel like we're not bringing enough."

Geneva shrugged. "This is what we all agreed to. Just the basics, so wouldn't have to haul too much with us."

"It kind of takes me back to when I first started," Drake said. "I'd go out looking for geocaches with only my Garmin and a pen. None of all the fancy things we carry today."

"I started out the same, but I have to admit, I don't know what I'd do without some of these things."

Geneva picked the mirror off the bed and opened it. "Do you know how many times I've almost blindly put my hand into a spider's web or a hornet's nest and this simple thing saved me from a nasty bite or worse? I also never go out geocaching anymore without a pair of tweezers in my pocket. So much better than trying to use a small stick to extract a stuck log from a container. Honestly, if it were just me, I'd just take these two things and leave the rest."

"Same," Drake said. "But Allie insisted we all have a multi-tool, a compass, and a flashlight with us."

"And you'll be glad you do if you get lost in the woods again," Allie said, peeking over the laptop.

Drake rolled his eyes. "It was only the one time. One!"

"Yeah. For six hours."

"I made it back eventually," Drake said in his own defense.

Geneva glanced at Allie and raised an eyebrow. "Is that true?"

Allie grinned. "That's his story to tell, not mine. Go ahead, Drake, you've got the floor."

Everyone's attention turned to Drake, and when he'd had enough of the uncomfortable silence, he broke it.

"Okay, so I wandered around for a while. I made it to a clearing, climbed over a fence, and found myself in a pasture. Then I found a kind farmer, and his wife gave me a ride to the trailhead."

"You left a couple things out there, Duck-man. Care to fill in the blanks, or shall I?" Allie said.

Drake's cheeks reddened. "Okay, okay. So, I climbed over the fence and made it halfway across the pasture when I spotted a bull with a full head of steam running toward me. Seeing that rampaging beast, I took off like a shot and ran as fast as I could toward the barn I'd spotted. I was about at the gate when I slipped on a fresh bull patty, spun around, and caught the butt of my jeans on the barbed wire fence. I heard someone call out and when I turned around to face the angry farmer who was in the middle of accusing me of stealing his prize bull, I ripped the seat from my jeans."

Geneva, while listening to the story, attempted to appear supportive, but couldn't hold her laughter anymore and it came gushing out. Ingrid and Allie joined in as well, and Drake didn't think it was funny at all.

Geneva wiped the tears from her eyes and stopped laughing long enough to press him to finish the story.

"Well, the farmer opened the gate for me, and walked me to the farmhouse with my torn jeans and my butt exposed to the world. He wanted to call the sheriff and have me arrested for trespassing, but lucky for me, his wife was a kind soul and offered to give me a ride off the property."

The women laughed again and kept at it until the titters finally died down.

"And that's why we'll carry the compass and the other stuff," Allie inserted.

"Yeah, yeah. I got you," Drake said as he shoved the items back into his bag.

After he returned the items to his bag, Drake grabbed the next one in line, which turned out to be Ingrid's. Besides the same items as were in his, she also carried hand sanitizer, lotion, lip balm, and eyeliner. He checked out Allie's bag next, and in hers he discovered a baseball cap and a Garmin for their rental car. Geneva's bag contained the same items as Drake, except she also had a small sandwich baggie filled with euros.

"What about other gear? Shouldn't we have packed for cold weather? Boots, gloves, that sort of thing?" Drake asked.

"No need," Geneva answered. "I checked the local

weather for everywhere we intend on visiting in the next few days, and all the snow is gone for the year, and they expect the temperatures to be warm for our entire visit."

Drake shrugged. "Okay. If you say so, I'm not going to worry about it. Are you two finished with the plan yet?"

"Almost," Ingrid said. "Hold your horses."

"I can't. I'm too excited. You know I've never been to Italy before," Drake said.

"No big deal," Geneva said. "It's just like going to Pennsylvania, except the pasta is better."

"Pennsylvania?" Drake asked. "Really?"

Geneva winked at him, then gave him a kiss on the forehead. "You're so gullible. One of the many things I love about you."

"Here's what we have," Allie said. "Tomorrow, we fly to Milan, then pick up our rental and head to Como. The following morning, we can grab a couple of local caches in Como, then head up into the mountains for the good stuff."

"Why can't we start caching right away," Drake said. "Why waste an entire day?"

"Because we don't land in Milan until almost nine at night," Ingrid said. "And then there's the long drive. I'm sure we'll all be dead tired and ready for bed by the time we get to Como. If you really feel the need to find a geocache, there seems to be an easy one only three blocks from the hotel."

Drake leaned over and took Geneva's hand in his. "I'm really looking forward to taking this trip with you. I had hoped for something more romantic, like Paris or Rome, but I'm sure this will be a great experience for us."

"Come on, Drake, what could be more romantic than the two of us together in the beauty of the Italian Alps?"

Ingrid coughed to get their attention. "Other than your best friends along for the ride? Right Allie?"

Allie smiled. "Who's saying that those two aren't going

to spoil our romantic vacation? I've always wanted to visit the Alps. I hope we'll have time to do some sightseeing too. Catch a few museums, or some art galleries?"

"I may have accidentally researched a few of those. Along with a romantic boat tour for two on Lake Como," Ingrid said.

"Don't you mean romantic boat tour for four?" Drake asked.

Ingrid smiled. "Sorry. From what I understand, it's a small boat."

Geneva laughed. "We'll just have to find a way to amuse ourselves while they're gone, Drake."

Drake kissed the back of Geneva's hand. "I think that's doable." His voice turned serious. "Have you thought about what we talked about? You moving to Nashville to be with me?"

"To be honest, I haven't had much of a chance to mull it over. I've been so busy with planning the new season of the symphony. It would be a tremendous change for me, Drake. Moving from Boston to Nashville. What would I do there? Does Nashville even have a symphony?"

Drake shrugged. "We've got an Opry. That's pretty much the same."

"Drake Decker, that's nowhere near the same thing," Allie scolded. "And to answer your question, Geneva, Nashville, has an excellent symphony orchestra. To be honest, if you're considering his offer, you should come visit us for a while, see how you'd like the small-town vibes."

"Nashville is hardly a small town," Geneva said.

"True, but neither of us live right in the city. I'm about twenty minutes out. Drake's probably thirty-five, depending on traffic. I think you'd like it. There's a more laid-back way of life, plenty of places to park, and people don't lean on their car horns."

It was Ingrid's turn to get angry. "So, what, you two would take my best friend from me and leave me here all alone in this metropolis?"

"Of course not, dear. I've already cleared some space for you in my house," Allie said. "You can have the guest room. It has its own bathroom, an empty closet, and my granddaddy's dresser just waiting for your things."

Ingrid pouted again. "So, you'd just shove me in the guest room, like a common…guest?"

"No. I said I had plenty of room for your things in the guest room," Allie answered.

"This is getting much too sappy for my tastes," Drake said. "Perhaps we should save all the big life-changing decisions for after this trip. After all, I've heard that you don't really get to know a person until you've traveled internationally with them."

Geneva raised her eyebrow, not buying a word. "Is that even true?"

"I don't know. It could be. Either way, we should all get some rest. It's a long flight and a busy day tomorrow."

CHAPTER TWO

By the time the group arrived at their small boutique hotel in Como, checked in, and found their rooms, the clock showed just after midnight. Geneva, Ingrid, and Allie had all managed to stay awake for the entire flight and were ready for bed. Drake, on the other hand, had slept on and off, lulled to sleep by the constant drone of the airplane's engine. Used to only seven hours of sleep a night, he was all ready to start the day.

"What's up with you?" Geneva asked as she slipped into bed and covered herself with a blanket.

"I'm too pumped up. I'm going out for a walk," Drake said.

"Hold on, I'll come with you."

Drake wanted to argue, but Geneva held up her open hand to stop him. She folded the covers back, got out of bed, and dressed within five minutes. Together, they slipped from the room and quietly left the small hotel.

The chill of the early morning air assaulted the couple as they stepped away from the entrance and walked along the ancient sidewalk. Drake reached out for Geneva's hand. It felt warm and inviting in his hand.

"Where are we headed? To find that geocache Ingrid mentioned?" Geneva asked.

Drake considered it for a moment, then sensed a shiver from Geneva. "No. Let's just go around the block. I'll get a little fresh air, then we'll head back."

Geneva nodded. "It's a little nippy out here. I should have brought a warmer coat."

Drake drew Geneva closer to him, hoping some of his body heat would transfer to her, but her shiver said otherwise. He stopped when they got to the corner of the block.

Drake faked a shiver of his own. "Come on, let's go back. I've had enough for tonight, and I'm more tired than I thought I was."

Geneva didn't argue and turned around without another word.

"What are you doing out here?" Drake asked.

"You said you needed to take a walk."

"I did. That explains what I'm doing out here. What are you doing out here?"

Geneva squeezed his hand. "Just thought I'd come along and make sure you stay out of trouble. You know I can't leave you alone. Who knows what trouble you'd get into on your own? Are you good? I'm freezing out here."

Without answering, Drake upped his speed and soon they arrived back at the hotel. Once back in the room, it took Geneva less than two minutes to change out of her clothes and slip back into bed.

Drake took his time going through his before bed ritual, shut off the light, and slipped between the sheets. He put an arm over Geneva and moved close to her.

"Are you awake?" Drake whispered. Beneath his arm,

Geneva's rhythmic breathing never fluctuated, and she started to snore softly. Drake moved a little closer to her and kissed her shoulder. "I can't imagine my life without you. You are the only one I'll ever love."

Allie and Ingrid were already in the breakfast room chatting away while eating Frosted Flakes and toast when Drake and Geneva entered.

"Y'all sleep well?" Allie asked as the couple took seats at the table.

"I slept like a rock, and I'm certainly ready to go today," Geneva answered. "Well, I need some coffee, and then I'll be ready."

Ingrid raised her spoon and pointed it toward the back wall. "It's a serve yourself situation. They have cereal, breads, yogurt, and fruit back there."

"You stay here. I'll get you some coffee. You want any food?" Drake asked.

"A bowl of cereal would be good enough, and the coffee, of course. With milk and sugar," Geneva answered.

"I'll take a banana if they have one over there," Allie added.

Drake left the table and headed to the breakfast bar.

"What's going on with him?" Allie asked once he'd gotten out of earshot.

"Why?"

"He's being overly…nice. I mean, he's a good guy, but I've never seen him offer to bring anyone breakfast before."

"Shh. He's returning," Ingrid warned.

Drake placed a small tray on the table overloaded with two bowls of cereal, a mug of steaming coffee, two slices of toast, and a bowl of assorted fruit. He unloaded the tray, returned it to the breakfast nook, and rejoined his friends at the table.

"Are you happy to see me?" Allie asked.

"What?" The question confused Drake, but then he got it. He extracted the banana from his pocket and handed it over.

"I guess not," Allie said as she took the fruit and peeled it open.

Geneva picked up the coffee and cradled the hot mug in her hands. She inhaled the potent brew, then blew on the liquid to cool it before attempting to take a sip. "My, this is good. Nice and strong. What's on the agenda for today?"

"Not much. Exploring the town, finding some caches, hitting up a couple of museums, and a sunset lake tour," Ingrid said.

"Sounds like a full day," Geneva said.

"What do we have for geocaches?" Drake asked.

"There's that one near here, if you didn't already find it. There's a virtual cache, a mystery, and two multi-caches nearby," Ingrid answered.

"That's it? Only five?"

"For today. Those are the ones that are easily walkable from here. There are plenty of others if we wanted to get in the car and leave town, but we thought it would give us a good taste of what we're in for."

"Are you done with that banana?" Drake asked Allie.

Allie nodded and handed over the half she hadn't eaten. Drake unpeeled the rest and sliced off half-dollar sized sections and let them drop into his cereal. Allie and Ingrid had finished eating and engaged in small talk while Drake and Geneva finished their breakfast. Thirty minutes later, they all stepped into the early morning Italian sun.

"I'll take point," Drake said as he pulled his phone from his pocket and opened his geocaching app. "Closest one is the traditional. It's only a few blocks from here."

Drake led the group along the main road for two blocks, then turned onto a side street.

"Is this right? It looks like an alley," Ingrid said.

Drake checked his app, spun in a circle to make sure he stood in the correct spot, and nodded. "Yep. This is it, the street we need. And notice a half a block down, there's a sign for a shop."

The friends continued up the narrow passageway. The one-way, brick lined lane was just wide enough for two cars, including a parking lane. As they walked, a friendly honk from a passing Fiat encouraged them to stop and move to the side as the vehicle passed.

"How far to the geocache?" Ingrid asked.

Drake stopped, checked the app, and watched as the numbers jumped from three feet, all the way to one hundred, and went back down again. "I'm not sure. There's too much interference from the buildings here. I can't get a good satellite fix."

Geneva looked up and saw the buildings in the lane stood at a minimum of three stories, and most times four, which would easily affect reception.

"Is there a hint?" Geneva asked.

Drake found the info. "Yes. But it's in Italian. Hold on, I'll translate it. Okay. The hint is 'it's piped in'."

"That's not a lot to go on," Ingrid said.

Drake shrugged. "That's all there is. Why don't you two take that side of the street, and we'll take this side?"

Allie and Ingrid stepped ten feet across the lane and started their search. The buildings along the lane shared common walls, making it appear as if a single structure spanned the entire length of the block. Other than doorways and windows, there seemed no place to hide a geocache of any size.

While Drake, Ingrid, and Geneva checked the metal grilles attached to windows for tiny nano containers, Allie strolled up the street, apparently not searching at all. She spotted a metal conduit that ran along the side of a building from the ground to the second floor, stepped off to the side, and found her quarry.

"It's over here."

Allie pulled the small magnetic key holder from behind the pipe, opened it, and retrieved a piece of paper from inside. She added her geocaching nickname just below the last name on the sheet. Allie passed the log to Geneva, the first one to reach her, and waited. Once Drake and Ingrid added their names as well, Allie put everything back together and replaced the geocache where she found it.

"That was easy. What's next?" Allie asked.

Drake glanced at his app. "The virtual and one of the multi-caches are about equidistant from here. Any suggestions?"

"Let's do the virtual," Ingrid said.

"Okay. Let's go."

Drake led the group from the lane, through the streets, and to the Basilica di San Fedele.

"It's beautiful," Allie said when they arrived at the site.

"According to the geocache description, they built it in the late eleven-hundreds," Drake said.

"It's a virtual?" Ingrid asked. "What do we need to get credit for this cache?"

"This is a pretty easy one. There's a door with a dragon on it somewhere here, and we only need to take a selfie with the dragon."

"That's not too bad," Geneva said. "I like those better than answering questions."

"You know where the door is?" Ingrid asked.

Drake shrugged. "Somewhere along the perimeter of this church."

"Can I go inside and look around? Y'all can look for the door while I take a quick peek at the interior, okay?" Allie

said.

"Fine by me," Drake said. "The rest of us will find the door, and you come find us when you're done inside."

"Anyone else want to come?" Allie asked.

"I will," Geneva said.

Allie and Geneva walked through the main door and did a quick tour of the chapels inside before approaching the main altar. Allie took a seat in a pew, and Geneva slid in next to her. From her seat, Allie looked around, and enjoyed the views of the frescoes painted on the ceiling above her.

"I really love stuff like this," Allie whispered.

"I didn't know you were religious," Geneva said.

"No. I'm not. But I can still appreciate the artwork and the architecture, right?"

Geneva nodded. "Can you imagine getting married in a place like this? Headed down that aisle with an organ the size of a house playing. With a white dress, a full bouquet of roses, and a train the length of a bedspread."

Allie dropped her gaze and met Geneva's eyes. "Not really. If it ever happens to me, I'd prefer a simple, outdoor wedding. Sounds like this is something you'd go for, though."

Geneva smiled. "Perhaps not this extravagant. But doesn't every woman have the dream of living like a princess on her wedding day and be the center of attention?"

"Center of attention? Now you really talked me out of it," Allie said. "But I'm sure someday your dream will come. Now, let's go find Drake and Ingrid before they move on to the next cache without us."

Allie and Geneva left the church and walked halfway around the perimeter, where they finally caught up with the others.

"It's right over there. Stand by the dragon and I'll take your picture," Drake said.

Allie and Geneva stood on either side of the carving and gave their best smiles as Drake clicked off a couple of photos.

"Did you log it yet?" Geneva asked.

"We did. I'll send you the pic so you can," Drake said.

While Allie and Geneva logged the geocache as found, Drake looked up the next nearest cache and read through the description.

"What's next?" Allie asked.

"It's a four-step multi-cache," Drake said. "The first waypoint is about four-tenths of a mile from here. Should we do that one or look for something less involved?"

Ingrid, Allie, and Geneva huddled together and had a quick discussion without Drake, and after forty seconds, they broke ranks and gave Drake the answer.

"Lead the way," Geneva said.

Drake took Geneva's hand, and the four friends stepped into the street, and soon they made their way along Via Bernadino Luini. The pedestrian traffic had picked up, and they had to navigate around the throngs of people stepping into markets and restaurants. Since the group wasn't in any great hurry, they took their time on the brick-inlaid street and enjoyed the smells emitted from bakeries and stopped occasionally to window shop.

Drake led them straight when the street name changed to Via Pietro Boldoni, and after twenty minutes and a couple of direction changes, the closed in feeling of the cramped streets disappeared when the friends stepped into a piazza. In the center of the square stood a tall, white statue of Alessandro Volta, and Drake guided the group right to it.

"What do we need?" Allie asked.

Drake read the description, then lifted his head, and looked at the giant marble monument. "We need twelve numbers that make up the date and perform some math to come up with the coordinates for the first stage."

Geneva scratched her nose. "Doesn't sound too hard, although I'm not sure how we find twelve numbers for one date."

Ingrid took the initiative and circled the statue. Two minutes later, she returned to the group with her notebook in hand. "Found it. There are twelve numbers because it's in Roman numerals. I jotted them down."

Ingrid passed her pad to Drake, and he passed his phone to Allie. As Allie read what he needed to do to determine the new coordinates, Drake worked on the numbers.

"Got it!" Drake announced.

"Good, let's go," Ingrid said.

"Nope. Hold on just a second. Read me those coordinates, Drake," Allie said. "I'll map them out and see where they lead. If stage two is too far away, we may want to skip it or come back to this one when we're out in the car."

Drake read off the numbers, and Allie mapped it on her phone.

"Yeah. I think you may have made an error there, Duckman," Allie said once she'd seen the results of her plotting.

Drake frowned. "Why?"

Allie turned her phone around. "Because the coordinates you just gave me are somewhere in the Adriatic Sea off the coast of Croatia. Geneva, would you mind?"

Geneva took the pad from Drake and Allie repeated her directions. Within a minute, they had a solution that took them only a quarter mile away. Allie input the waypoint into the phone and handed it back to Drake.

The group took off, and Drake led them from the monument north to Lake Como, then traveled along the lakefront until they reached the European Resistance Monument. While Allie stopped to explore the monument, the remainder of the group found a sign near the marina with the two sets of years they needed for the next step.

"Geneva, if you don't mind, why don't I read the description and tell you what you need to do to get the next waypoint?" Drake said.

Geneva pulled out the notebook and got her pen ready. While listening to Drake, she compared his instructions with the sign and soon had the next set of coordinates ready. Drake entered them into his app and projected the waypoint which wasn't far away.

"How was it?" Ingrid asked, noticing that Allie had returned to them.

"Both amazing and sad at the same time," Allie said. "They have stones from concentration camps and Hiroshima. There are also metal plates inscribed with excerpts of letters written by people sentenced to death during the war. Can you imagine how horrible that must have been?" Allie's words trailed off, and she sniffed twice to hold back the tears. She cleared her throat and spoke again. "Did y'all figure out where to go next?"

"Yep. A tenth of a mile that way," Drake said, pointing toward an enormous park.

Drake took Geneva's hand, and the pair walked ahead of Ingrid and Allie.

"Are you doing okay, Allie?" Ingrid asked.

"Me, sure. Sometimes when I visit places like this, I get too wrapped up in imagining what life must have been like. Then I get trapped in my thoughts. I'm sure that's seems silly to you."

"It's not silly to me. Did you forget my family is from Denmark? Although the country tried to stay neutral during the war, the Germans still occupied my country, and they killed many Danes," Ingrid said.

"I'm sorry. That must have been horrible for your family." Allie moved closer and took Ingrid's arm in hers.

"It was. Although I asked many times, my grandparents never spoke of it. Both claimed they were too young to remember that war, but when I would stay with them during the summer, friends of theirs would visit and I'd overhear the stories they told."

"I hope something as terrible as that war never happens again," Allie said.

"Me too. I think I know where we're headed."

"Where?"

Ingrid pointed off in the distance. Allie looked forward and spotted an old black locomotive sitting on a small section of track.

"You're probably right," Allie said.

The pair had fallen behind Geneva and Drake, and by the time they got to the train, Drake was searching for something while Geneva waited for the women.

"What's he up to?" Allie asked.

"He's looking for a plate with a date on it," Geneva said.

"I found it," Drake said. "It was on the back. Here."

Drake handed the pad to Geneva, then read off what Geneva needed to do to get the coordinates. Once she double-checked her work, she gave the numbers to Drake, and soon the party was back on the move.

They followed the stone path through the park until they came to an area where several concrete columns stood.

"Okay, everyone spread out," Drake said when they arrived at ground zero. Near the columns stood several large trees, a sign directing people to the restrooms, and a half dozen green park benches.

Geneva headed straight for the sign. Drake and Allie started inspecting the trees, and Ingrid made for the nearest bench. There, she slipped her Converse from her right foot, picked up the shoe, and examined the inside until she at last found the item that had annoyed her foot for most of the day.

"Where did you come from?" she asked the toothpick-sized stick that had hitched a ride with her. She tossed the stick away, then ran her fingers inside her shoe to ensure she'd gotten everything. Satisfied, she replaced the shoe. By sure happenstance, she looked down and noticed one bolt securing the bench to the ground didn't look the same as the others. She bent, inspected the odd one, and discovered she had found the cache, a tiny magnetic container the approximate size of her fingertip.

"Got it," she yelled to the others.

Ingrid remained where she was as the others joined her. "It's a nano," she said, holding the dark green cache between her forefinger and thumb.

"Nice job. How in the world did you find that?" Geneva asked.

Ingrid shrugged. "Either luck or skill, so I'm going with skill."

CHAPTER THREE

Drake heard a knock on the door and quickly finished tying his shoe before he answered it. Allie stood on the other side, smiling at him.

"Y'all ready to go?" she asked.

"Sure thing," Drake said. "I'll grab Geneva."

"Get a jacket, too. It might be chilly," Allie said. "We'll meet you outside, okay?"

Drake nodded and closed the door. He grabbed his jacket from the closet, and Geneva's as well, and he waited patiently for her to exit the tiny bathroom.

"Do I look okay?" Geneva asked.

"Like an angel. Come on, the others are waiting for us."

Drake helped Geneva into her coat and held the door as she passed through. As they left the hotel, Drake spotted Allie standing next to a car.

"What's this?" Drake asked.

"It's a taxi, silly."

"No, I meant why don't we take our rental?"

"Ingrid's idea. She didn't want us to drink too much at dinner and have to drive back. Besides, they have little parking at the restaurant."

Drake didn't argue. Instead, he and Geneva slid into the vehicle where Ingrid sat waiting for them. Allie got in next to the driver, and the cab pulled away from the hotel. It was a fast ride, and a few short minutes later, the taxi pulled over and let the group out at the marina.

"What's this?" Geneva asked.

"Dinner. Let's go. I've been looking forward to this all day," Ingrid answered.

The group walked to the end of the pier, where a hostess graciously greeted them and escorted them to a table next to a wide window on the port side of the boat.

"Is this your romantic cruise?" Geneva asked.

"Yep," Allie answered.

"You said there was only room for two on the boat," Drake said.

Allie grinned. "Did I? I misspoke. I meant there was only space for two on this side of the table. And room for two on that side."

Drake rolled his eyes and shook his head. He looked out the window. His eyes focused on a fishing boat coming in for the evening, the people on board waving as they passed the boat he was on.

"Drake, he asked you a question," Geneva said, tapping him on the shoulder.

Drake's view moved from the lake water lapping gently against the hull to the server standing next to the table.

"I'm so sorry," Drake apologized.

"Could I offer you some champagne, sir?"

"Yes, please. And I apologize, I didn't catch your name."

"It is Luca, sir."

Luca nodded once and left the table and returned two minutes later. From his tray, he handed out glasses of champagne to everyone except Allie, who received a glass of lemonade.

"Here's a toast to great friends and a great vacation!" Ingrid said, raising her glass.

The friends clinked glasses, and each took a sip.

"This is your aperitivo course," Luca said when he dropped off several small dishes filled with green and red olives, nuts, and cheese.

The friends dug in, except for Ingrid, who selected a single cube of cheese from the dish.

"Not hungry?" Allie asked.

Ingrid finished the cheese. "I'm famished. I'm waiting for the good stuff."

From the bridge, a horn tooted and a minute later, the boat pulled away from the dock and headed toward the center of the channel. The friends stared out the window as the boat cleared the marina, then followed the shoreline.

The view outside the window was rich in color. Lake Como contained deep blue water, with white wisps of spray that sprung up as the bow cut across the gentle waves. The majestic mountains wore the deep green coat of late spring, the trees awake after a long winter's rest. On the lowest quarter of the hills nearest the shore, Drake spotted small towns, and higher in the hills, an occasional large villa stood sentry over the water. All the buildings had a similar manner to them regardless of size or purpose, done in shades of white or beige, with roofs of red brown that reminded him of terracotta. Above them, the only mark in the bright blue sky was the white contrail of a passing plane.

After fifteen minutes of small talk, Luca returned and cleared away the empty dishes. He returned with fresh plates for the table, and after everyone had one, he brought out the next course.

"What is it?" Ingrid asked as Luca served.

"This is the antipasti course. I present to you a crostino, topped with sausage and stracchino cheese."

"I've never heard of that cheese," Allie said.

Luca smiled. "It's made from whole cow's milk and is like mozzarella or ricotta. It is fresh and used no more than three days after it's made. Please, enjoy."

Drake, Ingrid, and Geneva waited and observed as Allie picked up the bread, sniffed it, and took a bite.

Allie moaned, chewed, and swallowed. "Oh, my, that's delicious. I'm a fan. I wonder if we can get that cheese in Nashville."

"If we can't, I'm sure we can ship it in from somewhere," Drake said.

"Excellent. Now stop scrutinizing me. You're making me self-conscious," Allie said just before taking another bite.

The rest of the group ate, and all agreed with Allie that the newly discovered cheese was a keeper. Once they'd finished, Luca returned and replaced the dirty plates with clean ones.

"I wonder what's next," Drake said.

"The *primo piatto*. The first course, sir," Luca answered as he removed the empty glasses. "We normally serve it with a Pinot Grigio, unless you'd prefer something else."

"First course? We've already had two," Drake said.

Luca smiled. "No, sir, consider those pre-courses."

"Could I have some water, please?" Allie asked.

"Of course. Gas or no gas?"

Allie thought for half a second. "No gas, please."

Luca nodded, then left the table.

"Gas or no gas?" Drake asked.

Allie laughed. "Even I knew that one. He was asking if I wanted still or carbonated water. I don't like the bubbles in water, so I asked for still. Like plain tap water."

Luca returned a moment later and served the beverages

and made another trip and passed out the next course. "I serve to you potato gnocchi, with a pesto."

Drake glanced at the tiny, pillow-shaped pasta in his bowl. "I'm not typically a fan of pesto," he said, stabbing a sample and eating it. "However, this I'm a fan of."

"It's probably freshly made, and not the jarred stuff from the supermarket," Geneva said.

Drake nodded, and with enthusiasm, cleared the remainder of the gnocchi from his bowl in short order. He downed half of his wine, then wiped his mouth with his napkin.

"That was excellent. I wonder what's next," Drake said.

"I don't know, but I can't wait to find out," Geneva said.

Luca returned and acknowledged the empty dishes and gathered them. "We serve the next dish with a Chianti. May I recommend that for you?"

Drake glanced around the table and saw no dissents from Geneva or Ingrid. "Of course."

He drained the last of the wine and set the glass close to the table's edge for easy retrieval.

Luca left with the dirty dishes and silverware and returned with the wine, and a refreshed glass of water for Allie, and then he appeared with a platter, and as he passed out the plates, he explained the dish. "I present a veal osso buco, served over a bed of mashed potatoes, served with carrots, celery, and onions." Once everyone received a plate, he returned with a small basket of Italian bread, which he placed in the center of the table before he retreated.

Drake searched the table. "He forgot the butter."

Ingrid laughed. "The bread is for the marrow. Watch." Ingrid fished a slice of bread from the basket. Then, with her knife, she removed a bit of marrow from the veal bone's center. She spread it over the bread, then took a bite. "Oh my. I haven't had that in so long I'd forgotten how good it is."

Drake watched as Ingrid finished the treat, then repeated what he'd seen her do. He bit into the bread, then made a sour face, and set the bread next to his plate. "Nope. Not for me."

Ingrid shrugged. "It's an acquired taste."

"I hope we don't eat like this over the entire trip. I'd have to buy new pants," Geneva said as she cut off a slice of veal.

"That's why I brought two pairs of sweatpants along. So that I can eat all I want and not worry about it," Drake said.

"Excellent, I'll borrow a pair," Geneva said.

The conversation remained light as the four ate the main meal, and in the end, nothing remained on any of the four plates except the veal bones and the celery sections that Ingrid skipped.

Drake noticed and smiled. "You'll eat bone marrow, but not celery?"

Ingrid shook her head. "It's a texture thing. I don't like the little strings that break off. They always get stuck in my teeth."

"All is well here?" Luca said as he appeared to clear away the plates.

"That was the best thing I've ever eaten," Allie said. "I don't think I'll eat for days after this."

Luca grinned. "You mean after this entire meal is complete, correct?"

"Wait, what?" Allie said.

"I'll be right back."

Luca left, then returned in short order, and placed a white ceramic tray filled with fruit and cheese on the table.

"What's this?" Ingrid asked.

"The cheese and fruit course. With this, I will serve you a crisp, white wine. My personal favorite, okay?" Luca said.

"Okay," Ingrid said.

"How much more can there possibly be?" Geneva asked.

"Only three more courses to go. A nice panna cotta for dessert, then a coffee service, and finally, a fresh limoncello, which I recommend you take on the deck as you watch the sunset."

By the time the friends finished dinner, pushed away from the table, and made it to the boat's open air upper deck, the sun started to descend. The bright blue sky from earlier in the day faded as the sun did, replaced by hues of peach and lavender.

The captain turned the boat, so it faced west, back toward Como, and pulled back the throttle so they barely moved. A breeze, light as a dandelion wish, traveled through the sky.

The four friends sat on benches at the bow. Below them, the boat lazily cut through the water.

"Check those out over there," Geneva said, pointing off toward the north.

The friends watched as a dozen ducks swooped in mere feet over the boat and landed in the water not far away.

Drake draped his arm over Geneva's shoulder. "This is beautiful, isn't it?"

"Magical is more like it," Geneva whispered. "Did you know about this dinner cruise and not tell me?"

"Nope. This was all Allie and Ingrid's doing. I'm just as surprised that you are."

The boat engines hummed a little louder, and the captain picked up enough speed to adjust the vessel, so the bow pointed directly at the setting sun. From their position, they got the illusion that the orange ball headed directly into the lake, right in the valley's midpoint where the opposing mountains met.

The sky had shifted from the lighter hues, chased by

darker blues and purples as the sun descended.

Drake looked toward the shore. The green of the trees was gone, replaced by black of the encroaching night, and across the land, dots of lights appeared upon the shore like the bulbs on a Christmas tree. Even the sounds of daytime seemed to silence as the darkness draped over the lake.

The sun touched the far end of the lake, appearing to dip its first rays into the water, like a hesitant swimmer dipping in a toe to test the temperature of a pool.

As the sun dipped farther into the lake and the sky darkened, the stars emerged, one by one. They looked dim at first, but as the night encroached, they grew brighter, as if someone turned a knob to increase the power.

"Look at those stars," Allie said. "I've never seen the Big Dipper so pronounced."

"Me neither," Ingrid said. "Those stars seem like diamonds pressed into black velvet."

The captain engaged the engines just a bit, and the boat continued its leisurely journey toward the sun, which was half-gone, looking more like an animation than an actual event.

Drake watched as Geneva closed her eyes. "This is no time for a nap," he teased.

"I wouldn't think of it. I'm taking in the serenity of this perfect moment. The cool wind on my cheeks, the scent of the lake, the feel of the rocking boat. Try it."

Drake closed his eyes as well, and experienced all that and, as an added pleasure, the warmth of Geneva's body as they sat hip to hip.

The sun at last took her last gasp of air and dipped beneath the water before them.

"That was amazing," Allie said. "I'm so happy we did this."

Ingrid, Geneva, and Drake all agreed with the

sentiment.

"I'm getting chilly," Geneva said. "Should we go back inside?"

"Let's stay a couple more minutes and look at that," Drake said.

"What?"

Drake pointed to Geneva's left. To the south, the moon was starting to spring up from behind the mountain.

"Okay, we can stay a bit longer," Geneva agreed.

"Eh, I've seen the moon before," Allie said, waving her hand as if she could swat it from the sky. She stood and reached for Ingrid's hand. "Come on, Ingrid. Let's go see if they have any hot chocolate, or at the least, any more of that limoncello."

Ingrid took Allie's hand and Drake turned and watched them head for the stairs.

"I thought Allie didn't drink," Geneva said.

"She's not opposed to it," Drake said. "She just doesn't like to go overboard with it. Why, I don't know. It's a story she's yet to tell me, and I've known her forever."

"At least we always have a dependable designated driver," Geneva said.

"Oh, don't ever call her that. She's happy to do it, but she doesn't like the stigma of being a stick in the mud that comes with it."

"Have you ever seen the moon so bright?" Geneva asked.

Drake took a good, long look. The orb had risen above the shadows of the mountain and glowed brightly in the sky. It looked close enough to touch, and he easily appreciated the different shades of whites, grays, and blacks across its surface.

"No, I don't think I have," Drake said. "Are you still cold?"

"A bit, but I don't mind."

"Let's get downstairs. No sense getting a case of pneumonia the first full day of vacation."

Drake found his feet, and helped Geneva to hers, and together, they made their way to the lower level, where they found Allie and Ingrid back at the table. Both had cordial glasses filled with a light-yellow liquid and mugs of a vibrant scented hot chocolate.

"Bad news, Drake," Allie said. "They don't have the packet stuff with the dehydrated marshmallows like you enjoy."

"What is that then?" Drake asked, pointing at the mug.

"The freshest bit of heaven you'll ever taste."

Drake reached for Allie's mug, and she playfully slapped his hand. "Oh, no, mister. You need to get your own."

Drake looked around the room, searching for Luca. "Have you seen the server?"

"He'll be back any moment," Allie said. She drew the mug to her lips, blew on the hot liquid, and sipped. "Oh, my, I'm getting spoiled."

"That's the whole idea of this dinner," Luca said as he approached Drake and Geneva with a tray topped with mugs. Drake handed one to Geneva and took one for himself.

"Thank you, Luca."

"My pleasure, sir. Do you require anything else?"

Drake smiled. "You wouldn't happen to have a bag of marshmallows in the galley, would you?"

"I'll go check right away," Luca said.

As Luca headed toward the kitchen, Ingrid nodded toward him. "Any chance we could hire him for the week? I think he's the best server I've ever had."

"Thank you, ma'am. I appreciate the sentiment," Luca said. "I was unable to find a bag of them, sir, but I found these."

Luca picked the cover from the dish he carried. Drake looked in and saw several white blocks, each twice the size of the average sugar cube.

"What are those?" Drake asked.

"Marshmallows, sir. Made fresh this morning," Luca said. "Please, try one."

"You're kidding me, right?"

Luca shook his head and handed Drake a pair of tiny tongs, and Drake used them to extract a cube from the dish. He dropped it directly into his mouth. He chewed for a moment, then closed his eyes, and smiled as he swallowed.

"Luca. My man! I think I love you."

Luca's cheeks reddened, and he stayed silent.

"Hey," Geneva said, jabbing Drake in the ribs.

"Sorry dear. I meant to say I love his marshmallows."

"Better, but you're still in trouble."

"Here, I'll make it up to you." Drake used the tongs to extract more of the tender goodies from the dish and dropped two each into each of the mugs. "Thank you, Luca. It's been a pleasure having you with us for the night. Can we offer you a tip?"

Luca smiled and waved his hand in front of him like he was fending off an angry dog. "No, thank you, sir. We include the gratuity within the cost of the cruise. Enjoy those. We should reach the dock in fifteen minutes or so."

Luca gave the group a formal bow, then turned and left the friends to their treats.

Allie sighed. "I'm going to miss that man."

Drake rubbed her back. "I think we all will."

A horn sounded, and Drake looked out the window. The lights of the town twinkled in the distance, and he realized the voyage had come to an end.

"If any bit of our trip turns out as good as this, I'm sure

this will be a vacation to remember." Drake said.

CHAPTER FOUR

O h, man, it's early," Drake said to Ingrid as they waited in the hotel lobby.
"If I'm not mistaken, that was your idea, remember? Get out early, and I quote, geocache our faces off." Ingrid said.

Drake took off his Tennessee Titans baseball cap and ran his fingers through his hair. "Perhaps I shouldn't have been so eager. Besides, I hoped to get some push back on that from at least one of you."

"Not going to happen. We billed this trip as a geocaching adventure in Italy, remember? Not a let's sleep until noon every day and then see what there is to see a kind of vacation. If we wanted that, we could have gone to Florida."

"Good point," Drake admitted. "Where's Allie? Is she still in your room?"

"She went to get the car from the parking lot."

Drake frowned. "That's a four-block walk from here. I should have gone with her."

"Why?" Ingrid asked.

Drake hesitated but didn't answer.

"So that you could protect her?" Ingrid asked. "You know how Allie is. If anything, you'd have to protect anyone who hassles her from her."

Drake smiled. "True enough. She's as tough as a grizzly bear when she needs to be."

"Are you talking about Allie?" Geneva said as she joined the others.

"How could you tell?" Drake asked.

"Because you used the words, she, tough, and grizzly bear in the same sentence. Nothing against you, Drake, but if I ever got in a bar fight, I'd want that girl right by my side."

Drake laughed. "Me, too."

From inside they heard a couple of friendly toots from a car horn, and Ingrid stepped to the front window and glanced out.

"She's here," Ingrid said. "Everyone ready?"

Ingrid opened the door and held it while Geneva and Drake left the building and wedged themselves into the red Fiat 500X.

"Good morning," Allie said in a chipper tone. "Everyone ready for a fun day?"

"Why are you in such a good mood?" Drake asked.

"I don't know. Excited to be here? Not bogged down by too much wine? You tell me. Everyone buckled in?"

A chorus of yeses came from inside the subcompact SUV.

"Oh, shoot. I almost forgot Luna," Allie said.

"Luna?" Geneva asked.

Allie reached into her jacket pocket and retrieved her Garmin Nuvi GPS and held it up for all to see. "Luna. What do you call yours?"

"I don't have one of those. I use my phone."

"Ah," Allie said as she attached the unit to a holder,

plugged the external cord into the auxiliary power outlet near her knee, and turned it on. "Who's my navigator today?"

"What does all that entail?" Ingrid asked.

"Bring up the geocache on the Nuvi and hit the go button. Also, help find parking at the final location if need be. Also, make sure I don't go down the wrong way of one-way streets or drive off a cliff. I have a bad habit of not paying attention to the machine as I drive."

"Has Drake done it before?" Ingrid asked.

"Of course. All the time."

"Good. He's experienced. Let's switch seats, buddy."

Ingrid and Drake swapped seats, and they were ready to go. Almost.

"Why aren't we moving?" Drake asked.

Allie looked over at him and raised her eyebrows. "Because…"

"Because someone didn't enter a cache into Luna?" Drake asked.

Allie nodded.

"Who has the list for today?" Drake asked.

Ingrid rummaged through her backpack and produced the paper. "Here you go, Drake."

Drake took the list, glanced at it, and found the geocache in Luna. He pressed the green button, and Allie nodded at him, checked her side mirror, and pulled out into the early morning traffic.

"Twenty minutes to the destination. Where are we headed?" Allie asked.

"A little town called Moltrosio," Ingrid said. "There might be parking coordinates for this one."

Drake looked at the list of geocaches in his hand. "How can I tell? By these extra letters next to the geocache name?"

"You got it," Ingrid said. "Caches with parking

coordinates have a P, a virtual cache has a V, a multi-cache has an M, a mystery cache has a question mark."

"That's a nice system," Drake said.

"It should be familiar to you too. I got it from Allie."

"Did you put in the parking coordinates, or the cache coordinates?" Allie asked.

"Let me double check. Are you good on this road?" Drake asked.

Allie checked Luna and saw she had no turns for eight minutes. "Go ahead."

Drake retrieved Luna and checked for waypoints. He selected the correct one and placed Luna back into the holder. "I've got it now. Headed for the parking coordinates."

"Great, thanks."

Allie continued driving on the two-lane road that ran parallel to the north side of Lake Como. The farther she drove, the higher up the mountain they went. Soon, they came to a split in the road, and Luna directed Allie to take the left path toward the village. To their right, down the side of the mountain, were the blue cool waters of the lake. To their left, a twenty-foot stone wall fortified the mountain above them.

"Parking should be another half mile straight, then turn left," Drake said, taking the lead from Luna.

"Heard," Allie said, not taking her eyes from the road. When she got to within a hundred yards, she slowed, noticed a blue and white parking space, and pulled into a spot. "Where's the cache from here?"

"A block back the other way," Ingrid said.

"Okay. Everyone out," Allie said.

The group exited the Fiat, checked traffic, and walked in the direction from which they'd come. There, on a side street, they discovered a tall stone wall.

"Well, I guess it's time to get looking," Drake said.

The four spread out, and each started to search a three-foot-wide section of wall. Allie stood back a foot from the wall and scanned each crevice without touching it. Whenever she spotted something that appeared suspicious to her, she touched it, and attempted to extract it, but she found nothing but stone.

Ingrid, who stood to Allie's left, used a similar method, but she checked far more spaces than Allie did. Although she examined twice as many places, she found nothing either.

Geneva watched Ingrid and Allie for a moment. She rummaged through her backpack until she found a cheap ballpoint pen. Geneva removed the cap, turned it upside down, and ran the plastic clip along the joints in the stone. She quickly traced around the edges of one stone after another, and halfway down the wall, an inch above her knee, she felt something give.

"I think I have something here," Geneva said. She crouched and ran her pen clip into the joint again. With a little finesse and a bit of determination, she removed the small item from the wall.

"What is it?" Drake asked.

Geneva held up a small three-inch by two-inch flat plastic bag wrapped in black duct tape. She opened one end and removed the small plastic log. She signed it and passed it around. Once everyone had their nicknames on the sheet, Geneva put the cache back together and set it back into the wall.

"Nice job, girlfriend," Drake said. He kissed Geneva, took her hand, and began the walk back to the car.

"Can we stop for gelato?" Allie asked as they passed the shop. Allie stopped in front of the window and gave a friendly wave to a worker inside.

"That depends on whether you want to stand there drooling in the window for two hours," Ingrid said.

"Huh?"

"That's when the shop opens, dear."

Allie stepped away from the window and pushed her lower lip out in a pout. "Can we stop on the way home?"

"I think we can manage that," Drake said. "Come on, let's go. The faster we finish the day, the quicker you get your treat."

"Back to the car, everyone!" Allie joked, then took off in a slow jog toward the parking area.

"Where are we going next?" Allie asked as she started the car and the others buckled up for safety.

Drake consulted the list. "Hey Ingrid, why are there two letter Ps here?"

"It probably has two different parking areas," Ingrid answered. "What's the cache and I'll check out the description."

Drake gave her the number, and Ingrid looked up the details of the cache on her phone. "Yeah, okay, there are two sets of parking coordinates for two different trailheads. Do you want to have more or less of a hike?"

"I'd vote for less," Geneva said.

"Then go with the set that ends with three hundred."

Drake scoured through Luna until he found the correct set of coordinates. He entered them in, and they were finally good to go.

Allie followed Luna's directions as they left the village. Two miles from town, Allie turned north and followed a series of switchback roads that climbed higher into the mountains, then back down into a green valley, flushed with clover and livestock. The road traversed the valley, and near the end, they came to a crossroads. There, Allie stopped the car and shifted into Park.

"What's going on?" Drake asked.

"There's a geocache near here. Look." Allie pointed at

Luna. There, on the screen, not far away, was a small blue square that showed a waypoint. "Should we do this one first, then move on?"

"Which one is it?" Drake asked.

Allie pushed the box, the name displayed on the screen, and Allie read it to Drake.

"That's about six down on the list. Ingrid, I thought y'all put these in some sort of order."

"I did. Luna's route from the last cache must have differed from the one I mapped out manually," Ingrid said.

Drake nodded. "I get it. Happens all the time back home. Should we go after this one first, then?"

"Might as well, since we're here," Geneva answered for the group.

Allie shrugged, then pushed the button. Luna recalculated, and instead of heading straight, had Allie turn right at the crossroads. After a mile they ascended another mountain, and when the road turned from a two-lane, well-maintained road, to a gravel road that looked wide enough to accommodate only a car and a half, Allie stopped again.

"Are we sure about this?" Allie asked.

Drake glanced at Luna. "It's only another half mile. We've come this far, might as well go the rest of the way."

Allie shrugged. "Okay, then. Here we go."

Allie put the car back into gear and drove. For the first three-tenths of a mile, it was smooth going, but once they got to the edge of a meadow and into tree cover, the road climbed dramatically, like the initial climb of a roller coaster. Allie, unrealistically afraid she'd start sliding backwards, kept feathering the gas and climbing higher. The gravel road turned into dirt tire tracks with a strip of grass in the middle. When they had nearly gone up as far as they could, the road veered to the left and ended abruptly where a downed tree blocked the way.

Allie looked at Luna, which proclaimed they only had sixty feet until they reached their intended destination.

"I guess we walk from here," Allie said. She put the car in Park and turned off the car. After a second of hesitation, she applied the parking brake as well.

"That was a fun little hill," Ingrid said.

"You're more than welcome to drive the way back," Allie said, holding up the keys.

Ingrid shrugged. "Wouldn't be a problem. The way back from somewhere is always easier somehow."

Allie nodded. "True enough. Let's go. Drake, you got a bead on this one?"

Drake had his phone open and brought the geocache up on his app. "Yep, it's that way," he said, pointing in the same direction Luna wanted to go.

The four walked around the fallen tree and followed the remainder of the road until the claustrophobic trees opened and they found themselves at the top of the mountain, with a bright blue sky overhead.

"Oh wow, look at that!" Geneva exclaimed, pointing straight ahead.

She needn't have spoken, since all four friends were standing shoulder to shoulder, all looking in the same direction at the remains of a stone structure a hundred feet ahead of them.

Drake checked his phone. "I think they hid the cache at the building."

"You sure it's safe to go into an old building like that?" Geneva asked.

"I hope so," Drake said.

Drake looked at the stone structure, which, to him, appeared to be the remains of an ancient one-story house. From where he stood, he saw only the back, which contained a single cutout for a small window, and one side, which was nothing but stone. All around the building, the spring grasses were already growing tall around the foundation, and nature completely covered one corner in a blue-green moss.

"Let's check it out," he said.

He took three steps toward the building before the women followed him, and it didn't take long to close the distance. As they got to the corner, Drake reached out and brushed his fingers against the wall.

"I wonder how old this is," he said.

They moved around to the other side and discovered a doorway with no door, and Allie took the lead and stepped into the space. In its day, the interior of the home must have seemed shrouded in darkness considering there was but a single door and a small window for light, but since the house had no roof, the bright sun fully illuminated the inside.

The single room was perhaps fifty feet in length by twenty feet wide, and except for a built-in fireplace and a pile of brown leaves in one corner, it was completely empty.

Drake stepped to the fireplace, crouched, and brushed some dirt away from the hearth.

"There's some writing here, cut into the stone. It says CNG 1630."

"1630?" Geneva asked. "Someone built this place ten years after the Mayflower left for the New World? That's amazing."

"Or it could be this is even older, and that's just graffiti," Drake said.

Geneva rolled his eyes at him. "Funny. Where's the cache supposed to be?"

Drake checked the app. "Within 20 feet of here. Probably right here in the fireplace." Drake returned his attention to the fireplace, and although he found several loose stones that he could move that provided for potential hiding places, he found nothing but four hundred years' worth of soot and dirt. "Not here."

"Is there a hint for this one?" Ingrid asked.

Drake stood and clapped his hands to remove the loose dirt. He dug the phone from his back pocket and checked it. "It's in Italian. Can you translate it, Ingrid?"

"I could if I were Italian, but I've never studied the language," she said.

Ingrid retrieved her phone, and a single glance confirmed her suspicions. "I've got no cell service up here, so I won't be able to run it through a translator. We'll just have to try finding it the old-fashioned way by looking for it. I'll start on the outside."

As Ingrid left the building, Allie, Geneva, and Drake searched the inside, but other than the fireplace, there was no other place to look. Even the floor comprised hand cut flat stones, and Drake did a quick walk around seeing if there was a loose one, but there wasn't.

"Got to admit, whoever built this did a great job for it to stand for four centuries," Geneva said.

"Except for the roof, of course," Drake said.

"My guess is that they made it from wood or thatch and rotted away or burned off a long time ago," Allie said. "I'm going to go check on Ingrid."

Allie left the house and spotted Ingrid a few feet ahead, sitting in the grass.

"Hey, what are you doing?" Allie asked as she approached her friend.

"Looking," Ingrid answered.

"I don't think you're going to find the cache this way," Allie teased.

Ingrid pulled at Allie's arm. "Sit down here with me," she said.

Allie sat on the ground next to Ingrid, legs crossed. She leaned over, extracted a rock from beneath her, tossed it aside, and reset her position.

"Okay, now look," Ingrid said, pointing out ahead of her.

Allie stopped for a moment and for the first time since they'd arrived, gazed out across the horizon. From where they sat, they had an open view of the entire valley below them. Green patches in various shades cascaded across the valley. Wildflowers that ranged in color from red to yellow to purple provided contrast to the growing grass. The mountains surrounding the valley were alive in green, except for one small patch to her left that looked to be the remains of a wildfire. The tallest peak she saw had a cap of white at the top.

"It's beautiful here," Allie said.

Ingrid nodded. "Can you imagine finding this place, then building a home here? Especially back when they built this home? No technology, fewer people. Nothing to do but survive. Find food, water, shelter. I'll bet they had a small garden up here somewhere. And I'll bet they sat right here at some point every day and just enjoyed the splendor of this view."

Allie stayed silent for a moment, then agreed. "It's one of the things I like best about geocaching, finding out of the way places like this that time forgot. Magnificent views like this, forgotten history. Those are the real treasures to find."

A small plastic box appeared in Allie's line of sight, and she looked up and saw Geneva standing over her. "Are you two sitting down on the job?"

"Just enjoying this view," Allie said.

Geneva looked out toward the valley, then took a seat next to Allie. "It's spectacular, isn't it?" Geneva opened the box, retrieved the log, signed it, and passed it to Allie, who passed it to Ingrid. Once it returned to Geneva, she returned it to the box, and set the box in the grass next to her.

"Where's Drake?" Allie asked.

"Still looking for the cache inside the house. He's convinced it's in a secret wall somewhere."

"Where did you find it?"

"In the old dead tree on the far side of the house."

"Should we tell him you found it?" Allie asked.

"In a bit," Geneva said. "For now, I'm just enjoying the company and the view."

"Good plan," Allie agreed.

CHAPTER FIVE

I think we're in Switzerland," Drake said.

"What? Why would you say that?" Geneva asked.

"Because we passed a sign that said welcome to Switzerland. Ingrid, did you put and Swiss caches on the list?"

"We talked about that. It wasn't all that far away, and none of us have ever geocached in Switzerland before, so one or two may have slipped onto that list."

"Oh, good," Drake said. "For a moment, I thought we were in trouble. You good over there, Allie? Need me to drive?"

Allie glanced at Luna to get her bearings and over at Drake. "No. I'm good. We'll be at the waypoint in just under fifteen minutes."

Allie slowed, turned off the highway, and onto a local road. She followed the valley for six miles, then saw a large metal gate extending across the road. "Hey Ingrid, what does this sign mean?"

"I can't read it from back here. What does it look like?"

"It looks like a red-letter O with white space in the

middle," Allie said.

"Is there anything inside the white part?"

"No."

"Okay. That means no entry. The road is closed," Ingrid said.

"And that would explain the big metal gate as well," Drake said.

"How far is the cache from here? Can we walk it?" Geneva asked.

"It's another five miles to the parking coordinates," Allie said.

"And another quarter of a mile after that to the cache," Drake added. "Should I put in the other parking coordinates?"

"Might as well give it a try," Allie said. "If we can't get to that parking area, we'll talk about skipping this cache."

Drake reset Luna while Allie did a U-turn and backtracked to the main road. She turned left and headed into the heart of the Swiss Alps. After fifteen minutes, Luna told her to turn left, and Allie found herself back on a local road. It wound itself around the base of a mountain and afterward followed a river for several miles. Another right turn, and they began to ascend on another series of switchbacks.

"Are you doing okay?" Drake asked Allie after several minutes of watching her.

"I'm fine. Why do you ask?"

"You're driving in the middle of the road ten kilometers an hour under the speed limit, and your knuckles are white. Relax, it's only a mountain."

Allie exhaled. "I guess I'm a little stressed. I don't really like the big ones." Allie inched back into her own lane, then took her right hand off the wheel and flexed her fingers.

"Simply pretend you're back home driving through the

Smoky Mountains. You've done that a million times with no problem."

Allie flexed her left hand. "Yeah, but I know that road pretty well. It's always a touch intimidating when you don't recognize the road."

"You drove us through that canyon in New Mexico once. And through the Colorado Rockies, and it snowed during half of that trip," Drake said.

"That's true. That wasn't as bad, though."

"Why not? It's the same thing. Except this road is nice and dry. It's a nice day out, and there's hardly any traffic."

Allie smiled. "Thanks for the words of encouragement. I'm fine now. I got in my own head for a bit, and we're almost there."

"As long as this road isn't closed, too," Ingrid said.

"Thanks for giving me something else to worry about," Allie said. She looked in the rear-view mirror and saw Ingrid smile and wink at her.

Luna ordered a left turn, and Allie pulled into a wide-open parking lot.

"We made it!" Allie said.

"Excellent," Drake said. "I'm ready for a little walk."

"How far is the thing from here?" Geneva asked.

Drake did a quick check. "About over half a mile as the crow flies, but I'm guessing it's hidden off one of the park trails, which, of course, are never in a straight line."

"Trails?" Geneva asked as she exited the Fiat.

Drake pointed to the informational sign he spotted nearby. There were several trails displayed on the map, with corresponding colors to designate how difficult they were.

Once she left the car, Ingrid stepped over to the sign and looked at it.

"It would be nice to understand what that says," Drake said.

"Well," Ingrid started, "don't leave the marked trails. Don't gather any plants, including flowers or mushrooms. There's also don't hunt or disturb the animals or fish."

"How would you disturb a fish?" Drake asked. "Play loud music?"

Ingrid ignored him. "Don't make any fires. Don't bring animals into the park, including dogs. We can't use tents or stay in the park overnight, and we have to pack out all our waste. There's a five hundred Swiss franc fine for violations."

"How much is that in American dollars?" Drake asked.

"Close to six hundred," Geneva answered.

Ingrid kept reading. "Also, regarding the colors, the yellow is a regular trail that anyone should be able to handle. The red trail is a mountain trail on which you should wear your hiking boots, and the blue is the alpine trail which would probably kill us in our current physical conditions."

"Wait a second, Ingrid. I thought you didn't understand Italian," Drake said.

"I don't." Ingrid pointed at a specific part of the sign. "But that's in French, and that I learned as a child."

"The terrain on this cache is only two and a half, so should we assume it's off of a yellow trail?" Allie asked.

"Probably a good assumption," Geneva said. "Ingrid, can you figure out where we are on that map and where the yellow trail runs?"

"Of course," Ingrid said, putting her finger on the map. "There's a little X with the words 'you are here'. If I have the orientation figured out correctly, the trailhead for the yellow trail should be right behind us."

Drake left the board, walked across the parking lot, and surveyed the area. He returned within a few minutes. "Yeah, she's right. There are yellow trail markers over there."

"So, about a mile round trip. Shouldn't take us more than an hour, right? Everyone okay with that or want to stay in the car?" Allie asked.

"Nope. I'm good to go," Ingrid said.

"Me too," Geneva and Drake said simultaneously.

Allie glanced over at Ingrid. "Oh, boy, they're talking in unison now."

Ingrid grinned. "I know. How gross! Come on, let's go track down that cache before they go into full-on cute mode."

Ingrid and Allie turned and headed for the trail.

"Wait for us!" Drake called after them. "Come on, Geneva."

Drake and Geneva broke into a jog and caught up with Allie and Ingrid as they were about to enter the trail, and everyone stopped as they got there.

"Are you going to be able to handle this?" Drake asked Allie. "Looks like it might be a challenge for your bad knee."

"I wrecked that thing two years ago. It's fine. Go. Take the lead. We're burning daylight," Allie answered.

Drake shrugged. "Okay, if you say so. Come single file, though. The trail isn't wide enough for two here."

Drake moved out first, walked for six easy feet, then descended a set of stairs cut into the earth and reinforced with railroad ties. As he moved, he counted them under his breath. When he reached twenty-one, the last stair, he moved forward on the trail, then turned around and waited for the group to catch up to him.

"Looks scary, doesn't it?" Allie said. "Reminds me of those forests in those old-time fairy tales."

Drake looked around and caught what Allie was talking about. All around them, spruce trees that rose like giants from the forest floor dominated the area. The trees cast off the scent that transported Drake back to childhood when they'd go out into the forest every early December to find the year's Christmas tree. The trees littered the forest floor with needles, giving it a spongy feel, like walking on a waterbed.

There were other trees interspersed with the conifers, including clusters of beech, maple, and oak, and a couple Drake couldn't identify by sight alone.

"Should we leave a trail of breadcrumbs?" Geneva asked.

Allie waved her GPS in the air. "No need. I've got my handheld on. I marked the car with a waypoint, and I've got the route tracking on, so we'll have no problem getting back here. Much better than breadcrumbs."

Drake moved forward, careful to watch his step to avoid slipping.

"Should have brought hiking poles. I love having one when on a trek like this," Drake said.

"I usually have one too," Geneva said. "Too bad the TSA doesn't allow them as a carry-on item."

"Don't forget to find a spider stick, Drake," Allie said from the back.

"Spider stick?" Geneva asked.

"Drake believes that the entire arachnid species is out to get him and every time he walks through any trees, the spiders run ahead of him and build webs between trees at face height for him to walk into. So, he waves a stick in front of him to knock the webs down before he face-plants into them."

Geneva and Ingrid laughed.

"I'd like to see that," Geneva said.

"You'd like it. He looks like he's conducting an orchestra when he does it."

Drake stopped and turned around. He put his hands on his hips and an angry expression on his face. "Hey, I don't…" he started. He stopped speaking, stepped off the trail, and returned with a length of branch three feet long and two inches in diameter. "See what I found? A perfect spider stick!"

He spun back around and pointed his spider stick in the air in front of him. "Onward!" he directed.

The trail remained flat and straight for a hundred yards, and then they came to a T. Attached to a spruce tree were three arrows. A yellow one pointed right, the red and blue ones pointed left. Drake turned right, and twenty yards later, the trail bent around a boulder the size of the Fiat and started downhill for a short stretch before it leveled out again.

Drake stopped abruptly, and Geneva, not looking ahead of her at the moment, bumped right into him.

"Hey," Geneva said as she stepped back.

"Sorry. Look at that." Drake pointed his stick ahead of them and off to the right, up the mountain.

"Where?" Geneva asked as she moved closer to Drake.

"See this tree just off the trail here? Follow that like six trees up the hill, then five trees to the left."

The women followed his orders. Ingrid spotted it first.

"What's that?" she asked.

"I don't know," Drake said. "It almost looks like a goat. Why would there be a goat here?"

Allie hadn't seen it yet. "Is it brown and cute and has long horns that curve so far it looks like he could use them to scratch his own back?"

"I don't know about cute, but the rest of it tracks," Drake said.

"It's an ibex." Allie stepped off the trail and moved around Ingrid and Geneva so she could be next to Drake. "Where is it?"

Drake repeated his directions, then pointed directly at the animal. A tree partially obscured the beast, but it moved, and Allie saw it at last.

"That's amazing," Allie said.

"Are they dangerous?" Ingrid asked.

"No. It'll run away if we bother with it too much."

"Anything else we should keep in mind while on this little adventure?" Drake asked.

Allie shrugged. "Just the usual stuff we'd watch for back home. Birds, bears, deer, wolves. The common stuff. Like foxes, hedgehogs, marmots, and chamois."

"What's a chamois?" Geneva asked.

"Looks like that ibex, except with shorter horns," Allie answered.

"What's a marmot?" Ingrid asked.

"Large ground squirrel. Looks a little like a groundhog." Allie removed her camera from her pocket, got the ibex in the center of the viewfinder, and snapped a picture. "That was an excellent picture. He's looking right at us."

"How do you know so much about these animals?" Drake asked.

Allie took the lead and headed down the trail. "Animal Planet," she said over her shoulder.

With Allie in the lead, she picked up the pace of the group, and walked faster than the casual saunter that Drake had the group traveling by. As she walked, she examined the ground, on the lookout for any outcroppings of rocks, roots, or anything else that would trip them. The part of the trail they currently traversed seemed relatively free of debris and looked well maintained. She led the pack for ten minutes before she stopped and turned around.

"Everyone good yet?" she asked as she fished her water bottle from her backpack and took a drink. No one said otherwise. "How much farther, Drake?"

Drake checked and pointed down the ridge. "Three-tenths of a mile. Not too bad."

"Take point," Allie said.

Drake retook the lead position and marched on, once again slowing the pace. After two hundred feet, he stopped.

"We've got a problem here," he said.

"What?" Allie asked.

"Which way do we go?" he asked.

Allie looked around and realized there were two trails ahead of them. One went straight along the ridge, the other snaked down the mountain. She found and pointed to a yellow trail marker three feet straight ahead of them. "Follow the yellow."

Drake stepped onto the other trail, walked four feet, and pointed to another trail marker attached to a tree. It, too, contained a bright yellow coat of paint. "Which one?"

Allie glanced at the marker near her, then at Drake's. "I'm not sure."

"Hold on, let me check the trail map," Ingrid said.

"Where did you get a map?" Geneva asked.

"I took a picture of the one on the sign." Ingrid brought up the gallery on her phone and examined it for a moment. "I don't see the trail on there."

Ingrid handed her phone to Geneva, who took it, looked at it for twenty seconds before she passed it off to Allie. Allie scrutinized the image, stepped away from the group, and faced the direction from which they'd come. Everyone watched as she performed a lot of pointing and pirouetting, and, and last, rejoined the group. She gave Ingrid her phone back.

"I think it's a new trail, and they haven't updated the map yet," Allie said.

"So, which one do we follow?" Geneva asked.

"Where's the cache?" Allie asked.

Drake looked at the phone and lined up the arrow. He pointed in a direction that bisected both trails. "I think this trail does a loop. Why don't we split up, each take a direction, and meet at the cache? Allie, you and Ingrid take the straight trail, which looks easier from here, and Geneva and I will take the other."

"Okay. It shouldn't take more than another ten minutes to find that cache, so let's meet back here in twenty if we don't meet before then," Allie said. "Let's go, Ingrid. We'll beat them to it and get the names on the log first."

"I doubt it. Come on, Geneva," Drake said.

Drake stepped back down to the lower trail and waited for Geneva, watching her as she walked.

"Wait. Why are you limping?"

"It's nothing. I stepped on a rock a while ago and twisted my ankle," Geneva said.

Drake returned to the main trail and saw Allie and Ingrid had already slipped out of view. "Allie! Come back here!" Drake called. He waited a few moments, then exhaled when they saw them on their way back.

"What's up, buttercup?" Allie asked.

"Geneva broke her ankle," Drake said.

Geneva pushed him aside. "I did not break it. I rolled it on a rock. No big deal."

"Let Allie take a peek at it," Drake said.

Geneva looked from Drake to Allie and finally capitulated. "Okay, fine. What do you need me to do?"

Allie looked around and spotted a downed tree pushed off to the edge of the trail. "Can you make it to that tree and have a seat?"

Geneva turned, and Drake grabbed her arm for support. Allie stopped him.

"Let her do it. I want to see how she moves."

Geneva limped ten feet to the tree, pivoted, and sat. "See. No problem."

"You've got a slight limp," Allie said as she approached Geneva. "Does it hurt?"

"Nothing a couple aspirin wouldn't take care of."

"Can I look at it?"

"Do whatever you need to do to make Drake feel better," Geneva said.

Allie smiled. She crouched and removed Geneva's shoe and sock and examined her foot and ankle. "It's a little aggravated but doesn't seem swollen or broken. I think she twisted it and should be able to walk it off."

"That was the same conclusion I came to. You better now, Drake?" Geneva asked as she put her sock.

Drake nodded. "Just trying to be careful out here. You never know what will happen."

"I'll tell you what. You take Ingrid with you down the harder trail, and I'll take Geneva with me. I'll keep my eye on her and make sure she's okay. If she gets any worse, I'll wait with her here until y'all get back, and then we'll head back to the car together."

Drake nodded. "Sounds like a plan to me. You okay with it, Geneva? Ingrid?"

"Sure," the women said as one.

"Okay. Be good, and don't be afraid to take it easy," Drake said.

Drake nodded at Ingrid, and they stepped back onto the trail and headed down the trail branch he'd found.

"She'll be fine, Drake. Allie will take excellent care of her," Ingrid said as they stepped around a large boulder.

"I know. We'll probably get to that cache and find their names already on it, and them back on that tree, lounging around and waiting for us."

The pair followed the trail as it curved back on itself and down the mountain before it returned to the direction of the cache. The trail was a rough one and contained parts that had them walking across sections of rock, around boulders, over tree roots, and in one case, they needed to climb over a tree that blocked the entire path.

After fifteen minutes of walking, Drake stopped and

wiped the sweat from his forehead.

"Ever go out for a cache you later regret?" he asked.

Ingrid nodded. "You mean like this one?"

Drake smiled. "Come on. We're already running late."

"Should we go back?"

Drake checked his position. "No. We're only four hundred feet away. Let's keep moving forward and hope we pick up the easier trail at the cache."

Drake took his next step just as a rumble of thunder rolled up the mountain. "That didn't sound good."

Drake barely finished his sentence when the rain began. It started as a few lazy drops, then the skies opened, and the deluge began; drenching the pair in seconds.

"Let's go back," Ingrid pleaded.

"It will be faster going straight ahead," Drake said.

He moved forward thirty feet, then stopped.

"What is it?" Ingrid said.

Drake inched over so she could look. A tree had fallen parallel to the trail, leaving mere inches between the path and the edge. Where the path remained, the falling rainwater mixed with the runoff from up the hill, making a small puddle that was growing larger by the second.

"Take it slow through here," Drake said. "Watch how I do this and follow my steps."

Drake took a step, placing his foot as close to the tree as he could, then did the same with the next step. He walked slowly and intentionally, and using his method, he'd already made it halfway past the obstacle.

Lightning flashed above them, followed by a crack of thunder that resembled an exploding bomb. Drake, surprised by the event, wedged his foot underneath an inch of exposed branch. He pulled his foot out too hard. Drake pinwheeled his arms, trying to maintain his balance, but it didn't work. He did an awkward somersault, and disappeared down the mountain, leaving Ingrid alone on the trail.

Ingrid stared at the spot where Drake had stood a second before, and toward where he'd gone. The rain increased in velocity. Ingrid wiped the rain from her eyes and clenched her fists in frustration.

"Shit!" she screamed to the trees.

CHAPTER SIX

Ingrid stood alone in the rain, undecided on what to do. She remained still for a moment getting drenched, decided on a course of action, and grabbed her phone from her back pocket. She leaned over, attempting to protect it from the rain, brought up her contacts, and attempted to call Allie. Ingrid didn't even need to place the phone next to her ear to determine that the call wouldn't go through. Next, she tried to send texts to both Allie and Geneva and noticed neither one was delivered.

"Shit," she repeated.

Ingrid removed her backpack and dropped the phone inside to protect it from the elements and returned the pack to her shoulders. She turned around and checked out the trail they'd come in on and spotted a full-fledged stream flowing from the mountain above. As she watched, the water streamed faster, blocking her way.

Ingrid faced the other direction and eyed the spot where Drake had gone off the side. The puddle had grown deeper.

Ingrid hesitated, unable to move like a rabbit spotting a distant fox. She wiped the water from her face again, waited until a peal of thunder rose from the valley, and took one step forward. At first, she placed her foot next to the downed tree, just like she watched Drake do. Suddenly, she changed her mind and sat on the tree. An unpleasant sensation attacked her backside, the combination of cold water and rough bark. Ingrid used her hands to steady herself and slid halfway down the length of the tree, stopping where Drake had gone over the edge. She brushed her hair back with her hand and leaned forward as far as she dared, hoping to catch some sight of Drake.

"Drake? Drake! Can you hear me? Drake?" she screamed down the mountain. She stopped calling and listened for half a minute, but all she picked up was the pounding of raindrops against the leaves and ground.

Ingrid looked to her right and, two inches at a time, moved her away across the remainder of the tree. Once she got across, she struggled to her feet and started jogging up the trail. She made it twenty feet down the path before the toe of her right foot caught a rock, and she splayed forward like a baseball runner stealing second base. Ingrid wasn't running fast, but the mud and water lessened the resistance when she hit the ground. She slid forward, getting a face full of grime and muddying the entire front of her body in the process. Undaunted, she attempted to get to her feet, slipped once again, and fell onto her backside. Finally, she stood erect, used the bottom of her T-shirt to wipe the mud from her face, and regained her run along the trail.

She ran for fifty more years and stopped when the trail, which she expected to bend off to the right, meandered off to the left instead. Ingrid moved six feet along the path and encountered a steep descent before her.

"Geneva! Allie!" Ingrid screamed. She stopped but heard nothing but rain and thunder in response. She yelled again, and a third and fourth time, each time putting more effort in than the time before. After the fifth time, she retrieved her phone and once again tried to call for help. Ingrid's shoulders slumped when she saw she had no service in the area.

"Shit," Ingrid said.

She put her hands on her hips and looked down the trail again, watching the water flow steadily off the side of the steep hill, taking the path of least resistance.

"Okay, Ingrid, think this out. I've got three choices here. Try to guess where Allie and Geneva are and attempt to head off trail to find them, check where this trail leads and hope it goes somewhere, or go back and try to find Drake. Option one is idiotic. I'd end up getting myself lost, I'm sure. Option two is a long shot, so that only leaves me with option three, which is almost as idiotic as option one."

Ingrid drew in a deep breath, exhaled, and made her way back to the downed tree. Applying the same process she did before, Ingrid sat on the tree trunk and made her way to the center. She looked as far as she could down the mountain, but it wasn't far. All she saw was a muddy patch that resembled a slide, trees, and a dense fog that had appeared since she'd been gone. The gray and white fog rose from below like the boil from a witch's cauldron.

"Drake?" she yelled. "Are you down there? Drake?"

She hoped for an answer from him, or at least a sound other than the constant rain, but no answer came.

"Okay. Let's figure this out," Ingrid said to the universe. "I don't want to go the same way down that Drake did. That seems like a stupid idea, so let's find a better way."

Ingrid looked down to her left. The stream that had blocked her from going back to the main trail had widened, expanded, flooded more trail toward her, and added a second branch to the mini waterfall that dropped from the mountain not far from where she sat. To her right, things looked a little more promising, but only a little. Ingrid backtracked to the end of the trunk, searched for a steady spot to put her foot on, and stepped off the trail.

With care, Ingrid put her weight on the large rock she'd selected and put her left foot next to her right. Below her she discovered a half dozen stones that outcropped like steps, and she cautiously took them, one at a time, testing each one before she fully committed. The last step was two feet behind a large spruce, so her next move was to leave the rock and embrace the tree in a hug. She couldn't see around the giant tree without taking a few baby steps to the left, and once she did, she noticed the fog was getting closer and the next tree was ten feet down the mountain.

The pitch was steep, but not vertical, so Ingrid leaned against the tree and stepped forward. She crouched, took a sideway step down with her right foot, then followed it with her left. Another two steps, and she committed to the plan. The rain picked up a little harder, and she felt her back get pelted with large drops. Ingrid stepped again and the second she applied weight, the wet pine needles beneath her feet shifted. Ingrid fell on her hip, and she screamed as she slid the rest of the way until she slammed feet first into the tree she'd been aiming for.

The impact jarred the scream from her throat, and she worried she'd miss the tree and tumble down the valley, but she stopped when she slammed into the trunk. Ingrid rolled onto her back, moaned, and rubbed the hip she'd landed hard on. Without looking, she assumed the rough ride had torn her pants, and when she glanced at her fingers, she noticed bright red blood that washed away one raindrop at a time.

She gritted her teeth and slowly got back to her feet, battered but not broken. The tree she'd crashed against was only half as wide as the previous one, so she held on easily while she looked around it. Eight feet below her looked to flow a two-foot-wide stream produced by the heavy rain that ran parallel to the hill she found herself on. Two feet past the stream was the next drop off down the mountain, and below that, she couldn't tell, since the fog was almost at that level.

Ingrid stood stone still for a moment, considering her best option forward, and as she did, an ibex came along, walking from left to her right as if out on a summer stroll.

"Son of a bitch," Ingrid said. "It's a deer path."

The ibex spotted Ingrid, looked in her direction and took off running.

Ingrid sat on the wet ground and pushed out from the tree, her heels digging into the earth. She released the tension in her legs, slid a foot down the mountain and dug her heels in again to stop her momentum. Slowly, she descended until at last her feet hit the path. Once she was down, she stood, then, having a flat surface to tread on, followed the path until she came to a ten-foot drop that resembled a mud waterfall.

"I'm guessing you went that way, Drake," she said knowing full well he wouldn't respond.

Next to the path was a broken sapling. Ingrid looked as far down the hill as she could before the fog obscured her view. Three quarters of the way below her, she spotted other saplings the same size as the one next to her.

"Okay. I hope this works," she said.

Ingrid rubbed her hands on her pants and grabbed the sapling and tugged. It hadn't broken all the way through, so although she expected it to snap off in her hands, it didn't. She moved toward the edge of the cliff, and using the sapling as a makeshift rope, descended. When she got close enough to reach a sapling that wasn't already bent in half, she transferred from the original one. Ingrid held tight to the new tree, then used it as a guide until she reached the next one. The second sapling led to a third, and before she knew it,

Ingrid found herself on top of a rock outcropping. She got onto her stomach, crawled to the edge, and peered over. From where she was, she couldn't see a thing with the deep fog.

Ingrid moved to the side of the ledge and found it connected with the mountain and sloped down. Watching her step as she proceeded, she stepped from place to place until she found herself on yet another deer trail. When she turned around and looked behind her, she realized the outcropping she had been laying on top of moments earlier was actually a cave. Cold, wet, sore, and tired, she stepped inside the cave a few feet to get out of the rain.

"Hello?" she said into the cave. "Anyone in here?"

Ingrid heard nothing except her voice echoing back at her. The cave cut into the mountainside far enough that Ingrid didn't see the back of it, but having no desire to explore, she instead selected a large rock and sat down.

"Okay. I'll rest for a minute, and then get back at it," she said aloud.

Ingrid watched the rain fall outside the cave for a moment and shivered when a cold breeze wrapped its essence around her. She took her backpack from her shoulders, retrieved her phone, and checked to see if she had any service or if any of her messages had gone through. The answer being no to both, Ingrid placed it back in her backpack. As she zipped up the bag, she caught sight of her hands. They looked wrinkled and white, and she had a cut on her left hand that ran from the base of her thumb all the way to the wrist.

"There goes my career as a hand model," she said as loud as she could, trying to get a response from someone who wasn't there.

She yawned and stretched, trying to work the knots from her spine.

"I should have stayed in bed. Okay, girl, let's do this."

With a groan, Ingrid pushed herself to a standing position and then stepped into the cave's mouth. She stopped for a moment, not wanting to leave the relative comfort of the dry cave, took a deep breath and stepped out into the elements. She turned left and followed the deer trail. After fifty yards, Ingrid found Drake's waterfall, and she got close to the side, and leaned over. She expected to see rocks, trees, random puddles, and mud, but she missed a breath when she spotted a Titans blue baseball cap hanging from a short branch like someone had placed it there. The cap dangled only four feet from her, and the terrain gently sloped, so she easily stepped down to the hat and plucked it from the tree.

She turned the hat over in her hands. Other than being dirty and wrinkled, it didn't look like it had just fallen off a mountain. Ingrid inspected the inside and found it to be relatively clean. She brushed her hair back with her hands, then put the cap on and pulled the bill low to protect her eyes from the rain.

"Drake? Drake, can you hear me?" Ingrid yelled.

She paused. Nothing. Ingrid repeated the calls over and over again, waiting for a response in between, but nothing answered but storm sounds.

"Dammit, Drake," Ingrid said as she stepped down the slope. For twenty-five feet, she followed the impromptu stream as it veered gently to the left, then it disappeared from sight. Ingrid crept to the edge and peered over. Although the fog still swirled, she estimated the drop was at least thirty vertical feet. She shuddered, happy she couldn't see what was waiting for her at the bottom of the drop, but she knew she had to get down there.

Ingrid moved away from the edge, intending to find a less dramatic way to the bottom. As she stepped around a spruce, her foot caught on something, and she crashed to the ground. She got to her hands and knees, then pushed herself up and stood. Ingrid brushed the pine needles and dirt from her hands, then turned to see what she'd tripped over.

It was a leg, and attached to the leg was the rest of Drake, sitting with his back to the spruce tree. Ingrid stepped over and dropped to her knees before him.

"Drake? You alive, buddy?"

Ingrid grabbed Drake's arm, felt for a pulse, and found it beating steady and strong. She tapped gently on his right cheek as she repeated his name.

Finally, his eyes opened. "Hey, you. What took you so long to find me?"

Ingrid shrugged. "You know me. I like to take my time with things."

It took quite an effort, but Drake smiled. It faded quickly from his face.

"How are you doing?" Ingrid asked.

"That was the worst water slide ride ever," Drake said, his voice weak.

"Anything broken?"

Drake's eyes shut again. Rather than wake him right away, Ingrid gave him a rough inspection and checked his extremities and head for injuries.

"What are you going, Allie?" Drake muttered.

"It's Ingrid. I'm not going anywhere. I'm checking you for broken bones."

"Under shirt," Drake said. He tried to pull his shirt up but he didn't have the strength.

Ingrid lifted his shirt for him.

"Holy shit!" Ingrid exclaimed when she saw the three-inch piece of wood sticking out of Drake's stomach, just left of his navel. It was as thick as her thumb. She took it between two fingers to check the resistance, and it refused to come out easily, so Ingrid left it alone and replaced Drake's shirt.

"How bad is it?" Drake asked.

"I wouldn't want one. Drake, listen to me. I can't leave you here alone. We need to get you out of this rain. I know a place not far from here, but I can't carry you. You'll have to walk, okay?"

Ingrid looked at Drake's closed eyes and assumed he'd passed out again. She prepared to tap him on the cheek when he answered.

"Okay. We should go slow. It's slippers out there," he mumbled.

"That's right, Drake, slippers out here indeed. Can you open your eyes?"

Ingrid waited.

"Drake?"

Drake's eyes fluttered but failed to open.

Ingrid crouched and got close to Drake's ear. "Drake!" she yelled with all her might.

Drake's eyes snapped open as if spring-loaded. He shook his head, confused. "What?"

"Come on. Time to get up. Let's go."

Before Drake could answer, Ingrid grabbed his belt and started to lift him. Although she wasn't strong enough to pull him to his feet, he got the idea, struggled to get his feet beneath him, and stood. Ingrid propped him against the tree and held onto his belt so he wouldn't fall.

"You see me, Drake?" Ingrid asked.

"Yes," he mumbled.

"Here's the plan. We're going up that little hill, then we're going to take a path to a cave I found. It's no more than three hundred feet, okay? And once we get going, we're not going to stop. Got it?"

Drake nodded.

"Tell me the plan, Drake."

Drake raised his arm halfway and pointed up the

mountain. "Go up the hill, then path, then cave."

"Right. And no stopping. That's the important part. We're going on the count of three, so put your arm around my neck."

Drake did as he was told, and Ingrid counted. At three, she pulled him away from the tree. Drake's full body weight rested on Ingrid's shoulders, and she felt him pulling her to the ground.

"Hey, come on, man, move your feet."

Drake did, reluctantly, the left foot first, then the right. It wasn't more than a shuffle, but they moved, and as a bonus, he held his own weight.

"Let's get out of the open," Ingrid said. By using his belt more like a guide than for support, Ingrid prompted him to walk with her, and to her surprise, they ambled up the soft slope and made it to the deer trail in just over twelve minutes. Ingrid's back ached from supporting most of Drake's weight, but she said no breaks, so she needed to stick to that plan. She knew if she let him sit now, it would take more effort than she had in her to get him off the ground again.

"Come on, it's not much farther," Ingrid said. "Fifty more steps, Drake. You can do it."

Drake murmured something Ingrid couldn't pick up. Instead, she stepped forward and pulled him along the best that she could, but eventually she worked into a rhythm. Step, pull. Another step, another pull. Using her improvised method, one foot traveled turned into a yard, and then another. Ingrid desired to pick up the pace, but had neither the strength nor Drake's cooperation, so she kept it nice and easy. One yard at a time. Step. Pull. Step. Pull.

At last, they reached the cave opening, and Ingrid helped Drake inside. She considered setting him on the rock she's sat on earlier, but didn't want him to fall over, so instead she opted to sit him down on the ground with his back against the wall.

Ingrid took off Drake's hat, set it in his lap, and ran her fingers through her long hair, squeezing the water from it as she did. She looked at Drake, who was unconscious again.

"Okay, you're right. Let's rest up for a moment before we decide what to do next," she said as she closed her eyes.

CHAPTER SEVEN

W here do you think they are?" Allie asked, shifting in her seat to attempt to get more comfortable.

"It beats me," Geneva said. "You don't think they're waiting back at that tree you said we'd wait by, do you?"

"I would hope not. It wouldn't make sense to stand out in this downpour when we could hang in the nice dry car."

"Speaking of nice and dry, would you mind turning on the heat?" Geneva asked.

Allie glanced at her friend in the passenger seat. Geneva's hair was wet, and her forehead glistened like she'd recently come out of the shower.

"Of course." Allie started the car, turned the heat to the maximum setting, and adjusted the vents so the upcoming warm air blew on them. "This good?"

Geneva adjusted the vent closest to her. "Yes, thank you. What's the plan now? We sit and wait?"

Allie watched the rain buffet on the windshield. She activated the wipers, and they did their job momentarily, but in the short time between when they rose and fell again, the windshield got covered with twice as much water.

"Is it me, or is this rain like going through a car wash?" Geneva asked.

"I had that same image run through my head, complete with that massive rotating brush overhead. I'm not sure what we should do. Wait for the rain to taper off? Go out and try to find them? How long have they been gone?"

Geneva checked the time on her phone. "It's been an hour since we've been back, and it probably took us what, a half hour hike from when it started raining?"

Allie nodded. "Sounds about right."

"So, where do you imagine they are?" Geneva asked.

"I really don't have the faintest idea. At best, they found some shelter and hunkered in until the rain lets up. At worst…"

"No need to give me the worst case."

Allie patted Geneva's knee. "Stop worrying. I'm sure they're fine."

"Yeah, but doesn't Drake have a habit of getting himself into trouble?"

"Oh, trust me, he does. He'll do some extremely questionable things when looking for a geocache, but to his credit, he's never put anyone else's safety in jeopardy. He wouldn't do anything stupid with Ingrid in tow," Allie said.

"I know. I'm only getting nervous for both of them."

"Me too."

"We should try calling them again," Geneva said, holding up her phone.

Allie dialed Drake, noticed the call never connected, and tried Ingrid and received the same result. Next, she tried sending messages to both, and shook her head when those didn't go through, either.

"Did you have any luck?" Geneva asked.

Allie shook her head. "Nope. The call I made to you didn't go through, either, and you're sitting right next to me."

"I understood these international phone plans we got were supposed to work everywhere," Geneva said.

"I don't think it's the plan. My guess is it's the location. I can't imagine there's a lot of coverage where we are," Allie answered.

"So, what are we going to do if we need help? Drive down the mountain?"

As much as she hated the prospect of driving all the way back to town in the pouring rain, Allie didn't see another solution. "I guess so. But I don't like the idea of leaving here until we have to. I'd hate it if Drake and Ingrid came up the trail and found this parking lot empty."

The friends stopped talking. Other than the patter of rain on the windshield and roof, and the constant hum of the heater, silence settled over the car like a blanket. After a few minutes, the thermostat ticked, and the car got warmer inside. Allie flipped on the radio, found nothing to listen to, and switched it off again. To amuse herself, she tapped out a rhythm on the steering wheel.

"That's super annoying," Geneva said.

Allie stopped in mid-beat and looked over at her friend. "Sorry. I don't know what to do with my hands."

"Why don't we give it fifteen more minutes, and we'll go out and look for them?" Geneva said.

Allie looked down at her phone and checked the current time. "Screw that. I'm going now. Do you want to come with, or wait here in the nice warm and dry car?"

Geneva smiled. "Of course, I'd prefer to wait here. But I'll go with you. They're my friends, too. Besides, I don't want you to disappear into the wilderness, too."

Allie exhaled. "Thank goodness. I wasn't looking forward to heading out there by myself. Do you have an umbrella or a rain jacket with you?"

Geneva shook her head. "Not with me. I have both

packed away in my luggage back at the hotel."

"And you didn't think to bring them along with us today?" Allie scolded.

"Why would I? The weather looked to be perfect everywhere in the area. I didn't think I'd need them. Anyway, where's your umbrella and rain jacket?"

Allie looked from Geneva, out the side window, and back at Geneva. A smile spread across her face. "In my room, hanging in the closet."

Geneva waved a finger at her. Then both women broke out in authentic, mind-clearing laughter. Once she finished, Allie turned off the car.

"You ready to do this?" Allie asked. "I mean, are you sure you can make it with that ankle? We barely made it back here the last time."

Geneva let loose a loud sigh. "I need to try. I can't sit here and do nothing."

Allie shook her head. "No. I'm serious, Geneva. If that ankle is going to be a problem, then you shouldn't go. If we got halfway down the trail and it gave out, that wouldn't do any of us any good."

"I tell you I'm fine," Geneva said. "The second my foot starts to bother me, I'll come right back to the car. Honestly."

Allie looked her in the eyes, then nodded. "Okay. Any problem and you come right back."

Allie and Geneva reached for the door handles at the same time, popped open the doors, and stepped out in unison.

"Are we taking the packs?" Geneva asked.

"Yeah, we probably should," Allie said. She opened the back door, retrieved both backpacks, and waited for Geneva to get to her, then passed Geneva her backpack. Allie shut the door, locked the car, and shoved the keys into her front pocket.

As one, they turned, stepped across the parking lot, and started down the trail, Allie in the lead. Moving ahead, Allie stepped down the first five stairs, then stopped and turned to wait for Geneva. Allie spotted her at the top, looking like she was trying to negotiate the first step down.

Allie trudged back up the steps and joined Geneva at the top.

"What's going on?" Allie asked.

"I'm not sure," Geneva said. "I thought I could go, but I'm not sure."

"All right let's go back," Allie said.

Allie let Geneva walk ahead of her, and when they returned to the Fiat, Allie had Geneva get in the back seat behind the passenger. Geneva leaned up against the closed door and put her feet up on the seat. Allie removed Geneva's shoe and sock and inspected her ankle.

"It's more swollen than it was before," Allie said. "And it's redder. I still think it's a mild sprain, but obviously you shouldn't be walking around the mountainside in a rainstorm on it. You stay here, and I'll go looking for them."

Geneva reached out and grabbed Allie's hand. "No. I'm not good with you going out there alone."

"I can appreciate that, but someone needs to go. Can you honestly tell me you'd make it even a hundred yards down that trail without doing more damage to that ankle and putting the rest of us at risk?"

Geneva's eyes dropped to her lap, and she let go of Allie's hand.

"Look, Geneva, it's not worth you hurting yourself, too. Remember that fall I took in Arizona? I'm still not fully recovered from that, and that was over two years ago. You need to be smart and stay here. In fact, that's probably for the best. If anyone comes into the parking lot, you can tell them what's going on and see if they can get some help for us, okay?"

Geneva hesitated, then eventually nodded. "Okay, okay. I'll wait here."

Allie helped Geneva back into her sock and shoe and then propped Geneva's foot up on her backpack.

"Keep your ankle elevated as much as you can. I'll be back soon."

Allie removed the keys from her pocket and held them out for Geneva. As Geneva took the keys, she grasped Allie's hand firmly in hers.

"Be careful, Allie. Please."

Allie nodded, stepped back, and closed the door.

Alone, Allie wandered to the trailhead, took a deep breath, and carefully moved down the steps.

Since it was still raining hard, the trail was a muddy mess in places interspersed with deep puddles. She did what she could to stay out of the water and away from anything on the ground that would cause her to lose her footing. Although it took her twice the time to cover the same ground as before, she eventually made it to the downed tree they had all agreed to meet at a thousand hours earlier.

"Drake? Ingrid?" Allie called out, hoping the pair were within earshot. "Drake! Ingrid!"

Allie turned in a circle, calling out names, listening, then repeating the action until she kept moving. In a few steps she made it to the break in the trail and without hesitation, stepped onto the trail she had last seen Drake and Ingrid on.

In the rain, the lower trail seemed twice as perilous as the upper trail she and Geneva had taken earlier. Half the trail turned into a small, fast-flowing stream fed by rain and gravity, and Allie did her best to avoid the deepest depressions since she knew that once she stepped into a puddle, she really had no idea where she was placing her foot. Allie feared she'd end up in the back of the Fiat with

Geneva, sharing a backpack to keep their broken ankles elevated.

The path was no simple walk in the park, and Allie moved with a purpose, checking her footholds, and using the surrounding items, be they boulders or trees, to steady herself. After many elongated minutes, Allie turned a corner and found herself on a wider trail. The trail seemed flat and relatively free of obstructions and puddles, so Allie picked up the pace and trudged on for a hundred feet before she came to a stop.

Before her, the path was gone and in its place was a torrent of water rushing down from the mountain above her. She looked up and saw that time had eroded away a section of the mountainside and created a funnel that appeared at least twenty feet wide at the top and narrowed down to four feet where she currently stood. The water rushed fast and free before her.

"No way I'm getting across that," Allie said.

Allie stepped as close as she could to the water without getting the tops of her shoes splashed and looked past the water. Through the intermittent fog, she saw the path beyond, and then, a few feet farther on, an area that looked like a mudslide.

"Drake! Ingrid!" Allie called out. She tried to listen, but all she heard was the water racing by at her feet. She screamed the names again, and louder, but heard nothing in return.

Not able to go on, Allie turned around and made her way back to the meeting tree. She sat and pulled her GPS from her backpack. She brought up the tracking map and followed where she had gone with Geneva to find the geocache, their return to the car, and the little side trip where she tried to follow Drake and Ingrid's path.

"I really need a map of this park," Allie said.

She exhaled, stood, and began her trek back to the parking lot. When she arrived there, she took a picture of the park sign, then got back into the car.

"Did you find them?" Geneva asked.

"Nope. I continued down the trail they did, but it turned into a waterfall with this rain. Were you able to call them?"

"Nope," Geneva said. "I can't get through to anyone. And before you ask, no one else has come through while you were gone."

"You're telling me that mountain climbing during a monsoon isn't on people's lists of fun things to do? I'm shocked!" Allie said with added snark in her voice. "Sorry. Can I have the keys?"

Allie turned around and Geneva passed her the car keys. Allie fired up the engine and turned the heat on high. Then she retrieved her handheld and compared the tracking map to the picture she'd taken with her phone.

"What are you doing?" Geneva asked.

"I'm trying to get a feel for these trails. I'm wondering if the one we were on would have circled back around. Oh, crap."

"What?"

"I cut off half of the sign. I have to go take another picture."

Allie got out of the car and walked back to the sign. There was a large puddle between her and the sign that she needed to give a wide berth to avoid, and when she did, she went way past the sign and noticed for the first time there was a plastic box attached to the rear of the original sign. She stepped up to the box, opened it up, and pulled out a sheet of paper.

"Son of a bitch," Allie said as she noticed what was on the paper.

Allie slid back into the driver's seat, huffed loudly, and

slammed the door.

"What?" Geneva asked.

"Look what I found." Allie passed a copy of an updated trail map to Geneva.

"Where'd you get this from?"

"A box on the sign we all somehow overlooked. It looks recent, at least as of two months ago."

Allie studied the new map and compared it to the tracks on her handheld. "Yep. It would have taken seven kilometers, but that trail would have eventually looped around and met up with the branch Drake and Ingrid took."

"Seven kilometers? What's that in American?"

Allie thought for a second. "Four and a half, perhaps. I know a 5K run is just over three miles."

"Now what? Are you going back out there to take a four-mile walk in the rain?" Geneva asked.

"I don't see like there's another choice," Allie said. "And it would be more like nine miles, since I can't complete the loop with the trail blocked by water. I'd have to go back the way I came."

"That's too much. I should go with you," Geneva said.

Allie turned and looked Geneva in the eyes. "We just had a big fight about that. You should stay here, and you know it."

"Maybe we should go for help. Go back to town."

Allie considered it. "What time is it?"

"One-thirty."

"Okay. The average person can walk four miles an hour, right? That's over an hour there and an hour back, so, three hours tops and I can be back."

"That statistic, if I'm not mistaken, is for even terrain under sunny skies. And I heard it's only three miles an hour, not four."

"Okay, three miles an hour is nine miles in three hours. And I'll add another hour. Let's say that if I'm not back in four hours, then you drive the car to town and get help."

Geneva considered it. "Okay. If you're not back by six, I'll run for the calvary."

Allie nodded. "Good. Just remember that this isn't Boston, so don't drive a hundred down the mountain and try to avoid honking at everyone and everything you see."

Geneva chuckled. "Ha, ha. Hold on a second before you go."

Geneva bent over and retrieved her pack from under her ankle, and rummaged through it until she found a few things. "Here. I have a bottle of water and three protein bars. Take it all."

"You sure?"

"Yes, I'm sure. I'm not the one going to be hungry and thirsty out there. And you might need something for Drake and Ingrid."

"Good point. I wish we had more. I've only got a bottle of water on me," Allie said. She took the items from Geneva and stuffed them in her pack. "We should have packed more food and water."

"Why would we? I think this was the only hard cache on the list and everything else was relatively close to a town where we could get food, water, and gelato anytime we wanted," Geneva said.

"You had to mention the gelato?" Allie said.

Geneva smiled. "You get moving, find our friends, and before you know it, we'll be back at the shop. Maybe I'll buy you a double scoop of something."

"Okay, I'm going to hold you to that," Allie said.

"Hey, you forgot this," Geneva said, holding out the map.

"That's your copy. If someone comes by, you can tell

them what happened and where I went."

"Yellow trail?"

"Yep, that easy-peasy yellow trail anyone could do."

"Wait!" Geneva said. "What if someone comes and they don't speak English?"

Allie thought for a moment, then shrugged. "I don't know, Geneva. I'm sure you'll figure something out. If I don't leave now, I might never, so I'm going now."

Allie shut off the engine, dropped the key fob into the cup holder next to the driver's seat, and left the car. Outside in the rain, she donned the backpack and adjusted the straps for a better fit. She took a deep breath, then, for the third time that day, headed toward the trailhead.

A bolt of lightning flashed off to her side, followed shortly by a rumble of thunder.

"I should have picked up a different hobby, like painting watercolors or knitting scarves," Allie muttered as she stepped onto the trail.

CHAPTER EIGHT

"Well, hello there," Drake said as Ingrid opened her bright blue eyes.

"Hello yourself. How are you doing?" Ingrid asked.

"Not too bad. I'm thirsty. I have a lump on the back of my head the size of a baseball, and I seem to be growing a tree from my stomach."

Ingrid nodded. "That about sums it up. And one of those three I can actually do something about."

Ingrid retrieved Drake's backpack, opened it up, and withdrew a bottle of water. She cracked the seal, then handed it to him.

"Thanks. How did I get here?" Drake asked. "Come to think of it, where is here? I don't remember seeing this cave during the hike."

"Well, I don't know exactly where we are. Do you remember anything about what happened?"

Drake gave his head half a shake. He winced and stopped. "No, I don't."

"Well, the short version of the story is, you thought it would be a good idea to keep going on the trail, and from what I saw, you snagged your foot on something. When you pulled it loose, you lost your balance and headed ass over teakettle down the mountain."

"You're kidding."

"If I were, we'd be in a nice bistro somewhere drinking coffee and eating whatever the Italian version of scones is," Ingrid gathered her backpack, found her own water within, and had a swallow. "Allie would probably tell us."

"Tell us what?"

"What the Italian version of a scone is," Ingrid said.

Drake thought for a moment. "I don't know what it could be. You're right, though. Allie would. She knows a remarkable amount of random trivia. How did you say we got here?"

Ingrid clambered to her feet and stretched her hands overhead and cracked her neck and back. Once she limbered up, she sat back down next to Drake.

"It was no big deal. Once you disappeared over the cliff, I made my way down the mountain, found you, and single-handedly carried you into this dark, damp cave."

"You? Carried me?" Drake asked. "Thank you. I take it I was in a bit of trouble?"

A grave expression passed over Ingrid's face. "Let's just say I expected to find you dead, or never find you at all. I suspect if you'd continued on another twenty feet, it would have been both."

"Thanks for finding me and for getting me to safety," Drake said.

Ingrid shook her head and frowned. "Neither one of us is safe quite yet. All I did was get us under shelter from the rain. We're a way off from the main trail, and I'm not sure if I can get back the way I came. And I know you wouldn't be able to do it with a branch sticking out of you."

"I'm sure I could yank it out and be fine," Drake said,

lifting his shirt and looking at the protrusion.

"I'm equally sure that would be the last stupid thing you'd ever do. You know better than I do. It should stay where it is until you can get professional help."

"You're a professional," Drake said.

"I'm an English teacher. If you want to write an essay about it, then I'll be of help to you. Otherwise, let it go."

Drake grinned. "Got you."

Ingrid rolled her eyes. "Jerk."

"I'm tired," Drake said. "Really tired."

"I'll bet. I shouldn't have fallen asleep and let you doze off. You might have a concussion."

"First off, based purely on the lump on my head, it would surprise me if I don't have one. Second, I'm pretty sure experts debunked the whole don't go to sleep with a concussion thing."

"You sure about that?" Ingrid asked.

Drake shrugged. "Sixty percent."

Ingrid smiled. "Such confidence. I love that in a man."

"Sorry, I'm already taken."

"Yeah, me too. So, before you go off into dreamland, what are we going to do here?"

"I assume you already tried to call for help and couldn't reach anyone?"

"Correct. We have no service."

Drake took a drink of water as he pondered their situation further. "You sure we're off the trail?"

Ingrid nodded.

"How far? Can you tell?"

Ingrid retrieved her GPS from her pack and booted it up.   "That geocache had parking coordinates, right? I should be able to tell how far we are from those. The only problem is, they'd be straight up the mountain. I don't know how far I traveled to find you, but most of it was downhill. I passed one deer trail somewhere above us, and then there's this one we're on now, but I don't know where they lead, if anywhere."

"Would you guess we're a half mile off the main trail?" Drake asked.

"For sure. Probably more. Hold on, I've got no signal here in the cave. I'm going to step outside and see if I can get better reception."

Ingrid got to her feet and headed toward the cave's mouth.

"Hey, wait," Drake said. "Are you bleeding?"

Ingrid stopped and looked down at her leg. It was the first time she had stopped for a good look. She had shredded the pants in several strips, each at least six inches in length. The jeans contained dark ribbons of blood, but it didn't seem fresh.

"You should let me take a gander at that," Drake said.

"No, way, mister. There's no way I'm dropping my pants for you. I got us this far, so I'm sure I'll live. I'll be right back."

Ingrid stepped from the cave and found the largest open spot she could find. Eventually, the geocache list came up, and she selected the closest one and started to drill into the parking coordinates when the unit blinked rapidly several times and the screen grew dark.

"Shit," Ingrid said. She pressed the power button, but nothing happened. Standing in the rain, she flipped it over, opened the back, and dug out the batteries. Ingrid inspected them, saw nothing wrong, then shoved them back into place and button the unit back up. Again, the power button failed to work, so she hit the unit several times, knowing full well that objects often responded to brute force. Dejected, she headed back to Drake.

"My GPS isn't working. Can I try yours?"

"My unit is your unit," Drake said. "Should be in my pack."

Ingrid went through his pack and found it. She looked at it once, then shook her head.

"What?" Drake asked.

Ingrid turned the unit around. The screen looked cracked, and although it shouldn't happen, a chunk of the top corner was missing.

"And with my luck, the warranty period expired," Drake said.

"I guess it's back to the question of what we should do," Ingrid said.

"Well, experts say that if you get lost in the woods, you should stay put and wait for help to get to you," Drake said.

"True. But I wouldn't call this a normal woods situation. It's not like there's going to be a lot of hunters or hikers where we are."

"I think we have to try to walk out of here when the rain stops," Drake said. "It can't rain forever, can it?"

Ingrid smiled. "No more than forty days and nights at one time."

"I heard that somewhere once, too. Can you help me up?"

Ingrid stepped in front of Drake. With a grunt, helped him to his feet.

"Let me go," Drake said.

"Are you sure?"

Drake passed her a look, and Ingrid released him and backed away two feet. Drake took a step forward, then hesitated. Instead of moving forward, he stepped back again.

"Help me back down."

Ingrid did as she was told, and Drake rested his back against the cave wall.

"How did that feel?" Ingrid asked.

"Like someone had stabbed me with one of those wooden lances that knights jousted with. I think I could walk, but not far, and there's no way I can climb anywhere, other than into a bed."

"Okay," Ingrid said. "What's the plan?"

"Well, survival in the woods is usually about shelter, food, water, and fire," Drake said. "We're a quarter finished already, thanks to you."

"More if you count the water we have on us," Ingrid said. "How much do you have?"

Drake held out his half-filled bottle. "This much. You?"

Ingrid held hers up. It was three-quarters full.

"Okay. The first step of the plan is to put mine outside and let the rain fill it. See if there's a spot where you can use a palm leaf to funnel more water into the bottle."

"Palm leaf?" Ingrid asked.

"Wishful thinking. Find something that isn't poison ivy, oak, or sumac."

"Okay."

Ingrid grabbed his bottle and stepped outside. Off to the cave's side, opposite from the direction they'd come, she found a spot where the rain fell almost straight down at a steady rate. She looked up, following the source, and guessed it was a twist of fate that had the water dripping down through the trees as it did. She placed the bottle on the ground beneath the stream, and stacked rocks around the bottle so it wouldn't tip over. Ingrid watched the flow for a moment and estimated the bottle would fill to the brim within fifteen minutes if the rain kept up.

"What's next?" Ingrid asked as she stepped back into the cave.

"Food or fire. What do we have for food?" Drake said.

Drake dumped out his backpack. He had a chocolate bar and a pack of gum. Ingrid rooted through her pack and added two granola bars.

"Not much," Ingrid said.

"No matter. Water's the important thing. We can worry about food later. Now, what about fire?" Drake asked.

"Oh, I got that one handled," Ingrid said. "I'll be right back. I need to do a little exploring."

Ingrid dumped the contents from her backpack in a pile next to Drakes, then picked up his pack as well.

"You got your phone on you, or did you lose it?" Ingrid asked.

Drake leaned over and pulled his phone from the front pocket of his jeans. "Fortunately, I was smart enough to tuck this away before I fell."

He handed the phone to Ingrid, and she took a look at it. Like his GPS, the phone was trash. The screen appeared shattered, and there was a hairline crack along the backside. Ingrid shook it and water dripped out of the charging port. She tossed it back to him.

"You're kind of hard on electronics, Drake."

Drake caught the phone one-handed, looked it over, and threw it on the pile of stuff.

"I'll be back in a minute," Ingrid said. She turned and walked farther into the cave.

Once she got away from the wide cave mouth, the light dropped from dark gray to black in an instant. Ingrid dug out her phone and turned on the flashlight function. A foot off to her left, she found a bunch of dry pine needles on the cave floor. She gathered them into a pile, then brushed them into a backpack. Near the needles, she scored big time and found a brittle branch at least eight feet long. She dragged the branch all the way back to Drake, asked him to break it into smaller pieces, and headed back into the cave again.

Ingrid took her time exploring the cave. Every piece of wood or kindling she could cram into the backpacks, she did.

Needles, leaves, or branches. If she thought it would burn, she collected it. Whatever wouldn't fit into the bags, she carried back to Drake and built a pile.

Satisfied she'd collected enough for the moment, Ingrid went back to Drake, emptied her bags, and sorted her stash by type and size.

"What are you doing?" Drake asked.

"Magic. Sit tight, buddy."

Ingrid stepped into the rain, looked around, and started throwing rocks into the cave, just inside the entrance. Since she was already out and getting wet, she checked Drake's bottle, found it full, and returned it to him.

"Here's some fresh water. Hopefully, you don't get any bugs," Ingrid said as she handed him the bottle. Drake looked at the contents, shook the bottle to see what debris was floating in it, and then set the bottle aside.

Ingrid gathered up the stones and formed them into a rough circle, approximately two feet across. Then she added a small pile of pine needles to the center of the pile, along with several twigs.

"You have a match on you?" Ingrid asked.

"What?"

Ingrid grinned. "Never mind. Throw me your handheld and that gum."

Drake brushed through the pile, located the items Ingrid wanted, and tossed them over to her.

"What are you up to?" Drake asked.

"I already told you that. It's magic."

Ingrid extracted a piece of gum from the pack and put the stick in her mouth. Then she carefully folded the wrapper lengthwise and folded it back over itself. She unfolded the wrapper, then carefully tore the wrapper into three thin strips. Then, working as deliberately as she could, Ingrid tore pieces away from the center of a strip until only a thin segment remained. She repeated the process with the other strips, and when she finished, she had three nearly identical strips that resembled little foil hourglasses.

Ingrid set the wrappers down, cracked open Drake's GPS, retrieved the AA batteries from inside, and tossed the rest of the broken unit away. Ingrid placed one of the batteries inside the fire ring, right next to the pile of needles.

"I hope this works," Ingrid said.

"What?" Drake asked.

Without answering, Ingrid grabbed one of the small strips of gum wrapper, folded it over so the foil ends were on the inside, and depressed them around the positive and negative terminals of the battery.

"Ouch!" Ingrid said as a tiny spark erupted from the wrapper and lit the pine needles. Ingrid licked her forefinger and thumb, then quickly pulled the battery from the fire, and tossed it into the cave. It rolled for a foot and stopped right in front of Drake.

"You've got to be kidding me," Drake said. "That's amazing. Where did you learn to do that?"

Ingrid smiled as she fed the fire a few of the twigs and began to scatter them atop the building flames.

"All Danes are natural arsonists," she said. She caught Drake's shocked look and smiled. "Okay, strike that. When I was little, I spent a few years in the Girl Scouts. Can you come over and tend the fire?"

"Sure thing," Drake said. He had four feet of ground to cover, but rather than attempt to stand and walk, he got on his hands and knees and approached the fire that way. Ingrid moved the firewood pile, so it was closer to Drake. She rubbed her hands over the fire, enjoying the warmth.

"You know how to do this?" Ingrid asked.

"Yep," Drake said. "I have enough camping trips under my belt to give me the experience."

Ingrid nodded. "Okay. You keep an eye on the fire, and I'm going to see if I can find any more fuel. Since I don't know how long we'll be here, I want to gather as much as I can now."

"Good idea," Drake said. "And good luck."

Ingrid nodded, grabbed the empty backpacks, and headed back inside the cave.

She had a mental image of where she walked, so she didn't bother turning on the light until she was a good ten feet into the cave. Once again, she scoured the cave for fire materials, and finally, she reached the end of the cave where it came to a T junction.

Closer to the right wall, she turned right and immediately the walls closed in, the cave sides no farther than three feet apart from each other. She followed the path, but found it void of burnable material except for one three-foot-long stick. After fifteen feet, she came to a dead end and turned around.

Ingrid returned to the junction and continued straight. After four feet, the walls closed in on her, forcing Ingrid to turn sideways to fit in the corridor. She side-shuffled her way for twenty feet when the walls blew out again and Ingrid found herself in a large cavern.

She lifted her phone above her head, hoping to illuminate the area, but the darkness absorbed the light after six feet. Ingrid walked with the wall to her right, finding nothing until she spotted something that looked like a jacket. As she stepped closer, she realized the item was not a coat at all, but rather an old wool blanket. As she picked it up, the stiff fibers scratched against her arms, and by chance she looked at where the blanket had laid on the floor. There, on the floor, was a pile of stones laid out in the shape of an arrow.

Curious, Ingrid moved forward and another twenty-five feet later, she encountered a wall. Sitting on the floor before her were a couple of hand tools she didn't recognize. She picked them up and placed one in each back pocket. When she ran her light over the wall, she spotted something she didn't expect. Crudely cut into the wall was a bas-relief of an elephant.

"What in the world?" Ingrid asked to the empty room.

The sculpture showed the elephant in profile, and although some of the detail had worn away with time, the large body, rectangle legs, gigantic head, floppy ears, and tusks were unmistakably those of an elephant.

On either side of the elephant were two-foot-high curved tusks carved into the wall, covered in mosaic tiles, some of which were missing.

Ingrid couldn't help herself, so she ran her fingertips over the elephant, feeling the intricate detail. When she finished, her fingers drifted over to the tusk to her right. The tactile differences in the tile were striking. Some were polished smooth, like glass. Others seemed pitted and craggy, like stone. As Ingrid ran her fingers over one tile in particular, the cold sensation of its surface felt to her like a metal of some sort. Not intending to, she applied a little pressure, and the tile slipped from the sculpture and clattered when it hit the stone floor.

Ingrid looked around like security had caught her vandalizing an art museum, then bent and retrieved the piece she'd dropped. She attempted to place the piece where she'd knocked it from, but it dropped again. Ingrid caught it in midair and held it in her palm for a minute, thinking about what to do.

At last, she got an idea. From her mouth, she took the gum she'd been chewing on the entire time and placed it on the inside of the tile. Then she placed the tile where it belonged and pushed.

What Ingrid expected was that the gum would stick to the wall, holding the tile in place. Instead, Ingrid heard a loud click, and suddenly the elephant before her slid back into the wall, and off to the side, revealing a secret compartment.

Ingrid moved closer, brought the light up, and shined it in the hole.

CHAPTER NINE

I should have never agreed to the plan. We should have gone as a group. Together. Never, ever should have split up," Allie mumbled as she stepped down the initial stairs leading to the main trail. "Nothing good ever happens when the group splits up."

Allie reached the bottom stair, stopped, yawned, and moved on.

"We should all be in a nice, warm, dry museum somewhere. Looking at four-thousand-year-old art and listening to Drake whine about how he wants to leave. Or in a little cafe in some little town where they only speak Italian, eating pasta and drinking wine and telling stories until the rain lets up. But no. I'm out here in that rain, trudging around a mountainside, looking for my lost people."

Since she'd covered the same section of trail several times already, she recognized the area as she walked. Allie moved swiftly, aware of where to step, and less afraid that she'd make a misstep along the way. She still avoided the puddles where she could, but her mission had long drifted from worrying about remaining dry and clean. That train had blown well past the station.

"Nine miles. That's a long way, Allie," she said to herself. "Are you even ready for nine miles? In reality, probably not. Will your bad knee hold up for nine miles? Again, probably not. The smart thing to do would go back to the car, overcome your fear of the road, drive down the stupid mountain, and find a big St. Bernard, preferably carrying a little barrel of brandy. Let the dog find Drake and Ingrid. But today isn't about doing smart things, is it?"

The thunder rumbled in answer, and Allie glanced up toward the sky, although she couldn't see it. She thought perhaps the rain had lessened, but realized the section she currently sped-walked through contained a dense section of trees that prevented a good amount of rain from falling directly to the ground.

"Perhaps geocaching the Alps wasn't a good idea, after all. It's my fault we're here. Drake warned me about this, about going crazy with ideas, but I didn't listen. I could have written down a tropical beach location. Hawaii. That would have been a better idea. No, wait. That has jungles. And volcanoes. No. Not Hawaii."

Allie stopped for a second, realizing she'd been walking without bothering to track her surroundings. She turned around and glanced at the scenery behind her. Everything still looked familiar, so she restarted her walk. She plodded on in silence for several minutes, and at last she came to the downed tree where they all should have reunited hours prior. Rather than pull the paper map from her backpack and risk it getting drenched, she brought up the picture of it she'd taken with her phone. Up ahead a few yards, the trail split into the upper and lower sections, which looped around and returned to the junction.

She resized the image, making the section she was on bigger, and focused on that. With her finger, she traced the lower section she believed she'd already seen when she went to find her missing friends for the first time. She studied the curves and came to a conclusion.

"See, it's not as bad as you thought, Allie. Based on my estimate, I checked a good couple of kilometers already before that blockage. That's a third of the path I've covered."

Rejuvenated by her own pep talk, Allie headed for the upper trail. The trail followed a ridge and stayed relatively level for almost a mile. The trail appeared well groomed, free of rocks, limbs, and other debris, so even in the rain, Allie had no difficulties moving at a swift pace. After only ten minutes, she came to a section where the mountain overhung the trail. It was there were Allie and Geneva had initially waited undercover to see if the rain was going to let up.

Inside the cutout, someone had long ago carved out a five-foot length of rock, making a primitive seating area.

"Let's take a brief break," Allie announced as she slipped her backpack from her shoulders. She put the pack on the cutout and took a seat next to it. It actually wasn't a bad spot. With the falling rain going over the edge of the cutout, she got the impression that she was sitting inside a waterfall. Allie fought the urge to take off her shoes, and instead she massaged her left calf, and then her right. Once she'd relieved the tension in both legs, she withdrew a water bottle and had a mouthful of liquid, then stowed it back in her pack.

"You ready to go on, Allie?" she asked herself.

She thought for a moment, then answered. "No. Not really. I'd much prefer to stay here until it stops raining, and I dry up and get warm. I never thought much about the expression chilled to the bone, but I'm certainly feeling that way today."

Allie groaned as she pushed her way to her feet. "Time to go."

Allie returned the backpack to her shoulders, then stepped back into the rain. After another hundred yards, she recognized the fir tree where she and Geneva had turned around when the downpour started. The spruce was easy to recognize. It was right beside the trail, and someone had pruned away the bottom six feet of branches on the trail side. Allie walked on into the unknown.

She plodded for another quarter mile when she came to an area with several steps cut into the mountainside, supported by railroad ties, similar to the beginning of the trailhead. In this case, there appeared to be twice as many steps.

"Okay, let's take this one nice and easy, Allie. No missteps. No broken ankles."

Allie took the first step down and determined it was steep, but otherwise, wasn't too bad. The step slanted slightly, so the water ran to the edge, and from there, a channel carried the water down the slope. Allie stepped down the subsequent stairs with equal parts confidence and awareness, and she counted each step as she went.

"Lucky twenty-one," Allie said when she finally reached the bottom. "Whew, my legs are burning. I can't wait to go back up these."

Allie walked ten yards, found a downed tree stripped of bark bordering the trail and sat for a moment to rest. The tree was a long one, just over seven feet, and it tapered smaller in diameter toward Allie's left. As Allie leaned back to stretch, she looked to the left and then to the right. She returned to her normal sitting position, then leaned back again. There, about four feet to her right, sat an unnatural pile of rocks, otherwise known as a UPR. The UPR, a common way to hide a geocache in the woods, closely resembled its cousin, the UPS, or unnatural pile of sticks. The unnatural part came in because nature never stacked sticks or rocks in nice, symmetrical piles and then attempted to make them look natural. Only people did that.

Allie stood, moved over, sat back down, and began moving rocks. Sure enough, underneath the makeshift cairn was a plastic ammo box with a geocaching sticker on the side. Allie picked up the box, opened it, and squealed with delight. She removed an item from the ammo can, closed the box, and set it on the ground before her. Then she opened the package and donned the cheap florescent blue rain poncho she'd found in the geocache. She made sure the poncho cleared her backpack, then she put on the hood. Although the plastic was about the same quality Allie was familiar with from packing her own groceries at her local supermarket, it was good enough for the current situation.

Covered, Allie picked up the ammo can and checked to see if there was anything else useful inside. She found the paper log in a small plastic baggie, a string of plastic beads, two toy cars, one Euro coin, one American quarter, and a rock. The rock she took from the cache and dropped it at her feet. Then she closed up the ammo box, returned it to its spot, and covered it with the rocks.

"That was exciting. Score one for me," Allie said when she got back to her feet.

As Allie walked on, she discovered the lower loop seemed nowhere near as well-groomed as the upper trail. She found potholes galore to avoid, tree roots, and rocks to keep aware of, and her pace slowed considerably.

After an arduous twenty minutes of hiking, Allie came to a fork in the road. The marker attached to the tree nearby told Allie to stay on the upper trail where she was, but to her right, a well-used and pronounced deer trail branched down the mountainside. Allie retrieved her phone and checked the map. The yellow trail made a single loop, and where the group had divided earlier in the day was the only sanctioned trail. Allie shoved the phone back in her pocket and continued on the upper trail.

"I've got to be getting close by now. Ingrid! Drake!" Allie called out. She heard nothing back, so she kept walking. Fifteen minutes later, she came to a place she recognized. In front of her was a downed tree next to the trail, not unlike the several others she'd discovered on the trail. In front of this log stood a puddle of mud and water. Beyond the log was a short section of clear trail, and beyond that was the rushing water that blocked her path earlier.

Allie cupped her hands around her mouth and screamed. "Ingrid! Drake! Can you hear me? Drake! Ingrid!"

Allie stopped and waited, hearing nothing but the water near her and the sound of the rain hitting the earth.

Allie screamed their names repeatedly for five minutes, disheartened she hadn't heard a response. Although she wanted to cry, both for her missing friends, and from pure exhaustion, she didn't. Instead, Allie dropped her head and rubbed her temple. As she moved her hand, she looked down and spotted something unusual. She crouched and got as close to the ground as she could without sitting. There, she ran her fingertips over the shoe print in the mud.

Although only the back half of the print was visible, Allie still recognized it immediately. There was a stamp in the mud, and although it was backward, she read it easily.

"Converse All Star." Allie said. "From Ingrid's brand-new Chuck Taylors."

Allie's sense of relief was short-lived when it occurred to her that the front half of the footprint would have put Ingrid over the side.

"Oh, crap," Allie said.

She leaned as far forward over the side as she could without falling and looked for any evidence of Ingrid or Drake but spotted nothing. She backed away from the edge.

"Okay, Allie, think about this a minute. You didn't pass them on the trail, and there weren't many opportunities or a reason to go anywhere else but the trail."

Allie turned to her left and shoved the puzzle pieces into place.

"They came this way and got caught. Couldn't go back because of the water, so tried to make it to this side of the trail to loop around when something happened here." Her eyes drifted from the log to the muddy path to the edge. "Oh, double crap."

Allie spent several minutes screaming the names of Drake and Ingrid into the void, and got nothing in return for it.

"Okay, down it is, I guess," Allie said. She looked for a way down, starting with the spot where she found Ingrid's shoe print. Allie moved up the trail a few feet and found a place where she thought she could start down the mountain. She moved her foot off the trail, found the rock she wanted, hesitated for two long breaths, and pulled her foot back to the trail.

"Always wanting to do things the hard way," Allie said as she turned around and started jogging down the trail.

She almost ran past what she was looking for, and had to stop, turn herself around, and backtrack to where she found the deer trail that broke away from the main trail.

"I hope this leads somewhere," Allie said as she stepped onto the trail.

Unlike the main trail, the deer trail was, in a word, precarious. The trail ranged from between eight to twelve inches wide with prevalent rocks, tree roots, and the occasional section of underbrush that Allie needed to push through in order to move forward. All the while having to deal with slippery mud underfoot.

Still, Allie pressed on even though her speed had

dropped to a leisurely walk, bordering on a stroll. In several places, the trail came to spots where nothing but a few inches of ground separated the mountain's wall and the drop off.

A half hour later, Allie came to another branch. She flipped a mental coin, and rather than veer right and farther down the mountain, she continued on straight. For the first fifty yards, the walk was easy going. The path widened and flattened out, and the tree cover lessened, so although that meant less protection from the rain, Allie could at least enjoy the sky for a little while as she walked.

Then, the trees closed back in, the mountain slope grew steep, and the trail narrowed to nothing wider than a shoe. Allie carried on for another twenty yards, stepped around a boulder, and came to a spot where the trail ended at a sheer drop that started twenty feet over her head, and fell another forty feet below her. Had Allie been an ibex or a chamois, she easily might have pressed on forward, but since she was neither animal, she needed to pivot on one foot to turn around.

Before she did, she paused.

"Ingrid? Drake?" Allie called out, hoping for an answer. She repeated her calls and waited for a few minutes. When she felt her feet cramp, she recognized it was time to move on.

Slowly, Allie made her way back to where the trail split, then turned left and stopped. The trail sloped down a good sixty degrees and it was at least a six-foot drop between where she stood and the bottom.

Allie noticed a sapling to her right, and bent it over, intending to use it as an anchor as she descended the short section of trail. The first two steps worked fine, but on the third, her foot slipped. As she struggled for purchase with her feet, the young branch separated from the tree. Allie landed on her backside and slid to the bottom of the short hill. Allie stopped when she reached the bottom, then got to her feet. Thin mud coated the entire back of her pants, and only the poncho had saved her top half from being the same. Allie didn't even bother to brush herself. Instead, she looked around until she found the next section of trail and moved forward.

"This isn't so bad," Allie noted as she trudged on.

The current trail was much wider, contained actual green space on both sides of the trail, and remained relatively flat. Five minutes later, Allie stopped.

"Seriously?" she asked.

Before her, blocking the way ahead, was a deadfall. The giant spruce covered the entire width of the trail and had fallen in such a way that the massive root ball had wedged itself between two trees above the trail. The tree had then bent in on itself, and the top three feet had snapped in half, but remained connected to the tree by strips of bark. It dangled over the edge of the cliff like mistletoe. Between Allie and the opposite side of the trail were nine feet of thick fir branches, along with the debris it had brought along on its slide down the mountain.

Allie stepped back from the monster and analyzed the situation. She doubted she could go up and over, and she recognized that going the other way was out of the question, so it left her with no choice but picking her way right through the branches.

She stepped to the tree and moved the nearest branch. When she did, yellow and brown pine needles dropped from the branch and fell to the ground. As a test to see if the tree was old and brittle, Allie attempted to break off the branch. She couldn't. She moved out farther where the branch was narrower, and with some effort, snapped the branch.

"Clearly I'd need a chainsaw for this," Allie said under her breath. "Come on, girl, you can do this. Think of it as looking for a pine tree cache. You've found plenty of those before."

Instead of walking directly into the tree, Allie found a small gap in between boughs and stepped into that. There, she grabbed the branch in front of her, pulled it back until it was past her, then stepped through, letting the branch settle back in its original position. If the branch was pliable and small enough, Allie draped it over or under an adjacent branch to hold it in place. Regardless of the method, it made for slow going, and it took Allie ten minutes to gain eight feet of forward movement.

Once past the tree, Allie was able to gain speed again. Although the path grew narrower and the green space lessened, the terrain remained flat, and she hustled full speed ahead.

Allie stopped.

On the trail ahead, Allie saw a cave, and within the cave, she saw a flicker that implied a fire was burning. Her heart jumped, and she picked up the pace. She stopped in her tracks when she got to the mouth. A wide grin crossed her face when she saw Drake sitting on the floor, poking at the fire with a stick.

"Are you roasting chestnuts there, Duck-man?"

CHAPTER TEN

Drake looked up, and his demeanor changed in a microsecond.

"Allie!" He tried to get to his feet, lost his balance, and fell on his backside.

Allie rushed over and wrapped her arms around his neck. "Drake! I can't tell you how happy I am to see you."

"How did you know we were down here?" Drake asked.

"Are you kidding me? I'm three-quarters bloodhound," Allie said.

Drake's expression told Allie he wasn't buying it.

Allie stripped off the poncho and sat down cross-legged in front of the fire opposite Drake. She leaned forward, warming her hands.

"Okay, you got me. I spotted Ingrid's footprint in the mud, made a few general assumptions, ran into both good and bad luck and viola. Here I am. Speaking of whom, where is Ingrid? What happened to you guys?"

Drake threw a thumb over his shoulder. "She's back in the cave looking for stuff to burn. I suspect she's convinced we're never going to get out of here."

"She's safe, then?" Allie asked.

Drake nodded. "She saved me, Allie. I almost died out here, and she pulled me up the mountain and into this cave."

"No way," Allie said.

"Way."

"Tell me all about it," Allie said.

As Drake tended the fire, he spent several minutes giving Allie the story, at least, as much of it as he remembered.

"That's the worst story I've ever heard," Allie said when Drake finished.

"Ingrid would tell it much better. I think she was awake for more of this adventure than I was."

"How are you feeling? Anything broken?" Allie asked.

"No breaks, so far as I can tell. I've got a lump on my head, and this."

Drake lifted his shirt, exposing the protrusion.

"Holy cow, Drake, what did you do?" Allie asked.

Allie got to her feet and rushed to Drake's side, where she inspected his injury.

"What do you think, doc?" Drake asked after she checked his head and settled back down by the fire.

"Well, you're in need of an actual doctor. I don't imagine you have any internal bleeding, so I'm not even going to entertain the idea of ripping that wood out of your stomach. And as for your head, you'll need a scan for that. Thankfully, it was your head, so you couldn't have done too much damage."

Drake stuck his tongue out at Allie and laughed despite himself.

"Hey, Ingrid's injured, too. Her leg looks messed up, but she wouldn't let me check it out."

"Thanks for the heads up. She ventured into that cave,

you said? To search for wood?"

Drake nodded. "Yeah. She's been gone a while now. I don't know what's up."

"I'd better go track her down. Can you wait here?"

Drake smiled. "I'm pretty sure I can handle that."

Allie grabbed her backpack and fished out a flashlight.

"You hungry?" Allie asked Drake.

"Do you have a T-bone steak in there? Medium-rare? Baked potato with the works, and a side of fried shrimp?" Drake asked.

"No, but I have a granola bar," Allie said, waving the bar in the air.

"I'll pretend," Drake said. "Thanks."

Allie tossed Drake the bar, who caught it in mid-air.

"We'll be back in a bit," Allie said.

Drake waved her off. "Take your time. I'm not going anywhere."

Allie clicked on the flashlight and stepped deeper into the cave.

Although Allie's flashlight was less than six inches in length, the LEDs illuminated a vast area within the cave. Nearby, she spotted a pile of longer branches she assumed was Ingrid's work and saw lots of tinder and fuel material that Ingrid had bypassed for some reason. Allie made it all the way to the cave's rear without finding Ingrid, but it wasn't long before Allie spotted the same corridors that Ingrid had. Like her friend, she tried the right one first and retraced her steps when she arrived at the dead end.

Once she backtracked and headed in the other direction, Allie quickly found the other room, and at the far wall, she spotted Ingrid.

When Ingrid saw her own shadow on the wall, she turned around and faced the light. She held up a hand to shield her eyes from the glare.

"Who's there?" Ingrid asked, her voice projecting a slight tremor of fear.

"The Ghost of Christmas Past," Allie said.

"What? Who?"

"Ingrid, it's me. Allie."

Allie dropped the light, so the beam struck the floor instead of her friend. She rushed across the room and caught Ingrid in a hug.

"I've gathered you've had a long day," Allie said.

Ingrid exhaled. "You could say that again."

"I also understand you're injured."

Ingrid waved it off. "It's nothing. Simply a tiny scrape."

"Maybe. I still want to glance at your leg when we get back to the sunlight. Speaking of which, why have you been gone for so long?"

"I found something. Let me have your flashlight."

Allie handed over the light without question, and Ingrid took it and turned back toward the wall.

"What are you doing?" Allie asked as Ingrid shined the light into the hole.

"Seeing what's in here," Ingrid answered. "I found this secret compartment, and I think there's something in here."

Ingrid set the flashlight on the edge of the compartment, stood on her tiptoes, and reached in as far as she could. Her arm disappeared past the elbow.

"I almost got it. I can feel it. It's just out of reach," Ingrid said. "Arrrghh!" she screamed. Ingrid went silent, her mouth opening and closing like a carp in a koi pond. Her eyelids fluttered, and her eyes rolled back in her head.

"Ingrid?" Allie said, stepping forward. She put her hand on Ingrid's shoulder. "What's going on? Ingrid?"

Ingrid's eyes focused on Allie's, and a wide grin spread across her face. "Gotcha."

Allie gave Ingrid's shoulder a push. "Not funny. Really.

Not funny."

"Sure, it was. I've waited my entire life to do that to someone. I'm glad it was you."

"Would you quit messing around?" Allie said.

"Can you reach in there for me? My arm is like an inch too short," Ingrid said.

Allie stared at her without speaking.

"Seriously, Allie. It's an inch out of my reach. I can feel it, but I can't grab it."

Allie and Ingrid stood about the same height, but Allie's arms were a touch longer than Ingrid's.

Allie gave her a double take and switched positions with Ingrid. She put her arm in the hole and looked back at Ingrid.

"Don't think about it," Ingrid said.

Allie smiled. "Little old me? I would never. I got it."

Allie removed her arm from the chamber, and in her hand was an item, and she handed it to Ingrid.

"Anything else in there?" Ingrid asked.

"Nope, it's empty."

"Okay. Watch this." Ingrid located the proper tile on the tusk and pressed it. There was a clunk, a hiss, and the bas-relief pushed back into place.

"Is that an elephant?" Allie asked.

"Amazing, isn't it?"

"Sure is." Allie pulled her phone from her pocket and snapped pictures of the elephant and the tusks.

"Anything else to see in here?" Allie asked.

"Don't know. I didn't have a flashlight. You can look around if you like."

"Let's do it."

Allie took the flashlight and together, the women walked around the room. Allie focused the flashlight on the walls and floor, and soon they covered the entire area, finding nothing.

"Satisfied?" Allie asked.

"Yeah. I'll grab the blanket I found, and we'll head back to Drake."

Allie lit the way, and Ingrid picked up her treasure, and together, they headed back to the entrance. Near the fire, they found Drake lying on his side, softly snoring, the empty granola bar wrapper in his hand.

Ingrid covered him with her newly found blanket, then returned to Allie and embraced her in a bear hug.

"Did I tell you how happy I am to see you?" Ingrid asked.

"Not yet, but I'm ready." Allie wrapped her arms around Ingrid, and her hands moved down to Ingrid's back pockets. "What's this? You have something in your pocket, or are you happy to see me?"

"Oh, yeah." Ingrid broke away from the hug and stepped back. From her back pockets, she extracted the tools she'd found. In her left hand, she held a wood-handled trowel, the blade of which was crusted with rust, and looked like they salvaged it from the sea. In her right hand, she held a wood handle. Whatever was connected to the head had disappeared over time.

Allie took the tools and set them on the ground. "Can I take a look at that leg now?"

"It's not a big deal, just a little scrape," Ingrid argued.

Allie shook her head. "Don't argue. Just drop your pants and let me look."

"What about Drake?"

Allie looked over Ingrid's shoulder and noticed Drake hadn't moved an inch. "Drake is sleeping. Come on, let's get this over with."

Ingrid sighed, but complied. She undid her jeans and gritted her teeth while she inhaled as she slowly lowered her pants. She turned so Allie could have access to her leg.

"Oh, man. You're lucky I consider scars are sexy because I expect you're going to have a couple."

"Is it bad?" Ingrid asked.

"You look like you were either dragged by a horse across Oklahoma or slid down a mountain in Switzerland. Why don't you lay down on your side and try to get comfortable? I'll be right back."

Ingrid looked around for a comfortable place to settle in, and while she did, Allie retrieved her poncho and laid it down on the ground and spread it out as much as she could.

"Here, lay your butt on this," Allie said.

Allie went and retrieved her backpack. From it, she pulled her water and a pair of white socks in a plastic sandwich baggie.

"What are you doing?" Ingrid asked.

"Lay still and try not to move."

Allie removed the socks from the bag and put one over her hand like a glove. She wet the sock with the water, then gently wiped away the dirt and dried blood from Ingrid's hip, careful not to reopen any wounds.

"Drake told me you saved him. I'd like to hear your side of the story," Allie said as she worked on Ingrid's leg.

"There's not much to tell. We were on the yellow trail when the rain came. Then got cut off by a flood, and when Drake tried to carry on, he slipped and toppled over the edge. I climbed down the mountain and found him, then got us into this cave."

Allie chuckled. "This is going to be an amazing story once you learn how to expand the details and add a little more drama."

"Ouch," Ingrid said as she flinched.

"Sorry. You've got a stone about the size of a dime embedded in your leg that I'm trying to get out."

Ingrid flinched again. "That hurts. Leave it in there. I'll tell people it's a piercing."

"Oh, hush. I've almost got it." Allie picked at the stone a third time, and finally it let go of Ingrid's leg and dropped onto the poncho. A small trickle of blood came from the site, so Allie applied pressure to stem its flow. With her other hand, she picked up the stone and placed it into Ingrid's palm. "Here. You can keep this as a souvenir."

Ingrid eyed the stone for a moment, then closed her hand around it. "Thanks. How's it looking back there?"

"Well, it doesn't seem as bad as it did before I started. I do think you'll need to see a doctor and get a better cleaning than I can give you with a sock. You might also take a course of antibiotics just to be safe. For now, though, I've done all I can do."

Ingrid rolled onto her butt, and Allie helped her up. While Ingrid got back into her pants, Allie cleaned up the area and stowed her supplies in her pack. When they finished, they both sat back near the fire.

"How did you find us?" Ingrid asked as she opened the protein bar Allie had given to her.

"I found an updated trail map. It turns out that the trail loops around just like we assumed it did. I found your footprint up top and pieced together what happened."

"So you climbed down the mountain, too?"

Allie shook her head. "Didn't have to. Down the trail, the part you didn't get to yet, I found a deer trail that branched off down here. That's the way we're going to get back."

"Where was it?"

Allie pointed in the direction from where she'd come. "That way."

Ingrid shook her head. "I checked that way. There's a big pine blocking the road. Can't get through there."

"I got through. Took some effort, but I did it. After that, there are only a couple of spots that are a little difficult."

Ingrid took a bite, chewed, and swallowed. She washed it down with a drink of water before she spoke again. "What I meant was, I don't think Drake can get through there. He's got a bump on the noggin and a tree growing from his stomach."

"Yes, I saw them both."

"I can't get him through that tree by myself. Earlier, he had trouble talking and walking."

"He was talking pretty good when I got here. It's probably a result of the ding on his head. We'll let him rest for a bit. Together, I'm sure we can get him out of here," Allie said.

"Should we move him? Would that be the best thing to do here? Why not just go back and get some help?" Ingrid asked.

Allie stayed quiet and considered the question for several minutes until she finally answered.

"I gave that a lot of thought, actually. Even when I hadn't found you guys yet. From here, it would take me about an hour and a half to get back to the parking lot. Then another, what, half an hour to the nearest town? Then time to get the professionals organized, then get back to the parking lot, then more time to get back here. I think it would be best to move him if we can and save the time."

"Couldn't you call for help from the parking lot?" Ingrid asked.

"Nope. No service up there, just as there's no service down here."

"Speaking of the parking lot, where's Geneva?"

Allie smiled. "She's the smartest of all of us. Geneva is back in our nice, warm car. Probably napping like a cat in the backseat."

"She didn't want to go with you?" Ingrid said. A frown fell across her face.

"No, it wasn't like that at all. She tried, but I wouldn't let her. She would never have made this trip on that ankle. Geneva made it as far as the trailhead before I noticed she was hurting, too. Her heart was in it, but her body wasn't. We have a plan, though. If I'm not back by six, she's heading down the mountain to call in the professionals."

Ingrid nodded and checked her phone. "It's three-thirty now. Think we can make it back in time?"

"I do. As long as we keep moving and keep breaks to a minimum."

Ingrid glanced over at Drake. He'd wrapped himself in the blanket, and looked snug as a bug in a rug. "Is it worth the risk of moving him?"

"I think it's the best thing. We'll wake him up in a minute and see how mobile he is. If he can walk and talk like a normal human, we'll go. If he can't, we'll stay and wait for Geneva and whatever the Swiss calvary is called."

Ingrid looked at Drake again and noticed his eyes were open. "I don't know about that plan. Maybe we should leave him here and trek out ourselves. We can say we never found him. I'm sure the bears will take care of him for us."

Allie looked confused, but it cleared when Ingrid gestured toward Drake with her chin. Allie nodded her understanding.

"But what will we tell poor Geneva?" Allie asked.

"Well, when we found that treasure last year, we put all the reward money in that account for us to split equally, right?"

"Yeah, so?"

"So even though I'm not good at math, I'm pretty certain a gazillion dollars split three ways is better than a split four ways," Ingrid teased.

Allie smiled. "Excellent point. And you know what? Geneva is young, pretty, smart, and talented. I'm sure she'd have no trouble finding another beau. In fact, I've always believed she was way out of Drake's league, anyway."

"I can hear you jerks, you know," Drake said as he rolled over and sat up.

The women laughed.

"We were kidding," Ingrid said. "Besides, who knows how hard it would be to get a bear in here?"

"Good point. Perhaps we should push him over the cliff instead," Allie said.

"Hey. No bears, and no cliffs," Drake argued. "I like the other plan. The one where we get going and get out of here."

"Are you sure? You looked awfully comfortable sleeping there," Allie said.

"That was only an illusion. This blanket is scratchy and smells like old cheese."

"Okay, Drake. We can go, but first I'm going to test your mental acuity, and then walk you around a bit to see how you do. If you fail either of those tests, we're going to hunker down and wait for outside assistance. Deal?"

"Deal," Drake said without hesitation. "What do you want to do first?"

While Allie asked Drake a bunch of random questions, Ingrid sat still and stayed out of the way. Satisfied in the answers, Allie helped Drake to his feet. With a woman on each arm to prevent him from falling, Drake did several laps around the cave until he could walk on his own.

"Well, what's the verdict, doc?" Drake asked.

"I say we pack up, put out the fire, and hit the road," Allie said.

CHAPTER ELEVEN

Y'all ready to do this?" Allie asked.

Ingrid and Drake both nodded.

"I'll take the front. Drake, you stay on my tail, and Ingrid, you have the back. If anything happens, yell."

"Will do, captain," Ingrid said.

Allie looked around the cave one last time. They divided everything Ingrid had found and all the items they had brought with them among the three backpacks.

"By the way, you look adorable, Drake," Allie teased.

To protect his head and stomach, Allie had given the poncho to him.

"I agree," Ingrid said. "You look like a radioactive blueberry."

"I still say you guys are jerks. Can we get on with this already?"

The three got in line and stepped out from the cave and started down the trail.

"I think the rain has let up some," Ingrid said. "It's less of a tropical downpour, and more of a spring shower."

"I think you're right," Allie said. "Perhaps this day is

looking up after all."

Allie kept a steady pace and looked back after every fourth step she took. When she determined Drake and Ingrid had no trouble keeping up with her, she changed to looking back every eight steps.

The fresh rain mixed with the pine and produced a scent that permeated the area, and Allie breathed in the moist air with equal parts enjoyment and gratitude.

"Are you doing okay back there, Drake?" Allie asked over her shoulder.

"I am. You can even pick up the pace a little if you prefer," he answered.

"I prefer not to, but thank you, anyway."

Allie stepped around a large puddle and carried on for another fifty yards until they came to the downed tree. She waited for the others to catch up to her.

"The path continues on the other side of this tree. I got here by pushing my way through it. We'll need to take this slow. There are plenty of places to get caught up here."

Drake studied the large obstacle. "You know I hate pine tree geocaches, right?"

Allie smiled. "This is better. There's nothing to find except the trail, and that's straight on ahead. Besides, this tree is dead, so other than the annoying feeling of getting pine needles down the back of your shirt, this should be easy."

"You wouldn't happen to have a saw in your pack, would you?" Drake asked.

"Sorry. I left my saw at the hotel. I wasn't planning on doing any forestry today. Everyone ready?"

Hearing no objections, Allie stepped up to the giant, trying to remember the path she'd taken through the thing. She picked one of the large branches at waist height and pulled it toward them as far as the branch would bend, hoping it would break off. She detected no snap and determined she wouldn't get lucky with it after all.

"Ingrid, can you step in front of this and hold it until we're through?"

Ingrid nodded and walked around Allie and stood in front of the bough. "Okay, let it go, I got it."

Allie slowly released her grip, and the branch, wanting to spring back into place, caught on Ingrid's hip and stopped.

"Got it," Ingrid said. "It's pulling me, and I don't know how long I can hold it, so don't dawdle."

Allie stepped into the tree and grabbed the next branch in her way. She pulled and bent it back as far as she could, and as she was determining what to do with it, she heard a crack. She looked down at the bough and saw it splintered in half, although it remained attached to the trunk. Allie bent it back the opposite way, hoping to break it off completely, but it didn't. Instead, she pulled it back again, and tucked it behind another bough as if she were tucking a stray strand of hair behind her ear.

The next branch was only two feet off the ground, so Allie simply stepped over it, and as simple as that, she made it to the trunk. There, she stopped, wondering how she'd made it past it the first time she'd come through. The trunk was mere inches over three feet in diameter and leaned against a cliff wall the same way people often leaned against trees.

"Under, I must have gone under," Allie mumbled.

"What?" Drake asked.

"Only talking to myself. Hold on there."

"Not too long, Allie. This is getting heavy," Ingrid said. She shifted her body to regain her footing and stood still.

Allie spotted a broken branch, then it came to her, and suddenly she remembered. She'd squatted and duck-walked her way under the trunk close to the cliff wall.

"You think you can squat, Drake?"

Drake shrugged and tried it. He only got halfway down when the color drained from his face, and he grabbed his stomach. He stopped and stood as straight as he could.

"That's what I was afraid of. Okay. New plan," Allie said.

Allie got to work, snapping off the smaller branches from the trunk in the space between the path and the wall.

"Here. Toss these," she said when she got a handful and passed them to Drake. Drake backed out from the tree and threw the branches over the cliff, and headed back for a second round.

Satisfied she had removed all the impediments she could, Allie crouched and made her way under the tree. There, she removed what smaller branches she could from the other side and managed to push one of the larger boughs out of her way and secure it between two nearby branches. She nodded and returned to Drake.

"Come on in here, Ingrid," Allie said.

"All right," Ingrid said as she slowly walked toward her friends, careful not to let the branch she held snap fiercely back into place. As she joined the others, there was just enough room for the three of them, although Allie had to slump over slightly, and a nearby branch jabbed Ingrid in the ribs.

"Can you get the blanket?" Allie asked Ingrid.

"Drake has it."

Drake faced Allie, and Ingrid raised the poncho to get access to his backpack. The blanket didn't completely fit in the backpack, so it took no effort to find and remove it. When it was in hand, she passed it over to Allie.

"Okay, here's the plan. We're going to lay this on the ground, then you lay on it on your back and we'll pull you under the tree."

"That's the plan?" Drake asked.

Allie nodded. "The best one I can come up with." She folded the blanket in half the long way, then placed it on the ground. "Hop on. Put your head on the end closest to me."

To Drake's credit, he complied without a word.

"Ingrid, come with me and help me pull him through," Allie said. Once she finished, she made her way to the opposite side and waited for Ingrid to join her.

When Ingrid got to the other side, the women got on their hands and knees, hip to hip. They reached under the tree trunk, and each took a corner of the blanket.

"You ready?" Allie asked.

"I think so. Although it's still not too late to leave him."

"I can still hear you," Drake said.

"Okay. Count of three."

Allie gave the countdown, and with matching grunts, the women pulled on the blanket and Drake slid six inches toward them. They redoubled their efforts, yanked again, and Drake's head cleared the tree.

"Hi," he said. He smiled. "I kind of like this. Could you drag me the rest of the way back?"

"Okay, if I can knock you unconscious first," Allie answered.

She did another countdown, and on the third pull, Drake was clear of the tree up to his waist.

"You think you can sit up? We're running short of room in here," Allie said.

"You should have built a bigger fort," Drake answered as he sat up.

Rather than tug on the blanket again, Allie and Ingrid each took one of Drake's arms and pulled him backwards, free of the tree.

"Sit right there for a second," Allie said. "Ingrid, let's get you the rest of the way out of here."

Ingrid turned around and did a quick assessment. She

stepped to her left, bent over slightly, and easily stepped around a branch, then pushed her way through the last one and held the branch still while she waited for the others.

Allie helped Drake to his feet, and Drake followed the path Ingrid had taken. Allie grabbed the blanket, and within a few seconds, joined her friends. Once everyone was out, Ingrid stepped away from the branch, and it snapped back into place, showering the area with raindrops and pine needles.

"Well, that was fun," Drake said. "Where to next?"

Allie pointed up the trail. "That way. Should be relatively easy from here. You're in front, Ingrid, head on out."

Allie waited as Ingrid and Drake lined up and began hiking the trail. She recognized both were hurting to some degree. Ingrid was favoring her bad leg, and Drake was shuffling more than walking. But to their credit, neither of them uttered a word of complaint.

They marched in silence for several minutes until Ingrid stopped.

"Um. Yeah," she said.

"I forgot about this," Allie said. She stepped next to Ingrid and looked up at the short section of trail that she'd slid down earlier in the day.

Allie stepped forward, dug her feet in, and attempted to scramble up the short hill, but her foot slipped from beneath her the second she put her full weight on it. She tried a second time and failed.

"It's not that high. We could probably boost you up, and you could grab on to that tree right there," Drake said.

"Then how would you get up there?" Allie asked.

"Ingrid would give me a boost," Drake said.

Allie looked at Ingrid, who rolled her eyes and shook her head.

"That's not happening," Ingrid said.

Allie stepped back to better assess the situation. To her right, there was a sheer wall that rose past the height of where the trail picked up again. To her left stood several boulders, each the size of their Fiat that were lined up like marbles. The top of the one closest to the crest of the hill was just a few inches taller than the upper part of the trail.

Allie pointed. "What if we got on those boulders there? We could go from one to another until we got to the trail."

"What's on the far side of the boulders?" Drake asked.

Ingrid stepped down the trail a few yards until she could see past the last boulder in line. "Looks like a straight fall down to the next outcropping of trees."

"How far is the fall?" Drake asked.

Ingrid shrugged. "I don't know. Thirty feet, maybe forty. Certainly far enough that it would hurt if you hit the bottom."

"And then there's how we'd actually get up there," Drake said. "We have the same problem getting to the boulder top as we do getting up to the trail."

"Okay, okay," Allie said, conceding. "Poor plan."

"I got one. Give me a boost up," Ingrid said.

Without asking, Allie put her back to the slope, interlaced her fingers, and crouched. Ingrid stepped into Allie's hands, and Allie lifted her.

"A little more. I can't quite reach," Ingrid said.

"You're getting heavy," Allie huffed.

Drake stepped over and put his hands under Ingrid's flailing free foot and pushed. When Ingrid's weight shifted to the leg Drake was supporting, Allie spun around and pushed up on Ingrid's other foot. Together, Allie and Drake had enough strength to propel Ingrid to the upper trail.

"I made it!" Ingrid squealed with delight. "Toss your backpacks up here."

Allie and Drake removed their backpacks and tossed them up to Ingrid, who caught them and set them on the ground. Ingrid rummaged through them quickly, removing the blanket and anything else she deemed too bulky. She went to work on the shoulder straps next. Ingrid unbuckled the straps on her backpack and threaded one of the straps through an arm of Drake's, then attached the opposite strap to Allie's.

"Ta-dah," Ingrid said. She held up the interlaced backpacks that now resembled a rope ladder. "You can climb up this."

"You're not going to be able to pull us up," Drake said.

"Don't need to." Ingrid turned to the sapling Allie had busted in half earlier. She bent the sapling as far down as she could, then looped one of the backpack arms over the top. Ingrid worked on threading the flexible branches through until the backpack was on the ground. She flipped the end backpack over the hill, and the three dangled down and stopped just above knee height.

"No way that holds," Drake said.

"Come on, Mr. Negative, get on up there and give it a try," Allie said. She grabbed the bottom backpack and steadied it.

Drake stepped forward and put his foot on one of the shoulder straps. He put his full weight into it, and although the whole thing stretched, it held. Drake took the next step and grew more confident as he moved on to the next step. Within a minute, he joined Ingrid at the top.

"I told you this would hold," Drake said. "You think we should leave her here?"

Ingrid laughed, but Allie didn't think it was funny.

"I can hear you, you know," Allie said in her best imitation of Drake as she put her foot into the strap and began her climb.

Once she climbed to the top, they worked backward to remove the backpacks from the tree, separate the backpacks, and put everything back in order.

"That's the hardest part of this trail," Allie said.

"That's what you said about the tree," Ingrid said.

Ingrid took point, pushed on, and kept the party moving. After walking for several minutes, Ingrid stopped and groaned.

"You've got to be kidding me," Ingrid said, staring at the dozen stairs before them. "And if you dare say this is the hardest part of the trail, we're not stopping for gelato on the way back."

Drake moved to the nearby log and sat without saying anything, and Allie sat down to his left.

"Are you hanging in there?" she asked.

"Honestly, I don't know how much farther I can go," he said.

Allie gently patted his knee. "We're almost out of here. We only need to go up these stairs to get to the upper trail, then it's a quarter mile to the trailhead. You can make it."

Drake nodded. "Can I at least rest a bit?"

"Sure thing."

Ingrid, seeing the other sit, took a spot next to Drake.

"I sure wish this rain would end," Ingrid said.

"I think it will soon. There's a break in the clouds and a little blue sky," Allie said.

"Where?" Drake asked.

Allie pointed to a break in the trees off to their right. It wasn't a large spot of blue, just enough to hint that the warm sun might still be up in the sky somewhere.

Ingrid sighed. "And to think we went through all this trouble and never found the geocache we came all the way out here for."

Allie smiled. "I don't know about that. Behind you,

about a foot to your right, you'll find an ammo can under a pile of rocks."

"Ha. Ha. Now you're just being mean," Ingrid said.

Allie shrugged. "Okay. Don't get it then. I will after I sit for another minute."

"I don't think she's kidding, Ingrid," Drake said.

Ingrid leaned back and noticed there was indeed a pile of rocks next to the log. She undid the pile, exposing the ammo can beneath. She opened it and pulled out the plastic baggie holding the paper log.

"How did you know this was here?" Ingrid asked as she opened the baggie and fished out the log with her little finger.

"I found it by accident, just resting here on this log, like we're doing now."

Ingrid opened the front pocket of her backpack and extracted a black gel pen, attached her name to the log, and passed it to Drake. Drake signed and passed it to Allie, and Allie added her name and sent everything back to Ingrid.

Once Ingrid had everything back in order, she returned it to its hiding place.

"You ready to go, Drake?" Allie asked.

"Give me another minute, will you?"

"Sure, take all the time you need."

Allie got up and moved over to Ingrid's right, sat down, and took her hand.

"How are you holding up?" Allie asked.

Ingrid brushed a strand of wet hair away from her eyes. "I've had better days. I need a long, hot bath. And some food, and a nap. Perhaps all at the same time."

"Me too. As soon as we get Drake to a hospital and get that leg of yours looked at, we'll get those other needs of yours worked out."

"Great. Oh, and some gelato," Ingrid said. "That's for you."

"You said the magic word. Let's get a move on."

Allie turned to Drake. "You ready? Drake?"

Drake's eyes were closed, and he didn't move. Allie feared the worst, but then his chest hitched and he took a deep breath. Allie gently shook Drake's shoulder and his eyes opened.

"Come on, tough guy. Your girlfriend is waiting for you."

Drake nodded and accepted Allie's help to his feet. He lurched forward to the bottom stair, then with notable effort put his left foot on it. With Allie's help and a loud grunt, he made it up one step. They repeated the process almost a dozen times until, at last, they climbed the final stair.

While Allie waited for Ingrid to ascend the steps, Drake lurched on ahead.

"He's not looking so good," Ingrid said. She accepted Allie's hand for the boost up to the last step.

Allie turned around and watched Drake for a few seconds. "We need to get him medical attention as soon as possible. Let's go help him along."

Allie and Ingrid jogged ahead, and although the trail didn't comfortably accommodate three people walking side by side, each woman took one of Drake's arms over their shoulder, and together, they powered down the trail.

When they reached the final stairs, Ingrid supported Drake from behind while Allie pulled him up the final steps. Finally, back at the trailhead, the three looked out across the parking lot to see the Fiat pulling away.

"I guess we missed our ride," Ingrid said.

Drake's knees buckled, and he dropped to the ground, pulling Allie with him. Ingrid leaned down to help the others up, and no one saw the Fiat's brake lights illuminate bright red against the dreary day.

CHAPTER TWELVE

Allie tried to read an old John Grisham novel that she had owned forever. It had stood in her bookcase in her living room, along with a hundred other books on her pile of books to be read that she never seemed to get to. She had tackled the first few chapters on the plane ride over and vowed to finish it by the time she touched down back in America. Allie's eyes darted from the page to the door and she lost her place again. Frustrated, she turned back exactly one page to where the chapter began, shoved a dollar bill there to mark her place, and set the book in the empty chair next to her.

Instead of the book, she picked up a magazine on the table next to her and began to page through it. Since it was in Italian, she couldn't read the words, and since worry distracted her, she barely noticed the images as she flipped the pages.

Allie heard someone coming, and she looked toward the door just in time to watch an orderly rolling a wheelchair into the room. Ingrid sat in the seat, and when she saw Allie, her face lit up and she giggled and waved. As soon as the nurse parked the chair and applied the brakes, Allie and Ingrid both stood and embraced.

"Hey, you." Allie said. "How are you doing?"

"Much better. You smell so good," Ingrid said as she broke the hug. "And thanks for the clothes."

"You're welcome. When we got here, the hospital staff wasn't all that happy with me tracking mud everywhere, so they strongly encouraged me to clean up. And I figured everyone needed a change of clothes, so I brought extra sets in for everyone from the hotel. How's the leg?"

"Feels fine, but that might be the pain medication they gave me before they cleaned me out and dressed the leg. They said I should have only a couple of small scars, but I had no major damage," Ingrid said. "And you were right about the antibiotics. Those are waiting for me at the pharmacy."

Allie moved the novel from the chair to the table, and Ingrid took the seat next to Allie.

"Have you gotten any news about the others yet?" Ingrid asked.

"Nope. You're the first. Drake needed surgery, and I think Geneva should be out any time now."

Ingrid yawned and reached for the ceiling with both of her arms.

"Tired, sweetie?" Allie asked.

"I think it's a combination of the drugs they gave me and coming off the adrenaline high. I'm hungry, too. What time is it?"

Allie activated her phone that sat on the table right next to her novel. "A little after nine. Should we go get something to eat?"

Ingrid shook her head. "No. I can hold out for a while. Let's wait for the others."

"Geneva's back," Allie said.

Ingrid turned to the door in time to see the same orderly that brought her out wheeling out Geneva. Geneva had a white plastic bag in her lap, and a cane in her hand. Like Ingrid, Geneva looked tired and ready for the day to end. The orderly rolled the wheelchair to the spot next to Ingrid and helped Geneva from the wheelchair and into the seat.

"You're still waiting for one more?" the orderly asked Allie.

"Yes. Drake Decker. The last update I received; he was still in surgery."

"I will go check on him for you," the orderly said.

"Thank you," Allie said.

Before the orderly left, she glanced at Ingrid and at Geneva. A smile crossed her Roman face. "It must be dangerous to be your friend."

Allie laughed. "Only when they don't feed me."

The orderly smiled, removed the brakes from the chair, and left the waiting room.

"What's your story, Geneva?" Ingrid asked.

Geneva placed her plastic bag next to the identical one Ingrid had on the floor and shifted in her seat to get comfortable. "There's not much to tell. Had an x-ray and found nothing was broken. From what I understand from the doctor, it's not even a sprain, more like a strain. I should be fine in a day or two."

"What's with the cane?" Allie asked.

"Simply a precaution. I insisted I didn't really need it, but they gave it to me, anyway. They suggest I use it for a couple of days if I refuse to sit in the hotel room the entire time I'm on vacation."

Ingrid smiled. "That's probably a wise choice. Unless you'd like to stay at the hotel while the rest of us are out having fun."

Geneva swatted Ingrid's leg. "No way. I didn't fly

halfway around the world to sit in the room."

"We should take it easy for a few days." Allie said. "No more mountain climbing for the rest of this trip."

"Did either of you eat?" Geneva asked. "I could go for some pasta. What are those little pillow things called we had last night?"

"Gnocchi?" Ingrid offered.

"That's the one. I liked those. Let's get some once Drake comes out."

"Excellent idea," Allie said.

"You really think we should go to a restaurant looking like we do?" Ingrid asked.

"There's nothing wrong with the way you look," Allie said.

Allie turned her head and looked initially into Ingrid's eyes, then she expanded her view and saw what Ingrid was talking about. Ingrid's hair, normally a shade of blond so light it was almost white, had streaks of mud in it, and although Ingrid had done her best to wash up when she changed into fresh clothes, there was a smudge of mud behind her left ear, and a bit of grit beneath her right eye.

"Hold still," Allie said. She licked her thumb and wiped away the dirt from Ingrid's face. "There. You're good to go."

"What about her?" Ingrid asked, pointing a thumb in Geneva's direction.

Allie leaned over so she could get a better view of her friend. Geneva had escaped the mud tumbles that everyone else had taken, but not the downpour, so her short brown hair stuck out like hedgehog fur and was in need of dire attention from a brush.

"Hey, Geneva, you look great, too."

Geneva opened her mouth to protest, then closed it when the orderly entered the room.

"Your friend is out of surgery and recovery and moved

to a room. If you follow me, I'll take you to him," the orderly said.

The three friends rose as one. Allie collected her phone and book from the table and then grabbed the three white plastic bags at their feet. Together, they followed the orderly to the elevator, up to the fifth floor, and down the corridor.

"General visiting hours are over at ten," the orderly said as she turned and left the area.

"Go on in," Allie said to Geneva, who was standing closest to the door.

Geneva stepped over the threshold, followed by Allie and Ingrid.

Drake was sitting propped up in bed when the women entered. "Hi!" he said with equal parts excitement and fatigue. He wore a white and blue hospital gown, and an I.V. line stretched from his left arm to a machine next to the bed. On the machine hung two bags of medication.

Geneva headed over and gave Drake an extended kiss.

"What's that for?" Drake asked.

"Surviving," Geneva said.

"Then you need to kiss those two, too. I wouldn't be here without them."

Geneva turned and gave air kisses to Ingrid and Allie, then swung back around. "What's your prognosis?"

Before Drake could answer, Allie interrupted the couple as she lugged a chair from the room's corner to Drake's bedside. She nodded, and Geneva took the seat, still holding Drake's hand.

"I'm actually pretty well off for someone who fell off a mountain. Surprisingly, I don't have a concussion, just a big goose egg. And they took the tree out of my stomach. According to the surgeon, it didn't pierce any organs, so I got lucky there."

"What's with the drugs?" Geneva asked.

"A course of antibiotics, and a painkiller if I need one."

"When are you going to get out of here?" Ingrid asked.

"Probably tomorrow, unless my head gets wonky, or I have any post-surgical complications, which should be rare."

"Is there anything I can do for you?" Geneva asked.

"No darling, I'm fine. Although I don't think it was worth all this to find one cache."

A look of confusion crossed Geneva's face like an eclipse. "Wait, what? You found that cache?"

"No one told you?" Drake said. "Allie found it on the way to rescue us."

Geneva turned to Allie, a flash of anger in her eyes. "Our loved ones, lost and in danger out in the forest, and you stopped to find a geocache while looking for them?"

Allie waved her hands in front of her like she was trying to ward off a swarm of flies. "No, no. It wasn't like that at all. I found it on accident when I stopped for a rest. Tell her."

Allie looked from Drake to Ingrid, and back to Geneva.

Ingrid broke the tension with a laugh. "It's true. There was a log next to the trail, and the cache was behind the log. We practically sat on it when Drake needed to take a break. Since I was sitting right on top of it, I grabbed it and passed the log around. Sorry you can't get credit for it."

"Why not?" Geneva asked, her voice rising.

"You didn't sign the log. You know the rules, no sign, no find."

It was Geneva's turn to glance from Ingrid to Allie, trying to determine if they were serious. When she looked at Drake, she saw him trying to keep a chortle to himself. Finally, he broke.

"I wrote your name on the log," Drake said. "Even though technically it broke the rules, but we'll all consider it extenuating circumstances."

Geneva threw her arms in the air. "Not funny, you

three. What am I supposed to do with you?"

"I know what you can do for me," Drake said.

Geneva turned to him and saw a sly smile on his face. "Drake. You're injured and have visitors. This is neither the time nor the place."

"No, not that," Drake protested. "Well, yes, that, but not now. Would you three be okay with leaving? I've had a really long day and I feel myself falling asleep."

"Are you sure? I can stay with you tonight," Geneva said.

"No. You can go. You have your own injury to tend to. I'll be fine here."

"Okay, honey. If you need anything, just call." Geneva stood, leaned over, and gave Drake a soft kiss. She squeezed his hand, then stepped away from the bed.

Allie held up a plastic bag. "I brought you a change of clothes. I'll put them in the closet over here." Allie unpacked the clothes into the closet, then folded the bag and put it on a shelf. "Get good rest, Drake. I'll see you tomorrow."

"Thanks, Allie. I appreciate it. Hey, Ingrid?"

Ingrid stepped to Drake's bedside, and when she got there, he reached out for her hand.

"I owe you everything, Ingrid. I wouldn't be here not if it weren't for you. Because of that, I owe you a debt I'll never be able to repay."

Ingrid smiled, then leaned over and kissed Drake's forehead. "Take good care of yourself, and good care of Geneva. That will be payment enough."

The pair extended the moment in silence, then Ingrid squeezed Drake's hand. "Go to sleep. We'll see you tomorrow."

Drake nodded and turned off his overhead light while Ingrid and Allie stepped from his room.

"I'm glad he'll be okay," Ingrid said.

Allie put her arm around Ingrid's shoulders. "Me too. What do you say we find some gnocchi for Geneva?"

An hour later, the three women sat around a table at a busy restaurant a block from the hotel. Ingrid and Geneva shared a bottle of wine between them while Allie sipped at a glass of water.

"Here's to finally getting to eat," Geneva said as she raised her glass and touched it to the rims of the glasses of the two friends.

"I'll toast to that. You can't grasp how famished I am," Ingrid said. "I hope this place has good food."

Allie felt her stomach rumble. "At this rate, I'll take any food."

Like magic, a server appeared wearing black linen pants and a royal blue shirt with the restaurant's name embroidered above the pocket.

"Buonasera, ladies. Italian or English?" he asked.

"English, please," Allie said.

"Perfect. My name is Lorenzo. I see you're already situated on drinks. Do you know what you'd like to eat?"

Geneva handed Lorenzo her menu. "I'm going to have the potato gnocchi."

"Excellent," Lorenzo said as he took the menu. "What type of sauce would you like with that? I would recommend the pesto, tomato, or we have a nice sage butter sauce tonight."

Geneva thought for a moment. "I'll go with the butter sauce. Oh, and a salad, please."

"Excellent."

"I'll have the exact same thing," Ingrid said as she handed Allie her menu.

"Make it three," Allie said, handing the menus to Lorenzo.

"Perfect. Makes it easy for me. I'll return shortly."

"With Drake out of commission for the day, what should we do tomorrow?" Ingrid asked. "Geocaching as planned? Visit a museum or two? A spa day?"

Lorenzo stopped by the table and dropped off two small bottles. "For your salads. Olive oil and balsamic vinegar," he explained, then disappeared.

"A spa day sounds fantastic," Geneva said. "Manicure. Pedicure. Perhaps a mud mask."

Ingrid was in the middle of a drink when she started shaking her head, almost spilling her wine. "Uh, no. No mud. I've had enough of mud for this trip."

The women enjoyed a quick laugh, and as they finished, Lorenzo returned with the salads and meals. Starved, they quickly dove into their food.

Geneva took one bite of her gnocchi, chewed, swallowed, and picked up another tender potato pillow. "This is exquisite. I think it's even better than the ones we had last night."

"They are delicious," Ingrid said. "You know what would go real good with this sauce?"

"Bread?" Lorenzo asked as he swung by the table and dropped off a basket of Italian bread. "Careful, it's just out of the over and still hot."

"No way," Geneva said. She reached into the basket, then withdrew her fingers quickly. "Oh, yes, it is." Using her fork, she extracted a slice, then blew on it until it cooled a bit. She took the slice between her fingers and dipped it into the butter sauce. Geneva took a bite and slowly savored the taste. "Hello, heaven. I think I'm in love."

Ingrid and Allie extracted slices themselves and copied Geneva's process. Casual conversation ground to a halt as the friends devoured their meals. Over the next half an hour, the only sounds at the table were the clinking of silverware on plates. Finally, all three of the women set their plates aside.

"So, back to tomorrow's plan," Geneva said.

"I'd be interested in finding out what this is. Maybe a trip to a library or something?" Allie said.

"What?"

Allie held up her phone and showed the others the picture. "The thing you found in the cave. When you were in the shower before, I cleaned out our backpacks and found it. This writing was on parchment."

"I just thought it was some animal hide. I didn't even bother to check," Ingrid said.

Allie finished her water and set the empty glass on the table. "I don't know what you found, but it must be something special if they hid it like they did." Allie zoomed in and held out the phone for all to see. "Look. It has what appears to be Egyptian writing on it."

"Pardon my looking over your shoulder, but that's not Egyptian. It's Punic," Lorenzo said as he topped off Allie's water.

"Punic? Never heard of it." Ingrid said. "Looks like hieroglyphics to me."

"Punic is an offshoot of the Phoenician language. When I'm not waiting tables, I'm a student of ancient history in Rome. I specialize in ancient Carthage, but since it was a Phoenician settlement, I'm familiar with the culture overall."

"Can you translate this? Tell us what it means?"

"Do you mind?" Lorenzo asked, pointing at her phone.

Allie handed him the phone, and he studied the image for almost a minute, zooming in and out of the picture.

"Where did you get this?" Lorenzo asked. "I've seen several artifacts and photographs, but never anything quite like this."

Allie looked at Geneva and Ingrid, and both of them nodded.

"We found it in a cave in the mountains," Allie said.

"Was there anything else in the cave? Like wall carvings?" Lorenzo asked.

Ingrid retrieved her phone from her pocket, brought up the photos, and passed it to Lorenzo. He handed Allie back her phone, took Ingrid's, and only looked at it for a few seconds before recognition struck.

"These tusks, this elephant. I've seen images like this before. What you found looks related to Hannibal," said, returning the phone.

"Hannibal who?" Geneva asked.

Lorenzo hesitated before he answered, as if he'd misheard the question. "You've never heard of Hannibal? The Carthaginian general who led the Carthage army against the Roman Republic?"

"Wait, he was the one who took the elephants over the Alps, right?" Ingrid said.

"That's correct," Lorenzo said.

"Can you translate the whole thing or not?" Allie asked.

Lorenzo looked down. On his belt was something that looked like an old-fashioned beeper. He pushed a button to silence the buzzing.

"I'm sorry, I must go. I have other customers to attend to. Tomorrow, I have the day off. If you meet me at the park near the marina at ten in the morning, I will give you exactly what you need." Lorenzo turned to leave.

"And what's that?" Allie asked.

He looked back. "A history lesson. What else?"

CHAPTER THIRTEEN

At half-past ten, Allie, Geneva, and Ingrid sat together on a bench in the same park where they found the multi-cache the first day they arrived. They'd been on the bench for forty-five minutes, people watching and waiting for Lorenzo.

"I still don't think he's coming," Ingrid said as she impatiently kicked at the ground with the toe of her shoe.

"I don't either. He's late. Let's go," Geneva said.

"Hold on. Why can't you two have a little more patience?" Allie asked.

Geneva turned to Ingrid. "Did your girlfriend just ask the two of us why we can't have a little more patience? Isn't she the one who's always wanting to go so bad she cuts time into half-seconds?"

Ingrid laughed, then nodded. "Yep, that's her. Patience is way outside of her character."

Geneva lowered her voice. "Maybe that's not her."

"Are you thinking pod person? An imperfect duplicate of the Allie we know?"

"Exactly that."

Ingrid and Geneva both leaned forward and looked to

their left, and found Allie glaring at them.

"Y'all aren't funny," Allie said.

"Ah. No sense of humor," Geneva joked. "Perhaps this is our Allie after all."

Ingrid got the attention of her friends and pointed to a man in the distance. "Is that him? I can't tell."

The women watched as the man with the scarecrow build covered the hundred yards in short order. When he got to within twenty feet, he waved and made a beeline for them.

"Good morning," Lorenzo said. "I apologize for my tardiness. I know the Americans value punctuality. Did you bring the original item with you?"

"We did," Allie said.

"Excellent. Let's move over in that direction. There are tables we can use and spread out more comfortably."

"Lead the way," Allie said.

The women got to their feet and allowed Lorenzo to take the lead. He moved with purpose and had a high energy gait that included a bounce in his step. He didn't wait, and soon outpaced the friends by several steps.

"You go and keep up with him, Allie," Geneva said. "Ingrid and I will get there when we get there."

Allie, who had hung back with the others, increased her speed, and jogged a few feet until she pulled even with Lorenzo.

"We are almost there," Lorenzo said. He raised his hand and pointed. "See, over there in that glade is where we will stop."

Allie looked ahead and saw a half dozen picnic tables. Since the sun was out, and the weather was pleasant, three of the tables already contained occupants. One by a young blond woman reading a book, one with a young mother breastfeeding a baby, and one with two ancient men playing chess.

Lorenzo led Allie to the table farthest away from the others and swung his long legs over the seat and sat. From over his head, he took a weathered brown satchel and placed it on the table.

"Your friends, are they coming?" he asked.

Allie glanced off into the distance and saw Geneva and Ingrid making their way toward her. She watched them for a few seconds. Geneva had brought her cane and relied on it heavily, and Ingrid had a slight limp that was barely perceptible.

"They'll be here shortly. You were too fast for them," Allie said.

"For that, I apologize. I've always been in a rush."

As Lorenzo opened his bag, Allie checked him out. He had thick, long, sandy brown hair that he wore pulled back into a ponytail she hadn't noticed the night before. His eyes were a shade darker than his hair and still had the glint of youth in them. Lorenzo's face had a perfectly straight and slanted nose between his high and prominent cheekbones. His lips were full, yet thin, and when he smiled, he displayed shining white teeth. The only flaw Allie noticed was a slight indention on his front left incisor.

"How are you enjoying Italy?" Lorenzo asked as he cleared out his bag. From it, he extracted two textbooks, a notepad, and two pencils. He checked the tip of one, noticed it had a broken point, and rummaged inside his bag for a sharpener.

"It's a beautiful country," Allie said. "I've never been here before."

"Never been to Italy, and you come to Como? Most first-timers go to Rome or Venice, or Florence. Never to Como."

Allie hesitated for a second before answering. "We were looking for something with fewer tourists, and it's been a long-time dream of mine to visit the Alps."

"And so here you are," Lorenzo said. He finished with the pencil, tapped a finger on the lead to check the point, then, satisfied, set it next to its twin.

"What are you talking about?" Geneva asked as she at last made it to the table and sat down next to Allie. Ingrid took the remaining seat next to Lorenzo.

"Not much. Small talk while waiting for you," Allie said.

"Can I see it?" Lorenzo asked, getting right down to business.

Allie nodded at Ingrid. Ingrid slipped her backpack from her shoulders, undid the zipper, and pulled the parchment from its hiding spot. She handed it to Lorenzo, who took it and gently unrolled it onto the table.

"This is amazing. I've never seen anything like it." He had a giddy quality to his voice, much like a four-year-old on Christmas morning.

"What is it?" Geneva asked.

"Something that should be in a museum if it's authenticated to be real. What it appears to be, based on the writing and the markings on this one side, is an ancient document related to Hannibal," Lorenzo said.

"You mentioned him yesterday," Geneva said. "You have a quick summary you can give us?"

"Sure. Hannibal, like I said, was from Carthage, which is today in Tunisia. He was famous for taking elephants over the Alps to fight the Romans during the Second Punic War."

"Where did he get the elephants from?" Allie asked.

"North Africa. He took them across the Strait of Gibraltar, and attacked Saguntum, in modern day Spain, which touched off the war. Hannibal went through Iberia, then right down Italy's boot. He wreaked havoc in Italy for a decade before he got recalled back to Carthage. He's considered one of the greatest military tacticians in the ancient world."

"Sounds fascinating," Ingrid said.

"It is, actually. And the more I study that period, the more fascinated I am."

"Can you tell us what this says?" Allie asked.

"I can certainly try. Give me a few minutes, and I'll see what I can do."

Lorenzo opened his notebook to a blank page and transferred the writing on the parchment to the notebook. When he finished, he carefully rolled up the item and passed it back to Ingrid. Then he checked the spines of the two books he brought and selected the volume from the bottom of the pile. Without speaking, he worked. To not bother him, the friends remained silent as well, so the only sound came from the turning of pages and scratching of pencil lead across the page.

Several times, Lorenzo seemed to get stuck, and on those occasions, he put the pencil between his teeth as he pulled the book closer and examined the contents. At one point, he pushed the original tome aside and perused the other from cover to almost cover before he found what he sought.

At last, after almost an hour, Lorenzo snapped both books closed and stacked them, then placed his pencils on top of the small pile.

"I've got good news, and bad news, and a bit of a mystery for you," Lorenzo said as he set down his pencil.

"Tell us," Geneva said.

Lorenzo cleared his throat. "Well, the bad news is, although this appears written in Punic and everything appears to point to Hannibal, it isn't from his time."

"How did you determine that?" Geneva asked.

"This isn't all Punic writing on here. There's some neo-Punic, as well as some Latin, and even some Italian thrown in for good measure," Lorenzo said.

"This is all someone's idea of a practical joke?" Ingrid asked.

"Oh, I doubt that. Based on the pictures you showed me of the location where you found this, I doubt anyone would put that much effort into a joke. Besides, this leads to the good news. I would guess this document is from much later, not long ago. In fact, perhaps the early fifteen-hundreds."

"That's not that long ago?" Allie asked.

Lorenzo smiled. "To an Italian, it is practically yesterday. Italy is the home of the Eternal City, after all."

"So where does the mystery part come from?" Geneva asked.

"From the text. I've translated what I could. My Latin isn't really strong, and I might not have the Italian properly translated since it's a much older dialect than I'm familiar with. Either way, if you want to figure the rest of this message, there's a small local museum in Milan I suggest you visit." Lorenzo referenced his phone and from it jotted down the museum name and address on the page. He tore the entire page from the notebook and handed it to Allie.

Allie looked at the sheet. "Really?"

Lorenzo nodded. "Yes. The text clearly references him by name. Leonardo di ser Piero. Or as we all know him, Leonardo da Vinci."

"I don't understand," Allie said. "Why would an old document written in an ancient language point to Leonardo?"

Lorenzo shrugged, the palms of his hands pointing to the sky. "I don't know. That is your mystery to solve." He looked at his phone and noticed the time. "I'm sorry, but I must go. Good luck with your quest."

Lorenzo gathered his things back into his bag, then shook hands with each of the women before he nodded, turned, and walked away.

Allie looked at the paper, then set it in the center of the table. Ingrid picked it up and read through it before handing it off to Geneva.

"I don't understand any of this," Ingrid said. "What does Leonardo have to do with Hannibal, mountain passes, and heaven valleys?"

"I think you misread that," Geneva said as she looked at the paper. "It says seven valleys, not heaven valleys."

"Okay, then, same question, though," Ingrid said. "None of those things makes sense to me. I mean, they would if they stood separated logically, but if one of my students handed this in as an essay assignment, I'd take one look at it and hand it right back to them."

"Maybe that's the point," Geneva said. "A bit of a riddle to figure out, like a mystery cache. If this thing said to go to this address to locate this thing, that would probably defeat the purpose in the elaborate hiding place in the cave."

Ingrid nodded. "Point taken. So where do we go from here? To Milan? How far is that from here?"

"Only an hour," Allie said. "I'd hate to go down there while Drake is in the hospital. I'd hate for him to get released, only to find out we've skipped town. Why don't we walk back to the hotel and from there we can make a plan of what to do with our day?"

"Can we get lunch? I'm hungry," Geneva said as she rubbed her stomach.

Allie gave two quick nods and was about to speak when her phone rang. She didn't recognize the number, but answered anyway. "Hello?"

As she listened, she smiled. "Sure thing. See you soon then." Allie ended the call, then shoved her phone into her pocket. "Lunch will have to wait. That was Drake. They're releasing him."

*

"Are you done with those? Mind if I have them?" Drake asked Allie. He reached forward and grabbed a few French fries from her plate and devoured them without waiting for an answer. "These are fantastic. What do they call them here?"

Allie shrugged as she pushed her plate across the table. "No clue. I asked for French fries, and that's what they gave me. Didn't they feed you in the hospital?"

"They did. Some sort of eggplant thing. Tasted weird to me, but then, I'm not the biggest fan of eggplant. Tell me again what your waiter told you." Drake dipped one fry into a small container of sauce, leaving a drip on the table as he did.

Geneva related the story as she sopped up Drake's mess before he ran his elbow into it. Although he stayed engrossed in his meal, he gave her enough attention to fully take in the story.

"What are we going to do, then?" Drake asked when she finished. Drake wiped his fingers, then pushed the plate aside. "Is there any terrible food in this country? I mean, other than the eggplant?"

"Probably not," Allie said, answering his questions out of order. "Well, we can either continue on our vacation as originally planned, or we can follow this Leonardo thing and see where it goes."

"Couldn't we do both?" Drake asked. "There are geocaches down in Milan, right?"

"Sure there are," Geneva said. "More than there are around here, actually."

"Any virtual caches?" Ingrid asked.

Geneva shrugged, then retrieved her phone and checked her geocaching app for them. "A dozen or so."

"I vote for both, with an emphasis on virtual caches,"

Ingrid said.

"Are those virtual caches in the city? No chance of me rolling down a hill or getting mud caked into places where it's impossible to get out without help?" Drake asked.

"I can't tell for sure about the mud part, but they're all within the city. There are a few clustered around the city center, and they radiate out from there."

"What are we waiting for? Let's go," Ingrid said, with a tone that suggested more of an order than a suggestion.

No one argued as they got up from the table and exited the restaurant. Once in the Fiat, Drake climbed into the passenger seat and entered the museum address into Luna and pressed go.

"Are you certain this museum is open?" Drake asked as they pulled away from the curb. "It would be a shame if we drove all the way down there and found out it was closed."

"We called on the way to get you," Allie said. "They're a small museum and usually close by three, but will let us in if we're late."

"Can we do this virtual on the way?" Ingrid called from the backseat.

Allie looked in the rear-view mirror and saw Ingrid nodding vigorously at her. Ingrid met her eyes and smiled.

"How complicated is it?" Allie asked.

"There are three sundials on the same block, and we only need to take a selfie with them to get the smiley," Ingrid answered.

"What time is it now?" Allie asked.

"Almost one-thirty."

"Why don't we hit the museum first, then we'll have plenty of daylight left to do all the virtuals you want?"

"Okay, deal," Ingrid said. "You were going to the museum first regardless of what I said, weren't you?" Ingrid added after a few seconds' delay.

Allie grinned, refocused on the road in front of her, and punched the accelerator.

*

"Welcome," the curator said as Allie walked in the door, with Geneva, Ingrid, and finally Drake right behind her.

"Hi. We called earlier today," Allie said.

The curator took her glasses off and placed them on the display case she was sitting behind. She got off her stool, walked around the case, and offered her hand. The woman was short in statue, but her long golden copper hair and infectious smile more than made up for her diminutive size.

"Hello, I'm Victoria. You are Allison?"

"Allie. Yes, we spoke on the phone. We, um, found something that we would like you to take a look at."

Ingrid stepped forward and handed Victoria the parchment. Victoria eyed the item before she took it, turned around, and unrolled it on the display case.

"This is amazing. I've never seen anything like it," she said. "Where did you find it?"

Ingrid took a few moments to explain geocaching and tell the story of how she found the parchment. Victoria listened intently and nodded her understanding, never removing her gaze from the item.

"I don't know what much of this means. I can only read the Italian parts."

"It's written mostly in Punic," Allie said. She removed the sheet from her pocket, unfolded it, and placed it next to the parchment. "We ran into someone who translated it for us. He says there's also Latin and Italian on there as well."

Victoria nodded. "The Italian pieces are here, and here," she said, pointing to the writing on the parchment. She picked up the paper and studied it. "May I write on this?"

"Sure," Allie answered.

Victoria leaned over a case and grabbed a pencil from a

coffee mug featuring a facsimile of Leonardo's *Vitruvian Man*. She leaned over and jotted a few notes, adding in the Italian pieces that Lorenzo had omitted.

"Are you sure that's the correct translation?" Allie asked. "I don't mean to sound rude, but the person who translated the Punic for us said the Italian parts were in an older dialect than he was comfortable with."

Victoria beamed. "Of course it's correct. I've studied Leonardo da Vinci and that time period quite extensively."

"What about the Latin parts?" Geneva asked.

"No, sorry. That I can't help with, but it doesn't look like the missing information obscures the overall message much."

"Can you give us the gist?" Allie asked.

"Certainly. Overall, this document refers to Leonardo di ser Piero da Vinci, or, translated, Leonardo, son of ser Piero from Vinci. It also mentions something about following the seven valleys to the glorious gift."

"What does that mean?" Drake asked.

Victoria shrugged. "That I can't tell you."

"Does da Vinci have anything to do with this area?" Geneva asked.

Victoria smiled. "Oh, yes. He spent over twenty years in Milan. He painted many important pieces here. In fact, if you go over to the Church of Holy Mary of Grace, you'll find his *Last Supper* in the refectory."

"Really?" Allie asked.

Victoria nodded. "It's only three kilometers from here."

"Does it say anything else about the treasure? Any directions or anything?" Drake asked, jumping to the point.

Victoria studied the writing again. "It says in the next valley, look toward the man in the mountain to guide you."

"You mentioned valleys before," Geneva said. "If there are seven, how would we know which one is the next?"

"Please, wait a moment." Victoria left the room.

While waiting for Victoria to return, Allie took an opportunity to look around at what she could see without leaving the group. Based on a brochure on the counter, the museum featured Leonardo da Vinci's time in Milan, including a historical timeline. It included several photos of the museum's displays on the brochure. Next to the stack of brochures was a map highlighting the different places in Milan where da Vinci roamed, lived, or worked. Allie shoved the brochure and map into her back pocket when she saw Victoria returning.

"I found it," Victoria said. She handed Ingrid the parchment and notepaper, then on the clear countertop, she laid out a topographical map of Italy. "Can you point to where you found this?"

Allie stepped up to the map, found Como, then used her finger to trace the route they'd taken and stopped when she arrived at the mountain trail. "Right about here."

Victoria leaned over and studied the map for a moment. "Okay, yes. In this area, the seven valleys line up almost perfectly from west to east. You were at the far western one, so I suspect it referred to the next closest valley."

"Where would that be?" Drake asked.

Victoria looked again, then put her finger on a location. "The answer you seek would be right here."

CHAPTER FOURTEEN

Allie rose early the following morning, got dressed, and left the room carrying her shoes, closing the door behind her like a whisper. To the east, the sun had already cleared the two-story building across the street. Despite talking about getting a sunrise start, like the group normally did when out, Allie could tell simply by body language alone that none of her comrades were looking forward to an early morning. By the end of a lengthy discussion, she managed to convince everyone to sleep in for a bit.

While the others slept, Allie took a chair in the lobby and slipped into her favorite hiking boots, laced them up, and headed out the door. She walked to the street, looked to her left and right, and turned to the left. Allie walked down two blocks and took a right, and found the bookstore she remembered passing the day before. When she entered the shop, a little brass bell above her rang.

"May I help you?" the shopkeeper asked.

Allie looked to her left and saw the little man with closely cropped white hair and deep blue eyes. "How did you know I spoke English?"

The shopkeeper tugged at his collar. "I can always recognize a fellow American."

Allie smiled. "Really? Where are you from?"

"Tulsa, Oklahoma originally. I've been in Italy for thirty years. My name is Joseph."

Allie stepped forward and shook his hand. "Nice to meet you. I'm Allie, from Nashville. How did you end up here?"

"Met the love of my life while on a trip to Rome. Got married. Had kids. Opened this little shop. Now, what can I do for you, Allie, from Nashville?"

"I'd like a detailed map, topographic if you have one, specific to northern Italy if you can get that detailed. And a book on Leonardo da Vinci."

Joseph nodded. "The Leonardo section is right behind you. I've got perhaps a dozen titles in English. I'll have to check the map section to check if I have what you want."

Joseph excused himself and headed toward the store's rear, and Allie stepped over to the shelves to check out the Leonardo da Vinci books. When she got there, she found a complete row of them, mostly in Italian, but also in German, English, French, and Chinese. Joseph was correct, and she counted a dozen titles in English. Allie began to page through the options to determine which one gave her a good mix of biographical detail and da Vinci's exploits in Milan. She narrowed it down to two choices and took both books to the counter.

"I have several maps by region. Do you know which regions you're interested in?" Joseph said as he returned to his place, carrying several maps.

"Which region are we in?"

"Lombardy."

"Where does it extend to?" Allie asked.

Joseph opened the map and spread it on his counter.

"We are here," he said, pointing at Como. "This region covers about nine-thousand square miles, and most of this part of the country."

"I think this will do nicely. Which one of these two books is the best?" Allie asked, pointing to the tomes on the counter.

Joseph glanced at the titles and picked one up immediately. "This one. It's easier to read, it's a tad more factual, and two euros cheaper."

"I'll take it," Allie said.

Joseph rang her up, and a few minutes later Allie left the shop with her new purchases. She spotted a pastry shop across the street. There, she selected a brioche, a croissant-like pastry filled with custard and a bottle of orange juice and found an empty table. After she had a bite of pastry, she set it to the side and spread open the map before her.

The map was similar to the one that Victoria had, so she quickly found the park location from their previous adventures, as well as the next valley to the east. Allie determined the best road to take there, then retrieved her phone to determine if there were any geocaches in the area. She noticed there was and noted the codes, put her phone away, and closed the map.

Allie took another bite of her brioche and paged through the book on Leonardo da Vinci. The publisher had laid the book out in sections, the first quarter covering the biography of the man, then half the book highlighting the art and inventions he created. The last quarter contained detailed information about his time in Milan. She flipped back to page one and was about to dig in when she heard a muffled ping and felt her table vibrate. Allie extracted the phone and read the text from Ingrid, who was wondering where Allie had slipped off to.

Allie returned the text, stating she'd be back shortly,

then scarfed down the rest of her treat and drained the small bottle of juice. Once she'd sufficiently cleaned up the area, Allie headed back to the hotel.

"Where have you been?" Ingrid asked as Allie stepped into the room.

"Went out for a paper map so we don't get lost again," Allie said.

"Good idea." Ingrid said as she retrieved a brush and started running it through her hair, still wet from the shower she'd just finished.

"Can I take a peek at your leg?" Allie asked.

Ingrid nodded, had a seat on the edge of the bed, and rolled onto her side to give Allie a good view. Allie bent over to inspect Ingrid's leg. The angry redness had lessened to a pinkish color, and there were a couple of quarter-inch lines Allie suspected would be permanent, and one dimple in Ingrid's thigh that looked to be around for the long term.

Allie ran a fingertip gently up Ingrid's thigh, and Ingrid pulled her leg back and laughed in response.

"Stop! That tickles," Ingrid said. She got up from the bed and started to dress.

"Looks like you're fine to me," Allie said.

"I wasn't worried about me," Ingrid said. "I'm more concerned about the other two."

"We'll have to keep a close eye on them today. I think Geneva will be back to normal in a day or two, but Drake is the strong, silent type to a fault and wouldn't complain about his injuries if he had a hole right through his body."

Ingrid nodded as she buttoned her jeans. "I noticed."

Just under two hours later, Allie crested a hill and pulled into a scenic overlook. She stopped the car an inch before she hit the short rock wall before her, and everyone left the Fiat.

"This is an amazing view," Geneva said.

Allie joined Geneva and looked to the horizon. The valley stood lush and green below them, and Allie noticed the road they were currently on wound down the pass and into a small town in the center of the valley. The valley itself appeared to be ten miles long and half as wide.

"You guys want to help us find this cache, or just enjoy the scenery?" Drake asked.

"I guess both," Geneva answered.

Allie turned to her right and caught Drake and Ingrid examining the wall. The rock wall stood three feet high, just high enough to remind drivers to stop the car, and offer an uncomfortable place to sit if someone was so inclined.

"Any hints on this one?" Allie asked.

"No," Ingrid answered. "It has to be somewhere on this wall, though."

Allie glanced around the overlook. It held only four cars, but their Fiat was the only one currently in the lot. There was one sign in Italian, and although she couldn't read it, Allie headed for it anyway and checked behind it, hoping to find a magnetic container of some kind.

"I already checked there," Drake said.

That only left the wall itself. Ingrid, Drake, and Geneva had spread out, looking for gaps or loose rocks within the structure. Allie was about to select a spot to search for herself when Geneva stood up. In her hand, she had a black film container.

"Found it!" Geneva said.

"That wasn't so bad," Drake said.

Geneva passed the log around for signatures and returned it to its hiding spot. When she stood back up, she saw Allie scanning the area.

"What are you looking for?"

"A man in a mountain. Do you see anything?" Allie asked.

Geneva stopped for a moment and looked across the valley. "Nope. Perhaps someone in town can help us out."

Allie slid back behind the wheel and once everyone got strapped in, she navigated down the mountain and into the little town that comprised a gas station with an attached small store and a post office. Out of habit, Allie checked her fuel gauge as she neared the station and pulled into a pump.

"You want me to pump the gas?" Drake asked Allie.

"No. I got it."

"Good. I need to use the restroom. Do you need anything from inside?"

"No."

As Allie filled the tank, the other three headed into the gas station. Geneva was the first one out and she approached Allie with a smile on her face.

"What?" Allie asked.

"I got you a postcard," Geneva said.

The automatic shutoff clicked, so Allie removed the handle, returned it to the pump, and screwed the gas cap back on before accepting the postcard Geneva held out the entire time.

"Thanks," she said as she glanced at it. Allie intended to shove it into her pocket, then took a closer look at it. The picture was black and white and showed an old-time hiker standing in front of a cave entrance. The entrance curled up at either end, making it appear that it was smiling at the photographer. Above the cave were two round boulders that resembled eyeballs.

"The man in the mountain," Allie said in wonder. "Did you ask where this is?"

"Flip the card over."

Allie did and found handwritten directions in Geneva's familiar scrawl.

"Should take us about fifteen minutes from here,"

Geneva said.

Allie handed the postcard back to Geneva. "You're riding shotgun so you can read these directions as I drive."

Allie and Geneva got into the car and waited impatiently for the others. When Ingrid and Drake finally returned to the car, Allie pulled away a mere second after the final seatbelt clicked into place. Allie followed Geneva's directions, following the main road for almost a mile and then turning right on an unpaved road.

Allie followed the dirt road until it ended at the base of the mountain. The four left the Fiat and walked around a steel barrier that prevented vehicle traffic, and headed up the hill on a narrow dirt path. They arrived at a junction. Geneva checked her directions and led the group to the left. Within a hundred yards, they came to a set of stairs built into the mountain, complete with a wooden handrail broken in several places.

Rather than attempt to use the rotten handrail, they relied on each other to climb the steep stairs. At the top, they found an old sign, too weathered to read. All that remained in print was an outline of a black arrow pointed to the left.

"Well? Shall we?" Geneva asked as she stepped off the path and onto an overgrown trail.

"I'm not so sure we should do this," Ingrid said. "Isn't this the way we got into trouble the other day?"

"It's not raining, so this is a completely different type of trouble," Drake joked.

No one commented on the poor joke. Instead, Geneva focused on the trail before her and kept moving. They progressed up and over a small ridge, then the trail dipped down below a small cliff, and there, staring at them, was the man in the mountain.

"Well, we're here. Now what?" Geneva said.

"That's easy. Now we go in," Drake said.

The group looked at the cave before them. It was just over six feet high in the center and tapered upward on either end and joined with the mountainside. Since no one moved, Drake took the initiative and stepped up to the cave. He stayed just outside and peered in.

"Allie, I don't suppose you brought your flashlight?"

"Of course, I did." Allie, well prepared, took the tiny tool from her pocket, met Drake at the mouth, and turned it on.

Allie shined the light into the cave and saw it was nothing like she anticipated. The previous cave was expansive, with corridors and alternate areas to explore. From the outside, the man on the outside was an interesting sight. The man on the inside, not so much. The interior wasn't so much as a cave than an overhanging shelf, not more than four feet deep on the inside.

"This isn't what I expected," Drake said.

"Me either," Allie admitted. She shone the light from left to right and found nothing but a single offset boulder to the left, one crumpled beer can, and a hastily scribbled heart with the names Marco and Maria in the center. Allie clicked off the light and stowed it in her pocket. She and Drake turned away from the cave and rejoined their friends.

"There's nothing to see," Drake said. "If there ever was in the first place."

"You checked everything? It didn't seem like you were going long enough to check everything," Geneva said.

Allie shook her head. "You can go look for yourself, but there's nothing there."

"Maybe we're missing something," Ingrid said.

"Like what?" Drake asked.

Ingrid shrugged. "I don't know. Maybe we need to read the thing again. What did she say? Look at the mountain man?"

Allie bit her bottom lip and thought for a moment. "No. She said, look toward the man. Toward him. Not at him, or in him. Toward him. Spread out and see if you can find anything that faces this direction."

"I'll bet it's up there," Drake said without moving a muscle. Off to the side was a short, slanted hill that rose forty feet above them. "It's the only possible vantage point from here."

"But there's nothing up there," Geneva said. "It's just trees and brush."

"Sure. It is now, but I'm sure those have grown up sometime over the last five hundred years. I think it's worth a try. Who's with me?"

Drake looked at the women, but no one spoke.

"Actually, No. You're not going up there," Allie said. "I'll go. You shouldn't be scrambling up that hill in your condition."

"But," Drake started.

Geneva held up a single finger in front of his face. "Allie's right. You're grounded, mister. I'll go with her."

"Me too," Ingrid said.

Drake huffed, but everyone ignored him as Allie took point and walked fifty feet to the bottom of the rise. She stopped and looked up at the hill, which appeared a little steeper than it did from the original vantage point.

"Okay, let's do this," she said to the women as she found a spot between two large rocks and started the climb.

Allie followed her usual method of climbing hills, picking out a path visually before moving an inch. Slowly, she made her way up the slope, avoiding rocks, boulders, and trees as she ascended. She stopped after a few yards and looked behind her. Allie spotted Geneva following her exact path, and Ingrid was only a few steps behind Geneva. She turned back around and plowed forward, stopping only once when she deemed the path she'd chosen to be too hard on Geneva and Ingrid.

Allie made a final push, and the ground evened out on an outcropping eight feet wide by ten feet long. She turned around once she got settled on her feet and offered a hand to Geneva and finally Ingrid.

"Splendid view," Geneva said.

Allie stood and looked out across the area. Through the trees, she picked out half of the mountain man, and saw Drake standing on the trail waiting for them. He paced back and forth, which Allie knew from experience was from impatience.

"Can I have your flashlight?" Ingrid asked Allie. Without thinking, Allie handed it to her, and Ingrid switched it on and stepped away.

Allie turned and saw Ingrid headed for the back wall of the outcropping. There, she saw not so much of a cave as an unnaturally round hole in the stone, the approximate size of a sewer hole cover.

Ingrid got to her knees and shined the light into the hole.

"There's a little opening in here," she said.

Without a second of hesitation, Ingrid crawled into the hole.

"There's no way I would have done that," Geneva said to Allie.

Allie shook her head. "That girl does some odd things sometimes."

From outside, Allie and Geneva watched as Ingrid moved her legs and pushed farther in. Only the soles of Ingrid's shoes remained in sight. After a few minutes, Ingrid's feet wiggled, and Allie heard a muffled noise from inside. She stepped closer to the hole.

"What?" Allie called in. Allie got the message and nodded. "She wants us to pull her out."

Allie took Ingrid's right leg, and Geneva stepped up and took the left, and on the count of three, Allie and Geneva slowly pulled their friend from the breach.

"Thanks for the hand," Ingrid said as she stood. The front of her clothes were a mix of tan and gray from the dust, and when she patted herself down, she produced a cloud that Allie and Geneva had to step back from.

"How was that?" Geneva asked. "Did you find anything in there?"

"Not much. There were mostly rocks, a couple of old spider webs, and a really interesting skeleton of some small animal. Might have been a raccoon or squirrel or something, but all that's left is bone."

"That's it? Bones and rocks?" Geneva said. "I guess we struck out again."

"Oh, wait, there was this in there, too," Ingrid said. She bent over, reached into the hole, and from it extracted a bronze box that glinted in the sunlight.

CHAPTER FIFTEEN

Ingrid shoved the box into her backpack, and the women picked up Drake on the hike back to the car. Once there, Ingrid retrieved the box and set it on the hood of the Fiat.

"This is amazing, isn't it?" Ingrid said. A layer of tarnish in warm brown tones covered the box, but that didn't affect the beauty. There were intricate designs of common animals on every side. One side featured a horse, one a chicken, one a dog, and the fourth a cow. The top had an etching of all four animals together.

"Open it," Drake said.

Ingrid picked up the shoebox-sized box and attempted to lift the lid. It didn't budge. She made a second attempt, failed, and handed the box to Drake.

"You do it," Ingrid said.

Drake tried to lift the lid, but couldn't. He brought the box to eye height and scrutinized it.

"I don't see any seams or hinges at all. Are you sure this is a box?" he said.

Ingrid took it back and tipped it from side to side. Everyone heard the sound of something shifting from within.

"There's something in it," Ingrid said. "It must be a box of some kind. We just need to figure out how we open it."

"Might I suggest a hammer?" Drake asked.

Ingrid pulled the box back. "No way. You're not taking a hammer to this relic. It's probably priceless. What should we do?"

"Let's go back to the museum," Geneva suggested.

At four-thirty, Allie parked the car in the tiny lot attached to the museum. Ingrid had called along the way, so Victoria stood waiting by the door to let them in. She led the group into the small room that functioned as half break room and half storage room. There was a long table in the room, half-covered with papers. Victoria cleaned up the area and scavenged enough chairs for everyone to sit. Once everyone had a seat, Victoria removed her glasses and set them down before her.

"You said on the phone you had something exciting to show me?" Victoria said, leaning over the table.

Ingrid retrieved the box and set in on the table in front of Victoria.

Victoria's hands covered her mouth. "Oh, my. Do you know what this is?"

"A box," Ingrid answered. "We don't know how to open it, though."

Victoria laughed. "A box. No, dear. This is more than just a simple box."

Without excusing herself, Victoria pushed away from the table and stood up with such force that the chair she sat in toppled backward and hit the floor with a clatter. She left the room in a hurry while the four remained at the table, seated and silent. After a matter of several minutes, Victoria returned carrying a large book that she set down at her place. She picked up her chair and settled back into it.

"What do you have there?" Drake asked.

"In this volume are sketches of objects and inventions attributed to Leonardo da Vinci. I say attributed because none were ever confirmed. In here is a box similar to yours."

Victoria turned the book around so everyone could see it. The sketch on the page showed a three-dimensional box, and around the edges were clouds with faces, puffed cheeks blowing wind outward.

"These are clouds," Geneva said, pointing to the book. "Ours has animals."

"Yes. This one represents the direction of the four winds. But rumor has it there were different etchings. Like these clouds, or your animals, or stars in the sky. The method for entry was all the same. All you needed was a…." Victoria looked around the table and didn't find what she looked for. She lifted the book to check underneath, then replaced the book and left the room again. She returned a few minutes later, carrying something between her fingers that looked like a thin knitting needle.

"In theory, this should work the same as the one in the book."

Victoria put on her glasses and turned the box on its side so the chicken was facing up. She lined up the needle with the chicken's eye, then pushed down. There was a barely audible click, and Victoria grinned. She turned the box, so the next animal was facing up, then shoved the needle into the eye. Once she'd finished every animal, she flipped the box, so the bottom was up. She pulled on the bottom, and it released. Remaining on the table was the box top and four slats with tiny pegs that lined up perfectly with the animal eyes.

"Do you want to do the honors? It's your box," Victoria said.

Ingrid stepped forward and picked the small piece of parchment from the box and gently unrolled it on the table.

For comparison, Allie found the sheet from the previous parchment and laid that to the side.

"It looks the same as the other one to me," Allie said after studying the two documents.

Victoria leaned over the table to get a better view. "Similar, yes, but different in places. And this one is all in Italian. No Punic, no Latin."

"Can you translate it for us?" Allie asked.

"I can. Give me a few minutes," Victoria said. She took the parchment and stood. "Do you mind if I take this with me to my desk?"

"Not at all. Do you mind if I come with you?" Allie said. "I won't get in the way."

Victoria nodded. "Of course, follow me."

Allie followed Victoria from the room, through the museum, and to a small office close to the front door. Victoria took a seat behind an oak desk, cluttered with papers, books, a half-empty coffee cup, and a laptop.

Allie looked around for a chair, didn't spot one, and instead found a seat on a gray metal two-drawer file cabinet. From her position, it was easy to look over Victoria's shoulder to see what she was up to.

The first thing Victoria did was copy the text from the parchment to a legal pad, skipping two lines as she did so. When she had the lines copied, she rolled up the parchment and handed it over to her shoulder to Allie, who took it and placed it in her lap. Then, she went to work on the translation.

"Hand me that book you're almost sitting on, will you?" Victoria said.

Allie moved forward, reached behind her, and found the book wedged back behind her. She glanced briefly at the title, but as it was in Italian, she didn't know what it said. Allie handed it to Victoria.

Victoria opened the book and shuffled through a few

pages until she found the page she wanted. With her index finger as a guide, she traced it down the page until she arrived at the word she needed. She copied the word to the page, closed the book, and pushed it aside. For twenty minutes, Victoria worked on the translation while Allie shifted on top of the cabinet, trying to get comfortable. At last, Victoria dropped her pencil and turned her seat to face Allie.

"I'm finished. This is quite fascinating. Should we rejoin your friends?"

Victoria didn't wait for an answer. Instead, she rose and exited the room. Allie followed close on her tail, and although Victoria made only a slight detour within the museum to track down a book, she rushed right back to the conference room.

"We thought you guys left," Drake said as Allie and Victoria entered the room.

"Sorry, that took me longer than I expected," Victoria said as she took her chair. "This dialect is five hundred years old, so it takes a little while to get it correct."

Allie stretched, then dropped into her chair. She passed the parchment to Ingrid, who set it back in the box, then aligned the lid, and closed it.

"How familiar are you with the lost treasures of Leonardo?" Victoria asked.

Victoria looked around the table. No one reacted to the question.

"Tell us," Geneva said.

Victoria held up the book she'd retrieved. "This book is called *Mysteries of the Masters*. In essence, it is a compilation of random theories, secrets, and legends of the classical Italian painters. Caravaggio, Michelangelo, Raphael, Donatello, Leonardo."

"So, all the turtles?" Drake asked.

Victoria cocked her head and looked at him. "Turtles?"

"Forgive his poor joke," Geneva said. "Please go on. He won't interrupt again."

"Among the author's claims is that Leonardo, during his last years in Milan, hid away much of his art, journals, and inventions, and to this day, no one has ever found them."

Allie raised an eyebrow. "How can that be? Wasn't Leonardo one of the most prolific renaissance men of the times? Didn't he produce like hundreds of things over his lifetime?"

"Yes, but although the public knows about many of them, there's really no way to tell what he created over the course of his lifetime."

"But why hide things?" Ingrid asked.

Victoria shrugged. "I don't know. The answer to that question is long lost to history. And there's always the more certain answer, that there is nothing hidden, and they already found everything there is to find."

"That doesn't explain this, though," Ingrid said, placing her hand on top of the box. "Why go through all the trouble of hiding these clues if they didn't lead somewhere?"

"It could be a hoax," Drake said. "I mean, it's not like we've had any of these things authenticated. Someone could have made those parchments last month and found a way to make them look aged. And anyone with a basic working knowledge of metals could have cobbled that box together."

"But what about the cave where I found the first parchment?" Ingrid asked. "That seemed too elaborate and involved to be a simple prank. That would be like building an entire house to hide a geocache in a brick within the foundation."

Drake considered the point for a moment. "Okay, I think you have me there."

"There is a way to get your answer," Victoria said. "I

have a colleague who can test those items for you, and you'll know if they're authentic or not."

"When?" Allie asked.

"Please wait here while I make a phone call," Victoria said. She excused herself from the room.

Allie leaned over and picked up the legal pad.

"What does it say? Is there any clue to find the next stop?" Geneva asked.

"Past two, the master's mind awaits beneath the witch's cap," Allie read.

"That's it? You guys were gone for a half hour for a single line?" Drake asked.

"No. There's other stuff in here about glory and riches and having to be worthy to walk in the footsteps of the greatest man ever. But I skipped all that stuff. There's only one line about where to go next."

"What does 'past two' mean?" Ingrid asked. "Past two what?"

"Valleys, I imagine," Victoria said while she entered the room, catching the last part of the conversation. "My friend can meet with you soon if you're willing to stay longer."

"We'll stay," Drake said. "Why skip two valleys?"

"I mentioned there are seven valleys, correct? The first where you found the parchment, and the second where you found this box? That suggests you are supposed to be headed west to east, and the next two valleys in the line are unsettled by man."

"Why is that?" Allie asked.

"The third valley is nothing but a lake during the summer months, fed by snowmelt from the north."

"The entire valley?" Drake asked.

"Yes. It's not a large one, perhaps two or three kilometers square."

"And it's always been that way? Someone building a

dam somewhere did not create the lake?" Allie asked.

"No. It's been like that for as long as people have been in this region," Victoria said.

"What about the fourth valley?" Drake asked.

"That valley is impassible. It's more of a bowl than a valley. The mountains on every side are almost vertical. You can't get in there without climbing gear, and climbers are the only people who generally visit there.

"So, we can't drive there?" Geneva asked.

Victoria shook her head. "No. You can't access that valley without ropes, a parachute, or a helicopter."

"And thus, we skip two and go to the fifth valley?" Allie asked.

Victoria nodded. "Yes. It's a valley much like the one you've just returned from. There's a medium-sized village there. It has a restaurant, several houses within town, a store, and a church. It's quite a lovely town. It's not a large valley, smaller than where you were today." Victoria glanced at a clock on the wall above the coffeemaker. "We should go if you want to meet with my friend. Her place is only a few blocks from here, so we can walk."

The group rose as one and while the friends moved toward the front door, Victoria circled around the museum and turned out the lights. Once they were all outside, Victoria pointed in the direction they needed to go.

Allie walked ahead with Victoria while Drake, Geneva, and Ingrid trailed behind.

"There are a lot of Leonardo da Vinci sites in Milan?" Allie asked, more like a statement than a question.

"Oh, yes. There are many places here you can go to see his work. There's a fresco of his at the castle, although that's been under restoration for many years and not often open for viewing. You can see his *Codex Atlanticus* at the Biblioteca Ambrosiana. It's quite fascinating, although they only display a few pages at a time. And if you go to the National Museum of Science and Technology, you can see several models based on his designs."

"That doesn't sound like a lot," Allie said.

"Sadly, Leonardo's work is spread all over the world, so no one has access to the entire breadth of it. But what we do have access to here in Italy is remarkable."

Allie nodded in agreement and stopped speaking. As they crossed the street, she spotted a square. It was a patch of green surrounded by the bustle of the city, lined with waist-high bushes. A sidewalk divided the grass and led to a statue of someone Allie didn't recognize. Bordering the grass were four park benches, spread out equally to maintain an esthetic balance, and on one bench sat a man engrossed in a book. Somehow, on the busy road filled with speeding cars and beeping mopeds, the man found a quiet spot to read. Allie thought of her book back at the hotel.

Allie paid so much attention to the reading man she didn't notice Victoria had turned a corner and almost walked right onto the street into the path of an oncoming bus. She felt a sudden jerk on her jacket collar, one that pulled her back, startled.

"Where are you going?" Drake asked, releasing the grip on her coat.

The bus sped up, leaving a puff of exhaust behind.

"Thanks. I was daydreaming, I guess," Allie said.

"Come on. We're falling behind."

Allie looked around the corner and saw Victoria was almost a half block ahead of them, unaware the rest of the group had stopped. As if by telepathy, she halted, turned around, and waited. Once the group caught up, Victoria pointed to a nondescript door.

"We're here," Victoria said. She reached for the bell.

The bell shrilled, and the group waited for almost a full

minute before the door opened. A tall woman with brown hair flowing down to her waist stepped outside and swept Victoria in her arms. The friends greeted each other with kisses on each cheek.

"These are your people?" the woman asked. "Please come inside."

"I'm Lucia," the woman said, greeting Allie with kisses as well.

"I'm Allie. That's Geneva, Drake, and Ingrid," Allie said, introducing her friends who had instinctively lined up to enter the building.

Allie followed Victoria, fully expecting to be led into the interior of a house, but instead the main room looked more like a chemistry lab than a house. There was a giant dining table in the middle, and Lucia had the walls lined with file cabinets, storage cabinets, and workstations topped with clusters of beakers, microscopes, and several things that looked like microwave ovens.

"So, what do you have for me?" Lucia said when she'd ushered Ingrid into the room.

"We have some things we found, and we'd like to know if you can authenticate them," Allie said.

Lucia laughed in a pitch that resembled a meadowlark song. "I can. It is what I do, among my other tasks."

Allie nodded at Ingrid, who slipped her backpack from her shoulders, undid the straps, and pulled out the parchment and the box.

"Where did you get these?" Lucia asked.

"The parchment we found accidentally while out hiking. The box we found based on what was on the parchment," Allie said.

Lucia stared at Allie for a moment, and when Allie didn't provide further information, Lucia grinned. "Let's see what we can find out."

Lucia stepped to the corner near the door, where she put an oversized lab coat over the dark blue dress she wore and donned a pair of thin gloves. She pulled out a stool from under the table, sat down, and carefully unrolled the parchment.

"Oh, this is lovely," Lucia said. "You have quite the find here."

Lucia stretched to her left and retrieved a container stuffed with long cotton swabs and an unmarked white plastic bottle filled with a liquid.

"This won't damage your piece, okay?" Lucia said to no one in particular. She selected a swab, put two drops of liquid on the swab's cotton tip. She rubbed the tip on the parchment, blackening the cotton.

Satisfied, Lucia moved to one of her workstations, where she prepared her sample and dropped it into a machine.

"What is that?" Drake asked.

"It is a mass spectrometer. It will help determine what they made this ink from."

"How long will that take?" Drake asked.

Lucia smiled again. "It works quickly, and I should have the results in only a day or two. In the meantime, let's check the parchment itself."

With a pair of scissors and permission, Lucia snipped a tiny sample from the document and placed it beneath a microscope. "Ah, yes. They made this from ibex hide."

Lucia returned to the table and turned her attention to the box.

"You'll need something thin, like a needle, to open that," Victoria said.

Lucia rose and checked around the lab until she found something to use, then handed it to Victoria, who opened the box. Once inside, Lucia repeated the tests with the second parchment. Once she finished, she examined the box itself.

"Do you need to run that through the machine, too?" Geneva asked.

"No. There are more practical tests I can do," Lucia said.

Lucia circled the room again and returned with several items to the table.

"This is a magnet," she said, holding up the object for all to see. She placed it against the box, and it didn't stick. "That is a good sign. Bronze is non-magnetic."

Next, she took a small silver hammer, held the box lid loosely by a corner, and tapped the lid. A tone, not unlike a bell, resounded in the room for a few seconds.

"Pleasant, yes?" Lucia said. "I'm quite certain this is bronze."

For her last test, Lucia took several minutes to examine the box with a magnifying glass, while the rest of the group stayed silent and waited.

"This is remarkable construction. It is definitely hand etched," Lucia said.

She went into another bout of silence for several minutes, then she looked up, her eyes wild with excitement.

"Oh, my goodness!" Lucia exclaimed. "Yes!" She jumped from the stool and circled the table, unable to control her emotions.

"What is it?" Victoria asked.

Lucia returned to the box and held the magnifying glass for her. "What do you see?"

Victoria moved the glass to focus it better, then sat straight up. "Look at this," she said to Allie.

Allie came forward, looked through the glass and saw what looked like four little loops connected to each other. "Yeah? So?"

Victoria grinned. "Leonardo never signed his artwork. Instead, he used a symbol of intertwining knots. I believe this to be genuine."

CHAPTER SIXTEEN

The group headed out before sunrise the next morning.

"I hope this isn't a sign of things to come," Ingrid said as she looked out the window at the falling rain. "Usually I like the rain, but for this trip, I'm pretty much over it."

"I second that," Drake said. "Rain, rain, go away, and don't come back until I'm back home in my living room."

"Oh, come one. It's barely a sprinkle. Just a passing cloud, really," Allie said. "If it makes you feel any better, it should stop raining in an hour or so. The weather segment on the news this morning said it will be warmer and sunny today."

"How far is it to the valley?" Drake asked.

"If we take the straight shot, it will be just under three hours. If we stop for the caches that Geneva researched for us, we could easily add another hour to that time. The question becomes, should we do the caches along the way, or just head straight for the valley?"

"How hard are the caches?" Drake asked.

"You'd have to ask Geneva that question," Allie said.

"Geneva? How hard are they?" Drake asked from the

passenger seat. When he received no answer, he repeated her name. "Ingrid, is everything okay back there?"

Ingrid glanced over at her seatmate. Geneva reclined back in her seat, her head pressed against the window, and had her jacket covering her like an impromptu jacket. As they drove under a streetlight, Ingrid noticed Geneva's chest rise and fall.

"She's napping, Drake. Did you keep her up too late?" Ingrid asked.

"I don't know. She stayed up reading while I drifted off to sleep. Actually, a nap sounds nice," Drake said.

"You can't nap, you're the navigator," Allie whispered in a low tone. "You know the rules."

"Ingrid can do it," Drake said.

"I can do it," Ingrid offered.

Allie didn't answer, and instead pulled into the parking lot of a closed business. Once stopped, Ingrid and Drake switched seats. Allie listened for Ingrid's seatbelt to click and then watched in the rearview as Drake got settled. Like Geneva, he rested his head against the window and closed his eyes.

"Those guys are no fun," Allie said as she pulled back onto the road.

"I think they're both still messed up from a few days ago. Drake was barely keeping up with us yesterday. Did you notice?"

"I did. Is there something going on that he's hiding from us? Surgery complications, perhaps? Has Geneva said anything about him?"

"No," Ingrid said. "Well, yes. She mentioned he's been sleeping more, but she blew that off to jet lag and all the running around we've been doing."

"Funny, I think we've been running around less here than we would be back home. Has he been taking his antibiotics?" Allie asked.

"I don't know. We'll have to remember to ask him. Do you think he'll tell us the truth about it?"

"Good question. He's as honest as anyone can be, but occasionally he gets that macho-induced dose of irrationality,"

"Maybe we should steal his pills and count them. That would tell us right away if he's taking them or not," Ingrid said.

"Although that's a great idea, it's dishonest. We'll ask him and trust that he'll tell us the truth."

"What if we had Geneva steal and count? They're in the same room. He wouldn't even notice."

Allie smiled. "That's an even better idea. You want to ask her, or should I?"

"I will, first chance I get. So, back to the initial question. Do we stop for the geocaches along the way, or head directly to the valley?"

"She has the list, so let's see how far we get before she wakes up. Personally, I'd like to find one on the way, if only to get out of the car and stretch the legs."

Allie approached the highway she needed, flipped on her signal, turned right, and began the slow climb into the mountains. Through the raindrops and the intermittent windshield wipers, Allie noticed the first sign of the approaching sun, a swatch of brightening colors attempting to climb the mountains before her.

"I love sunrises," Allie blurted.

"Me too," Ingrid said. "Especially over the mountains, or a large body of water."

Allie retreated into her own thoughts and split her concentration between the road and the sunrise. As the miles dropped behind her, the sun advanced in the sky. The rays stretched over the mountaintops, and the rain ended for good as shades of pink, orange, and gold chased away the drops and replaced them with the promise of a bright day. During her trance, the miles and night sky drifted away as lazy as a napping cat.

"The rain stopped," Drake said.

Allie glanced into the mirror and caught him rubbing his nap from his eyes. "I told you it would."

"There's a geocache at a gas station two miles up the road. Can we stop there?" Geneva asked.

"No problem," Allie said, straightening her posture. "It's a perfect time for a break."

As she entered into the station, Allie determined she had plenty of gas, so she pulled into a parking space rather than a pump.

"I have to go use the restroom," Ingrid said as she exited the car.

Drake accompanied Ingrid into the building while Allie followed Geneva. Geneva's GPS guided them around the side of the building, and there, Geneva spotted the geocache right away. The geocache stood out in plain sight, a flat magnet a little larger than a bumper sticker attached to the side of the air compressor. The magnet looked official and although it contained words in Italian neither woman recognized, it also held the identification number of the geocache.

Geneva removed the magnet and flipped it over. There she found the long flat log tucked inside a plastic bag taped to the magnet. She fished it out, signed it, and handed it to Allie.

"How's Drake doing?" Allie asked as she penned her nickname on the log.

Geneva's eyes met Allie's. "He seems a little off. I've asked him about it several times, but he just waves me away and tells me he's fine."

Allie nodded. "Has he been taking his meds?"

Geneva hesitated before answering. "I'm not sure. I think he took his pills yesterday. He's supposed to take the antibiotics twice a day with meals."

"We've spent all our meals together, and I've yet to see him take a pill," Allie said.

"I usually take them after," Drake said.

Allie and Geneva turned around, not realizing Drake and Ingrid had joined them.

Drake got the bottle out of his pocket and shook it. Inside, the pills rattled. "Trust me, the last thing I want is an infection."

"We're just concerned. Have you been doing okay?" Allie asked.

"Sure. Other than being a little more tired than usual, but my doctor said I should expect that."

Allie stood, unresponsive. "Okay, if you say so," she said at last, passing the log and pen to Drake. Allie shivered, regretting she'd left her jacket in the car rather than putting it on. Geneva and Ingrid were wearing theirs to ward off the early morning chill.

"I'm heading back to the car," Allie said. "I need to put on my coat, so I'll meet y'all back there." As she looked up, Allie noticed a bead of sweat on Drake's forehead.

Over an hour later, the road wound its way around a bend, and before them, the valley they'd searched for came into view. Even though they were a few miles from town, they could easily spot the church steeple towering over the rest of the town. They passed a sign announcing the village limits when Ingrid's phone rang.

"Hello? I'm sorry I don't speak… Yes? Okay. Yes, I understand. Thank you." Ingrid disconnected the call. "That was Lucia. She said her analysis is done, and the ink is consistent with what they made during Leonardo's lifetime.

She says that although she can't a hundred percent validate the results without further tests, she's about eighty percent confident in her assessment."

"I'll take eighty," Allie said. "Anyone have an idea of how to find the witch's cap?"

"I do. Enter these coordinates into Luna," Geneva said. She relayed the numbers and Ingrid entered them into the machine and pressed go.

"What is this?" Allie asked.

"There's a geocache there. In the description, it mentions that the cache is located along a popular hiking trail that leads to one of the unique geological features in the area. It turns out that there's a geological feature there that looks like an isosceles triangle. To me, if you put an isosceles triangle on top of a wide brim, what does that look like?"

Ingrid grinned. "A witch's hat."

Geneva nodded. "Exactly. That's what I thought of as well."

"I'm just worried that if there's a geocache there and it is a popular hiking spot, that someone would have discovered the cave a long time ago," Allie said.

"The cache itself is an Earthcache, so there's no physical container to find," Geneva said.

"How hard are the questions?" Drake asked.

"Not bad, actually. We should be able to figure it out once we get there."

Allie continued the drive, and once she got to the far side of town, the road followed a small river. Luna advised Allie to turn right, and when she did, Allie drove over a stone bridge, turned left, and continued following the river from the opposite side of the main road. Eventually, the river curled away from the main road, and Allie followed the path they were on until they reached a marked parking area. Allie pulled in and shut down the Fiat.

"Okay, Geneva, where do we go from here?" Allie asked once they were all outside and ready to go.

Geneva checked her GPS and pointed at the only trail leading from the parking lot and toward the mountainside. "I think we go that way. It's not far, only four hundred feet or so."

"It's always the 'or so' part that makes me nervous," Drake said.

Geneva grabbed Drake's arm and dragged him forward. "Let's go, hero. I'm sure this won't be any trouble at all."

Ingrid laughed. "Always the famous last words, right?"

Geneva walked to the trailhead and stepped into the trees. Unlike the previous trails they'd been on recently, this one had a layer of asphalt paving the way. In several spots, wooden horse fences kept the hikers from venturing off the trail. At one point the trail veered off toward the river, and the slope changed, forcing the friends to trudge uphill for a hundred feet. Once the climb ended, the trees cleared away, and they came to an open area.

"Wow, that's cool," Drake said, looking at the geological features before them.

Carved by nature into the mountain was a shape that looked like a perfect triangle. It stood forty feet high and, on either side, water flowed from the mountain above. Before them, the trail continued on beneath the triangle. One side of the path butted up against the mountain, and on the opposite side, a black steel fence prevented anyone from falling over the edge.

"Should we do the Earthcache first, or look for a cave?" Drake asked.

"Let's get the questions out of the way. They'll only take a couple of minutes," Geneva suggested. "The questions are: what are the angle of the two long sides of the triangle, what color are the vertical veins of stone beneath the triangle with the number of each, and what happens to the water that falls on either side of the hat?"

"I'll take the angle question," Ingrid said.

"I'll do the vein count," Allie offered.

"So then, I guess I'll check out the water," Drake said.

Ingrid took her phone from her pocket and found the protractor app she wanted. She held her phone up before her with the phone lined up with the triangle's side, then walked beneath the triangle and took the measurement from the other side. She returned to Geneva.

"I've got seventy-five degrees on both sides, give or take," Ingrid said.

Geneva nodded and typed the information into her phone. "Got it."

As Ingrid stepped away to help Allie, Drake returned.

"The water on both sides falls from here and joins into the main river," Drake said.

Geneva recorded his answer, then they moved to the thirty-foot-wide area beneath the triangle.

"Do you have an answer, Allie?" Geneva asked.

Allie stood at the opposite end from Geneva. "I'm doing a third count. I came up with difference numbers on the first two."

Allie looked at the wall behind her, and she scanned the vertical stripes in alternating black and red-brown in the shaded area beneath the triangle. The stripes had different widths, and Allie touched each stripe as she counted them aloud and walked in Geneva's direction.

"I've got forty black and thirty-eight in whatever you would call this reddish-brown," Allie said.

"Okay, got it."

"What do you suppose those stripes are?" Ingrid asked.

"I don't know," Allie said. "Probably exposed mineral

veins or something. Take a picture of them and we'll figure it out later."

"You know what I didn't see in here anywhere? A cave," Drake said.

"I didn't either," Allie said.

"That last one I found wasn't in a cave. It was just a hole, remember?" Ingrid said. "Everyone spread out and see if you can find anything at all."

Ingrid, Drake, and Geneva started to examine the wall behind them while Allie stepped to the fence, leaned over, and looked below. She saw a drop of fifteen feet, and then the river as it meandered its way toward the village. She leaned over farther and looked to the left and right to see if there was a way down to the ground and spotted the remnants of an old trail.

Allie followed the main trail to the opposite side of the triangle. There, the trail ended, enclosed by more steel fencing. She went to the river's side of the fence and looked down the mountain. There, she spotted a set of long disused stone steps carved into the granite. The steps were rugged, covered with gray-green lichen, and looked perilous from where she stood. Allie looked back at her friends who were still examining the back wall, then shrugged, and slipped easily through the fence rails.

The first stair down was wide and dry, and Allie had no difficulty stepping down. The next step, although dry, was barely the width of one sideways foot, so Allie held on to the bottom fence rail to help her down. From there, Allie carefully climbed down another two stairs before she decided it seemed safer to sit and go down one step at a time. Feet, then butt. She repeated the process a dozen times, and then the steps made a turn toward the river. She looked ahead and, to her delight, saw the steps led to an outcropping wide enough to support not only her, but all of her friends if they chose to join her.

Allie turned and faced the vertical wall behind her, looking for any caves, holes, or indents in the wall. She found nothing, so she stepped backward three feet, making sure she was well enough from the edge, and scanned the area with her eyes, looking for any visual clues. She was about to give up and head back to her friends when she spotted something where the third step intersected with the wall, something that resembled a patterned scar.

Allie crouched and ran her finger over the postage-stamp shaped spot. Something about it seemed familiar, so she found a flat stone and used it to scrape away the collected dirt and algae. When the surface seemed somewhat clean, she dropped to her knees and looked at it closer.

"I found something, I think," Allie called out.

"Allie? Where are you?" Ingrid yelled back.

"I'm down below. Look over the edge."

Allie stood and looked up, and after a couple of seconds, Ingrid's face beamed down at her.

"What are you doing down there?" Ingrid asked.

"I found something," Allie yelled, pointing at the mark. "Come down here. No wait. Stay there."

Allie retrieved a phone, snapped a picture, then sent it to Ingrid via a text, added a brief message and waited for the response. She looked above her and saw Ingrid's head disappear. After a few moments, Ingrid returned.

"Yes, that looks like the knots. Geneva and Drake think so too. Should one of us come down?" Ingrid yelled.

"No. Give me a minute," Allie yelled.

Allie found the car keys and used them to scrape away the caked-in dirt from the knots, and as she did, the small indent grew deeper. She dropped to her knees, leaned forward and blew on the symbol. Eventually, enough of the dirt cleared out and the details within the pattern became obvious. A hole was in the center of the intertwined knots. Allie used her little finger to clear the dirt from the hole, then looked around and found a stick that looked small enough to fit in the void. Allie continued working on the dirt, then put the stick in the hole to determine how deep it went. She felt some resistance, pushed harder, and heard something click. When she tried to remove the stick, it stuck. She pulled harder, and to her surprise, the entire section of wall around the symbol broke away.

Allie turned, switched on her phone light and shone it in the hole. Inside, she spotted a leather bag. She removed it, opened the bag, and withdrew a parchment. Allie unrolled it and saw it was similar to the two others in their possession, so she returned it to the bag and returned to her feet.

She looked up and saw everyone watching her with interest.

"I'm coming back up," Allie yelled to the group. She felt their gaze on her as she carefully ascended each step. When she got to the top, she handed Geneva the bag, and Drake helped her back through the fence.

"Another parchment?" Ingrid asked.

"Yes. Of course, it looks like it's all in Italian again," Allie said.

"We should have brought Victoria along. That way, we could have saved time running all the way back to Milan," Drake said.

"There's no reason to run. We'll send her a picture of the parchment, and she can work from that. We can stay out here and head over to the next valley," Geneva said.

"Let's head back to the village. We'll get something to eat while we wait for Victoria's answer," Ingrid said.

Allie nodded. "I hope it's somewhere that sells gelato. "

CHAPTER SEVENTEEN

I'm sorry they didn't have any gelato," Ingrid said to Allie. "Are you sure you don't want a bite of this cannoli? It's quite delicious."

Allie shook her head while she bit into the last of her sandwich. She swallowed and washed it down with a drink of orange soda that tasted more like an orange than anything she'd ever experienced in America.

"Did you get the translation back yet?" Allie asked as she capped her bottle.

Ingrid put down her dessert and picked up her phone. "Nope. She said it would be a bit. Perhaps a bit hasn't elapsed yet."

Allie wiped her hands with a napkin and dropped it onto her plate. "All this waiting is maddening for me. I feel like I should be doing something."

"You can do something. Be patient. I'm trying to finish my lunch," Ingrid said. "Perhaps you should go out for a walk like the other two did."

Allie looked out the restaurant window, but didn't spot her friends. The only people in view were an old man walking a dog and the woman he was talking to. "Where did you say they headed?"

"I didn't say, and neither did they. Geneva said they would be back within a half hour."

"How long have they been gone?" Allie asked.

Ingrid consulted her phone. "Twenty-one minutes. Chill out. You're driving me nuts." Ingrid placed her phone to her right and returned to her cannoli. "You sure you don't want the last bite? You don't know what you're missing."

"I do. I'm missing gelato," Allie said. "Chocolate. Strawberry. Mint. Peach. Whatever. Gelato is what I'm missing the most."

Ingrid smiled. "We'll get you some. I promise." She slowly ate the last of her dessert and followed it with the last of a glass of milk. "Hey, I have an idea. Why don't we head over to the next valley? We know the clue is going to lead there anyway, so why not get a jump on it? We might see if there are any geocaches over there and collect those while we wait on Victoria."

Allie nodded. "That's a good idea. And you've got milk on your chin."

While Ingrid wiped her mouth, Allie opened her backpack and fished out the map. It took her a moment to find their current position and the next valley to the east. "It's about fifteen miles from here," she said.

"Where?" Ingrid asked.

"We are here and the next one is there," Allie said as she placed a saltshaker on their current spot and the pepper shaker on where they needed to go next.

Without disturbing the shakers, Ingrid turned the map around so she could read it better. Once she had her bearings, she looked up the area on her phone and plunged in to locate any geocaches that might be in the area.

"You have a pen and paper on you? I left mine in the

car." Ingrid asked without looking up.

Allie dipped into her backpack and pulled out the requested items and slid them across the table. While she twisted in her seat, trying hard not to seem impatient, Allie looked out the window. The woman was gone and the man with the dog had made it only another twenty feet before stopping to chat with another man, also with a dog in tow. She checked in the other direction and saw no sign of her friends.

"I suppose any geocaches with a high terrain rating are out?" Ingrid asked.

"Let's try to stick to two or less. Preferably less," Allie answered.

Allie watched as Ingrid jotted down geocache ID numbers and coordinates for each. When she dropped the pen and sat back, there were four on the notepad.

"I think these are the most interesting. Especially the third one on the list," Ingrid said.

"What's so special about it?"

"The description says it's a petrified tree in the middle of nowhere."

"That does sound interesting. Should we go?" Allie said.

Ingrid nodded. "The only question that remains is whether to find Geneva and Drake and bring them along."

Allie dipped into her pocket and pulled out a euro coin. "The side with the man on it, we pick them up. The side with the number on it, we leave them here."

Allie flipped the coin high in the air, caught it on the way down, and slammed it onto the table. She smiled and removed her hand.

"Oh crap," Ingrid said when she saw the result.

*

"I can't believe you wanted to leave us behind," Geneva

said, breaking almost a half hour of silence.

"Believe me, it wasn't us. It was the coin," Ingrid said. "It's pure good luck that you guys showed up when you did. Where did you disappear to, anyway?"

"We walked over to the church to check it out. It's beautiful inside. You should have seen the thing."

"Did you take lots of pictures?" Ingrid asked.

"Yes, I did. It was a beautiful church, wasn't it, honey?" Geneva asked. She elbowed Drake in the ribs when he didn't respond right away.

"Yes, dear. Beautiful church."

Allie caught Drake's eyes in the mirror, and when he rolled them, she couldn't suppress her smile.

"Wish I had been there," Allie said.

Luna told Allie to turn, and she did. After the turn, Allie drove another mile and parked in a small lot. The group emerged from the Fiat and stood in front of the car.

"That's not what I expected," Allie said. "I thought you said petrified tree."

"Yes, I did."

"I've visited the Petrified Forest in Arizona, and I've never seen a tree like that," Drake said.

"Me either," Geneva added.

Before the group stood a petrified tree unlike anything they'd ever experienced. The tree looked like a Saguaro cactus from the American southwest desert. The main trunk stood arrow straight and fifteen feet tall. Offshoots of branches, much thinner than the main trunk, spread out a few inches from the trunk and reached for the bright blue sky.

Geneva stopped to snap a picture while Ingrid brought up the cache description and looked for clues.

"The cache page says it's not on the tree, yet not far from it. Search for something similar, yet different," Ingrid said.

"How could you read that?" Drake asked. "Did you learn fluent Italian in the last couple of days?"

Ingrid smiled and held up her phone. "I didn't need to. The cache owner has Italian and English descriptions on the page. It should be within ten feet of where we're standing."

The four spread out and looked for the geocache.

"There's a pile of rocks over here," Drake said as he pointed at the ground.

"I've got one here, too," Geneva said.

Ingrid was closest to Drake, so she decided to help him sort through his pile while Allie joined Geneva for hers.

"I really dislike these," Allie said, looking down at the fifty or sixty rocks that made up a tiny hill.

Geneva toed a rock and pushed it aside. "Yeah, me too. I usually skip these. Why don't we wait and see if they find it over there?"

Allie nodded. "That's a great idea. If they don't, we can ask for help here. Drake loves these things."

Geneva crouched and picked up a rock, looked underneath it, and placed it to the side. "We should at least pretend that we're looking hard for it."

Allie nodded, then picked up the rock closest to her. She examined it, found it to be an ordinary rock, and put it down. The second rock yielded nothing as well.

"Eureka!" Drake exclaimed.

Allie and Geneva looked over at Drake, where he held a small box above his head like he'd just pulled Excalibur from a stone. Allie dropped the rock she held, and she and Geneva joined the others.

Ingrid's phone rang, and she answered on the fourth ring. "Hello? Hold on, let me put you on speaker." Ingrid fumbled with the buttons and then nodded. "Okay. Go ahead."

"Hello, this is Victoria. Can you hear me?"

"Sure can," Allie said. "Go ahead."

"I translated what I could of the parchment you found today. There were some things I couldn't make out because the picture wasn't clear. If I had the parchment with me, I would have been able to do it all."

"Did you get anything helpful to our quest?" Allie asked.

"Oh, yes. If you go to the sixth valley, you'll find something that shouldn't exist in nature. Steadfast and still."

"You mean like, for example, a large, petrified tree in the middle of a field?" Drake said.

The line went silent.

"Did we lose her?" Geneva asked after a few seconds of no one speaking.

"No. I'm still here. A petrified tree would fit what's written here. How did you know that?"

"Because we're already here," Allie said.

"Oh. Well, then I would search that tree for the next clue if I were you," Victoria said.

"Okay. Thanks Victoria. I'll call you back if we need anything else," Ingrid said. She disconnected the call and stowed her phone.

As one, the group turned around and faced the tree. Allie stepped close to it and ran her hand along the surface. Although it looked smooth, she detected a complex texture beneath her fingertips. She marveled at the palette of colors, from the various hues of brown and gray to the stripes of yellow and orange, to the pink patches within.

"I can't believe Leonardo da Vinci hid a clue here. How would someone even do that with the technology available five hundred years ago?" Drake said.

"I don't know, but let's check it over anyway," Allie said. "Since the intertwined knots led me to the last clue, it would be a good bet that this one would be the same. Look for the knots."

Each person took a side of the tree and began the search.

"How high up should we look?" Geneva asked.

"I don't know," Allie said. "Start with anything at eye level and below. If we need to search higher, we'll figure it out."

Allie stood before the tree, three inches away. She scanned the tree for marks, working her way from left to right. When she reached the far right, she dropped her gaze a few inches and searched the tree in the opposite direction. Allie followed the same pattern until she got close to the ground. When she couldn't look down any farther, she got to her knees, and eventually ended up on hands and knees, like she was a gardener picking weeds by hand.

"I got nothing," Allie said.

"Crawl over here and help me out, then," Ingrid said.

Allie moved forward and around the trunk. Ingrid stepped back two feet to make room for Allie.

"You make your way up, and I'll meet you in the middle," Ingrid said.

While Ingrid worked from the top-down, Allie scanned the tree from the bottom-up. Both women came up with the same results. Nothing.

Already close to the ground, Allie moved forward again, where Geneva was just about finished with her section.

"This is hopeless," Geneva said.

"Hey, I think I have something," Drake said. "Allie, crawl on over here and take a look."

Allie did as requested and moved around to Drake's side of the tree. There, he pointed at something near where the trunk met the ground. Allie strained to see and then touched the spot.

"I don't think that's anything," Allie said.

"No. Go lower, where that little nub comes out of the ground."

Allie found the spot Drake alluded to. Nub was the correct term, as it looked like someone had dropped a rock the size of a plum on the ground. She leaned over to check it out, and sure enough, peeking out above the grass, was the top half of the intertwined knots they'd been searching for.

"Can you find me a stick or something to dig with?" Allie asked.

Geneva, Drake, and Ingrid scoured the area, and together they found two flat rocks, a stick, and a plastic spoon. Allie looked at the options available and selected the spoon from Drake's hand. She went to work on the grass around the nub and uncovered it one spoonful at a time. The nub turned out to be the part of an exposed petrified root from the tree. Allie dug out as much as she could until the entirety of the knots symbol was clear of dirt and debris. Unlike the one from earlier in the day, this one didn't have a hole in the center. Allie pushed on the knots, and nothing happened.

"I don't understand," Allie said. "When I put pressure on the last one, the hole opened."

"Maybe you need to dig down farther. It could be it's underneath the tree," Drake said.

"Well, then grab something and get down here and help me."

Drake looked at the items available to him and selected a rock in the shape of an arrowhead and the stick. He moved to the side opposite Allie and began to dig with the rock, pushing the dirt to the side as he released it.

"You need more help down there?" Geneva asked.

"Yes, but there's not really any room for you. Why don't y'all take a break, and when one of us gets tired, you can take our place," Allie said.

Geneva nodded and stayed standing where she was. Ingrid moved a few feet away and sat cross-legged on the grass, watching as Allie and Drake worked to uncover the root.

Everyone stayed silent as Drake and Allie pawed at the dirt. As if a cruel joke, a cool wind blew through the valley, and off in the distance, a peal of rumble echoed through the mountains.

"My guess is you guys should dig a little faster," Geneva said.

Drake stopped, looked at the sky, and then back at Geneva. "Maybe it's time for you guys to jump in and help. I'd hate to do this in the rain."

Ingrid kneeled next to Allie and Geneva crowded in beside Drake and four hands working on the single task became eight.

The thunder rumbled again, and the sky darkened as more storm clouds rolled in.

The four quickly got into a rhythm, with Allie and Drake loosening the dirt while Ingrid and Geneva pushed it aside. After ten minutes, Allie reached under the root and touched Drake's fingertips.

"We're through. We need to expand the hole," Allie said.

The group redoubled the effort, and soon the hole doubled, then quadrupled in size.

"Hold on, I think I have something. Someone give me a phone," Allie said as she rubbed the underside of the root.

"Here," Ingrid said, passing her phone to Allie.

Allie took the phone, set the camera to rear-facing, and moved it under the root. There, plain as day, she saw another set of intertwined knots on the screen. Like the previous find, this set had a hole in the center.

"Pass me that stick, Drake," Allie said.

Drake gave up the wood, and realizing it was too long to fit, Allie broke the stick in half. She placed the stick under the root, used her index finger to guide her over the hole, then inserted the stick and pushed. When she felt resistance, she pushed harder, and a chunk of the tree dropped into her hand.

Allie pulled the stick and tree from the hole, then without looking, reached underneath into the hole.

"I got something. Feels like a string or something," Allie said.

Allie caught the item between two fingers and pulled. A leather strap dropped from the hole, so Allie wrapped her fingers around it and gave it a hearty yank. She spotted the edge of a parchment and eventually wiggled it free.

"Got it," Allie said, holding the find in the air. As soon as she finished speaking, the first of the big, lazy raindrops began plopping to the ground.

"I guess it's time to get going," Ingrid said as she got to her feet.

"Let's cover this back up first," Drake said.

As one, they pushed the dirt into the hole until they'd covered even the nub, and then Drake took some time and set the disrupted grass back in place. Once everything looked as natural as could be, the four friends jogged back to the car.

Once they all entered the Fiat and closed the doors, Allie fired up the engine just as a flash of lightning streaked across the sky.

"It really is time to go," Allie said. She put the car into gear, did a U-turn in the small parking area, and headed for the road.

"Are you going to send Victoria a picture of this new parchment?" Allie had the parchment on the seat next to her, and Ingrid leaned over and grabbed it.

Ingrid unrolled the parchment, propped it up against

the glove compartment and snapped a picture. She opened her texts, then realized she had a problem. "I can't do it. I lost service," she said.

"Must be the storm," Geneva said from the back.

As they drove on, the rain grew harder, forcing Allie to slow down and set the windshield wipers on high.

"How far is town?" Allie asked.

"Only three or four miles," Ingrid said.

"Okay. If this rain doesn't let up by then, I'm going to pull in somewhere until it eases. I have no desire to drive four hours through this downpour."

As Allie stopped speaking, she noticed the windshield had started to fog.

"Ingrid, can you mess with the fan and clear that out?"

Ingrid flipped on the defroster, and as she did, a gust of wind came through the valley like an oncoming train. It caught Allie off guard, and it pushed the Fiat into the oncoming lane until Allie regained control and navigated back where she belonged. The rain picked up, and Allie slowed even further, unable to see only three feet beyond the hood. She took her hand off the steering wheel just long enough to flip on the hazard lights and struggled to keep the car on the pavement. She hadn't realized she'd been holding her breath until she passed the village limits sign. Allie exhaled, flexed her hands over the steering wheel, and pulled into the first parking lot she came to.

CHAPTER EIGHTEEN

Allie?"

Allie opened her eyes and noticed Ingrid's perfect face in front of hers.

"Good morning," Ingrid said.

Allie smiled. "Good morning. What's up?"

"Everything but you. Drake wants to know what the plan is for today. Are we going to the seventh valley?"

"Yes. What time is it?"

Ingrid checked. "It's a bit after nine. I hated waking you. I can't imagine how tired you are."

Allie nodded and closed her eyes. Tired was an understatement. The day before, they'd waited in the parking lot for an hour for the rain to let up, and when it didn't, they returned to the restaurant to hunker down somewhere warmer and more comfortable than the car. The sunset took the rain with it, and only afterward did they begin the four-hour drive back to the hotel.

"Allie?"

"No, I'm getting up right now." Allie threw the blanket off and managed to swing her legs over the edge of the bed.

"Would you like some tea?" Ingrid asked.

"I'd love a cup. I'll be down to the dining room in ten minutes." Allie rubbed her eyes and ran her fingers through her tangled hair. "Actually, I'd love a shower, too, so I'll be down in fifteen."

"Here," Ingrid said.

Allie accepted what Ingrid handed her without question. It was a mug, steam coming off the top. Allie sniffed.

"Is this cinnamon?" Allie asked.

Ingrid nodded. "Yep. With a dollop of honey, the way you like it."

Allie smiled and took a sip. "This is wonderful. I love you so much right now."

Ingrid grinned. "How could you not? I'm adorable. I'll catch you downstairs in a bit."

Sixteen minutes later, Allie strolled into the dining room. Her hair was still wet from the shower, and she'd revived the bounce in her step. "Good morning, everyone," she said as she placed her empty mug on the table. "What's good for breakfast today?"

"The sandwiches aren't bad," Drake said.

For breakfast, the hotel laid out a variety of meats, breads, and cheeses, in addition to the common breakfast fare. Rather than go for the cereal or oatmeal, Drake had taken to making sandwiches instead, usually salami, ham, and cheese between thick slices of fresh-baked Italian bread.

"Did you send the picture off to Victoria for translation?" Allie asked Ingrid.

"Yep, I did that first thing. She reached out and asked for closeups and additional shots of some things, so I sent those off too. She should get back to us within the hour."

"Do you guys mind if I eat something before we head out?"

Drake pointed toward the food. "Go ahead. I highly recommend the salami stuff and that white cheese."

Allie headed over to the breakfast bar, made herself a plate, and returned to the table. She put her plate on the table and slid into a chair next to Ingrid.

"This will be the seventh valley. Perhaps this is the day we get to the end of the mystery," Allie said.

"It would be nice," Geneva said. "Not so much from the standpoint of becoming rich and famous, but more like getting back to our normally scheduled vacation."

"Is all the driving getting to you?" Drake asked.

Geneva thought for a moment, finishing a corner of toast before she answered. "It's not that. I enjoy the adventure, and don't mind the rides. I'd simply like to get more immersed in the culture. Visit more of the city sites? You get what I'm saying."

Allie nodded. "I do. I was hoping to get a few museums in, and we haven't stepped inside a single one."

"And I won't. I'll wait outside, or do something else," Drake said.

"We've got another ten days here. Why don't we take the day off and do something else?" Ingrid asked.

Allie pointed her oatmeal spoon in Ingrid's direction. "That's a good idea. We could all split up for the day, do our own things. Have a down day. If there is a hidden pile of artifacts out there, they've been there for five hundred years. Another day won't change that. We can go to the valley tomorrow. Or the day after, or whenever."

Geneva sat fiddling with a spoon. "No. I think we should go for it today. I'm sure it's on all our minds, so we get it out of the way. And then we return to the scheduled programming."

"Are you sure, honey?" Drake asked.

"Yes. Let's do it and get it out of the way," Geneva said.

"That's it then. We'll go for it as soon as we get the translation back from Victoria," Allie said.

Everyone had finished breakfast and Allie barely finished her third mug of cinnamon tea when Ingrid received the call they'd been waiting for. She jotted down the information and closed out the call.

"The parchment leads to the seventh valley, like we all assumed. There, beneath the tallest peak, we'll find what we've been looking for," Ingrid said.

"I don't like the idea of being under the tallest peak," Drake said. "Does that mean at the mountaintop? Or at the base?"

"We won't know until we get there," Allie said. "Y'all get your stuff, and I'll go get the car. Ingrid, can you grab my backpack? I think I left it on the chair next to the window."

"Sure thing."

"Okay, then. I'll be back in five minutes," Allie said.

Twenty minutes later, Allie returned to the hotel on foot to find her friends standing outside the hotel waiting for her.

"Where's the car?" Drake asked.

"Won't start," Allie said.

"For real?"

"No, Drake. Not for real. I spent the last half hour waiting around the corner to play a practical joke on you. So, the laughs are on you! Of course, it's real. The starter clicks when I turn the key, but it won't turn over."

"What's wrong with it?" Ingrid asked.

"I don't know."

"Did you check under the hood?" Geneva asked.

"Okay," Allie said, holding up her hands in defense. "Everyone come with me."

Allie turned around and led the group away from the hotel. Together, they walked in the bright morning sun three blocks to a public parking garage. Rather than wait for the old, slow elevator, Allie guided them up a flight of steps to the first floor, and walked halfway across the garage. There, the Fiat sat in its spot, right where they'd left it the night before.

"Okay, pop the hood," Drake said.

"Drake, you know nothing about cars. What good is popping the hood going to do?" Allie asked.

"It's something they always do on television. Just do it. I had a problem once where I thought I was having major car trouble, and I took it in and found that my battery cables were loose. I admit I'm not exactly a mechanic, but even I can wiggle a cable to check if it's loose."

Allie unlocked the doors, opened hers, and leaned in and activated the hood release. Drake opened the hood and set the strut in place to hold it open. He dipped his head over the engine, then looked around to the side of the car where the three women waited for his report.

"I found the problem," Drake said.

"Loose cable?" Geneva asked.

"You might say that. Come and take a look."

Drake stepped aside to make room for everyone else. The women lined up in front of the engine compartment and looked in.

"Yeah, I can tell where the problem is," Allie said. "Son of a bitch. Who? Why?"

Inside the engine compartment, someone had sliced clean in half every accessible hose and wire.

"How does something like that happen?" Ingrid asked.

"I know. I've heard of catalytic converters being ripped off a car, but this is way beyond that," Drake said. "It doesn't even look like anything is missing, just vandalized."

"So, what do we do now?" Geneva asked.

"Head back to our hotel, call the rental car place, and hope I get someone who speaks really good English," Allie

said.

"You seem remarkably composed about this," Drake said. "I'm not sure I'd be the same way if something like this happened to my truck."

Allie shrugged. "It's not my car. And I got the full additional insurance package. I guess this time it was well worth the extra money. Step back."

Once her friends moved aside, Allie released the strut, tucked it back into place, and slammed the hood shut. Silently, she led the group from the parking structure and returned to the hotel. Allie stopped at the desk and her friends continued to the breakfast area.

"What did they say?" Geneva asked when Allie returned. She looked around the table, everyone was waiting for her response with interest.

"Well, thanks to the front desk clerk who helped translate our situation, the rental company will send us a replacement car and pick this one up," Allie said.

"That's it?" Drake asked.

"Yep. We should get it sometime this afternoon."

"Another problem solved," Geneva said.

"And we get a little downtime you wanted," Ingrid said. "What should we do with the day?"

"I wouldn't mind returning to that big park we visited a few days ago. The one by the water. There are a few other monuments I wouldn't mind seeing, and they have the Volta Museum I'd like to walk though," Allie said.

"Who's Volta?" Drake asked.

"He invented the electric battery," Allie said.

"And you want to go to that museum because?"

"Because, unlike you, Drake Decker, I have an appreciation for history."

"What do you want to do?" Drake asked Geneva.

"I'm not sure. Walk around, maybe visit a few shops.

Maybe we can check about getting a replacement phone for you."

"That's actually an excellent idea. I propose a free day. Geneva and I will hit the shops, and you two can do what you two do," Drake said.

Allie nodded. "That works for me. Ingrid, would you prefer to go shopping with them or hang with me?"

Ingrid looked from Allie to Geneva. "I'm not big on shopping, so I'll come with you. Although I may wait outside the museum for you if I decide to pass."

"Okay. That's a deal," Allie said. "I'll give Geneva a call later this afternoon and we'll discuss what we want to do about dinner."

"Great," Drake said. "I guess until later, then. Enjoy your day."

Allie and Ingrid watched as the couple took their leave and headed toward the front door.

"You ready?" Allie asked.

"Let me go dump my backpack in the room first. I don't want to haul it around all day," Ingrid said.

"Good idea. I'll come with you. I don't feel like carrying around anything I don't need to today. Why lug it if you don't need it, right?"

An hour later, Ingrid and Allie were walking along the waterfront, hand in hand. Off in the distance, the Volta Museum stood visible, its neoclassical style and four stately columns on display.

"Are you upset we didn't go to the valley today?" Ingrid asked.

"No. Not for a minute," Allie said. "Look at us. Enjoying a gorgeous day and taking it easy for a change. Regardless of what y'all think, sometimes I like a slower pace. This stuff isn't too boring for you, is it?"

"Of course not. I enjoy taking in the history just like you

do."

They stopped when they got in front of the museum.

"Are you coming in with me?" Allie asked.

Ingrid let loose a deep exhale.

Allie laughed. "Just say no, sweetheart. It's fine. We're not joined at the hip or anything. Besides, you'd be more help to me if you did me a favor while I'm in there."

"Sure. What?"

Allie pointed at a park bench off to the side of the museum next to the water. "You see that bench over there? Can you go grab that bench, so I have a place to sit down when I'm done exploring inside the building?"

"That, I can do." Ingrid said.

The women parted ways, and Allie watched as Ingrid headed for the bench. She took a moment to snap a picture of the building, then headed for the door. Once she paid her admission fee, Allie stepped into the rotunda of the building and spun in a circle, marveling at the marble columns and floor. Each direction led to an alcove featuring an original invention or other aspect of Alessandro Volta's life and career.

Allie took her time exploring the exhibits, and after a while she ended back at the first exhibit she viewed. She glanced at her phone and it shocked her to see that she'd spent just over an hour inside the space.

She rushed outside, working on her apology to Ingrid for taking so long, turned the corner, and where she expected to spot only Ingrid waiting for her on the bench, she noticed the backs of two heads instead. Allie picked up her pace and rounded the bench. There, sitting on the opposite side of the bench Ingrid, was Lorenzo.

"I'm so sorry I took so long, Ingrid," Allie said when Ingrid noticed her.

"Don't worry about it. I know how you get lost in those

things. Besides, Lorenzo's been keeping me company."

"Lorenzo," Allie said. "Nice to see you again." Allie put out her hand for Lorenzo to shake, but Lorenzo got to his feet and kissed both of Allie's cheeks in a traditional greeting.

"Please, sit next to your friend," Lorenzo said, offering his seat to Allie. "Ingrid said you were inside the museum? Some fascinating things in there."

"There are," Allie agreed. "What are you doing here?"

"I live near to here, so I always walk along the lakefront and through the park. I'm here usually five days a week. While on my journey today, I spotted Ingrid sitting along, and I stopped to say hello, and she invited me to sit with her until you returned."

"Thank you for keeping her company while I was away," Allie said. "Ingrid—"

"Lorenzo was telling me about his life and desire to visit America," Ingrid said, interrupting.

"You've never been to America?" Allie asked.

"No, but it's always been my dream to visit. Tell me, where do you two come from?"

"Well," Allie said, "I'm from Nashville, and Ingrid is from Boston."

"Nashville and Boston? Those are by New York City?" Lorenzo asked.

"No. I'm about four hours away from New York by car," Ingrid said.

"And I'm about fourteen hours away," Allie said.

"Fourteen hours? By auto? That is like going from here to London."

"The United States is a big country," Allie said.

"If Ingrid is four hours away and you are fourteen, then you don't live near each other?"

"No," Allie said. "I'm more from the middle of the country. Do you know of any cities in the middle?"

"Like Chicago?"

"Yes. Exactly. My city is about five hundred miles south of Chicago."

"And so then, where is Los Angeles?"

Allie thought for a second. "L.A. is roughly two thousand miles to the west of me."

"Two thousand miles? How many kilometers is that?" Lorenzo asked.

"It would be like going from here to Minsk," Ingrid said. "From my home to L.A. is like going from Rome to Moscow."

Lorenzo's jaw dropped. "That far? In one country?"

Ingrid laughed. "Yes. The United States is large. You could spend a year there and not see everything there is to see."

"I would like to try," Lorenzo said. "I would like to see the entire world."

"You live in Europe. There isn't enough to see here?" Ingrid said. "There are so many places I would visit if I lived here. I'd love to see France, Germany, Spain. I've been here before, but only to England and Scandinavia."

"Bah. I've traveled around here, and I'm ready to leave. I'd like to visit everywhere. Africa, Australia, China, Brazil. Anywhere but here," Lorenzo said.

"But you said it was your dream to study. What was it, Hannibal?" Ingrid said.

"Actually, that was more my father's dream than mine. Since I was a boy, he told me stories about Hannibal and his great journey across the mountains. And I admit, I grew fascinated by those stories early on, but the more I studied them, the less they appealed to me."

"So, what do you want?" Ingrid asked.

"Like I said. I want to see the world for myself, not just learn about it in some classroom or dusty old library. Even this museum, as beautiful and historic as it is, isn't for me. I'd die if I had to spend my entire life inside one like my father wants."

"What does your father do now?" Allie asked.

"He's a merchant. Selling goods to the locals and trinkets to the tourists. He dreams of a better life for me, but I think he secretly dreams that if I had the money, I would help him get by and he could close his shop for good. That's another reason I'd like to go to America."

"Why?"

"So that I could be rich, of course. You're rich, aren't you?"

Ingrid and Allie looked into each other's eyes, an unsaid understanding growing between them not to say anything about finances.

"The idea that all Americans are rich is only a story. Most of us live paycheck to paycheck or work multiple jobs just to make ends meet," Ingrid said. "The big houses and lavish lifestyles you see in the movies or on television shows only show a small percentage of how most Americans really live. Unlike what you've heard, the streets aren't really paved with gold."

"But there are wealthy people there, right?" Lorenzo asked.

"Yes. Just like most everywhere," Allie said.

"I would take my chances there, where I could do anything, or be anything I wanted to be. Make a fortune several times over."

Allie prepared to deliver a response when she got literally saved by the bell, in this case her phone ring tone.

"I'm sorry, I need to get this," Allie said as she reached for the answer button. "Hello? Yes, this is she. Okay, how long? Right. See you then." Allie disconnected the phone and turned to Ingrid. "That was the rental company. I need to get back to the car so we can swap it out."

Ingrid nodded and stood without saying anything.

"I'm sorry, Lorenzo, but we need to go. It's been a pleasure speaking with you," Allie said. She reached out for Ingrid's hand, then pulled her into a swift walk.

Ingrid turned and waved goodbye.

"What's he doing?" Allie asked.

"Staring at us," Ingrid said.

"What's the level on your creepy mete?"

"Out of ten? Twelve. Let's walk a little faster."

CHAPTER NINETEEN

At fourteen minutes after eleven the next morning, Allie drove the replacement Fiat into the seventh valley. Unlike the other valleys, this one contained no towns, shops, houses, or people. It was also the smallest valley by far. A river ran through the middle, and other than the two-lane road that followed the banks, each side of the river measured at most two hundred yards before the slopes climbed into mountaintops.

Alongside the road were pullouts every few hundred yards that offered spots for fishermen and others to park, but as they traveled through the valley, all the parking areas were empty.

The day before, Allie and Geneva had worked out which peak along the four-mile-long valley was the tallest and determined it was the one at the farthest end.

"I think this is the most beautiful one yet," Geneva said as she stared out the window, watching the natural wonder pass by.

"Me too. I like the spooky, claustrophobic vibe of it," Ingrid said.

"You would," Geneva said. "How long until we get there?"

Allie snuck a peek at Luna. "Couple of minutes yet. We're almost there."

"I hope there's a place to park," Drake said.

"If there's not, we can take the next closest spot and hike in," Allie said.

Allie smiled when Drake let out a groan that filled the entire car for everyone to enjoy.

"It'll be fine. If there's no spot there, I can drop the three of you off and park the car and hike back myself."

"How is it you're the one with the busted-up knee, yet you're the one having to do all the hard walks on this trip?" Drake asked.

"I'm not the only one with an excuse anymore. You, Geneva, and Ingrid are all injured, too."

"Actually, I'm like my old self. I completely forgot about twisting my ankle," Geneva said.

"I'm fine, too," Ingrid added. "You know, I think even the few scars I had are starting to fade."

"What I'm hearing is Drake is the only one here with a problem?" Allie teased. "Any objections to dropping him off and hiking in ourselves?"

"I'm down for it," Ingrid said.

"Me, too. It would be nice to have some girl time," Geneva added.

"We're only a few hundred yards away," Allie said. "Hold on to those hopes."

Allie slowed down as they reached the destination and pulled into an area that seemed large enough to fit three cars. Once they were out into the open, Ingrid found a path that led across the road to the river, and Geneva found one that headed up the slope toward the mountain peak.

"I guess we go this way," Geneva said, pointing up the

path.

"Lead the way," Allie said.

Geneva took point and led the group along the narrow path that climbed straight up the slope for ten feet, then started a steep ascent diagonally across the hill. They trudged on one stride at a time. After fifteen minutes, Geneva stopped, turned around, and looked at the group behind her. Each of them was breathing heavily, and although it was a cool day, Drake, unlike the rest of them, had beads of sweat sliding down his forehead.

"Why did you stop?" Ingrid asked.

"Because the trail did," Geneva said. "Check it out."

Ingrid was next in line and was facing Geneva. She leaned to her left and saw that the trail ended at the sheer side of the mountain.

"There's nowhere to go?" Ingrid asked.

Geneva turned back around and studied her options. "Well, there are two. If you can climb a wall, you can go up, and if you want to fall, you can take a step to your right and slide down to the car."

"There's no entrance there?" Allie asked from the back.

"Not one that's readily apparent. You're welcome to come up here and look."

"Okay, I will."

Drake had a large flat rock to his right big enough to accommodate him, so he stepped onto that and let Allie take his spot in line. Then he stepped off and walked down the trail a few feet to make room for Ingrid and Geneva. By using the same technique Drake did, Ingrid and Geneva took turns stepping on his rock to allow Allie to move to the front of the line.

Once she faced the mountain, Allie got a better idea of what Geneva described. Directly in front of her, the trail ended at the face. To her left was the mountain, and to her right, the mountain dropped away. Allie scanned the surface for Leonardo's knots, but after a futile search, she had to admit to herself that there was nothing to be found.

She turned around and faced her friends. "There's nothing here."

"That's what I said," Geneva said. "What should we do?"

"Head back down, I guess," Allie said.

Drake led the group back down the path and to the car. When they got to the parking area, they spotted an ancient pickup truck that displayed so much rust it was hard to determine if the original color was brown or red.

Allie unlocked the back of the Fiat, and from a shopping bag, retrieved four bottles of water. She passed them out to everyone, then sat on the SUV's bumper and took a deep drink.

"I'm sorry, you guys. I thought for sure it would be up there," Allie said.

"It's not your fault," Drake said. "We're playing a five-century game here. It would be foolish to expect that everything would work out."

"Perhaps the translation was wrong somehow," Ingrid said. "I'll give Victoria a call." Ingrid made an attempt, but the call didn't go through.

"What now?" Drake asked.

"We head back. Return to our geocaching and touring." Allie said.

"It's a shame. I like it here," Ingrid said. "Do you mind if I take a few pictures before we go?"

Allie shrugged. "Knock yourself out. We're in no hurry."

Ingrid grinned like a child being offered an ice cream cone, then checked the road for traffic and headed to the path leading to the river. Allie watched as Ingrid plodded down the path, then turned left and disappeared down the bank. She had another drink of water and shifted her butt to get comfortable while waiting for her friend. She heard a door open, then felt someone sit in the car.

"What's going on up there?" Allie asked.

"We're having sex!" Drake yelled, a note of triumph in his voice.

Geneva let loose a loud sigh. "We are not. I'm taking a stone out of my shoe."

"Is that what they're calling it these days?" Allie said. She laughed, and Drake joined her.

"That's not funny," Geneva said.

Drake stepped to the rear of the van and faced Allie. "She didn't like that."

"Are you okay? You're sweating up a storm."

Drake wiped his forehead with his hand, then looked at his glistening palm. "I guess so."

"Sit down here. Drink some water," Allie said. She jumped off the bumper and Drake took her place.

Drake unscrewed the cap from his water and lifted the bottle to his lips. He hesitated for the briefest of seconds, then his eyes rolled back into his head, and he fell forward and landed face down in the dirt.

"Oh, shit, Drake!" Allie yelled. She dropped to her knees beside her fallen friend.

"What happened?" Geneva asked when she got to the scene.

"He fainted. Can you call for help? Drake? Can you hear me?"

Allie checked for his pulse in his neck, then in his arm. She dropped her ear to near his mouth. "He's got a pulse, and he's breathing. I don't know what the problem is. Did you get through?"

"No," Geneva said.

"Help me get him in the car."

Allie got under one of Drake's arms, and Geneva got the other one, and together they struggled to get Drake into the back seat of the Fiat. Geneva got into the backseat with Drake and rested his head on her lap.

"Okay, let's go," Allie said, opening the driver's door.

"No! You forgot Ingrid," Geneva yelled.

"Oh, shit. Don't tell her. I'll be right back."

Allie left the car, ran across the road without looking, and jogged down the only path available to her. She ran without observing her environment, and at one point kicked a rock and sprawled to the ground. She jumped up without brushing herself off and picked up her pace.

The path followed the river and bent inward toward the mountain. Allie didn't even realize she'd entered a cave until she'd taken four strides inside and slid to a stop when she found Ingrid standing still right before her.

Allie reached out for Ingrid's hand. "Come on. Drake's sick. We need to go right now."

Ingrid didn't move or speak. Allie looked into her eyes and saw a look of concern that she guessed wasn't for Drake alone. She watched as Ingrid slowly lifted her chin.

Allie pivoted to face the cave entrance and stopped. Lorenzo blocked the way, holding a shotgun.

"What is this?" Allie asked.

"A stick-up," Lorenzo sneered. "You don't think I knew what you were looking for? I could tell the second I spotted that scroll."

"You said you couldn't read the old Italian on there," Allie said.

"I lied. I knew if I got someone else to help you, I could follow you without you suspecting me."

"What do you want from us?" Allie asked.

"The treasure, of course. My father didn't tell me stories

only of Hannibal crossing the Alps. He also told me the legends of the lost treasure of Leonardo."

"Look, we have to go," Allie growled. "Our friend is sick."

Allie took a step toward Lorenzo, and he responded by holding out the shotgun.

"I will shoot if you move again. Put your hands up."

Allie and Ingrid both complied.

"What are you going to do with us?" Ingrid asked.

"First thing I'm going to do is have you explore this cave for me and find the treasure. After that, who's to say? Get going."

Allie and Ingrid turned around and faced the inner cave.

"It's dark in there. We'll never be able to find anything," Allie said.

Allie detected two thunks at her feet and turned around. There, she spotted two flashlights. She picked them up, turned one on, and handed the other to Ingrid.

"Happy?" Lorenzo asked. "Go on."

Allie swept the light through the cave. At most it was eight feet deep, but she saw a black hand-painted arrow on the back wall that pointed to the left. She walked in that direction with Ingrid right on her heels and Lorenzo two yards behind Ingrid.

Allie followed the arrows deeper into the cave. Not that she needed to, since there was only one way to go. There were no alternate branches to explore at all, so she moved as quickly as she dared, hoping to find a way to ditch Lorenzo and get back to Drake. Allie noticed the temperature drop at first as they ventured deeper into the labyrinth, and then it evened out.

"How far should I go?" Allie asked.

"As far as it takes. Keep moving. Don't stop."

Allie continued following the black arrows and eventually they led to a large cavern the size of an ice rink. Stalactites and stalagmites added an ambiance that other circumstances would have been quite enjoyable, but instead they added a dreary, damp feel.

"Ingrid, stop," Lorenzo said. "Your friend stays with me. You check around here and let me know what you find. You come back empty-handed, and Ingrid will have a problem."

Allie nodded that she understood, then stepped farther into the cavern. She found the sweet spot where the light would reach the walls, yet she could stay closer to the center of the room and navigate the rock formations. She got a quarter way around the room when she got to an area where the stalagmites were a few feet offset from the wall, forming a gap not easily noticed.

Inside the gap sat two large chests, not unlike the type Allie had seen in countless pirate movies. She opened the one closest to her and shined the flashlight inside. Empty. Allie opened the next one and this time the light found a large leather satchel covered in dust. She opened the bag, and from within withdrew a journal made of parchment, covered in leather. When she shined the light on the pages, she recognized hand-drawn blueprints similar to those associated with Leonardo da Vinci. Allie turned page after page, then set the journal down and extracted another from the satchel. Satisfied she'd found the treasure, she stowed everything away and closed both chests.

Now that she had what she needed, Allie continued her way around the cavern, looking for something to use as a weapon. She stopped briefly to check something that caught her eye, but since it was neither a weapon nor a way out, she continued her journey around the room. When she completed the circle, she stepped in front of Lorenzo.

"It's back there," Allie said, shining the light in the general direction of the chests.

"Go. Show me," Lorenzo ordered.

Allie led the way, and when they arrived at the chests, Lorenzo pushed the women against the wall, and while keeping one eye on them, opened both chests. Like Allie had done, Lorenzo extracted a journal from the satchel and opened it. As he did, he lowered the shotgun slightly and Allie took a hesitant step forward.

"No," Lorenzo said, returning the shotgun to chest height. Keeping the women in his sights, Lorenzo removed a bag from his shoulder and tossed it to Ingrid. "There's rope in there. Tie up your friend."

Ingrid didn't move. Lorenzo stepped forward and placed the barrel of the shotgun on Allie's forehead.

"Tie her or lose her. Your choice."

"Okay, okay," Ingrid said, bending over to find the rope. When she found it, she bound Allie's wrists behind her back as directed, and then secured Allie to a nearby stalagmite. Once Ingrid tied up Allie tight, Lorenzo tied Ingrid to Allie. Once he trussed up the women, Lorenzo turned his full attention to the chests.

"This discovery will make me rich beyond comprehension," Lorenzo said as he cleared items from the chest.

"Take the treasure, let us go," Allie said.

"Oh, no, I can't do that. You'll tell the authorities. Did you look in here? Journals. Art. Gold. No. You'll need to stay right where you are."

"Our friends will come and find us," Ingrid said.

Her comment gave Lorenzo pause, and he dropped the gold coins he had in his hand back into the chest.

"Yes. The other two. I'll deal with them as well. I thank you for the reminder. Now, if you'll excuse me, I'll go tend to them."

Lorenzo took a moment to shove as many items from the chest as he could fit into his shoulder bag. Then he did the same with two satchels from the chest. Confident he couldn't carry any more, he took Ingrid's flashlight, turned it off, and put it into his pocket. Allie's flashlight he picked up and left the cavern, leaving Allie and Ingrid in the pitch black.

Neither woman spoke, and in the quiet somewhere, Allie heard a drop of water fall into a puddle, followed thirty seconds later by another.

"How are we going to get out of this one?" Ingrid asked.

"I was just thinking about that very thing. I don't suppose calling for help will do any good."

"Probably not. You don't happen to have a knife in your pocket, do you?"

"No," Allie said. "Even if I did, it wouldn't do much good since I can't reach my pocket. You tied me too tight."

"Sorry. I thought he would check it."

"He did. You did the right thing. Can you move at all?"

Allie felt Ingrid make an attempt, but she could tell Ingrid struggled against her bonds.

"Not much," Ingrid said. "Maybe if we worked together, we could break this rock thing and get some slack."

Allie counted to three, and despite their best efforts, they didn't move more than a half inch.

"I think he's coming back," Allie said. "I can see light coming this way."

"Can we kick him or something?" Ingrid asked.

"I can't move my legs," Allie said.

The light got closer, and when it was within three feet, it shined directly into their faces.

"You're still here. Good," Lorenzo said. "One more trip, I think, and then I can take care of your friends."

The light moved from the women to the chest, and once

again Lorenzo filled his bag and the three remaining satchels from the chest. When he finished, he shined the light into the bottom of both chests. Then he tipped over a chest and checked for a false compartment, and finding none, repeated the action with the remaining chest.

"And now, I'll say goodbye for now. Don't worry, though. I'll be back within twenty or thirty minutes to let you go."

The light turned and grew smaller as Lorenzo left the cavern.

"You really believe he's going to let us go?" Ingrid asked.

"Not a chance. We need to escape from here. Let's try moving back and forth and see if that helps. Maybe we can press the rope against the rock and cut through it," Allie said.

Since Ingrid's hands were in front, she could make sure part of her rope contacted the stalagmite, and together, they produced a slight rocking motion, moving side to side an inch at a time. For what seemed like hours, they worked in silence trying to break their bonds. The rope held.

"He's coming back," Allie said, noticing the light dancing toward them.

"Great," Ingrid said. "I guess this is it. Going out trapped like this was something I never envisioned for myself. I had hoped to die in bed as an old woman, with my great-great-great grandchildren at my side."

"Shh, he's almost here."

The light stopped a few feet from them and hung still, illuminating the faces of Ingrid and Allie.

"So do you gals want to leave here, or what?" Geneva asked from behind the light.

CHAPTER TWENTY

A llie, do you have any threes?" Ingrid asked.

"Crap. Here." Allie passed the three of diamonds to Ingrid, who paired it with the three of spades in her hand and placed them on the table in front of her.

"I'm telling you, she's an expert at this game. She could go pro," Geneva said.

"What game?" Drake asked.

The women stopped their game and looked over toward the bed.

"Go, Fish," Geneva said as she stood and moved to Drake's bedside. "How are you feeling?"

"Tired. What happened?"

"When you had surgery, they didn't get all the wood out of your stomach, so you got an infection. They had to operate on you again."

"Am I better?" Drake asked.

Geneva brought his hand to her lips and kissed his fingers. "Yes, thankfully. You had us all scared."

"How long have I been here?"

"Three days. You've been sleeping a lot, though. Don't you remember anything from recently?"

Drake shook his head no. Near his bed was a large cup of water. He reached for it, and Geneva held it steady while he drank.

"I suppose we should catch you up. What's the last thing you remember?"

"We climbed up and down that mountain, and you wanted to have sex in the car," Drake said.

"Close enough. Well, in a nutshell, you passed out. Allie and Ingrid got kidnapped, I caught the culprit, and Allie discovered Leonardo da Vinci's hidden stockpile."

Drake struggled to sit up, so Geneva found the controls and lifted the bed's head until he reached a comfortable position.

"Perhaps instead of only the nutshell, you should give me the whole nut."

"Okay. You passed out, so Allie and I got you into the car. Allie was ready to race you back to civilization when I realized we were about to leave Ingrid behind."

"Wait, really? You were going to leave me there?" Ingrid said, dropping the cards in her hand onto the table.

"No, of course not, honey," Allie said. "We would have come back for you, eventually."

Ingrid made a face of mock anger and waved her fist in the air.

"Calm down, you two," Geneva scolded. "Anyway, we noticed Ingrid was still missing, so Allie decided to look for her. She was gone for a long time, so I headed out to search for both of them. I followed the path that ran along the river and had just stepped around the bend when I saw Lorenzo bent over, emptying bags of something on the ground. When he disappeared back into the cave, I ran over and discovered that he had all kinds of interesting things."

"Why didn't you come for us?" Ingrid asked.

"I tried to, but I only made it like three feet into the cave until it got too dark, and I didn't have a flashlight on me. I also saw Lorenzo had a rifle on him, so I didn't want to get too close to him."

"Valid points," Ingrid conceded.

"Then what?" Drake asked.

"Then I rushed back to our back to our car. I considered driving for help, since the keys were dangling from the ignition, but I didn't want to leave you guys. I assumed Lorenzo was the one who disabled our other car, so I wanted to return the favor."

"That was probably a good assumption," Allie said. "He followed us for days, apparently. Must be good at it, too, because I never spotted him."

"Me neither," Ingrid said.

"What did you do? Cut all his wires?" Drake asked.

"I thought about it, but I had nothing to cut with. I got the tire iron from our trunk and used it like a pry bar to dislodge a few things in his engine. Even though I didn't know what I was doing. I just figured if I could disconnect something, anything, then he'd be stuck there," Geneva said.

"So, you wanted the guy with the gun there with us?" Ingrid asked.

Geneva shrugged. "Perhaps I didn't think that part through too clearly. I was under a lot of stress at the time, so sue me."

"Stop interrupting her," Drake scolded. "Go on."

"I didn't want him to find me, so I climbed up the mountain trail and hid behind a boulder. When he came back, he wasn't carrying any of his treasure, so I assumed he was looking for us. First, he headed to our car and saw you passed out in the back seat. He must not have considered you a threat, because he let you be."

"Wait, so you went to hide and left me in the car?" Drake asked.

Geneva shrugged again. "What was I going to do with you? I couldn't carry you up the mountain by myself, and I guessed since you were already unconscious, he wouldn't mess with you."

"Stop interrupting her," Ingrid scolded. "We haven't heard any of this story." Ingrid grinned at Drake, and he smiled in return.

"Okay," Drake said. "You hid up the mountain, and?"

"And after Lorenzo found you, he started looking for me. He checked in and around both vehicles, and actually walked a few feet up the mountain path before he stopped. I thought for sure I'd get caught. Although he couldn't see me from the ground, he'd easily spot me if he came more than fifteen feet up the trail. Anyway, when he couldn't find me, he left to get the treasure. It must have been a lot, because he made two trips. The first time, he dumped several old leather bags into the bed of his pickup. That's when he made his mistake."

"What was that?" Drake asked.

"Before he put the bags in the truck, he leaned his gun against the back tire. When he left for the rest of the loot, he forgot to take it with him. When he disappeared down the hill, I ran down the trail, grabbed the shotgun and waited on the far side of our Fiat. When he came back, I threatened him with his own weapon."

Ingrid clapped. "That's incredible!"

"What happened next?" Drake asked.

"Next was mostly luck. As I stood there pointing a gun at Lorenzo, trying to decide what to do about him, an off-duty cop, who just happened to be out for a joyride on his new motorcycle, took an interest in us. Of course, he pulled his gun on me, and when he did, I dropped the one I had. It took about three minutes for me to tell him what happened, and when he looked in the pickup bed and saw the goods, he put Lorenzo in handcuffs. Then he radioed in for backup and told me to find Ingrid and Allie."

"We thought you were him coming back to finish us off," Ingrid admitted. "I almost wet myself. I was so scared."

"So, then they got an ambulance for me and drove me all the way back here?" Drake asked.

"Not at all," Allie said. "They brought in a helicopter for you. Landed it right in the middle of the road."

"It was a beautiful flight. The scenery was marvelous," Geneva said.

"You got to enjoy the ride, and I slept through the whole thing?" Drake asked.

Geneva laughed. "Don't worry. I took pictures."

Ingrid gathered all the playing cards and shoved them back into the box while Allie put on her coat.

"Where are you two going?" Drake asked.

Allie walked over to Drake's bedside, leaned over, and kissed him on the forehead. "Ingrid and I are going to help a friend with a project. Geneva will stay here to keep you company, and we'll be back later."

"Maybe," Ingrid said.

Allie nodded vigorously. "Right. If you're lucky, we'll be back later. Or we might go to the spa."

"You girls are such jerks," Drake said.

"That's why you love us," Allie said.

Allie and Ingrid left the room, leaving the couple to themselves.

*

Four days later, Allie parked the Fiat in an open spot right in front of Victoria's Leonardo da Vinci Museum. Before the four got out of the car, Victoria stood outside, waiting to welcome the group.

"Thank you for coming!" Victoria said as she greeted each person with cheek kisses and welcomed them into the museum.

"This is coming along nicely," Allie said as she stepped into the main room. All the exhibit cases had moved into the center of the room and sat covered with drop cloths. A fresh coat of paint covered all the walls, and murals representing Leonardo's drawings were penciled in over the fresh paint. "This will look fantastic when it's finished."

"Let's go sit," Victoria said. She led the group to the same small break room they'd occupied.

"When do the new exhibits open?" Allie asked.

Drake's attention perked up. "You're putting the things Lorenzo stole on display here?"

Victoria laughed. "Oh, no. Everything he found was fake."

"Fake?" I don't understand.

"Everything in those chests were reproductions," Allie said. "A few of the visitor bureaus around Northern Italy got the idea of doing a scavenger hunt of sorts based on the works of well-known Italian artists. Since the legend of the lost treasures of Leonardo da Vinci is so prevalent in this area, they thought it only natural to use that cave to 'hide' the Leonardo stuff."

"Are you saying we were chasing around the country for nothing? None of that was real?" Drake asked.

"Come with me," Victoria said.

Victoria led the group from the storeroom to a side room. The only things in the room were eight crates. The two largest were the size of an easy chair, the rest the average size of a piano bench.

"What's all this?" Drake asked.

"The lost works of Leonardo da Vinci," Victoria said.

"But where did you get it?"

Victoria pointed at Allie. "From her."

Drake passed Allie a look that she'd seen plenty of times before and knew she needed to offer an explanation.

"Let's go sit back down and I'll explain," Allie said.

Once everyone took their seats back in the breakroom, Allie began speaking.

"Two days after our encounter with Lorenzo, Ingrid and I drove back out to the valley."

"Why?" Drake asked.

"Because when Lorenzo had me search the cavern, I found this," Allie said, pulling out her phone. She opened her photos and showed everyone the picture of the intertwined knots embedded in the cave wall. "I figured since I'd already found the chests, I could withhold this little nugget from Lorenzo. I already knew the stuff in the trunk was fake."

"How?"

"The journal I picked up had the company's stamp on the back cover. Anyway, the symbol concealed the hiding spot of all those things that Victoria has in those crates. We contacted Victoria, and she took it from there."

Victoria waved her hand. "It was no effort on my part, I just hired movers."

"Won't there be some question of ownership?"

"Well, I have the good news and the bad news for you regarding that," Victoria said. "The bad news is, according to law, the state owns everything you found. The good news is, you will receive a splendid finder's fee based on the value of the items recovered. I suspect you will get more money than you've ever dreamed of."

"What happens to the artifacts?" Drake asked.

"That is the good news for me. Since I already have connections within the antiquities bureau, I've arranged to catalog the items and display many of them here. Of course, I don't have the room for everything, so I'll share with other museums in Milan, but the entire trove will stay in this region."

"That's good," Drake said. "I was, however, hoping to add something to my personal collection."

"You don't have a collection," Allie said.

Drake shrugged. "Just dreaming."

Victoria smiled. "Well, perhaps I can convince the government to let you hold on to a little something for us, just as a loan, of course."

"Of course."

"Now, would you like to see what you found?" Victoria asked.

Drake erupted in a wide grin. "How is that even a question?"

*

The next morning, after breakfast, the four walked along the lakeshore.

"Can you believe all that stuff?" Drake said. "Journals, art, inventions, sketches. It's going to take Victoria years to catalog all of those items."

"I can tell you she's looking forward to it. She can't wait to get started. It will be a boon to this region, and Italy in general," Ingrid said.

"So, with this all behind us, what do we do now?" Drake asked.

"We get back to vacationing like normal people," Geneva said. "With geocaching, and shopping, and taking pictures of all the things we encounter."

Drake stopped and looked out over the water. It was a perfect day. The sun glowed in the sky, causing a reflection of diamonds on the surface of the lake. The bright blue sky carried but a single lazy cloud.

"I wasn't thinking about vacation. I've been thinking more about the future, and the future I want to have is one with you." Drake removed an object from his pocket and dropped to a knee. "Geneva, I've loved you since the day we met. I can't picture a future without you. Will you marry me?"

Geneva stared into Drake's eyes for a moment, and then focused on the engagement ring he held between his fingers. Her eyes went from the ring, to Drake, to Ingrid, to Allie, and back to Drake.

"Of course, I'll marry you," Geneva said. "Get up here."

Drake stood and placed the ring on her finger. The couple embraced and then kissed.

"That was sweet, wasn't it?" Allie asked.

"Sure was," Ingrid said.

"Did you get it all on video?"

"Every moment."

"It's about time he asked her. He's been walking around this entire trip with that ring in his pocket like an idiot," Allie said.

"I'm surprised it didn't end up at the bottom of the mountain," Ingrid said.

The couple broke their embrace, and Drake looked at his other two friends. "We can hear you."

Allie shrugged, then leaned in and gave Ingrid a quick kiss. "Let's leave the lovebirds alone for a while. Now that everything else is out of the way, can we finally go find some gelato?"

ABOUT THE AUTHOR

Dan DeKoning was born and raised in Milwaukee, Wisconsin, and currently lives in Knoxville, Tennessee with his wife and their cats.

He is a storyteller and poet who loves to write in a variety of genres and themes. He is also a voracious reader who loves to read anything he can get his hands on.

When he's not writing, you can find him hunting for treasures in used bookstores, or out exploring the planet, or geocaching, or searching for adventures and stories to tell.

ALSO BY DAN DEKONING

This is Dan DeKoning's complete library at the time of publication, but Dan has new books coming out all the time. Sign up for his newsletter at DanDeKoning.com to stay up to date on new releases.

<u>Fiction</u>
Déjà Vu
The Haunting of Hyacinth House
How Deep the Darkness

<u>Geocaching Mystery Series</u>
The Cacheland Conspiracy
The Quincy Bay Quandary
The Secret of the Seven Valleys
The Geocaching Mystery Omnibus – Volume 1

<u>Codi Cassidy Cozy Mystery Series</u>
Acoustics and Alibis
Ballads and Bloodshed
Codas and Calibers
Codi Cassidy Omnibus – Volume 1

<u>Poetry Collections</u>
Lost and Found
Random Thoughts

www.ingramcontent.com/pod-product-compliance
Lightning Source LLC
Chambersburg PA
CBHW061847310726
48972CB00004B/917